Will Ohio

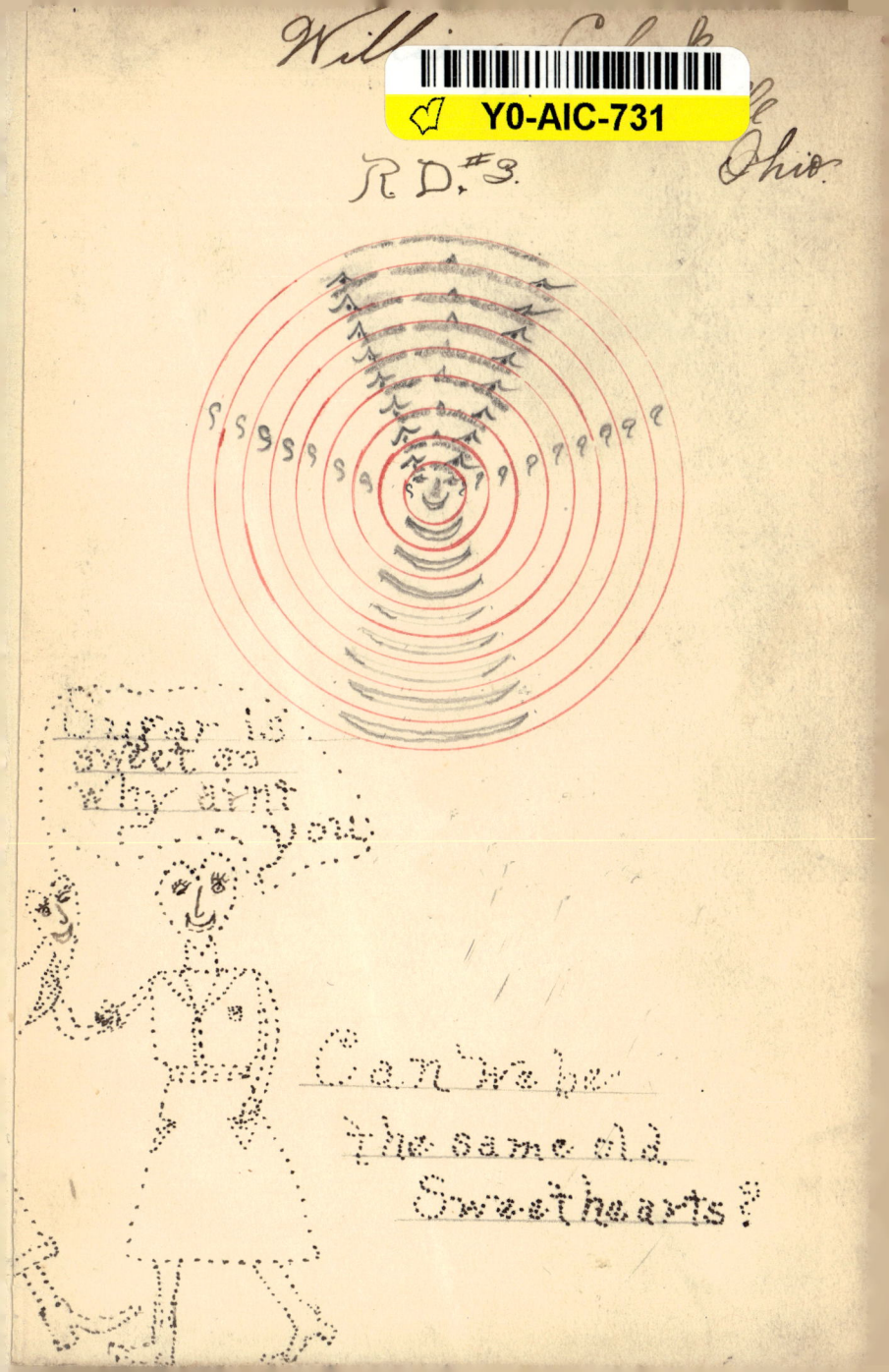

R.D. #3.

Sugar is
sweet so
why aint
you

Can we be
The same old
Sweethearts?

THE FORTUNE THEATER
During the Performance of an Elizabethan Play

(Drawing based on an architectural model in Columbia University.)

HALLECK'S NEW ENGLISH LITERATURE

BY

REUBEN POST HALLECK, M.A., LL.D.

AUTHOR OF "HISTORY OF ENGLISH LITERATURE"
"HISTORY OF AMERICAN LITERATURE"

AMERICAN BOOK COMPANY

NEW YORK   CINCINNATI   CHICAGO

Copyright, 1913, by
REUBEN POST HALLECK.

Copyright, 1913, in Great Britain.

HAL. NEW ENG. LIT.

W. P. 13

PREFACE

In this *New English Literature* the author endeavors to preserve the qualities that have caused his former *History of English Literature* to be so widely used; namely, suggestiveness, clearness, organic unity, interest, and the power to awaken thought and to stimulate the student to further reading.

The book furnishes a concise account of the history and growth of English literature from the earliest times to the present day. It lays special emphasis on literary movements, on the essential qualities that differentiate one period from another, and on the spirit that animates each age. Above all, the constant purpose has been to arouse in the student an enthusiastic desire to read the works of the authors discussed. Because of the author's belief in the guide-book function of a history of literature, he has spent much time and thought in preparing the unusually detailed *Suggested Readings* that follow each chapter.

It was necessary for several reasons to prepare a new book. Twentieth century research has transformed the knowledge of the Elizabethan theater and has brought to light important new facts relating to the drama and to Shakespeare. The new social spirit has changed the critical viewpoint concerning authors as different as Wordsworth, Keats, Ruskin, Dickens, and Tennyson. Wordsworth's treatment of childhood, for instance, now requires an amount of space that would a short time ago have seemed disproportionate. Later Victorian writers, like Meredith, Hardy, Swinburne, and Kipling, can no longer be accorded the usual brief perfunctory treatment. Increased modern interest in contemporary life is also demanding some account of the literature already produced by the twentieth century. An entire chapter is devoted to showing how this new literature reveals the thought and ideals of this generation.

Other special features of this new work are the suggestions and references for a literary trip through England, the historical introductions to the chapters, the careful treatment of the modern drama, the latest bibliography, and the new illustrations, some of which have been specially drawn for this work, while others have been taken from original paintings in the National Portrait Gallery, London, and elsewhere. The illustrations are the result of much individual research by the author during his travels in England.

The greater part of this book was gradually fashioned in the classroom, during the long period that the author has taught this subject. Experience with his classes has proved to him the reasonableness of the modern demand that a textbook shall be definite and stimulating.

The author desires to thank the large number of teachers who have aided him by their criticism. Miss Elizabeth Howard Spaulding and Miss Sarah E. Simons deserve special mention for valuable assistance. The entire treatment of Rudyard Kipling is the work of Miss Mary Brown Humphrey. The greater part of the chapter, *Twentieth-Century Literature*, was prepared by Miss Anna Blanche McGill. Some of the best and most difficult parts of the book were written by the author's wife.

R. P. H.

CONTENTS

		PAGE
INTRODUCTION — LITERARY ENGLAND		1

CHAPTER		
I.	FROM 449 A.D. TO THE NORMAN CONQUEST, 1066	7
II.	FROM THE NORMAN CONQUEST, 1066, TO CHAUCER'S DEATH, 1400	53
III.	FROM CHAUCER'S DEATH, 1400, TO THE ACCESSION OF ELIZABETH, 1558	99
IV.	THE AGE OF ELIZABETH, 1558–1603	119
V.	THE PURITAN AGE, 1603–1660	220
VI.	FROM THE RESTORATION, 1660, TO THE PUBLICATION OF PAMELA, 1740	256
VII.	THE SECOND FORTY YEARS OF THE EIGHTEENTH CENTURY, 1740–1780	304
VIII.	THE AGE OF ROMANTICISM, 1780–1837	351
IX.	THE VICTORIAN AGE, 1837–1900	449
X.	TWENTIETH-CENTURY LITERATURE	587
SUPPLEMENTARY LIST OF AUTHORS AND THEIR CHIEF WORKS		625
INDEX		633

LIST OF ILLUSTRATIONS

		PAGE
1.	Woden	12
2.	Exeter Cathedral	18
3.	Anglo-Saxon Gleeman. (From the tapestry designed by H. A. Bone)	21
4.	Facsimile of Beginning of Cotton MS. of Beowulf. (British Museum)	25
5.	Facsimile of Beginning of Junian MS. of Cædmon	32
6.	Anglo-Saxon Musicians. (From illuminated MS., British Museum)	35
7.	The Beginning of Alfred's Laws. (From illuminated MS., British Museum)	45
8.	The Death of Harold at Hastings. (From the Bayeux tapestry)	53
9.	What Mandeville Saw. (From Edition of 1725)	73
10.	John Wycliffe. (From an old print)	74
11.	Treuthe's Pilgryme atte Plow. (From a MS. in Trinity College, Cambridge)	77
12.	Gower Hearing the Confession of a Lover. (From Egerton MS., British Museum)	79
13.	Geoffrey Chaucer. (From an old drawing in the MS. of Occleve's Poems, British Museum)	80
14.	Canterbury Cathedral	84
15.	Pilgrims Leaving the Tabard Inn. (From Urry's Chaucer)	86
16.	Facsimile of Lines Describing the Franklyn. (From the Cambridge University MS.)	87
17.	Franklyn, Friar, Knight, Prioress, Squire, Clerk of Oxford. (From the Ellesmere MS.)	87–89
18.	Morris Dancers. (From MS. of Chaucer's Time)	92
19.	Henry VIII, giving Bibles to Clergy and Laity. (From frontispiece to Coverdale Bible)	101
20.	Book Illustration, Early Fifteenth Century. (British Museum)	105
21.	Facsimile of Caxton's Advertisement of his Books. (Bodleian Library, Oxford)	106
22.	Malory's *Morte d'Arthur*. (From DeWorde's Edition, 1529)	107
23.	Early Title Page of *Robin Hood*. (Copland Edition, 1550)	110
24.	William Tyndale. (From an old print)	113
25.	Sir Thomas Wyatt. (After Holbein)	114
26.	Facsimile of Queen Elizabeth's Signature	119
27.	Sir Philip Sidney. (After the miniature by Isaac Oliver, Windsor Castle)	125
28.	Francis Bacon. (From the painting by Van Somer, National Portrait Gallery)	128
29.	Title page of *Bacon's Essays*, 1597	131
30.	John Donne. (From the painting by Jansen, South Kensington Museum)	137
31.	Edmund Spenser. (From a painting in Duplin Castle)	139
32.	Miracle Play at Coventry. (From an old print)	148
33.	Hell Mouth in the Old Miracle Play. From a Columbia University Model	149
34.	Fool's Head	152
35.	Air-Bag Flapper and Lath Dagger	153
36.	Fool of the Old Play	154
37.	Thomas Sackville	157
38.	Theater in Inn Yard. (From Columbia University model)	159
39.	Reconstructed Globe Theater, Earl's Court, London, 1912	160
40.	The Bankside and its Theaters. (From the Hollar engraving, about 1620)	162
41.	Contemporary Drawing of Interior of an Elizabethan Theater	164
42.	Marlowe's Memorial Statue at Canterbury	170
43.	William Shakespeare. (From the Chandos portrait, National Portrait Gallery)	174
44.	Shakespeare's Birthplace, Stratford-on-Avon	175
45.	Classroom in Stratford Grammar School	176
46.	Anne Hathaway's Cottage, Shottery	178
47.	View of Stratford-on-Avon	182
48.	Inscription over Shakespeare's Tomb	183

LIST OF ILLUSTRATIONS

		PAGE
49.	Shakespeare — The D'Avenant Bust. (Discovered in 1845)	190
50.	Henry Irving as Hamlet	191
51.	Ellen Terry as Lady Macbeth. (From the painting by Sargent)	192
52.	Falstaff and his Page. (From a drawing by B. Westmacott)	193
53.	Ben Jonson. (From the portrait by Honthorst, National Portrait Gallery)	199
54.	Ben Jonson's Tomb in Westminster Abbey	201
55.	Francis Beaumont	206
56.	John Fletcher	207
57.	Cromwell Dictating Dispatches to Milton. (From the painting by Ford Madox Brown)	222
58.	Thomas Fuller	225
59.	Izaak Walton	227
60.	Jeremy Taylor	227
61.	John Bunyan. (From the painting by Sadler, National Portrait Gallery)	228
62.	Bedford Bridge, Showing Gates and Jail. (From an old print)	230
63.	Bunyan's Dream. (From Fourth Edition *Pilgrim's Progress*, 1680)	231
64.	Woodcut from the First Edition of Mr. Badman	232
65.	Robert Herrick	234
66.	John Milton. (After a drawing by W. Faithorne, at Bayfordbury)	238
67.	John Milton, Æt. 10	239
68.	Milton's Visit to Galileo in 1638. (From the painting by T. Lessi)	240
69.	Facsimile of Milton's Signature, 1663	241
70.	Title Page to *Comus*, 1637	242
71.	Milton's Motto from *Comus*, with Autograph, 1639	244
72.	Milton Dictating *Paradise Lost* to his Daughter. (From the painting by Munkacsy)	250
73.	Samuel Butler	257
74.	John Dryden. (From the painting by Sir Godfrey Kneller, National Portrait Gallery)	265
75.	Birthplace of Dryden. (From a print)	266
76.	Daniel Defoe. (From a print by Vandergucht)	272
77.	Jonathan Swift. (From the painting by C. Jervas, National Portrait Gallery)	277
78.	Moor Park. (From a drawing)	278
79.	Swift and Stella. (From the painting by Dicksee)	279
80.	Joseph Addison. (From the painting by Sir Godfrey Kneller, National Portrait Gallery)	285
81.	Birthplace of Addison	287
82.	Richard Steele	288
83.	Sir Roger de Coverley in Church. (From a drawing by B. Westmacott)	290
84.	Alexander Pope. (From the portrait by William Hoare)	293
85.	Pope's Villa at Twickenham. (From an old print)	294
86.	Rape of the Lock. (From a drawing by B. Westmacott)	296
87.	Alexander Pope. (From a contemporary portrait)	297
88.	Horace Walpole	311
89.	Thomas Gray	314
90.	Stoke Poges Churchyard	315
91.	A Blind Beggar Robbed of his Drink. (From a British Museum MS.)	317
92.	Samuel Richardson. (From an original drawing)	320
93.	Henry Fielding. (From the drawing by Hogarth)	322
94.	Laurence Sterne	324
95.	Uncle Toby and Corporal Trim. (From a drawing by B. Westmacott)	324
96.	Tobias Smollett	325
97.	Edward Gibbon. (From the painting by Sir Joshua Reynolds)	328
98.	Edmund Burke. (From the painting by Sir Joshua Reynolds, National Portrait Gallery)	330
99.	Oliver Goldsmith. (From the painting by Sir Joshua Reynolds, National Portrait Gallery)	332
100.	Goldsmith and Dr. Johnson. (From a drawing by B. Westmacott)	333
101.	Goldsmith's Lodgings, Canonbury Tower, London	334

LIST OF ILLUSTRATIONS

		PAGE
102.	Dr. Primrose and his Family. (From a drawing by G. Patrick Nelson)	336
103.	Samuel Johnson. (From the painting by Sir Joshua Reynolds)	339
104.	Samuel Johnson's Birthplace. (From an old print)	341
105.	James Boswell	343
106.	Cheshire Cheese Inn To-day	344
107.	Robert Southey	358
108.	Charles Lamb. (From a drawing by Maclise)	359
109.	Bo-Bo and Roast Pig. (From a drawing by B. Westmacott)	360
110.	William Cowper. (From the portrait by Sir Thomas Lawrence)	364
111.	Cowper's Cottage at Weston	365
112.	John Gilpin's Ride. (From a drawing by R. Caldecott)	365
113.	Robert Burns. (From the painting by Nasmyth, National Portrait Gallery)	368
114.	Birthplace of Burns	369
115.	Burns and Highland Mary. (From the painting by James Archer)	371
116.	Sir Walter Scott. (From the painting by William Nicholson)	375
117.	Abbotsford, Home of Sir Walter Scott	376
118.	Scott's Grave in Dryburgh Abbey	377
119.	Loch Katrine and Ellen's Isle	378
120.	Walter Scott. (From a life sketch by Maclise)	379
121.	Scott's Desk and "Elbow Chair" at Abbotsford	381
122.	Jane Austen. (From an original family portrait)	383
123.	Jane Austen's Desk	385
124.	William Wordsworth. (From the portrait by B. R. Haydon)	387
125.	Boy of Winander. (From the painting by H. O. Walker, Congressional Library)	388
126.	Wordsworth's Home at Grasmere — Dove Cottage	391
127.	Grasmere Lake	393
128.	William Wordsworth. (From a life sketch in *Fraser's Magazine*)	396
129.	Rydal Mount near Ambleside	397
130.	Samuel Taylor Coleridge. (From a pencil sketch by C. R. Leslie)	399
131.	Coleridge's Cottage at Nether-Stowey	401
132.	Coleridge as a Young Man. (From a sketch made in Germany)	405
133.	Lord Byron. (From a portrait by Kramer)	407
134.	Byron at Seventeen. (From a painting)	408
135.	Newstead Abbey, Byron's Home	409
136.	Castle of Chillon	410
137.	Byron's Home at Pisa	414
138.	Percy Bysshe Shelley. (From the portrait by Amelia Curran, National Portrait Gallery)	417
139.	Shelley's Birthplace, Field Place	418
140.	Grave of Shelley, Protestant Cemetery, Rome	420
141.	Facsimile of Stanza from *To a Skylark*	421
142.	John Keats. (From the painting by Hilton, National Portrait Gallery)	426
143.	Keats's Home, Wentworth Place	428
144.	Grave of Keats, Rome	429
145.	Facsimile of Original MS. of *Endymion*	430
146.	Endymion. (From the painting by H. O. Walker, Congressional Library)	431
147.	Thomas de Quincey. (From the painting by Sir J. W. Gordon, National Portrait Gallery)	436
148.	Room in Dove Cottage	437
149.	Charles Darwin	452
150.	John Tyndall	453
151.	Thomas Huxley. (From the painting by John Collier, National Portrait Gallery)	454
152.	Dante Gabriel Rossetti. (From the drawing by himself, National Portrait Gallery)	463
153.	Thomas Babington Macaulay. (From the painting by Sir F. Grant, National Portrait Gallery)	466
154.	Cardinal Newman. (From the painting by Emmeline Deane)	473
155.	Thomas Carlyle. (From the painting by James McNeill Whistler)	477
156.	Craigenputtock	478

LIST OF ILLUSTRATIONS

		PAGE
157.	Mrs. Carlyle. (From a miniature portrait)	479
158.	John Ruskin. (From a photograph)	488
159.	Charles Dickens. (From a photograph taken in America, 1868)	496
160.	Dickens's Home, Gads Hill	498
161.	Facsimile of MS. of *A Christmas Carol*	501
162.	William Makepeace Thackeray. (From the painting by Samuel Laurence, National Portrait Gallery)	504
163.	Caricature of Thackeray by Himself	505
164.	Thackeray's Home where *Vanity Fair* was Written	506
165.	George Eliot. (From a drawing by Sir F. W. Burton, National Portrait Gallery)	511
166.	George Eliot's Birthplace	512
167.	Robert Louis Stevenson. (From a photograph)	517
168.	Stevenson as a Boy	518
169.	Edinburgh Memorial of Robert Louis Stevenson. (By St. Gaudens)	522
170.	George Meredith. (From the painting by G. F. Watts, National Portrait Gallery)	524
171.	Thomas Hardy. (From the painting by Winifred Thompson)	530
172.	Max Gate. (The Home of Hardy)	532
173.	Matthew Arnold. (From the painting by G. F. Watts, National Portrait Gallery)	534
174.	Robert Browning. (From the painting by G. F. Watts, National Portrait Gallery)	541
175.	Elizabeth Barrett Browning. (From the painting by Field Talfourd, National Portrait Gallery)	542
176.	Facsimile of MS. from *Pippa Passes*	550
177.	Alfred Tennyson. (From a photograph by Mayall)	554
178.	Farringford	555
179.	Facsimile of MS. of *Crossing the Bar*	561
180.	Algernon Charles Swinburne. (From the painting by Dante Gabriel Rossetti)	564
181.	Rudyard Kipling. (From the painting by John Collier)	569
182.	Mowgli and his Brothers. (From *The Jungle Book*)	572
183.	The Cat That Walked. (From Kipling's drawing for *Just-So Stories*)	573
184.	Joseph Conrad	589
185.	Arnold Bennett	590
186.	John Galsworthy	592
187.	Herbert George Wells	593
188.	William Butler Yeats	598
189.	John Masefield	601
190.	Alfred Noyes	604
191.	Henry Arthur Jones	607
192.	Arthur Wing Pinero	607
193.	George Bernard Shaw. (From the bust by Rodin)	609
194.	James Matthew Barrie	610
195.	Stephen Phillips	612
196.	Lady Gregory	615
197.	John Synge	618

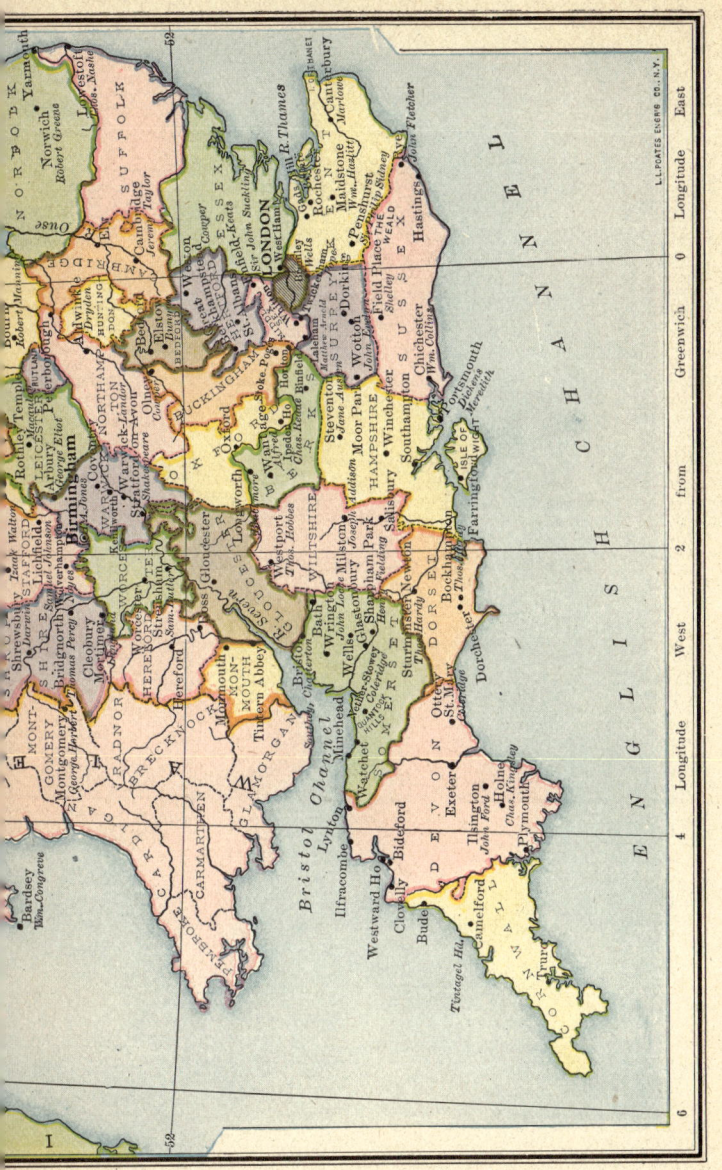

NEW ENGLISH LITERATURE

INTRODUCTION

LITERARY ENGLAND

Some knowledge of the homes and haunts of English authors is necessary for an understanding of their work. We feel in much closer touch with Shakespeare after merely reading about Stratford-on-Avon; but we seem to share his experiences when we actually walk from Stratford-on-Avon to Shottery and Warwick. The scenery and life of the Lake Country are reflected in Wordsworth's poetry. Ayr and the surrounding country throw a flood of light on the work of Burns. The streets of London are a commentary on the novels of Dickens. A journey to Canterbury aids us in recreating the life of Chaucer's Pilgrims.

Much may be learned from a study of literary England. Whether one does or does not travel, such study is necessary. Those who hope at some time to visit England should acquire in advance as much knowledge as possible about the literary associations of the places to be visited; for when the opportunity for the trip finally comes, there is usually insufficient time for such preparation as will enable the traveler to derive the greatest enjoyment from a visit to the literary centers in which Great Britain abounds.

INTRODUCTION

Whenever an author is studied, his birthplace should be located on the literary map, page xii. Baedeker's *Great Britain* will be indispensable in making an itinerary. The *Reference List for Literary England* (p. 4) is sufficiently comprehensive to enable any one to plan an enjoyable literary pilgrimage through Great Britain and to learn the most important facts about the places connected with English authors.

The following suggestions from the author's experience are intended to serve merely as an illustration of how to begin an itinerary. The majority of east-bound steamships call at Plymouth, a good place to disembark for a literary trip. From Plymouth, the traveler may go to Exeter (a quaint old town with a fine cathedral, the home of *Exeter Book*, p. 19), thence by rail to Camelford in Cornwall and by coach four miles to the fascinating Tintagel (King Arthur), where, as Tennyson says in his *Idylls of the King:* —

> "All down the thundering shores of Bude and Bos,
> There came a day as still as heaven, and then
> They found a naked child upon the sands
> Of dark Tintagil by the Cornish sea,
> And that was Arthur."

Next, the traveler may go by coach to Bude (of which Tennyson remarked, "I hear that there are larger waves at Bude than at any other place. I must go thither and be alone with God") and to unique Clovelly and Bideford (Kingsley), by rail to Ilfracombe, by coach to Lynton (Lorna Doone), and the adjacent Lynmouth (where Shelley passed some of his happiest days and alarmed the authorities by setting afloat bottles containing his *Declaration of Rights*), by coach to Minehead, by rail to Watchet, driving past Alfoxden (Wordsworth) to Nether-Stowey (Coleridge) and the Quantock Hills (p. 401), by motor and rail to Glastonbury (Isle of Avalon, burial place of King Arthur and Queen Guinevere), by rail to Wells (cathedral), to Bath (many literary associations), to Bristol (Chatterton, Southey), to Gloucester (fine cathedral, tomb of Edward II), and to Ross, the starting point for a remarkable all day's row down the river Wye to Tintern Abbey (Wordsworth), stopping for dinner at Monmouth (Geoffrey of Monmouth, p. 66).

After a start similar to the foregoing, the traveler should begin to make an itinerary of his own. He will enjoy a trip more if he has a share in planning it. From Tintern Abbey he might proceed, for instance, to Stratford-on-Avon (Shakespeare); then to Warwick, Kenilworth, and the George Eliot Country in North Warwickshire and Staffordshire.

For natural beauty, there is nothing in England that is more delightful than a coaching trip through Wordsworth's Lake Country (Cumberland and Westmoreland). From there it is not far to the Carlyle Country (Ecclefechan, Craigenputtock), to the Burns Country (Dumfries, Ayr), and to the Scott Country (Loch Katrine, The Trossachs, Edinburgh, and Abbotsford). In Edinburgh, William Sharp's statement about Stevenson should be remembered, "One can, in a word, outline Stevenson's own country as all the region that on a clear day one may in the heart of Edinburgh descry from the Castle walls."

If the traveler lands at Southampton, he is on the eastern edge of Thomas Hardy's Wessex, Dorchester in Dorsetshire being the center. The Jane Austen Country (Steventon, Chawton) is in Hampshire. To the east, in Surrey, is Burford Bridge near Dorking, where Keats wrote part of his *Endymion*, where George Meredith had his summer home, and where "the country of his poetry" is located.

INTRODUCTION

In London, it is a pleasure to trace some of the greatest literary associations in the world. We may stand at the corner of Monkwell and Silver streets, on the site of a building in which Shakespeare wrote some of his greatest plays. Milton lived in the vicinity and is buried not far distant in St. Giles Church. In Westminster Abbey we find the graves of many of the greatest authors, from Chaucer to Tennyson. London is not only Dickens Land and Thackeray Land, but also the "Land" of many other writers. We may still eat in the Old Cheshire Cheese (p. 344), where Johnson and Goldsmith dined.

Those interested in literary England ought to include the cathedral towns in their itinerary, so that they may visit the wonderful "poems in stone," some of which, *e.g.*, Canterbury (Chaucer), Winchester (Izaak Walton, Jane Austen), Lichfield (Johnson), have literary associations. For this reason, all of the cathedral towns in England have been included in the literary map.

REFERENCE LIST FOR LITERARY ENGLAND

Baedeker's *Great Britain* (includes England and Scotland).
Baedeker's *London and its Environs*.
Adcock's *Famous Houses and Literary Shrines of London*.
Lang's *Literary London*.
Hutton's *Literary Landmarks in London*.
Lucas's *A Wanderer in London*.
Shelley's *Literary By-Paths in Old England*.
Baildon's *Homes and Haunts of Famous Authors*.
Bates's *From Gretna Green to Land's End*.
Masson's *In the Footsteps of the Poets*.
Wolfe's *A Literary Pilgrimage among the Haunts of Famous British Authors*.
Salmon's *Literary Rambles in the West of England*.
Hutton's *A Book of the Wye*.
Headlam's *Oxford (Medieval Towns Series)*.
Winter's *Shakespeare's England*.

READING REFERENCES

Murray's *Handbook of Warwickshire*.
Lee's *Stratford-on-Avon, from the Earliest Times to the Death of Shakespeare*.
Tompkins's *Stratford-on-Avon* (Dent's *Temple Topographies*).
Brassington's *Shakespeare's Homeland*.
Winter's *Grey Days and Gold* (Shakespeare).
Collingwood's *The Lake Counties* (Dent's County Guides).
Wordsworth's *The Prelude* (Books I.–V.).
Rawnsley's *Literary Associations of the English Lakes*.
Knight's *Through the Wordsworth Country*.
Bradley's *Highways and Byways in the English Lakes*.
Jerrold's *Surrey* (Dent's County Guides).
Dewar's *Hampshire with Isle of Wight* (Dent's County Guides).
Ward's *The Canterbury Pilgrimage*.
Harper's *The Hardy Country*.
Snell's *The Blackmore Country*.
Melville's *The Thackeray Country*.
Kitton's *The Dickens Country*.
Sloan's *The Carlyle Country*.
Dougall's *The Burns Country*.
Crockett's *The Scott Country*.
Hill's *Jane Austen: Her Homes and Her Friends*.
Cook's *Homes and Haunts of John Ruskin*.
William Sharp's *Literary Geography and Travel Sketches* (Vol. IV. of *Works*) contains chapters on *The Country of Stevenson, The Country of George Meredith, The Country of Carlyle, The Country of George Eliot, The Brontë Country, Thackeray Land, The Thames from Oxford to the Nore*.
Hutton's *Literary Landmarks of Edinburgh*.
Stevenson's *Picturesque Notes on Edinburgh*.
Loftie's *Brief Account of Westminster Abbey*.
Parker's *Introduction to the Study of Gothic Architecture*.
Stanley's *Memorials of Westminster Abbey*.
Kimball's *An English Cathedral Journey*.
Singleton's *How to Visit the English Cathedrals*.
Bond's *The English Cathedrals* (200 illustrations).
Cram's *The Ruined Abbeys of Great Britain* (65 illustrations).
Home's *What to See in England*.
Boynton's *London in English Literature*.

GENERAL REFERENCE LIST FOR THE STUDY OF ENGLISH LITERATURE[1]

Cambridge History of English Literature, 14 vols.
Garnett and Gosse's *English Literature*, 4 vols.
Morley's *English Writers*, 11 vols.
Jusserand's *Literary History of the English People*.
Taine's *English Literature*.
Courthope's *History of English Poetry*, 6 vols.
Stephens and Lee's *Dictionary of National Biography* (dead authors).
New International Cyclopedia (living and dead authors).
English Men of Letters Series (abbreviated reference, E. M. L.)
Great Writers' Series (abbreviated reference, G. W.).
Poole's *Index* (and continuation volumes for reference to critical articles in periodicals).
The United States Catalogue and *Cumulative Book Index*.

SELECTIONS FROM ENGLISH LITERATURE[2]

* Pancoast and Spaeth's *Early English Poems*. (P. & S.) [3]
* Warren's *Treasury of English Literature, Part I.* (Origins to Eleventh Century: London, One Shilling.) (Warren.)
* Ward's *English Poets*, 4 vols. (Ward.)
* Bronson's *English Poems*, 4 vols. (Bronson.)
Oxford Treasury of English Literature, Vol. I., *Beowulf to Jacobean*;
* Vol. II., *Growth of the Drama*; Vol. III., *Jacobean to Victorian*. (*Oxford Treasury*.)
* *Oxford Book of English Verse*. (*Oxford*.)
* Craik's *English Prose*, 5 vols. (Craik.)
* Page's *British Poets of the Nineteenth Century*. (Page.)
Chambers's *Cyclopedia of English Literature*. (Chambers.)
Manly's *English Poetry* (from 1170). (Manly I.)
Manly's *English Prose* (from 1137). (Manly II.)
Century Readings for a Course in English Literature. (*Century*.)

---

[1] For special references to authors, movements, and the history of the period, see the lists under the heading, *Suggestions for Further Study*, at the end of each chapter. [2] School libraries should own books marked *.

[3] The abbreviation in parentheses after titles will be used in the *Suggested Readings* in place of the full title.

CHAPTER I

FROM 449 A.D. TO THE NORMAN CONQUEST, 1066

Subject Matter and Aim. — The history of English literature traces the development of the best poetry and prose written in English by the inhabitants of the British Isles. For more than twelve hundred years the Anglo-Saxon race has been producing this great literature, which includes among its achievements the incomparable work of Shakespeare.

This literature is so great in amount that the student who approaches the study without a guide is usually bewildered. He needs a history of English literature for the same reason that a traveler in England requires a guidebook. Such a history should do more than indicate where the choicest treasures of literature may be found; it should also show the interesting stages of development; it should emphasize some of the ideals that have made the Anglo-Saxons one of the most famous races in the world; and it should inspire a love for the reading of good literature.

No satisfactory definition of "literature" has ever been framed. Milton's conception of it was "something so written to after times, as they should not willingly let it die." Shakespeare's working definition of literature was something addressed not to after times but to an eternal present, and invested with such a touch of nature as to make the whole world kin. When he says of Duncan: —

"After life's fitful fever he sleeps well,"

he touches the feelings of mortals of all times and opens the door for imaginative activity, causing us to wonder why life should be a fitful fever, followed by an incommunicable sleep. Much of what we call literature would not survive the test of Shakespeare's definition; but true literature must appeal to imagination and feeling as well as to intellect. No mere definition can take the place of what may be called a feeling for literature. Such a feeling will develop as the best English poetry and prose are sympathetically read. Wordsworth had this feeling when he defined the poets as those: —

"Who gave us nobler loves and nobler cares."

The Mission of English Literature. — It is a pertinent question to ask, What has English literature to offer?

In the first place, to quote Ben Jonson: —

"The thirst that from the soul doth rise
Doth ask a drink divine."

English literature is of preëminent worth in helping to supply that thirst. It brings us face to face with great ideals, which increase our sense of responsibility for the stewardship of life and tend to raise the level of our individual achievement. We have a heightened sense of the demands which life makes and a better comprehension of the "far-off divine event" toward which we move, after we have heard Swinburne's ringing call: —

" . . . this thing is God,
To be man with thy might,
To grow straight in the strength
of thy spirit, and live out thy life
as the light."

We feel prompted to act on the suggestion of —

> " . . . him who sings
> To one clear harp in divers tones,
> That men may rise on stepping-stones
> Of their dead selves to higher things."[1]

In the second place, the various spiritual activities demanded for the interpretation of the best things in literature add to enjoyment. This pleasure, unlike that which arises from physical gratification, increases with age, and often becomes the principal source of entertainment as life advances. Shakespeare has Prospero say : —

> " . . . my library
> Was dukedom large enough."

The suggestions from great minds disclose vistas that we might never otherwise see. Browning truly says : —

> " . . . we're made so that we love
> First when we see them painted, things we have passed
> Perhaps a hundred times nor cared to see."

Sometimes it is only after reading Shakespeare that we can see —

> " . . . winking Mary buds begin
> To ope their golden eyes,
> With everything that pretty is,"

and only after spending some time in Wordsworth's company that the common objects of our daily life become invested with —

> "The glory and the freshness of a dream."

In the third place, we should emphasize the fact that one great function of English literature is to bring deliverance to souls weary with routine, despondent, or suffering

[1] Tennyson's *In Memoriam*.

the stroke of some affliction. In order to transfigure the everyday duties of life, there is need of imagination, of a vision such as the poets give. Without such a vision the tasks of life are drudgery. The dreams of the poets bring relief and incite to nobler action.

> "The soul hath need of prophet and redeemer.
>   Her outstretched wings against her prisoning bars,
> She waits for truth, and truth is with the dreamer
>   Persistent as the myriad light of stars."[1]

We need to listen to a poet like Browning, who —

> "Never doubted clouds would break,
>   Never dreamed, tho' right were worsted, wrong would triumph,
> Held we fall to rise, are baffled to fight better,
>   Sleep to wake."

In the fourth place, the twentieth century is emphasizing the fact that neither happiness nor perpetuity of government is possible without the development of a spirit of service, — a truth long since taught by English literature. We may learn this lesson from *Beowulf*, the first English epic, from Alfred the Great, from William Langland, and from Chaucer's *Parish Priest*. All Shakespeare's greatest and happiest characters, all the great failures of his dramas, are sermons on this text. In *The Tempest* he presents Ariel, tendering his service to Prospero: —

> "All hail, great master! grave sir, hail! I come
> To answer thy best pleasure."

Shakespeare delights to show Ferdinand winning Miranda through service, and Caliban remaining an abhorred creature because he detested service. Much of modern literature is an illuminated text on the glory of service. Coleridge

---

[1] Florence Earle Coates's *Dream the Great Dream.*

voiced for all the coming years what has grown to be almost an elemental feeling to the English-speaking race: —

> "He prayeth best who loveth best
> All things both great and small."

The Home and Migrations of the Anglo-Saxon Race. — Just as there was a time when no English foot had touched the shores of America, so there was a period when the ancestors of the English lived far away from the British Isles. For nearly four hundred years prior to the coming of the Anglo-Saxons, Britain had been a Roman province. In 410 A.D. the Romans withdrew their legions from Britain to protect Rome herself against swarms of Teutonic invaders. About 449 a band of Teutons, called Jutes, left Denmark, landed on the Isle of Thanet (in the northeastern part of Kent), and began the conquest of Britain. Warriors from the tribes of the Angles and the Saxons soon followed, and drove westward the original inhabitants, the Britons or Welsh, *i.e.* foreigners, as the Teutons styled the natives.

Before the invasion of Britain, the Teutons inhabited the central part of Europe as far south as the Rhine, a tract which in a large measure coincides with modern Germany. The Jutes, Angles, and Saxons were different tribes of Teutons. These ancestors of the English dwelt in Denmark and in the lands extending southward along the North Sea.

The Angles, an important Teutonic tribe, furnished the name for the new home, which was called Angle-land, afterward shortened into England. The language spoken by these tribes is generally called Anglo-Saxon or Saxon.

The Training of the Race. — The climate is a potent factor in determining the vigor and characteristics of a race. Nature reared the Teuton like a wise but not indulgent parent. By every method known to her, she endeavored to render him fit to colonize and sway the world. Summer paid him but a brief visit. His companions were the frost, the fluttering snowflake, the stinging hail. For music, instead of the soft notes of a shepherd's pipe under blue Italian or Grecian skies, he listened to the north wind whistling among the bare branches, or to the roar of an angry northern sea upon the bleak coast.

The feeble could not withstand the rigor of such a climate, in the absence of the comforts of civilization. Only the strongest in each generation survived; and these transmitted to their children increasing vigor. Warfare was incessant, not only with nature, but also with the surrounding tribes. Nature kept the Teuton in such a school until he seemed fit to colonize the world and to produce a literature that would appeal to humanity in every age.

The Early Teutonic Religion. — In the early days on the continent, before the Teuton had learned of Christianity, his religious beliefs received their most pronounced coloring from the rigors of his northern climate, from the Frost Giants, the personified forces of evil, with whom he battled. The kindly, life-bringing spring and summer, which seemed to him earth's redeeming divinity, were soon slain by the arrows that came from the winter's quivers. Not even Thor, the wielder of the thunderbolt, nor Woden, the All-Father, delayed the inevitable hour when the dusk of winter came, when the voice of Baldur

WODEN

could no longer be heard awaking earth to a new life. The approach of the "twilight of the gods," the *Götterdämmerung*, was a stern reality to the Teuton.

Although instinct with gloomy fatalism, this religion taught bravery. None but the brave were invited to Valhalla to become Woden's guest. The brave man might perish, but even then he won victory; for he was invited to sit with heroes at the table of the gods. "None but the brave deserves the fair," is merely a modern softened rendering of the old spirit.

The Christian religion, which was brought to the Teuton after he had come to England, found him already cast in a semi-heroic mold. But before he could proceed on his matchless career of world conquest, before he could produce a Shakespeare and plant his flag in the sunshine of every land, it was necessary for this new faith to develop in him the belief that a man of high ideals, working in unison with the divinity that shapes his end, may rise superior to fate and be given the strength to overcome the powers of evil and to mold the world to his will. The intensity of this faith, swaying an energetic race naturally fitted to respond to the great moral forces of the universe, has enabled the Anglo-Saxon to produce the world's greatest literature, to evolve the best government for developing human capabilities, and to make the whole world feel the effect of his ideals and force of character. At the close of the nineteenth century, a French philosopher wrote a book entitled *Anglo-Saxon Superiority, In What Does It Consist?* His answer was, "In self-reliance and in the happiness found in surmounting the material and moral difficulties of life." A study of the literature in which the ideals of the race are most artistically and effectively embodied will lead to much the same conclusion.

The History of Anglo-Saxon England. — The first task of the Anglo-Saxons after settling in England was to subdue the British, the race that has given King Arthur and his Knights of the Round Table to English literature. By 600 A.D., after a century and a half of struggle, the Anglo-Saxons had probably occupied about half of England.

They did not build on the civilization that Rome had left when she withdrew in 410, but destroyed the towns and lived in the country. The typical Englishman still loves to dwell in a country home. The work of Anglo-Saxon England consisted chiefly in tilling the soil and in fighting.

The year 597 marks an especially important date, the coming of St. Augustine, who brought the Christian faith to the Anglo-Saxons. Education, literature, and art followed, finding their home in the monasteries.

For nearly 400 years after coming to England, the different tribes were not united under one ruler. Not until 830 did Egbert, king of the West Saxons, become overlord of England. Before and after this time, the Danes repeatedly plundered the land. They finally settled in the eastern part above the Thames. Alfred (849–900), the greatest of Anglo-Saxon rulers, temporarily checked them, but in the latter part of the tenth century they were more troublesome, and in 1017 they made Canute, the Dane, king of England. Fortunately the Danes were of the same race, and they easily amalgamated with the Saxons.

These invasions wasted the energies of England during more than two centuries, but this long period of struggle brought little change to the institutions or manner of life in Anglo-Saxon England. The *witan*, or assembly of wise men, the forerunner of the present English parliament,

I. Founder of Eng. Drama
  1. Success of Blank verse
  2. Cast aside Classical unities

II. General Characteristics
  1. Reflects spirit of the Renaissance
  2. Adopt for hearts the impossible
  3. Each restoration
  4. Very little sense of humor
  5. Does not deserve attention
     Characters do not grow in the drama

Kinds of plays used in Eng. Drama
  (comparatively few in Eng. Drama)
  Founder of the Greek Drama

I. Miracle
II. Mystery
III. Morality

Christopher Marlowe 1564-1593

I. Birthplace — Canterbury

II. Education — Cambridge

III. Occupation —
   1. Actor
   2. Writer of plays.

IV. Works
  A. Dramas
    1. Tamburlaine, Lover of Conquest
    2. Dr. Faustus, Love of Knowledge
    3. The Jew of Malta, Love of Wealth.
    4. Edward II.

  B. Lyrical Poem:
    Hero and Leander

met in 1066 and chose Harold, the last Anglo-Saxon king.

During these six hundred years, the Anglo-Saxons conquered the British, accepted Christianity, fought the Danes, finally amalgamating with them, brought to England a lasting representative type of government, established the fundamental customs of the race, surpassed all contemporary western European peoples in the production of literature, and were ready to receive fresh impetus from the Normans in 1066.

The Anglo-Saxon Language. — Our oldest English literature is written in the language spoken by the Angles and the Saxons. This at first sight looks like a strange tongue to one conversant with modern English only; but the language that we employ to-day has the framework, the bone and sinew, of the earlier tongue. Modern English is no more unlike Anglo-Saxon than a bearded man is unlike his former childish self. A few examples will show the likeness and the difference. "The noble queen" would in Anglo-Saxon be *sēo æðele cwēn;* "the noble queen's," *ðære æðelan cwēne.* *Sēo* is the nominative feminine singular, *ðære* the genitive, of the definite article. The adjective and the noun also change their forms with the varying cases. In its inflections Anglo-Saxon resembles its sister language, the modern German.

After the first feeling of strangeness has passed away, it is easy to recognize many of the old words. Take, for instance, this from *Beowulf:* —

> ". . . ðȳ hē ðone fēond ofercwōm,
> gehnægde helle gāst."

Here are eight words, apparently strange, but even a novice soon recognizes five of them: *hē, fēond* (fiend), *ofercwōm* (overcame), *helle* (hell), *gāst* (ghost). The word *ðone*, strange as it looks, is merely the article "the."

> . . . therefore he overcame the fiend,
> Subdued the ghost of hell.

Let us take from the same poem another passage, containing the famous simile: —

> ". . . lēoht inne stōd,
> efne swā of hefene hādre scīneð
> rodores candel."

Of these eleven words, seven may be recognized: *lēoht* (light), *inne* (in), *stōd* (stood), *of*, *hefene* (heaven), *scīneð* (shineth), *candel* (candle).

> . . . a light stood within,
> Even so from heaven serenely shineth
> The firmament's candle.

Some prefer to use "Old English" in place of "Anglo-Saxon" in order to emphasize the continuity of the development of the language. It is, however, sometimes convenient to employ different terms for different periods of development of the same entity. We do not insist on calling a man a "grown boy," although there may be no absolute line of demarcation between boy and man.

Earliest Anglo-Saxon Literature. — As with the Greeks and Romans, so with the Teutons, poetry afforded the first literary outlet for the feelings. The first productions were handed down by memory. Poetry is easily memorized and naturally lends itself to singing and musical accompaniment. Under such circumstances, even prose would speedily fall into metrical form. Poetry is, furthermore, the most suitable vehicle of expression for the emotions. The ancients, unlike modern writers, seldom undertook to make literature unless they felt so deeply that silence was impossible.

The Form of Anglo-Saxon Poetry. — Each line is divided into two parts by a major pause. Because each of these parts was often printed as a complete line in old texts, *Beowulf* has sometimes been called a poem of 6368 lines, although it has but 3184.

A striking characteristic of Anglo-Saxon poetry is consonantal alliteration; that is, the repetition of the same consonant at the beginning of words in the same line: —

> "Grendel gongan; Godes yrre bær."
> Grendel going; God's anger bare.

The usual type of Anglo-Saxon poetry has two alliterations in the first half of the line and one in the second. The lines vary considerably in the number of syllables. The line from *Beowulf* quoted just above has nine syllables. The following line from the same poem has eleven: —

> "Flota fāmig-heals, fugle gelīcost."
> The floater foamy-necked, to a fowl most like.

This line, also from *Beowulf*, has eight syllables: —

> "Nīpende niht, and norðan wind."
> Noisome night, and northern wind.

Vowel alliteration is less common. Where this is employed, the vowels are generally different, as is shown in the principal words of the following line: —

> "On ēad, on ǣht, on eorcan stān."
> On wealth, on goods, on precious stone.

End rime is uncommon, but we must beware of thinking that there is no rhythm, for that is a pronounced characteristic. Anglo-Saxon verse was intended to be sung, and hence rhythm and accent or stress are important. Stress and the length of the line are varied; but we usually find that the four most important words, two in each half of the line, are stressed on their most important syllable. Alliteration usually shows where to place three stresses. A fourth stress generally falls on a word presenting an emphatic idea near the end of the line.

EXETER CATHEDRAL

The Manuscripts that have handed down Anglo-Saxon Literature. — The earliest Anglo-Saxon poetry was transmitted by the memories of men. Finally, with the slow growth of learning, a few acquired the art of writing, and transcribed on parchment a small portion of the current songs. The introduction of Christianity ushered in prose translations and a few original compositions, which were taken down on parchment and kept in the monasteries.

THE ANGLO-SAXON SCOP AND GLEEMAN

The study of Anglo-Saxon literature is comparatively recent, for its treasures have not been long accessible. Its most famous poem, *Beowulf*, was not printed until the dawn of the nineteenth century. In 1822 Dr. Blume, a German professor of law, happened to find in a monastery at Vercelli, Italy, a large volume of Anglo-Saxon manuscript, containing a number of fine poems and twenty-two sermons. This is now known as the *Vercelli Book*. No one knows how it happened to reach Italy. Another large parchment volume of poems and miscellany was deposited by Bishop Leofric at the cathedral of Exeter in Devonshire, about 1050 A.D. This collection, one of the prized treasures of that cathedral, is now called the *Exeter Book*.

Many valuable manuscripts were destroyed at the dissolution of the monasteries in the time of Henry VIII., between 1535 and 1540. John Bale, a contemporary writer, says that "those who purchased the monasteries reserved the books, some to scour their candlesticks, some to rub their boots, some they sold to the grocers and soap sellers, and some they sent over sea to the bookbinders, not in small numbers, but at times whole ships full, to the wondering of foreign nations."

The Anglo-Saxon Scop and Gleeman. — Our earliest poetry was made current and kept fresh in memory by the singers. The kings and nobles often attached to them a *scop*, or maker of verses. When the warriors, after some victorious battle, were feasting at their long tables, the banquet was not complete without the songs of the *scop*. While the warriors ate the flesh of boar and deer, and warmed their blood with horns of foaming ale, the *scop*, standing where the blaze from a pile of logs disclosed to him the grizzly features of the men, sang his most stirring songs, often accompanying them with the music of a rude harp. As the feasters roused his enthusiasm with their applause, he would sometimes indulge in an outburst of eloquent extempore song. Not infrequently the imagination of some king or noble would be fired, and he would sing of his own great deeds.

We read in *Beowulf* that in Hrothgar's famous hall —

> ". . . ðær wæs hearpan swēg,
> swutol sang scopes."

> . . . there was sound of harp
> Loud the singing of the scop.

In addition to the *scop*, who was more or less permanently attached to the royal court or hall of a noble, there was a craft of gleemen who roved from hall to hall. In the song of *Widsið* we catch a glimpse of the life of a gleeman : —

> " Swā scriðende gesceapum hweorfað
> glēomen gumena geond grunda fela."

> Thus roving, with shapéd songs there wander
> The gleemen of the people through many lands.

The *scop* was an originator of poetry, the gleeman more often a mere repeater, although this distinction in the use of the terms was not observed in later times.

The Songs of Scop and Gleeman. — The subject matter of these songs was suggested by the most common experiences of the time. These were with war, the sea, and death.

The oldest Anglo-Saxon song known, which is called *Widsið* or the *Far Traveler*, has been preserved in the *Exeter Book*. This song was probably composed in the older Angle-land on the continent and brought to England in the memories of the singers. The poem is an account of the wanderings of a gleeman over a great part of Europe. Such a song will mean little to us unless we can imaginatively represent the circumstances under which it was sung, the long hall with its tables of feasting, drinking warriors, the firelight throwing weird shadows among the smoky rafters. The imagination of the warriors would be roused as similar experiences of their own were suggested by these lines in Widsið's song: —

From the tapestry designed by H. A. Bone.
ANGLO-SAXON GLEEMAN

> "Ful oft of ðām hēape hwīnende flēag
> giellende gār on grome ðēode."
>
> Full oft from that host hissing flew
> The whistling spear on the fierce folk.

The gleeman ends this song with two thoughts characteristic of the poets of the Saxon race. He shows his love for noble deeds, and he next thinks of the shortness of life, as he sings: —

> "In mortal court his deeds are not unsung,
> Such as a noble man will show to men,
> Till all doth flit away, both life and light."

A greater *scop*, looking at life through Saxon eyes, sings : —

> "We are such stuff
> As dreams are made on; and our little life
> Is rounded with a sleep."[1]

The *scop* in the song called *The Wanderer* (*Exeter Book*) tells how fleeting are riches, friend, kinsman, maiden, — all the "earth-stead," and he also makes us think of Shakespeare's "insubstantial pageant faded" which leaves "not a rack behind."

Another old song, also found in the *Exeter Book*, is the *Seafarer*. We must imagine the *scop* recalling vivid experiences to our early ancestors with this song of the sea : —

> "Hail flew in hard showers,
> And nothing I heard
> But the wrath of the waters,
> The icy-cold way;
> At times the swan's song;
> In the scream of the gannet
> I sought for my joy,
> In the moan of the sea whelp
> For laughter of men,
> In the song of the sea-mew
> For drinking of mead."[2]

To show that love of the sea yet remains one of the characteristics of English poetry, we may quote by way of comparison a song sung more than a thousand years later, in Victoria's reign : —

> "The wind is as iron that rings,
>   The foam heads loosen and flee;
> It swells and welters and swings,
>   The pulse of the tide of the sea.

---

[1] Shakespeare's *The Tempest*, Act IV., Scene 1.
[2] Morley's translation, *English Writers*, Vol. II., p. 21.

THE SONGS OF SCOP AND GLEEMAN

> " Let the wind shake our flag like a feather,
>   Like the plumes of the foam of the sea!
>
> . . . .
>
> In the teeth of the hard glad weather,
>   In the blown wet face of the sea." [1]

Kipling in *A Song of the English* says of the sea: —

> " . . . there's never a wave of all her waves
>   But marks our English dead."

Another song from the *Exeter Book* is called *The Fortunes of Men*. It gives vivid pictures of certain phases of life among the Anglo-Saxons: —

> " One shall sharp hunger slay;
>   One shall the storms beat down;
>   One be destroyed by darts,
>   One die in war.
>   One shall live losing
>   The light of his eyes,
>   Feel blindly with fingers;
>   And one lame of foot,
>   With sinew-wound wearily
>   Wasteth away,
>   Musing and mourning,
>   With death in his mind.
>
> . . . . . .
>
> One shall die by the dagger,
>   In wrath, drenched with ale,
>   Wild through wine, on the mead bench
>   Too swift with his words;
>   Too lightly his life
>   Shall the wretched one lose." [2]

The songs that we have noted, together with *Beowulf*, the greatest of them all, will give a fair idea of *scopic* poetry.

[1] Swinburne's *A Song in Time of Order*.
[2] Morley's *English Writers*, Vol. II., pp. 33, 34.

BEOWULF

The Oldest Epic of the Teutonic Race. — The greatest monument of Anglo-Saxon poetry is called *Beowulf*, from the name of its hero. His character and exploits give unity and dignity to the poem and raise it to the rank of an epic.

The subject matter is partly historical and partly mythical. The deeds and character of an actual hero may have furnished the first suggestions for the songs, which were finally elaborated into *Beowulf*, as we now have it. The poem was probably a long time in process of evolution, and many different *scops* doubtless added new episodes to the song, altering it by expansion and contraction under the inspiration of different times and places. Finally, it seems probable that some one English poet gave the work its present form, making it a more unified whole, and incorporating in it Christian opinions.

We do not know when the first *scop* sang of Beowulf's exploits; but he probably began before the ancestors of the English came to England. We are unable to ascertain how long *Beowulf* was in process of evolution; but there is internal evidence for thinking that part of the poem could not have been composed before 500 A.D. Ten Brink, a great German authority, thinks that Beowulf was given its present form not far from 700 A.D. The unique manuscript in the British Museum is written in the West Saxon dialect of Alfred the Great's time (849–901).

The characters, scenery, and action of *Beowulf* belong to the older Angle-land on the continent of Europe; but the poem is essentially English, even though the chief action is laid in what is now known as Denmark and the southern part of Sweden. Hrothgar's hall, near which the hero performed two of his great exploits, was probably on the island of Seeland.

> Hƿæt ƿe Gardena in geardagum. þeod cyninga
> þrym gefrunon huða æþelingas elle
> fremedon. oft scyld scefing sceaþer
> þreatum monegū mægþum meodo setla

British Museum.
FACSIMILE OF BEGINNING OF COTTON MS. OF BEOWULF

TRANSLATION

> Lo! we, of the Gar-Danes in distant days,
> The folk-kings' fame have found,
> How deeds of daring the æthelings did.
> Oft Scyld-Scefing from hosts of scathers,
> From many men the mead seats [reft].

The student who wishes to enter into the spirit of the poem will do well to familiarize himself with the position of these coasts, and with a description of their natural features in winter as well as in summer. Heine says of the sea which Beowulf sailed: —

"Before me rolleth a waste of water . . . and above me go rolling the storm clouds, the formless dark gray daughters of air, which from the sea in cloudy buckets scoop up the water, ever wearied lifting and lifting, and then pour it again in the sea, a mournful, wearisome business. Over the sea, flat on his face, lies the monstrous, terrible North Wind, sighing and sinking his voice as in secret, like an old grumbler; for once in good humor, unto the ocean he talks, and he tells her wonderful stories."

Beowulf's Three Great Exploits. — The hero of the poem engaged in three great contests, all of which were prompted by unselfishness and by a desire to relieve human misery. Beowulf had much of the spirit that animates the social worker to-day. If such a hero should live in our time, he would probably be distinguished for social service, for fighting the forces of evil which cripple or destroy so many human beings.

Hrothgar, the king of the Danes, built a hall, named Heorot, where his followers could drink mead, listen to the scop, enjoy the music of the harp, and find solace in social intercourse during the dreary winter evenings.

> "So liv'd on all happy the host of the kinsmen
> In game and in glee, until one night began,
> A fiend out of hell-pit, the framing of evil,
> And Grendel forsooth the grim guest was hight,
> The mighty mark-strider the holder of moorland,
> The fen and the fastness."[1]

This monster, Grendel, came from the moors and devoured thirty of the thanes. For twelve winters he visited Heorot and killed some of the guests whenever he heard the sound of festivity in the hall, until at length the young hero Beowulf, who lived a day's sail from Hrothgar, determined to rescue Heorot from this curse. The youth selected fourteen warriors and on a "foamy-necked floater, most like to a bird," he sailed to Hrothgar.

Beowulf stated his mission, and he and his companions determined to remain in Heorot all night. Grendel heard them and came.

> ". . . he quickly laid hold of
> A soldier asleep, suddenly tore him,

[1] *Beowulf*, translated by William Morris and A. J. Wyatt.

Bit his bone-prison, the blood drank in currents,
Swallowed in mouthfuls."[1]

Bare-handed, Beowulf grappled with the monster, and they wrestled up and down the hall, which was shaken to its foundations. This terrible contest ended when Beowulf tore away the arm and shoulder of Grendel, who escaped to the marshes to die.

In honor of the victory, Hrothgar gave to Beowulf many presents and a banquet in Heorot. After the feast, the warriors slept in the hall, but Beowulf went to the palace. He had been gone but a short time, when in rushed Grendel's mother, to avenge the death of her son. She seized a warrior, the king's dearest friend, and carried him away. In the morning, the king said to Beowulf: —

"My trusty friend Æschere is dead. . . . The cruel hag has wreaked on him her vengeance. The country folk said there were two of them, one the semblance of a woman; the other, the specter of a man. Their haunt is in the remote land, in the crags of the wolf, the wind-beaten cliffs, and untrodden bogs, where the dismal stream plunges into the drear abyss of an awful lake, overhung with a dark and grizzly wood rooted down to the water's edge, where a lurid flame plays nightly on the surface of the flood — and there lives not the man who knows its depth! So dreadful is the place that the hunted stag, hard driven by the hounds, will rather die on the bank than find a shelter there. A place of terror! When the wind rises, the waves mingle hurly-burly with the clouds, the air is stifling and rumbles with thunder. To thee alone we look for relief."[2]

Beowulf knew that a second and harder contest was at hand, but without hesitation he followed the bloody trail of Grendel's mother, until it disappeared at the edge of a terrible flood. Undaunted by the dragons and serpents that made their home within the depths, he grasped a

[1] Translated by J. L. Hall.   [2] Earle's translation.

sword and plunged beneath the waves. After sinking what seemed to him a day's space, he saw Grendel's mother, who came forward to meet him. She dragged him into her dwelling, where there was no water, and the fight began. The issue was for a time doubtful; but at last Beowulf ran her through with a gigantic sword, and she fell dead upon the floor of her dwelling. A little distance away, he saw the dead body of Grendel. The hero cut off the head of the monster and hastened away to Hrothgar's court. After receiving much praise and many presents, Beowulf and his warriors sailed to their own land, where he ruled as king for fifty years.

He engaged in his third and hardest conflict when he was old. A firedrake, angered at the loss of a part of a treasure, which he had for three hundred years been guarding in a cavern, laid waste the land in the hero's kingdom. Although Beowulf knew that this dragon breathed flames of fire and that mortal man could not long withstand such weapons, he sought the cavern which sheltered the destroyer and fought the most terrible battle of his life. He killed the dragon, but received mortal hurt from the enveloping flames. The old hero had finally fallen; but he had through life fought a good fight, and he could say as the twilight passed into the dark: —

"I have ruled the people fifty years; no folk-king was there of them that dwelt about me durst touch me with his sword or cow me through terror. I bided at home the hours of destiny, guarded well mine own, sought not feuds with guile, swore not many an oath unjustly."[1]

The poem closes with this fitting epitaph for the hero: —

"Quoth they that he was a world-king forsooth,
The mildest of all men, unto men kindest,
To his folk the most gentlest, most yearning of fame."[2]

[1] Translated by Childs.   [2] Translated by Morris and Wyatt.

Wherein Beowulf is Typical of the Anglo-Saxon Race. — *Beowulf* is by far the most important Anglo-Saxon poem, because it presents in the rough the persistent characteristics of the race. This epic shows the ideals of our ancestors, what they held most dear, the way they lived and died.

I. We note the love of liberty and law, the readiness to fight any dragon that threatened these. The English *Magna Charta* and *Petition of Right* and the American *Declaration of Independence* are an extension of the application of the same principles embodied in *Beowulf*. The old-time spirit of war still prevails in all branches of the race; but the contest is to-day directed against dragons of a different type from Grendel, — against myriad forms of industrial and social injustice and against those forces which have been securing special privileges for some and denying equal opportunity for all.

II. *Beowulf* is a recognition in general of the great moral forces of the universe. The poem upholds the ideals of personal manliness, bravery, loyalty, devotion to duty. The hero has the ever-present consciousness that death is preferable to dishonor. He taught his thane to sing: —

> "Far better stainless death
> Than life's dishonored breath."

III. In this poem, the action outweighs the words. The keynote to *Beowulf* is deeds. In New England, more than a thousand years later, Thoreau wrote, "Be not simply good; be good for something." In reading other literatures, for instance the Celtic, we often find that the words overbalance the action. The Celt tells us that when two bulls fought, the "sky was darkened by the turf thrown up by their feet and by the foam from their mouths. The province rang with their roar and the inhabitants hid in caves or climbed the hills."

Again, more attention is paid to the worth of the subject matter and to sincerity of utterance than to mere form or polish. The literature of this race has usually been more distinguished for the value of the thought than for artistic presentation. Prejudice is felt to-day against matter that relies mainly on art to secure effects.

IV. Repression of sentiment is a marked characteristic of *Beowulf*, and it still remains a peculiarity of the Anglo-Saxon race. Some people say vastly more than they feel. This race has been inclined to feel more than it expresses. When it was transplanted to New England, the same characteristic was prominent, the same apparent contradiction between sentiment and stern, unrelenting devotion to duty. In *Snow Bound*, the New England poet, Whittier, paints this portrait of a New England maiden, still Anglo-Saxon to the core: —

> "A full, rich nature, free to trust,
> Truthful and almost sternly just,
> Impulsive, earnest, prompt to act,
> And make her generous thought a fact,
> Keeping with many a light disguise
> The secret of self-sacrifice."

No matter what stars now shine over them, the descendants of the English are still truthful and sternly just; they still dislike to give full expression to their feelings; they still endeavor to translate thoughts into deeds, and in this world where all need so much help, they take self-sacrifice as a matter of course. The spirit of *Beowulf*, softened and consecrated by religion, still persists in Anglo-Saxon thought and action.

THE CÆDMONIAN CYCLE

Cædmon. — In 597 St. Augustine began to teach the Christian religion to the Anglo-Saxons. The results of this teaching were shown in the subsequent literature. In what is known as Cædmon's *Paraphrase*, the next great Anglo-Saxon epic, there is no decrease in the warlike spirit. Instead of Grendel, we have Satan as the arch-enemy against whom the battle rages.

Cædmon, who died in 680, was until middle life a layman attached to the monastery at Whitby, on the northeast coast of Yorkshire. Since the *Paraphrase* has been attributed to Cædmon on the authority of the Saxon historian Bede, born in 673, we shall quote Bede himself on the subject, from his famous *Ecclesiastical History:* —

"Cædmon, having lived in a secular habit until he was well advanced in years, had never learned anything of versifying; for which reason, being sometimes at entertainments, where it was agreed for the sake of mirth that all present should sing in their turns, when he saw the instrument come toward him, he rose up from table and returned home.

"Having done so at a certain time, and gone out of the house where the entertainment was, to the stable, where he had to take care of the horses that night, he there composed himself to rest at the proper time; a person appeared to him in his sleep, and, saluting him by his name, said, 'Cædmon, sing some song to me.' He answered, 'I cannot sing; for that was the reason why I left the entertainment, and retired to this place, because I could not sing.' The other who talked to him replied, 'However, you shall sing.' 'What shall I sing?' rejoined he. 'Sing the beginning of created beings,' said the other. Hereupon he presently began to sing verses to the praise of God."

Cædmon remembered the poetry that he had composed in his dreams, and repeated it in the morning to the inmates of the monastery. They concluded that the gift of song was divinely given and invited him to enter the monastery and devote his time to poetry.

Of Cædmon's work Bede says: —

"He sang the creation of the world, the origin of man, and all the history of Genesis: and made many verses on the departure of the children of Israel out of Egypt, and their entering into the land of promise, with many other histories from Holy Writ; the incarnation, passion, resurrection of our Lord, and his ascension into heaven; the coming of the Holy Ghost, and the preaching of the Apostles; also the terror of future judgment, the horror of the pains of hell, and the delights of heaven."

The Authorship and Subject Matter of the Cædmonian Cycle. — The first edition of the *Paraphrase* was published in 1655 by Junius, an acquaintance of Milton. Junius attributed the entire *Paraphrase* to Cædmon, on the authority of the above quotations from Bede.

FACSIMILE OF BEGINNING OF JUNIAN MANUSCRIPT OF CÆDMON

TRANSLATION

For us it is mickle right that we should praise with words, love with our hearts, the Lord of the heavens, the glorious King of the people. He is the mighty power, the chief of all exalted creatures, Lord Almighty.

The *Paraphrase* is really composed of three separate poems: the *Genesis*, the *Exodus*, and the *Daniel;* and these are probably the works of different writers. Critics are not agreed whether any of these poems in their present form can be ascribed to Cædmon. The *Genesis* shows internal evidence of having been composed by several different writers, but some parts of this poem may be Cædmon's own work. The *Genesis*, like Milton's *Paradise Lost*, has for its subject matter the fall of man and its consequences. The *Exodus*, the work of an unknown writer, is a poem of much originality, on the escape of the children of Israel from Egypt, their passage through the Red Sea, and the destruction of Pharaoh's host. The *Daniel*, an uninteresting poem of 765 lines, paraphrases portions of the book of *Daniel* relating to Nebuchadnezzar's dreams, the fiery furnace, and Belshazzar's feast.

Characteristics of the Poetry. — No matter who wrote the *Paraphrase*, we have the poetry, a fact which critics too often overlook. Though the narrative sometimes closely follows the Biblical account in *Genesis*, *Exodus*, and *Daniel*, there are frequent unfettered outbursts of the imagination. The *Exodus* rings with the warlike notes of the victorious Teutonic race.

The *Genesis* possesses special interest for the student, since many of its strong passages show a marked likeness to certain parts of Milton's *Paradise Lost* (p. 244). As some critics have concluded that Milton must have been familiar with the Cædmonian *Genesis*, it will be instructive to note the parallelism between the two poems. Cædmon's hell is "without light and full of flame." Milton's flames emit no light; they only make "darkness visible." The following lines are from the *Genesis:* —

> "The Lord made anguish a reward, a home
> In banishment, hell groans, hard pain, and bade
> That torture house abide the joyless fall.
> When with eternal night and sulphur pains,

> Fullness of fire, dread cold, reek and red flames,
> He knew it filled."[1]

With this description we may compare these lines from Milton: —

> "A dungeon horrible, on all sides round,
>   As one great furnace flamed; yet from those flames
> No light; but rather darkness visible.
>   . . . a fiery deluge, fed
> With ever burning sulphur unconsumed."[2]

In Cædmon "the false Archangel and his band lay prone in liquid fire, scarce visible amid the clouds of rolling smoke." In Milton, Satan is shown lying "prone on the flood," struggling to escape "from off the tossing of these fiery waves," to a plain "void of light," except what comes from "the glimmering of these livid flames." The older poet sings with forceful simplicity: —

> "Then comes, at dawn, the east wind, keen with frost."

Milton writes: —

> ". . . the parching air
> Burns frore, and cold performs the effect of fire."[3]

When Satan rises on his wings to cross the flaming vault, the *Genesis* gives in one line an idea that Milton expands into two and a half: —

> "Swang ðæt fȳr on twā   fēondes cræfte."
> Struck the fire asunder with fiendish craft.

> ". . . on each hand the flames,
> Driven backward, slope their pointing spires, and, rolled
> In billows, leave i' th' midst a horrid vale."[4]

It is not certain that Milton ever knew of the existence of the Cædmonian *Genesis;* for he was blind three years

---

[1] Morley's translation. [2] *Paradise Lost,* Book I., lines 61–69.
[3] *Paradise Lost,* II., 594. [4] *Ibid.,* I., 222–224.

before it was published. But whether he knew of it or not, it is a striking fact that the temper of the Teutonic mind during a thousand years should have changed so little toward the choice and treatment of the subject of an epic, and that the first great poem known to have been written on English soil should in so many points have anticipated the greatest epic of the English race.

THE CYNEWULF CYCLE

Cynewulf is the only great Anglo-Saxon poet who affixed his name to certain poems and thus settled the question of their authorship. We know nothing of his life except what we infer from his poetry. He was probably born near the middle of the eighth century, and it is not unlikely that he passed part of his youth as a thane of some noble. He became a man of wide learning, well skilled in "word-craft" and in the Christian traditions of the time. Such learning could then hardly have been acquired outside of some monastery whither he may have retired.

Illuminated MS., British Museum.
ANGLO-SAXON MUSICIANS

In variety, inventiveness, and lyrical qualities, his poetry shows an advance over the Cædmonian cycle. He has a poet's love for the beauty of the sun and the moon (*heofon-condelle*), for the dew and the rain, for the strife of the waves (*holm-ðræce*), for the steeds of the sea (*sund-hengestas*), and for the "all-green" (*eal-grēne*) earth. "For Cynewulf," says a critic, "'earth's crammed with heaven and every common bush afire with God.'"

Cynewulf has inserted his name in runic characters in four poems: *Christ, Elene, Juliana,* a story of a Christian martyr, and the least important, *The Fates of the Apostles.* The *Christ,* a poem on the Savior's Nativity, Ascension, and Judgment of the world at the last day, sometimes suggests Dante's *Inferno* or *Paradiso,* and Milton's *Paradise Lost.* We see the —

> "Flame that welters up and of worms the fierce aspect,
> With the bitter-biting jaws — school of burning creatures."[1]

Cynewulf closes the *Christ* with almost as beautiful a conception of Paradise as Dante's or Milton's, — a conception that could never have occurred to a poet of the warlike Saxon race before the introduction of Christianity: —

> "... Hunger is not there nor thirst,
> Sleep nor heavy sickness, nor the scorching of the Sun;
> Neither cold nor care."[1]

Elene is a dramatic poem, named from its heroine, Helena, the mother of the Roman emperor Constantine. A vision of the cross bearing the inscription, "With this shalt thou conquer," appeared to Constantine before a victorious battle and caused him to send his mother to the Holy Land to discover the true cross. The story of her successful voyage is given in the poem *Elene*. The miraculous power of the true cross among counterfeits is shown in a way that suggests kinship with the fourteenth century miracle plays (p. 147). A dead man is brought in contact with the first and the second

---

[1] Brooke's translation.

cross, but the watchers see no divine manifestation until he touches the third cross, when he is restored to life.

Elene and the *Dream of the Rood*, also probably written by Cynewulf, are an Anglo-Saxon apotheosis of the cross. Some of this Cynewulfian poetry is inscribed on the famous Ruthwell cross in Dumfriesshire.

Andreas and Phœnix. — Cynewulf is probably the author of *Andreas*, an unsigned poem of special excellence and dramatic power. The poem, "a romance of the sea," describes St. Andrew's voyage to Mermedonia to deliver St. Matthew from the savages. The Savior in disguise is the Pilot. The dialogue between him and St. Andrew is specially fine. The saint has all the admiration of a Viking for his unknown Pilot, who stands at the helm in a gale and manages the vessel as he would a thought.

Although the poet tells of a voyage in eastern seas, he is describing the German ocean : —

> " Then was sorely troubled,
> Sorely wrought the whale-mere. Wallowed there the Horn-fish,
> Glode the great deep through ; and the gray-backed gull
> Slaughter-greedy wheeled. Dark the storm-sun grew,
> Waxed the winds up, grinded waves ;
> Stirred the surges, groaned the cordage,
> Wet with breaking sea."[1]

Cynewulf is also the probable author of the *Phœnix*, which is in part an adaptation of an old Latin poem. The *Phœnix* is the only Saxon poem that gives us the rich scenery of the South, in place of the stern northern landscape. He thus describes the land where this fabulous bird dwells : —

> "Calm and fair this glorious field, flashes there the sunny grove;
> Happy is the holt of trees, never withers fruitage there.

[1] Brooke's translation.

Bright are there the blossoms. . . .
In that home the hating foe houses not at all,

. . . .

Neither sleep nor sadness, nor the sick man's weary bed,
Nor the winter-whirling snow. . . .
. . . but the liquid streamlets,
Wonderfully beautiful, from their wells upspringing,
Softly lap the land with their lovely floods."[1]

GENERAL CHARACTERISTICS OF ANGLO-SAXON POETRY

Martial Spirit. — The love of war is very marked in Anglo-Saxon poetry. This characteristic might have been expected in the songs of a race that had withstood the well-nigh all-conquering arm of the vast Roman Empire.

Our study of *Beowulf* has already shown the intensity of the martial spirit in heathen times. These lines from the *Fight at Finnsburg*, dating from about the same time as *Beowulf*, have only the flash of the sword to lighten their gloom. They introduce the raven, for whom the Saxon felt it his duty to provide food on the battlefield: —

". . . hræfen wandrode
sweart and sealo-brūn; swurd-lēoma stōd
swylce eal Finns-buruh fȳrenu wǣre."

. . . the raven wandered
Swart and sallow-brown; the sword-flash stood
As if all Finnsburg were afire.

The love of war is almost as marked in the Christian poetry. There are vivid pictures of battle against the heathen and the enemies of God, as shown by the following selection from one of the poems of the Cædmonian cycle: —

"Helmeted men went from the holy burgh,
  At the first reddening of dawn, to fight:

[1] Brooke's translation.

> Loud stormed the din of shields.
> For that rejoiced the lank wolf in the wood,
> And the black raven, slaughter-greedy bird."[1]

Judith, a fragment of a religious poem, is aflame with the spirit of war. One of its lines tells how a bird of prey —

> "Sang with its horny beak the song of war."

This very line aptly characterizes one of the emphatic qualities of Anglo-Saxon poetry.

The poems often describe battle as if it were an enjoyable game. They mention the "play of the spear" and speak of "putting to sleep with the sword," as if the din of war were in their ears a slumber melody.

One of the latest of Anglo-Saxon poems, *The Battle of Brunanburh*, 937, is a famous example of war poetry. We quote a few lines from Tennyson's excellent translation: —

> "Grimly with swords that were sharp from the grindstone,
> Fiercely we hack'd at the flyers before us.
> . . . .
> Five young kings put asleep by the sword-stroke
> Seven strong earls of the army of Anlaf
> Fell on the war-field, numberless numbers."

Love of the Sea. — The Anglo-Saxon fondness for the sea has been noted, together with the fact that this characteristic has been transmitted to more recent English poetry. Our forefathers rank among the best seamen that the world has ever known. Had they not loved to dare an unknown sea, English literature might not have existed, and the sun might never have risen on any English flag.

[1] Morley's translation.

The *scop* sings thus of Beowulf's adventure on the North Sea:—

> "Swoln were the surges, of storms 'twas the coldest,
> Dark grew the night, and northern the wind,
> Rattling and roaring, rough were the billows."[1]

In the *Seafarer*, the *scop* also sings:—

> "My mind now is set,
> My heart's thought, on wide waters,
> The home of the whale;
> It wanders away
> Beyond limits of land.
>
> . . . . . .
>
> And stirs the mind's longing
> To travel the way that is trackless."[2]

In the *Andreas*, the poet speaks of the ship in one of the most charming of Saxon similes:—

> "Foaming Ocean beats our steed: full of speed this boat is;
> Fares along foam-throated, flieth on the wave,
> Likest to a bird."[3]

Some of the most striking Saxon epithets are applied to the sea. We may instance such a compound as *ār-ge-bland* (*ār*, "oar"; *blendan*, "to blend"), which conveys the idea of the companionship of the oar with the sea. From this compound, modern poets have borrowed their "oar-disturbéd sea," "oaréd sea," "oar-blending sea," and "oar-wedded sea." The Anglo-Saxon poets call the sun rising or setting in the sea the *mere-candel*. In *Beowulf*, *mere-strǣta*, "sea-streets," are spoken of as if they were the easily traversed avenues of a town.

Figures of Rhetoric. — A special characteristic of Anglo-Saxon poetry is the rarity of similes. In Homer they are

---

[1] Brooke's translation.   [2] Morley's translation.
[3] Brooke's translation.

frequent, but Anglo-Saxon verse is too abrupt and rapid in the succession of images to employ the expanded simile. The long poem of *Beowulf* contains only five similes, and these are of the shorter kind. Two of them, the comparison of the light in Grendel's dwelling to the beams of the sun, and of a vessel to a flying bird, have been given in the original Anglo-Saxon on pages 16, 17. Other similes compare the light from Grendel's eyes to a flame, and the nails on his fingers to steel: while the most complete simile says that the sword, when bathed in the monster's poisonous blood, melted like ice.

On the other hand, this poetry uses many direct and forcible metaphors, such as "wave-ropes" for ice, the "whale-road" or "swan-road" for the sea, the "foamy-necked floater" for a ship, the "war-adder" for an arrow, the "bone-house" for the body. The sword is said to sing a war song, the slain to be put to sleep with the sword, the sun to be a candle, the flood to boil. War is appropriately called the sword-game.

Parallelisms. — The repetition of the same ideas in slightly differing form, known as parallelism, is frequent. The author, wishing to make certain ideas emphatic, repeated them with varying phraseology. As the first sight of land is important to the sailor, the poet used four different terms for the shore that met Beowulf's eyes on his voyage to Hrothgar: *land, brimclifu, beorgas, sænæssas* (land, sea-cliffs, mountains, promontories).

This passage from the *Phœnix* shows how repetition emphasizes the absence of disagreeable things: —

">. . . there may neither snow nor rain,
Nor the furious air of frost, nor the flare of fire,
Nor the headlong squall of hail, nor the hoar frost's fall,
Nor the burning of the sun, nor the bitter cold,

> Nor the weather over-warm, nor the winter shower,
> Do their wrong to any wight."[1]

The general absence of cold is here made emphatic by mentioning special cold things: "snow," "frost," "hail," "hoar frost," "bitter cold," "winter shower." The absence of heat is emphasized in the same way.

Saxon contrasted with Celtic Imagery. — A critic rightly says: "The gay wit of the Celt would pour into the song of a few minutes more phrases of ornament than are to be found in the whole poem of *Beowulf*." In three lines of an old Celtic death song, we find three similes: —

> "Black as the raven was his brow;
> Sharp as a razor was his spear;
> White as lime was his skin."

We look in Anglo-Saxon poetry in vain for a touch like this: —

> "Sweetly a bird sang on a pear tree above the head of Gwenn before they covered him with a turf."[2]

Celtic literature shows more exaggeration, more love of color, and a deeper appreciation of nature in her gentler aspects. The Celt could write: —

> "More yellow was her head than the flower of the broom, and her skin was whiter than the foam of the wave, and fairer were her hands and fingers than the blossoms of the wood anemone amidst the spray of the meadow fountain."[3]

King Arthur and his romantic Knights of the Round Table are Celtic heroes. Possibly the Celtic strain persisting in many of the Scotch people inspires lines like these in more modern times: —

> "The corn-craik was chirming
> His sad eerie cry[4]

---

[1] Brooke's translation.   [2] *Llywarch's Lament for his Son Gwenn.*
[3] Guest's *Mabinogion*.   [4] William Motherwell's *Wearie's Well.*

And the wee stars were dreaming
Their path through the sky."

In order to produce a poet able to write both *A Midsummer Night's Dream* and *Hamlet*, the Celtic imagination must blend with the Anglo-Saxon seriousness. As we shall see, this was accomplished by the Norman conquest.

ANGLO-SAXON PROSE

When and where written. — We have seen that poetry normally precedes prose. The principal part of Anglo-Saxon poetry had been produced before much prose was written. The most productive poetic period was between 650 and 825. Near the close of the eighth century, the Danes began their plundering expeditions into England. By 800 they had destroyed the great northern monasteries, like the one at Whitby, where Cædmon is said to have composed the first religious song. As the home of poetry was in the north of England, these Danish inroads almost completely silenced the singers. What prose there was in the north was principally in Latin. On the other hand, the Saxon prose was produced chiefly in the south of England. The most glorious period of Anglo-Saxon prose was during Alfred's reign, 871–901.

Bede. — This famous monk (673–735) was probably the greatest teacher and the best known man of letters and scholar in all contemporary Europe. He is said to have translated the *Gospel of St. John* into Saxon, but the translation is lost. He wrote in Latin on a vast range of subjects, from the *Scriptures* to natural science, and from grammar to history. He has given a list of thirty-seven works of which he is the author. His most important work is the *Ecclesiastical History of the English People*, which is really a history of England from Julius Cæsar's invasion to 731. The quotation from Bede's work relative to Cædmon (p. 31) shows that Bede could relate things simply and well. He passed almost all his useful life at the monastery of Jarrow on the Tyne.

Alfred (849–901). — The deeds and thoughts of Alfred, king of the West Saxons from 871 until his death in 901, remain a strong moral influence on the world, although he died more than a thousand years ago. Posterity rightly gave him the surname of "the Great," as he is one of the comparatively few great men of all time. E. A. Freeman, the noted historian of the early English period, says of him : —

"No man recorded in history seems ever to have united so many great and good qualities. . . . A great part of his reign was taken up with warfare with an enemy [the Danes] who threatened the national being; yet he found means personally to do more for the general enlightenment of his people than any other king in English history."

After a Danish leader had outrageously broken his oaths to Alfred, the Dane's two boys and their mother fell into Alfred's hands, and he returned them unharmed. "Let us love the man," he wrote, "but hate his sins." His revision of the legal code, known as *Alfred's Laws*, shows high moral aim. He does not forget the slave, who was to be freed after six years of service. His administration of the law endeavored to secure the same justice for the poor as for the rich.

Alfred's example has caused many to stop making excuses for not doing more for their kind. If any one ever had an adequate excuse for not undertaking more work than his position absolutely demanded, that man was Alfred; yet his ill health and the wars with the Danes did not keep him from trying to educate his people or from earning the title, "father of English prose." Freeman even says that England owes to Alfred's prose writing and to the encouragement that he gave to other writers the "possession of a richer early literature than any other people of western Europe" and the maintenance of the habit of writing after the Norman conquest, when English was no longer used in courtly circles.

Although most of his works are translations from the Latin, yet he has left the stamp of his originality and sterling sense upon them all. Finding that his people needed textbooks in the native tongue, he studied Latin so that he might consult all accessible authorities and translate the most helpful works, making alterations and additions to suit his plan. For example, he found a Latin work on history and geography by Orosius, a Spanish Christian of the fifth century; but as this book contained much material that was unsuited to Alfred's purposes, he omitted some parts, changed others, and, after interviewing travelers from the far North, added much original matter. These additions, which even now are not uninteresting reading, are the best material in the book. This work is known as Alfred's *Orosius*.

Alfred also translated Pope Gregory's *Pastoral Rule* in order to show the clergy how to teach and care for their flocks. Alfred's own words at the beginning of the volume show how great was the need for the work. Speaking of the clergy, he says:—

"There were very few on this side Humber who would know how to render their services in English, or so much as translate an epistle out of Latin into English; and I ween that not many would be on the other side Humber. So few of them were there, that I cannot think of so much as a single one, south of Thames, when I took to the realm."[1]

Alfred produced a work on moral philosophy, by altering and amending the *De Consolatione Philosophiæ* of Bœthius, a noble Roman who was brutally thrown into prison and executed about 525 A.D. In simplicity and moral power, some of Alfred's original matter in this volume was not surpassed by any English writer for several hundred years. We frequently find such thoughts as, "If it be not in a man's power to do good, let him have the good intent." "True high birth is of the mind, not of the flesh." His *Prayer* in the same work makes us feel that he could see the divine touch in human nature:—

"No enmity hast Thou towards anything . . . Thou, O Lord, bringest together heavenly souls and earthly bodies, and minglest them in this world. As they came hither from Thee, even so they also seek to go hence to Thee."

Ælfric, 955 ?–1025 ?— The most famous theologian who followed Alfred's example in writing native English prose, and who took Alfred for his model, was a priest named Ælfric. His chief works are his *Homilies*, a series of sermons, and the *Lives of the Saints*. Although much of his writing is a compilation or a translation from the Latin Fathers, it is often remarkably vigorous in expression and stimulating to the reader. We find such thoughts as:—

"God hath wrought many miracles, and He performs them every day, but these miracles have become much less important in the sight of men

[1] Earle's translation.

because they are very common. . . . Spiritual miracles are greater than the physical ones."

To modern readers the most interesting of Ælfric's writings is his *Colloquium*, designed to teach Latin in the monastery at Winchester. The pupils were required to learn the Latin translation of his dialogues in the Anglo-Saxon vernacular. Some of these dialogues are to-day valuable illustrations of the social and industrial life of the time. The following is part of the conversation between the Teacher and the Plowman: —

"*Teacher*. What have you to say, plowman? How do you carry on your work?

"*Plowman*. O master, I work very hard; I go out at dawn, drive the oxen to the field, and yoke them to the plow. There is no storm so severe that I dare to hide at home, for fear of my lord, but when the oxen are yoked, and the share and coulter have been fastened to the plow, I must plow a whole acre or more every day.

. . . .

"*Teacher*. Oh! oh! the labor must be great!
"*Plowman*. It is indeed great drudgery, because I am not free."[1]

The Anglo-Saxon Chronicle. — This is the first history of any branch of the Teutonic people in their own tongue. The *Chronicle* has come down to us in several different texts, according as it was compiled or copied at different monasteries. The *Chronicle* was probably begun in Alfred's reign. The entries relating to earlier events were copied from Bede's *Ecclesiastical History* and from other Latin authorities. The *Chronicle* contains chiefly those events which each year impressed the clerical compilers as the most important in the history of the nation. This work is a fountainhead to which writers of the history of those times must turn.

[1] Cook and Tinker's *Select Translations from Old English Prose.*

A few extracts (translated) will show its character:—

"A.D. 449. This year ... Hengist and Horsa, invited by Vortigern, King of Britons, landed in Britain, on the shore which is called Wappidsfleet; at first in aid of the Britons, but afterwards they fought against them."

"806. This year the moon was eclipsed on the Kalends of September; and Eardulf, King of the Northumbrians, was driven from his kingdom; and Eanbert, Bishop of Hexham, died."

Sometimes the narrative is extremely vivid. Those who know the difficulty of describing anything impressively in a few words will realize the excellence of this portraiture of William the Conqueror:—

"1087. If any would know what manner of man King William was, the glory that he obtained, and of how many lands he was lord; then will we describe him as we have known him. ... He was mild to those good men who loved God, but severe beyond measure to those who withstood his will. ... So also was he a very stern and a wrathful man, so that none durst do anything against his will, and he kept in prison those earls who acted against his pleasure. He removed bishops from their sees, and abbots from their offices, and he imprisoned thanes, and at length he spared not his own brother, Odo. ... Amongst other things, the good order that William established is not to be forgotten; it was such that any man, who was himself aught, might travel over the kingdom with a bosom-full of gold, unmolested; and no man durst kill another. ... He made large forests for the deer, and enacted laws therewith, so that whoever killed a hart or a hind should be blinded ... and he loved the tall stags as if he were their father."

SUMMARY

The Anglo-Saxons, a branch of the Teutonic race, made permanent settlements in England about the middle of the fifth century A.D. Like modern German, their language is highly inflected. The most flourishing period of Anglo-Saxon poetry was between 650 and 825 A.D. It was produced for the most part in the north of England, which was overrun by the Danes about 800. These marauders destroyed many of the monasteries and silenced the voices of the singers. The prose was written chiefly in the south of England after the greatest poetic masterpieces had been produced. The Norman Conquest of England, beginning in 1066, brought the period to a close.

Among the poems of this age, we may emphasize: (1) the shorter *scopic* pieces, of which the *Far Traveler*, *The Wanderer*, *The Seafarer*, *The Fortunes of Men*, and *The Battle of Brunanburh* are important examples; (2) *Beowulf*, the greatest Anglo-Saxon epic poem, which describes the deeds of an unselfish hero, shows how the ancestors of the English lived and died, and reveals the elemental ideals of the race; (3) the *Cædmonian Cycle* of scriptural paraphrases, some of which have Miltonic qualities; and (4) the *Cynewulf Cycle*, which has the most variety and lyrical excellence. Both of these *Cycles* show how the introduction of Christianity affected poetry.

The subject matter of the poetry is principally war, the sea, and religion. The martial spirit and love of the sea are typical of the nation that has raised her flag in every clime. The chief qualities of the poetry are earnestness, somberness, and strength, rather than delicacy of touch, exuberance of imagination, or artistic adornment.

The golden period of prose coincides in large measure with Alfred's reign, 871–901, and he is the greatest prose writer. His translations of Latin works to serve as textbooks for his people contain excellent additions by him. Ælfric, a tenth century prose writer, has left a collection of sermons, called *Homilies*, and an interesting *Colloquium*, which throws strong lights on the social life of the time. The *Anglo-Saxon Chronicle* is an important record of contemporaneous events for the historian.

REFERENCES FOR FURTHER STUDY

HISTORICAL

In connection with the progress of literature, students should obtain for themselves a general idea of contemporary historical events from any of the following named works: —

Gardiner's *Students' History of England*, Green's *Short History of the English People*, Walker's *Essentials in English History*, Cheney's *A Short History of England*, Lingard's *History of England*, Traill's *Social England*, Vol. I., Ramsay's *The Foundations of England*.

LITERARY

Cambridge History of English Literature, Vol. I.

Brooke's *History of Early English Literature to the Accession of King Alfred*.

Morley's *English Writers*, Vols. I. and II.

Earle's *Anglo-Saxon Literature*.

Ten Brink's *Early English Literature*, Vol. I.

The Exeter Book, edited and translated by Gollancz (Early English Text Society).

Gurteen's *The Epic of the Fall of Man: A Comparative Study of Cædmon, Dante, and Milton*.

Cook's *The Christ of Cynewulf*. (The *Introduction* of 97 pages gives a valuable account of the life and writings of Cynewulf.)

Kennedy's *Translation of the Poems of Cynewulf*.

Bede's *Ecclesiastical History of England and the Anglo-Saxon Chronicle*, 1 vol., translated by Giles in Bohn's *Antiquarian Library*.

Snell's *The Age of Alfred*.

Pauli's *Life of Alfred* (Bohn's *Antiquarian Library*).

Gem's *An Anglo-Saxon Abbot: Ælfric of Eynsham*.

Mabinogion (a collection of Welsh fairy tales and romances, *Everyman's Library*), translated by Lady Charlotte Guest.

Pancoast and Spaeth's *Early English Poems* (abbreviated reference) ("P. & S.").

Cook and Tinker's *Select Translations from Old English Poetry* ("C. & T.").

Cook & Tinker's *Select Translations from Old English Prose* ("C. & T. *Prose*").

SUGGESTED READINGS

WITH QUESTIONS AND SUGGESTIONS

The student who is not familiar with the original Anglo-Saxon should read the translations specified below: —

Scopic Poetry.[1] — *Widsið* or the *Far Traveler*, translated in Morley's *English Writers*, Vol. II., 1–11, or in C. & T.,[2] 3–8.

The Wanderer, translated in P. & S., 65–68; C. & T., 50–55; Brooke, 364–367.

The Seafarer, translated in P. & S., 68–70; C. & T., 44–49; Morley, II., 21–26; Brooke, 362, 363.

The Fortunes of Men, trans. in P. & S., 79–81; Morley, II., 32–37.

Battle of Brunanburh, Tennyson's translation.

What were the chief subjects of the songs of the scop? How do they reveal the life of the time? Is there any common quality running through them? What qualities of this verse appear in modern poetry?

Beowulf. — This important poem should be read entire in one of the following translations: Child's *Beowulf* (*Riverside Literature Series*); Earle's *The Deeds of Beowulf, Done into Modern Prose* (Clarendon Press); Gummere's *The Oldest English Epic*; Morris and Wyatt's *The Tale of Beowulf*; Hall's *Beowulf, Translated into Modern Metres*; Lumsden's *Beowulf, an Old English Poem, Translated into Modern Rhymes* (the most readable poetic translation).

Translations of many of the best parts of *Beowulf* may be found in P. & S., 5–29; C. & T., 9–24; Morley, I., 278–310; Brooke, 26–73.

Where did the exploits celebrated in the poem take place? Where was Heorot? What was the probable time of the completion of *Beowulf*? Describe the hero's three exploits. What analogy is there between the conflict of natural forces in the Norseland and Beowulf's fight with Grendel? What different attitude toward nature is manifest in modern poetry? What is the moral lesson of the poem? Show that its chief characteristics are typical of the Anglo-Saxon race.

Cædmonian Cycle. — Some of the strongest passages may be found in P. & S., 30–45; C. & T., 104–120; Morley, II., 81–101; Brooke, 290–340. Read at the same time from Milton's *Paradise Lost*, Book I., lines 44–74, 169–184, 249–263, and *passim*.

---

[1] In his *Education of the Central Nervous System*, Chaps. VII.–X., the author has endeavored to give some special directions for securing definite ideas in the study of poetry.   [2] For full titles, see page 50.

What evidence do we find in this cycle of the introduction of Christianity? Who takes the place of Grendel? What account of Cædmon does Bede give? What is the subject matter of this cycle?

Cynewulf Cycle. — *The Poems of Cynewulf*, translated by C. W. Kennedy. Translations of parts of this cycle may be found in Whitman's *The Christ of Cynewulf*, and *The Exeter Book*, translated by Gollancz. Good selections are translated in P. & S., 46-55; C. & T., 79-103; and 132-142; Morley, II., 206-241; Brooke, 371-443. For selections from the *Phœnix*, see P. & S., 54-65; C. & T., 143-163.

What new qualities does this cycle show? What is the subject matter of its most important poems? What is especially noticeable about the *Andreas* and the *Phœnix?*

General Characteristics of the Verse. — What is its usual form? What most striking passages (*a*) in *Beowulf*, (*b*) elsewhere, show the Saxon love of war and of the sea? Instance some similes and make a list of vivid metaphors. What are the most striking parallelisms found in your readings? What conspicuous differences are there between Saxon and Celtic imagery? (See Morley, I., 165-239, or Guest's *Mabinogion*, also p. 42 of this volume.) What excellencies and defects seem to you most pronounced in Anglo-Saxon verse?

Prose. — The *Anglo-Saxon Chronicle* and Bede's *Ecclesiastical History* are both translated in one volume of Bohn's *Antiquarian Library*. The most interesting part of Bede for the student of literature is the chapter relating to Cædmon (Chap. XXIV., pp. 217-220).

In the *Chronicle*, read the entries for the years 871, 878, 897, 975, 1087, and 1137.

Alfred's *Orosius* is translated into modern English in the volume of Bohn's *Antiquarian Library* entitled, *Alfred the Great, his Life and Anglo-Saxon Works*, by Pauli. Sedgefield's translation of the *Consolations of Boethius* distinguishes the original matter by Alfred from the translation. Selections from Alfred's works are given in C. & T. (*Prose*), 85-146, and in Earle's *Anglo-Saxon Literature*, 186-206.

For selections from Ælfric, see C. & T. (*Prose*), 149-192. Read especially the *Colloquies*, 177-186.

What was Bede's principal work? Why has Alfred been called the "father of English prose"? What were his ideals? Mention his chief works and their object. What is the character of Ælfric's work? Why are modern readers interested in his *Colloquium?*

Why is the *Anglo-Saxon Chronicle* important?

CHAPTER II

FROM THE NORMAN CONQUEST, 1066, TO CHAUCER'S DEATH, 1400

From the Bayeaux tapestry.

THE DEATH OF HAROLD AT HASTINGS

The Norman Conquest. — The overthrow of the Saxon rule in England by William the Conqueror in 1066 was an event of vast importance to English literature. The Normans (Norsemen or Northmen), as they were called, a term which shows their northern extraction, were originally of the same blood as the English race. They settled in France in the ninth century, married French wives, and adopted the French language. In 1066 their leader, Duke William, and his army crossed the English Channel and won the battle of Hastings, in which Harold, the last Anglo-Saxon king, was killed. William thus became king of England.

Characteristics of the Normans. — The intermixture of Teutonic and French blood had given to the Normans the best qualities of both races. The Norman was nimble-witted, highly imaginative, and full of northern energy. The Saxon possessed dogged perseverance, good common sense, if he had long enough to think, and but little imagination. Some one has well said that the union of Norman with Saxon was like joining the swift spirit of the eagle to the strong body of the ox, or, again, that the Saxon furnished the dough, and the Norman the yeast. Had it not been for the blending of these necessary qualities in one race, English literature could not have become the first in the world. We see the characteristics of both the Teuton and the Norman in Shakespeare's greatest plays. A pure Saxon could not have turned from Hamlet's soliloquy to write: —

"Where the bee sucks, there suck I."[1]

Progress of the Nation, 1066-1400. — The Normans were specially successful in giving a strong central government to England. The feudal system, that custom of parceling out land in return for service, was so extended by William the Conqueror, that from king through noble to serf there was not a break in the interdependence of one human being on another. At first the Normans were the ruling classes and they looked down on the Saxons; but intermarriage and community of interests united both races into one strong nation before the close of the period.

There was great improvement in methods of administering justice. Accused persons no longer had to submit to the ordeal of the red-hot iron or to trial by combat, relying on heaven to decide their innocence. Ecclesiastical courts

[1] *The Tempest*, V., I.

lost their jurisdiction over civil cases. In the reign of Henry II. (1154–1189), great grandson of William the Conqueror, judges went on circuits, and the germ of the jury system was developed.

Parliament grew more influential, and the first half of the fourteenth century saw it organized into two bodies, — the Lords and the Commons. Three kings who governed tyrannically or unwisely were curbed or deposed. King John (1199–1216) was compelled to sign the *Magna Charta*, which reduced to writing certain foundation rights of his subjects. Edward II. (1307–1327) and Richard II. (1377–1399) were both deposed by Parliament. One of the reasons assigned for the deposition of Richard II. was his claim that " he alone could change and frame the laws of the kingdom."

The ideals of chivalry and the Crusades left their impress on the age. One English monarch, Richard the Lion-Hearted (1189–1199), was the popular hero of the Third Crusade. In *Ivanhoe* and *The Talisman*, Sir Walter Scott presents vivid pictures of knights and crusaders.

We may form some idea of the religious spirit of the Middle Ages from the Gothic cathedrals, which hold the same relative position in the world's architecture as Shakespeare's work does in literature. Travelers often declare that there is to-day nothing in England better worth seeing than these cathedrals, which were erected in the twelfth, thirteenth, and fourteenth centuries.[1]

The religious, social, and intellectual life of the time was profoundly affected by the coming of the friars (1220), who included the earnest followers of St. Francis (1182–1226), that Good Samaritan of the Middle Ages. The

[1] For the location of all the English cathedral towns, see the *Literary Map*, p. XII.

great philosopher and scientist, **Roger Bacon** (1214-1294), who was centuries in advance of his time, was a Franciscan friar. He studied at Oxford University, which had in his time become one of the great institutions of Europe.

The church fostered schools and learning, while the barons were fighting. Although William Langland (p. 76), a fourteenth-century cleric, pointed out the abuses which had crept into the church, he gave this testimony in its favor: —

"For if heaven be on this earth or any ease for the soul, it is in cloister or school. For in cloister no man cometh to chide or fight, and in school there is lowliness and love and liking to learn."

The rise of the common people was slow. During all this period the tillers of the soil were legally serfs, forbidden to change their location. The Black Death (1349) and the Peasants' Revolt (1381), although seemingly barren of results, helped them in their struggle toward emancipation. Some bought their freedom with part of their wages. Others escaped to the towns where new commercial activities needed more labor. Finally, the common toiler acquired more commanding influence by overthrowing even the French knights with his long bow. This period laid the foundation for the almost complete disappearance of serfdom in the fifteenth century. France waited for the terrible Revolution of 1789 to free her serfs. England anticipated other great modern nations in producing a literature of universal appeal because her common people began to throw off their shackles earlier.

This period opens with a victorious French army in England, followed by the rule of the conquerors, who made French the language of high life. It closes with the **ascendancy** of English government and speech at home and with the mid-fourteenth century victories of English armies on French soil, resulting in the capture of Calais, which remained for more than two hundred years in the possession of England.

At the close of this period we find Wycliffe, "the morning star of the Reformation," and Chaucer, the first great singer of the welded Anglo-Norman race. His wide interest in human beings and his knowledge of the new Italian literature prefigure the coming to England of the Revival of Learning in the next age.

It will now be necessary to study the changes in the language, which were so pronounced between 1066 and Chaucer's death.

THE EMERGENCE OF MODERN ENGLISH

Three Languages used in England. — For three hundred years after the Norman Conquest, three languages were widely used in England. The Normans introduced French, which was the language of the court and the aristocracy. William the Conqueror brought over many Norman priests, who used Latin almost exclusively in their service. The influence of this book Latin is generally underestimated by those who do not appreciate the power of the church. The Domesday survey shows that in 1085 the church and her dependents held more than one third of some counties.

In addition to the Latin and the French (which was itself principally of Latin origin), there was, thirdly, the Anglo-Saxon, to which the middle and the lower classes of the English stubbornly adhered.

The Loss of Inflections. — Anglo-Saxon was a language with changing endings, like modern German. If a Saxon wished to say, "good gifts," he had to have the proper case endings for both the adjective and the noun, and his expression was *gōde giefa*. For "the good gifts," he said *ðā gōdan giefa*, inflecting "the" and at the same time changing the case ending of "good."

The Norman Conquest helped to lop off these endings, which German has never entirely lost. We, however, no longer decline articles or ordinary adjectives. Instead of having our attention taken up with thinking of the proper endings, we are left free to attend to the thought rather than to the vehicle of its expression. Although our pronouns are still declined, the sole inflection of our nouns, with the exception of a few like *ox*, *oxen*, or *mouse*, *mice*, is the addition of *'s*, *s*, or *es* for the possessive and the plural. Modern German, on the other hand, still retains these troublesome case endings. How did English have the good fortune to lose them?

Whenever two peoples, speaking different languages, are closely associated, there is a tendency to drop the terminations and to use the stem word in all grammatical relations. If an English-speaking person, who knows only a little German, travels in Germany, he finds that he can make himself understood by using only one form of the noun or adjective. If he calls for "two large glasses of hot milk," employing the incorrect expression, *zwei gross Glass heiss Milch*, he will probably get the milk as quickly as if he had said correctly, *zwei grosse Gläser heisse Milch*. Neglect of the proper case endings may provoke a smile, but the tourist prefers that to starvation. Should the Germans and the English happen to be thrown together in nearly equal numbers on an island, the Germans would begin to drop the inflections that the English could not understand, and the German language would undergo a change.

If there were no books or newspapers to circulate a fixed form of speech, the alteration in the spoken tongue would be comparatively rapid.

Such dropping of terminations is precisely what did happen before the Norman Conquest in those parts of England most overrun by the Danes. There, the adjectives lost their terminations to indicate gender and case, and the article "the" ceased to be declined.

Even if the Normans had not come to England, the dropping of the inflections would not have ceased. Many authorities think that the grammatical structure of English would, even in the absence of that event, have evolved into something like its present form. Of course the Norman Conquest hastened many grammatical changes that would ultimately have resulted from inherent causes, but it did not exercise as great an influence as was formerly ascribed to it. Philologists find it impossible to assign the exact amount of change due to the Conquest and to other causes. Let us next notice some changes other than the loss of inflections.

Change in Gender. — Before any one could speak Anglo-Saxon correctly, he had first to learn the fanciful genders that were attached to nouns: "trousers" was feminine; "childhood," masculine; "child," neuter. During this period the English gradually lost those fanciful genders which the German still retains. A critic thus illustrates the use of genders in that language: "A German gentleman writes a masculine letter of feminine love to a neuter young lady with a feminine pen and feminine ink on masculine sheets of neuter paper, and incloses it in a masculine envelope with a feminine address to his darling, though neuter, Gretchen. He has a masculine head, a feminine hand, and a neuter heart."

Prefixes, Suffixes, and Self-explaining Compounds. — The English tongue lost much of its power of using prefixes. A prefix joined to a well-known word changes its meaning and renders the coining of a new term unnecessary. The Anglo-Saxons, by the use of prefixes, formed ten compounds from their verb *flōwan*, "to flow." Of these, only one survives in our "overflow." From *sittan*, "to sit," thirteen compounds were thus formed, but every one has perished. A larger percentage of suffixes was retained, and we still have many words like "wholesomeness," "child-hood," "sing-er."

The power of forming self-explaining compounds was largely lost. The Saxon compounded the words for "tree," and "worker," and said *trēow-wyrhta*, "tree-wright," but we now make use of the single word "carpenter." We have replaced the Saxon *bōc-cræft*, "book-art," by "literature"; *æfen-glōm*, "evening-gloom," by "twilight"; *mere-swīn*, "sea-swine," by "porpoise"; *ēag-wræc*, "eye-rack," by "pain in the eye"; *leornung-cild*, "learning-child," by "pupil." The title of an old work, *Ayen-bite of In-wit*, "Again-bite of In-wit," was translated into "Remorse of Conscience." *Grund-weall* and *word-hora* were displaced by "foundation" and "vocabulary." The German language still retains this power and calls a glove a "hand-shoe," a thimble a "finger-hat," and rolls up such clumsy compound expressions as *Unabhängigkeits-erklärung*.

We might lament this loss more if we did not remember that Shakespeare found our language ample for his needs, and that a considerable number of the old compounds still survive, as *home-stead, man-hood, in-sight, break-fast, house-hold, horse-back, ship-man, sea-shore, hand-work,* and *day-light.*

Introduction of New Words and Loss of Old Ones. — Since the Normans were for some time the governing race, while many of the Saxons occupied comparatively menial positions, numerous French words indicative of rank, power, science, luxury, and fashion were introduced. Many titles were derived from a French source. English thus obtained words like "sovereign," "royalty," "duke," "marquis," "mayor," and "clerk." Many terms of government are from the French; for instance, "parliament," "peers," "commons." The language of law abounds in French terms, like "damage," "trespass," "circuit," "judge," "jury," "verdict," "sentence," "counsel," "prisoner." Many words used in war, architecture, and medicine also have a French origin. Examples are "fort," "arch," "mason," "surgery." In fact, we find words from the French in almost every field. "Uncle" and "cousin," "rabbit" and "falcon," "trot" and "stable," "money" and "soldier," "reason" and "virtue," "Bible" and "preach," are instances in point.

French words often displaced Saxon ones. Thus, the Saxon *Hælend*, the Healer, gave way to the French *Savior*, *wanhope* and *wonstead* were displaced by *despair* and *residence*. Sometimes the Saxon stubbornly kept its place beside the French term. The English language is thus especially rich in synonyms, or rather in slightly differentiated forms of expression capable of denoting the exact shade of thought and feeling. The following words are instances: —

SAXON	FRENCH	SAXON	FRENCH
body	corpse	green	verdant
folk	people	food	nourishment
swine	pork	wrangle	contend
calf	veal	fatherly	paternal
worth	value	workman	laborer

English was enriched not only by those expressions gained from the daily speech of the Normans, but also by words that were added from literary Latin. Thus, we have the Saxon "ask," the Norman-French "inquire" and "question," and the Latin "interrogate." "Bold," "impudent," "audacious"; "bright," "cheerful," "animated"; "earnings," "wages," "remuneration"; "short," "brief," "concise," are other examples of words, largely synonymous, from the Saxon, the Norman-French, and the Latin, respectively. These facts explain why modern English has such a wealth of expression, although probably more than one half of the Anglo-Saxon vocabulary has been lost.

The Superiority of the Composite Tongue. — While we insist on the truth that Anglo-Saxon gained much of its wonderful directness and power from standing in close relations to earnest life, it is necessary to remember that many words of French origin did, by an apprenticeship at the fireside, in the field, the workshop, and the laboratory, equally fit themselves for taking their place in the language. Such words from French-Latin roots as "faith," "pray," "vein," "beast," "poor," "nurse," "flower," "taste," "state," and "fool" remain in our vocabulary because they were used in everyday life.

Pure Anglo-Saxon was a forcible language, but it lacked the wealth of expression and the flexibility necessary to respond to the most delicate touches of the mastermusicians who were to come. When Shakespeare has Lear say of Cordelia : —

> "Her voice was ever soft,
> Gentle, and low; an excellent thing in woman,"

we find that ten of the thirteen words are Saxon, but the other three of Romance (French) origin are as necessary

THE EMERGENCE OF MODERN ENGLISH

as is a small amount of tin added to copper to make bronze. Two of these three words express varying shades of quality.

Lounsbury well says: "There result, indeed, from the union of the foreign and native elements, a wealth of phraseology and a many-sidedness in English, which give it in these respects a superiority over any other modern cultivated tongue. German is strictly a pure Teutonic speech, but no native speaker of it claims for it any superiority over the English as an instrument of expression, while many are willing to concede its inferiority."

The Changes Slowly Accomplished. — For over a hundred years after the Conquest, but few French words found their way into current English use. This is shown by the fact that the *Brut*, a poem of 32,250 lines, translated from a French original into English about 1205, has not more than a hundred words of Norman-French origin.

At first the Normans despised the tongue of the conquered Saxons, but, as time progressed, the two races intermarried, and the children could hardly escape learning some Saxon words from their mothers or nurses. On the other hand, many well-to-do Saxons, like parents in later times, probably had their children taught French because it was considered aristocratic.

Until 1204 a knowledge of French was an absolute necessity to the nobles, as they frequently went back and forth between their estates in Normandy and in England. In 1204 King John lost Normandy, and in the next reign both English and French kings decreed that no subject of the one should hold land in the territory of the other. This narrowing of the attention of English subjects down to England was a foundation stone in building up the supremacy of the English tongue,

In 1338 began the Hundred Years' War between France and England. In Edward the Third's reign (1327-1377), it was demonstrated that one Englishman could whip six Frenchmen; and the language of a hostile and partly conquered race naturally began to occupy a less high position. In 1362 Parliament enacted that English should thereafter be used in law courts, "because the laws, customs, and statutes of this realm, be not commonly known in the same realm, for that they be pleaded, shewed, and judged in the French tongue, which is much unknown in the said realm."

LITERATURE OF THE PERIOD 1066-1400

Metrical Romances. — For nearly three hundred years after the Norman Conquest the chief literary productions were metrical romances, which were in the first instance usually written by Frenchmen, but sometimes by Englishmen (*e.g.* Layamon, p. 67) under French influence. There were four main cycles of French romance especially popular in England before the fifteenth century. These were tales of the remarkable adventures of King Arthur and his Knights, Charlemagne and his Peers, Alexander the Great, and the heroes at the siege of Troy. At the battle of Hastings a French minstrel is said to have sung the *Song of Roland* from the Charlemagne cycle.

These long stories in verse usually present the glory of chivalry, the religious faith, and the romantic loves of a feudal age. In *Beowulf*, woman plays a very minor part and there is no love story; but in these romances we often find woman and love in the ascendancy. One of them, well known to-day in song, *Tristram and Iseult* (Wagner's *Tristan und Isolde*), "a possession of our composite race," is almost entirely a story of romantic love.

The romances of this age that have most interest for English readers are those which relate to King Arthur and his Knights of the Round Table. The foundation suggestions for the most of this cycle are of British (Welsh) origin. This period would not have existed in vain, if it had given to the world nothing but these Arthurian ideals of generosity, courage, honor, and high endeavor, which are still a potent influence. In his *Idylls of the King*, Tennyson calls Arthur and his Knights: —

> "A glorious company, the flower of men,
> To serve as model for the mighty world,
> And be the fair beginning of a time."

The *Quest of the Holy Grail* belongs to the Arthurian cycle. Percival (Wagner's Parsifal), the hero of the earlier version and Sir Galahad of the later, show the same spirit that animated the knights in the Crusades. Tennyson introduces Sir Galahad as a knight whose strength is as the strength of ten because his heart is pure, undertaking "the far-quest after the divine." The American poet Lowell chose Sir Launfal, a less prominent figure in Arthurian romance, for the hero of his version of the search for the Grail, and had him find it in every sympathetic act along the common way of life.

The story of *Gawayne and the Green Knight*, "the jewel of English medieval literature," tells how Sir Gawayne, Arthur's favorite, fought with a giant called the Green Knight. The romance might almost be called a sermon, if it did not reveal in a more interesting way a great moral truth, — that deception weakens character and renders the deceiver vulnerable in life's contests. In preparing for the struggle, Sir Gawayne is guilty of one act of deceit. But for this, he would have emerged unscathed from the battle. One wound, which leaves a lasting scar, is the result of an apparently trivial deception. His purity and honor in all things else save him from death. This story, which reminds us of Spenser's *Faerie Queene*, presents in a new garb one of the oft-recurring ideals of the race, "keep troth" (truth). Chaucer sings in the same key:—

> "Hold the hye wey, and let thy gost thee lede,
> And trouthe shall delivere, it is no drede."

We should remember that these romances are the most characteristic literary creations of the Middle Ages, that they embody the new spirit of chivalry, religious faith, and romantic love in a feudal age, that they had a story to tell, and that some of them have never lost their influence on human ideals.

A Latin Chronicler. — One chronicler, **Geoffrey of Monmouth**, although he wrote in Latin, must receive some attention because of his vast influence on English poetry. He probably acquired his last name from being archdeacon of Monmouth. He was appointed Bishop of St. Asaph in 1152 and died about 1154. Unlike the majority of the monkish chroniclers, he possessed a vivid imagination, which he used in his so-called *History of the Kings of Britain*.

Geoffrey pretended to have found an old manuscript which related the deeds of all British kings from Brutus, the mythical founder of the kingdom of Britain, and the great-grandson of Æneas, to Cæsar. Geoffrey wrote an account of the traditionary British kings down to Cadwallader in 689 with as much minuteness and gravity as Swift employed in the *Voyage to Lilliput* (p. 281). Other chroniclers declared that Geoffrey lied saucily and shamelessly, but his book became extremely popular. The monks could not then comprehend that the world's greatest literary works were to be products of the imagination.

In Geoffrey of Monmouth's *History of the Kings of Britain* we are given vivid pictures of King Lear and his daughters, of Cymbeline, of King Arthur and his Knights, of Guinevere and the rest of that company whom later poets have immortalized. It is probable that Geoffrey was not particular whether he obtained his materials from old chroniclers, Welsh bards, floating tradition, or from his own imagination. His book left its impress on the historical imagination of the Middle Ages. Had it not been for Geoffrey's *History*, the dramas of *King Lear* and *Cymbeline* might never have been suggested to Shakespeare.

Layamon's Brut. — About 1155 a Frenchman named Wace translated into his own language Geoffrey of Monmouth's works. This translation fell into the hands of Layamon, a priest living in Worcestershire, who proceeded to render the poem, with additions of his own, into the Southern English dialect. Wace's *Brut* has 15,300 lines; Layamon's, 32,250. As the matter which Layamon added is the best in the poem, he is, in so far, an original author of much imaginative power. He is certainly the greatest poet between the Conquest and Chaucer's time.

A selection from the *Brut* will give the student an opportunity of comparing this transition English with the language in its modern form: —

" And Ich wulle varan to Avalun:	And I will fare to Avalon,
To vairest alre maidene,	To the fairest of all maidens,
To Argante ðere quene,	To Argante the queen,
Alven swiðe sceone;	Elf surpassing fair;
And heo scal mine wunden	And she shall my wounds
Makien alle isunde,	Make all sound,
Al hal me makien	All hale me make
Mid halweige drenchen.	With healing draughts.

And seoðe Ich cumen wulle	And afterwards I will come
To mine kineriche	To my kingdom
And wunien mid Brutten	And dwell with Britons
Mid muchelere wunne."	With much joy.

With this, compare the following lines from Tennyson's *The Passing of Arthur*: —

> ". . . I am going a long way
>
> . . . .
>
> To the island-valley of Avilion,
> Where falls not hail, or rain, or any snow,
> Nor ever wind blows loudly; but it lies
> Deep-meadow'd, happy, fair with orchard lawns
> And bowery hollows crown'd with summer sea,
> Where I will heal me of my grievous wound.
>
> . . . .
>
> He passes to be King among the dead,
> And after healing of his grievous wound
> He comes again."

Layamon employed less alliteration than is found in Anglo-Saxon poetry. He also used an occasional rime, but the accent and rhythm of his verse are more Saxon than modern. When reading Tennyson's *Idylls of the King*, we must not forget that Layamon was the first poet to celebrate in English King Arthur's deeds. The *Brut* shows little trace of French influences, not more than a hundred French words being found in it.

Orm's Ormulum. — A monk named Orm wrote in the Midland dialect a metrical paraphrase of those parts of the *Gospels* used in the church on each service day throughout the year. After the paraphrase comes his metrical explanation and application of the *Scripture*.

He says: —

> "Þiss boc iss nemmnedd Orrmulum
> Forrði ðatt Ormm itt wrohhte."
>
> This book is named Ormulum
> For that Orm it wrote.

There was no fixed spelling at this time. Orm generally doubled the consonant after a short vowel, and insisted that any one who copied his work should be careful to do the same. We shall find on counting the syllables in the two lines quoted from him that the first line has eight; the second, seven. This scheme is followed with great precision throughout the poem, which employs neither rime nor regular alliteration. Orm used even fewer French words than Layamon. The date of the *Ormulum* is probably somewhere between 1200 and 1215.

The Ancren Riwle. — About 1225 appeared the most notable prose work in the native tongue since the time of Alfred, if we except the *Anglo-Saxon Chronicle*. Three young ladies who had secluded themselves from the world in Dorsetshire, wished rules for guidance in their seclusion. An unknown author, to oblige them, wrote the *Ancren Riwle* (Rule of Anchoresses). This book not only lays down rules for their future conduct in all the affairs of life, but also offers much religious consolation.

The following selection shows some of the curious rules for the guidance of the anchoresses, and furnishes a specimen of the Southern dialect of transitional English prose in the early part of the thirteenth century: —

"ȝe, mine leoue sustren,	Ye, my beloved sisters,
ne schulen habben no best	shall have no beast
bute kat one. . . . ȝe schulen	but one cat. . . . Ye shall
beon i-dodded four siðen	be cropped four times
iðe ȝere, uorto lihten ower	in the year for to lighten your
heaued. . . . Of idelnesse awakeneð	head. . . . Of idleness ariseth
muchel flesshes fondunge. . . .	much temptation of the flesh. . . .
Iren ðet lið stille gedereð	Iron that lieth still soon gathereth
sone rust."	rust.

The keynote of the work is the renunciation of self. Few productions of modern literature contain finer pictures

" Þe sixte kunfort is ðet ure Louerd, hwon he iðoleð ðet we beoð itented, he plaieð mid us, ase ðe moder mid hire ȝunge deorlinge; vlihð from him, and hut hire, and let hit sitten one, and loken ȝeorne abuten, and cleopien Dame! dame! and weopen one hwule; and ðeonne mid i-spredde ermes leapeð lauhwinde vorð, and cluppeð and cusseð and wipeð his eien. Riht so ure Louerd let us one iwurðen oðer hwules, and wiðdraweð his grace and his kunfort, ðet we ne ivindeð swetnesse in none ðinge ðet we wel doð, ne savur of heorte; and ðauh, iðet ilke point ne luveð he us ure leove veder never ðe lesce, auh he deð hit for muchel luve ðet he haveð to us."

The sixth comfort is that our Lord, when he suffers that we be tempted, he plays with us, as the mother with her young darling; she flees from it, and hides herself, and lets it sit alone and look anxiously about and cry "Dame! dame!" and weep awhile; and then with out-spread arms leaps laughing forth and clasps and kisses it and wipes its eyes. Exactly so our Lord leaves us alone once in a while and withdraws his grace and his comfort, that we find sweetness in nothing that we do well, no relish of heart; and notwithstanding, at the same time, he, our dear Father, loves us nevertheless, but he does it for the great love that he has for us.

Professor Sweet calls the *Ancren Riwle* "one of the most perfect models of simple, natural, eloquent prose in our language." For its introduction of French words, this work occupies a prominent place in the development of the English language. Among the words of French origin found in it, we may instance: "dainty," "cruelty," "vestments," "comfort," "journey," "mercer."

Lyrical Poetry. — A famous British Museum manuscript, known as *Harleian MS., No. 2253*, which was transcribed about 1310, contains a fine anthology of English lyrics, some of which may have been composed early in the thirteenth century. The best of these are love lyrics, but they are less remarkable for an expression of the tender passion than for a genuine appreciation of nature. Some of them are full of the joy of birds and flowers and warm spring days.

A lover's song, called *Alysoun*, is one of the best of these lyrics:—

> "Bytuene Mershe ant [1] Averil [2]
> When spray biginneth to spring,
> The lutel [3] foul hath hire wyl
> On hyre lud [4] to synge."

A famous spring lyric beginning:—

> "Lenten [5] ys come with love to toune,[6]
> With blosmen ant with briddes [7] roune," [8]

is a symphony of daisies, roses, "lovesome lilies," thrushes, and "notes suete of nyhtegales."

The refrain of one love song is invigorating with the breath of the northern wind:—

> "Blou, northerne wynd!
> Send thou me my suetyng!
> Blou, northerne wynd! blou, blou, blou!"

The *Cuckoo Song*, which is perhaps older than any of these, is the best known of all the early lyrics:—

"Sumer is i-cumen in	Summer is a-coming in,
Lhude sing cuccu	Loud sing cuckoo,
Groweth sed and bloweth med	Groweth seed and bloometh mead,
And springeth the wde nu.	And springeth the wood now.
Sing cuccu, cuccu."	Sing cuckoo, cuckoo.

A more somber note is heard in the religious lyrics:—

> "Wynter wakeneth al my care,
> Nou this leves waxeth bare;
> Ofte I sike [9] ant mourne sare [10]
> When hit cometh in my thoht
> Of this worldes joie, hou hit goth al to noht."

---

[1] and.   [2] April.   [3] little.   [4] in her language.   [5] Spring.
[6] in its turn.   [7] birds.   [8] song.   [9] sigh.   [10] sorely.

We do not know the names of any of these singers, but they were worthy forerunners of the later lyrists of love and nature.

Robert Manning of Brunne. — We have now come to fourteenth-century literature, which begins to wear a more modern aspect. Robert Manning, generally known as Robert of Brunne, because he was born at Brunne, now called Bourn, in Lincolnshire, adapted from a Norman-French original a work entitled *Handlyng Synne* (*Manual of Sins*). This book, written in the Midland dialect in 1303, discourses of the Seven Deadly Sins and the best ways of living a godly life.

A careful inspection of the following selection from the *Handlyng Synne* will show that, aside from the spelling, the English is essentially modern. Most persons will be able to understand all but a few words. He was the first prominent English writer to use the modern order of words. The end rime is also modern. A beggar, seeing a beast laden with bread at the house of a rich man, asks for food. The poem says of the rich man: —

"He stouped down to seke a stone,	He stooped down to seek a stone,
But, as hap was, than fonde he none.	But, as chance was, then found he none.
For the stone he toke a lofe,	For the stone he took a loaf,
And at the pore man hyt drofe.	And at the poor man it drove.
The pore man hente hyt up belyue,	The poor man caught it up quickly,
And was thereof ful ferly blythe,	And was thereof full strangely glad,
To hys felaws fast he ran	To his fellows fast he ran
With the lofe, thys pore man."	With the loaf, this poor man.

Oliphant says: "Strange it is that Dante should have been compiling his *Inferno*, which settled the course of Italian literature forever, in the selfsame years that Robert of Brunne was compiling the earliest pattern of well-formed

New English. . . . Almost every one of the Teutonic changes in idiom, distinguishing the New English from the Old, the speech of Queen Victoria from the speech of Hengist, is to be found in Manning's work."

Mandeville's Travels. — Sir John Mandeville, who is popularly considered the author of a very entertaining work of travels, states that he was born in St. Albans in 1300, that he left England in 1322, and traveled in the East for thirty-four years. His *Travels* relates what he saw and heard in his wanderings through Ethiopia, Persia, Tartary, India, and Cathay. What he tells on his own authority, he vouches for as true, but what he relates as hearsay, he leaves to the reader's judgment for belief.

No such single traveler as Mandeville ever existed. The work attributed to him has been proved to be a compilation from the writings of other travelers. A French critic says wittily: "He first lost his character as a truthful writer; then out of the three versions of his book, French, English, and Latin, two were withdrawn from him, leaving him only the first. Existence has now been taken from him, and he is left with nothing at all." No matter, however, who the author was, the book exists. More manuscripts of it survive than of any other work except the *Scriptures*. It is the most entertaining volume of English prose that we have before 1360. The sentences are simple and direct, and they describe things vividly: —

Old print from Edition of 1725.
WHAT MANDEVILLE SAW

"In Ethiope ben many dyverse folk: and Ethiope is clept [1] Cusis In that contree ben folk, that han but o foot: and thei gon so fast, that it is marvaylle: and the foot is so large, that it schadewethe alle the body azen [2] the Sonne whanne thei wole [3] lye and reste hem." [4]

From an old print.

JOHN WYCLIFFE

Mandeville also tells of a bird that used to amuse itself by flying away with an elephant in its talons. In the land of Prester John was a valley where Mandeville says he saw devils jumping about as thick as grasshoppers. Stories like these make the work as interesting as *Gulliver's Travels.*

The so-called Mandeville's *Travels* was one of the few works that the unlearned of that age could understand

[1] called.   [2] against.   [3] will.   [4] them.

and enjoy. Consequently its popularity was so great as to bring a large number of French words into familiar use. The native "againbought" is, however, used instead of the foreign "redeemed."

John Wycliffe. — Wycliffe (1324–1384) was born at Hipswell, near Richmond, in the northern part of Yorkshire. He became a doctor of divinity and a master of one of the colleges at Oxford. Afterward he was installed vicar of Lutterworth in Leicestershire, where he died. In history he is principally known as the first great figure in the English Reformation. He preceded the other reformers by more than a century. In literature he is best known for the first complete translation of the *Bible*,— a work that exerted great influence on English prose. All the translation was not made by him personally, but all was done under his direction. The translation of most of the *New Testament* is thought to be his own special work. He is the most important prose writer of the fourteenth century. His prose had an influence as wide as the circulation of the *Bible*. The fact that it was forced to circulate in manuscript, because printing had not then been invented, limited his readers; but his translation was, nevertheless, read by many. To help the cause of the Reformation, he wrote argumentative religious pamphlets, which are excellent specimens of energetic fourteenth-century prose.

Of his place in literature, Ten Brink says: "Wycliffe's literary importance lies in the fact that he extended the domain of English prose and enhanced its powers of expression. He accustomed it to terse reasoning, and perfected it as an instrument for expressing rigorous logical thought and argument; he brought it into the service of great ideas and questions of the day, and made it the medium of polemics and satire. And above all, he raised it to the dignity of the national language of the *Bible*."

The following is a specimen verse of Wycliffe's translation. We may note that the strong old English word "againrising" had not then been displaced by the Latin "resurrection."

"Jhesu seith to hir, I am agenrisyng and lyf; he that bileueth in me, he, if he schal be deed, schall lyue."

Piers Plowman. — *The Vision of William Concerning Piers the Plowman*, popularly called *Piers Plowman*, from its most important character, is the name of an allegorical poem, the first draft ("A" text) of which was probably composed about 1362. Later in the century two other versions, known as texts "B" and "C" appeared. Authorities differ in regard to whether these are the work of the same man. *The Vision* is the first and the most interesting part of a much longer work, known as *Liber de Petro Plowman* (*The Book of Piers the Plowman*).

The authorship of the poem is not certainly known, but it has long been ascribed to William Langland, born about 1322 at Cleobury Mortimer in Shropshire. The author of *Piers Plowman* seems to have performed certain functions connected with the church, such as singing at funerals.

Piers Plowman opens on a pleasant May morning amid rural scenery. The poet falls asleep by the side of a brook and dreams. In his dream he has a vision of the world passing before his eyes, like a drama. The poem tells what he saw. Its opening lines are : —

"In a *s*omer *s*eson · whan *s*oft was the *s*onne
I *sh*ope[1] me in *sh*roudes[2] · as I a *sh*epe[3] were

[1] arrayed.   [2] garments.   [3] shepherd.

In *h*abite as an *h*eremite[1] · un*h*oly of workes
*W*ent *w*yde in þis *w*orld · *w*ondres to here
Ac on a *M*ay *m*ornynge · on *M*aluerne hulles[2]
Me by*f*el a *f*erly[3] · of *f*airy me þouȝ te
I *w*as *w*ery for*w*andred[4] · and *w*ent me to reste
Under a *b*rode *b*ank · *b*i a *b*ornes[5] side,
And as I *l*ay and *l*ened[6] · and *l*oked in þe waters
I *s*lombred in a *s*lepyng · it *s*weyved[7] so merye."

The language of *Piers Plowman* is a mixture of the Southern and the Midland dialects. It should be noticed

From a manuscript in Trinity College, Cambridge.

TREUTHE'S PILGRYME ATTE PLOW

that the poem employs the old Anglo-Saxon alliterative meter. There is no end rime. *Piers Plowman* is the last great poem written in this way.

The actors in this poem are largely allegorical. Abstractions are personified. Prominent characters are Conscience, Lady Meed or Bribery, Reason, Truth, Gluttony,

[1] hermit.   [2] hills.   [3] wonder.   [4] tired out with wandering.
[5] brook.   [6] reclined.   [7] sounded.

Hunger, and the Seven Deadly Sins. In some respects, the poem is not unlike the *Pilgrim's Progress* (p. 230), for the battle in passing from this life to the next is well described in both; but there are more humor, satire, and descriptions of common life in Langland. Piers is at first a simple plowman, who offers to guide men to truth. He is finally identified with the Savior.

Throughout the poem, the writer displays all the old Saxon earnestness. His hatred of hypocrisy is manifest on every page. His sadness, because things are not as they ought to be, makes itself constantly felt. He cannot reconcile the contradiction between the real and the ideal. In attacking selfishness, hypocrisy, and corruption; in preaching the value of a life of good deeds; in showing how men ought to progress toward higher ideals; in teaching that "Love is the physician of life and nearest our Lord himself,—" *Piers Plowman* proved itself a regenerating spiritual force, a stepping-stone toward the later Reformation.

The author of this poem was also a fourteenth-century social reformer, protesting against the oppression of the poor, insisting on mutual service and "the good and loving life." In order to have a well-rounded conception of the life of the fourteenth century, we must read *Piers Plowman*. Chaucer was a poet for the upper classes. *Piers Plowman* gives valuable pictures of the life of the common people and shows them working—

> "To kepe kyne in þe field, þe corne fro þe bestes,
> Diken[1] or deluen[2] or dyngen[3] vppon sheues,[4]
> Or helpe make mortar or bere mukke a-felde."

We find in the popular poetry of *Piers Plowman* almost as many words of French derivation as in the work of the

[1] to make dykes or ditches.　[2] to dig.　[3] to thrash (ding).　[4] sheaves.

more aristocratic Chaucer. This fact shows how thoroughly the French element had become incorporated in the speech of all classes. The style of the author of *Piers Plowman* is, however, remarkable for the old Saxon sincerity and for the realistic directness of the bearer of a worthy message.

John Gower. — Gower, a very learned poet, was born about 1325 and died in 1408. As he was not sure that English would become the language of his cultivated countrymen, he tried each of the three languages used in England. His first important work, the *Speculum Meditantis*, was written in French; his second, the *Vox Clamantis*, in Latin; his third, the *Confessio Amantis*, in English.

The *Confessio Amantis* (*Confession of a Lover*) is principally a collection of one hundred and twelve short tales.

From the Egerton MS., British Museum.

EARLY PORTRAIT OF GOWER HEARING THE CONFESSION OF A LOVER (CONFESSIO AMANTIS)

An attempt to unify them is seen in the design to have the confessor relate, at the lover's request, those stories which reveal the causes tending to hinder or to further love. Gower had ability in story-telling, as is shown by the tales about Medea and the knight Florent; but he lacked Chaucer's dramatic skill and humor. Gower's influence has waned because, although he stood at the threshold of the Renaissance, his gaze was chiefly turned backward toward medievalism. His contemporary, Chaucer, as we shall see (p. 92), was affected by the new spirit.

From an old drawing in Occleve's Poems, British Museum.
GEOFFREY CHAUCER

GEOFFREY CHAUCER, 1340?-1400

Life. — Chaucer was born in London about 1340. His father and grandfather were vintners, who belonged to the upper class of merchants. Our first knowledge of Geoffrey Chaucer is obtained from the household accounts of the Princess Elizabeth, daughter-in-law of Edward III., in whose family Chaucer was a page. An entry shows that she bought him a fine suit of clothes, including a pair of red and black breeches. Such evidence points to the fact that he was early accustomed to associating with the nobility, and enables us to understand why he and the author of *Piers Plowman* regard life from different points of view.

In 1359 Chaucer accompanied the English army to France and was taken prisoner. Edward III. thought enough of the youth to pay for his ransom a sum equivalent to-day to about $1200. After his return he was made valet of the king's chamber. The duties of that office "consisted in making the royal bed, holding torches, and carrying messages." Later, Chaucer became a squire.

In 1370 he was sent to the continent on a diplomatic mission. He seems to have succeeded so well that during the next ten years he was repeatedly sent abroad in the royal service. He visited Italy twice and may thus have met the Italian poet Petrarch. These journeys inspired Chaucer with a desire to study Italian literature, — a literature that had just been enriched by the pens of Dante and Boccaccio.

We must next note that Chaucer's life was not that of a poetic dreamer, but of a stirring business man. For more than twelve years he was controller of customs for London. This office necessitated assessing duties on wools, skins, wines, and candles. Only a part of this work could be performed by deputy. He was later overseeing clerk of the king's works. The repeated selection of Chaucer for foreign and diplomatic business shows that he was considered sagacious as well as trustworthy. Had he not kept in close touch with life, he could never have become so great a poet. In this connection we may remark that England's second greatest writer, Milton, spent his prime in attending to affairs of state. Chaucer's busy life did not keep him from attaining third place on the list of England's poets.

There are many passages of autobiographical interest in

his poems. He was a student of books as well as of men, as is shown by these lines from the *Hous of Fame:*—

> "For whan thy labour doon al is,
> And hast y-maad thy rekeninges,
> In stede of rest and newe thinges,
> Thou gost hoom to thy hous anoon,
> And, also domb as any stoon,
> Thou sittest at another boke,
> Til fully daswed [1] is thy loke,
> And livest thus as an hermyte." [2]

Chaucer was pensioned by three kings, — Edward III., Richard II., and Henry IV. Before the reign of Henry IV., Chaucer's pensions were either not always regularly paid, or they were insufficient for certain emergencies, as he complained of poverty in his old age. The pension of Henry IV. in 1399 must have been ample, however; since in that year Chaucer leased a house in the garden of a chapel at Westminster for as many of fifty-three years as he should live. He had occasion to use this house but ten months, for he died in 1400.

He may be said to have founded the Poets' Corner in Westminster Abbey, as he was the first of the many great authors to be buried there.

Chaucer's Earlier Poems. — At the age of forty, Chaucer had probably written not more than one seventh of a total of about 35,000 lines of verse which he left at his death. Before he reached his poetic prime, he showed two periods of influence, — French and Italian.

During his first period, he studied French models. He learned much from his partial translation of the popular French *Romaunt of the Rose*. The best poem of his

---

[1] dazed.   [2] hermit.

French period is *Dethe of Blanche the Duchesse*, a tribute to the wife of John of Gaunt, the son of Edward III.

Chaucer's journey to Italy next turned his attention to Italian models. A study of these was of especial service in helping him to acquire that skill which enabled him to produce the masterpieces of his third or English period. This study came at a specially opportune time and resulted in communicating to him something of the spirit of the early Renaissance (p. 102).

The influence of Boccaccio and, sometimes, of Dante is noticeable in the principal poems of the Italian period, — the *Troilus and Criseyde*, *Hous of Fame*, and *Legende of Good Women*. The *Troilus and Criseyde* is a tale of love that was not true. The *Hous of Fame*, an unfinished poem, gives a vision of a vast palace of ice on which the names of the famous are carved to await the melting rays of the sun. The *Legende of Good Women* is a series of stories of those who, like Alcestis, are willing to give up everything for love. In *A Dream of Fair Women* Tennyson says: —

> "'The Legend of Good Women,' long ago
>   Sung by the morning star of song, who made
> His music heard below;
>   Dan Chaucer, the first warbler, whose sweet breath
> Preluded those melodious bursts that fill
>   The spacious times of great Elizabeth
> With sounds that echo still."

In this series of poems Chaucer learned how to rely less and less on an Italian crutch. He next took his immortal ride to Canterbury on an English Pegasus.

General Plan of the Canterbury Tales. — People in general have always been more interested in stories than in any other form of literature. Chaucer probably did not

CANTERBURY CATHEDRAL

realize that he had such positive genius for telling tales in verse that the next five hundred years would fail to produce his superior in that branch of English literature.

All that Chaucer needed was some framework into which he could fit the stories that occurred to him, to make them something more than mere stray tales, which might soon be forgotten. Chaucer's great contemporary Italian storyteller, Boccaccio, conceived the idea of representing some of the nobility of Florence as fleeing from the plague, and telling in their retirement the tales that he used in his *Decameron*. It is not certain that Chaucer received from the *Decameron* his suggestions for the *Canterbury Tales*, although he was probably in Florence at the same time as Boccaccio.

In 1170 Thomas à Becket, Archbishop of Canterbury, was murdered at the altar. He was considered both a martyr and a saint, and his body was placed in a splendid mausoleum at the Cathedral. It was said that miracles were worked at his tomb, that the sick were cured, and that the worldly affairs of those who knelt at his shrine prospered. It became the fashion for men of all classes to go on pilgrimages to his tomb. As robbers infested the highways, the pilgrims usually waited at some inn until there was a sufficient band to resist attack. In time the journey came to be looked on as a holiday, which relieved the monotony of everyday life. About 1385 Chaucer probably went on such a pilgrimage. To furnish amusement, as the pilgrims cantered along, some of them may have told stories. The idea occurred to Chaucer to write a collection of such tales as the various pilgrims might have been supposed to tell on their journey. The result was the *Canterbury Tales*.

Characters in the Tales. — Chaucer's plan is superior to Boccaccio's; for only the nobility figure as story-tellers in the *Decameron*, while the Canterbury pilgrims represent all ranks of English life, from the knight to the sailor.

The *Prologue* to the *Tales* places these characters before us almost as distinctly as they would appear in real life. At the Tabard Inn in Southwark, just across the Thames from London, we see that merry band of pilgrims on a pleasant April day. We look first upon a manly figure who strikes us as being every inch a knight. His cassock shows the marks of his coat of mail.

> "At mortal batailles hadde he been fiftene.
> . . . .
> And of his port as meke as is a mayde.
> He never yet no vileinye ne sayde

> In al his lyf, un-to no maner wight.
> He was a verray parfit gentil knight."

His son, the Squire, next catches our attention. We notice his curly locks, his garments embroidered with gay flowers, and the graceful way in which he rides his

From Urry's Chaucer.

PILGRIMS LEAVING THE TABARD INN

horse. By his side is his servant, the Yeoman, "clad in cote and hood of grene," with a sheaf of arrows at his belt. We may even note his cropped head and his horn suspended from a green belt. We next catch sight of a Nun's gracefully pleated wimple, shapely nose, small mouth, "eyen greye as glas," well-made cloak, coral beads, and brooch of gold. She is attended by a second Nun and three Priests. The Monk is a striking figure:—

> "His heed was balled, that shoon as any glas,
> And eek his face, as he hadde been anoint.
> He was a lord ful fat and in good point."

There follow the Friar with twinkling eyes, "the beste beggere in his hous," the Merchant with his forked beard, the Clerk (scholar) of Oxford in his threadbare garments, the Sergeant-at-Law, the Franklyn (country gentleman), Haberdasher, Carpenter, Weaver, Dyer, Tapycer (tapestry

A frankeleyn was in hese cumpanye
whit was hese berd as is þe daysie
Of complexioū he was sanguyn
Wel louede he þe morwe a soppe in wyn
To leuyn in delit was euere hese wone

From the Cambridge University MS.

FACSIMILE OF LINES DESCRIBING THE FRANKLYN[1]

maker), Cook, Shipman, Physician, Wife of Bath, Parish Priest, Plowman, Miller, Manciple (purchaser of provisions), Reeve (bailiff of a farm), Summoner (official of an ecclesiastical court), and Pardoner. These characters, exclusive of Baily (the host of the Tabard Inn) and Chaucer himself, are alluded to in the *Prologue* to the *Tales* as —

"Wel nyne and twenty in a companye,
Of sondry folk, by aventure y-falle
In felawshipe, and pilgrims were they alle,
That toward Caunterbury wolden ryde."

THE FRANKLYN[2]

The completeness of the picture of fourteenth century English life in the *Canterbury Tales* makes them absolutely necessary reading for the historian as well as for the student of literature. Certainly no one who has ever read the *Prologue* to the *Tales* will question Chaucer's right to be considered a great *original*

THE FRIAR

[1] *The Prologue*, Lines 331-335.
[2] The cuts of the Pilgrims are from the Fourteenth Century Ellesmere MS. of *Canterbury Tales*.

poet, no matter how much he may have owed to foreign teachers.

The Tales. — Harry Baily, the keeper of the Tabard Inn, who accompanied the pilgrims, proposed that each member of the party should tell four tales, — two going and two returning. The one who told the best story was to have a supper at the expense of the rest. The plan thus outlined was not fully executed by Chaucer, for the collection contains but twenty-four tales, all but two of which are in verse.

THE KNIGHT

The *Knightes Tale*, which is the first, is also the best. It is a very interesting story of love and chivalry. Two young Theban noblemen, Palamon and Arcite, sworn friends, are prisoners of war at Athens. Looking through the windows of their dungeon, they see walking in the garden the beautiful sister of the queen. Each one swears that he will have the princess. Arcite is finally pardoned on condition that he will leave Athens and never return, on penalty of death; but his love for Emily lures him back to

THE PRIORESS

the forbidden land. Reduced almost to a skeleton, he disguises himself, goes to Athens, and becomes a servant in the house of King Theseus. Finally, Palamon escapes from prison, and by chance encounters Arcite. The two men promptly fight, but are interrupted by Theseus, who at first

THE SQUIRE condemns them to death, but later relents and

directs them to depart and to return at the end of a year, each with a hundred brave knights. The king prescribes that each lover shall then lead his forces in mortal battle and that the victor shall wed the princess.

On the morning of the contest, Palamon goes before dawn to the temple of Venus to beseech her aid in winning Emily, while Arcite at the same time steals to the temple of Mars to pray for victory in war. Each deity not only promises but actually grants the suppliants precisely what they ask; for Arcite, though fatally wounded, is victorious in the battle, and Palamon in the end weds Emily. Although Boccaccio's *Teseide* furnished the general plot for this *Knightes Tale*, Chaucer's story is, as Skeat says, "to all intents, a truly original poem."

THE CLERK OF OXFORD

The other pilgrims tell stories in keeping with their professions and characters. Perhaps the next best tale is the merry story of *Chanticleer and the Fox*. This is related by the Nun's Priest. The Clerk of Oxford tells the pathetic tale of *Patient Griselda*, and the Nun relates a touching story of a little martyr.

Chief Qualities of Chaucer. — I. Chaucer's descriptions are unusually clear-cut and vivid. They are the work of a poet who did not shut himself in his study, but who mingled among his fellow-men and noticed them acutely. He says of the Friar: —

> "His eyen twinkled in his heed aright,
> As doon the sterres in the frosty night."

Our eyes and ears distinctly perceive the jolly Monk, as he canters along: —

> "And, whan he rood, men might his brydel here
> Ginglen in a whistling wind as clere,
> And eek as loude as dooth the chapel-belle."

II. Chaucer's pervasive, sympathetic humor is especially characteristic. We can see him looking with twinkling eyes at the Miller, "tolling thrice"; at the Monk, "full fat and in good point," hunting with his greyhounds, "swift as fowl in flight," or smiling before a fat roast swan; at the Squire, keeping the nightingale company; at the Doctor, prescribing by the rules of astrology. The Nun feels a touch of his humor: —

> "Ful wel she song the service divyne,
> Entuned in hir nose ful semely."

Of the lawyer, he says: —

> "No-wher so bisy a man as he ther nas,
> And yet he semed bisier than he was."

Sometimes Chaucer's humor is so delicate as to be lost on those who are not quick-witted. Lowell instances the case of the Friar, who, "before setting himself softly down, drives away the cat," and adds what is true only of those who have acute understanding: "We know, without need of more words, that he has chosen the snuggest corner."

His humor is often a graceful cloak for his serious philosophy of existence. The humor in the *Prologue* does not impair its worth to the student of fourteenth-century life.

III. Although Chaucer's humor and excellence in lighter vein are such marked characteristics, we must not forget his serious qualities; for he has the Saxon seriousness as well as the Norman airiness. As he looks over the struggling world, he says with sympathetic heart: —

> "Infinite been the sorwes and the teres
> Of olde folk, and folk of tendre yeres." [1]

In like vein, we have: —

> "This world nis but a thurghfare ful of wo,
> And we ben pilgrimes, passinge to and fro;
> Deeth is an ende of every worldly sore." [1]

> "Her nis non hoom, her nis but wildernesse.
> Forthe, pylgrime, forthe! forthe, beste out of thi stal!
> Knowe thi contree, look up, thank God of al!" [2]

The finest character in the company is that of the Parish Priest, who attends to his flock like a good Samaritan: —

> "But Cristes lore, and his apostles twelve,
> He taughte, and first he folwed it him-selve."

IV. The largeness of his view of human nature is remarkable. Some poets, either intentionally or unintentionally, paint one type of men accurately and distort all the rest. Chaucer impartially portrays the highest as well as the lowest, and the honest man as well as the hypocrite. The pictures of the roguish Friar and the self-denying Parish Priest, the Oxford Scholar and the Miller, the Physician and the Shipman, are painted with equal fidelity to life. In the breadth and kindliness of his view of life, Chaucer is a worthy predecessor of Shakespeare. Dryden's verdict on Chaucer's poetry is: "Here is God's plenty."

V. His love of nature is noteworthy for that early age. Such lines as these manifest something more than a desire for rhetorical effect in speaking of nature's phenomena: —

> "Now welcom somer, with thy sonne softe,
> That hast this wintres weders over-shake,
> And driven awey the longe nightes blake [3] !" [4]

---

[1] *Knightes Tale.*
[2] *Truth: Balade de bon Conseyl.*
[3] black.
[4] *The Parlement of Foules.*

His affection for the daisy has for five hundred years caused many other people to look with fonder eyes upon that flower.

VI. He stands in the front rank of those who have attempted to tell stories in melodious verse. Lowell justly says: "One of the world's three or four great storytellers, he was also one of the best versifiers that ever made English trip and sing with a gayety that seems careless, but where every foot beats time to the tune of the thought."

VII. He is the first great English author to feel the influence of the Renaissance, which did not until long

From a Manuscript of Chaucer's Time.
MORRIS DANCERS

afterward culminate in England. Gower has his lover hear tales from a confessor in cloistered quiet. Chaucer takes his Pilgrims out for jolly holidays in the April sunshine. He shows the spirit of the Renaissance in his joy in varied life, in his desire for knowledge of all classes of men as well as of books, in his humor, and in his general reaching out into new fields. He makes us feel that he lives in a merrier England, where both the Morris dancer and the Pilgrim may show their joy in life.

What Chaucer did for the English Language. — Before Chaucer's works, English was, as we have seen, a language of dialects. He wrote in the Midland dialect, and aided in making that the language of England. Lounsbury says of Chaucer's influence: " No really national language could exist until a literature had been created which would be admired and studied by all who could read, and taken as a model by all who could write. It was only a man of genius that could lift up one of these dialects into a preëminence over the rest, or could ever give to the scattered forces existing in any one of them the unity and vigor of life. This was the work that Chaucer did." For this reason he deserves to be called our first modern English poet. At first sight, his works look far harder to read than they really are, because the spelling has changed so much since Chaucer's day.

SUMMARY

The period from the Norman Conquest to 1400 is remarkable (1) for bringing into England French influence and closer contact with the continent; (2) for the development of (*a*) a more centralized government, (*b*) the feudal system and chivalry, (*c*) better civil courts of justice and a more representative government, *Magna Charta* being one of the steps in this direction; (3) for the influence of religion, the coming of the friars, the erection of unsurpassed Gothic cathedrals; (4) for the struggles of the peasants to escape their bondage, for a striking decline in the relative importance of the armored knight, and for Wycliffe's movement for a religious reformation.

This period is also specially important because it gave to England a new language of greater flexibility and power. The old inflections, genders, formative prefixes, and capacity of making self-explaining compounds were for the most part lost. To supply the places of lost words and to express those new ideas which came with the broader experiences of an emancipated, progressive nation, many new words were adopted from the French and the Latin. When the time for literature came, Chaucer found ready for his pen the strongest, sincerest, and most flexible language that ever expressed a poet's thought.

In tracing the development of the literature of this period, we have noted (1) the metrical romances; (2) Geoffrey of Monmouth's (Latin) *History of the Kings of Britain*, and Layamon's *Brut*, with their stories of Lear, Cymbeline, and King Arthur; (3) the *Ormulum*, a metrical paraphrase of those parts of the *Gospels* used in church service; (4) the *Ancren Riwle*, remarkable for its natural eloquent prose and its noble ethics, as well as for showing the development of the language; (5) the lyrical poetry, beginning to be redolent of the odor of the blossom and resonant with the song of the bird; (6) the *Handlyng Synne*, in which we stand on the threshold of modern English; (7) Mandeville's *Travels*, with its entertaining stories; (8) Wycliffe's monumental translation of the *Bible* and vigorous religious prose pamphlets; (9) *Piers Plowman*, with its pictures of homely life, its intense desire for higher ideals and for the reformation of social and religious life; (10) Gower's *Confessio Amantis*, a collection of tales about love; and (11) Chaucer's poetry, which stands in the front rank for the number of vivid pictures of contemporary life, for humor, love of nature, melody, and capacity for story-telling.

REFERENCES FOR FURTHER STUDY

HISTORICAL

An account of the history of this period may be found in either Gardiner,[1] Green, Lingard, Walker, or Cheney. Volumes II. and III. of the *Political History of England*, edited by Hunt (Longmans), give the history in greater detail. For the social side, consult Traill, I. and II. See also Rogers's *Six Centuries of Work and Wages*. Freeman's *William the Conqueror*, Green's *Henry II.*, and Tout's *Edward I.* (*Twelve English Statesmen Series*) are short and interesting. Kingsley's *Hereward the Wake* deals with the times of William the Conqueror and Scott's *Ivanhoe* with those of Richard the Lion-Hearted. Archer and Kingsford's *The Story of the Crusades*, Cutt's *Parish Priests and their People in the Middle Ages in England*, and Jusserand's *English Wayfaring Life in the Fourteenth Century* are good works.

LITERARY

Cambridge History of English Literature, Vols. I. and II.
Bradley's *Making of English*.
Schofield's *English Literature from the Conquest to Chaucer*.
Ker's *Epic and Romance*.
Saintsbury's *The Flourishing of Romance and the Rise of Allegory*.
Lawrence's *Medieval Story* (excellent).
Weston's *The Romance Cycle of Charlemagne and his Peers*.
Weston's *King Arthur and his Knights*.
Maynadier's *The Arthur of the English Poets*.
Nutt's *The Legends of the Holy Grail*.
Jusserand's *Piers Plowman*.
Warren's *Langland's Vision of Piers the Plowman, Done into Modern Prose*.
Savage's *Old English Libraries*.
Schofield's *Chivalry in English Literature*.
Snell's *The Age of Chaucer*.
Root's *The Poetry of Chaucer*.
Tuckwell's *Chaucer* (96 pp.).
Pollard's *Chaucer* (142 pp.).

---

[1] For full titles, see p. 50.

96   FROM 1066 TO CHAUCER'S DEATH, 1400

Legouis's *Chaucer*.
Coulton's *Chaucer and his England*.
Lowell's *My Study Windows* contains one of the best essays ever written on Chaucer.
Mackail's *The Springs of Helicon* (Chaucer).

SUGGESTED READINGS
WITH QUESTIONS AND SUGGESTIONS

Romances. — The student will be interested in reading from Lawrence's *Medieval Story*, Chapters III., *The Song of Roland*; IV., *The Arthurian Romances*; V., *The Legend of the Holy Grail*; VI., *The History of Reynard the Fox*. Butler's *The Song of Roland* (*Riverside Literature Series*) is an English prose translation of a popular story from the Charlemagne cycle. *Sir Gawayne and the Green Knight* has been retold in modern English prose by J. L. Weston (London: David Nutt). A long metrical selection from this romance is given in Bronson,[1] I., 83-100, in *Oxford Treasury*, I., 60-81, and a prose selection in *Century*, 1000-1022.

Stories from the Arthurian cycle may be found in Newell's *King Arthur and the Table Round*. See also Maynadier's *The Arthur of the English Poets*, and Tennyson's *The Idylls of the King*.

Geoffrey of Monmouth's *History of the Kings of Britain* is translated in Giles's *Six Old English Chronicles* (Bohn Library).

Selections from Layamon's *Brut* may be found in Bronson, I.; P. & S.; and Manly, I.

What were the chief subjects of the cycles of Romance? Were they mostly of English or French origin? What new elements appear, not found in Beowulf? Which of these cycles has the most interest for English readers? How does this cycle still influence twentieth-century ideals? In what respect is the romance of *Gawayne* like a sermon?

What Shakespearean characters does Geoffrey of Monmouth introduce? How is Layamon's *Brut* related to Geoffrey's chronicle? Point out a likeness between the *Brut* and the work of a Victorian poet.

Ormulum, Lyrics, and Robert Manning of Brunne. — Selections may be found in P. and S.; Bronson, I.; *Oxford* (lyrics, pp. 1-10); **Manly, I.**; Morris's *Specimens of Early English*. Among the lyrics,

[1] For full titles, see p. 6.

read specially, "Sumer is i-cumen in," "Alysoun," "Lenten ys come with love to toune," and "Blow, Northern Wind."

What was the purpose of the *Ormulum?* What is its subject matter? Does it show much French influence?

What new appreciation of nature do the thirteenth-century lyrics show? Point out at least twelve definite concrete references to nature in "Lenten ys come with love to toune." How many such references are there in the *Cuckoo Song?*

What difference do you note between the form of Robert Manning of Brunne's *Handlyng Synne* and Anglo-Saxon poetry? Can you find an increasing number of words of French derivation in his work?

Prose. — Manly's *English Prose*, Morris's *Specimens of Early English*, Parts I. and II., Chambers, I., Craik, I., contain specimens of the best prose, including Mandeville and Wycliffe. Mandeville's *Travels* may be found in modern English in Cassell's *National Library* (15¢). Bosworth and Waring's edition of the *Gospels* contains the Anglo-Saxon text, together with the translations of Wycliffe and Tyndale. No. 107 of Maynard's *English Classics* contains selections from both Wycliffe's *Bible* and Mandeville's *Travels*.

What is the subject matter of the *Ancren Riwle?* What is the keynote of the work? Mention some words of French origin found in it.

What is the character of Mandeville's *Travels?* Why was it so popular?

In what does Wycliffe's literary importance consist? Compare some verses of his translation of the *Bible* with the 1611 version.

Piers Plowman and Gower. — Selections are given in P. and S.; Bronson, I.; Ward, I.; Chambers, I.; and Manly, I. Skeat has edited a small edition of *Piers the Plowman* ("B" text) and also a larger edition, entitled *The Vision of William concerning Piers the Plowman, in Three Parallel Texts*. G. C. Macaulay has a good volume of selections from Gower's *Confessio Amantis*.

What is the difference between the form of the verse in *Piers Plowman* and *Handlyng Synne?* Who is Piers? Who are some of the other characters in the poem? What type of life is specially described? In what sort of work are the laborers engaged? Why may the author of *Piers Plowman* be called a reformer?

Why was Gower undecided in what language to write? What is the subject matter of the *Confessio Amantis?*

Chaucer. — Read the *Prologue* and if possible also the *Knightes*

Tale (Liddell's, or Morris-Skeat's, or Van Dyke's, or Mather's edition). Good selections may be found in Bronson, I.; Ward, I.; P. and S., and *Oxford Treasury*, I. Skeat's Complete Works, 6 vols., is the best edition. Skeat's *Oxford Chaucer* in one volume has the same text. The *Globe Edition of Chaucer*, edited by Pollard, is also a satisfactory single volume edition. Root's *The Poetry of Chaucer*, 292 pp., is a good reference work in connection with the actual study of the poetry.

Give a clear-cut description of the six of Chaucer's pilgrims that impress you most strongly. How has the *Prologue* added to our knowledge of life in the fourteenth century? Give examples of Chaucer's vivid pictures. What specimens of his humor does the *Prologue* contain? Do any of Chaucer's lines in the *Prologue* show that the Reformation spirit was in the air, or did Wycliffe and Langland alone among contemporary authors afford evidence of this spirit? Compare Chaucer's verse with Langland's in point of subject matter. What qualities in Chaucer save him from the charge of cynicism when he alludes to human faults? Does the *Prologue* attempt to portray any of the nobler sides of human nature? Is the *Prologue* mainly or entirely concerned with the personality of the pilgrims? Has Chaucer any philosophy of life? Are there any references to the delights of nature? Note any passages that show special powers of melody and mastery over verse. Does the poem reveal anything of Chaucer's personality? In your future reading see if you can find another English story-teller in verse who can be classed with Chaucer.

CHAPTER III

FROM CHAUCER'S DEATH, 1400, TO THE ACCESSION OF ELIZABETH, 1558

The Course of English History. — The century and a half that followed the death of Chaucer appealed especially to Shakespeare. He wrote or helped to edit five plays that deal with this period, — *Henry IV.*, *Henry V.*, *Henry VI.*, *Richard III.*, and *Henry VIII.* While these plays do not give an absolutely accurate presentation of the history of the time, they show rare sympathy in catching the spirit of the age, and they leave many unusually vivid impressions.

Henry IV. (1399–1413), a descendant of John of Gaunt, Duke of Lancaster, one of the younger sons of Edward III., and therefore not in the direct line of succession, was the first English king who owed his crown entirely to Parliament. Henry's reign was disturbed by the revolt of nobles and by contests with the Welsh. Shakespeare gives a pathetic picture of the king calling in vain for sleep, "nature's tired nurse," and exclaiming: —

"Uneasy lies the head that wears a crown."

Henry V. (1413–1422) is one of Shakespeare's romantic characters. The young king renewed the French war, which had broken out in 1337 and which later became known as the Hundred Years' War. By his victory over the French at Agincourt (1415), he made himself a national hero. Shakespeare has him say: —

"I thought upon one pair of English legs
Did march three Frenchmen."

In the reign of Henry VI. (1422-1461), Joan of Arc appeared and saved France.

The setting aside of the direct succession in the case of Henry IV. was a pretext for the Wars of the Roses (1455-1485) to settle the royal claims of different descendants of Edward III. While this war did not greatly disturb the common people, it occupied the attention of those who might have been patrons of literature. Nearly all the nobles were killed during this prolonged contest; hence when Henry VII. (1485-1509), the first of the Tudor line of monarchs, came to the throne, there were no powerful nobles with their retainers to hold the king in check. He gave a strong centralized government to England.

The period following Chaucer's death opens with religious persecution. In 1401 the first Englishman was burned at the stake for his religious faith. From this time the expenses of burning heretics are sometimes found in the regular accounts of cities and boroughs. Henry VIII. (1509-1547) broke with the Pope, dissolved the monasteries, proclaimed himself head of the church, and allowed the laity to read the *Bible*, but insisted on retaining many of the old beliefs. In Germany, Martin Luther (1483-1546) was in the same age issuing his famous protests against religious abuses. Edward VI. (1547-1553) espoused the Protestant cause. An order was given to introduce into all the churches an English prayer book, which was not very different from that in use to-day in the Episcopal churches. Mary (1553-1558) sought the aid of fagots and the stake to bring the nation back to the old beliefs.

While this period did not produce a single great poet or a statesman of the first rank, it witnessed the destruction of the majority of the nobility in the Wars of the Roses, the increase of the king's power, the decline of feudalism, the final overthrow of the knight by the yeoman with his long bow at Agincourt (1415), the freedom of the serf, and the growth of manufactures, especially of wool. English trading vessels began to displace even the ships of Venice.

From frontispiece to Coverdale Bible.

HENRY VIII. GIVING BIBLES TO CLERGY AND LAITY

In spite of the religious persecution with which the period began and ended, there was a remarkable change in religious belief, the dissolution of the monasteries and the subordination of church to state being striking evidences of this change. An event that had far-reaching consequences on literature and life was the act of Henry VIII. in ordering a translation of the *Bible* to be placed in every parish church in England. The death of Mary may in a measure be said to indicate the beginning of modern times.

Contrast between the Spirit of the Renaissance and of the Middle Ages. — One of the most important intellectual movements of the world is known as the Renaissance or Revival of Learning. This movement began in Italy about the middle of the fourteenth century and spread slowly westward. While Chaucer's travels in Italy and his early contact with this new influence are reflected in his work, yet the Renaissance did not reach its zenith in England until the time of Shakespeare. This new epoch followed a long period, known as the Middle Ages, when learning was mostly confined to the church, when thousands of the best minds retired to the cloisters, when many questions, like those of the revolution of the sun around the earth or the cause of disease, were determined, not by observation and scientific proof, but by the assertion of those in spiritual authority. Then, scientific investigators, like Roger Bacon (p. 56), were thought to be in league with the devil and were thrown into prison. In 1258 Dante's tutor visited Roger Bacon, and, after seeing his experiments with the mariner's compass, wrote to an Italian friend: —

"This discovery so useful to all who travel by sea, must remain concealed until other times, because no mariner dare use it, lest he fall under imputation of being a magician, nor would sailors put to sea with one who carried an instrument so evidently constructed by the devil."

Symonds says: "During the Middle Ages, man had lived enveloped in a cowl. He had not seen the beauty of the world, or had seen it only to cross himself and turn aside, to tell his beads and pray." Before the Renaissance, the tendency was to regard with contempt mere questions of earthly progress and enjoyment, because they were considered unimportant in comparison with the eternal future

THE RENAISSANCE 103

of the soul. It was not believed that beauty, art, and literature might play a part in saving souls.

The Schoolmen of the Middle Ages often discussed such subjects as these: whether the finite can comprehend the infinite at any point, since the infinite can have no finite points; whether God can make a wheel revolve and be stationary at the same time; whether all children in a state of innocence are masculine. Such debates made remarkable theologians and metaphysicians, developed precision in defining terms, accuracy in applying the rules of deductive logic, and fluency in expression. As a result, later scientists were able to reason more accurately and express themselves with greater facility.

The chief fault of the studies of the Middle Ages consisted in neglecting the external world of concrete fact. The discussions of the Schoolmen would never have introduced printing or invented the mariner's compass or developed any of the sciences that have revolutionized life.

The coming of the Renaissance opened avenues of learning outside of the church, interested men in manifold questions relating to this world, caused a demand for scientific investigation and proof, and made increasing numbers seek for joy in this life as well as in that to come.

Causes and Effects of the Renaissance. — Some of the causes of this new movement were the weariness of human beings with their lack of progress, their dissatisfaction with the low estimate of the value of this life, and their yearning for fuller expansion of the soul, for more knowledge and joy on this side of the grave.

Another cause was the influence of Greek literature newly discovered in the fifteenth century by the western world. In 1423 an Italian scholar brought 238 Greek manuscripts to Italy. In 1453 the Turks captured Constantinople, the capital of the Eastern Roman Empire and the headquarters of Grecian learning. Because of the remoteness of this capital, English literature had not been greatly influenced by Greece. When Constantinople fell, many of her scholars went to Italy, taking with them precious Grecian manuscripts. As Englishmen often visited Italy, they soon began to study Grecian masterpieces, and to fall under the spell of Homer and the Athenian dramatists.

The renewed study of Greek and Latin classics stimulated a longing for the beautiful in art and literature. Fourteenth-century Italian writers, like Petrarch and Boccaccio, found increasing interest in their work. Sixteenth-century artists, such as Leonardo da Vinci, Michael Angelo, and Raphael show their magnificent response to a world that had already been born again.

Many of the other so-called causes of the Renaissance should strictly be considered its effects. The application of the modern theory of the solar system, the desire for exploration, the use of the mariner's compass, the invention and spread of printing, were more effects of the new movement than its causes.

Sir Thomas More (1478–1535), inspired by the spirit of the Renaissance, wrote in Latin a remarkable book called *Utopia* (1516), which presents many new social ideals. In the land of Utopia, society does not make criminals and then punish them for crime. Every one worships as he pleases. Only a few hours of work a day are necessary, and all find genuine pleasure in that. In Utopia life is given to be a joy. No advantage is taken of the weak or the unfortunate. Twentieth-century dreams of social justice are not more vivid and absorbing than Sir Thomas More's. It is pleasant to think that the Roman Catholic church in

1886 added to her list of saints this lovable man, "martyr to faith and freedom."

When the full influences of the Renaissance reached England, Shakespeare answered their call, and his own creations surpass the children of Utopia.

The Invention of Printing. — In 1344, about the time of Chaucer's birth, a *Bible* in manuscript cost as much as three oxen. A century later an amount equal to the wages of a workman for 266 days was paid for a manuscript *Bible*. At this time a book on astronomy cost as much as 800 pounds of butter. One page of a manuscript book cost the equivalent of from a dollar to a dollar and a half to-day. When a member of the Medici family in Florence desired a library, he sent for a book contractor, who secured forty-five copyists. By rigorous work for nearly two years they produced two hundred volumes.

British Museum.
BOOK ILLUSTRATION, EARLY FIFTEENTH CENTURY

One of the most powerful agencies of the Renaissance was the invention of printing, which multiplied books indefinitely and made them comparatively cheap. People were alive with newly awakened curiosity, and they read books to learn more of the expanding world.

About 1477 William Caxton, who had set up his press at the Almonry, near Westminster Abbey, printed the first book in England, *The Dictes and Notable Wise Sayings of the Philosophers*. Among fully a hundred different volumes that he printed were Chaucer's *Canterbury Tales*, Malory's *Morte d'Arthur*, and an English translation of Vergil's *Æneid*.

> If it plese ony man spirituel or temporel to bye ony pyes of two and thre comemoracios of salisburi vse enprentid after the forme of this preset lettre whiche ben wel and truly correct, late hym come to westmonester in to the almonesrye at the reed pale and he shal haue them good chepe

> Supplico stet cedula

Bodleian Library, Oxford.

FACSIMILE OF CAXTON'S ADVERTISEMENT OF HIS BOOKS

Malory's Morte d'Arthur. — The greatest prose work of the fifteenth century was completed in 1470 by a man who styles himself Sir Thomas Malory, Knight. We know nothing of the author's life; but he has left as a monument a great prose epic of the deeds of King Arthur and his Knights of the Round Table. From the various French legends concerning King Arthur, Malory selected his materials and fashioned them into the completest Arthuriad that we possess. While his work cannot be called original, he displayed rare artistic power in arranging, abridging, and selecting the various parts from different French works.

Malory's prose is remarkably simple and direct. Even in the impressive scene where Sir Bedivere throws the dying King Arthur's sword into the sea, the language tells the story simply and shows no straining after effect:—

"And then he threw the sword as far into the water as he might, and there came an arm and an hand above the water, and met it, and caught it, and so shook it thrice and brandished, and then vanished away the hand with the sword in the water. . . . 'Now put me into the barge,' said the King; and so he did softly. And there received him three queens with great mourning, and so they set him down, and in one of their laps King Arthur laid his head, and then that queen said, 'Ah, dear brother, why have ye tarried so long from me?'"

After the dusky barge has borne Arthur away from mortal sight, Malory writes: "Here in this world he changed his life." A century before, Chaucer had with equal simplicity voiced the Saxon faith:—

"His spirit chaunged hous."[1]

Sometimes this prose narrative, in its condensation and expression of feeling, shows something of the poetic spirit. When the damsel on the white palfrey sees that her knightly lover has been killed, she cries:—

"'O Balin! two bodies hast thou slain and one heart, and two hearts in one body, and two souls thou hast lost.' And therewith she took the sword from her love that lay dead, and as she took it, she fell to the ground in a swoon."

From De Worde's Ed., 1529.

MALORY'S MORTE D'ARTHUR

Malory's work, rather than Layamon's *Brut*, has been the storehouse to which later poets have turned. Many nineteenth-century poets are indebted to Malory. Tennyson's *Idylls of the King*, Matthew Arnold's *Death of Tristram*, Swinburne's *Tristram of Lyonesse*, and William Morris's *Defense of Guinevere* were inspired by the *Morte*

[1] *Knightes Tale.*

d'Arthur. Few English prose works have had more influence on the poetry of the Victorian age.

Scottish Poetry. — The best poetry of the fifteenth century was written in the Northern dialect, which was spoken north of the river Humber. This language was just as much English as the Midland tongue in which Chaucer wrote. Not until the sixteenth century was this dialect called Scotch.

James I. of Scotland (1406-1437) spent nineteen years of his youth as a prisoner in England. During his captivity in Windsor Castle, he fell in love with a maiden, seen at her orisons in the garden, and wrote a poem, called the *King's Quair*, to tell the story of his love. Although the *King's Quair* is suggestive of *The Knightes Tale* (p. 88), and indeed owes much to Chaucer, it is a poetic record of genuine and successful love. These four lines from the spring song show real feeling for nature: —

> "Worshippe, ye that lovers be, this May,
> For of your bliss the kalends are begun,
> And sing with us, 'Away, Winter, away,
> Come, Summer, come, the sweet season and sun!'"

Much of this Scotch poetry is remarkable for showing in that early age a genuine love of nature. Changes are not rung on some typical landscape, copied from an Italian versifier. The Northern poet had his eye fixed on the scenery and the sky of Scotland. About the middle of the century, Robert Henryson, a teacher in Dunfermline, wrote: —

> "The northin wind had purifyit the air
> And sched the misty cloudis fra the sky."[1]

This may lack the magic of Shelley's rhythm (p. 424), but the feeling for nature is as genuine as in the later poet's lines: —

[1] *Testament of Cresseid.*

> "For after the rain when, with never a stain
> The pavilion of heaven is bare."[1]

William Dunbar, the greatest poet of this group, who lived in the last half of the fifteenth century, was a loving student of the nature that greeted him in his northland. No Italian poet, as he wandered beside a brook, would have thought of a simile like this: —

> "The stonés clear as stars in frosty night."[2]

Dunbar takes us with him on a fresh spring morning, where —

> "Enamelled was the field with all coloúrs,
> The pearly droppés shook in silver showers,"[2]

where we can hear the matin song of the birds hopping among the buds, while —

> "Up rose the lark, the heaven's minstrel fine."[2]

Both Dunbar and **Gawain Douglas** (1474?–1522), the son of a Scotch nobleman, had keen eyes for all coloring in sky, leaf, and flower. In one line Dunbar calls our attention to these varied patches of color in a Scotch garden: "purple, azure, gold, and gulés [red]." In the verses of Douglas we see the purple streaks of the morning, the bluish-gray, blood-red, fawn-yellow, golden, and freckled red and white flowers, and —

> "Some watery-hued, as the blue wavy sea."[3]

Outside the pages of Shakespeare, we shall for the next two hundred years look in vain for so genuine a love of scenery and natural phenomena as we find in fifteenth-century Scottish poetry. These poets obtained many of

---

[1] *The Cloud.*   [2] *The Golden Targe.*
[3] *Prologue to Æneid,* Book XII.

their images of nature at first hand, an achievement rare in any age.

"**Songs for Man or Woman, of All Sizes.**" — When Shakespeare shows us Autolycus offering such songs at a rustic festival,[1] the great poet emphasizes the fondness for the ballad which had for a long time been developing a taste for poetry. While it is difficult to assign exact dates to the composition of many ballads, we know that they flourished in the fifteenth century. They were then as much prized as the novel is now, and, like it, they had a story to tell. The verse was often halting, but it succeeded in conveying to the hearer tales of love, of adventure, and of mystery. These ballads were sometimes tinged with pathos; but there was an energy in the rude lines that made the heart beat faster and often stirred the listeners to find in a dance an outlet for their emotions. Even now, with all the poetry of centuries from which to choose, it is refreshing to turn to a Robin Hood ballad and look upon the greensward, hear the rustle of the leaves in Nottingham forest, and follow the adventures of the hero. We read the opening lines:—

EARLY TITLE PAGE OF ROBIN HOOD

"There are twelve months in all the year,
  As I hear many say,

[1] *The Winter's Tale*, IV., 4.

> But the merriest month in all the year
> Is the merry month of May.
>
> "Now Robin Hood is to Nottingham gone,
> With a link a down, and a day,
> And there he met a silly old woman
> Was weeping on the way."

Of our own accord we finish the ballad to see whether Robin Hood rescued her sons, who were condemned to death for shooting the fallow deer. The ballad of the *Nut-Brown Maid* has some touches that are almost Shakespearean.

Some of the carols of the fifteenth century give a foretaste of Elizabethan song. One carol on the birth of the Christ-child contains stanzas like these, which show artistic workmanship, imaginative power, and, above all, rare lyrical beauty: —

> "He cam also stylle
> to his moderes bowr,
> As dew in Aprille
> that fallyt on the flour.
>
> "He cam also stylle
> ther his moder lay,
> As dew in Aprille
> that fallyt on the spray."[1]

We saw that the English tongue during its period of exclusion from the Norman court gained strength from coming in such close contact with life. Although the higher types of poetry were for the most part wanting during the fifteenth century, yet the ballads multiplied and sang their songs to the ear of life. Critics may say that the rude stanzas seldom soar far from the ground, but we are again reminded of the invincible strength of Antæus

[1] Wright's *Songs and Carols of the Fifteenth Century*, p. 30.

so long as he kept close to his mother earth. English poetry is so great because it has not withdrawn from life, because it was nurtured in such a cradle. When Shakespeare wrote his plays, he found an audience to understand and to appreciate them. Not only those who occupied the boxes, but also those who stood in the pit, listened intelligently to his dramatic stories. The ballad had played its part in teaching the humblest home to love poetry. These rude fireside songs were no mean factors in preparing the nation to welcome Shakespeare.

William Tyndale, 1490?–1536.— The Reformation was another mighty influence, working side by side with all the other forces to effect a lasting change in English history and literature. In the early part of the sixteenth century, Martin Luther was electrifying Germany with his demands for church reformation. In order to decide which religious party was in the right, there arose a desire for more knowledge of the *Scriptures*. The language had changed much since Wycliffe's translation of the *Bible*, and, besides, this was accessible only in manuscript. William Tyndale, a clergyman and an excellent linguist, who had been educated at both Oxford and Cambridge, conceived the idea of giving the English people the *Bible* in their own tongue. As he found that he could not translate and print the *Bible* with safety in England, he went to the continent, where with the help of friends he made the translation and had it printed. He was forced to move frequently from place to place, and was finally betrayed in his hiding place near Brussels. After eighteen months' imprisonment without pen or books, he was strangled and his body was burned at the stake.

Of his translation, Brooke says: "It was this *Bible* which, revised by Coverdale, and edited and reëdited as

WILLIAM TYNDALE

From an old print.

Cromwell's Bible, 1539, and again as *Cranmer's Bible*, 1540, was set up in every parish church in England. It got north into Scotland and made the Lowland English more like the London English. It passed over into the Protestant settlements in Ireland. After its revival in 1611 it went with the Puritan Fathers to New England and fixed the standard of English in America. Many millions of people now speak the English of Tyndale's *Bible*, and there is no other book which has had, through the *Authorized Version*, so great an influence on the style of English literature and on the standard of English prose."

The following verses from Tyndale's version show its simplicity, directness, and similarity to the present version:—

"Jesus sayde unto her, Thy brother shall ryse agayne.

"Martha sayde unto hym, I knowe wele, he shall ryse agayne in the resurreccion att the last day.

"Jesus sayde unto her, I am the resurreccion and lyfe; whosoever beleveth on me, ye, though he were deed, yet shall he lyve."

Italian Influence: Wyatt and Surrey. — During the reign of Henry VIII. (1509–1547), the influence of Italian poetry made itself distinctly felt. The roots of Elizabethan poetry were watered by many fountains, one of the chief of which flowed from Italian soil. To Sir Thomas Wyatt (1503–1542) and to the Earl of Surrey (1517–1547) belongs the credit of introducing from Italian sources new influences, which helped to remodel English poetry and give it a distinctly modern cast.

These poets were the first to introduce the sonnet, which Shakespeare, Milton, and Wordsworth employed with such power in after times. Blank verse was first used in England by the Earl of Surrey, who translated a portion of Vergil's *Æneid* into that measure. When Shakespeare took up his pen, he found that vehicle of poetic expression ready for his use.

After Holbein.
SIR THOMAS WYATT

Wyatt and Surrey adopted Italian subject matter as well as form. They introduced the poetry of the amorists, that is, verse which tells of the woes and joys of a lover. We find Shakespeare in his *Sonnets* turning to this subject, which he made as broad and deep as life. In 1557, the year before Elizabeth's accession, the poems of Wyatt and Surrey appeared in Tottel's *Miscellany*, one of the earliest printed collections of modern English poetry.

SUMMARY

The first part of the century and a half following the death of Chaucer saw war with France and the Wars of the Roses, in which most of the nobles were killed. The reign of Henry VII. and his successors in the Tudor line shows the increased influence of the crown, freed from the restraint of the powerful lords. The period witnessed the passing of serfdom and the extension of trade and manufactures.

The changes in religious views were far-reaching. Henry VIII. superseded the Pope as head of the English church, dissolved the monasteries, and placed an English translation of the *Bible* in the churches. Henry's son and successor, Edward VI., established the Protestant form of worship, but his half-sister Mary used persecution in an endeavor to bring back the old faith.

The influences of the Renaissance, moving westward from Italy, were tending toward their culmination in the next period. The study of Greek literature, the discovery of the new world, the decline of feudalism, the overthrow of the armed knight, the extension of the use of gunpowder, the invention of printing, the increased love of learning, the demand for scientific investigation, the decline of monastic influence, shown in the new interest in this finite world and life, — all figured as causes or effects of the new influence.

The most important prose works are Sir Thomas Malory's *Morte d'Arthur*, a masterly retelling of the Arthurian legends; Sir Thomas More's *Utopia*, a magnificent Renaissance dream of a new social world; and Tyndale's translation of the *Bible*. The best poetry was written in Scotland, and this verse anticipates in some measure that love of nature which is a dominant characteristic of the last part of the eighteenth century. The age is noted for its ballads, which aided in developing among high and low a liking for poetry. At the close of the period, we find Italian influences at work, as may be seen in the verse of Wyatt and Surrey.

REFERENCES FOR FURTHER STUDY

HISTORICAL

An account of the history of this period may be found in either Gardiner,[1] Green, Lingard, Walker, or Cheney. Vols. IV. and V. of *The Political History of England*, edited by Hunt (Longmans), gives the history in greater detail. For the social side, consult Traill's *Social England*, Vols. II. and III., also Cheney's *Industrial and Social History of England*, Field's *Introduction to the Study of the Renaissance*, Einstein's *The Italian Renaissance in England*, Symonds's *A Short History of the Renaissance*.

LITERARY

The Cambridge History of English Literature, Vol. II.
Snell's *The Age of Transition*, 1400-1580.
Morley's *English Literature*, Vols. VI. and VII.
Minto's *Characteristics of English Poets*, pp. 69-130.
Saintsbury's *Short History of English Literature*, pp. 157-218.
Dictionary of National Biography, articles on *Malory, Caxton, Henryson, Gawain Douglas, Dunbar, Tyndale, Wyatt*, and *Surrey*.
Veitch's *The Feeling for Nature in Scottish Poetry*.
Percy's *Reliques of Ancient English Poetry*.
Gummere's *Old English Ballads*.
Child's *The English and Scotch Popular Ballads*.
Collins's *Greek Influence on English Poetry*.
Tucker's *The Foreign Debt of English Literature*.

[1] For full titles, see p. 50.

SUGGESTED READINGS
WITH QUESTIONS AND SUGGESTIONS

Malory.— Craik,[1] 72–74; *Century*, 19–33; Swiggett's *Selections from Malory*; Wragg's *Selections from Malory*,— all contain good selections. The Globe Edition is an inexpensive single volume containing the complete text. The best edition is a reproduction of the original in three volumes with introductions by Oscar Sommer and Andrew Lang (London: David Nutt). Howard Pyle has retold Malory's best stories in simple form (Scribner).

Compare the death (or passing) of Arthur in Malory with Tennyson's *The Passing of Arthur*. What special qualities do you notice in the manner of Malory's telling a story? Is his work original? Why has it remained so popular? What age specially shows its influence?

More. — The English translation of the *Utopia* may be found entire in *Everyman's Library* (35 ¢). There are good selections in Craik, I., 162–167.

What is the etymological meaning of *Utopia?* What is its modern significance? Did More really give a new word to literature and speech? The *Utopia* should be read for an indication of the influence of the Renaissance and for comparison with twentieth-century ideas of social improvement.

Tyndale. — Bosworth and Waring's *Gospels*, containing the Anglo-Saxon, Wycliffe, and Tyndale versions. Specimens of Tyndale's prose are given in Chambers, I., 130; Craik, I., 185–187.

Why is Tyndale's translation of the *Bible* important to the student of literature? What are some special qualities of this translation?

Early Scottish Poetry. — Selections from fifteenth-century Scottish poetry may be found in Bronson, I., 170–197; Ward, I., *passim*; P. & S., 246–277; *Oxford*, 16–33.

From the *King's Quair* and the poems of Henryson, Dunbar, and Gawain Douglas, select passages that show first-hand intimacy with nature. Compare these with lines from any poet whose knowledge of nature seems to you to be acquired from books.

Ballads. — Ward, I., *passim*, contains among others three excellent ballads, -- *Sir Patrick Spens, The Twa Corbies, Robin Hood Rescuing the Widow's Three Sons*. Bronson, I., 203–254; P. & S., 282–301; *Oxford*, 33–51; and Maynard's *English Classics*, No. 96, *Early English Ballads*

---

[1] For full titles, see p. 6.

also have good selections. The best collection is Child's *The English and Scotch Popular Ballads*, 5 vols.

What are the chief characteristics of the old ballads? Why do they interest us to-day? Which of those indicated for reading has proved most interesting? What influence impossible for other forms of literature was exerted by the ballad? What did Autolycus mean (*Winter's Tale*, IV., 4) when he offered "songs for man or woman, of all sizes"? Have any ballads been written in recent times?

Wyatt and Surrey. — Read two characteristic love sonnets by Wyatt and Surrey, P. & S., 313-319; Ward, I., 251, 257; Bronson, II., 1-4. A specimen of the first English blank verse employed by Surrey in translating Vergil's *Æneid*, is given in Bronson, II., 4, 5; in P. & S., 322, 323; and Chambers, I., 162.

Why are Wyatt and Surrey called amourists? What contributions did they make to the form of English verse? What foreign influences did they help to usher in?

CHAPTER IV

THE AGE OF ELIZABETH, 1558-1603

The Reign of Elizabeth. — Queen Elizabeth, who ranks among the greatest of the world's rulers, was the daughter of Henry VIII. and his second wife Anne Boleyn. Elizabeth reigned as queen of England from 1558 until her death in 1603. The remarkable allowances which she made for difference of opinion showed that she felt the spirit of the Renaissance. She loved England, and her most important acts were guided, not by selfish personal motives, but by a strong desire to make England a great nation.

She had a law passed restoring the supremacy of the monarch, "as well in all spiritual or ecclesiastical things as temporal." The prayer book of Edward VI. was again introduced and the mass was forbidden. She was broad enough not to inquire too closely into the private religious opinions of her subjects, so long as they went to the established church. For each absence they were fined a shilling. Next to churchgoing and her country, she loved and encouraged plays.

FACSIMILE OF ELIZABETH'S SIGNATURE TO A LICENSE FOR THE EARL OF LEICESTER'S COMPANY OF PLAYERS, 1574

For more than twenty years she was worried by the fear that either France or Spain would put her Catholic cousin, Mary Queen of Scots, on the English throne. With masterly diplomacy, Elizabeth for a long time managed to retain the active friendship of at least one of these great powers, in order to restrain the other from interfering. She had kept Mary a prisoner for nineteen years, fearing to liberate her. At last an active conspiracy was discovered to assassinate Elizabeth and put Mary on the throne. Elizabeth accordingly had her cousin beheaded in 1587. Spain thereupon prepared her fleet, the Invincible Armada, to attack England. When this became known, the outburst of patriotic feeling was so intense among all classes in England that the queen did not hesitate to put Lord Howard, a Catholic, in command of the English fleet. The Armada was utterly defeated, and England was free to enter on her glorious period of influencing the thought and action of the world.

In brief, Elizabeth's reign was remarkable for the rise of the middle classes, for the growth of manufactures, for the appearance of English ships in almost all parts of the world, for the extension of commerce, for greater freedom of thought and action, for what the world now calls Elizabethan literature, and for the ascendancy of a great mental and moral movement to which we must next call attention.

Culmination of the Renaissance and the Reformation. — We have seen (p. 102) that the Renaissance began in Italy in the fourteenth century and influenced the work of Chaucer. In the same century, Wycliffe's influence (p. 75) helped the cause of the Reformation. Elizabethan England alone had the good fortune to experience the culmination of these two movements at one and the same time. At no other period and in no other country have two forces, like the Renaissance and the Reformation, combined at the height of their ascendancy to stimulate the human mind. One result of these two mighty influences was the work of William Shakespeare, which speaks to the ear of all time.

The Renaissance, having opened the gates of knowledge, inspired the Elizabethans with the hope of learning every secret of nature and of surmounting all difficulties. The Reformation gave man new freedom, imposed on him the gravest individual responsibilities, made him realize the importance of every act of his own will, and emphasized afresh the idea of the stewardship of this present life, for which he would be held accountable. In Elizabethan days, these two forces coöperated; in the following Puritan age they were at war.

Some Characteristics of Elizabethan Life. — It became an ambition to have as many different experiences as possible, to search for that variety craved by youth and by a youthful age. Sir Walter Raleigh was a courtier, a writer, a warden of the tin mines, a vice admiral, a captain of the guard, a colonizer, a country gentleman, and a pirate. Sir Philip Sidney, who died at the age of thirty-two, was an envoy to a foreign court, a writer of romances, an officer in the army, a poet, and a courtier. Shakespeare left the little town where he was born, to plunge into the more complex life of London. The poet, Edmund Spenser, went to turbulent Ireland, where he had enough experiences to suggest the conflicts in the *Faerie Queene*.

The greater freedom and initiative of the individual and the remarkable extension of trade with all parts of the world naturally led to the rise of the middle class. The nobility were no longer the sole leaders in England's rapid progress. Many of Elizabeth's councilors were said to have sprung from the masses, but no reign could boast of wiser ministers. It was then customary for the various classes to mingle much more freely than they do now. There was absence of that overspecialization which to-day keeps people in such sharply separated groups. This mingling was further aided by the tendency to try many different pursuits and by the spirit of patriotism in the air. All classes were interested in repelling the Spanish Armada and in maintaining England's freedom. It was fortunate for Shakespeare that the Elizabethan age gave him unusual opportunity to meet and to become the spokesman of all classes of men. The audience that stood in the pit or sat in the boxes to witness the performance of his plays, comprised not only lords and wealthy merchants, but also weavers, sailors, and country folk.

Initiative and Love of Action. — The Elizabethans were distinguished for their initiative. This term implies the possession of two qualities: (1) ingenuity or fertility in ideas, and (2) ability to pass at once from an idea to its suggested action. Never did action habitually follow more quickly on the heels of thought. The age loved to translate everything into action, because the spirit of the Renaissance demanded the exercise of youthful activity to its fullest capacity in order that the power which the new knowledge promised could be acquired and enjoyed before death. As the Elizabethans felt that real life meant activity in exploring a new and interesting world, both physical and mental, they demanded that their literature should present this life of action. Hence, all their greatest poets, with the exception of Spenser, were dramatists. Even Spenser's *Faerie Queene*, with its abstractions, is a poem of action, for the **virtues** fight with the vices.

ELIZABETHAN PROSE LITERATURE

Variety in the Prose. — The imaginative spirit of the Elizabethans craved poetry, and all the greatest authors of this age, with the exception of Francis Bacon, were poets. If, however, an Elizabethan had been so peculiarly constituted as to wish to stock his library with contemporary prose only, he could have secured good works in many different fields. He could, for instance, have obtained (1) an excellent book on education, the *Scholemaster* of **Roger Ascham** (1515-1568); (2) interesting volumes of travel, such as the *Navigations, Voyages, and Discoveries of the English Nation*, by **Richard Hakluyt** (1552-1616); and *The Discovery of Guiana*, by **Sir Walter Raleigh** (1552-1618); (3) history, in the important *Chronicles of England, Ireland, and Scotland* (1578), by **Raphael Holinshed**; the *Chronicle* (*Annals of England*) and *Survey of London*, by **John Stow** (1525-1604); and the *Brittania*, by **William Camden** (1551-1623); (4) biography, in the excellent translation of *Plutarch's Lives*, by **Sir Thomas North** (1535-1601?); (5) criticism, in *The Apologie for Poetrie*, by Sir Philip Sidney; (6) essays on varied subjects by Francis Bacon; (7) works dealing with religion and faith: (*a*) **John Foxe's** (1516-1587) *Book of Martyrs*, which told in simple prose thrilling stories of martyrs and served as a textbook of the Reformation; (*b*) Hooker's *Of the Laws of Ecclesiastical Polity*, a treatise on theology; (8) fiction,[1] in John Lyly's *Euphues* (1579), Robert Greene's *Pandosto* (1588), Sir Philip Sidney's *Arcadia* (1590), Thomas Lodge's *Rosalynde* (1590), Nashe's *The Unfortunate Traveler* (1594), and **Thomas Deloney's** *The Gentle Craft* (1597).[2]

---

[1] For additional mention of Elizabethan novelists, see p. 317.

[2] For references to selections from all these prose writers, see p. 215.

Shakespeare read Holinshed, North, Greene, Sidney, and Lodge (see p. 187) and turned some of their suggestions into poetry, which we very much prefer to their prose. We are nearly certain that Shakespeare studied Lyly's *Euphues*, because we can trace the influence of that work in his style.

It was the misfortune of Elizabethan prose to be almost completely overshadowed by the poetry. This prose was, however, far more varied and important than that of any preceding age. The books mentioned on page 123 constitute only a small part of the prose of this period.

Lyly, Sidney, Hooker. — In 1579, when Shakespeare was fifteen years old, there appeared the first part of an influential prose work, John Lyly's (1554?–1606) *Euphues, the Anatomy of Wit*, followed in 1580 by a second part, *Euphues and his England*. Much of Lyly's subject matter is borrowed, and his form reflects the artificial style then popular over Europe.

Euphues, a young Athenian, goes to Naples, where he falls in love and is jilted. This is all the action in the first part of the so-called story. The rest is moralizing. In the second part, Euphues comes to England with a friend, who falls in love twice, and finally marries; but again there is more moralizing than story. Euphues returns to Athens and retires to the mountains to muse in solitude.

In its use of a love story, *Euphues* prefigures the modern novel. In *Euphues*, however, the love story serves chiefly as a peg on which to hang discussions on fickleness, youthful follies, friendship, and divers other subjects.

Lyly aimed to produce artistic prose, which would render his meaning clear and impressive. To achieve this object, he made such excessive use of contrast, balanced words and phrases, and far-fetched comparisons, that his style seems highly artificial and affected. This quotation is typical:—

After the miniature by Isaac Oliver, Windsor Castle.

Philippe Sidney.

"Achilles spear could as well heal as hurt, the scorpion though he sting, yet he stints the pain, though the herb *Nerius* poison the sheep, yet is a remedy to man against poison. . . . There is great difference between the standing puddle and the running stream, yet both water: great odds between the adamant and the pomice, yet both stones, a great distinction to be put between *vitrum* and the crystal, yet both glass: great contrariety between Lais and Lucretia, yet both women."

Although this selection shows unnatural or strained antithesis, there is also evident a commendable desire to vary the diction and to avoid the repetition of the same word. To find four different terms for nearly the same idea: "difference," "odds," "distinction," and "contrariety," involves considerable painstaking. While it is true that the term "euphuism" has come to be applied to any stilted, antithetical style that pays more attention to the manner of expressing a thought than to its worth, we should remember that English prose style has advanced because some writers, like Lyly, emphasized the importance of artistic form. Shakespeare occasionally employs euphuistic contrast in an effective way. The sententious Polonius says in *Hamlet:*—

"Give every man thy ear, but few thy voice."

Sir Philip Sidney (1554–1586) wrote for his sister, the Countess of Pembroke, a pastoral romance, entitled *Arcadia* (published in 1590). Unlike Lyly, Sidney did not aim at precision, emphatic contrast, and balance. For its effectiveness, the *Arcadia* relies on poetic language and conceptions. The characters in the romance live and love in a Utopian Arcadia, where "the morning did strow Roses and Violets in the heavenly floor against the coming of the Sun," and where the shepherd boy pipes "as though he should never be old."

Passages like the following show Sidney's poetic style and as much exuberant fancy as if they had been written by a Celt (see p. 42):—

"Her breath is more sweet than a gentle southwest wind, which comes creeping over flowery fields and shadowed waters in the extreme heat of summer; and yet is nothing compared to the honey-flowing speech that breath doth carry."

The *Arcadia* furnished Shakespeare's *King Lear* with the auxiliary plot of Gloucester and his two sons and inspired Thomas Lodge to write his novel *Rosalynde*, which in turn suggested Shakespeare's *As You Like It*.

To Sidney belongs the credit of having written the first meritorious essay on criticism in the English language, *The Apologie for Poetrie*. This defends the poetic art, and shows how necessary such exercise of the imagination is to take us away from the cold, hard facts of life.

Richard Hooker's (1554?–1600) *Of the Laws of Ecclesiastical Polity* shows a third aim in Elizabethan prose, — to express carefully reasoned investigation and conclusion in English that is as thoroughly elaborated and qualified as the thought. Lyly's striking contrasts and Sidney's flowery prose do not appeal to Hooker, who uses Latin inversions and parenthetical qualifications, and adds clause after clause whenever he thinks it necessary to amplify the thought or to guard against misunderstanding. Hooker's prose is as carefully wrought as Lyly's and far more rhythmical. Both were experimenting with English prose in different fields, serving to teach succeeding writers what to imitate and to avoid.

Unlike *Euphues* and the *Arcadia*, *Of the Laws of Ecclesiastical Polity* is more valuable for its thought than for its form of expression. This work, which is still studied as an authority, is an exposition of divine law in its relations to both the world and the church. Hooker was personally a compound of sweetness and light, and his philosophy is marked by sweet reasonableness. He was a clergyman of the Church of England, but he shows a spirit of toleration toward other churches. He had much of the modern idea of growth in both government and religion, and he "accepts no system of government either in church or state as unalterable."

From the painting by Van Somer, National Portrait Gallery.

FRANCIS BACON, 1561-1626

Life. — A study of Bacon takes us beyond the limits of the reign of Elizabeth, but not beyond the continued influences of that reign. Francis Bacon, the son of Sir Nicholas Bacon, Lord Keeper of the Great Seal under Elizabeth, was born in London and grew up under the influences of the court. In order to understand some of Bacon's actions in later life, we must remember the influences that helped to fashion him in his boyhood days. Those with whom he early associated and who unconsciously molded him were not very scrupulous about the way in which they secured the favor of the court or the means which they took to outstrip an adversary. They also encouraged in him a taste for expensive luxuries. These unfortunate influences were intensified when, at the age of sixteen, he went with the English ambassador to Paris, and remained there for two and a half years, studying statecraft and diplomacy.

When Bacon was nineteen, his father died. The son, being without money, returned from Paris and appealed to his uncle, Lord Burleigh, one of Elizabeth's ministers, for some lucrative position at the court. In a letter to his uncle, Bacon says: "I confess I have as vast contemplative ends as I have moderate civil ends; for I have taken all knowledge to be my province." This statement shows the Elizabethan desire to master the entire world of the New Learning. Instead of helping his nephew, however, Lord Burleigh seems to have done all in his power to thwart him. Bacon thereupon studied law and was admitted to the bar in 1582.

Bacon entered Parliament in 1584 and distinguished himself as a speaker. Ben Jonson, the dramatist, says of him: "There happened in my time one noble speaker who was full of gravity in his speaking. No man ever spoke more neatly, more presly, more weightily, or suffered less emptiness, less idleness, in what he uttered. His hearers could not cough or look aside from him without loss. The fear of every man that heard him was lest he should make an end." This speaking was valuable training for Bacon in writing the pithy sentences of his *Essays*. A man who uses the long, involved sentences of Hooker can never become a speaker to whom people will listen. The habit of directness and simplicity, which Bacon formed in his speaking, remained with him through life.

Among the many charges against Bacon's personal code of ethics, two stand out conspicuously. The Earl of Essex, who had given Bacon an estate then worth £1800, was influential in having him appointed to the staff of counselors to Queen Elizabeth. When Essex was accused of treason, Bacon kept the queen's friendship by repudiating him and taking an active part in the prosecution that led to the earl's execution. After James I. had made Bacon Lord High Chancellor of England, he was accused of receiving bribes as a judge. He replied that he had accepted only the customary presents given to judges and that these made no difference in his decisions. He was tried, found guilty, fined £40,000, and sentenced to be imprisoned in the Tower during the king's pleasure. After a few days, however, the king released him, forgave the fine, and gave him an annual pension of £1200.

The question whether he wrote Shakespeare's plays needs almost as much discussion on the moral as on the intellectual side (p. 195). James Spedding, after studying Bacon's life and works for thirty years, said: "I see no reason to suppose that Shakespeare did not write the plays. But if somebody else did, then I think I am in a position to say that it was not Lord Bacon."

After his release, Bacon passed the remaining five years of his life in retirement, — studying and writing. His interest in observing natural objects and experimenting with them was the cause of his death. He was riding in a snowstorm when it occurred to him to test snow as a preservative agent. He stopped at a house, procured a fowl, and stuffed it with snow. He caught cold during this experiment and, being improperly cared for, soon died.

The Essays. — The first ten of his *Essays*, his most popular work, appeared in the year 1597. At the time of his death, he had increased them to fifty-eight. They deal with a wide range of subjects, from *Studies* and *Nobility*, on the one hand, to *Marriage and Single Life* and *Gardens*, on the other. The great critic Hallam says: "It would be somewhat derogatory to a man of the slightest claim to polite letters, were he unacquainted with the *Essays* of Bacon. It is, indeed, little worth while to read this or any other book for reputation's sake; but very few in our language so well repay the pains, or afford more nourishment to the thoughts."

TITLE PAGE OF BACON'S ESSAYS, 1597

The following sentence from the essay *Of Studies* will show some of the characteristics of his way of presenting thought: —

"Reading maketh a full man, conference a ready man, and writing an exact man; and, therefore, if a man write little, he had need have a great memory; if he confer little, he had need have a present wit; and if he read little, he had need have much cunning to seem to know that he doth not."

We may notice here (1) clearness, (2) conciseness, (3) breadth of thought and observation.

A shrewd Scotchman says: "It may be said that to men wishing to rise in the world by politic management of their fellowmen, Bacon's *Essays* are the best handbook hitherto published." In justification of this criticism, we need only quote from the essay *Of Negotiating:* —

"It is generally better to deal by speech than by letter. . . . Letters are good, when a man would draw an answer by letter back again, or when it may serve, for a man's justification, afterwards to produce his own letter, or where it may be danger to be interrupted or heard by pieces. To deal in person is good, when a man's face breedeth regard, as commonly with inferiors, or in tender cases, where a man's eye upon the countenance of him with whom he speaketh may give him a direction how far to go, and generally, where a man will reserve to himself liberty either to disavow or to expound."

Scientific and Miscellaneous Works. — *The Advancement of Learning* is another of Bacon's great works. The title aptly expresses the purpose of the book. He insists on the necessity of close observation of nature and of making experiments with various forms of matter. He decries the habit of spinning things out of one's inner consciousness, without patiently studying the outside world to see whether the facts justify the conclusions. In other words, he insists on induction. Bacon was not the father of the inductive principle, as is sometimes wrongly stated; for prehistoric man was compelled to make inductions before he could advance one step from barbarism. The trouble was that this method was not rigorously applied. It was currently believed that our valuable garden toad is venomous and that frogs are bred from slime. For his knowledge of bees, Lyly consulted classical authors in preference to watching the insects. Bacon's writings exerted a powerful influence in the direction of exact inductive method.

Bacon had so little faith in the enduring qualities of the English language, that he wrote the most of his philosophical works in Latin. He planned a Latin work in six parts, to cover the whole field of the philosophy of natural science. The most famous of the parts completed is the *Novum Organum*, which deals with certain methods for searching after definite truth, and shows how to avoid some ever present tendencies toward error.

Bacon wrote an excellent *History of the Reign of Henry VII.*, which is standard to this day. He is also the author of *The New Atlantis*, which may be termed a Baconian Utopia, or study of an ideal commonwealth.

General Characteristics. — In Bacon's sentences we may often find remarkable condensation of thought in few words. A modern essayist has taken seven pages to express, or rather to obscure, the ideas in these three lines from Bacon: —

"Men of age object too much, consult too long, adventure too little, repent too soon, and seldom drive business home to the full period, but content themselves with a mediocrity of success."[1]

His works abound in illustrations, analogies, and striking imagery; but, unlike the great Elizabethan poets, he appeals more to cold intellect than to the feelings. We are often pleased with his intellectual ingenuity, for instance, in likening the Schoolmen to spiders, spinning such stuff as webs are made of "out of no great quantity of matter."

He resembles the Elizabethans in preferring magnificent to commonplace images. It has been often noticed that if he essays to write of buildings in general, he prefers to describe palaces. His knowledge of the intellectual side of human nature is especially remarkable, but, unlike Shakespeare, Bacon never drops his plummet into the emotional depths of the soul.

[1] *Of Youth and Age.*

THE NON-DRAMATIC POETRY — LYRICAL VERSE

A Medium of Artistic Expression. — No age has surpassed the Elizabethan in lyrical poems, those "short swallow flights of song," as Tennyson defines them. The English Renaissance, unlike the Italian, did not achieve great success in painting. The Englishman embodied in poetry his artistic expression of the beautiful. Many lyrics are merely examples of word painting. The Elizabethan poet often began his career by trying to show his skill with the ingenious and musical arrangement of words, where an Italian would have used color and drawing on an actual canvas.

We have seen that in the reign of Henry VIII. Wyatt and Surrey (p. 114) introduced into England from Italy the type of lyrical verse known as the sonnet. This is the most artificial of lyrics, because its rules prescribe a length of exactly fourteen lines and a definite internal structure.

The sonnet was especially popular with Elizabethan poets. In the last ten years of the sixteenth century, more than two thousand sonnets were written. Even Shakespeare served a poetic apprenticeship by writing many sonnets as well as semi-lyrical poems, like *Venus and Adonis*.

We should, however, remember that the sonnet is only one type of the varied lyric expression of the age. Many Elizabethan song books show that lyrics were set to music and used on the most varied occasions. There were songs for weddings, funerals, dances, banquets, — songs for the tinkers, the barbers, and other workmen. If modern readers chance to pick up an Elizabethan novel, like **Thomas Lodge's** *Rosalynde* (1590), they are surprised to find that prose will not suffice for the lover, who must "evaporate" into song like this: —

> "Love in my bosom like a bee,
>   Doth suck his sweet,
> Now with his wings he plays with me,
>   Now with his feet."

There are large numbers of Elizabethan lyrics apparently as spontaneous and unfettered as the song of the lark. The seeming artlessness of much of this verse should not blind us to the fact that an unusual number of poets had really studied the art of song.

Love Lyrics. — The subject of the Elizabethan sonnets is usually love. Sir Philip Sidney wrote many love sonnets, the best of which is the one beginning: —

> "With how sad steps, O Moon, thou climb'st the Skies!"

Edmund Spenser composed fifty-eight sonnets in one year to chronicle his varied emotions as a lover. We may find among Shakespeare's 154 sonnets some of the greatest love lyrics in the language, such, for instance, as CXVI., containing the lines: —

> "Love is not love
> Which alters when it alteration finds";

or, as XVIII.: —

> "Shall I compare thee to a summer's day?
>   Thou art more lovely and more temperate:
> Rough winds do shake the darling buds of May,
>   And summer's lease hath all too short a date.
>   .   .   .   .
>   But thy eternal summer shall not fade."

Sonnets came to be used in much the same way as a modern love letter or valentine. In the latter part of Elizabeth's reign, sonnets were even called "merchantable ware." **Michael Drayton** (1563-1631), a prolific poet, author of the *Ballad of Agincourt*, one of England's greatest war songs, tells how he was employed by a lover to write a sonnet which won the lady. Drayton's best sonnet is, *Since there's no help, come let us kiss and part.*

Outside of the sonnets, we shall find love lyrics in great variety. One of the most popular of Elizabethan songs is Ben Jonson's: —

> "Drink to me only with thine eyes,
> And I will pledge with mine;
> Or leave a kiss but in the cup,
> And I'll not look for wine."

The Elizabethans were called a "nest of singing birds" because such songs as the following are not unusual in the work of their minor writers: —

> "Sweet air, blow soft; mount, lark, aloft
> To give my love good morrow!
> Wings from the wind to please her mind,
> Notes from the lark I'll borrow."[1]

Pastoral Lyrics. — In Shakespeare's early youth it was the fashion to write lyrics about the delights of rustic life with sheep and shepherds. The Italians, freshly interested in Vergil's *Georgics* and *Bucolics*, had taught the English how to write pastoral verse. The entire joyous world had become a Utopian sheep pasture, in which shepherds piped and fell in love with glorified shepherdesses. A great poet named one of his productions, *Shepherd's Calendar* (p. 141) and Sir Philip Sidney wrote in poetic prose the pastoral romance *Arcadia*.

Christopher Marlowe's *The Passionate Shepherd to his Love* is a typical poetic expression of the fancied delight in pastoral life: —

> ". . . we will sit upon the rocks,
> Seeing the shepherds feed their flocks
> By shallow rivers, to whose falls
> Melodious birds sing madrigals."

[1] Thomas Heywood's *Matin Song*.

Miscellaneous Lyrics. — As the Elizabethan age progressed, the subject matter of the lyrics became broader. Verse showing consummate mastery of form expressed the most varied emotions. Some of the greatest lyrics of the period are the songs interspersed in the plays of the dramatists, from Lyly (p. 167) to Beaumont and Fletcher (p. 205). The plays of Shakespeare, the greatest and most varied of Elizabethan lyrical poets, especially abound in such songs. Two of the best of these occur in his *Cymbeline*. One is the song —

"Hark! hark! the lark at heaven's gate sings,"

and the other is the dirge beginning: —

"Fear no more the heat o' the sun."

Ariel's songs in *The Tempest* fascinate with the witchery of untrammeled existence. Two lines of a song from *Twelfth Night* give an attractive presentation of the Renaissance philosophy of the present as opposed to an elusive future: —

"What is love? 'tis not hereafter;
Present mirth hath present laughter."

Two of the later Elizabethan poets, Ben Jonson and **John Donne** (1573–1631), specially impress us by their efforts to secure ingenious effects in verse.

From the painting ascribed to Cornelius Jansen, South Kensington Museum.

JOHN DONNE

Ben Jonson often shows this tendency, as in trying to give a poetic definition of a kiss as something —

"So sugar'd, so melting, so soft, so delicious,"

and in showing so much ingenuity of expression in the cramping limits of an epitaph: —

> "Underneath this stone doth lie
> As much beauty as could die,
> Which in life did harbor give
> To more virtue than doth live."

The poet most famous for a display of extreme ingenuity in verse is John Donne, a traveler, courtier, and finally dean of St. Paul's Cathedral, who possessed, to quote his own phrase, an "hydroptic immoderate desire of human learning." He paid less attention to artistic form than the earlier Elizabethans, showed more cynicism, chose the abstract rather than the concrete, and preferred involved metaphysical thought to simple sensuous images. He made few references to nature and few allusions to the characters of classical mythology, but searched for obscure likenesses between things, and for conceits or far-fetched comparisons. In his poem, *A Funeral Elegy*, he shows these qualities in characterizing a fair young lady as: —

> "One, whose clear body was so pure and thin,
> Because it need disguise no thought within;
> 'Twas but a through-light scarf her mind to enroll,
> Or exhalation breathed out from her soul."

The idea in Shakespeare's simpler expression, "the heavenly rhetoric of thine eye," was expanded by Donne into: —

> "Our eye-beams twisted, and did thread
> Our eyes upon one double string."

Donne does not always show so much fine-spun ingenuity, but this was the quality most imitated by a group of his successors (p. 234). His claim to distinction rests on the originality and ingenuity of his verse, and perhaps still more on his influence over succeeding poets.[1]

[1] Suggestions for additional study of Elizabethan lyrics are given on p. 215.

From a painting in Duplin Castle

EDMUND SPENSER, 1552-1599

Life and Minor Poems. — For one hundred and fifty-two years after Chaucer's death, in 1400, England had no great poet until Edmund Spenser was born in London in 1552. Spenser, who became the greatest non-dramatic poet of the Elizabethan age, was twelve years older than Shakespeare.

His parents were poor, but fortunately in Elizabethan times, as well as in our own days, there were generous men who found their chief pleasure in aiding others. Such a man assisted Spenser in going to Cambridge. Spenser's benefactor was sufficiently wise not to give the student enough to dwarf the growth of self-reliance. We know that Spenser was a sizar at Cambridge, that is, one of those students who, to quote Macaulay, "had to perform some menial services. They swept the court; they carried up the dinner to the fellows' table, and changed the plate and poured out the ale of the rulers of society." We know further that Spenser was handicapped by ill health during a part of his course, for we find records of allowances paid "Spenser *ægrotanti.*"

After leaving Cambridge Spenser went to the north of England, probably in the capacity of tutor. While there, he fell in love with a young woman whom he calls Rosalind. This event colored his after life. Although she refused him, she had penetration enough to see in what his greatness consisted, and her opinion spurred him to develop his abilities as a poet. He was about twenty-five years old when he fell in love with Rosalind; and he remained single until he was forty-two, when he married an Irish maiden named Elizabeth. In honor of that event, he composed the *Epithalamion*, the noblest marriage song in any literature. So strong are early impressions that even in its lines he seems to be thinking of Rosalind and fancying that she is his bride.

After returning from the north, he spent some time with Sir Philip Sidney, who helped fashion Spenser's ideals of a chivalrous gentleman. Sidney's influence is seen in Spenser's greatest work, the *Faerie Queene*. Sir Walter Raleigh was another friend who left his imprint on Spenser.

In 1579 Spenser published the *Shepherd's Calendar*.

This is a pastoral poem, consisting of twelve different parts, one part being assigned to each of the twelve months. Although inferior to the *Faerie Queene*, the *Shepherd's Calendar* remains one of the greatest pastoral poems in the English language.

In 1580 he was appointed secretary to Lord Gray, Lord Lieutenant of Ireland. In one capacity or another, in the service of the crown, Spenser passed in Ireland almost the entire remaining eighteen years of his life. In 1591 he received in the south of Ireland a grant of three thousand acres, a part of the confiscated estate of an Irish earl. Sir Walter Raleigh was also given forty-two thousand acres near Spenser. Ireland was then in a state of continuous turmoil. In such a country Spenser lived and wrote his *Faerie Queene*. Of course, this environment powerfully affected the character of that poem. It has been said that to read a contemporary's account of "Raleigh's adventures with the Irish chieftains, his challenges and single combats, his escapes at fords and woods, is like reading bits of the *Faerie Queene* in prose."

In 1598 the Irish, infuriated by the invasion of their country and the seizure of their lands, set fire to Spenser's castle. He and his family barely escaped with their lives. He crossed to England and died the next year, according to some accounts, in want. He was buried, at the expense of Lord Essex, in Westminster Abbey, near Chaucer.

The Faerie Queene. — In 1590 Spenser published the first three books of the *Faerie Queene*. The original plan was to have the poem contain twelve books, like Vergil's *Æneid*, but only six were published. If more were written, they have been lost.

The poem is an allegory with the avowed moral purpose of fashioning "a gentleman or noble person in vertuous and gentle discipline." Spenser says: "I labour to pourtraict in Arthure, before he was King, the image of a brave knight, perfected in the twelve private morall vertues, as Aristotle hath devised." Twelve Knights personifying twelve Virtues were to fight with their opposing Vices, and the twelve books were to tell the story of the conflict. The Knights set out from the court of Gloriana, the Faerie Queene, in search of their enemies, and meet with divers adventures and enchantments.

The hero of the tale is Arthur, who has figured so much in English song and legend. Spenser makes him typical of all the Virtues taken together. The first book, which is really a complete poem by itself, and which is generally admitted to be the finest, contains an account of the adventures of the Red Cross Knight who represents Holiness. Other books tell of the warfare of the Knights who typify Temperance, Chastity, Friendship, Justice, and Courtesy.

The poem begins thus: —

"A gentle Knight was pricking[1] on the plaine,
  Ycladd in mightie armes and silver shielde,
Wherein old dints of deepe woundes did remaine,
  The cruell markes of many' a bloody fielde;
Yet armes till that time did he never wield.

.   .   .   .

"And on his brest a bloodie Crosse he bore,
  The deare remembrance of his dying Lord,
For whose sweete sake that glorious badge he wore.

.   .   .   .

"Upon a great adventure he was bond,
  That greatest Gloriana to him gave,
That greatest glorious Queene of Faerie lond."

The entire poem really typifies the aspirations of the human soul for something nobler and better than can be gained

[1] riding.

without effort. In Spenser's imaginative mind, these aspirations became real persons who set out to win laurels in a fairyland, lighted with the soft light of the moon, and presided over by the good genius that loves to uplift struggling and weary souls.

The allegory certainly becomes confused. A critic well says: "We can hardly lose our way in it, for there is no way to lose." We are not called on to understand the intricacies of the allegory, but to read between the lines, catch the noble moral lesson, and drink to our fill at the fountain of beauty and melody.

Spenser a Subjective Poet. — The subjective cast of Spenser's mind next demands attention. We feel that his is an ideal world, one that does not exist outside of the imagination. In order to understand the difference between subjective and objective, let us compare Chaucer with Spenser. No one can really be said to study literature without constantly bringing in the principle of comparison. We must notice the likeness and the difference between literary productions, or the faint impression which they make upon our minds will soon pass away.

Chaucer is objective; that is, he identifies himself with things that could have a real existence in the outside world. We find ourselves looking at the shiny bald head of Chaucer's Monk, at the lean horse and threadbare clothes of the Student of Oxford, at the brown complexion of the Shipman, at the enormous hat and large figure of the Wife of Bath, at the red face of the Summoner, at the hair of the Pardoner "yelow as wex." These are not mere figments of the imagination. We feel that they are either realities or that they could have existed.

While the adventures in the Irish wars undoubtedly gave the original suggestions for many of the contests between good and evil in the *Faerie Queene*, Spenser intentionally idealized these knightly struggles to uphold the right and placed them in fairyland. This great poem is the work of a mind that loved to elaborate purely subjective images. The pictures were not painted from gazing at the outside world. We feel that they are mostly creations of the imagination, and that few of them could exist in a real world. There is no bower in the bottom of the sea, "built of hollow billowes heaped hye," and no lion ever follows a lost maiden to protect her. We feel that the principal part of Shakespeare's world could have existed in reality as well as in imagination. Spenser was never able to reach this highest type of art.

The world, however, needs poets to create images of a higher type of beauty than this life can offer. These images react on our material lives and cast them in a nobler mold. Spenser's belief that the subjective has power to fashion the objective is expressed in two of the finest lines that he ever wrote: —

> "For of the soule the bodie forme doth take;
> For soule is forme, and doth the bodie make."[1]

Chief Characteristics of Spenser's Poetry. — We can say of Spenser's verse that it stands in the front rank for (1) melody, (2) love of the beautiful, and (3) nobility of the ideals presented. His poetry also (4) shows a preference for the subjective world, (5) exerts a remarkable influence over other poets, and (6) displays a peculiar liking for obsolete forms of expression.

Spenser's melody is noteworthy. If we read aloud correctly such lines as these, we can scarcely fail to be impressed with their harmonious flow: —

[1] *An Hymne in Honour of Beautie.*

> "A teme of Dolphins raunged in aray
>   Drew the smooth charett of sad Cymoent:
> They were all taught by Triton to obay
>   To the long raynes at her commaundement:
>   As swifte as swallowes on the waves they went.
>
>   .   .   .   .
>
> "Upon great Neptune's necke they softly swim,
> And to her watry chamber swiftly carry him.
> Deepe in the bottome of the sea her bowre
> Is built of hollow billowes heaped hye."[1]

The following lines will show Spenser's love for beauty, and at the same time indicate the nobility of some of his ideal characters. He is describing Lady Una, the fair representative of true religion, who has lost through enchantment her Guardian Knight, and who is wandering disconsolate in the forest:—

> "... Her angel's face,
>   As the great eye of heaven, shyned bright,
> And made a sunshine in the shady place;
> Did never mortall eye behold such heavenly grace.
>
> "It fortuned out of the thickest wood
>   A ramping Lyon rushed suddeinly,
> Hunting full greedy after salvage blood.
>   Soone as the royall virgin he did spy,
>   With gaping mouth at her ran greedily,
> To have att once devoured her tender corse;
>   But to the pray when as he drew more ny,
>   His bloody rage aswaged with remorse,
> And with the sight amazd, forgat his furious forse.
>
> "In stead thereof he kist her wearie feet,
>   And lickt her lilly hands with fawning tong,
> As he her wronged innocence did weet.
>   O, how can beautie maister the most strong,
>   And simple truth subdue avenging wrong!"[2]

---

[1] *Faerie Queene*, Book III., Canto 4.   [2] *Ibid.*, Book I., Canto 3.

The power of beauty has seldom been more vividly described. As we read the succeeding stanzas and see the lion following her, like a faithful dog, to shield her from harm, we feel the power of both beauty and goodness and realize that with Spenser these terms are interchangeable. Each one of the preceding selections shows his preference for the subjective and the ideal to the actual.

Spenser searched for old and obsolete words. He used "eyne" for "eyes," "fone" for "foes," "shend" for "shame." He did not hesitate to coin words when he needed them, like "mercify" and "fortunize." He even wrote "wawes" in place of "waves" because he wished it to rime with "jaws." In spite of these peculiarities, Spenser is not hard reading after the first appearance of strangeness has worn away.

A critic rightly says that Spenser repels none but the anti-poetical. His influence upon other poets has been far-reaching. Milton, Dryden, Byron, Wordsworth, Keats, and Shelley show traces of his influence. Spenser has been called the poet's poet, because the more poetical one is, the more one will enjoy him.

THE ENGLISH DRAMA

The Early Religious Drama. — It is necessary to remember at the outset that the purpose of the religious drama was not to amuse, but to give a vivid presentation of scriptural truth. On the other hand, the primary aim of the later dramatist has usually been to entertain, or, in Shakespeare's exact words, "to please." Shakespeare was, however, fortunate in having an audience that was pleased to be instructed, as well as entertained.

Before the sixteenth century, England had a religious drama that made a profound impression on life and thought. The old religious plays helped to educate the public, the playwrights, and the actors for the later drama.

Any one may to-day form some idea of the rise of the religious drama, by attending the service of the Catholic church on Christmas or Easter Sunday. In many Catholic churches there may still be seen at Christmas time a representation of the manger at Bethlehem. Sometimes the figures of the infant Savior, of Joseph and Mary, of the wise men, of the sheep and cattle, are very lifelike.

The events clustering about the Crucifixion and the Resurrection furnished the most striking material for the early religious drama. Our earliest dramatic writers drew their inspiration from the *New Testament*.

Miracle and Mystery Plays. — A Miracle play is the dramatic representation of the life of a saint and of the miracles connected with him. A Mystery play deals with gospel events which are concerned with any phase of the life of Christ, or with any Biblical event that remotely foreshadows Christ or indicates the necessity of a Redeemer. In England there were few, if any, pure Miracle plays, but the term "Miracle" is applied indiscriminately to both Miracles and Mysteries.

The first Miracle play in England was acted probably not far from 1100. In the fourteenth, fifteenth, and sixteenth centuries these plays had become so popular that they were produced in nearly every part of England. Shakespeare felt their influence. He must have had frequent opportunities in his boyhood to witness their production. They were seldom performed in England after 1600, although visitors to Germany have, every ten years, the opportunity of seeing a modern production of a Mystery in the *Passion Play* at Oberammergau.

The Subjects. — Four great cycles of Miracle plays have

been preserved: the York, Chester, and Coventry plays, so called because they were performed in those places, and the Towneley plays, which take their name from

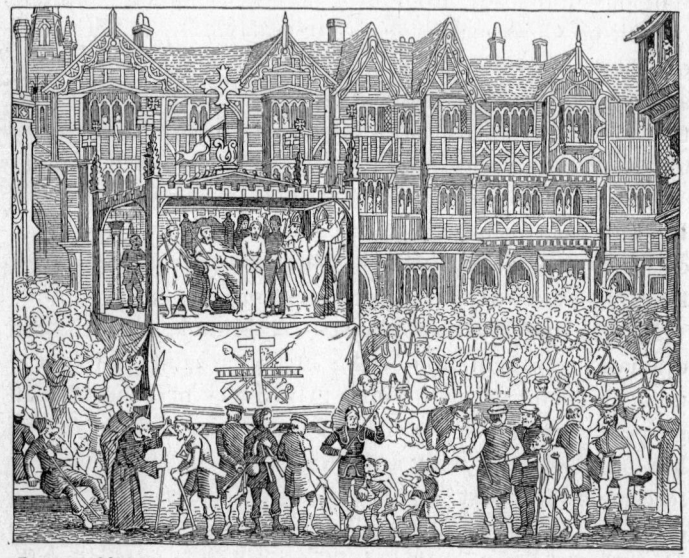

From an old print

MIRACLE PLAY AT COVENTRY

Towneley Hall in Lancashire, where the manuscript was kept for some time. It is probable that almost every town of importance had its own collection of plays.

The York cycle contains forty-eight plays. A cycle or circle of plays means a list forming a complete circle from Creation until Doomsday. The York collection begins with Creation and the fall of Lucifer and the bad angels from Heaven,—a theme which was later to inspire the pen of one of England's greatest poets. The tragedies of Eden and the Flood, scenes from the lives of Abraham, Isaac, and Moses, the manger at Bethlehem, the slaughter of the Innocents, the Temptation, the resurrection of Lazarus, the Last Supper, the Trial, the Crucifixion, and the Easter triumph are a few of the Miracle plays that were acted in the city of York.

The Actors and Manner of Presentation. — At first the actors were priests who presented the plays either in the church or in its immediate vicinity on sacred ground. After a while the plays became so popular that the laity presented them. When they were at the height of their popularity, that is, during the fourteenth and fifteenth centuries, the actors were selected with great care from the members of the various trades guilds. Each guild undertook the entire responsibility for the presentation of some one play, and endeavored to surpass all the other guilds.

Considerable humor was displayed in the allotment of various plays. The tanners presented the fall of Lucifer and the bad angels into the infernal regions; the ship carpenters, the play of Noah and the building of the ark; the bakers, the Last Supper; the butchers, the Crucifixion. In their prime, the Miracle plays were acted on wooden platforms mounted on wheels. There were two distinct stories in these movable stages, a lower one in which

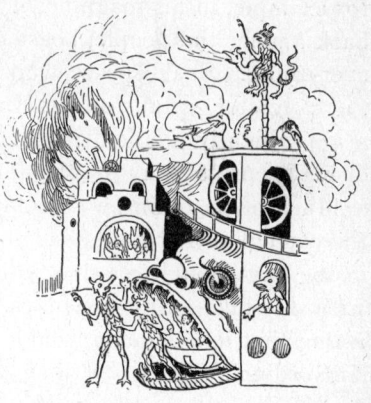

From a Columbia University Model.
HELL MOUTH

the actors dressed, and an upper one in which they played. The entrance to the lower story, known as Hell Mouth, consisted of a terrible pair of dragonlike jaws, painted red. From these jaws issued smoke, flame, and horrible outcries. From the entrance leaped red-coated devils to tempt the Savior, the saints, and men. Into it the devils would disappear with some wicked soul. They would torture it and make it roar with pain, as the smoke poured faster from the red jaws.

In York on Corpus Christi Day, which usually fell in the first week in June, the actors were ordered to be in their places on these movable theaters at half past three in the morning. Certain stations had been selected throughout the city, where each pageant should stop and, in the proper order, present its own play. In this way the enormous crowds that visited York to see these performances were more evenly scattered throughout the city.

The actors did not always remain on the stage. Herod, for example, in his magnificent robes used to ride on horseback among the people, boast of his prowess, and overdo everything. Shakespeare, who was evidently familiar with the character, speaks of out-Heroding Herod. The Devil also frequently jumped from the stage and availed himself of his license to play pranks among the audience.

Much of the acting was undoubtedly excellent. In 1476 the council at York ordained that four of the best players in the city should examine with regard to fitness all who wished to take part in the plays. So many were desirous of acting that it was much trouble to get rid of incompetents. The ordinance ran: " All such as they shall find sufficient in person and cunning, to the honor of the City and worship of the said Crafts, for to admit and able; and all other insufficient persons, either in cunning, voice, or person, to discharge, ammove and avoid." A critic says that

THE ENGLISH DRAMA

this ordinance is "one of the steps on which the greatness of the Elizabethan stage was built, and through which its actors grew up."[1]

Introduction of the Comic Element in the Miracle Plays. — While the old drama generally confined itself to religious subjects, the comic element occasionally crept in, made its power felt, and disclosed a new path for future playwrights. In the *Play of Noah's Flood*, when the time for the flood has come, Noah's wife refuses to enter the ark and a domestic quarrel ensues. Finally her children pull and shove her into the ark. When she is safe on board, Noah bids her welcome. His enraged wife deals him resounding blows until he calls to her to stop, because his back is nearly broken.

The *Play of the Shepherds* includes a genuine little comedy, the first comedy worthy of the name to appear in England. While watching their flocks on Christmas Eve, the shepherds are joined by Mak, a neighbor whose reputation for honesty is not good. Before they go to sleep, they make him lie down within their circle; but he rises when he hears them begin to snore, steals a sheep, and hastens home. His wife is alarmed, because in that day the theft of a sheep was punishable by death. She finally concludes that the best plan will be to wrap the animal in swaddling clothes and put it in the cradle. If the shepherds come to search the house, she will pretend that she has a child; and, if they approach the cradle, she will caution them against touching it for fear of waking the child and causing him to fill the house with his cries. She speedily hurries Mak away to resume his slumbers among the shepherds. When they wake, they miss the sheep, suspect Mak, and go to search his house. His wife allows

[1] Smith's *York Plays*.

them to look around thoroughly, but she keeps them away from the cradle. They leave, rather ashamed of their suspicion. As they are going out of the door, a thought strikes one of them whereby they can make partial amends. Deciding to give the child sixpence, he returns, lifts up the covering of the cradle, and discovers the sheep. Mak and his wife both declare that an elf has changed their child into a sheep. The shepherds threaten to have the pair hanged. They seize Mak, throw him on a canvas, and toss him into the air until they are exhausted. They then lie down to rest and are roused with the song of an angel from Bethlehem.

To produce this comedy required genuine inventive imagination; for there is nothing faintly resembling this incident in the sacred narrative. These early exercises of the imagination in our drama may resemble the tottering footsteps of a child, but they were necessary antecedents to the strength, beauty, and divinity of movement in Elizabethan times.

The Morality. — The next step in the development of the drama is known as the Morality play. This personified abstractions. Characters like Charity, Hope, Faith, Truth, Covetousness, Falsehood, Abominable Living, the World, the Flesh, and the Devil, — in short, all the Virtues and the Vices, — came on the stage in the guise of persons, and played the drama of life.

FOOL'S HEAD[1]

Critics do not agree about the precise way in which the Morality is related to the Miracle play. It is certain that the Miracle play had already introduced some abstractions.

[1] Stage properties of the Vice and Fool.

THE ENGLISH DRAMA

In one very important respect, the Morality marks an advance, by giving more scope to the imagination. The Miracle plays had their general treatment absolutely predetermined by the Scriptural version of the action or by the legends of the lives of saints, although diverting incidents could be introduced, as we have seen. In the Morality, the events could take any turn which the author chose to give.

In spite of this advantage, the Morality is in general a synonym for what is uninteresting. The characters born of abstractions are too often bloodless, like their parents. The Morality under a changed name was current a few years ago in the average Sunday-school book. Incompetent writers of fiction to-day often adopt the Morality principle in making their characters unnaturally good or bad, mere puppets who do not develop along the line of their own emotional prompting, but are moved by machinery in the author's hands.

AIR-BAG FLAPPER[1]

A new character, the Vice, was added as an adjunct to the Devil, to increase the interest of the audience in the Morality play. The Vice represented the leading spirit of evil in any particular play, sometimes Fraud, Covetousness, Pride, Iniquity, or Hypocrisy. It was the business of the Vice to annoy the Virtues and to be constantly playing pranks. The Vice was the predecessor of the clown and the fool upon the stage. The Vice also amused the audience by tormenting the Devil, belaboring him with a sword of lath, sticking thorns into him, and making him roar with pain. Sometimes the Devil would be kicked down Hell Mouth by the offended

LATH DAGGER[1]

[1] Stage properties of the Vice and Fool.

Virtues; but he would soon reappear with saucily curled tail, and at the end of the play he would delight the spectators by plunging into Hell Mouth with the Vice on his back.

Court Plays. — In the first part of the sixteenth century, the court and the nobility especially encouraged the production of plays whose main object was to entertain. The influence of the court in shaping the drama became much more powerful than that of the church. Wallace says of the new materials which his researches have disclosed in the twentieth century:—

FOOL OF THE OLD PLAY

"They throw into the lime-light a brilliant development of this new drama through the Chapel Royal, a development that took place primarily under the direction of the great musicians who served as masters of the children of the Chapel and as court entertainers, the first true poets-laureate, through the reigns of Henry VIII., Edward VI., Mary, and Elizabeth."[1]

In 1509 Henry VIII. appointed William Cornish (died 1523) to be Master of the Children of the Chapel Royal. This court institution with its choral body of men and boys not only ministered "by song to the spiritual well-being of the sovereign and his household," but also gave them "temporal" enjoyment in dances, pageants, and plays. We must not forget, however, that the Chapel Royal was

[1] C. W. Wallace's *The Evolution of the English Drama up to Shakespeare.*

THE ENGLISH DRAMA 155

originally, as its name implies, a religious body. Cornish was a capable dramatist, as well as a musician and a poet; and he, unlike the author of *Everyman*, wrote plays simply to amuse the court and its guests. He has even been called the founder of the secular English drama.[1]

The court of Henry VIII. became especially fond of the Interlude, which was a short play, often given in connection with a banquet or other entertainment. Any dramatic incident, such as the refusal of Noah's wife to enter the ark, or Mak's thievery in *The Play of the Shepherds*, might serve as an Interlude. **Cornish** and **John Heywood** (1497?–1580?), a court dramatist of much versatility, incorporated in the Interlude many of the elements of the five-act drama. *The Four P's*, the most famous Interlude, shows a contest between a Pardoner, Palmer, Pedlar, and Poticary, to determine who could tell the greatest lie. Wallace thinks that the best Interludes, such as *The Four P's* and *The Pardoner and the Frere*, were written by Cornish, although they are usually ascribed to Heywood.

Cornish had unusual ability as a deviser of masques and plays. One of his interludes for children has allegorical characters that remotely suggest some that appear in the modern *Bluebird*, by Maeterlinck. Cornish had Wind appear "in blue with drops of silver"; Rain, "in black with silver honeysuckles"; Winter, "in russet with flakes of silver snow"; Summer, "in green with gold stars"; and Spring, "in green with gold primroses." In 1522 Cornish wrote and presented before Henry VIII. and his guest, the Roman emperor, a political play, especially planned to indicate the attitude of the English monarch toward Spain and France. Under court in-

[1] Wallace, *op. cit.*, p. 37.

fluences, the drama enlarged its scope and was no longer chiefly the vehicle for religious instruction.

Early Comedies. — Two early comedies, divided, after the classical fashion, into acts and scenes, show close approximation to the modern form of English plays.

Ralph Royster Doyster was written not far from the middle of the sixteenth century by **Nicholas Udall** (1505–1556), sometime master of Eton College and, later, court poet under Queen Mary. This play, founded on a comedy of Plautus, shows the classical influence which was so powerful in England at this time. Ralph, the hero, is a conceited simpleton. He falls in love with a widow who has already promised her hand to a man infinitely Ralph's superior. Ralph, however, unable to understand why she should not want him, persists in his wooing. She makes him the butt of her jokes, and he finds himself in ridiculous positions. The comedy amuses us in this way until her lover returns and marries her. The characters of the play, which is written in rime, are of the English middle class.

Gammer Gurton's Needle, the work of **William Stevenson**, a little-known pre-Shakespearean writer, was acted at Christ's College, Cambridge, shortly after the middle of the sixteenth century. This play borrows hardly anything from the classical stage. Most of the characters of *Gammer Gurton's Needle* are from the lowest English working classes, and its language, unlike that of *Ralph Royster Doyster*, which has little to offend, is very coarse.

Gorboduc and the Dramatic Unities. — The tragedy of *Gorboduc*, the first regular English tragedy written in blank verse, was acted in 1561, three years before the birth of Shakespeare. This play is in part the work of **Thomas Sackville** (1536–1608), a poet and diplomat, the author of two powerful somber poems, the *Induction* and *Complaint of the Duke of Buckingham.* In spite of their heavy narrative form, these poems are in places even more dramatic than the dull tragedy of *Gorboduc*, which was fashioned after the classical rules of Seneca and the Greeks. *Gorboduc* requires little action on the stage. There is considerable bloodshed in the play; but the spectators are informed of the carnage by a messenger, as they are not permitted to witness a bloody contest on the stage.

THOMAS SACKVILLE

If *Gorboduc* had been taken for a model, the English drama could never have attained Shakespearean greatness. Our drama would then have been crippled by following the classical rules, which prescribed unity of place and time in the plot and the action. The ancients held that a play should not represent actions which would, in actual life, require much more than twenty-four hours for their performance. If one of the characters was a boy, he had to be represented as a boy throughout the play. The next act could not introduce him as one who had grown to manhood in the interval. The classical rules further required that the action should be performed in one place, or near it. Anything that happened at a great distance had to be related by a messenger, and not acted on the stage.

Had these rules been followed, the English drama could never have painted the growth and development of character, which is not the work of a day. The genius of

Marlowe and Shakespeare taught them to disregard these dramatic unities. In *As You Like It*, the action is now at the court, and now in the far-off Forest of Arden. Shakespeare knew that the imagination could traverse the distance. At the beginning of the play Oliver is an unnatural, brutal brother; but events change him, so that in the fourth act, when he is asked if he is the man who tried to kill his brother, Oliver replies: —

> "'Twas I; but 'tis not I."

THE PRESENTATION OF ELIZABETHAN PLAYS

The Elizabethan Theater. — Before considering the work of the Elizabethan dramatists, we should know something of the conditions which they had to meet in order to produce plays for the contemporary stage. The courtyard of London inns often served as a playhouse before sufficient regular theaters were built. The stage was in one end of the yard, and the unused ground space in front served as the pit. Two or three tiers of galleries or balconies around the yard afforded additional space for both actors and spectators. These inn yards furnished many suggestions which were incorporated in the early theaters.

The first building in England for the public presentation of plays was known as The Theater. It was built in London in 1576. In 1598 Shakespeare and his associates, failing to secure a lease of the ground on which this building stood, pulled it down, carried the materials across the river, and erected the famous Globe Theater on the Bankside, as the street running along the south side of the Thames was called. In late years a careful study of the specifications (1599) for building the Fortune Theater (see Frontispiece) has thrown much light on the Globe, which

From Columbia University model.

THEATER IN INN YARD

is unusually important from its association with Shakespeare. Although the Fortune was square, while the Globe was octagonal, the Fortune was in many essentials modeled after the Globe. A part of the specifications of the Fortune read as follows: —

". . . the frame of the saide howse to be sett square and to conteine fowerscore foote of lawful assize everye waie square, without, and fiftie five foote of like assize square, everye waie within . . . and the saide frame to conteine three stories in heigth . . . [the] stadge shall conteine in length fortie and three foote of lawfull assize, and in breadth to extende to the middle of the yarde of the said howse: the same stadge to be paled in belowe with goode stronge and sufficyent new oken boardes. . . . And the said stadge to be in all other proportions contryved and fashioned like unto the stadge of the saide Playhowse called the Globe."

The first part of the twentieth century has made a detailed study of the stage on which the great Elizabethan plays were acted. G. F. Reynolds says: —

From an original drawing.

RECONSTRUCTED GLOBE THEATER, "SHAKESPEARE'S ENGLAND," EARL'S COURT, LONDON, 1912

"Most students agree that the 'typical' Elizabethan stage consisted of a platform, uncurtained in front, open as well at the sides, carpeted, it is generally said, with rushes, and surrounded with a railing, a space behind this platform closed by a sliding curtain, and a balcony with its own curtains and entrances. There were also a space below the stage reached by trap doors, a dressing room behind the stage, machinery by which characters ascended to and descended from some place above, and in some theaters at least, a 'heavens,' or roof over part or all of the stage."[1]

Possibly no single stage had every feature mentioned in the above description, which gives, however, a good general idea of a typical stage of the time. We must remember that no one has the right to assert that different Elizabethan stages did not differ in details. We are not sure that every stage was so planned as to be divided into two parts by a sliding curtain. The drawing of the Swan Theater (p. 164) shows no place for such a curtain, although

[1] *What We Know of the Elizabethan Stage.*

it is possible that the draftsman forgot to include it. The specifications of the stage of the Fortune Theater make no mention of a railing.

The Play and the Audience. — It is impossible to criticize Elizabethan plays properly from the point of view of the twentieth-century stage. Many modern criticisms are shown to be without reason when we understand the wishes of the audience and the manner of presenting the plays. The conditions of the entry or the reëntry of a player might explain some of those lengthy monologues that seem so inartistic to modern dramatists. The Elizabethan theaters and the tastes of their patrons had certain important characteristics of their own.

I. In the public theaters,[1] the play began in the early afternoon, usually between two and three o'clock, and lasted for about two hours. The audience was an alert one, neither jaded by a long day's business nor rendered impatient by waiting for the adjustment of scenery. The Elizabethans constituted a vigorous audience, eager to meet the dramatist and actors more than half way in interpreting what was presented.

II. In the case of such public theaters as the Globe and the Fortune, even their roofed parts, which extended around the pit and back of the stage and which contained the galleries and the boxes, were all exposed to the open air on the inner side. The pit, which was immediately in front of the stage, had the sky for a roof and the ground for a floor. The frequenters of the pit, who often jostled

---

[1] Performances were often given at night in private theaters. From the records in a lawsuit over the second Blackfriars Theater (p. 167, note), we learn that there were in 1608 only three private theaters in London, — Blackfriars, Whitefriars, and a St. Paul's Cathedral playhouse, in which boys acted.

each other for standing room, were sometimes called the "groundlings." Occasionally a severe rain would drive them out of the theater to seek shelter. Those who attended the Elizabethan public theater were in no danger of being made drowsy or sick by its bad air.

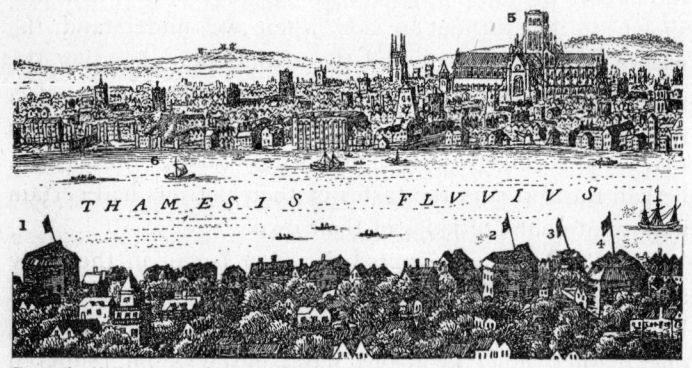

From the Hollar engraving, about 1620.

THE BANKSIDE AND ITS THEATERS

1. The Swan Theater.
2. The Bear Gardens.
3. The Hope Theater.
4. The Globe Theater.
5. Old St. Paul's.
6. The Temple.

III. The audiences did not attend merely for relaxation or amusement. They often came for information and education, and they were probably glad to learn about alchemy from one of Ben Jonson's plays. The audience doubtless welcomed long monologues if they were well delivered and presented ideas of worth. The theater took the place of lectures, newspapers, magazines, and, to a certain extent, of books. We know that in 1608 the Blackfriars Theater acted the part of a newspaper in presenting a scandal about the French king and that at another time it gave some humorous information concerning the English monarch's newly discovered silver mine in Scotland.

IV. The Elizabethans loved good poetry for its imaginative appeal. Shakespeare was a poet before he was a dramatist. Beautiful poetry presenting high ideals must have met with vigorous appreciation, or Shakespeare could not have continued to produce such great work.

V. The Elizabethans also demanded story and incident. Modern critics have often noticed that the characterization in Shakespeare's fourth acts, *e.g.*, in *Macbeth*, does not equal that in the preceding part of the play; but the fourth act of *Macbeth* interested the Elizabethans because there was progress in the complicated story. To modern theatergoers this fourth act seems to drag because they have acquired through novel reading a liking for analysis and dissection.

Shakespeare succeeded in interesting the Elizabethans by embodying in story and incident his portrayal of character. Because of admiration for the revelation of character in his greatest plays, modern readers forget their moving incidents, — for instance, the almost bloodcurdling appearances of a ghost, the actions of a crazed woman, the killing of an eavesdropper on the stage, two men fighting at an open grave, the skull and bones of a human being dug from a grave in full view of the audience, the fighting to the death on the stage, which is ghastly with corpses at the close. When we add to this the roar of cannon whenever the king drinks, as well as when there is some more noteworthy action, and remember that the very last words of *Hamlet* are: "Go, bid the soldiers shoot," we shall realize that there was not much danger of going to sleep even during a performance of *Hamlet*.

Scenery. — The conditions under which early Elizabethan plays were sometimes produced are thus described by Sir Philip Sidney: —

"You shall have Asia of the one side, and Africa of the other, and so many other under-kingdoms, that the player when he comes in, must ever begin with telling you where he is, or else the tale will not be conceived. Now shall you have three ladies walk to gather flowers, and then we must believe the stage to be a garden. By and by we hear news of a shipwreck in the same place, then we are to blame if we accept it not for a rock."

Those who remember this well-known quotation too often forget that Sidney wrote before Shakespeare's plays were produced. We do not know whether Sidney was describing a private or a public stage, but the private theaters had the greater amount of scenery.

CONTEMPORARY DRAWING OF INTERIOR OF AN ELIZABETHAN THEATER[1]

Modern research has shown that the manner of presenting plays did not remain stationary while the drama was rapidly evolving. Before Shakespeare died, there were such stage properties as beds, tables, chairs, dishes, fetters, shop wares, and perhaps also some artificial trees, mossy banks, and rocks. A theatrical manager in an inven-

[1] This drawing of the Swan Theater, London, was probably made near the end of the sixteenth century by van Buchell, a Dutchman, from a description by his friend, J. de Witt. The drawing, found at the University of Utrecht, although perhaps not accurate in details, is valuable as a rough contemporary record of an impression communicated to a draftsman by one who had seen an Elizabethan play.

tory of stage properties (1598) mentions "the sittie of Rome," which was perhaps a cloth so painted as to present a perspective of the city. He also speaks of a "cloth of the Sone and Mone." The use of such painted cloths was an important step toward modern scenery. We may, however, conclude that the scenery of any Elizabethan theater would have seemed scant to one accustomed to the detailed setting of the modern stage.

The comparatively little scenery in Elizabethan theaters imposed strenuous imaginative exercise on the spectators. This effort was fortunate for all concerned — for the dramatist and for the actor, but especially for the spectator, who became accustomed to give an imaginative interpretation and setting to a play that would mean little to a modern theatergoer.

Actors. — Those who have seen some of the recent performances of plays under Elizabethan conditions, on a stage modeled after that of Shakespeare's time (see Frontispiece and p. 164), have been surprised at the increase of the actors' power. The stage projects far enough into the pit to bring the actors close to the audience. Their appeal thus becomes far more personal, direct, and forceful. The spectator more easily identifies himself with them and almost feels as if he were a part of the play. This has been the experience of those who have seen the old-time reproduction of plays as different as *The Tempest*, *A Midsummer Night's Dream*, *The Merchant of Venice*, and *Much Ado About Nothing*. In the case of *The Tempest*, a very interesting act was presented when all the scenery consisted of a board on which was painted "Prospero Isle."

In Shakespeare's times, the plays were probably well acted. While the fame of Elizabethan actors like Edward

Alleyn and Richard Burbage has come down to modern times, the success of plays did not depend on single stars. Shakespeare is said to have played in minor rôles. The audience discouraged bad acting. The occupants of the pit would throw apples or worse missiles at an unsatisfactory player, and sometimes the disgusted spectators would suddenly leap on the stage and chase an incompetent actor off the boards.

Prior to the Restoration in 1660, the women's parts were taken by boys. While this must have hampered the presentation of characters like Lady Macbeth, it is now known to have been less of a handicap than was formerly thought. The twentieth century has seen feminine parts so well played by carefully trained boys that the most astute women spectators never detected the deception. Boys, especially those of the Chapel Royal, had for a long time acted masculine, as well as feminine, parts. As late as the beginning of the seventeenth century, the choir boys were presenting some of the great Elizabethan plays in a private theater connected with St. Paul's Cathedral. Rosencrantz in the second act of *Hamlet* bears witness to the popularity of these boy actors, when he calls them "little eyases, that cry on the top of question and are most tyrannically clapped for it." Ben Jonson's touching lyrical epitaph on a boy actor, Salathiel Pavy, who had for "three fill'd zodiacs" been "the stage's jewel," shows how highly the Elizabethans sometimes regarded boy actors. The regular theaters found the companies of boys such strong rivals that, in 1609, Shakespeare and other theatrical managers used modern business methods to suppress competition and agreed to pay the master of the boys of St. Paul's enough to cause him to withdraw them permanently from competing with the other theaters.

PRE-SHAKESPEAREAN DRAMATISTS

The "University Wits" and Thomas Kyd. — Five authors, John Lyly, George Peele, Robert Greene, Thomas Lodge, and Thomas Nashe, all graduates of Oxford or Cambridge, were sufficiently versatile to be called "university wits." Amid various other activities, all of them were impelled by the spirit of the age to write plays. These intellectual aristocrats hurled the keen shafts of their wit at those dramatists, who, without a university education, were arrogant enough to think that they could write plays. Because Shakespeare had never attended a university, Greene called him "an upstart Crow beautified with our feathers."

On New Year's, 1584, **John Lyly** (p. 124), the author of *Euphues*, presented in the first Blackfriars Theater[1] his prose comedy, entitled *Campaspe*. This play relates the love story of Alexander the Great's fair Theban captive, Campaspe. The twenty-eight characters necessary to produce this play were obtained from the boys of the Chapel Royal (p. 154) and St. Paul's Cathedral. Two months later Lyly's *Sapho and Phao* was given in the

[1] The lease of the building for the first Blackfriars Theater, on Ludgate Hill, London, was taken in 1576 by Richard Farrant, master of the boys of Windsor Chapel, and canceled in 1584. In 1595 James Burbage bought a building for the second Blackfriars Theater, near the site of the first. This was a private theater, competing with the Globe, with which Shakespeare was connected. The chief dramatists for the second Blackfriars were Ben Jonson, George Chapman, and John Marston. James I. suppressed the second Blackfriars in 1608 because its actors satirized him and the French king. A few months later, Shakespeare and his associates assumed the management of the Blackfriars and gave performances there as well as at the Globe.

These facts explain Wallace's discovery (see p. 181) that Shakespeare at the time of his death owned a one-seventh interest in the second Blackfriars, a theater that had formerly been a rival to the Globe.

same theater with a cast of seventeen boys. It should be remembered that these plays, so important in the evolution of the drama, were acted by boys under royal patronage. *Campaspe* is little more than a series of episodes, divided into acts and scenes, but, unlike *Gorboduc*, *Campaspe* has many of the characteristics of an interesting modern play.

Lyly wrote eight comedies, all but one in prose. In the history of the drama, he is important for (1) finished style, (2) good dialogue, (3) considerable invention in the way he secured interest, by using classical matter in combination with contemporary life, (4) subtle comedy, and (5) influence on Shakespeare. It is doubtful whether Shakespeare could have produced such good early comedies, if he had not received suggestions from Lyly's work in this field.

The chapel boys also presented at Blackfriars in the same year **George Peele's** (1558–1597) *The Arraignment of Paris*, a pastoral drama in riming verse. In Juno's promise to Paris, Peele shows how the possibilities of the New World affected his imagination: —

> "Xanthus shall run liquid gold for thee to wash thy hands;
> And if thou like to tend thy flock and not from them to fly,
> Their fleeces shall be curlèd gold to please their master's eye."

While *The Arraignment of Paris* and his two other plays, *David and Bathsabe* and *The Old Wives' Tale*, are not good specimens of dramatic construction, the beauty of some of Peele's verse could hardly have failed to impress both Marlowe and Shakespeare with the poetic possibilities of the drama. Peele writes without effort —

> "Of moss that sleeps with sound the waters make,"

and has David build —

> " . . . a kingly bower,
> Seated in hearing of a hundred streams."

Robert Greene (1560–1592) showed much skill in (1) the construction of plots, (2) the revelation of simple and genuine human feeling, and (3) the weaving of an interesting story into a play. His best drama is the poetic comedy *Friar Bacon and Friar Bungay*. In this play, he made the love story the central point of interest.

Thomas Lodge (1558–1625), author of the story *Rosalynde*, which Shakespeare (p. 190) used to such good advantage, wrote in collaboration with Greene, *A Looking Glass for London and England*, and an independent play, *The Wounds of Civil War*. **Thomas Nashe** (1567–1601), best known for his picaresque novel, *The Unfortunate Traveler* (p. 317), wrote a play, *Summer's Last Will and Testament*, but he and Lodge had little dramatic ability.

Thomas Kyd (1558–1594), although lacking a university education, succeeded in writing, about 1586, the most popular early Elizabethan play, *The Spanish Tragedy*, a blank verse drama, in which blood flows profusely. Although this play is not free from classical influences, yet its excellence of construction, effective dramatic situations, vigor of movement, and romantic spirit helped to prepare the way for the tragedies of Marlowe and Shakespeare.

CHRISTOPHER MARLOWE, 1564–1593

Life. — The year 1564 saw the birth of the two greatest geniuses in the English drama, Marlowe and Shakespeare. Marlowe, the son of a shoemaker, was born at Canterbury, and educated at Cambridge. When he was graduated, the dramatic profession was the only one that gave full scope to genius like his. He became both playwriter and actor. All his extant work was written in about six years. When he was only twenty-nine he was fatally stabbed in a tavern quarrel. Shakespeare had at that age not produced his greatest plays. Marlowe unwittingly wrote his own epitaph in that of Dr. Faustus: —

> "Cut is the branch that might have grown full straight,
> And burnèd is Apollo's laurel-bough."

Works. — Marlowe's great tragedies are four in number: *Tamburlaine*, *Dr. Faustus*, *The Jew of Malta*, and *Edward II*. No careful student of English literature can afford to be unacquainted with any of them. Shakespeare's work appears less miraculous when we know that a predecessor at the age of twenty-four had written plays like *Tamburlaine* and *Dr. Faustus*.

Tamburlaine shows the supreme ambition for conquest, for controlling the world with physical force. It is such a play as might have been suggested to an Elizabethan by watching Napoleon's career. *Dr. Faustus*, on the other hand, shows the desire for knowledge that would give universal power, a desire born of the Renaissance. *The Jew of Malta* is the incarnation of the passion for the world's wealth, a passion that towers above common greed only by the magnificence of its immensity. In that play we see that Marlowe —

MARLOWE'S MEMORIAL STATUE AT CANTERBURY

> "Without control can pick his riches up,
> And in his house heap pearl like pebble stones,
> . . . .
> Infinite riches in a little room."

Edward II. gives a pathetic picture of one of the weakest of kings. This shows more evenness and regularity of construction than any of Marlowe's other plays; but it is the one least characteristic of him. The others manifest more intensity of imagination, more of the spirit of the age.

Dr. Faustus shows Marlowe's peculiar genius at its best. The legend on which the play is based came from Germany, but Marlowe breathed his own imaginative spirit into the tragedy. Faustus is wearied with the barren philosophy of the past. He is impatient to secure at once the benefits of the New Learning, which seems to him to have all the powers of magic. If he can immediately enjoy the fruits of such knowledge, he says: —

> "Had I as many souls as there be stars,
> I'd give them all."

In order to acquire this knowledge and the resulting power for twenty-four years, he sells his soul to Mephistopheles. Faustus then proceeds to enjoy all that the new order of things promised. He commands Homer to come from the realm of shades to sing his entrancing songs. He summons Helen to appear before him in the morning of her beauty. The apostrophe to her shows the vividness and exuberance of his imagination: —

> "Was this the face that launched a thousand ships
> And burnt the topless towers of Ilium?
> Sweet Helen, make me immortal with a kiss.
> . . . .
> Oh! thou art fairer than the evening air
> Clad in the beauty of a thousand stars."

Marlowe left a fragment of a lyrical poem, entitled *Hero and Leander*, which is one of the finest productions of its kind in the language. Shakespeare accorded him the unusual honor of quoting from this poem.

In What Sense is Marlowe a Founder of the English Drama? — His success with blank verse showed Shakespeare that this was the proper versification for the drama. Before Marlowe, rime or prose had been chiefly employed in writing plays. Sackville had used blank verse in *Gorboduc*, but his verse and Marlowe's are as unlike as the movements of the ox and the flight of the swallow. The sentences of *Gorboduc* generally end with the line, and the accents usually fall in the same place. Marlowe's blank verse shows great variety, and the major pause frequently does not come at the end of the line.

Marlowe cast the dramatic unities to the wind. The action in *Dr. Faustus* occupies twenty-four years, and the scene changes from country to country. He knew that he was speaking to a people whose imaginations could accompany him and interpret what he uttered. The other dramatists followed him in placing imaginative interpretation above measurements by the foot rule of the intellect. Symonds says of him: "It was he who irrevocably decided the destinies of the romantic drama; and the whole subsequent evolution of that species, including Shakespeare's work, can be regarded as the expansion, rectification, and artistic ennoblement of the type fixed by Marlowe's epoch-making tragedies. In very little more than fifty years from the publication of *Tamburlaine*, our drama had run its course of unparalleled energy and splendor."

General Characteristics. — As we sum up Marlowe's general qualities, it is well to note that they exhibit in a striking way the characteristics of the time. In the morning of that youthful age the superlative was possible. *Tamburlaine*, *The Jew of Malta*, and *Dr. Faustus* show in the superlative degree the love of conquest, of wealth, and of knowledge. Everything that Marlowe wrote is stamped with a love of beauty and of the impossible.

Tamburlaine speaks like one of the young Elizabethans —

> "That in conceit bear empires on our spears,
> Affecting thoughts co-equal with the clouds."

Marlowe voices the new sense of worth of enfranchised man : —

> "Thinkest thou heaven is such a glorious thing?
> I tell thee, 'tis not half so fair as thou,
> Or any man that breathes on earth.
> . . . .
> 'Twas made for man, therefore is man more excellent." [1]

Marlowe's faults are the faults of youth and of his time. Exaggeration and lack of restraint are shown in almost all his work. In *Tamburlaine*, written when he was twenty-two, he is often bombastic. He has hardly any sense of humor. He does not draw fine distinctions between his characters.

On the other hand, using the words of Tamburlaine, we may say of all his dramatic contemporaries, excepting Shakespeare —

> "If all the heavenly quintessence they still
> From their immortal flowers of poesy,"

were gathered into one vial, it could not surpass the odor from patches of flowers in Marlowe's garden.

These seven lines represent better than pages of description the aspiring spirit of the new Elizabethan Renaissance.

> "Our souls whose faculties can comprehend
> The wondrous architecture of the world,
> And measure every wandering planet's course,
> Still climbing after knowledge infinite,
> And always moving as the restless spheres,
> Will us to wear ourselves and never rest
> Until we reach the ripest fruit of all." [2]

---

[1] *Dr. Faustus*, Scene 6. [2] *Tamburlaine*, Act II., Scene 7.

From the Chandos portrait in the National Portrait Gallery.

WILLIAM SHAKESPEARE, 1564-1616

Birthplace and Parents.—William Shakespeare, the greatest of the world's writers, was born in Stratford-on-Avon, Warwickshire. The name originally meant one skilled in wielding a spear. The first William Shakespeare of

whom mention is made in the records was hanged for robbery near Stratford; but it is only fair to state that in those days hanging was inflicted for stealing even a sheep.

The great dramatist's birthplace lies in the midst of England's fairest rural scenery. When two Englishmen were asked to name the finest walk in England, one chose the walk from Stratford to Coventry, the other, the walk from Coventry to Stratford.

SHAKESPEARE'S BIRTHPLACE, STRATFORD-ON-AVON

A short distance northeast of Stratford are Warwick with its castle, the home of the famous king-maker, and Kenilworth Castle, whose historic associations were romantic enough to stir the imagination of a boy like Shakespeare.

He was the son of John Shakespeare, an influential merchant, who in 1571 was elected chief alderman of Stratford. The poet's mother was the daughter of Robert Arden, a well-to-do farmer. We are told that she was her father's favorite among seven children. Perhaps it was due to her influence that he had a happy childhood. His references to plays and sports and his later desire to return to Stratford are indicative of pleasant boyhood days.

Probably his mother was the original of some of her son's noblest conceptions of women. His plays have more heroines than heroes. We may fancy that it was his mother who first pointed out to him —

> ". . . daffodils,
> That come before the swallow dares, and take
> The winds of March with beauty; violets dim,
> But sweeter than the lids of Juno's eyes."[1]

We may imagine that from her teaching, as she walked with him over the Stratford fields, he obtained suggestions which enabled him to hold captive the ear of the world, when he sang of the pearl in the cowslip's ear, of the bank where the wild thyme blows, of the greenwood tree and the merry note of the bird. Many of the references to nature in his plays are unsurpassed in English verse.

What He Learned at School. — In all probability Shakespeare entered the Stratford Grammar School at about the

CLASSROOM IN STRATFORD GRAMMAR SCHOOL[2]

age of seven and continued there until he was nearly fourteen. The typical course in grammar schools of that

[1] *The Winter's Tale*, Act IV., Scene 4.
[2] Tradition says that Shakespeare occupied the desk in the farthest corner.

period consisted principally of various Latin authors. One school in 1583 had twenty-five Latin books on its list of studies, while the only required works in English were the *Catechism, Psalter, Book of Common Prayer*, and *New Testament*. Children were required to study Lilly's *Latin Grammar* instead of their mother tongue. Among the works that Shakespeare probably read in Latin, Æsop's *Fables* and Ovid's *Metamorphoses* may be mentioned.

Although English was not taught, Shakespeare shows wonderful mastery in the use of his mother tongue. We have the testimony of the schoolmaster, Holofernes, in *Love's Labor's Lost* to show that the study of Latin led to facility in the use of English synonyms: —

"The deer was, as you know, *sanguis*, in blood, ripe as the pomewater, who now hangeth like a jewel in the ear of *caelo*, the sky, the welkin, the heaven; and anon falleth like a crab on the face of *terra*, the soil, the land, the earth."

Three English equivalents are here given for each of the Latin terms *caelo* and *terra*. The same schoolmaster uses seven synonyms in describing the "fashion" of speech of the ignorant constable, — "undressed, unpolished, uneducated, unpruned, untrained, or, rather unlettered, or, ratherest, unconfirmed, fashion." When we remember that it was really Shakespeare who wrote this, we know that he had been led to study variety of expression. His large vocabulary (p. 196) could not have been acquired by any one without hard work.

A good translation of the English *Bible* was accessible to him. Scriptural phrases and references appear in his plays, and volumes have been written to show the influence of the *Bible* on his thought.

Financial Reverses of the Shakespeare Family. — It is probable that Shakespeare at about the age of fourteen was taken from school to assist his father in the store. The elder Shakespeare was then overtaken by financial reverses and compelled to mortgage his wife's land. His affairs went from bad to worse; he was sued for debt, but the court could not find any property to satisfy the claim. It is possible that he was for a short time even imprisoned for debt. Finally he was deprived of his alderman's gown.

These events must have made a deep impression on the sensitive boy, and they may have led him to an early determination to try to master fortune. In after years he showed a business sagacity very rare for a poet.

Marriage and Departure from Stratford. — The most famous lovers' walk in England is the footpath from Stratford, leading about one mile westward through meadows to the hamlet of Shottery. Perhaps William Shakespeare had this very walk in mind when he wrote the song: —

> "Journeys end in lovers' meeting
> Every wise man's son doth know."

ANNE HATHAWAY'S COTTAGE, SHOTTERY

The end of his walk led to Anne Hathaway's home in Shottery. She was nearly eight years his senior, but in 1582 at the age of eighteen he married her.

There is a record that Shakespeare's twin children, Hamnet and Judith, were baptized in 1585. From this we know that before he was twenty-one Shakespeare had a wife and family to support. We have no positive information to tell us what he did for the next seven years after the birth of his twins. Tradition says that he joined a group of hunters, killed some of the deer of Sir Thomas Lucy at Charlecote Park, and fled from Stratford to London in consequence of threatened prosecution. There is reason to doubt the truth of this story, and Shakespeare may have sought the metropolis merely because it offered him more scope to provide for his rapidly increasing family.

Connects Himself with the London Stage. — The next scene of Shakespeare's life is laid in London. In 1592 Robert Greene (p. 169), a London poet, dramatist, and hack-writer, wrote: —

"There is an upstart Crow, beautified with our feathers, that with his *Tyger's heart wrapped in a Player's hide*, supposes he is as well able to bumbast out a blank verse as the best of you; and being an absolute *Iohannes fac-totum*, is in his owne conceit the only Shake-scene in a countrie."[1]

The best critics agree that the "upstart Crow" and "Shake-scene" refer to Shakespeare. The allusion to "Tyger's heart" is from the third part of *King Henry VI.* and is addressed by the Duke of York to Queen Margaret of Anjou: —

"O tiger's heart wrapped in a woman's hide!"

Greene's satiric thrust shows that Shakespeare was becoming popular as a playwright. We can only imagine the steps by which he rose to his ascendancy as a dramatist. Perhaps he first served the theater in some menial capacity, then became an actor, and assisted others in revising or adapting plays before he acquired sufficient skill to write a play entirely by himself.

[1] Greene's *Groatsworth of Wit*, Grosart's edition of Greene's *Works*, Vol. XII., p. 144.

In 1593 he published the non-dramatic poem, *Venus and Adonis*, which he dedicated to the Earl of Southampton. This nobleman is said to have given Shakespeare, on one occasion, "a thousand pounds to enable him to make a purchase which he heard he had a mind to." This would show that Shakespeare had a capacity for attracting people and making lasting friendships. In 1597 he purchased "New Place," the stateliest house in Stratford, and we hear no more of his father's financial troubles.

Twentieth-century Discoveries. — In the first decade of the twentieth century, Professor C. W. Wallace discovered in the London Record Office a romantic story in which Shakespeare was an important figure. This story opens in the year 1598 in the London house of a French Huguenot, Christopher Mountjoy, wig-maker, with whom Shakespeare lived. Mountjoy took as apprentice for six years, Stephen Bellott, a young Frenchman. Beside him worked Mary Mountjoy, the proprietor's only daughter, who looked with favor upon the young apprentice. At the end of his apprenticeship Stephen left without proposing marriage to Mary; but on his return Mrs. Mountjoy asked Shakespeare to make a match between Stephen and Mary, — a task in which he was successful.

Seven and a half years later Shakespeare was called into court to testify to all the facts leading to the marriage. After a family quarrel, Mr. Mountjoy declared that he would never leave Stephen and Mary a groat, and the son-in-law brought suit for a dowry. Shakespeare's testimony shows that he remembered Mrs. Mountjoy's commission and the part that he played in mating the pair, but he forgot the amount of the dowry and when it was to be paid. The puzzled court turned the matter over for settlement to the French church in London, but it is not known what decision was reached.

The documents in the case show that Shakespeare was on familiar terms with tradesmen, that they thought well of him, that he was willing to undertake to try to make two people happy, and that he lived in the Mountjoy house at the corner of Silver and Monkwell streets. During the period of Stephen's apprenticeship (1598–1604), Shakespeare wrote some of his greatest plays, such as *Hamlet* and *Othello*. From its connection with Shakespeare, this is the most important corner in London for literary associations.

Wallace also found documents showing that Shakespeare owned at the time of his death a one-seventh interest in the Blackfriars Theater (p. 167) and a one-fourteenth interest in the Globe. The hitherto unknown fact that he continued to hold to the end of his life these important interests, requiring such skilled supervision, makes more doubtful the former assumption that he spent the last years of his life entirely at Stratford.

Last Years and Death. — Shakespeare probably bought New Place in Stratford as a residence for his family and a retreat for himself out of the theatrical season, but he doubtless continued to live in London for the greater part of his time until a few years before his death in 1616. The Mountjoy testimony proves that he was in London in May, 1612.

We are positive, however, that he was living in Stratford at the time of his death. He may for several years have taken only occasional trips to London to look after his interests in his theaters. It is not improbable that his health forced him to retire to Stratford, for it is difficult to see how any one could have produced nearly two Shakespearean plays a year for almost twenty years without breaking down under the strain. He had in addition almost certainly helped to manage the production of the plays, and tradition says that he was also an actor. Some of the parts which he is said to have played are the ghost in *Hamlet*, Adam in *As You Like It*, and Old Knowell in Ben Jonson's *Every Man in his Humor*.

In 1616, at the age of fifty-two, this master-singer of the world, who, in De Quincey's phrase, was "a little lower

STRATFORD-ON-AVON, SHOWING CHURCH WHERE SHAKESPEARE IS BURIED

than the angels," died and was buried in the parish church at Stratford. Shakespeare knew that in the course of time graves were often opened and the bones thrown into the charnel house. The world is thankful that he deliberately planned to have his resting place remain unmolested. His grave was dug seventeen feet deep and over it was placed the following inscription, intended to frighten those who might think of moving his bones : —

> Good frend for Iesvs sake forbeare,
> To digg the dvst encloased heare:
> Bleste be y̱ man y̱ spares thes stones,
> And cvrst be he y̱ moves my bones.

INSCRIPTION OVER SHAKESPEARE'S TOMB

Publication of his Plays. — It is probable that Shakespeare himself published only two early poems. Sixteen of his plays appeared in print during his lifetime; but the chances are that they were taken either from notes or from stage copies, more or less imperfect and surreptitiously obtained. The twentieth century has seen one of these careless reprints of a single play sell for more than three times as much as it cost to build a leading Elizabethan theater.[1] If Shakespeare himself had seen to the publication of his plays, succeeding generations would have been saved much trouble in puzzling over obscurities due to an imperfect text. We must remember, however, that publishing a play was thought to injure its success on the stage. One manager offered a printer a sum now equal to $100 not to publish a copy of a play that he had secured.

The *First Folio* edition of Shakespeare's works was published in 1623, seven years after his death, by two of his friends, John Heming and Henry Condell. In their dedication of the plays they say : —

"We have but collected them and done an office to the dead . . . without ambition either of self profit or fame, only to keep the memory of so worthy a friend and fellow alive, as was our Shakespeare, by humble offer of his plays."

If Shakespeare had not possessed the art of making

[1] The contract price for building the Fortune Theater was £440.

friends, we might to-day be without such plays as *Twelfth Night*, *As You Like It*, *The Winter's Tale*, *Cymbeline*, *The Tempest*, *Julius Cæsar*, *Antony and Cleopatra*, and *Macbeth*. These were printed for the first time in the 1623 *Folio*.

Amount and Classification of his Work. — The *First Folio* edition contained thirty-five plays, containing 100,120 lines. The Globe edition, one of the best modern texts of Shakespeare, has thirty-seven plays. Even if we give him no credit for the unknown dramas which he assisted in fashioning, and if we further deduct all doubtful plays from this number, the amount of dramatic work of which he is certainly the author is only less astonishing than its excellence. His non-dramatic poetry, comprising *Venus and Adonis*, *Lucrece*, 154 *Sonnets*, and some other short pieces, amounts to more than half as many lines as Milton's *Paradise Lost*.

Mere genius without wonderful self-control and a well-ordered use of time would not have enabled Shakespeare to leave such a legacy to the world. The pressure for fresh plays to meet exigencies is sufficient to explain why he did not always do his best work, even if we suppose that his health was never "out of joint."

The *First Folio* gives the current contemporary classification of the plays into "Comedies," "Histories," and "Tragedies." We indicate the following as some of the best in each class: —

Comedies: *A Midsummer Night's Dream, As You Like It, Twelfth Night, The Merchant of Venice, The Winter's Tale*, and *The Tempest*.

Histories: *Richard III., Henry IV., Henry V., Julius Cæsar.*

Tragedies: *Hamlet, Macbeth, Lear, Othello, Romeo and Juliet.*

Four Periods of his Life. — We may make another classification from a different point of view, according to the period of his development at the time of writing special plays. In order to study his growth and changing ideals, it will assist us to divide his work into four periods.

(1) There was the sanguine period, showing the exuberance of youthful love and imagination. Among the plays that are typical of these years are *The Comedy of Errors*, *A Midsummer Night's Dream*, *Romeo and Juliet*, *Richard II.*, and *Richard III.* These were probably all composed before 1595.

(2) The second period, from 1595 to 1601, shows progress in dramatic art. There is less exaggeration, more real power, and a deeper insight into human nature. There appears in his philosophy a vein of sadness, such as we find in the sayings of Jaques in *As You Like It*, and more appreciation of the growth of character, typified by his treatment of Orlando and Adam in the same play. Among the plays of this period are *The Merchant of Venice*, *Henry IV.*, *Henry V.*, and *As You Like It*.

(3) We may characterize the third period, from 1601 to 1608, as one in which he felt that the time was out of joint, that life was a fitful fever. His father died in 1601, after great disappointments. His best friends suffered what he calls, in *Hamlet*, "the slings and arrows of outrageous fortune." In 1601 Elizabeth executed the Earl of Essex for treason, and on the same charge threw the Earl of Southampton into the Tower. Even Shakespeare himself may have been suspected. The great plays of this period are tragedies, among which we may instance *Julius Cæsar*, *Hamlet*, *Othello*, *Macbeth*, and *King Lear*.

(4) The plays of his fourth period, 1608-1613, are remarkable for calm strength and sweetness. The fierce-

ness of *Othello* and *Macbeth* is left behind. In 1608 Shakespeare's mother died. Her death and the vivid recollection of her kindness and love may have been strong factors in causing him to look on life with kindlier eyes. The greatest plays of this period are *Cymbeline*, *The Winter's Tale*, and *The Tempest*.

While the dates of the composition of these plays are not exactly known, the foregoing classification is probably approximately correct. It should be followed in studying the development and the changing phases of Shakespeare's mind. (See table, pp. 188 and 189.)

Development as a Dramatist. — It is possible to study some of Shakespeare's plays with increased interest, if we note the reasons for assigning them to certain periods of his life. We conclude that *Love's Labor's Lost*, for instance, is an early play, because of its form, — excess of rime, small proportion of blank verse, lack of mastery of poetic expression, — and also because it suffers from the puns, conceits, and overdrawn wit and imagery of his early work. Almost one half of the 2789 lines of *Love's Labor's Lost* rime, while there are only 579 lines of blank verse. Of the 2064 lines in *The Tempest*, one of the last of his plays, 1458 are in blank verse. The plays of his first period show less freedom in the use of verse. He dislikes to let his meaning run over into the next line without a pause, and he hesitates to introduce those extra syllables which give such wonderful variety to his later work. As he grows older, he also uses more prose. *Romeo and Juliet* has 405 lines of prose in a total of 3052 lines, while *Hamlet*, a tragedy of 3931 lines, has 1208 lines of prose.

His treatment of his characters is even a more significant index to his growth than the form of his dramas. In the earlier plays, his men and women are more engaged with external forces than with internal struggles. In as excellent an early tragedy as *Romeo and Juliet*, the hero fights more with outside obstacles than with himself. In the great later tragedies, the internal conflict is more emphasized, as in the cases of Hamlet and Macbeth. "See thou character" became in an increasing degree Shakespeare's watchword. He grew to care less for mere incident, for plots based on mistaken identity, as in *The Comedy of Errors;* but he became more and more interested in the delineation of character, in showing the effect of evil on Macbeth and his wife, of jealousy on Othello, of indecision on Hamlet, as well as in exploring the ineffectual attempts of many of his characters to escape the consequences of their acts.

Sources of his Plots. — We should have had fewer plays from Shakespeare, if he had been compelled to take the time to invent new plots. The sources of the plots of his plays may usually be found in some old chronicle, novel, biography, or older play. Holinshed's *Chronicles of England, Scotland, and Ireland*, published when Shakespeare was fourteen years old, gives the stories of Lear, Cymbeline, Macbeth, and of all the English kings who are the heroes of the historical plays. As Holinshed is very dry reading, if Shakespeare had followed him closely, for instance, in *King Lear*, the play would have lost its most impressive parts. There is not in Holinshed even a suggestion of the Falstaff of *Henry IV.*, that veritable "comic Hamlet," who holds a unique place among the humorous characters of the world.

North's translation of Plutarch's *Lives*, published when Shakespeare was fifteen years old, became his textbook of ancient history and furnished him the raw material for plays like *Julius Cæsar* and *Antony and Cleopatra*.

TABLE OF SHAKESPEARE'S PLAYS[1]

Play	Total of Lines	Prose	Blank	Pentameter Rimes	Rimes, Short Lines	Songs	Published	Supposed Date
I.—PLAYS OF FIRST (RIMING) PERIOD							
Love's Labor's Lost	2789	1086	579	1028	54	32	1598	1588–9
Comedy of Errors	1778	240	1150	380	—	—	1623	1589–91[2]
Midsummer Night's Dream	2174	441	878	731	138	63	1600	1590–1
Two Gentlemen of Verona	2294	409	1510	116	—	15	1623	1590–2
Romeo and Juliet	3052	405	2111	486	—	—	1597	1591–3
Richard II.	2756	—	2107	537	—	—	1597	? 1593
Richard III.	3619	55?	3374	170	—	—	1597	? 1594–5
II.—HISTORIES AND COMEDIES OF SECOND PERIOD							
King John	2570	—	2403	150	—	—	1623	1594–5
Merchant of Venice	2660	673	1896	93	34	9	1600[2]	? 1595–6
1 Henry IV.	3176	1464	1622	84	—	—	1598	1596–7[3]
2 Henry IV.	3446	1860	1417	74	7	15	1600	1598–9
Henry V.	3380	1531	1678	101	2	8	1600	1598[8]
Merry Wives	3018	2703	227	69	—	19	1602	1599
Much Ado, &c.	2826	2106	643	40	18	16	1600	1599–1600
As You Like It	2857	1681	925	71	—	97	1623	1599–1600[8]
Twelfth Night	2690	1741	763	120	130	60	1623	1601[8]
All's Well	2966	1453	1234	280	2	12	1623	1601–2
(Love's Labor's Won, 1590).							

III.—TRAGEDIES AND COMEDY OF THIRD PERIOD

Julius Caesar	2478	165	2241	34	—	1623	1601[3]
Hamlet	3931	1208	2490	81	60	1603[2]	1602-3[8]
Measure for Measure	2821	1134	1574	73	6	1623	? 1603
Othello	3316	541	2672	86	25	1622	? 1604
Macbeth	2108	158	1588	118	—	1623	1605-68
King Lear	3334	903	2238	74	83	1608[2]	1605-68
Antony and Cleopatra	3063	255	2761	42	6	1623	1606-7
Coriolanus	3410	829	2521	42	—	1623	? 1607-8

IV.—PLAYS OF FOURTH PERIOD

Tempest	2064	458	1458	2	96	1623	1609-10
Cymbeline	3339	638	2585	107	32	1623	1609-10
Winter's Tale	3075	844	1825	—	57	1623	? 1611

V.—DOUBTFUL PLAYS

Titus Andronicus	2523	43	2338	144	—	1594	1588-90
1 Henry VI.	2677	—	2379	314	—	1623	1592-4
2 Henry VI.	3162	448	2562	122	—	1623	1592-4
3 Henry VI.	2904	—	2749	155	—	1623	1592-4
Contention	1952	381	1571	44	—	1594	1586-8
True Tragedy	2101	—	2035	66	—	1595	1586-8

VI.—PLAYS IN WHICH SHAKESPEARE WAS NOT SOLE AUTHOR

Taming of the Shrew	2649	516	1971	169	15	1623	1596-7
Troilus and Cressida	3496	1186	2025	196	16	1609	1603
Timon of Athens	2373	596	1560	184	18	1623	1607-8
Pericles	2389	418	1436	225	89	1609[2]	1608-9[3]
Henry VIII.	2822	67?	2613	16	12	1623	1610-12[3]

Poems published.—*Venus and Adonis*, 1593; *Lucrece*, 1594; *Passionate Pilgrim*, 1599; *Phœnix and Turtle* in Chester's *Loves Martyr*, 1601; *Sonnets*, 1609, with *A Lover's Complaint*.

[1] Adapted from Furnivall.   [2] Entered one year before at Stationers' Hall.   [3] May be looked on as fairly certain.

Shakespeare recognized the greatness of North's *Plutarch* and paid it the compliment of following its thought more closely than that of any other of his sources.

Shakespeare found suggestions for *As You Like It* in Thomas Lodge's contemporary novel *Rosalynde*, but Touchstone and Adam are original creations.

Our astonishment is often increased to find that the merest hint led to an imperishable creation, such as the character of Lady Macbeth, the reference to whom in Holinshed is confined to these twenty-eight words, ". . . specially his wife lay sore upon him to attempt the thing, as she that was very ambitious, burning in unquenchable desire to bear the name of a queen." His plays are almost as different from the old chronicles or tales as the rose from the soil which nourished it.

Discovered in 1845 on site of Duke's Theater.
SHAKESPEARE — THE D'AVENANT BUST

General Characteristics

Sympathy. — His most pronounced characteristic is the broadest sympathy ever shown by an author. He seems to have been able to sympathize with every kind of human soul in every emergency. He plays with the simple rustics in *A Midsummer Night's Dream*. The portrait of the serving man Adam, in *As You Like It*, is as kindly and as discriminating as that of king or nobleman. Though he is the scholar and philosopher in *Hamlet*, he can afterward roam the country with the tramp Autolycus in *The Winter's Tale*. Women have marveled at the ease with which his sympathy crosses the barriers of sex, at his portraits of Portia, Rosalind, Desdemona, Lady Macbeth, Miranda, Cleopatra, and Cordelia. Great actresses have testified to their amazement at his discovery of feminine secrets which they had thought no man could ever divine.

Universality. — Shakespeare's sympathy might have been broad enough to include all the people of his own time and their peculiar interests, but might have lacked the power to project itself into the universal heart of humanity.

HENRY IRVING AS HAMLET

Sometimes a writer voices the ideals and aspirations of his own day so effectively that he is called the spokesman of his age, but he makes slight appeal to future generations. Shakespeare was the spokesman of his own time, but he had the genius also to speak to all ages. He loved to present the eternal truths of the human heart and to invest them with such a touch of nature as to reveal the kinship of the entire world.

His contemporary, the dramatist, Ben Jonson, had the penetration to say of Shakespeare: —

"He was not of an age but for all time."

He meant that Shakespeare does not exhibit some popular conceit, folly, or phase of thought, which is merely the fashion of the hour and for which succeeding generations would care nothing; but that he voices those truths which appeal to the people of all ages. The grief of Lear over the dead Cordelia, the ambition of Lady Macbeth, the loves of Rosalind and Juliet, the questionings of Hamlet, interest us as much to-day as they did the Elizabethans. Fashions in literature may come and go, but Shakespeare's work remains.

From the painting by Sargent.
ELLEN TERRY AS LADY MACBETH

Humor. — Shakespeare had the most comprehensive sense of humor of any of the world's great writers, — a humor that was closely related to his sympathy. It has been said that he saved his tragedies from the fatal disease of absurdity, by inoculating them with his comic virus, and that his sense of humor kept him from ever becoming shrill. This faculty enabled him to detect incongruity, to keep from overstressing a situation, to enter into the personality of others, to recover quickly from "the slings and arrows of outrageous fortune," and in one of his last plays, *The Tempest*, to welcome the "brave young world" as if he would like to play the game of life again. It was largely because of his humor that the tragedies and pain of life did not sour and subdue Shakespeare.

He soon wearies of a vacant laugh. He has only one strictly farcical play, *The Comedy of Errors*. There are few intellects keen enough to extract all the humor from Shakespeare. For literal minds the full comprehension of even a slight display of his humor, such as the following dialogue affords, is better exercise than the solution of an algebraic problem. Dogberry, a constable in *Much Ado About Nothing*, thus instructs the Watch:—

"*Dogberry*. You shall comprehend all vagrom men; you are to bid any man stand in the prince's name.

"*Watch*. How if a' will not stand?

"*Dogberry*. Why, then, take no note of him, but let him go, and presently call the rest of the watch together, and thank God you are rid of a knave."

Of all Shakespeare's qualities, his humor is the hardest to describe because of its protean forms. Falstaff is his greatest humorous creation. So resourceful is he that even defeat enables him to rise like Antæus after a fall. His humor is almost a philosophy of existence for those who love to use wit and ingenuity in trying to evade the laws of sober, orderly living. Perhaps it was for this very reason that Shakespeare consented to send so early to "Arthur's bosom"[1] a character who had not a little of the complexity of Hamlet.

From a drawing by B. Westmacott.
FALSTAFF AND HIS PAGE

Much of Shakespeare's humor is delicately suffused

[1] *Henry V.*, Act II., Scene 3, line 10.

through his plays. Many of them either ripple with the laughter of his characters or are lighted with their smiles. We may pass pleasant hours in the company of his joyous creations, such as Rosalind in *As You Like It*, or Portia in *The Merchant of Venice*, or Puck as the spokesman for *A Midsummer Night's Dream*, who good naturedly exclaims: —

> "Lord, what fools these mortals be!"

or Viola and her companions in *Twelfth Night*, or Beatrice and Benedict in *Much Ado About Nothing*, or Ariel in *The Tempest* playing pranks on the bewildered mariners and singing of the joys of life which come as a reward for service: —

> "Merrily, merrily shall I live now
> Under the blossom that hangs on the bough."

Shakespeare is also the one English author who is equally successful in depicting the highest type of both comedy and tragedy. He has the power to describe even a deathbed scene so as to invest it with both humor and pathos. Dame Quickly's lines in *Henry V.*, on the death of Falstaff, show this capacity.

The next greatest English writer is lacking in this sense of humor. John Milton could write the tragedies of a *Paradise Lost* and a *Samson Agonistes*, but he could not give us the humor of *A Midsummer Night's Dream*, *The Comedy of Errors*, or *As You Like It*. We have seen that the next greatest dramatic genius, Marlowe, has little sense of humor. Mrs. Browning correctly describes the plays of Shakespeare as filled —

> "With tears and laughters for all time."

Moral Ideals. — To show the moral consequences of acts was the work which most appealed to him. Banquo voiced the comprehensiveness of moral law when he said, "In the great hand of God I stand." There is here great divergence between the views of Shakespeare and of Bacon. Dowden says:—

"While Bacon's sense of the presence of physical law in the universe was for his time extraordinarily developed, he seems practically to have acted upon the theory that the moral laws of the world are not inexorable, but rather by tactics and dexterity may be cleverly evaded. Their supremacy was acknowledged by Shakespeare in the minutest as well as in the greatest concerns of human life."

By employing "tactics" in sending Hamlet on a voyage to England, the king hoped to avoid the consequences of his crime. Macbeth in vain tried every stratagem to "trammel up the consequence." Goneril and Regan drove their white-haired father out into the storm; but even in *King Lear*, where the forces of evil seem to run riot, let us note the result:—

"Throughout that stupendous Third Act the good are seen growing better through suffering, and the bad worse through success. The warm castle is a room in hell, the storm-swept heath a sanctuary. . . . The only real thing in the world is the soul with its courage, patience, devotion. And nothing outward can touch that."[1]

Shakespeare makes no pessimists. He shows how misfortune crowns life with new moral glory. We rise from the gloom of *King Lear*, feeling that we would rather be like Cordelia than like either of her sisters or any other selfish character who apparently triumphs until life's close. And yet Cordelia lost everything, her portion of her father's kingdom and her own life. When we realize that Shakespeare found one hundred and ten lines in *King Lear* sufficient not only to confer immortality on Cordelia, but also to make us all eager to pay homage to her, in spite of the

[1] Bradley's *Shakespearean Tragedy*, p. 327.

fact that the ordinary standard of the world has not ceased to declare such a life a failure, we may the better understand that his greatest power consisted in revealing the moral victories possible for this rough-hewn human life.

Shakespeare made a mistake about the seacoast of Bohemia and the location of Milan with reference to the sea, but he was always sure of the relative position of right and wrong and of the ultimate failure of evil. In his greatest plays, for instance, in *Macbeth*, he sought to impress the incalculable danger of meddling with evil, the impossibility of forecasting the tragedy that might thereby result, the certainty that retribution would follow, either here or beyond "this bank and shoal of time."

Mastery of his Mother Tongue. — His wealth of expression is another striking characteristic. In a poem on Shakespeare, Ben Jonson wrote: —

"Thou had'st small Latin and less Greek."

Shakespeare is, however, the mightiest master of the English tongue. He uses 15,000 different words, while the second greatest writer in our language employs only 7000. A great novelist like Thackeray has a vocabulary of about 5000 words, while many uneducated laborers do not use over 600 words. The combinations that Shakespeare has made with these 15,000 words are far more striking than their mere number.

Variety of Style. — The style of Milton, Addison, Dr. Johnson, and Macaulay has some definite peculiarities, which can easily be classified. Shakespeare, on the contrary, in holding the mirror up to nature, has different styles for his sailors, soldiers, courtiers, kings, and shepherds, — for Juliet, the lover; for Mistress Quickly, the alewife; for Hamlet, the philosopher; and for Bottom, the weaver. To employ so many styles requires genius of a peculiar kind. In the case of most of us, our style would soon betray our individuality. When Dr. Samuel Johnson tried to write a drama, he made all his little fishes talk like whales, as Goldsmith wittily remarked.

In the same play Shakespeare's style varies from the dainty lyric touch of Ariel's song about the cowslip's bell and the blossoming bough, to a style unsurpassed for grandeur: —

> "The cloud-capp'd towers, the gorgeous palaces,
> The solemn temples, the great globe itself,
> Yea, all which it inherit, shall dissolve
> And, like this insubstantial pageant faded,
> Leave not a rack behind."

In the same passage his note immediately changes to the soft *vox humana* of —

> "We are such stuff
> As dreams are made on, and our little life
> Is rounded with a sleep."

His Influence on Thought. — With the exception of the *Scriptures*, Shakespeare's dramas have surpassed all other works in molding modern English thought. If a person should master Shakespeare and the *Bible*, he would find most that is greatest in human thought, outside of the realm of science.

Even when we do not read him, we cannot escape the influence of others who have been swayed by him. For generations, certain modes of thought have crystallized about his phrases. We may instance such expressions as these: "Brevity is the soul of wit." "What's in a name?" "The wish was father to the thought." "The time is out of joint." "There's the rub." "There's a divinity that shapes our ends." "Comparisons are odorous." It would, perhaps, not be too much to say that the play of *Hamlet* has affected the thought of the majority of the English-speaking race. His grip on Anglo-Saxon thought has been increasing for more than three hundred years.

Shakespeare's influence on the thought of any individual has only two circumscribing factors, — the extent of Shakespearean study and the capacity of interpreting the facts of life. No intelligent person can study Shakespeare without becoming a deeper and more varied thinker, without securing a broader comprehension of human existence, — its struggles, failures, and successes. If we have before viewed humanity through a glass darkly, Shakespeare will gradually lead us where we can see face to face the beauty and the grandeur of the mystery of existence. His most valuable influence often consists in rendering his students sympathetic and in making them feel a sense of kinship with life. Shakespeare's readers more quickly realize that human nature shows the shaping touch of divinity. They have the rare joy of discovering the world anew and of exclaiming with Miranda : —

> "How many goodly creatures are there here!
> How beauteous mankind is! O brave new world,
> That has such people in't!"[1]

When we have really become acquainted with Shakespeare, our lives will be less prosaic and restricted. After intimate companionship with him, there will be, in the words of Ariel, hardly any common thing in life —

> "But doth suffer a sea-change
> Into something rich and strange."[2]

[1] *The Tempest*, Act V., Scene 1.   [2] *Ibid.*, Act I., Scene 2.

From the portrait by Gerard Honthorst, National Portrait Gallery.

BEN JONSON, 1573?-1637

Life. — About nine years after the birth of Shakespeare his greatest successor in the English drama was born in London. Jonson outlived Shakespeare twenty-one years and helped to usher in the decline of the drama.

Ben Jonson, the son of a clergyman and the stepson of

a master bricklayer, received a good education at Westminster School. Unlike Shakespeare, Jonson learned much Latin and Greek. In one respect Jonson's training was unfortunate for a poet. He was taught to write prose exercises first and then to turn them into poetry. In this way he acquired the habit of trying to express unpoetical ideas in verse. Art could change the prose into metrical riming lines, but art could not breathe into them the living soul of poetry. In after times Jonson said that Shakespeare lacked art, but Jonson recognized that the author of *Hamlet* had the magic touch of nature. Jonson's pen rarely felt her all-embracing touch.

If Jonson served an apprenticeship as a bricklayer, as his enemies afterward said, he did not continue long at such work. He crossed the Channel and enlisted for a brief time as a soldier in the Netherlands. He soon returned to London and became a writer for the theater, and thenceforth lived the life of an author and a student. He loved to study and translate the classics. In fact, what a novice might think original in Jonson's plays was often borrowed from the classics. Of his relations to the classical writers, Dryden says, "You track him everywhere in their snow." Jonson was known as the most learned poet of the age, because, if his plays demanded any special knowledge, no subject was too hard, dry, or remote from common life for him to attempt to master it. He knew the boundaries of Bohemia, and he took pleasure in saying to a friend: "Shakespeare in a play brought in a number of men saying they had suffered shipwreck in Bohemia, where is no sea near, by some hundred miles."

Jonson's personal characteristics partly explain why he placed himself in opposition to the spirit of the age. He was extremely combative. It was almost a necessity

BEN JONSON

for him to quarrel with some person or with some opinion. He killed two men in duels, and he would probably have been hanged, if he had not pleaded benefit of clergy. For the greater part of his life, he was often occupied with pen and ink quarrels.

When James I. ascended the throne in 1603, Jonson soon became a royal favorite. He was often employed to write masques, a peculiar species of drama which called for magnificent scenery and dress, and gave the nobility the opportunity of acting the part of some distinguished or supernatural character. Such work brought Jonson into intimate association with the leading men of the day.

It is pleasant to think that he was a friend of Shakespeare. Jonson's pithy volume of prose, known as *Discoveries Made upon Men and Matter*, contains his famous criticism on Shakespeare, noteworthy because it shows how a great contemporary regarded him, "I loved the man and do honor his memory on this side idolatry as much as any." Few English writers have received from a great rival author such convincing testimony in regard to lovable personality.

BEN JONSON'S TOMB IN WESTMINSTER ABBEY

In 1616, the year in which Shakespeare died, Jonson was made poet laureate. When he died in 1637, he was buried in an upright position in Westminster Abbey. A plain stone with the unique inscription, "O Rare Ben Jonson," marks his grave.

Plays.—Ben Jonson's comedies are his best dramatic work. From all his plays we may select three that will best repay reading: *Volpone*, *The Alchemist*, and *The Silent Woman*. *Volpone* is the story of an old, childless, Venetian nobleman whose ruling passion is avarice. Everything else in the play is made tributary to this passion. The first three lines in the first act strike the keynote of the entire play. Volpone says:—

> "Good morning to the day; and next, my gold!—
> Open the shrine, that I may see my saint.
> Hail the world's soul and mine!"

The Alchemist makes a strong presentation of certain forms of credulity in human nature and of the special tricks which the alchemists and impostors of that day adopted. One character wants to buy the secret of the helpful influence of the stars; another parts with his wealth to learn the alchemist's secret of turning everything into gold and jewels. The way in which these characters are deceived is very amusing. A study of this play adds to our knowledge of a certain phase of the times. In point of artistic construction of plot, *The Alchemist* is nowhere excelled in the English drama; but the intrusion of Jonson's learning often makes the play tedious reading, as when he introduces the technical terms of the so-called science of alchemy to show that he has studied it thoroughly. One character speaks to the alchemist of—

> "Your lato, azoch, zernich, chibrit, heautarit,"

and another asks:—

> "Can you sublime and dulcify? calcine?
> Know you the sapor pontic? sapor stiptic,
> Or what is homogene, or heterogene?"

Lines like the following show that Jonson's acute mind had grasped something of the principle of evolution:—

> "... 'twere absurd
> To think that nature in the earth bred gold
> Perfect in the instant: something went before.
> There must be remote matter."

The Silent Woman is in lighter vein than either of the plays just mentioned. The leading character is called Morose, and his special whim or "humor" is a horror of noise. His home is on a street "so narrow at both ends that it will receive no coaches nor carts, nor any of these common noises." He has mattresses on the stairs, and he dismisses the footman for wearing squeaking shoes. For a long time Morose does not marry, fearing the noise of a wife's tongue. Finally he commissions his nephew to find him a silent woman for a wife, and the author uses to good advantage the opportunity for comic situations which this turn in the action affords. Dryden preferred *The Silent Woman* to any of the other plays.

Besides the plays mentioned in this section, Jonson wrote during his long life many other comedies and masques as well as some tragedies.

Marks of Decline. — A study of the decline of the drama, as shown in Jonson's plays, will give us a better appreciation of the genius of Shakespeare. We may change Jonson's line (see p. 191) so that it will state one reason for his not maintaining Shakespearean excellence:—

> "He was not for all time, but of an age."

His first play, *Every Man in his Humor*, paints, not the

universal emotions of men, but some special humor. He thus defines the sense in which he uses humor: —

> "As when some one peculiar quality
> Doth so possess a man, that it doth draw
> All his affects, his spirits and his powers,
> In their confluctions, all to run one way,
> This may be truly said to be a Humor."

Unlike Shakespeare, Jonson gives a distorted or incomplete picture of life. In *Volpone* everything is subsidiary to the humor of avarice, which receives unnatural emphasis. In *The Alchemist* there is little to relieve the picture of credibility and hypocrisy, while *The Silent Woman* has for its leading character a man whose principal "humor" or aim in life is to avoid noise.

No drama which fails to paint the nobler side of womanhood can be called complete. In Jonson's plays we do not find a single woman worthy to come near the Shakespearean characters, Cordelia, Imogen, and Desdemona. His limitations are nowhere more marked than in his inability to portray a noble woman.

Another reason why he fails to present life completely is shown in these lines, in which he defines his mission: —

> "My strict hand
> Was made to seize on vice, and with a gripe
> Squeeze out the humor of such spongy souls
> As lick up every idle vanity."

Since the world needs building up rather than tearing down, a remedy for an ailment rather than fault-finding, the greatest of men cannot be mere satirists. Shakespeare displays some fellow feeling for the object of his satire, but Jonson's satire is cold and devoid of sympathy.

Jonson deliberately took his stand in opposition to the romantic spirit of the age. Marlowe and Shakespeare had disregarded the classical unities (see p. 157) and had developed the drama on romantic lines. Jonson resolved to follow classical traditions and to adhere to unity of time and place in the construction of his plots. The action in the play of *The Silent Woman*, for instance, occupies only twelve hours.

General Characteristics. — Jonson's plays show the touch of a conscientious artist with great intellectual ability. His vast erudition is constantly apparent. He is the satiric historian of his time, and he exhibits the follies and the humors of the age under a powerful lens. He is also the author of dainty lyrics (p. 137), and forcible prose criticism.

Among the shortcomings of his plays, we may specially note lack of feeling and of universality. He fails to comprehend the nature of woman. He is not a sympathetic observer of manifold life, but presents only what is perceived through the frosted glass of intellect. His art is self-conscious. He defiantly opposed the romantic spirit of the age and weakened the drama by making it bear the burden of the classical unities.

MINOR DRAMATISTS

Beaumont and Fletcher. — Next to Marlowe, Shakespeare, and Ben Jonson, the two most influential dramatists were Francis Beaumont (1584–1616) and John Fletcher (1579–1625). They are usually mentioned together because they collaborated in writing plays. Fletcher had the great advantage of working with Shakespeare in producing *Henry VIII*. Beaumont died nine years before Fletcher, and it is doubtful whether he collaborated with Fletcher in more than fifteen of the fifty plays published under their joint names.

Two of their greatest plays, *Philaster* and *The Maid's Tragedy*, are probably their joint production. *The Faithful Shepherdess* and *Bonduca* are among the best of about eighteen plays supposed to have been written by Fletcher alone. After Beaumont's death, Fletcher sometimes collaborated with other dramatists.

FRANCIS BEAUMONT

Almost all the so-called Beaumont and Fletcher plays are well constructed. These dramatists also have, in common with the majority of their associates, the ability to produce occasional passages of exquisite poetry. A character in *Philaster* speaks of death in lines that suggest *Hamlet*: —

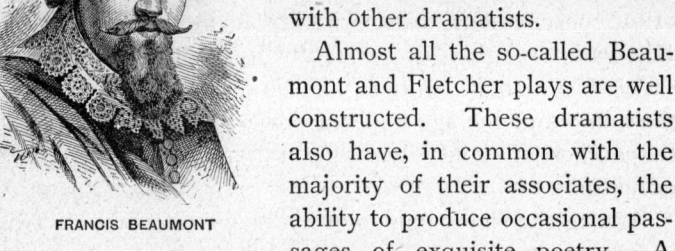

> " 'Tis less than to be born; a lasting sleep,
> A quiet resting from all jealousy;
> A thing we all pursue; I know besides
> It is but giving over of a game
> That must be lost."

Beaumont and Fletcher's work is noteworthy for its pictures of contemporary life and manners, for wealth of incident, rapidity of movement, and variety of characters.

Not long after the beginning of the seventeenth century there was a change in the taste of the patrons of the theater. Shakespeare declined in popularity. The playwrights tried to solve the problem of interesting audiences that wished only to be entertained. This attempt led to a change in dramatic methods.

Changed Moral Ideals. — Under Elizabeth's successors the Puritan spirit increased and the most religious part of the community seldom attended the theater. The later dramatists pay little attention to the moral development of character and its self-revelation through action. They often merely describe character and paint it from the outside. We have seen that Shakespeare's great plays are almost a demonstration in moral geometry, but Beaumont and Fletcher are not much concerned over the moral consequences of an action. The gravest charge against them is that they "unknit the sequence of moral cause and effect." After reading such plays, we do not rise with the feeling that there is a divinity that shapes our ends.

JOHN FLETCHER

Coleridge says, "Shakespeare never renders that amiable which religion and reason alike teach us to detest, or clothes impurity in the garb of virtue, like Beaumont and Fletcher." Much of the work of their contemporary dramatists is marred by such blemishes. Unpleasant as are numbers of these plays, they are less insidious than many which have appeared on the stage in modern times.

Love of Surprises. — The dramatists racked their inventive powers to introduce surprises to interest the audience. Here was a marked departure from Shakespeare's later method. He plans *Macbeth* so as to have his audience forecast the logical result. Consequences of the most tremendous import, beside which Beaumont and Fletcher's surprises seem trivial, follow naturally from Macbeth's actions. In his greatest plays, Shakespeare, unlike the later dramatists, never relies on illogical surprises to sustain the interest. The witch queen in one of the plays of Thomas Middleton (1570–1627) suddenly exclaims:—

> " . . . fetch three ounces of the red-haired girl
>   I kill'd last midnight."

Shakespeare's witches suggest only enough of the weird and the horrible to transfix the attention and make the beholder realize the force of the temptation that assails Macbeth. Charles Lamb truly observes that Middleton's witches "can harm the body," but Shakespeare's "have power over the soul."

Middleton could, however, write a passage like the following, which probably suggested to Milton one of the finest lines in *Lycidas*:—

> "Upon those lips, the sweet fresh buds of youth,
> The holy dew of prayer lies, like pearl
> Dropt from the opening eyelids of the morn
> Upon a bashful rose."

Large Number of Playwrights. — Beaumont and Fletcher were only two of a large number of dramatists who were born in the age of Elizabeth, and who, with few exceptions, lived into the second quarter of the seventeenth century. Their work was the result of earlier Elizabethan impulses, and it is rightly considered a part of the great dramatic movement of the Elizabethan age. The popularity of the drama continued to attract many authors who in a different age might have produced other forms of literature.

George Chapman (1559?–1634), who is best known for his fine translation of Homer's *Iliad*, turned dramatist in middle life, but found it difficult to enter into the feelings of characters unlike himself. His best two plays, *Bussy D'Ambois* and *The Revenge of Bussy D'Ambois*, are tragedies founded on French history. **Thomas Middleton**, gifted in dramatic technique and dialogue and noted for his comedy of domestic manners, was the author of *Michaelmas Term*, *A Trick to Catch the Old One*, *The Changeling* (in collaboration with **William Rowley**, 1585?-1640?). **John Marston** (1576?-1634) wrote *Antonio and Mellida*, a blood and thunder tragedy, and collaborated with Jonson and Chapman to produce *Eastward Hoe*, an excellent comic picture of contemporary life. *The Shoemaker's Holiday* of **Thomas Dekker** (1570?-1640) is also a good comedy of London life and manners. **Philip Massinger** (1584-1640), a later collaborator with Fletcher, wrote *A New Way to Pay Old Debts*, a play very popular in after times. **Thomas Heywood** (1572?-1650), one of the most prolific dramatists, claimed to have had "either an entire hand or at the least a main finger," in two hundred and twenty plays. His best work is *A Woman Killed with Kindness*, a domestic drama that appealed to the middle classes.

A Tragic Group. — Three dramatists: **John Webster** (1602-1624), **Cyril Tourneur** (1575?-1626), and **John Ford** (1586-1640?), had a love for the most somber tragedy. In tragic power, Webster approaches nearest to Shakespeare. Webster's greatest play, *The Duchess of Malfi* (acted in 1616), and *The White Devil*, which ranks second, show the working of a master hand, but Webster's genius comes to a focus only in depicting the horrible. He loves such gloomy metaphors as the following: —

> "You speak as if a man
> Should know what fowl is *coffined* in a baked meat
> Afore you cut it open."

Tourneur's *The Atheist's Tragedy* is in Webster's vein, but far inferior to *The Duchess of Malfi*.

Ford's *The Broken Heart* is a strong, but unpleasant, tragedy. He is so fascinated with the horrible that he introduces it even when it is not the logical outcome of a situation. His best but least characteristic play is *Perkin Warbeck*, which is worthy of ranking second only to Shakespeare's historical plays.

End of the Elizabethan Drama. — James Shirley (1596-1666), "the last of the Elizabethans," endeavored to the best of his ability to continue the work of the earlier dramatists. *The Traitor* and *The Cardinal* are two of the best of his many productions. He was hard at work writing new plays in 1642, when the Puritans closed the theaters. He was thus forced to abandon the profession that he enjoyed and compelled to teach in order to earn a livelihood.

The drama has never since regained its Elizabethan ascendancy. The coarse plays of the Restoration (1660) flourished for a while, but the treatment of the later drama forms but a minor part of the history of the best English literature. Few plays produced during the next two hundred years are much read or acted to-day. *She Stoops to Conquer* (1773), by Oliver Goldsmith, and *The Rivals* (1775) and *The School for Scandal* (1777), by Richard Brinsley Sheridan, are the chief exceptions before 1890.

SUMMARY

The Elizabethan age was a period of expansion in knowledge, commerce, religious freedom, and human opportunities. The defeat of the Armada freed England from fear of Spanish domination and made her mistress of the sea.

England was vivified by the combined influence of the Renaissance and the Reformation. Knowledge was expanding in every direction and promising to crown human effort with universal mastery. The greater feeling of individuality was partly due to the Reformation, which emphasized the direct responsibility of each individual for all acts affecting the welfare of his soul.

Elizabethans were noted for their resourcefulness, their initiative, their craving for new experiences, and their desire to realize the utmost out of life. As they cared little for ideas that could not be translated into action, they were particularly interested in the drama.

Although the prose covers a wide field, it is far inferior to the poetry. Lyly's *Euphues* suffers from overwrought conceits and forced antitheses, but it influenced writers to pay more attention to the manner in which thought was expressed. The flowery prose of Sidney's *Arcadia* presents a pastoral world of romance. His *Apologie for Poetrie* is a meritorious piece of early criticism. While Hooker indicates advance in solidity of matter and dignity of style, yet a comparison of his heavy religious prose with the prayer of the king in *Hamlet* or with Portia's words about mercy in *The Merchant of Venice* will show the vast superiority of the poetry in dealing with spiritual ideas. Bacon's *Essays*, celebrated for pithy condensation of striking thoughts, is the only prose work that has stood the test of time well enough to claim many readers to-day.

Poetry, both lyric and dramatic, is the crowning glory of the Elizabethan age. The lyric verse is remarkable for its wide range and for beauty of form and sentiment. The lyrics include love sonnets, pastorals, and miscellaneous verse. Shakespeare's *Sonnets* and the songs in his dramas are the best in this field, but many poets wrote exquisite artistic lyrics.

Edmund Spenser is the only great poet who was not

also a dramatist. His *Faerie Queene* fashions an ideal world dominated by a love of beauty and high endeavor.

The greatest literary successes of the age were won in writing plays for the stage. In England the drama had for centuries slowly developed through Miracle plays, Moralities, and Interludes to the plays of Marlowe, Shakespeare, and Ben Jonson. These three are the greatest Elizabethan dramatists, but they are only the central figures of a group.

The English drama in the hands of Sackville imitated Seneca and followed the rules of the classic stage. Marlowe and Shakespeare threw off the restraints of the classical unities; and the romantic drama, rejoicing in its freedom, speedily told the story of all life.

The innyards were used for the public presentation of plays before the erection of theaters in the last quarter of the sixteenth century. The theaters were a great educational force in Shakespeare's time. They not only furnished amusement, but they also took the place of periodicals, lectures, and books. The actors, coming into close contact with their audience and unable to rely on elaborate scenery as an offset to poor acting, were equal to the task of so presenting Shakespeare's great plays as to make them popular.

Shakespeare's plays, the greatest ever written, reveal wonderful sympathy, universality, humor, delineation of character, high moral ideals, mastery of expression, and strength, beauty, and variety of poetic form.

Great as is Ben Jonson, he hampered himself by observing the classical unities and by stressing accidental qualities. He lacks Shakespeare's universality, broad sympathy, and emotional appeal.

Other minor dramatists, like Beaumont and Fletcher,

show further decline, because they constructed their plays more from the outside, showed less development of character in strict accordance with moral law, and relied more for effect on sensational scenes. The drama has never since taken up the wand that dropped from Shakespeare's hands.

REFERENCES FOR FURTHER STUDY

HISTORICAL

In addition to the chapters on the time in the histories of Gardiner, Green, Lingard, Walker, and Traill (p. 50), see Stephenson's *The Elizabethan People*, Creighton's *Queen Elizabeth*, Wilson's *Life in Shakespeare's England*, Stephenson's *Shakespeare's London*, Warner's *English History in Shakespeare's Plays*.

LITERARY

General and Non-Dramatic

The Cambridge History of English Literature, Vols. IV., V., and VI.
Courthope's *A History of English Poetry*, Vol. II.
Schelling's *English Literature during the Lifetime of Shakespeare*.
Seccombe and Allen's *The Age of Shakespeare*, 2 vols.
Saintsbury's *A History of Elizabethan Literature*.
Dictionary of National Biography for lives of Lyly, Sidney, Hooker, Bacon, Spenser, and the minor dramatists.
Walton's *Life of Hooker*.
Church's *Life of Bacon*. (E. M. L.)
Church's *Life of Spenser*. (E. M. L.)
Mackail's *The Springs of Helicon* (Spenser).
Dowden's *Transcripts and Studies* (Spenser).
Lowell's *Among My Books* (Spenser).
Erskine's *The Elizabethan Lyric*.

The Drama[1]

Schelling's *Elizabethan Drama, 1558–1642*, 2 vols.
Ward's *A History of English Dramatic Literature*, 3 vols.

[1] For a list of books of selections from the drama, see p. 216.

Brooke's *The Tudor Drama*.
Chambers's *The Mediæval Stage*.
Allbright's *The Shakespearean Stage*.
Lawrence's *Elizabethan Playhouse and Other Studies*.
Smith's *York Plays* (Clarendon Press).
Symonds's *Shakespeare's Predecessors in the English Drama*.
Bates's *The English Religious Drama*.
Manly's *Specimens of the Pre-Shakespearean Drama*.
Wallace's *The Evolution of the English Drama up to Shakespeare*.
Ingram's *Christopher Marlowe and his Associates*.
Dowden's *Transcripts and Studies* (Marlowe).
Symonds's *Ben Jonson*.
Swinburne's *A Study of Ben Jonson*.

Shakespeare

Lee's *A Life of William Shakespeare*.
Furnivall and Munro's *Shakespeare: Life and Work*.
Harris's *The Man Shakespeare and his Tragic Life Story*.
Halliwell-Phillipps's *Outlines of the Life of Shakespeare*.
Raleigh's *Shakespeare*. (E. M. L.)
Baker's *The Development of Shakespeare as a Dramatist*.
MacCracken, Pierce, and Durham's *An Introduction to Shakespeare*.
Bradley's *Shakespearean Tragedy* (excellent).
Bradley's *Oxford Lectures on Poetry*.
Dowden's *Shakespeare, His Mind and Art*.
Coleridge's *Lectures on Shakespeare* (pp. 21–58 of Beers's *Selections from the Prose Writings of Coleridge*).
Lowell's *Shakespeare Once More*, in *Among My Books*.
Wallace's *Shakespeare, the Globe, and Blackfriars*.
How Shakespeare's Senses were Trained, Chap. X. in Halleck's *Education of the Central Nervous System*.
Rolfe's *Shakespeare the Boy*.
Boswell-Stone's *Shakespeare's Holinshed*.
Brooke's *Shakespeare's Plutarch*, 2 vols.
Madden's *The Diary of Master William Silence: A Study of Shakespeare and of Elizabethan Sport*.
Winter's *Shakespeare on the Stage*.

SUGGESTED READINGS
WITH QUESTIONS AND SUGGESTIONS

Elizabethan Prose. — Good selections from Ascham, Hakluyt, Raleigh, Holinshed, Stow, Camden, North, Sidney, Foxe, Hooker, Lyly, Greene, Lodge, and Nashe are given in Craik, I.[1] Chambers, I. and Manly, II. also give a number of selections. Deloney's *The Gentle Craft* may be found in the Clarendon Press edition of his *Works*. For Bacon, see Craik, II.

These selections will give the student a broader grasp of the Elizabethan age. The style and subject matter of Lyly's *Euphues*, Sidney's *Arcadia*, Hooker's *Of the Laws of Ecclesiastical Polity*, and Bacon's *Essays* should be specially noted. Which one of these authors exerted the strongest influence on his own age? Which one makes the strongest appeal to modern times? In what respects does the style of any Elizabethan prose writer show an improvement over that of Mandeville and Malory?

Lyrics. — For specimens of love sonnets, read Nos. 18, 33, 73, 104, 111, and 116 of Shakespeare's *Sonnets*. Compare them with any of Sidney's and Spenser's sonnets. Other love lyrics which should be read are Spenser's *Prothalamion*, Lodge's *Love in My Bosom Like a Bee*, and Ben Jonson's *To Celia*. Among pastoral lyrics, read from Spenser's *Shepherd's Calendar* for August, 1579, Perigo and Willie's duet, beginning: —

"It fell upon a holy eve,"

and Marlowe's *The Passionate Shepherd to His Love*. The best pastoral lyrics from the modern point of view are Shakespeare's two songs: "Under the Greenwood Tree" (*As You Like It*) and "When Icicles Hang by the Wall" (*Love's Labor's Lost*). The best miscellaneous lyrics are the songs in Shakespeare's *Cymbeline*, *The Tempest*, and *As You Like It*. Drayton's *Ballad of Agincourt* and *Sonnet* 61 are his best lyrical verse. Read Ben Jonson's *An Epitaph on Salathiel Pavy* and, from his Pindaric Ode, the stanza beginning: —

"It is not growing like a tree."

From John Donne, read either *The Funeral*, *The Canonization*, or *The Dream*.

[1] For full titles, see p. 6.

Good selections from all varieties of Elizabethan lyrics may be found in Bronson, II., Ward, I., *Oxford*, *Century*, Manly, I. Nearly all the lyrics referred to in this list, including the best songs from the dramatists, are given in Schelling's *Elizabethan Lyrics* (327 pp., 75 cents). This work, together with Erskine's *The Elizabethan Lyric* and Reed's *English Lyrical Poetry from its Origins to the Present Time*, will serve for a more exhaustive study of this fascinating subject.

From your reading, select from each class the lyric that pleases you most, and give reasons for your choice. Which lyric seems the most spontaneous? the most artistic? the most inspired? the most modern? the most quaint? the most and the least instinct with feeling?

Edmund Spenser. — The *Faerie Queene*, Book I., Canto I., should be read. Maynard's *English Classic Series*, No. 27 (12 cents) contains the first two cantos and the *Prothalamion*. Kitchin's edition of Book I. (Clarendon Press, 60 cents) is an excellent volume. The Globe edition furnishes a good complete text of Spenser's work. Ample selections are given in Bronson, II., Ward, I., and briefer ones in Manly, I., and *Century*.

THE DRAMA

The Best Volumes of Selections. — The least expensive volume to cover nearly the entire field with brief selections is Vol. II. of *The Oxford Treasury of English Literature*, entitled *Growth of the Drama* (Clarendon Press, 412 pp., 90 cents). Pollard's *English Miracle Plays, Moralities, and Interludes* (Clarendon Press, 250 pp., $1.90) is the best single volume of selections from this branch of the drama. *Everyman and Other Miracle Plays* (Everyman's Library, 35 cents) is a good inexpensive volume. Manly's *Specimens of the Pre-Shakespearean Drama* (three volumes, $1.25 each) covers this field more fully. Morley's *English Plays* (published as Vol. III. of Cassell's *Library of English Literature*, at eleven and one half shillings) contains good selections from nearly all the plays mentioned below, except those by Shakespeare and Jonson. Williams's *Specimens of the Elizabethan Drama, from Lyly to Shirley*, 1580–1642 (Clarendon Press, 576 pp., $1.90) is excellent for a comprehensive survey of the field covered. Lamb's *Specimens of English Poets Who Lived about the Time of Shakespeare* (Bohn's Library, 552 pp.) contains a large number of good selections.

Miracle Plays. — Read the Chester Play of *Noah's Flood*, Pollard,[1] 8-20, and the Towneley *Play of the Shepherds*, Pollard, 31-43; Manly's *Specimens*, I., 94-119; Morley's *English Plays*, 12-18. These two plays best show the germs of English comedy.

Moralities. — The best *Morality* is that known as *Everyman*, Pollard, 76-96; also in *Everyman's Library*. If *Everyman* is not accessible, *Hycke-Scorner* may be substituted, Morley, 12-18; Manly's *Specimens*, I., 386-420.

Court Plays, Early Comedies, and Gorboduc. — The best *Interlude* is *The Four P's*. Adequate selections are given in Morley, 18-20, and in Symonds's Shakespeare's *Predecessors in the English Drama*, 188-201. Pollard and Manly give several good selections from other *Interludes*.

Ralph Royster Doyster may be found in Arber's *Reprints*; in Morley's *English Plays*, pp. 22-46; in Manly's *Specimens*, II., 5-92; in *Oxford Treasury*, II., 161-174, and in *Temple Dramatists* (35 cents).

Gorboduc is given in *Oxford Treasury*, II. pp., 40-54 (selections); Morley's *English Plays*, pp. 51-64; and, under the title of *Ferrex and Porrex*, in Dodsley's *Old Plays*.

What were some of the purposes for which *Interludes* were written? How did they aid in the development of the drama?

In what different forms are *The Four P's*, *Ralph Royster Doyster*, and *Gorboduc* written? Why would Shakespeare's plays have been impossible if the evolution of the drama had stopped with *Gorboduc*?

Pre-Shakespearean Dramatists. — Selections from Lyly, Peele, Greene, Lodge, Nashe, and Kyd may be found in Williams's *Specimens*. Morley and *Oxford Treasury* also contain a number of selections. Peele's *The Arraignment of Paris* and Kyd's *The Spanish Tragedy* are in *Temple Dramatists*. Greene's best plays are in *Mermaid Series*.

What are the merits of Lyly's dialogue and comedy? What might Shakespeare have learned from Lyly, Peele, Greene, and Kyd? In what different form did these dramatists write? What progress do they show?

Marlowe. — Read *Dr. Faustus*, in *Masterpieces of the English Drama* (American Book Company) or in *Everyman's Library*. This play may also be found in Morley's *English Plays*, pp. 116-128, or in Morley's *Universal Library*. Selections from various plays of Marlowe may be found in *Oxford Treasury*, 61-85, 330-356; and in Williams's *Specimens*, 25-34.

---

[1] For full titles of books of dramatic selections, see the preceding paragraph.

Does *Dr. Faustus* observe the classical unities? In what way does it show the spirit of the Elizabethan age? Was the poetic form of the play the regular vehicle of dramatic expression? In what does the greatness of the play consist? What are its defects? Why do young people sometimes think Marlowe the greatest of *all* the Elizabethan dramatists?

Shakespeare. — The student should read in sequence one or more of the plays in each of Shakespeare's four periods of development (pp. 185, 188), such as *A Midsummer Night's Dream* and *Romeo and Juliet*, for the first period; *As You Like It* and *The Merchant of Venice*, for the second; *Hamlet* and *King Lear* or *Macbeth* or *Julius Cæsar*, for the third; and *The Winter's Tale* and *The Tempest*, for the fourth.

Among the many good annotated editions of separate plays are the Clark and Wright, Rolfe, Hudson, Arden, Temple, and Tudor editions. Furness's *Variorum Shakespeare* is the best for exhaustive study. The best portable single volume edition is Craig's *Oxford Shakespeare*, India paper, 1350 pages.

The student cannot do better than follow the advice of Dr. Johnson: "Let him who is unacquainted with the powers of Shakespeare, and who desires to feel the highest pleasure that the drama can give, read every play, from the first scene to the last, with utter negligence of all his commentators. ... Let him read on through brightness and obscurity, through integrity and corruption; let him preserve his comprehension of the dialogue and his interest in the fable. And when the pleasures of novelty have ceased, let him attempt exactness and read the commentators."

Shakespeare's three greatest tragedies, *Hamlet*, *King Lear*, and *Macbeth*, should be read several times. After becoming familiar with the story, the student should next determine the general aim of the play and analyze the personality and philosophy of each of the leading characters.

After reading some of all classes of Shakespeare's plays, point out his (*a*) breadth of sympathy, (*b*) humor, (*c*) moral ideals, (*d*) mastery of English and variety of style, and (*e*) universality. What idea of his personality can you form from his plays? If you have read them in sequence, point out some of the characteristics of each of his four periods. Why is Shakespeare often called a great dramatic artist? How did his audience and manner of presentation of his plays modify his treatment of a dramatic theme?

Ben Jonson and Minor Dramatists. — The best plays of Ben Jonson, Chapman, Beaumont and Fletcher, Middleton, Massinger, Webster, and Tourneur may be found in *Masterpieces of the English Drama* edited by Schelling (American Book Company). Selections from all the minor dramatists mentioned may be found in Williams's *Specimens*. The teacher will need to exercise care in assigning readings. Most of the minor dramatists are better suited to advanced students.

Read Jonson's *The Alchemist* or the selection in Williams's *Specimens*. A sufficient selection from *Philaster* may be found in Vol. II. of *The Oxford Treasury*, in Morley, and in Williams's *Specimens*.

What points of difference between Shakespeare and Jonson do you notice? What is his object in *The Alchemist*? Why is its plot called unusually fine? Wherein does Jonson show a decline in the drama?

Who were Beaumont and Fletcher? What movement in the drama do they illustrate? What are the characteristics of some other minor dramatists? What are the chief reasons why the minor dramatists fail to equal Shakespeare? When and why did this period of the drama close?

CHAPTER V

THE PURITAN AGE, 1603-1660

History of the Period. — James I. (1603-1625), son of Mary Stuart, Queen of Scots, and the first of the Stuart line to reign in England, succeeded Elizabeth. His stubbornness and folly not only ended the intense patriotic feeling of the previous reign, but laid the foundation for the deadly conflict that resulted. In fifty-four years after the defeat of the Armada, England was plunged into civil war.

The guiding belief of James I. was that kings governed by divine right, that they received from the Deity a title of which no one could lawfully deprive them, no matter how outrageously they ruled, and that they were not in any way responsible to Parliament or to the people. In acting on this belief, he first trampled on the religious liberty of his subjects. He drove from their churches hundreds of clergymen who would not take oath that they believed that the prayer book of the Church of England agreed in every way with the *Bible*. He boasted that he would " harry out of the kingdom " those who would not conform.

During the reign of James I. and that of his son, Charles I. (1625-1649), a worse ruler on the same lines, thousands of Englishmen came to New England to enjoy religious liberty. The Pilgrim Fathers landed at Plymouth in 1620. The exodus was very rapid during the next twenty years, since those who insisted on worshiping God as they chose were thrown into prison and sometimes had their ears cut off and their noses mutilated. In the sixteenth century, the religious struggle was between Catholics and Protestants, but in this age both of the contestants were Protestant. The Church of England (Episcopal church) was persecuting those who would not conform to its beliefs.

Side by side with the religious strife was a struggle for constitutional government, for legal taxes, for the right of freedom of speech in Parliament. James I. and Charles I. both collected illegal taxes. Finally, when Charles became involved in war with Spain, Parliament forced him in return for a grant of money to sign the *Petition of Right* (1628), which was in some respects a new *Magna Charta*.

Charles did not keep his promises. For eleven years he ruled in a despotic way without Parliament. In 1642 civil war broke out between the Puritans, on one side, and the king, nobles, landed gentry, and adherents of the Church of England, on the other. The Puritans under the great Oliver Cromwell were victorious, and in 1649 they beheaded Charles as a "tyrant, traitor and murderer." Cromwell finally became Protector of the Commonwealth of England. The greatest Puritan writer, John Milton, not only upheld the Commonwealth with powerful argumentative prose, but also became the government's most important secretary. Though his blindness would not allow him to write after 1652, he used to translate aloud, either into Latin or the language of the foreign country, what Cromwell dictated or suggested. Milton's undersecretary, Andrew Marvel, wrote down this translation.

The Puritans remained in the ascendancy until 1660,

From the painting by Ford Madox Brown.

CROMWELL DICTATING TO MILTON DISPATCHES TO THE KING OF FRANCE CONCERNING THE MASSACRE IN PIEDMONT[1]

when the Stuart line was restored in the person of Charles II.

The Puritan Ideals. — The Renaissance had at first seemed to promise everything, the power to reveal the secrets of Nature, to cause her to gratify man's every wish, and to furnish a perpetual fountain of happy youth. These expectations had not been fulfilled. There were still poverty, disease, and a longing for something that earth had not given. The English, naturally a religious race, reflected much on this. Those who concluded that life could never yield the pleasure which man anticipates, who determined by purity of living to win a perfect land be-

[1] See Milton's Sonnet: *On the Late Massacre in Piedmont.*

yond the shores of mortality, who made the New World of earlier dreams a term synonymous with the New Jerusalem, were called Puritans.

Their guide to this land was the *Bible*. Our *Authorized Version* (1611), the one which is in most common use to-day, was made in the reign of James I. From this time it became much easier to get a copy of the *Scriptures*, and their influence was now more potent than ever to shape the ideals of the Puritans. In fact, it is impossible to estimate the influence which this *Authorized Version* has had on the ideals and the literature of the English race. Had it not been for this *Version*, current English speech and literature would be vastly different. Such words and expressions as "scapegoat," "a labor of love," "the eleventh hour," "to cast pearls before swine," and "a howling wilderness" are in constant use because the language of this translation of the *Bible* has become incorporated in our daily speech, as well as in our best literature.

The Puritan was so called because he wished to purify the established church from what seemed to him great abuses. He accepted the faith of John Calvin, who died in 1564. Calvinism taught that no earthly power should intervene between a human soul and God, that life was an individual moral struggle, the outcome of which would land the soul in heaven or hell for all eternity, that beauty and art and all the pleasures of the flesh were dangerous because they tended to wean the soul from God.

The Puritan was an individualist. The saving of the soul was to him an individual, not a social, affair. Bunyan's Pilgrim flees alone from the wrath to come. The twentieth century, on the other hand, believes that the regeneration of a human being is both a social and an individual affair, — that the individual, surrounded by the forces of evil, often has little opportunity unless society comes to his aid. The individualism of the Puritan accomplished a great task in preparing the way for democracy, for fuller liberty in church and state, in both England and America.

Our study of the Puritan ideals embodied in literature takes us beyond 1660, the date of the Restoration, because after that time two great Puritan writers, John Milton and John Bunyan, did some of their most famous work, the one in retirement, the other in jail. Such work, uninfluenced by the change of ideal after the Restoration, is properly treated in this chapter. While a change may in a given year seem sufficiently pronounced to become the basis for a new classification, we should remember that literary influences never begin or end with complete abruptness.

THE PROSE OF THE PURITAN AGE

Variety of Subject. — Prose showed development in several directions during this Puritan age: —

I. The use of prose in argument and controversy was largely extended. Questions of government and of religion were the living issues of the time. Innumerable pamphlets and many larger books were written to present different views. We may instance as types of this class almost all the prose writings of **John Milton** (1608–1674).

II. English prose dealt with a greater variety of philosophical subjects. Shakespeare had voiced the deepest philosophy in poetry, but up to this time such subjects had found scant expression in prose.

Thomas Hobbes (1588–1679) is the great philosophical writer of the age. In his greatest work, *Leviathan; or, The Matter, Form, and Power of a Commonwealth*, he considers questions of metaphysical philosophy and of government in a way that places him on the roll of famous English philosophers.

III. History had an increasing fascination for prose writers. **Sir Walter Raleigh's** *History of the World* (1614) and Lord Clarendon's *History of the Great Rebellion*, begun in 1646, are specially worthy of mention.

IV. Prose was developing its capacity for expressing delicate shades of humor. In Chaucer and in Shakespeare, poetry had already excelled in this respect. **Thomas Fuller** (1608–1661), an Episcopal clergyman, displays an almost inexhaustible fund of humor in his *History of the Worthies of England*. We find scattered through his works passages like these: —

THOMAS FULLER

"A father that whipped his son for swearing, and swore at him while he whipped him, did more harm by his example than good by his correction."

Speaking of a pious short person, Fuller says: —

"His soul had but a short diocese to visit, and therefore might the better attend the effectual informing thereof."

Of the lark, he writes: —

"A harmless bird while living, not trespassing on grain, and wholesome when dead, then filling the stomach with meat, as formerly the ear with music."

Before Fuller, humor was rare in English prose writers, and it was not common until the first quarter of the next century.

V. Sir Thomas Browne (1605–1682), an Oxford graduate and physician, is best known as the author of three prose works: *Religio Medici* (*Religion of a Physician*, 1642), *Vulgar Errors* (1646), and *Hydriotaphia* or *Urn Burial* (1658). In imagination and poetic feeling, he has some kinship with the Elizabethans. He says in the *Religio Medici*: —

"Now for my life, it is a miracle of thirty years, which to relate were not a history but a piece of poetry, and would sound to common ears like a fable. . . . Men that look upon my outside, perusing only my condition and fortunes, do err in my altitude; for I am above Atlas's shoulders. . . . There is surely a piece of divinity in us — something that was before the elements and owes no homage unto the sun."

The *Religio Medici*, however, gives, not the Elizabethan, but the Puritan, definition of the world as "a place not to live in but to die in."

Urn Burial, which is Browne's masterpiece, shows his power as a prose poet of the "inevitable hour": —

"There is no antidote against the *opium* of time. . . . The greater part must be content to be as though they had not been, to be found in the register of God, not in the record of man. . . . But man is a Noble Animal, splendid in ashes, and pompous in the grave, solemnizing nativities and deaths with equal luster, not omitting ceremonies of bravery, in the infamy of his nature."

Browne's prose frequently suffers from the infusion of too many words derived from the Latin, but his style is rhythmical and stately and often conveys the same emotion as the notes of a great cathedral organ at the evening twilight hour.

VI. *The Complete Angler* of **Izaak Walton** (1593–1683) is so filled with sweetness and calm delight in nature and life, that one does not wonder that the book has passed through about two hundred editions. It manifests a genuine love of nature, of the brooks, meadows, flowers. In his pages we catch the odor from the hedges gay with wild flowers and hear the rain falling softly on the green leaves: —

"But turn out of the way a little, good scholar, towards yonder high honeysuckle hedge; there we'll sit and sing, whilst this shower falls so gently on the teeming earth, and gives yet a sweeter smell to the lovely flowers that adorn these verdant meadows."

IZAAK WALTON

VII. Of the many authors busily writing on theology, **Jeremy Taylor** (1613–1667), an Episcopal clergyman, holds the chief place. His imagination was so wide and his pen so facile that he has been called a seventeenth-century prose Shakespeare. Taylor's *Holy Living* and *Holy Dying* used to be read in almost every cottage. This passage shows his powers of imagery as well as the Teutonic inclination to consider the final goal of youth and beauty: —

JEREMY TAYLOR

"Reckon but from the sprightfulness of youth, and the fair cheeks and full eyes of childhood, from the vigorousness and strong texture of the joints of five-and-twenty, to the hollowness and dead paleness, to the loathsomeness and horror of a three days' burial, and we shall perceive the distance to be very great and very strange. But so have I seen a rose newly springing from the clefts of its hood, and at first it was fair as morning, and full with the dew of heaven as a lamb's fleece . . . and at night, having lost some of its leaves and all its beauty, it fell into the portion of weeds and outworn faces."

From the painting by Sadler, National Portrait Gallery.

JOHN BUNYAN, 1628-1688

Life. — The Bedfordshire village of Elstow saw in 1628 the birth of John Bunyan who, in his own peculiar field of literature, was to lead the world. His father, Thomas Bunyan, was a brazier, a mender of pots and pans, and he reared his son John to the same trade. In his autobiography, John Bunyan says that his father's house was of "that rank that is meanest and most despised of all the families in the land."

JOHN BUNYAN

The boy went to school for only a short time and learned but little from any books except the *Bible*. The father, by marrying a second time within a year after his wife's death, wounded the feelings of his sixteen-year-old son sufficiently to cause the latter to enlist as a soldier in the Civil War. At about the age of twenty, Bunyan married, though neither he nor his wife had at the time so much as a dish or a spoon.

Bunyan tells us that in his youth he was very wicked. Probably he would have been so regarded from the point of view of a strict Puritan. His worst offenses, however, seem to have been dancing on the village green, playing hockey on Sundays, ringing bells to rouse the neighborhood, and swearing. When he repented, his vivid imagination made him think that he had committed the unpardonable sin. In the terror that he felt at the prospect of the loss of his soul, he passed through much of the experience that enabled him to write the *Pilgrim's Progress*.

Bunyan became a preacher of God's word. Under trees, in barns, on the village green, wherever people resorted, he told them the story of salvation. Within six months after the Restoration, he was arrested for preaching without Episcopal sanction. The officers took him away from his little blind daughter. The roisterers of the Restoration thought a brazier was too coarse to have feelings; yet Bunyan dropped tears on the paper when he wrote of "the many hardships, miseries, and wants that my poor family were like to meet with, should I be taken from them, especially my poor blind child, who lay nearer to my heart than all besides. Oh, the thoughts of the hardship my poor blind one might undergo, would break my heart to pieces." In spite of his dependent family and the natural right of the freedom of speech, Bunyan was thrust into Bedford jail and kept a prisoner for nearly twelve years. Had it not been for his imprisonment in this "squalid den," of which he speaks in the *Pilgrim's Progress*, we should probably be without that famous work, a part of which, at least, was written in the jail.

In 1672, as a step toward restoring the Catholic religion, Charles II. suspended all penal statutes against the dissenting clergy; Bunyan was thereupon released from jail.

From an old print.

BEDFORD BRIDGE, SHOWING GATES AND JAIL

After his release, he settled down to his life's work of spreading the Gospel by both pen and tongue. When he visited London to preach, it was not uncommon for twelve hundred persons to come to hear him at seven o'clock in the morning of a week day in winter.

The immediate cause of his death was a cold caught by riding in the rain, on his way to try to reconcile a father and son. In 1688 Bunyan died as he uttered these words, "Take me, for I come to Thee."

His Work. — Bunyan achieved the distinction of writing the greatest of all allegories, the *Pilgrim's Progress*. This is the story of Christian's journey through this life, the story of meeting Mr. Worldly Wiseman, of the straight gate and the narrow path, of the Delectable Mountains of Youth, of the valley of Humiliation, of the encounter with Apollyon, of the wares of Vanity Fair, "kept all the year long," of my lord Time-server, of Mr. Anything, of imprisonment in Doubting Castle by Giant Despair, of the flowery land of Beulah, lying beyond the valley of the Shadow of Death, through which a deep, cold river runs, and of the city of All Delight on the other side. This story still has absorbing interest for human beings, for the child and the old man, the learned and the ignorant.

Bunyan wrote many other works, but none of them equals the *Pilgrim's Progress*. His *Holy War* is a powerful allegory, which has been called a prose *Paradise Lost*. Bunyan also produced a strong piece of realistic fiction, the *Life and Death of Mr. Badman*. This shows the descent of a soul along the broad road. The story is the counterpart of his great masterpiece, and ranks second to it in point of merit.

From Fourth Edition Pilgrim's Progress, 1680.

BUNYAN'S DREAM

General Characteristics. — Since the *Pilgrim's Progress* has been more widely read in England than any other book except the *Bible*, it is well to investigate the secret of Bunyan's power.

In the first place, his style is simple. In the second place, rare earnestness is coupled with this simplicity. He had something to say, which in his inmost soul he felt to be of supreme importance for all time. Only a great man can tell such truths without a flourish of language, or without straining after effect. At the most critical part of the journey of the Pilgrims, when they approach the river of death, note that Bunyan avoids the tendency to indulge in fine writing, that he is content to rely on the power of the subject matter, simply presented, to make us feel the terrible ordeal:—

"Now I further saw that betwixt them and the gate was a river; but there was no bridge to go over, and the river was very deep. . . . The Pilgrims then, especially Christian, began to despond in their minds, and looked this way and that, but no way could be found by them by which they might escape the river. . . . They then addressed themselves to the water, and entering, Christian began to sink. . . . And with that, a great darkness and horror fell upon Christian, so that he could not see before him. . . .

Let Badman's broken leg put check
To Badman's course of evil,
Lest, next time, Badman breaks his neck,
And so goes to the devil.

WOODCUT FROM THE FIRST EDITION OF MR. BADMAN

"Now, upon the bank of the river, on the other side, they saw the two shining men again, who there waited for them. . . . Now you must note that the city stood upon a mighty hill; but the Pilgrims went up that hill with ease, because they had these two men to lead them up by the arms; they had likewise left their mortal garments behind them in the river; for though they went in with them, they came out without them."

Of all the words in the above selection, eighty per cent are monosyllables. Few authors could have resisted the tendency to try to be impressive at such a climax. One has more respect for this world, on learning that it has set the seal of its approval on such earnest simplicity and has neglected works that strive with every art to attract attention.

Bunyan furthermore has a rare combination of imagination and dramatic power. His abstractions become living persons. They have warmer blood coursing in their veins than many of the men and women in modern fiction. Giant Despair is a living giant. We can hear the clanking of the chains and the groans of the captives in his dungeon. We are not surprised to learn that Bunyan imagined that he saw and conversed with these characters. The *Pilgrim's Progress* is a prose drama. Note the vivid dramatic presentation of the tendency to evil, which we all have at some time felt threatening to wreck our nobler selves: —

"Then Apollyon straddled quite over the whole breadth of the way, and said, 'I am void of fear in this matter; prepare thyself to die; for I swear by my infernal den that thou shalt go no further; here will I spill thy soul.'"

It would be difficult to find English prose more simple, earnest, strong, imaginative, and dramatic than this. Bunyan's style felt the shaping influence of the *Bible* more than of all other works combined. He knew the *Scriptures* almost by heart.

THE POETRY OF THE PURITAN AGE

Lyrical Verse. — The second quarter of the seventeenth century witnessed an outburst of song that owed its inspiration to Elizabethan lyrical verse.

Soon after 1600 a change in lyric poetry is noticeable. The sonnet fell into disfavor with the majority of lyrists. The two poets of greatest influence over this period, Ben Jonson and John Donne (p. 137), opposed the sonnet. Ben Jonson complained that it compels all ideas, irrespective of their worth, to fill a space of exactly fourteen lines, and that it therefore operates on the same principle as the bed of Procrustes. The lyrics of this period, with the exception of those by Milton, were usually less idealistic, ethereal, and inspired than the corresponding work of the Elizabethans. This age was far more imitative, but it chose to imitate Jonson and Donne in preference to Shakespeare. The greatest lyrical poet of this time thus addresses Jonson as a patron saint: —

> "Candles I'll give to thee,
> And a new altar;
> And thou, Saint Ben, shall be
> Writ in my psalter."[1]

Cavalier Poets. — Robert Herrick (1591–1674), Thomas Carew (1598?–1639?), Sir John Suckling (1609–1642), and Richard Lovelace (1618–1658) were a contemporary group of lyrists who are often called Cavalier poets, because they sympathized with the Cavaliers or adherents of Charles I.

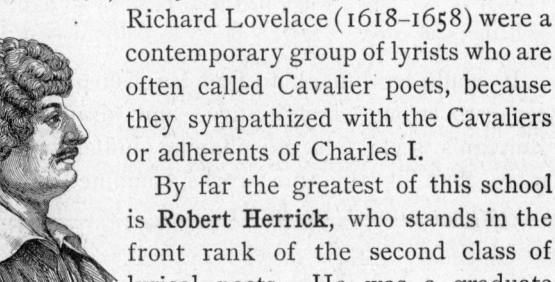

By far the greatest of this school is **Robert Herrick**, who stands in the front rank of the second class of lyrical poets. He was a graduate of Cambridge University, who by an accident of the time became a clergyman. The parish, or "living," given him by the king, was in the southwestern part of Devonshire. By affixing the title *Hesperides* to his volume of nearly thirteen hundred poems, Herrick doubtless meant to imply that they were chiefly composed in the western part

ROBERT HERRICK

---

[1] Robert Herrick's *Prayer to Ben Jonson*.

of England. In the very first poem of this collection, he announces the subject of his songs: —

> "I sing of brooks, of blossoms, birds, and bowers;
>   Of April, May, of June, and July flowers.
> I sing of May-poles, hock-carts, wassails, wakes;
>   Of bridegrooms, brides, and of their bridal cakes
> . . . .
> I write of groves, of twilights, and I sing
>   The court of Mab, and of the Fairie-king.
> I write of hell; I sing and ever shall,
>   Of heaven, and hope to have it after all."

His lyric range was as broad as these lines indicate. The most of his poems show the lightness of touch and artistic form revealed in the following lines from *To the Virgins*: —

> "Gather ye rose-buds while ye may:
>   Old Time is still a-flying;
> And this same flower that smiles to-day,
>   To-morrow will be dying."

His facility in melodious poetic expression is evident in this stanza from *The Litany*, one of the poems in *Noble Numbers*, as the collection of his religious verse is called: —

> "When the passing-bell doth toll
>   And the furies in a shoal
> Come to fright a parting soul,
>   Sweet Spirit, comfort me."

The lyric, *Disdain Returned*, of the courtier, **Thomas Carew**, shows both a customary type of subject and the serious application often given: —

> "He that loves a rosy cheek,
>   Or a coral lip admires,
> Or from starlike eyes doth seek
>   Fuel to maintain his fires,
> As old time makes these decay,
> So his flames must waste away."

Carew could write with facility on the subjects in vogue at court, but when he ventures afield in nature poetry, he makes the cuckoo hibernate! In his poem *The Spring*, he says:—

> ". . . wakes in hollow tree
> The drowsy Cuckoo and the Humble-bee."

In these lines from his poem *Constancy*, **Sir John Suckling** shows that he is a typical Cavalier love poet:—

> "Out upon it, I have loved
> Three whole days together;
> And am like to love three more,
> If it prove fair weather."

From **Richard Lovelace** we have these exquisite lines written in prison:—

> "Stone walls do not a prison make
> Nor iron bars a cage;
> Minds innocent and quiet take
> That for an hermitage."

To characterize the Cavalier school by one phrase, we might call them lyrical poets in lighter vein. They usually wrote on such subjects as the color in a maiden's cheek and lips, blossoms, meadows, May days, bridal cakes, the paleness of a lover, and —

> ". . . wassail bowls to drink,
> Spiced to the brink,"

but sometimes weightier subjects were chosen, when these lighter things failed to satisfy.

Religious Verse. — Three lyrical poets, George Herbert (1593–1633), Henry Vaughan (1622–1695), and Richard Crashaw (1612?–1650?), usually chose religious subjects. **George Herbert**, a Cambridge graduate and rector of

Bemerton, near Salisbury, wrote *The Temple*, a book of religious verse. His best known poem is *Virtue*: —

> "Sweet day, so cool, so calm, so bright,
> The bridal of the earth and sky:
> The dew shall weep thy fall to night;
> For thou must die."

The sentiment in these lines from his lyric *Providence* has the genuine Anglo-Saxon ring: —

> "Hard things are glorious; easy things good cheap.
> The common all men have; that which is rare,
> Men therefore seek to have, and care to keep."

Henry Vaughan, an Oxford graduate and Welsh physician, shows the influence of George Herbert. Vaughan would have been a great poet if he could have maintained the elevation of these opening lines from *The World*: —

> "I saw Eternity the other night,
> Like a great ring of pure and endless light,
> All calm, as it was bright."

Richard Crashaw, a Cambridge graduate and Catholic mystic, concludes his poem, *The Flaming Heart*, with this touching prayer to Saint Teresa: —

> "By all of Him we have in thee
> Leave nothing of myself in me.
> Let me so read my life that I
> Unto all life of mine may die."

His verse, like that of his contemporaries, is often marred by fantastic conceits which show the influence of Donne. Although much of Crashaw's poem, *The Weeper*, is beautiful, he calls the eyes of Mary Magdalene: —

> "Two walking baths, two weeping motions,
> Portable and compendious oceans."

After a drawing by W. Faithorne, at Bayfordbury.

JOHN MILTON, 1608-1674

His Youth. — The second greatest English poet was born in London, eight years before the death of Shakespeare. John Milton's father followed the business of a scrivener and drew wills and deeds and invested money for clients. As he prospered at this calling, his family did not suffer for want of money. He was a man of much culture and a musical composer of considerable note.

· A portrait of the child at the age of ten, the work of the painter to the court, still exists and shows him to have been "a sweet, serious, round-headed boy," who gave early promise of future greatness. His parents, seeing that he acted as if he was guided by high ideals, had the rare judgment to allow him to follow his own bent. They employed the best teachers to instruct him at home. At the age of sixteen he was fully prepared to enter Christ's College, Cambridge, where he took both the B.A. and M.A. degrees.

JOHN MILTON, ÆT. 10

His Early Manhood and Life at Horton. — In 1632 Milton left Cambridge and went to live with his father in a country home at Horton, about twenty miles west of London. Milton had been intended for the church; but he felt that he could not subscribe to its intolerance, and that he had another mission to perform. His father accordingly provided sufficient funds for maintaining him for over five years at Horton in a life of studious leisure. The poet's greatest biographer, David Masson, says: "Until Milton was thirty-two years of age, if even then, he did not earn a penny for himself." Such a course would ruin ninety-nine out of every hundred talented young men; but it was the making of Milton. He spent those years in careful study and in writing his immortal early poems.

In 1638, when he was in his thirtieth year, he determined to broaden his views by travel. He went to Italy, which the Englishmen of his day still regarded as the home of art, culture, and song. After about fifteen months abroad, hearing that his countrymen were on the

From the painting by T. Lessi.
VISIT OF MILTON TO THE BLIND GALILEO AT THE VILLA D'ARCETRI NEAR FLORENCE IN 1638

verge of civil war, he returned home to play his part in the mighty tragedy of the times.

Milton's "Left Hand." — In 1642 the Civil War broke out between the Royalists and the Puritans. He took sides in the struggle for liberty, not with his sword, but with his pen. During this time he wrote little but prose. He regretted that the necessity of the time demanded prose, in the writing of which, he says, "I have the use, as I may account it, but of my left hand."

With that "left hand" he wrote much prose. There is one common quality running through all his prose works, although they treat of the most varied subjects. Every one of these works strikes a blow for fuller liberty in some direction, — for more liberty in church, in state, and in home relations, for the freedom of expressing opinions, and for a system of education which should break away from the leading strings of the inferior methods of the past. His greatest prose work is the *Areopagitica: A Speech for the Liberty of Unlicensed Printing*.

Much of his prose is poetic and adorned with figures of rhetoric. He frequently follows the Latin order, and inverts his sentences, which are often unreasonably long. Sometimes his "left hand" astonishes us by slinging mud at his opponents, and we eagerly await the loosing of the right hand which was to give us *Paradise Lost*.

His Blindness. — The English government from 1649 to 1660 is known as the Commonwealth. The two most striking figures of the time were Oliver Cromwell, who in 1653 was styled the Lord Protector, and John Milton, who was the Secretary for Foreign Tongues.

One of the greatest of European scholars, a professor at Leyden, named Salmasius, had written a book attacking the Commonwealth and upholding the late king. The Council requested Milton to write a fitting answer. As his eyes were already failing him, he was warned to rest them; but he said that he would willingly sacrifice his eyesight on the altar of liberty. He accordingly wrote in reply his *Pro Populo Anglicano Defensio*, a Latin work,

From his application to wed Elizabeth Minshull, Feb. 11, 1663.

FACSIMILE OF MILTON'S SIGNATURE IN THE ELEVENTH YEAR OF HIS BLINDNESS which was published in 1651. This effort cost him his eyesight. In 1652, at the age of forty-three, he was totally blind. In his *Paradise Lost*, he thus alludes to his affliction: —

> "Thus with the year
> Seasons return; but not to me returns
> Day, or the sweet approach of even or morn,
> Or sight of vernal bloom or summer's rose,
> Or flocks, or herds, or human face divine;
> But clouds instead and ever-during dark
> Surrounds me, from the cheerful ways of men
> Cut off."

Life after the Restoration. — In 1660, when Charles II. was made king, the leaders of the Commonwealth had to flee for their lives. Some went to America for safety, while others were caught and executed. The body of Cromwell was taken from its grave in Westminster Abbey, suspended from the gallows, and left to dangle there. Milton was concealed by a friend until the worst of the storm had blown over. Then some influential friends interceded for him, and his blindness probably won him sympathy.

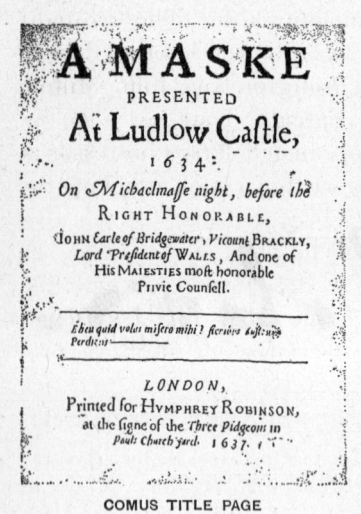

During his old age his literary work was largely dependent on the kindness of friends, who read to him, and acted as his amanuenses. His ideas of woman having been formed in the light of

COMUS TITLE PAGE

JOHN MILTON

the old dispensation, he had not given his three daughters such an education as might have led them to take a sympathetic interest in his work. They accordingly resented his calling on them for help.

During this period of his life, when he was totally blind, he wrote *Paradise Lost*, *Paradise Regained*, and *Samson Agonistes*. He died in 1674, and was buried beside his father in the chancel of St. Giles, Cripplegate, London.

Minor Poems. — In 1629, while Milton was a student at Cambridge, and only twenty-one years old, he wrote a fine lyrical poem, entitled *On the Morning of Christ's Nativity*. These 244 lines of verse show that he did not need to be taught the melody of song any more than a young nightingale.

Four remarkable poems were written during his years of studious leisure at Horton, — *L'Allegro*, *Il Penseroso*, *Comus*, and *Lycidas*. *L'Allegro* describes the charms of a merry social life, and *Il Penseroso* voices the quiet but deep enjoyment of the scholar in retirement. These two poems have been universal favorites.

Comus is a species of dramatic composition known as a Masque, and it is the greatest of its class. It far surpasses any work of a similar kind by Ben Jonson, that prolific writer of Masques (p. 201). Some critics, like Taine and Saintsbury, consider *Comus* the finest of Milton's productions. Its 1023 lines can soon be read; and there are few poems of equal length that will better repay careful reading.

Comus is an immortal apotheosis of virtue. While in Geneva in 1639, Milton was asked for his autograph and an expression of sentiment. He chose the closing lines of *Comus:* —

Written in an album at Geneva.
MILTON'S MOTTO FROM COMUS, WITH AUTOGRAPH

Lycidas, one of the world's great elegies, was written on the death of Milton's classmate, Edward King. Mark Pattison, one of Milton's biographers, says: "In *Lycidas* we have reached the high-water mark of English poesy and of Milton's own production."

He is one of the four greatest English sonnet writers. Shakespeare alone surpasses him in this field. Milton numbers among his pupils Wordsworth and Keats, whose sonnets rank next in merit.

Paradise Lost; Its Inception and Dramatic Plan. — Cambridge University has a list, written by Milton before he was thirty-five, of about one hundred possible subjects for the great poem which he felt it was his life's mission to give to the world. He once thought of selecting Arthur and his Knights of the Round Table; but his final choice was *Paradise Lost*, which stands first on this special list. There are in addition four separate drafts of the way in which he thought this subject should be treated. This proves that the great work of a man like Milton was planned while he was young. It is possible that he may even have written a very small part of the poem earlier than the time commonly assigned.

All four drafts show that his early intention was to make the poem a drama, a gigantic Miracle play. The closing of the theaters and the prejudice felt against them during the days of Puritan ascendancy may have influenced Milton to forsake the dramatic for the epic form, but he seems never to have shared the common prejudice against the drama and the stage. His sonnet on Shakespeare shows in what estimation he held that dramatist.

Subject Matter and Form. — About 1658, when Milton was a widower, living alone with his three daughters, he began, in total blindness, to dictate his *Paradise Lost*, sometimes relying on them but more often on any kind friend who might assist him. The manuscript accordingly shows a variety of handwriting. The work was published in 1667, after some trouble with a narrow-minded censor who had doubts about granting a license.

The subject matter can be best given in Milton's own lines at the beginning of the poem: —

> "Of man's first disobedience, and the fruit
> Of that forbidden tree, whose mortal taste
> Brought death into the World, and all our woe,
> With loss of Eden, till one greater Man
> Restore us, and regain the blissful seat,
> Sing, Heavenly Muse . . ."

The poem treats of Satan's revolt in heaven, of his conflict with the Almighty, and banishment with all the rebellious angels. Their new home in the land of fire and endless pain is described with such a gigantic grasp of the imagination, that the conception has colored all succeeding theology.

The action proceeds with a council of the fallen angels to devise means for alleviating their condition and annoying the Almighty. They decide to strike him through his child, and they plot the fall of man. In short, *Paradise Lost* is an intensely dramatic story of the loss of Eden. The greatest actors that ever sprang from a poet's brain appear before us on the stage, which is at one time the sulphurous pit of hell, at another the bright plains of heaven, and at another the Elysium of our first parents.

In form the poem is an epic in twelve books, containing a total of 10,565 lines. It is written in blank verse of wonderful melody and variety.

Paradise Regained and Samson Agonistes. — After finishing *Paradise Lost*, Milton wrote two more poems, which he published in 1671. *Paradise Regained* is in great part a paraphrase of the first eleven verses of the fourth chapters of *St. Matthew*. The poem is in four books of blank verse and contains 2070 lines. Although it is written with great art and finish, *Paradise Regained* shows a falling off in Milton's genius. There is less ornament and less to arouse human interest.

Samson Agonistes (Samson the Struggler) is a tragedy containing 1758 lines, based on the sixteenth chapter of *Judges*. This poem, modeled after the Greek drama, is hampered by a strict observance of the dramatic unities. It is vastly inferior to the *Paradise Lost*. *Samson Agonistes* contains scarcely any of the glorious imagery of Milton's earlier poems. It has been called "the most unadorned poem that can be found."

CHARACTERISTICS OF MILTON'S POETRY

Variety in his Early Work. — A line in *Lycidas* says: —

"He touched the tender stops of various quills,"

and this may be said of Milton. His early poems show great variety. There are the dirge notes in *Lycidas;* the sights, sounds, and odors of the country, in *L'Allegro;* the delights of "the studious cloister's pale," in *Il Penseroso;* the impelling presence of his "great Task-Master," in the sonnets.

Although Milton is noted for his seriousness and sublimity, we must not be blind to the fact that his minor poems show great delicacy of touch. The epilogue of the Spirit at the end of *Comus* is an instance of exquisite airy fancy passing into noble imagination at the close. In 1638 Sir Henry Wotton wrote to Milton this intelligent criticism of *Comus:* "I should much commend the tragical part, if the lyrical did not ravish me with a certain Doric delicacy in your Songs and Odes, whereunto I must plainly confess to have seen yet nothing parallel in our language: *Ipsa mollities.*"

Limitations. — In giving attention to Milton's variety, we should not forget that when we judge him by Elizabethan standards his limitations are apparent. As varied as are his excellences, his range is far narrower than Shakespeare's. He has little sense of humor and less sympathy with human life than either Shakespeare or Burns. Milton became acquainted with flowers through the medium of a book before he noticed them in the fields. Consequently, in speaking of flowers and birds, he sometimes makes those mistakes to which the bookish man is more prone than the child who first hears the story of Nature from her own lips. Unlike Shakespeare and Burns, Milton had the misfortune to spend his childhood in a large city. Again, while increasing age seemed to impose no limitations on Shakespeare's genius, his touch being as delicate in *The Tempest* as in his first plays, Milton's style, on the other hand, grew frigid and devoid of imagery toward the end of his life.

Sublimity. — The most striking characteristic of Milton's poetry is sublimity, which consists, first, in the subject matter. In the opening lines of *Paradise Lost* he speaks of his "adventurous song" —

> "That with no middle flight intends to soar
> Above the Aonian mount, while it pursues
> Things unattempted yet in prose or rhyme."

Milton succeeded in his intention. The English language has not another poem that approaches *Paradise Lost* in sustained sublimity.

In the second place, we must note the sublimity of treatment. Milton's own mind was cast in a sublime mold. This quality of mind is evident even in his figures of rhetoric. The Milky Way appears to him as the royal highway to heaven: —

> "A broad and ample road, whose dust is gold,
> And pavement stars."[1]

When Death and Satan meet, Milton wishes the horror of the scene to manifest something of the sublime. What other poet could, in fewer words, have conveyed a stronger impression of the effect of the frown of those powers?

> "So frowned the mighty combatants, that Hell
> Grew darker at their frown."[2]

George Saintsbury's verdict is approved by the majority of the greatest modern critics of Milton: "In loftiness —

[1] *Paradise Lost*, Book VII., lines 577–578. [2] *Ibid.*, Book II., lines 719–720.

sublimity of thought, and majesty of expression, both sustained at almost superhuman pitch, he has no superior, and no rival except Dante."

Mastery of Verse. — Milton's verse, especially in *Paradise Lost*, is such a symphony of combined rhythm, poetic expression, and thought; it is so harmonious, so varied, and yet so apparently simple in its complexity, that it has never been surpassed in kind.

His mastery of rhythm is not so evident in a single line as in a group of lines. The first sentence in *Paradise Lost* contains sixteen lines, and yet the rhythm, the pauses, and the thought are so combined as to make oral reading easy and the meaning apparent. The conception of the music of the spheres in their complex orbits finds some analogy in the harmony of the combined rhythmical units of his verse.

Denied the use of his eyes as a guide to the form of his later verse, he must have repeated aloud these groups of lines and changed them until their cadence satisfied his remarkably musical ear. Lines like these show the melody of which this verse is capable : —

> "Heaven opened wide
> Her ever-during gates, harmonious sound
> On golden hinges moving."[1]

To begin with, he had, like Shakespeare and Keats (p. 433), an instinctive feeling for the poetic value of words and phrases. Milton's early poems abound in such poetic expressions as "the frolic wind," "the slumbring morn," "linkèd sweetness," "looks commercing with the skies," "dewy-feathered sleep," "the studious cloister's pale," "a dim religious light," the "silver lining" of the cloud,

---

[1] *Paradise Lost*, Book VII., lines 207–209.

"west winds with musky wing," "the laureate hearse where Lycid lies." His poetic instinct enabled him to take common prosaic words and, by merely changing the position

From the painting by Munkacsy.
MILTON DICTATING PARADISE LOST TO HIS DAUGHTERS

of the adjective, transmute them into imperishable verse. His "darkness visible" and "human face divine" are instances of this power.

Twentieth century criticism is more fully recognizing the debt of subsequent poetic literature to Milton. Saintsbury writes: —

"Milton's influence is omnipresent in almost all later English poetry, and in not a little of later prose English literature. At first, at second, at third, hand, he has permeated almost all his successors." [1]

How the Paradise Lost has affected Thought. — Few people realize how profoundly this poem has influenced

---

[1] *The Cambridge History of English Literature*, Vol. VII., p. 156.

men's ideas of the hereafter. The conception of hell for a long time current was influenced by those pictures which Milton painted with darkness for his canvas and the lightning for his brush. Our pictures of Eden and of heaven have also felt his touch. Theology has often looked through Milton's imagination at the fall of the rebel angels and of man. Huxley says that the cosmogony which stubbornly resists the conclusions of science, is due rather to the account in *Paradise Lost* than to *Genesis*.

Many of Milton's expressions have become crystallized in modern thought. Among such we may mention: —

> "The mind is its own place, and in itself
> Can make a Heaven of Hell, a Hell of Heaven,
> What matter where, if I be still the same?"[1]

> "To reign is worth ambition, though in Hell:
> Better to reign in Hell, than serve in Heaven."[2]

> ". . . Who overcomes
> By force hath overcome but half his foe."[3]

The effect of *Paradise Lost* on English thought is more a resultant of the entire poem than of detached quotations. *L'Allegro* and *Il Penseroso* have furnished as many current quotations as the whole of *Paradise Lost*.

The Embodiment of High Ideals. — No poet has embodied in his verse higher ideals than Milton. When twenty-three, he wrote that he intended to use his talents —

> "As ever in my great Taskmaster's eye."[4]

Milton's poetry is not universally popular. He deliberately selected his audience. These lines from *Comus* show to whom he wished to speak:—

[1] *Paradise Lost*, Book I., line 254. [2] *Ibid.*, line 262. [3] *Ibid.*, line 649.
[4] Sonnet: *On His Having Arrived at the Age of Twenty-three*.

"Yet some there be that by due steps aspire
To lay their just hands on that golden key
That opes the palace of eternity.
To such my errand is."

He kept his promise of writing something which speaks for liberty and for nobility of soul and which the world would not willingly let die. His ideals react on us and raise us higher than we were. To him we may say with Wordsworth: —

"Thy soul was like a star and dwelt apart;
Thou hadst a voice whose sound was like the sea,
Pure as the naked heavens, majestic, free."[1]

SUMMARY

The Puritan age was one of conflict in religious and political ideals. James I. and Charles I. trampled on the laws and persecuted the Puritans so rigorously that many of them fled to New England. Civil war, in which the Puritans triumphed, was the result.

The Puritans, realizing that neither lands beyond the sea nor the New Learning could satisfy the aspirations of the soul, turned their attention to the life beyond. Bunyan's Pilgrim felt that the sole duty of life was to fight the forces of evil that would hold him captive in the City of Destruction and to travel in the straight and narrow path to the New Jerusalem. Life became a ceaseless battle of the right against the wrong. Hence, much of the literature in both poetry and prose is polemical. Milton's *Paradise Lost* is an epic of war between good and evil. The book that had the most influence in molding the thought of the time was the King James (1611) version of the *Bible*.

[1] *Milton: A Sonnet.*

The minor prose deals with a variety of subjects. There are argumentative, philosophical, historical, biographical, and theological prose works; but only the fine presentation of nature and life in *The Complete Angler* interests the general reader of to-day, although the grandeur of Milton's *Areopagitica*, the humor of Thomas Fuller, the stately rhythmical prose of Sir Thomas Browne, and the imagery and variety of Jeremy Taylor deserve more readers.

Bunyan's *Pilgrim's Progress* is the masterpiece of Puritan prose, written in the simple, direct language of the 1611 version of the *Bible*. The book is a prose epic of the journey of the Puritan Christian from the City of Destruction to the New Jerusalem.

The Cavalier poets wrote much lyrical verse, mostly in lighter vein, but the religious poets strike a deeper note. The work of these minor poets is often a reflection of the Elizabethan lyrics of Donne and Jonson.

John Milton, who has the creative power of the Elizabethans, is the only great poet of the period. His greatest poems are *L'Allegro, Il Penseroso, Lycidas, Comus*, and *Paradise Lost*. In sublimity of subject matter and cast of mind, in nobility of ideals, in expression of the conflict between good and evil, he is the fittest representative of the Puritan spirit in literature.

REFERENCES FOR FUTURE STUDY

HISTORICAL

Read the chapters on this period in Gardiner,[1] Walker, Cheney, Lingard, or Green. For the social life, see Traill, IV. The monumental history of this time has been written in eighteen volumes by Samuel Rawson Gardiner. His *Oliver Cromwell*, 1 vol., is excellent, as is also Frederick Harrison's *Oliver Cromwell*.

[1] For full titles, see list on p. 50.

LITERARY

The *Cambridge History of English Literature*, Vol. **VII.**
Courthope's *History of English Poetry*, Vol. III.
Masterman's *The Age of Milton*.
Saintsbury's *A History of Elizabethan Literature* (comes down to 1660).
Dowden's *Puritan and Anglican Studies in Literature*.
Dictionary of National Biography (for lives of minor writers).
Froude's *John Bunyan*.
Brown's *John Bunyan, his Life, Times, and Works*.
Macaulay's Life of Bunyan in *Encyclopedia Britannica* or in his *Essays*.
Macaulay's *Essay on Southey's Edition of the Pilgrim's Progress*.
Masson's *The Life of John Milton, Narrated in Connection with the Political, Ecclesiastical, and Literary History of his Time* (6 vols.).
Masson's *Poetical Works of John Milton*, 3 vols., contains excellent introductions and notes, and is the standard edition.
Raleigh's *Milton*.
Pattison's *Milton*. (E. M. L.)
Woodhull's *The Epic of Paradise Lost*.
Macaulay's *Essay on Milton*.
Lowell's *Milton* (in *Among My Books*).
Addison's criticisms on Milton, beginning in number 267 of *The Spectator*, are suggestive.

SUGGESTED READINGS
WITH QUESTIONS AND SUGGESTIONS

Prose. — The student will obtain a fair idea of the prose of this age by reading Milton's *Areopagitica*, Cassell's *National Library* (15 cents), or *Temple Classics* (45 cents); Craik,[1] II., 471–475; the selections from Thomas Hobbes, Craik, II., 214–221; from Thomas Fuller, Craik, II., 377–387; from Sir Thomas Browne, Craik, II., 318–335; from Jeremy Taylor, Craik, II., 529–542; and from Izaak Walton, Craik, II., 343–349. Manly, II., has selections from all these writers; the *Oxford Treasury* and *Century*, from all but Hobbes. The student who has the time will wish to read *The Complete Angler* entire (Cassell's *National Library*, 15 cents; or *Temple Classics*, 45 cents).

Compare (*a*) the sentences, (*b*) general style, and (*c*) worth of the

---
[1] For full titles, see p. 6.

subject matter of these authors; then, to note the development of English prose, in treatment of subject as well as in form, compare these works with those of (1) Wycliffe and Mandeville in the fourteenth century, (2) Malory in the fifteenth, and (3) Tyndale, Lyly, Sidney, Hooker, and Bacon (*e.g.* essay *Of Study*, 1597), in the sixteenth.

Bunyan's *Pilgrim's Progress* should be read entire (*Everyman's Library*, 35 cents; Cassell's *National Library*, 15 cents; *Temple Classics*, 45 cents). Selections may be found in Craik, III., 148–166; Manly, II., 139–143; *Oxford Treasury*, 83–85; *Century*, 225–235.

In what does the secret of Bunyan's popularity consist — in his style, or in his subject matter, or in both? What is specially noteworthy about his style? Point out some definite ways in which his style was affected by another great work. Suppose that Bunyan had held the social service ideals of the twentieth century, how might his idea of saving souls have been modified?

Lyrical Poetry. — Specimens of the best work of Herrick, Carew, Suckling, Lovelace, Herbert, Vaughan, and Crashaw may be found in Ward, II.; Bronson, II.; *Oxford Treasury*, III.; Manly, I.; and *Century*.

What is the typical subject matter of the Cavalier poets? What subject do Herbert, Vaughan, and Crashaw choose? Which lyric of each of these poets pleases you most? What difference do you note between these lyrics and those of the Elizabethan age? What Elizabethan lyrists had most influence on these poets? What are some of the special defects of the lyrists of this age?

John Milton. — *L'Allegro, Il Penseroso, Comus, Lycidas* (American Book Company's *Eclectic English Classics*, 20 cents), and *Paradise Lost*, Books I. and II. (same series), should be read. These poems, including his excellent *Sonnets*, may also be found in Cassell's *National Library*, *Everyman's Library*, and the *Temple Classics*. Selections are given in Ward, II., 306–379; Bronson, II., 334–423; *Oxford Treasury*, III., 34–70; Manly, I., and *Century, passim*.

Which is the greatest of his minor poems? Why? Is the keynote of *Comus* in accord with Puritan ideals? Are there qualities in *Lycidas* that justify calling it "the high-water mark" of English lyrical poetry? Which poem has most powerfully affected theological thought? Which do you think is oftenest read to-day? Why? What are the most striking characteristics of Milton's poetry? Contrast Milton's greatness, limitations, and ideals of life, with Shakespeare's.

CHAPTER VI

FROM THE RESTORATION, 1660, TO THE PUBLICATION OF PAMELA, 1740

History of the Period. — This chapter opens with the Restoration of Charles II. (1660–1685) in 1660 and ends before the appearance, in 1740, of a new literary creation, Richardson's *Pamela*, the novel of domestic life and character. This period is often called the age of Dryden and Pope, the two chief poets of the time. When Oliver Cromwell died, the restoration of the monarchy was inevitable. The protest against the Puritanic view of life (p. 223) had become strong. Reaction always results when excessive restraint in any direction is removed.

During his exile, Charles had lived much in France and had become accustomed to the dissolute habits of the French court. The court of Charles II. was the most corrupt ever known in England. The Puritan virtues were laughed to scorn by the ribald courtiers who attended Charles II. **John Evelyn** (1620–1706) and **Samuel Pepys** (1633–1703) left diaries, which give interesting pictures of the times. The one by Pepys is especially vivid.

In 1663 **Samuel Butler** (1612–1680) published a famous satire, entitled *Hudibras*. Its object was to ridicule everything that savored of Puritanism. This satire became extremely popular in court circles, and was the favorite reading of the king.

Charles II. excluded all but Episcopalians from holding office, either in towns or in Parliament. Only those who sanctioned the Episcopal prayer book were allowed to preach. In order to keep England's friendship and to be able to look to her for assistance in time of war, Louis XIV. of France paid Charles II. £100,000 a year to act as a French agent. In this capacity, Charles II. began war against Holland. From a position of commanding importance under Cromwell, England had become a third-rate power, a tail to a French kite.

SAMUEL BUTLER

James II. (1685-1688), who succeeded his brother, Charles II., undertook to suspend laws and to govern like a despot. He was driven out in the bloodless revolution of 1688 by his son-in-law, William (1689-1702), and his daughter Mary. William of Orange, who thus became king of England, was a prince of Holland. This revolution led to the *Bill of Rights* (1689), the "third pillar of the British Constitution," the two previous being *Magna Charta* and the *Petition of Right*. The foundations were now firmly laid for a strictly constitutional monarchy in England. From this time the king has been less important, sometimes only a mere figure-head.

This revolution, coupled with the increasing rivalry of France in trade and colonial expansion, altered the foreign policy of England. Holland was the head of the European coalition against France; and William III. was influential in having England join it. For the larger part of the eighteenth century there was intermittent war with France.

Under Anne (1702-1714) the Duke of Marlborough won many remarkable victories against France. The most worthy goal of French antagonism, expansion of trade, and displacement of the French in America and India, was not at this time clearly apparent.

Anne's successor was the Hanoverian Elector, George I. (1714-1727), a descendant of the daughter of James I., who had married a German prince. At the time of his accession, George I. was fifty-four years old and could speak no English. He seldom attended the meetings of his cabinet, since he could not understand the deliberations. This circumstance led to further decline of royal power, so that his successor, George II. (1727-1760), said: "Ministers are the king in this country."

The history of the rest of this period centers around the great prime minister, Robert Walpole, whose ministry lasted from 1715-1717 and from 1721-1742. His motto was, "Let sleeping dogs lie"; and he took good care to offend no one by proposing any reforms, either political or religious. "Every man has his price" was the succinct statement of his political philosophy; and he did not hesitate to secure by bribery the adoption of his measures in Parliament. He succeeded in three aims: (1) in making the house of Hanover so secure on the throne that it has not since been displaced, (2) in giving fresh impetus to trade and industry at home by reducing taxation, and (3) in strengthening the navy and encouraging colonial commerce.

Change in Foreign Influence. — Of all foreign influences from the beginning of the Renaissance to the Restoration, the literature of Italy had been the most important. French influence now gained the ascendancy.

There were several reasons for this change. (1) France under the great Louis XIV. was increasing her political importance. (2) She now had among her writers men who were by force of genius fitted to exert wide influence. Among such, we may instance Molière (1622–1673), who stands next to Shakespeare in dramatic power. (3) Charles II. and many Cavaliers had passed the time of their exile in France. They became familiar with French literature, and when they returned to England in 1660, their taste had already been influenced by French models.

Change in the Subject Matter of Literature. — The Elizabethan age impartially held the mirror up to every type of human emotion. The writers of the Restoration and of the first half of the eighteenth century, as a class, avoided any subject that demanded a portrayal of deep and noble feeling. In this age, we catch no glimpse of a Lady Macbeth in the grasp of remorse or of a Lear bending over a dead Cordelia.

The popular subjects were those which appealed to cold intellect; and these were, for the most part, satirical, didactic, and argumentative. The two greatest poets of the period, John Dryden and his successor, Alexander Pope, usually chose such subjects. John Locke (1632–1704), a great prose writer of this age, shows in the very title of his most famous work, *Of the Conduct of the Understanding*, what he preferred to discuss. That book opens with the statement, "The last resort a man has recourse to in the conduct of himself is his understanding." This declaration, which is not strictly true, embodies a pronounced tendency of the age, which could not understand that the world of feeling is no less real than that of the understanding.

One good result of the ascendancy of the intellect was seen in scientific investigation. The Royal Society was founded in 1662 to study natural phenomena and to penetrate into the hidden mysteries of philosophy and life.

The Advance of Prose. — In each preceding age, the masterpieces were poetry; but before the middle of the eighteenth century we find the prose far surpassing the poetry. Dryden, almost immediately after the Restoration, shows noteworthy advance in modern prose style. He avoids a Latinized inversion, such as the following, with which Milton begins the second sentence of his *Areopagitica* (1644):—

"And me perhaps each of these dispositions, as the subject was whereon I entered, may have at other times variously affected . . ."

Here, the object "me" is eighteen words in advance of its predicate. The sentence might well have ended with the natural pause at "affected," but Milton adds fifty-one more words. We may easily understand by comparison why the term "modern" is applied to the prose of Dryden (p. 269) and of his successors Addison and Steele (p. 289). To emphasize the precedence of these writers in the development of modern prose is no disparagement to Bunyan's style, which is almost as quaint and as excellent as that of the 1611 version of the *Bible*.

French influence was cumulative in changing the cumbersome style of Milton's prose to the polished, neatly-turned sentences of Addison. Matthew Arnold says: "The glory of English literature is in poetry, and in poetry the strength of the eighteenth century does not lie. Nevertheless the eighteenth century accomplished for us an immense literary progress, and its very shortcomings in poetry were an instrument to that progress, and served it. The example of Germany may show us what a nation loses from having no prose style. . . . French prose is marked in the highest degree by the qualities of regularity, uniformity, precision, balance. . . . The French made their poetry also conform to the law which was molding their prose. . . . This may have been bad for French poetry, but it was good for French prose."

The same influence which gave vigor, point, and definiteness to the prose, necessary for the business of the world, helped to dwarf the poetry. If both could not have advanced together, we may be thankful that the first part of the eighteenth century produced a varied prose of such high excellence.

The Classic School. — The literary lawgivers of this age held that a rigid adherence to certain narrow rules was the prime condition of producing a masterpiece. Indeed, the belief was common that a knowledge of rules was more important than genius.

The men of this school are called *classicists* because they held that a study of the best works of the ancients would disclose the necessary guiding rules. No style that did not closely follow these rules was considered good. Horace, seen through French spectacles, was the classical author most copied by this school. His *Epistles* and *Satires* were considered models.

The motto of the classicists was polished regularity. Pope struck the keynote of the age when he said: —

"True wit is nature to advantage dress'd,
What oft was thought, but ne'er so well express'd."[1]

These two lines show the form of the "riming couplet," which the classical poets adopted. There is generally a pause at the end of each line; and each couplet, when detached from the context, will usually make complete sense.

[1] *Essay on Criticism,* lines 297, 298.

Edmund Waller (1606–1687), remembered to-day for his single couplet: —

> "The soul's dark cottage, battered and decayed,
>   Lets in new light through chinks that time has made,"

had used this form of verse before 1630; but it was reserved for Dryden, and especially for Pope, to bring the couplet to a high degree of perfection. A French critic advised poets to compose the second line of the couplet first. No better rule could have been devised for dwarfing poetic power and for making poetry artificial.

Voltaire, a French classicist, said, "I do not like the monstrous irregularities of Shakespeare." An eighteenth-century classicist actually endeavored to improve Hamlet's soliloquy by putting it in riming couplets. These lines from *Macbeth* show that Shakespeare will not tolerate such leading strings nor allow the ending of the lines to interfere with his sense: —

> ". . . Besides, this Duncan
>   Hath borne his faculties so meek, hath been
>   So clear in his great office, that his virtues
>   Will plead like angels, trumpet-tongued against
>   The deep damnation of his taking-off."

A later romantic poet called the riming couplet "rocking-horse meter"; and said that the reading of many couplets reminded him of round trips on a rocking-horse.

Advances are usually made by overstressing some one point. The classicists taught the saving grace of style, the need of restraint, balance, clearness, common sense. We should therefore not despise the necessary lesson which English literature learned from such teaching, — a lesson which has never been forgotten.

The Drama. — The theaters were reopened at the time of the Restoration. It is interesting to read in the vivacious *Diary* of Samuel Pepys how he went in 1661 to see Shakespeare's *Romeo and Juliet*, "a play of itself the worst that I ever heard." The next year he characterizes *A Midsummer Night's Dream* as "the most ridiculous play that I ever saw." He liked the variety in *Macbeth*, and calls *The Tempest* "the most innocent play that I ever saw."

The Restoration dramatists, who were dominated by French influence, so often sneered at morality and the virtues of the home, that they have paid the penalty of being little read in after times. The theater has not yet entirely recovered from the deep-seated prejudice which was so intensified by the coarse plays which flourished for fifty years after the Restoration.

Although John Dryden is best known among a large number of Restoration dramatists,[1] he did better work in another field. **William Congreve** (1670–1729) made the most distinctive contribution to the new comedy of manners. Descended from an old landowning family in Staffordshire, he was for a while a mate of Jonathan Swift at Trinity College, Dublin. In 1691 Congreve was entered in the Middle Temple, London, to begin the study of law, but he soon turned playwright. His four comedies, — *The Old Bachelor, The Double Dealer, Love for Love, The Way of the World*, — and one tragedy, *The Mourning Bride*, were all written in the last decade of the seventeenth century. After 1700 he wrote no more plays, although he lived nearly thirty years longer. On his death, in 1729, he was buried in Westminster Abbey.

Congreve attempts to picture the manners of contemporary society, and he does not penetrate far below the surface of life. He is not read for the depth of his thought,

[1] For a list of the chief dramatists of the Restoration and their best work, see p. 626.

but for his humor and for the clear, pointed style of his prose comedies. George Meredith (p. 523) says:—

"Where Congreve excels all his English rivals is in his literary force, and a succinctness of style peculiar to him. . . . He is at once precise and voluble. If you have ever thought upon style, you will acknowledge it to be a signal accomplishment. In this he is a classic, and he is worthy of treading a measure with Molière."

Congreve's best comedies are *Love for Love* and *The Way of the World*. The majority of critics agree with Meredith in calling Miss Millimant, who is the heroine of the latter play, "an admirable, almost a lovable heroine." Meredith illustrates one phase of his own idea of the comic spirit, by the language which Miss Millimant uses in accepting her lover: "If I continue to endure you a little longer, I may by degrees dwindle into a wife." Congreve's peculiar genius is well shown in his ability to make her manner of speech reveal her characteristics. His plays are unfortunately disfigured with the coarseness of the age.

The blemishes in the drama did not exist, however, without an emphatic contemporary protest. **Jeremy Collier** (1650–1729), a non-conforming bishop, in his *Short View of the Immorality of the Stage* (1698), complains that the unworthy hero of one of Congreve's plays "is crowned for the man of merit, has his wishes thrown into his lap, and makes the happy exit."

Such attacks had their weight and prepared the way for the more moral sentimental comedies of Richard Steele and succeeding playwrights. The sacrifice of plot to moral purpose and the deliberate introduction of scenes designed to force an appeal to sentiment caused the later drama to deteriorate in a different way. We shall see (p. 337) that the natural hearty humor of Goldsmith's comedy, *She Stoops to Conquer* (1773), afforded a welcome relief from such plays.

From the painting by Sir Godfrey Kneller, National Portrait Gallery.

Jon: Dryden.

JOHN DRYDEN, 1631-1700

Life. — John Dryden was born in 1631 in the small village of Aldwinkle, in the northern part of Northamptonshire. Few interesting facts concerning his life have come down to us. His father was a baronet; his mother, the daughter of a rector. Young Dryden graduated from Cambridge in 1654.

During his entire life, Dryden was a professional literary man; and with his pen he made the principal part of his living. This necessity often forced him against his own better judgment to cater to the perverted taste of the Restoration. When he found that plays had more market

From a print.

BIRTHPLACE OF DRYDEN

value than any other kind of literature, he agreed to furnish three plays a year for the king's actors, but was unable to produce that number. For fifteen years in the prime of his life, Dryden did little but write plays, the majority of which are seldom read to-day. His only important poem during his dramatic period was *Annus Mirabilis* (*The Wonderful Year*, 1666), memorable for the great London fire and for naval victories over the Dutch.

By writing the greatest political satire in the language at the age of fifty, he showed the world where his genius lay. During the last twenty years of his life, he produced but few plays. His greatest satires, didactic poems, and lyrics belong to this period. In his last years he wrote a spirited translation of Vergil, and retold in his own inimitable way various stories from Chaucer and Boccaccio and *Ovid*. These stories were published in a volume entitled *Fables, Ancient and Modern*. Dryden died in 1700 and was buried in Westminster Abbey beside Chaucer.

It is difficult to speak positively of Dryden's character. He wrote a poem in honor of the memory of Cromwell, and a little later another poem, *Astræa Redux*, welcoming Charles II. He argued in stirring verse in favor of the Episcopal religion when that was the faith of the court; but after the accession of James II., who was a Catholic, Dryden wrote another poem to prove the Catholic Church the only true one. He had been appointed poet laureate in 1670, but the Revolution of 1688, which drove James from the throne, caused Dryden to lose the laureateship. He would neither take the oath of fealty to the new government nor change his religion. In spite of adversity and the loss of an income almost sufficient to support him, he remained a Catholic for the rest of his life and reared his sons in that faith.

He seems to have been of a forgiving disposition and ready to acknowledge his own faults. He admitted that his plays were disfigured with coarseness. He was very kind to young writers and willing to help them with their work. In his chair at Will's Coffee House, discoursing to the wits of the Restoration about matters of literary art, he was one of the most prominent figures of the age.

His Prose. — Although to the majority of people Dryden is known only as a poet, his influence on prose has been so far-reaching as to entitle him to be called one of the founders of modern prose style.

The shortening of sentences has been a striking feature in the development of modern English prose. Edmund Spenser averages about fifty words to each of his prose sentences; Richard Hooker, about forty-one. One of the most striking sentences in Milton's *Areopagitica* contains ninety-five words, although he crowds over three hundred words into some of his long sentences. The sentences in some of Dryden's pages average only twenty-five words in length. Turning to Macaulay, one of the most finished masters of modern prose, we find that his sentences average twenty-two words. Dryden helped also to free English prose from the inversions, involutions, and parenthetical intricacies of earlier times. His influence on both prose and poetry were much the same. In verse he adopted the short, easily understood unit of the classical couplet; and in prose, the short, direct sentence.

Dryden's prose deals chiefly with literary criticism. Most of his prose is to be found in the prefaces to his plays and poems. His most important separate prose composition is his *Essay of Dramatic Poesy*, a work which should be read by all who wish to know some of the foundation principles of criticism.

Satiric Poetry. — No English writer has surpassed Dryden in satiric verse. His greatest satire is *Absalom and Achitophel*, in which, under the guise of Old Testament characters, he satirizes the leading spirits of the Protestant opposition to the succession of James, the brother of Charles II., to the English throne. Dryden thus satirizes Achitophel, the Earl of Shaftesbury : —

> "Great wits are sure to madness near allied,
> And thin partitions do their bounds divide;
> Else, why should he, with wealth and honor blest,
> Refuse his age the needful hours of rest?
> Punish a body which he could not please,
> Bankrupt of life, yet prodigal of ease?
> And all to leave what with his toil he won

> To that unfeathered two-legged thing, a son.
>
> . . . .
>
> In friendship false, implacable in hate,
> Resolved to ruin or to rule the state."

Zimri, the Duke of Buckingham, is immortalized thus: —

> "Stiff in opinions, always in the wrong,
> Was everything by starts, and nothing long."

Mac Flecknoe is another satire of almost as great merit, directed against a certain Whig poet by the name of Shadwell. He would have been seldom mentioned in later times, had it not been for two of Dryden's lines: —

> "The rest to some faint meaning make pretence,
> But Shadwell never deviates into sense."

All for Love, one of Dryden's greatest plays, shows the delicate keenness of his satire in characterizing the cold-blooded Augustus Cæsar, or Octavius, as he is there called. Antony has sent a challenge to Octavius, who replies that he has more ways than one to die. Antony rejoins: —

> "He has more ways than one;
> But he would choose them all before that one.
> *Ventidius.* He first would choose an ague or a fever.
> *Antony.* No; it must be an ague, not a fever;
> He has not warmth enough to die by that."

Dryden could make his satire as direct and blasting as a thunderbolt. He thus describes his publisher: —

> "With leering looks, bull-faced, and freckled fair,
> With two left legs, and Judas-colored hair,
> And frowsy pores that taint the ambient air."

Argumentative or Didactic Verse. — Dryden is a master in arguing in poetry. He was not a whit hampered by the restrictions of verse. They were rather an advantage to him, for in poetry he could make more telling arguments in briefer compass than in prose. The best two examples of his power of arguing in verse are *Religio Laici*, written in 1682, to uphold the Episcopal religion, and *The Hind and the Panther*, composed in 1687, to vindicate the Catholic church. Verse of this order is called didactic, because it endeavors to teach or to explain something. The age of the Restoration delighted in such exercises of the intellect vastly more than in flights of fancy or imagination.

Lyrical Verse. — While most of Dryden's best poetry is either satiric or didactic, he wrote three fine lyrical poems: *Alexander's Feast, A Song for St. Cecilia's Day,* and *An Ode to Mrs. Anne Killigrew.* All are distinguished by remarkable beauty and energy of expression. *Alexander's Feast* is the most widely read of Dryden's poems. The opening lines of the *Ode to Mrs. Anne Killigrew* seem almost Miltonic in their conception, and they show great power in the field of lyrical poetry. Mistress Killigrew was a young lady of rare accomplishments in both poetry and painting, who died at the age of twenty-five. Dryden thus begins her memorial ode: —

> "Thou youngest virgin daughter of the skies,
>   Made in the last promotion of the blest;
> Whose palms, new plucked from Paradise,
> In spreading branches more sublimely rise,
>   Rich with immortal green above the rest:
>   . . . .
> Thou wilt have time enough for hymns divine,
> Since Heaven's eternal year is thine."

Some of his plays have songs and speeches instinct with lyrical force. The following famous lines on the worth of existence are taken from his tragedy of *Aurengzebe:* —

> "When I consider'd life, 'tis all a cheat,
>   Yet, fool'd with hope, men favor the deceit,
>   Trust on, and think to-morrow will repay:

>   To-morrow's falser than the former day;
>   Lies worse; and while it says, we shall be blest
>   With some new joys, cuts off what we possest.
>   Strange cozenage! none would live past years again;
>   Yet all hope pleasure in what yet remain.
>   And, from the dregs of life, think to receive
>   What the first sprightly running could not give.
>   I'm tir'd with waiting for this chemic gold,
>   Which fools us young and beggars us when old."

General Characteristics. — In point of time, Dryden is the first great poet of the school of literary artists. His verse does not tolerate the unpruned irregularities and exaggerations of many former English poets. His command over language is remarkable. He uses words almost as he chooses, but he does not invest them with the warm glow of feeling. He is, however, something more than a great word artist. Many of his ideas bear the stamp of marked originality.

In the field of satiric and didactic poetry, he is a master. The intellectual, not the emotional, side of man's nature appeals strongly to him. He heeds not the song of the bird, the color of the rose, nor the clouds of evening.

Although more celebrated for his poetry than for his prose, he is the earliest of the great modern prose stylists, and he displays high critical ability.

DANIEL DEFOE, 1659?–1731

Varied Experiences. — Daniel Defoe was born in London, probably the year before the Restoration. His father, a butcher in good circumstances, sent the boy to a school in which English, instead of Latin, was the medium of instruction. He was taught how to express himself in the simple, forceful English for which he became famous. His education was planned to make him a dissenting

From a print by Vandergucht.

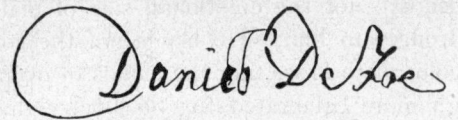

Daniel DeFoe

minister; but he preferred a life of varied activity. He became a trader, a manufacturer of tiles, a journalist, and a writer of fiction. By also serving as a government agent and spy, he incurred the severe criticism of contemporaries. It is doubtful if even Shakespeare had more varied experiences or more vicissitudes in life.

For writing what would to-day be considered a harmless piece of irony, *The Shortest Way with Dissenters*, in which Defoe, who was himself a dissenter, advocated banishment or hanging, he suffered the mortification of exposure for three days in the pillory and of imprisonment in the pestilent Newgate jail. His business of making tiles was consequently ruined. These experiences, with which his enemies taunted him, colored his entire life and made him realize that the support of his wife and six children necessitated care in his choice and treatment of subjects.

His life was a succession of changing fortunes. He died in poverty in 1731 and was buried in Bunhill Fields, London. His grave was marked by only a small headstone, but the English boys and girls who had read *Robinson Crusoe* in the Victorian age subscribed the money for a monument with a suitable inscription. It is remarkable that Bunhill Fields, which contains the graves of so many humble dissenters, should be the final resting place of both Bunyan and Defoe, the authors of the first two English prose works most often read to-day.

A Journalist and a Prolific Writer. — Defoe has at last come to be regarded as the first great English journalist. He had predecessors in this field, for as early as 1622 the *Coranto*, or journal of "current" foreign news, appeared. In 1641, on the eve of the civil war, the *Diurnall* of domestic news was issued. In 1643, when Parliament appointed a licenser, who gave copyright protection to the "catchword" or newspaper title, journalists became a "recognized body." "Newsbooks" and especially "newsletters" grew in popularity. Only a few years after the Restoration, there appeared *The London Gazette*, which has been continued to the present time as the medium through which the government publishes its official news.

From 1704 to 1713 Defoe issued *The Review*, which appeared triweekly for the greater part of the time, and gave the news current in England and in much of Europe. *The Review*, an unusual achievement for the age, shows Defoe to have been a journalist of great ability. This paper had one department, called *The Scandal Club*, which furnished suggestions for *The Tatler* and *The Spectator* (p. 288).

It has been computed that Defoe wrote for *The Review* during the nine years of its publication 5000 pages of essays, in addition to nearly the same amount of other matter. He also issued many pamphlets, which performed somewhat the same service as the modern newspaper with its editorials. It is probable that he was the most prolific of all English authors. Few have discussed as wide a range of matter. He wrote more than two hundred and fifty separate works on subjects as different as social conditions, the promotion of business, human conduct, travels in England, and ghosts.

Fiction. — Defoe was nearly sixty when he began to write fiction. In 1719 he published the first part of *Robinson Crusoe*, the story of the adventures of a sailor wrecked on a solitary island. The Frenchman Daudet said of this work: "It is as nearly immortal as any book can ever be." The nineteenth century saw more than one hundred editions of it published in London alone. It has been repeatedly issued in almost every language of Europe. The secret of the success of *Robinson Crusoe* has puzzled hundreds of writers who have tried to imitate it.

The world-wide popularity of *Robinson Crusoe* is chiefly due (1) to the peculiar genius of the author; (2) to his journalistic training, which enabled him to seize on the essential elements of interest and to keep these in the foreground; (3) to the skill with which he presents matter-of-fact details, sufficient to invest the story with an atmosphere of perfect reality; (4) to his style, which is as simple and direct as the speech of real life, and which is made vivid by specific words describing concrete actions, — such as hewing a tree, sharpening a stake, hanging up grapes to dry, tossing a biscuit to a wild cat, taking a motherless kid in his arms; and (5) to the skill with which he sets a problem requiring for its solution energy, ingenuity, self-reliance, and the development of the moral power necessary to meet and overcome difficulties.

Young and old follow with intense interest every movement of the shipwrecked mariner when he first swims to the stranded ship, constructs a raft, and places on it "bread, rice, three Dutch cheeses, five pieces of dried goat's flesh, a little remainder of European corn, and the carpenter's chest." Readers do not accompany him passively as he lands the raft and returns. They work with him; they are not only made a part of all Crusoe's experience, but they react on it imaginatively; they suggest changes; they hold their breath or try to assist him when he is in danger. Defoe's genius in making the reader a partner in Robinson Crusoe's adventures has not yet received sufficient appreciation. The author could never have secured such a triumph if he had not compelled readers to take an active part in the story.

It was for a long time thought that Defoe was ignorant, that he accidentally happened to write *Robinson Crusoe* because he had been told of the recent experience of Alexander Selkirk on a solitary island in the Pacific. It is now known that Defoe was well educated, versed in several languages, and the most versatile writer of his time. *Robinson Crusoe* was no more of an accident than any other creation of genius.

Defoe's other principal works of fiction are: *Memoirs of a Cavalier*, the story of a soldier's adventures in the seventeenth century; *The Life, Adventures, and Piracies of the Famous Captain Singleton*, a graphic account of adventures in a journey across Africa; *Moll Flanders*, a story of a well-known criminal; and *A Journal of the Plague Year*, a vivid, imaginative presentation, in the most realistic way, of the horrors of the London plague in 1665. These works are almost completely overshadowed by *Robinson Crusoe;* but they also show Defoe's narrative power and his ability to make fiction seem an absolute reality. In writing *Gulliver's Travels*, Swift received valuable hints from Defoe. Stevenson's *Treasure Island* (p. 521) is the most successful of the almost numberless stories of adventure suggested by *Robinson Crusoe*.

JONATHAN SWIFT, 1667-1745

Life. — Swift, one of the greatest prose writers of the eighteenth century, was born of English parents in Dublin in 1667. It is absolutely necessary to know something of his life in order to pass proper judgment on his writings. A cursory examination of his life will show that heredity and environment were responsible for many of his peculiarities. Swift's father died a few months before the birth of his son, and the boy saw but little of his mother.

Swift's school and college life were passed at Kilkenny School and Trinity College, Dublin. For his education he was indebted to an uncle, who made the boy feel the bitterness of his dependence. In after times he said that his uncle treated him like a dog. Swift's early experience seems to have made him misanthropic and hardened to consequences, for he neglected certain studies, and it was only by special concession that he was allowed to take his A. B. degree in 1686.

After leaving college, he spent almost ten years as the private secretary of Sir William Temple, at Moor Park in Surrey, about forty miles southwest of London.

From the painting by C. Jervas, National Portrait Gallery.

Temple had been asked to furnish some employment for the young graduate because Lady Temple was related to Swift's mother. Here Swift was probably treated as a dependent, and he had to eat at the second table. Finally, this life became so intolerable that he took holy orders and went to a little parish in Ireland; but after a stay of eighteen months he returned to Moor Park, where he remained until Temple's death in 1699. Swift then went to another little country parish in Ireland. From there he visited London on a mission in behalf of the Episcopal Church in Ireland. He quarreled with the Whigs, became a Tory, and assisted that party by writing many political pamphlets. The Tory ministry soon felt that it could scarcely do without him. He dined with ministers of state, and was one of the most

From a drawing.

MOOR PARK

important men in London; but he advanced the interests of his friends much better than his own, for he got little from the government except the hope of becoming a bishop. In 1713 he was made dean of St. Patrick's Cathedral, Dublin. In 1714, Queen Anne died, the Tories went out of power, and Swift returned to Ireland, a disappointed man. He passed the rest of his life there, with the exception of a few visits to England.

When English politicians endeavored to oppress Ireland with unjust laws, Swift championed the Irish cause. A man who knew him well, says: "I never saw the poor so carefully and conscientiously attended to as those of his cathedral." He gave up a large part of his income every year for the poor. In Dublin he was looked upon as a hero. When a certain person tried to be revenged on Swift for a satire, a deputation of Swift's neighbors proposed to thrash the man. Swift sent them home, but they boycotted the man and lowered his income £1200 a year.

During the last years of his life, Swift was hopelessly insane. He died in 1745, leaving his property for an asylum for lunatics and incurables.

From the painting by Dicksee.

SWIFT AND STELLA

The mysteries in Swift's life may be partly accounted for by the fact that during many years he suffered from an unknown brain disease. This affection, the galling treatment received in his early years, and the disappointments of his prime, largely account for his misanthropy, for his coldness, and for the almost brutal treatment of the women who loved him.

Swift's attachment to the beautiful Esther Johnson,

known in literature as Stella, led him to write to her that famous series of letters known as the *Journal to Stella*, in which he gives much of his personal history during the three sunniest years of his life, from 1710 to 1713, when he was a lion in London. Thackeray says: "I know of nothing more manly, more tender, more exquisitely touching, than some of these brief notes, written in what Swift calls his 'little language' in his *Journal to Stella*."

A Tale of a Tub and the Battle of the Books. — Swift's greatest satire, the greatest prose satire in English, is known as *A Tale of a Tub*. The purpose of the work is to uphold the Episcopalians and satirize opposing religious denominations. For those not interested in theological arguments, there is much entertaining philosophy, as the following quotation will show: —

"If we take an examination of what is generally understood by happiness, as it has respect either to the understanding or the senses, we shall find all its properties and adjuncts will herd under this short definition, — that it is a perpetual possession of being well deceived. And first, with relation to the mind or understanding, it is manifest what mighty advantages fiction has over truth; and the reason is just at our elbow, because imagination can build nobler scenes and produce more wonderful revolutions than fortune or nature will be at expense to furnish."

Swift's satiric definition of happiness as the art "of being well deceived" is a characteristic instance of a combination of his humor and pessimistic philosophy.

In the same volume with *A Tale of a Tub*, there was published a prose satire in almost epic form, *An Account of a Battle between the Ancient and Modern Books in St. James Library* (1704). Although this satire apparently aims to demonstrate the superior merits of the great classical writers, it is mainly an attack on pretentions to knowledge. Our greatest surprise in this satire comes not only from discovering the expression, "sweetness and light," made famous by Matthew Arnold in the Victorian age, but also from finding that a satirist like Swift assigned such high rank to these qualities. He says that the "Ancients" thus expressed an essential difference between themselves and the "Moderns":—

> "The difference is that, instead of dirt and poison, we have rather chosen to fill our lives with honey and wax, thus furnishing mankind with the two noblest of things, which are Sweetness and Light."

Gulliver's Travels. — The world is always ready to listen to any one who has a good story to tell. Neither children nor philosophers have yet wearied of reading the adventures of Captain Lemuel Gulliver in Lilliput and Brobdingnag. *Gulliver's Travels* is Swift's most famous work.

Gulliver makes four remarkable voyages to strange countries. He first visits Lilliput, which is inhabited by a race of men about six inches high. Everything is on a corresponding scale. Gulliver eats a whole herd of cattle for breakfast and drinks several hogsheads of liquor. He captures an entire fleet of warships. A rival race of pygmies endeavors to secure his services so as to obtain the balance of power. The quarrels between these little people seem ridiculous, and so petty as to be almost beneath contempt.

Gulliver next visits Brobdingnag, where the inhabitants are sixty feet tall, and the affairs of ordinary human beings appear petty and insignificant. The cats are as large as three oxen, and the dogs attain the size of four elephants. Gulliver eats on a table thirty feet high, and trembles lest he may fall and break his neck. The baby seizes Gulliver and tries to swallow his head. Afterward the hero fights a desperate battle with two rats. A monkey catches him and carries him to the almost infinite height of the house top. Certainly, the voyages to Lilliput and Brobdingnag merit Leslie Stephen's criticism of being "almost the most delightful children's book ever written."

The third voyage, which takes him to Laputa, satirizes the philosophers. We are taken through the academy at Lagado and are shown a typical philosopher: —

"He had been eight years upon a project for extracting sunbeams out of cucumbers, which were to be put in vials, hermetically sealed, and let out to warm the air in raw, inclement summers. He told me he did not doubt that in eight years more he should be able to supply the governor's gardens with sunshine at a reasonable rate."

In this voyage the Struldbrugs are described. They are a race of men who, after the loss of every faculty and of every tie that binds them to earth, are doomed to continue living. Dante never painted a stronger or a ghastlier picture.

On his fourth voyage, he visits the country of the Houyhnhnms and describes the Yahoos, who are the embodiment of all the detestable qualities of human beings. The last two voyages are not pleasant reading, and one might wish that the author of two such inimitable tales as the adventures in Lilliput and Brobdingnag had stopped with these.

Children read *Gulliver's Travels* for the story, but there is much more than a story in the work. In its pages the historian finds allusions that throw much light on the history of the age. Among the Lilliputians, for example, there is one party, known as the Bigendians, which insists that all eggs shall be broken open at the big end, while another party, called the Littleendians, contends that eggs shall be opened only at the little end. These differences typify the quarrels of the age concerning religion and politics. The *Travels* also contains much human philosophy. The lover of satire is constantly delighted with the keenness of the thrusts.

General Characteristics. — Swift is one of the greatest of English prose humorists. He is noted also for wit of that satiric kind which enjoys the discomfiture of the victim. A typical instance is shown in the way in which, under the assumed name of Isaac Bickerstaff, he dealt with an astrologer and maker of prophetic almanacs, whose name was Partridge. Bickerstaff claimed to be an infallible astrologer, and predicted that Partridge would die March 29, 1708, at 11 P.M. When that day had passed, Bickerstaff issued a pamphlet giving a circumstantial account of Partridge's death. Partridge, finding that his customers began to decrease, protested that he was alive. Bickerstaff promptly replied that Partridge was dead by his own infallible rules of astrology, and that the man now claiming to be Partridge was a vile impostor.

Swift's wit frequently left its imprint on the thought of the time. The results of this special prank with the astrologer were: first, to cause the wits of the town to join in the hue and cry that Partridge was dead; second, to increase the contempt for astrologers; and, third, in the words of Scott: "The most remarkable consequence of Swift's frolic was the establishment of the *Tatler*." Richard Steele, its founder, adopted the popular name of Isaac Bickerstaff (p. 287).

Taine says of Swift: "He is the inventor of irony, as Shakespeare of poetry." The most powerful instance of Swift's irony is shown in his attempt to better the condition of the Irish, whose poverty forced them to let their children grow up ignorant and destitute, or often even die of starvation. His *Modest Proposal* for relieving such distress is to have the children at the age of one year served as a new dish on the tables of the great. So apt is irony to be misunderstood and to fail of its mark, that for a time Swift was considered merely brutal; but soon he convinced the Irish that he was their friend, willing to contribute both time and money to aid them. His ironical remarks on *The Abolishing of Christianity* were also misunderstood.

His poems, such as *A Description of a City Shower*, and *Cadenus and Vanessa*, show the same general characteristics as his prose, but are inferior to it.

We shall search Swift's work in vain for examples of pathos or sublimity. We shall find his pages caustic with wit, satire, and irony, and often disfigured with coarseness. One of the great pessimists of all time, he is yet tremendously in earnest in whatever he says, from his *Drapier's Letters*, written to protect Ireland from the schemes of English politicians, to his *Gulliver's Travels*, where he describes the court of Lilliput. This earnestness and circumstantial minuteness throw an air of reality around his most grotesque creations. He pretended to despise Defoe; yet the influence of that great writer, who made fiction seem as real as fact, is plainly apparent in Gulliver's remarkable adventures.

Although sublimity and pathos are outside of his range, his style is remarkably well adapted to his special subject matter. While reading his works, one scarcely ever thinks of his style, unless the attention is specially directed to it. Only a great artist can thus conceal his art. A style so natural as this has especial merits which will repay study. Three of its chief characteristics are simplicity, flexibility, and energetic directness.

From the painting by Sir Godfrey Kneller, National Portrait Gallery.

JOSEPH ADDISON, 1672-1719

Life. — Joseph Addison was born in the paternal rectory at Milston, a small village in the eastern part of Wiltshire. He was educated at Oxford. He intended to become a clergyman, but, having attracted attention by his graceful Latin poetry, was dissuaded by influential court friends from entering the service of the church. They persuaded him to fit himself for the diplomatic service, and secured for him a yearly pension of £300. He then went to France, studied the language of that country, and traveled extensively, so as to gain a knowledge of foreign courts. The death of King William in 1702 stopped his pension, however, and Addison was forced to return to England to seek employment as a tutor.

The great battle of Blenheim was won by Marlborough in 1704. As Macaulay says, the ministry was mortified to see such a victory celebrated by so much bad poetry, and he instances these lines from one of the poems:

> "Think of two thousand gentlemen at least,
> And each man mounted on his capering beast;
> Into the Danube they were pushed by shoals."

The Chancellor of the Exchequer went to Addison's humble lodgings and asked him to write a poem in honor of the battle. Addison took the town by storm with a simile in which the great general was likened to the calm angel of the whirlwind. When people reflected how calmly Marlborough had directed the whirlwind of war, they thought that no comparison could be more felicitous. From that time Addison's fortunes rose. Since his day no man relying on literary talents alone has risen so high in state affairs. He was made assistant Secretary of State, Secretary for Ireland, and finally chief Secretary of State.

Though Addison was a prominent figure in the political world, it is his literary life that most concerns us. In his prime he wrote for *The Tatler* and *The Spectator*, famous newspapers of Queen Anne's day, many inimitable essays on contemporary life and manners. Most newspaper work is soon forgotten, but these essays are read by the most cultivated people of to-day. In his own age his most meritorious production was thought to be the dull tragedy of *Cato*, a drama observing the classical unities. Some of his *Hymns* are much finer. Lines like these, written of the stars, linger in our memories: —

"Forever singing as they shine,
 The hand that made us is divine."

Addison had a singularly pleasing personality. Though he was a Whig, the Tories admired and applauded him. He was a good illustration of the truth that if one smiles in the mirror of the world, it will answer him with a smile. Swift said he believed the English would have made Addison king, if they had been requested to place him on the throne. Pope's jealous nature prompted him to quarrel with Addison, but the quarrel was chiefly on one side. Men like Macaulay and Thackeray have exerted their powers to do justice to the kindliness and integrity of Addison.

THE BIRTHPLACE OF ADDISON

Addison died at the age of forty-seven, and was buried in Westminster Abbey.

Collaborates with Steele. — Under the pen name of Isaac Bickerstaff, Richard Steele (1672-1729), a former schoolmate and friend of Addison, started in 1709 *The Tatler*, a periodical published three times a week. This discussed matters of interest in society and politics, and occasionally published an essay on morals and manners. Steele was a good-natured, careless individual, with a varied experience as soldier, playwright, moralist, keeper of the official gazette, and pensioner. He says that he always "preferred the state of his mind to that of his fortune"; but his mental state was often fickle, and too much dependent on bodily luxuries, though he was patriotic enough to sacrifice his personal fortune for what he considered his country's interest.

We find Addison a frequent contributor to *The Tatler* after its seventeenth number. Steele says: "I fared like a distressed prince who calls in a powerful neighbor to his aid; I was undone by my auxiliary; when I had once called him in, I could not subsist without dependence on him."

The Tatler was discontinued in 1711, and Steele projected the more famous *Spectator* two months later. Addison wrote the first number, but the second issue, which came from Steele's pen, contains sketches of those characters which have become famous in the *Sir Roger de Coverley Papers*. Steele's first outline of Sir Roger is a creation of sweetness and light:—

RICHARD STEELE

"His tenants grow rich, his servants look satisfied, all the young women profess to love him, and the young men are glad of his company. When he comes into a house he calls the servants by their names, and talks all the way upstairs to a visit."

The influence of such a character must have been especially wholesome on the readers of the eighteenth century. Without the suggestive originality of Steele, we might never have had those essays of Addison, which we read most to-day; but while Steele should have full credit for the first bold sketches, the finished portraits in the De Coverley gallery are due to Addison. Steele says of his associate, "I claim to myself the merit of having extorted excellent productions from a person of the greatest abilities, who would not have let them appear by any other means."

It is well, however, to remember that Steele did much more work than is popularly supposed. Beginning with March 1, 1711, there were 555 issues of *The Spectator* published on succeeding week days. To these were added 80 more numbers at irregular intervals. Of these 635 numbers, Steele wrote 236 and Addison 274.

In many respects each seemed to be the complement of the other. Steele's writings have not the polish or delicate humor of Addison's, but they have more strength and pathos. Addison had the greater genius, and he was also more willing to spend time in polishing his prose and making it artistic. From the far greater interest now shown in Addison, the student should be impressed by the necessity of artistic finish as well as of excellence in subject matter.

Addison's Essays. — The greatest of Addison's *Essays* appeared in *The Spectator* and charmed many readers in Queen Anne's age. The subject matter of these *Essays* is extremely varied. On one day there is a pleasant paper on witches; on another, a chat about the new woman; on another, a discourse on clubs. Addison is properly a moral satirist, and his pen did much more than the pulpit to civilize the age and make virtue the fashion. In *The Spectator*, he says: "If I meet with anything in city, court, or country, that shocks modesty or good manners, I shall use my utmost endeavors to make an example of it." He accomplished his purpose, not by heated denunciations of vice, but by holding it up to kindly ridicule. He remembered the fable of the different methods employed by the north wind and the sun to make a man lay aside an ugly cloak.

Addison stated also that one of his objects was to bring "philosophy out of closets and libraries, schools and colleges, to dwell in clubs and assemblies, at tea tables and coffeehouses." His papers on Milton did much to diminish that great poet's unpopularity in an age that loved form rather than matter, art rather than natural strength.

The Sir Roger de Coverley Papers. — The most famous of Addison's productions are his papers that appeared in *The Spectator*, describing a typical country gentleman, Sir Roger de Coverley, and his friends and servants. Taine says that Addison here invented the novel without suspecting it. This is an overstatement; but these papers certainly have the interest of a novel from the moment Sir Roger appears until his death, and the delineation of character is far in advance of that shown in the majority of modern novels. We find ourselves rereading the *De Coverley Papers* more than once, a statement that can be made of but few novels.

From a drawing by B. Westmacott.
SIR ROGER IN CHURCH

General Characteristics. — Addison ranks among the greatest of English essayists. Some of his essays, like the series on *Paradise Lost*, deal with literary criticism; but most people to-day read little from his pen except the *Sir Roger de Coverley Papers*, which give interesting pictures of eighteenth-century life and manners.

Before we have read many of Addison's essays, we shall discover that he is a humorist of high rank. His humor is of the kind that makes one smile, rather than laugh aloud. Our countenance relaxes when we discover that his rules for an eighteenth-century club prescribe a fine for absence except in case of sickness or imprisonment. We are quietly amused at such touches as this in the delineation of Sir Roger: —

"As Sir Roger is landlord to the whole congregation, he keeps them in very good order, and will suffer nobody to sleep in it besides himself; for, if by chance he has been surprised into a short nap at sermon, upon recovering out of it, he stands up and looks about him, and, if he sees anybody else nodding, either wakes them himself, or sends his servants to them."

Addison is remarkable among a satiric group of writers because he intended his humor to be "remedial," — not merely to inflict wounds, but to exert a moral influence, to induce human beings to forsake the wrong and to become more kindly. We may smile at Sir Roger; but we have more respect for his kindliness, after reading in *Spectator* No. 383, how he selected his boatmen to row him on the Thames: —

"We were no sooner come to the Temple Stairs, but we were surrounded with a crowd of watermen, offering us their respective services. Sir Roger, after having looked about him very attentively, spied one with a wooden leg, and immediately gave him orders to get his boat ready. As we were walking towards it, 'You must know,' says Sir Roger, 'I never make use of anybody to row me, that has not either lost a leg or an arm. I would rather bate him a few strokes of his oar than not employ an honest man that had been wounded in the Queen's service. If I was a lord or a bishop, and kept a barge, I would not put a fellow in my livery that had not a wooden leg.'"

Such humor, which finds its chief point in a desire to make the world kindlier, must have appealed to the eighteenth century, or *The Spectator* could not have reached a circulation of ten thousand copies a day. Addison would not now have his legion of warm admirers if his humor had been personal, like Pope's, or misanthropical, like Swift's.

Of his style, Dr. Samuel Johnson says, "Whoever wishes to attain an English style, familiar but not coarse, and elegant but not ostentatious, must give his days and nights to the study of Addison." Benjamin Franklin, as we know from his *Autobiography*, followed this advice with admirable results. Addison's style seems as natural and easy as the manners of a well-bred person. When we have given some attention to dissecting his style, we may indeed discover that a prose model for to-day should have more variety and energy and occasionally more precision; but such a conclusion does not mean that any writer of this century would like the task of surpassing the *De Coverley Papers*.

ALEXANDER POPE, 1688–1744

Life. — Alexander Pope was born in London in 1688. His father, a devout Catholic, was a linen merchant, who gave his son little formal schooling, but allowed him to pick up his education by reading such authors as pleased his fancy.

He was a very precocious child. At the age of twelve he was writing an *Ode on Solitude*. He chose his vocation early, for writing poetry was the business of his life.

In his childhood, his parents removed from London to Binfield, a village in Berkshire, nine miles from Windsor. When he was nearly thirty years old, his translation of the *Iliad* enabled him to buy a house and grounds at Twickenham on the Thames, about twelve miles above London. He lived here for the rest of his life, indulging his taste

From the portrait by William Hoare.

A. Pope

for landscape gardening and entertaining the greatest men of the age.

After early middle life, his writings made him pecuniarily independent, but he suffered much from ill health. In his *Lives of the English Poets*, Dr. Samuel Johnson says of Pope : —

"By natural deformity, or accidental distortion, his vital functions were so much disordered that his life was a long disease. . . . When he rose, he was invested in a bodice made of stiff canvas, being scarce able to hold himself erect till they were laced, and he then put on a flannel waistcoat. One side was contracted. His legs were so slender that he enlarged their bulk with three pair of stockings. ...

"In all his intercourse with mankind, he had great delight in artifice, and endeavored to attain all his purposes by indirect and unsuspected methods. *He hardly drank tea without a stratagem.*"

The publication of his correspondence tangled him in a mesh of deceptions, because his desire to appear in a favorable light led him to change letters that he had sent to friends. His double-dealing, intense jealousy, and irritability, due to his physical condition, caused him to become involved in many quarrels, which gave him the opportunity to indulge to the utmost his own satiric tendency. In one of his late satires, *The Epistle to Dr. Arbuthnot*, he charged Addison with the inclination to —

"Damn with faint praise, assent with civil leer,
And without sneering, teach the rest to sneer."

On the basis of what he wrote, we may divide his life into three periods. During his first thirty years, he produced various kinds of verse, like the *Essay on Criticism* and *The Rape of the Lock*. The middle period of his life was marked by his translation of Homer's *Iliad* and *Odyssey*. In his third period, he wrote moral and didactic poems, like the *Essay on Man*, and satires, like the *Dunciad*.

From an old print.
POPE'S VILLA AT TWICKENHAM

Some Poems of the First Period : Essay on Criticism and The Rape of the Lock. — Pope's first published poem, *The Pastorals*, which appeared in 1709, was followed in

1711 by *An Essay on Criticism,* — an exquisite setting of a number of gems of criticism which had for a long time been current. Pope's intention in writing this poem may be seen from what he himself says: "It seems not so much the perfection of sense to say things that have never been said before, as to express those best that have been said oftenest."

From this point of view, the poem is remarkable. No other writer, except Shakespeare, has in an equal number of lines said so many things which have passed into current quotation. Rare perfection in the form of statement accounts for this. The poem abounds in such lines as these: —

> "For fools rush in where angels fear to tread."

> "To err is human, to forgive divine."

> "All seems infected that th' infected spy,
> As all looks yellow to the jaundiced eye."

> "In words, as fashions, the same rule will hold,
> Alike fantastic, if too new or old:
> Be not the first by whom the new are tried,
> Nor yet the last to lay the old aside."

The Rape of the Lock, which is Pope's masterpiece, is almost a romantic poem (p. 307), even though it is written in classical couplets. It was a favorite with Oliver Goldsmith, and James Russell Lowell rightly says: "The whole poem more truly deserves the name of a creation than anything Pope ever wrote." The poem is a mock epic, and it has the supernatural machinery which was supposed to be absolutely necessary for an epic. In place of the gods and goddesses of the great epics, however, the fairy-like sylphs help to guide the action of this poem.

The poem, which is founded on an actual incident, describes a young lord's theft of a lock of hair from the head of a court beauty. Pope composed *The Rape of the Lock* to soothe her indignation and to effect a reconciliation. The whole of this poem should be read by the student, as it is a vivid satiric picture of fashionable life in Queen Anne's reign.

Translation of Homer. — Pope's chief work during the middle period of his life was his translation of the *Iliad* and of the *Odyssey* of Homer. From a financial point of view, these translations were the most successful of his labors. They brought him in nearly £9000, and made him independent of bookseller or of nobleman.

From a drawing by B. Westmacott.
RAPE OF THE LOCK

The remarkable success of these works is strange when we remember that Pope's knowledge of Greek was very imperfect, and that he was obliged to consult translations before attempting any passage. The Greek scholar Bentley, a contemporary of Pope, delivered a just verdict on the translation: "A pretty poem, Mr. Pope, but you must not call it Homer." The historian Gibbon said that the poem had every merit except faithfulness to the original.

Homer is simple and direct. He abounds in concrete terms. Pope dislikes a simple term and loves a circumlocution and an abstraction. We have the concrete "herd of swine" translated into "a bristly care," "skins," into "furry spoils." The concrete was considered common and undignified. Homer says in simple language: "His father wept with him," but Pope translates this: "The father poured a social flood."

Pope used to translate thirty or forty verses of the *Iliad* before rising, and then to spend a considerable time in polishing them. But half of the translation of the *Odyssey* is his own work. He employed assistants to finish the other half; but it is by no means easy to distinguish his work from theirs.

Some Poems of his Third Period: "Essay on Man," and "Satires." — The *Essay on Man* is a philosophical poem with the avowed object of vindicating the ways of God to man. The entire poem is an amplification of the idea contained in these lines: —

> "All nature is but art unknown to thee;
> All chance, direction which thou canst not see;
> All discord, harmony not understood;
> All partial evil, universal good.
> And spite of pride, in erring reason's spite,
> One truth is clear, Whatever is, is right."

From contemporary portrait.

ALEXANDER POPE

The chief merit of the poem consists in throwing into polished form many of the views current at the time, so that they may be easily understood. Before we read very far we come across such old acquaintances as —

> "The proper study of mankind is man."

"An honest man's the noblest work of God."

"Vice is a monster of so frightful mien
As, to be hated, needs but to be seen;
Yet, seen too oft, familiar with her face,
We first endure, then pity, then embrace."

The *Epistle to Dr. Arbuthnot* and *The Dunciad* are Pope's greatest satires. In *The Dunciad*, an epic of the dunces, he holds up to ridicule every person and writer who had offended him. These were in many cases scribblers who had no business with a pen; but in a few instances they were the best scholars of that day. A great deal of the poem is now very tiresome reading. Much of it is brutal. Pope was a powerful agent, as Thackeray says, in rousing that obloquy which has ever since pursued a struggling author. *The Dunciad* could be more confidently consulted about contemporary literary history, if Pope had avoided such unnecessary misstatements as:—

"Earless on high, stood unabash'd De Foe."

This line is responsible for the current unwarranted belief that the author of *Robinson Crusoe* lost his ears in the pillory.

General Characteristics. — Pope has not strong imagination, a keen feeling for nature, or wide sympathy with man. Leslie Stephen says: "Pope never crosses the undefinable, but yet ineffaceable line, which separates true poetry from rhetoric." The debate in regard to whether Pope's verse is ever genuine poetry may not yet be settled to the satisfaction of all; but it is well to recognize the undoubted fact that his couplets still appeal to many readers who love clearness and precision and who are not inclined to wrestle with the hidden meaning of greater poetry. One of his poems, *The Rape of the Lock*, has become almost a universal favorite because of its humor, good-natured satire, and entertaining pictures of society in Queen Anne's time.

He is the poet who best expresses the classical spirit of the eighteenth century. He excels in satiric and didactic verse. He expresses his ideas in perfect form, and embodies them in classical couplets, sometimes styled "rocking-horse meter"; but he shows no power of fathoming the emotional depths of the soul.

In the history of literature, he holds an important place, because, more than any other writer, he calls attention to the importance of correctness of form and of careful expression. He is the prince of artificial poets. Though he erred in exalting form above matter, he taught his age the needed lesson of careful workmanship.

SUMMARY

The Restoration and the first part of the eighteenth century display a low moral standard in both church and state. This standard had its effect on literature. The drama shows marked decline. We find no such sublime outbursts of song as characterize the Elizabethan and Puritan ages. The writers chose satiric or didactic subjects, and avoided pathos, deep feeling, and sublimity. French influence was paramount.

The classical school, which loved polished regularity, set the fashion in literature. An old idea, dressed in exquisite form, was as welcome as a new one. Anything strange, irregular, romantic, full of feeling, highly imaginative, or improbable to the intellect, was unpopular. Even in *Gulliver's Travels*, Swift endeavored to be as realistic as if he were demonstrating a geometrical proposition.

Dryden and Pope are the two chief poets of the classical school. Both use the riming couplet and are distinguished for their satiric and didactic verse. Their poetry shows more intellectual brilliancy than imaginative power. They display little sympathy with man and small love for nature.

The age is far more remarkable for its prose than for its poetry. French influence helped to develop a concise, flexible, energetic prose style. The deterioration in poetry was partly compensated for by the rapid advances in prose, which needed the influences working toward artistic finish. Because of its cleverness, avoidance of long sentences, and of classical inversions, Dryden's prose is essentially modern. Defoe's *Robinson Crusoe* is the world's most popular story of adventure, told in simple and direct, but seemingly artless, prose. Of all the prose writers since Swift's time, few have equaled him and still fewer surpassed him in simplicity, flexibility, directness, and lack of affectation. The essays of Steele and Addison constitute a landmark. No preceding English prose shows so much grace of style, delicate humor, and power of awakening and retaining interest as do the *Sir Roger de Coverley Papers*.

The influence of this age was sufficient to raise permanently the standard level of artistic literary expression. The unpruned, shapeless, and extravagant forms of earlier times will no longer be tolerated.

SUGGESTIONS FOR FURTHER STUDY

HISTORICAL

An account of the history of this period may be found in either Gardiner,[1] Green, Walker, or Cheney. Vols. VIII. and IX. of the *Political History of England* give the history in greater detail. For the

---

[1] For full titles, see p. 50.

social side, consult Traill, Vols. IV. and V., and Cheney's *Industrial and Social History of England*. Lecky's *History of England in the Eighteenth Century* is an excellent work.

LITERARY

The Cambridge History of English Literature, Vols. VIII., IX., X.
Courthope's *A History of English Poetry*, Vols. III., IV., and V.
Stephen's *English Literature in the Eighteenth Century*.
Taine's *History of English Literature*, Book III., Chaps. I., II., III.
Gosse's *History of Eighteenth Century Literature* begins with 1660.
Garnett's *The Age of Dryden*.
Phillips's *Popular Manual of English Literature*, Vol. I.
Minto's *Manual of English Prose Literature*.
Saintsbury's *Life of Dryden*. (E. M. L.)
Macaulay's *Essay on Dryden*.
Lowell's *Essay on Dryden* in *Among My Books*.
Dryden's *Essays on the Drama*, edited by Strunk.
Fowler's *Life of Locke*. (E. M. L.)
Stephen's *History of Thought in the Eighteenth Century*.
Dennis's *The Age of Pope*.
Thackeray's *English Humorists* (Swift, Addison, Steele, Pope).
Stephen's *Life of Swift*. (E. M. L.)
Craik's *Life of Swift*.
Courthope's *Life of Addison*. (E. M. L.)
Macaulay's *Essay on Addison*.
Stephen's *Life of Pope*. (E. M. L.)
De Quincey's *Essay on Pope*, and *On the Poetry of Pope*.
Johnson's *Lives of the Poets* (Dryden, Pope, Addison).
Lowell's *My Study Windows* (Pope).

SUGGESTED READINGS
WITH QUESTIONS AND SUGGESTIONS

Dryden. — From his lyrical verse, read *Alexander's Feast* or *A Song for St. Cecilia's Day*. The opening lines of *Religio Laici* or of *The Hind and the Panther* will serve as a specimen of his argumentative or didactic verse and *Absalom and Achitophel* for his satire. (**Cassell's** *National Library*, 15 cents.)

Selections are given in Ward,[1] II., 454-483; Bronson, III., 20-58; Manly, I., 203-209; *Oxford Treasury*, III., 99-110; *Century*, 266-285.

For his critical prose, read *An Essay of Dramatic Poesy* (Strunk's edition of *Dryden's Essays on the Drama*). For selections see Craik, III., 148-154; Manly, II., 146-163; *Century*, 276-285.

What is the chief subject matter of Dryden's verse? Point out typical qualities in his argumentative and satiric verse. Give definite instances of his power in argument and satire.

Why is his prose called modern? Point out some of its qualities.

Defoe. — Read or reread *Robinson Crusoe* and point out where he specially shows the skill of the journalist in the presentation of his facts. Can you select passages that show the justice of the criticism on p. 274? How would the interest in the story have been affected, had Defoe, like the author of *Swiss Family Robinson*, caused the shipwreck to occur on an island where tropical fruits would have rendered unnecessary Crusoe's labor to secure food?

Swift. — Craik's *English Prose Selections*, Vol. III., pp. 391-424, contains representative selections from Swift's prose. The best of these are *The Philosophy of Clothes*, from *A Tale of a Tub* (Craik, III., 398); *A Digression concerning Critics*, from the same (Craik, III., 400); *The Emperor of Lilliput* (Craik, III., 417) and *The King of Brobdingnag* (Craik, III., 419), from *Gulliver's Travels*.

Selections may be found also in Manly, II., 184-198; *Oxford Treasury*, III., 125-129; *Century*, 299-323.

Is Swift's a good prose style? Does he use ornament? Can you find a passage where he strives after effect? In what respects do the subjects which he chooses and his manner of treating them show the spirit of the age? Why is *Gulliver's Travels* so popular? What are the most important lessons which a young writer may learn from Swift? In what is he specially lacking?

Addison and Steele. — From the *Sir Roger de Coverley Papers* the student should not fail to read *Spectator* No. 112, *A Country Sunday*. He may then read *Spectator* No. 2, by Steele, which sketches the De Coverley characters, and compare the style and characteristics of the two authors. The student who has the time at this point should read all the *De Coverley Papers* (*Eclectic English Classics*, American Book Company).

Good selections from both Addison and Steele may be found in Craik, III., 469-535; Manly, II., 198-216; *Century*, 324-349.

[1] For full titles, see p. 6.

In what did Addison and Steele excel? What qualities draw so many readers to the *De Coverley Papers?* Why may they be called a prelude to the modern novel?

Select passages which will serve to bring into sharp contrast the style and humor of Swift and of Addison.

Pope. — Read *The Rape of the Lock* (printed with the *Essay on Man* in *Eclectic English Classics*, American Book Company, 20 cents). Selections from this are given in Ward, III., 73-82. The *Essay on Man*, Book I. (Ward, III., 85-91), will serve as a specimen of his didactic verse. The *Epistle to Dr. Arbuthnot* (Ward, III., 103-105) will illustrate his satire, and the lines from the *Iliad* in Ward, III., 82, will show the characteristics of his translation.

The Rape of the Lock and full selections are given in Bronson, III., 89-144; *Century*, 350-368; Manly, I., 228-253.

How does Pope show the spirit of the classical school? What are his special merits and defects? Does an examination of his poetry convince you that Leslie Stephen's criticism (p. 298) is right? Select lines from six great poets of different periods. Place beside these selections some of Pope's best lines, and see if you have a clearer idea of the difference between rhetoric and true poetry.

CHAPTER VII

THE SECOND FORTY YEARS OF THE EIGHTEENTH CENTURY, 1740-1780

The Colonial Expansion of England. — The most important movements in English history during the second forty years of the eighteenth century are connected with colonial expansion. In 1739 friction between England and Spain over colonial trade forced Robert Walpole, the prime minister, into a war which was not successfully prosecuted, and which compelled him to resign in 1742. The humorous statement that he "abdicated," contains a large element of truth, for he had been a much more important ruler than the king. The contest with Spain was merged in the unprofitable war of the Austrian Succession (1740-1748), in which England participated.

The successors of Walpole were weak and inefficient; but in 1757 William Pitt, the Elder (1708-1778), although merely secretary of state, obtained the ascendancy in the government. Walpole had tried in vain to bribe Pitt, who was in politics the counterpart of Wesley in religious life. Pitt appealed to the patriotism and to the sense of honor of his countrymen, and his appeal was heard. His enthusiasm and integrity, coupled with good judgment of men, enabled him to lead England to become the foremost power of the world.

France had managed her colonial affairs in America and in India so well that it seemed as if she might in both places displace England. Pitt, however, selected good leaders and planned a comprehensive method of warfare against France, both in Europe and in the colonies. Between 1750 and 1760 Clive was making Great Britain mistress of the vast empire of India. The French and Indian War (1754-1760) in America resulted in favor of England. In 1759 Wolfe shattered the power of France in Canada, which has since remained an English colony. England was expanding to the eastward and the westward and taking her literature with her. As Wolfe advanced on Quebec, he was reading Gray's *Elegy*.

At the beginning of this century England owned one half of the island of Great Britain and a few colonial settlements. Not until 1707 were England and Scotland united. In 1763 England had vast dominions in North America and India. She had become the greatest colonial power in the world.

The New Religious Influence. — England could not have taken such a commanding position unless the patriotism and morals of her citizens had improved since the beginning of the century. The church had become too lukewarm and respectable to bring in the masses, who saw more to attract them in taverns and places of public amusement.

When religious influence was at the lowest ebb, two eloquent preachers, John Wesley and George Whitefield, started a movement which is still gathering force. Wesley did not ask his audience to listen to a sermon on the favorite bloodless abstractions of the eighteenth-century pulpit, such as Charity, Faith, Duty, Holiness, — abstractions which never moved a human being an inch heavenward. His sermons were emotional. They dealt largely with the emotion of love, — God's love for man.

He did not ask his listeners to engage in intellectual disquisitions about the aspects of infinity. He did not preach free-will metaphysics or trouble his hearers with a satisfactory philosophical account of the origin of evil. He spoke about things that reached not only the understanding but also the feelings of plain men.

About the same time, Whitefield was preaching to the miners near Bristol. As he eloquently told them the story of salvation he brought tears to the eyes of these rude men and made many resolve to lead better lives.

This religious awakening may have been accompanied with too much appeal to the feelings and unhealthy emotional excitement; but some vigorous movement was absolutely necessary to quicken the spiritual life of a decadent age.

The American Revolution. — The second forty years of the eighteenth century witnessed another movement of great importance to the world, — the revolt of the American colonies (1775). When George III. (1760–1820) came to the throne, he determined to be the real ruler of his kingdom, — to combine in himself the offices of king, prime minister, and cabinet. He undertook to coerce public opinion at home and abroad. He repeatedly offended the American colonies by attempts to tax them and to regulate their trade. They rebelled in 1775 and signed their Declaration of Independence in 1776. Under the leadership of George Washington, and with the help of France, they achieved their independence. The battle of Yorktown (1781), won by Washington and the French navy, was the last important battle of the American Revolution. In spite of her great loss, England still retained Canada and her West India possessions and remained the first colonial power.

CHANGE IN LITERARY STANDARDS: ROMANTICISM

What is Romanticism? — In order to comprehend the dominating spirit of the next age, it is important to understand the meaning of the romantic movement. Between 1740 and 1780 certain romantic influences were at work in opposition to the teaching of the great classical writer, Dr. Samuel Johnson (p. 338), who was almost the literary dictator of the age.

The best short definition of romanticism is that of Victor Hugo, who calls it "liberalism in literature." This has the merit of covering all kinds of romantic movements. "Liberalism" here means toleration of departures from fixed standards, such as the classical couplet and didactic and satiric subjects. Romanticism is characterized by less regard for form than for matter, by a return to nature, and by encouragement of deep emotion. Romanticism says: "Be liberal enough not to sneer at authors when they discard narrow rules. Welcome a change and see if variety and feeling will not add more interest to literature."

In this period and the far more glorious one that followed, romanticism made its influence felt for the better in four different ways. An understanding of each of these will make us more intelligent critics.

In the first place, the romantic spirit is opposed to the prosaic. The romantic yearns for the light that never was on sea or land and longs to attain the unfulfilled ambitions of the soul, even when these in full measure are not possible. Sometimes these ambitions are so unrelated to the possible that the romantic has in certain usage become synonymous with the impractical or the absurd; but this is not its meaning in literature. The romantic may not always be "of imagination all compact," but it has a tendency in that direction. To the romanticists a reality of the imagination is as satisfying as a reality of the prosaic reason; hence, unlike the classicists, the romanticists can enjoy *The Tempest* and *A Midsummer Night's Dream*. The imagination is the only power that can grasp the unseen. Any movements that stimulate imaginative activity must give the individual more points of contact with the part of the world that does not obtrude itself on the physical senses, and especially with many facts of existence that cold intellectual activity can never comprehend. Hence, romanticism leads to greater breadth of view.

In the second place, the romantic is the opposite of the hackneyed. Hence, too much repetition may take away a necessary quality from what was once considered romantic. The epithets "ivory" and "raven," when applied to "brow" and to "tresses," respectively, were at first romantic; but much repetition has deprived them of this quality. If an age is to be considered romantic, it must look at things from a point of view somewhat different from that of the age immediately preceding. This change may be either in the character of the thought or in the manner of its presentation, or in both. An example of the formal element of change which appeared, consists in the substitution of blank verse and the Spenserian stanza for the classical couplets of the French school. In the next age, we shall find that the subject matter is no longer chiefly of the satiric or the didactic type.

In the third place, the highest type of romanticism encourages each author to express himself in an individual way, to color the world according to his own moods. This individual element often appears in the ideals that we fashion and in our characteristic conceptions of the spiritual significance of the world and its deepest realities. Two writers of this period by investing nature with a spirit of melancholy (p. 314) illustrate one of the many ways in which romantic thought seeks individuality of expression.

In the fourth place, the romantic movement encouraged the portrayal of broader experiences and especially the expression of deeper feeling. The mid-eighteenth century novels of Richardson and Fielding were strong agencies in this direction; and they were followed in the next age by the even more intense appeal of the great romantic poets to those thoughts and feelings that lie too deep for tears.

The classic school shunned as vulgar all exhibitions of enthusiasm and strong emotion, such as the love of Juliet and the jealousy of Othello; but the romanticists, knowing that the feelings had as much value and power as the intellect, encouraged their expression. Sometimes this tendency was carried to an extreme, both in fiction and in the sentimental drama (pp. 264, 337); but it was necessary for romanticism to call attention to the fact that great literature cannot neglect the world of feeling.

Early Romantic Influences. — The readers and imitators of the great romantic poet, Edmund Spenser, were growing in number. Previous to 1750, there was only one eighteenth-century edition of Spenser's works published in England. In 1758 three editions of the *Faerie Queene* appeared and charmed readers with the romantic enchantment of bowers, streams, dark forests, and adventures of heroic knights.

James Thomson (1700–1748), a Scotch poet, used the characteristic Spenserian form and subject matter for his romantic poem, *The Castle of Indolence* (1748). He placed his castle in "Spenser land": —

> "A pleasing land of drowsy-head it was,
>   Of dreams that wave before the half-shut eye;
> And of gay castles in the clouds that pass,
>   Forever flushing round a summer sky."

The influence of Shakespeare increased. In 1741 the great actor David Garrick captivated London by his presentation of Shakespeare's plays.

Milton's poetry, especially his *Il Penseroso*, with its individual expression of melancholy, its studious spirit, "commercing with the skies and bringing all Heaven before the eyes," left a strong impress on the romantic spirit of the age. The subject matter of his *Paradise Lost* satisfied the romantic requirement for strangeness and strong feeling. In the form of his verse, James Thomson shows the influence of Milton as well as of Spenser. Thomson's greatest achievement is *The Seasons* (1730), a romantic poem, written in Miltonic blank verse. He takes us where —

> "The hawthorn whitens; and the juicy groves
>   Put forth their buds."

He was one of the earliest poets to place Nature in the foreground, to make her the chief actor. He reverses what had been the usual poetic attitude and makes his lovers, shepherds, and harvesters serve largely as a background for the reflection of her moods instead of their own. The spring shower, the gusts sweeping over fields of corn, the sky saddened with the gathering storm of snow, are the very fabric of his verse. Unlike Wordsworth, Thomson had not sufficient genius to invest Nature with an intelligent, loving, companionable soul; but his pictures of her were sufficiently novel and attractive to cause such a classicist and lover of the town as Dr. Samuel Johnson to say: —

"The reader of *The Seasons* wonders that he never saw before what Thomson shows him, and that he never yet has felt what Thomson impresses."

Ossian " and The Castle of Otranto." — Two contemporary works proved a romantic influence out of all proportion to the worth of their subject matter.

Between 1760 and 1764 **James Macpherson**, a Highland schoolmaster, published a series of poems, which he claimed to have translated from an old manuscript, the work of Ossian, a Gaelic poet of the third century. This so-called translation in prose may have been forged either in whole or in part; but the weirdness, strange imagery, melancholy, and "other-world talk of ghosts riding on the tempest at nightfall," had a pronounced effect on romantic literature.

The Castle of Otranto: A Gothic Romance (1765) by **Horace Walpole** (1717–1797) tells a story of a Gothic castle where mysterious labyrinths and trap doors lead to the strangest adventures. The term "Gothic" had been contemptuously applied to whatever was medieval or out of date, whether in architecture, literature, or any form of art. The unusual improbabilities of this Gothic romance were welcomed by readers weary of commonplace works where nothing ever happens. The influence of *The Castle of Otranto* was even felt across the Atlantic, by Charles Brockden Brown (1771–1810), the early American novelist. Some less pronounced traces of such influence are discernible also in the work of Edgar Allan Poe and Nathaniel Hawthorne.

HORACE WALPOLE

Mrs. Anne Radcliffe (1764–1823) was a successor of

Walpole in the field of Gothic romance. Her stories, *The Romance of the Forest* and *The Mysteries of Udolpho*, have their castle and their thrilling, unnatural episodes. Lack of portrayal of character and excess of supernatural incident were causing fiction to suffer severe deterioration.

Percy's Reliques and Translation of Mallet's Northern Antiquities. — In 1765 Thomas Percy (1729-1811) published *The Reliques of Ancient English Poetry*, an epoch-making work in the history of the romantic movement. The *Reliques* is a collection of old English ballads and songs, many of which have a romantic story to tell. Scott drew inspiration from them, and Wordsworth acknowledged his indebtedness to their influence. So important was this collection that it has been called "the Bible of the Romantic Reformation."

In 1770 appeared Percy's translation of Mallet's *Northern Antiquities*. For the first time the English world was given an easily accessible volume which disclosed the Norse mythology in all its strength and weirdness. As classical mythology had become hackneyed, poets like Gray rejoiced that there was a new fountain to which they could turn. Thor and his invincible hammer, the Frost Giants, Bifrost or the Rainbow Bridge, Odin, the Valkyries, Valhal, the sad story of Baldur, and the Twilight of the Gods, have appealed strongly to a race which takes pride in its own mythology, to a race which to-day loves to hear Wagner's translation of these myths into the music of *Die Walküre*, *Siegfried*, and *Götterdämmerung*.

Thomas Chatterton, 1752-1770. — This Bristol boy was early in his teens impressed with Percy's *Reliques* and with the fact that Macpherson's claim to having discovered *Ossian* in old manuscripts had made him famous. Chatterton spent much time in the interesting old church of St.

Mary Redcliffe, of which his ancestors had been sextons for several generations. He studied the manuscripts in an old chest and began to write a series of poems, which he claimed to have discovered among the parchments left by Thomas Rowley, a fifteenth-century monk.

Chatterton was unsuccessful in finding a publisher, and he determined to go to London, where he thought that, like other authors, he could live by his pen. In April, 1770, at the age of seventeen, he left Bristol for London, where he took poison in August of the same year to escape a slower death by starvation.

His romantic poetry and pathetic end appealed to all the great poets. Wordsworth spoke of him as "the marvelous boy"; Coleridge called him "young-eyed Poesy"; Shelley honored him in *Adonais;* and Keats inscribed *Endymion* to his memory. Traces of his influence may be found in Coleridge and Keats.

The greatest charm of Chatterton's verse appears in unusual epithets and unexpected poetic turns, such, for instance, as may be noted in these lines from his best "Rowley" poem, *Aella, a Tragycal Enterlude:* —

> "Sweet his tongue as the throstle's note;
> Quick in dance as thought can be."

> "Hark! the raven flaps his wing
>   In the briar'd dell below;
> Hark! the death-owl loud doth sing,
>   To the night-mares as they go."

While Chatterton did not leave enough verse of surpassing merit to rank him as a great poet, his work nevertheless entitles him to be chosen from among all his boyish peers to receive the laurel wreath for song.

The Literature of Melancholy. — The choice of subjects in which the emotion of melancholy was given full sway shows one direction taken by the romantic movement. Here, the influence of Milton's *Il Penseroso* can often be traced. The exquisite *Ode to Evening*, by **William Collins** (1721–1759), shows the love for nature's solitudes where this emotion may be nursed. Lines like these:—

> ". . . be mine the hut,
> That, from the mountain's side,
> Views wilds and swelling floods,
> And hamlets brown, and dim-discovered spires;
> And hears their simple bell; and marks o'er all
> Thy dewy fingers draw
> The gradual dusky veil,"

caused Swinburne to say: "Corot on canvas might have signed his *Ode to Evening*."

THOMAS GRAY

The high-water mark of the poetry of melancholy of this period was reached in **Thomas Gray's** (1716–1771) *Elegy Written in a Country Churchyard* (1751). The poet with great art selected those natural phenomena which cast additional gloom upon the scene. We may notice in the very first stanza that the images were chosen with this end in view:—

> "The curfew tolls the knell of parting day,
> The lowing herd winds slowly o'er the lea,
> The plowman homeward plods his weary way,
> And leaves the world to darkness and to me."

Then we listen to the droning flight of the beetle, to the drowsy tinklings from a distant fold, to the moping owl in an ivy-mantled tower. Each natural object, either directly or by contrast, reflects the mood of man. Nature serves as a background for the display of emotion.

Gosse says in his *Life of Gray:* "The *Elegy* has exercised an influence on all the poetry of Europe, from Denmark to Italy, from France to Russia. With the exception of certain works of Byron and Shakespeare, no English poem has been so widely admired and imitated abroad."

STOKE POGES CHURCHYARD (SCENE OF GRAY'S ELEGY)

The Conflict between Romanticism and Classicism. — The influences of this period were not entirely in the direction of romanticism. Samuel Johnson, the literary dictator of the age, was unsparing in his condemnation of the movement. The weight of his opinion kept many romantic tendencies in check. Even authors like Gray were afraid to adopt the new creed in its entirety. In one stanza of his *Hymn to Adversity* we find four capitalized abstractions, after the manner of the classical school: Folly, Noise, Laughter, Prosperity; and the following two lay figures, little better than abstractions: —

"The summer Friend, the flattering Foe."

These abstractions have little warmth or human interest. After Gray had studied the Norse mythology, we find him using such strong expressions as "iron-sleet of arrowy shower." Collins's ode on *The Passions* contains seventeen personified abstractions, from "pale Melancholy" to "brown Exercise."

The conflict between these two schools continues; and many people still think that any poetry which shows polished regularity must be excellent. To prove this statement, we have only to turn to the magazines and glance at the current poetry, which often consists of words rather artificially strung together without the soul of feeling or of thought.

THE DEVELOPMENT OF THE MODERN NOVEL

The Growth of Prose Fiction. — Authentic history does not take us back to the time when human beings were not solaced by tales. The *Bible* contains stories of marked interest. *Beowulf*, the medieval romances (p. 64), the *Canterbury Tales*, and the ballads relate stories in verse.

For a long time the knight and his adventures held the place of honor in fiction; but the time came when improbable or impossible achievements began to pall. The knight who meets with all kinds of adventures and rescues everybody, is admirably burlesqued in *Don Quixote* by the Spanish author Cervantes, which appeared at the beginning of the seventeenth century. This world-famous romance shows by its ridicule that the taste for the impossible adventures of chivalry was beginning to pall. The following title to one of the chapters of *Don Quixote* is sufficiently suggestive: "Chapter LVIII. — Which tells how Adventures came crowding on Don

Quixote in Such Numbers that they gave him No Breathing Time."

Much prose fiction was written during the Elizabethan Age. We have seen that Lyly's *Euphues* and Sidney's *Arcadia* contain the germs of romance. Two of the novelists of the sixteenth century, Robert Greene (1560?-1592) and Thomas Lodge (1558?-1625), helped to give to Shakespeare the plots of two of his plays. Greene's novel *Pandosto* suggested the plot of *The Winter's Tale*, and Lodge's *Rosalind* was the immediate source of the plot of *As You Like It*.

Although Greene died in want at the age of thirty-two, he was the most prolific of the Elizabethan novelists. His most popular stories deal with the passion of love as well as with adventure. He was also the pioneer of those realistic novelists who go among the slums to study life at first hand. Greene made a careful study of the sharpers and rascals of London and published his observations in a series of realistic pamphlets.

Thomas Nashe (1567-1601) was the one who introduced into England the picaresque novel in *The Unfortunate Traveller, or the Life of Jacke Wilton* (1594). The picaresque novel (Spanish, *picaro*, a rogue) is a story of adventure in which rascally tricks play a prominent part. This type of fiction came from Spain and attained great popularity in England. Jacke Wilton is page to a noble house. Many of his sharp tricks were doubtless drawn from real life. Nashe is a worthy prede-

From a British Museum MS.

A BLIND BEGGAR ROBBED OF HIS DRINK

cessor of Defoe in narrating adventures that seem to be founded on actual life.

In spite of an increasing tendency to picture the life of the time, Elizabethan prose fiction did not entirely discard the matter and style of the medieval romances. All types of prose fiction were then too prone to deal with exceptional characters or unusual events. Even realists like Greene did not present typical Elizabethan life. The greatest realist in the prose fiction of the Elizabethan Age was Thomas Deloney (1543?–1600), who chose his materials from the everyday life of common people. He had been a traveling artisan, and he knew how to paint "the life and love of the Elizabethan workshop." He wrote *The Gentle Craft*, a collection of tales about shoemakers, and *Jack of Newberry*, a story of a weaver.

The seventeenth century produced *The Pilgrim's Progress*, a powerful allegorical story of the journey of a soul toward the New Jerusalem. Mrs. Aphra Behn (1640–1689), dramatist and novelist, shows the faults of the Restoration drama in her short tales, which helped to prepare the way for the novelists of the next century. Her best story is *Oroonoko* (1658), a tale of an African slave, which has been called "the first humanitarian novel in English," and a predecessor of *Uncle Tom's Cabin*.

Fiction in the First Part of the Eighteenth Century. — Defoe's *Robinson Crusoe* (p. 274) shows a great advance over preceding fiction. In the hands of Defoe, fiction became as natural as fact. Leslie Stephen rightly calls his stories "simple history minus the facts." Swift's *Gulliver's Travels* (1726) is artfully planned to make its impossibilities seem like facts. *Robinson Crusoe* took another forward step in showing how circumstances and environment react on character and develop the power to grapple with difficulties and overcome them. Unlike the majority of modern novels, Defoe's masterpiece does not contain a love story.

The essay of life and manners at the beginning of the eighteenth century presents us at once with various pigments necessary for the palette of the novelist. Students on turning to the second number of *The Spectator* will find sketches of six different types of character, which are worthy to be framed and hung in a permanent gallery of English fiction. The portrait of Sir Roger de Coverley may even claim one of the places of honor on the walls.

Distinction between the Romance and the Modern Novel. — The romances and tales of adventure which had been so long in vogue differ widely from the modern novel. Many of them pay but little attention to probability; but those which do not offend in this respect generally rely on a succession of stirring incidents to secure attention. Novels showing the analytic skill of Thackeray's *Vanity Fair*, or the development of character in George Eliot's *Silas Marner* would have been little read in competition with stirring tales of adventure, if such novels had appeared before a taste for them had been developed by habits of trained observation and thought.

We may broadly differentiate the romance from the modern novel by saying that the romance deals primarily with incident and adventure for their own sake, while the novel concerns itself with these only in so far as they are necessary for a faithful picture of life or for showing the development of character.

Again, the novel gave a much more prominent position to that important class of human beings who do the most of the world's work, — a type that the romance had been inclined to neglect.

From an original drawing.

Samuel Richardson, the First Modern English Novelist. — Samuel Richardson (1689-1761) was born in Derbyshire. When he was only thirteen years old some of the young women of the neighborhood unconsciously began to train him for a novelist by employing him to conduct their love correspondence. This training partly accounts for the fact that every one of his novels is merely a collection of letters, written by the chief characters to each other and to their friends, to narrate the progress of events.

At the age of fifteen Richardson went to London and learned the printer's trade, which he followed for the rest of his life. When he was about fifty years old, some pub-

DEVELOPMENT OF THE MODERN NOVEL

lishers asked him to prepare a letter writer which would be useful to country people and to others who could not express themselves with a pen. The idea occurred to him of making these letters tell a connected story. The result was the first modern novel, *Pamela*, published in four volumes in 1740. This was followed by *Clarissa Harlowe*, in seven volumes, in 1747-48, and this by *Sir Charles Grandison*, in seven volumes, in 1753.

The affairs in the lives of the leading characters are so minutely dissected, the plot is evolved so slowly and in a way so unlike the astonishing bounds of the old romance, that one is tempted to say that Richardson's novels progress more slowly than events in life. One secret of his success depends on the fact that we feel that he is deeply interested in all his characters. He is as much interested in the heroine of his masterpiece, *Clarissa Harlowe*, as if she were his own daughter. He has the remarkable power of so thoroughly identifying himself with his characters that, after we are introduced to them, we can name them when we hear selections read from their letters.

The length and slow development of his novels repel modern readers, but there was so little genuinely interesting matter in the middle of the eighteenth century that many were sorry his novels were no longer. The novelty of productions of this type also added to their interest. His many faults are largely those of his age. He wearies his readers with his didactic aims. He is narrow and prosy. He poses as a great moralist, but he teaches the morality of direct utility.

The drama and the romance had helped to prepare the way for the novel of everyday domestic life. While this way seemed simple, natural, and inevitable, Richardson was the first to travel in it. Defoe had invested fictitious adventure with reality. Richardson transferred the real human life around him to the pages of fiction. The ascendancy of French influence was noteworthy for a considerable period after the Restoration. England could now repay some of her debt. Richardson exerted powerful influence on the literature of France as well as on that of other continental nations.

From the original sketch by Hogarth.
HENRY FIELDING

Henry Fielding, 1707-1754. — The greatest novelist of the eighteenth century, and one of the greatest that England ever produced, was Henry Fielding, who was born in Sharpham Park, Somersetshire. After graduating at the University of Leyden, he became a playwright, a lawyer, a judge of a police court, and, most important of all, a novelist, or a historian of society, as he preferred to style himself.

When Richardson's *Pamela* appeared, Fielding determined to write a story caricaturing its morality and sentiment, which he considered hypocritical. Before he had gone very far he discovered where his abilities lay, and, abandoning his narrow, satiric aims, he wrote *Joseph Andrews* (1742), a novel far more interesting than *Pamela*. *Jonathan Wild the Great* (1743) tells the story of a rogue who was finally hanged. In 1749 appeared Fielding's masterpiece, *Tom Jones*, and in 1751 his last novel, *Amelia*.

Richardson lacks humor, but Fielding is one of the greatest humorists of the eighteenth century. Fielding is also a master of plot. From all literature, Coleridge selected, for perfection of plot, *The Alchemist, Œdipus Tyrannus*, and *Tom Jones*.

Fielding's novels often lack refinement, but they palpitate with life. His pages present a wonderful variety of characters, chosen from almost all walks of life. He could draw admirable portraits of women. Thackeray says of Amelia, the heroine of the novel that bears her name: —

"To have invented that character, is not only a triumph of art, but it is a good action. They say it was in his own home that Fielding knew her and loved her, and from his own wife that he drew the most charming character in English fiction. . . . I admire the author of *Amelia*, and thank the kind master who introduced me to that sweet and delightful companion and friend. *Amelia*, perhaps, is not a better story than *Tom Jones*, but it has the better ethics; the prodigal repents at least before forgiveness,—whereas that odious broad-backed Mr. Jones carries off his beauty with scarce an interval of remorse for his manifold errors and shortcomings. . . . I am angry with Jones. Too much of the plum cake and rewards of life fall to that boisterous, swaggering young scapegrace." [1]

The "prodigal" to whom Thackeray refers is Captain Booth, the husband of Amelia, and "Mr. Jones" is the hero of *Tom Jones*. Fielding's wife, under the name of Sophia Western, is also the heroine of *Tom Jones*. It is probable that in the characters of Captain Booth and Tom Jones, Fielding drew a partial portrait of himself. He

[1] *The English Humorists of the Eighteenth Century.*

seems, however, to have changed in middle life, for his biographer, Austin Dobson, says of him: "He was a loving father and a kind husband; he exerted his last energies in philanthropy and benevolence; he expended his last ink in defence of Christianity."

Fielding shows the eighteenth-century love of satire. He hates that hypocrisy which tries to conceal itself under a mask of morality. In the evolution of the plots of his novels, he invariably puts such characters in positions that tear away their mask. He displays almost savage pleasure in making them ridiculous. Perhaps the lack of spirituality of the age finds the most ample expression in his pages; but Chaucer's Parish Priest and Fielding's Parson Adams are typical of those persisting moral forces that have bequeathed a heritage of power to England.

LAURENCE STERNE

Sterne and Smollett. — With Richardson and Fielding it is customary to associate two other mid-eighteenth century novelists, Laurence Sterne (1713–1768) and Tobias Smollett (1721–1771). Between 1759 and 1767 Sterne wrote his first novel, *The Life and Opinions of Tristram Shandy, Gentleman*, which presents the delight-

From a drawing by B. Westmacott.
UNCLE TOBY AND CORPORAL TRIM

fully comic and eccentric members of the Shandy family, among whom Uncle Toby is the masterpiece. In 1768 Sterne gave to the world that compound of fiction, essays, and sketches of travel known as *A Sentimental Journey through France and Italy.* The adjective "sentimental" in the title should be specially noted, for it defines Sterne's attitude toward everything in life. He is habitually sentimental in treating not only those things fitted to awaken deep emotion, but also those trivial incidents which ordinarily cause scarcely a ripple of feeling. Although he is sometimes a master of pathos, he frequently gives an exhibition of weak and forced sentimentalism. He more uniformly excels in subtle humor, which is his next most conspicuous characteristic.

TOBIAS SMOLLETT

Roderick Random (1748), *Peregrine Pickle* (1751), and *The Expedition of Humphrey Clinker* (1771) are Smollett's best novels. They are composed mainly of a succession of stirring or humorous incidents. In relying for interest more on adventure than on the drawing of character, he reverts to the picaresque (see p. 317) type of story.

The Relation of Richardson, Fielding, Sterne, and Smollett to Subsequent Fiction. — Although the modern reader frequently complains that these older novelists often seem heavy, slow in movement, unrefined, and too ready to draw a moral or preach a sermon, yet these four men hold an important place in the history of fiction. With varying degrees of excellence, Richardson, Fielding, and Sterne all have the rare power of portraying character from within, of interpreting real life. Some novelists resort to the far easier task of painting merely external characteristics and mannerisms. Smollett belongs to the latter class. His effective focusing of external peculiarities and caricaturing of exceptional individuals has had a far-reaching influence, which may be traced even in the work of so great a novelist as Charles Dickens. Fielding, on the other hand, had great influence on Thackeray, who has recorded in *The English Humorists of the Eighteenth Century* his admiration for his earlier fellow-craftsman.

Although subsequent English fiction has invaded many new fields, although it has entered the domain of history and of sociology, it is not too much to say that later novelists have advanced on the general lines marked out by these four mid-eighteenth century pioneers. We may even affirm with Gosse that "the type of novel invented in England about 1740-50 continued for sixty or seventy years to be the only model for Continental fiction; and criticism has traced in every French novelist, in particular, the stamp of Richardson, if not of Sterne, and of Fielding."

PHILOSOPHICAL, HISTORICAL, AND POLITICAL PROSE

Philosophy. — Although the majority of eighteenth-century writers disliked speculative thought and resolutely turned away from it, yet the age produced some remarkable philosophical works, which are still discussed, and which have powerfully affected later thought. **David Hume** (1711–1776) is the greatest metaphysician of the century. He took for his starting point the conclusions of a contemporary philosopher, George Berkeley (1685–1753).

Berkeley had said that ideas are the only real existing entities, that matter is merely another term for the ideas in the Mind of the Infinite and has no existence outside of mind. He maintained that if every quality should be taken away from matter, no matter would remain; *e.g.*, if color, sweetness, sourness, form, and all other qualities should be taken away from an apple, there would be no apple. Now, a quality is a mental representation based on a sensation, and this quality varies as the sensation varies; in other words, the object is not a stable immutable thing. It is only a thing as I perceive it. Berkeley's idealistic position was taken to crush atheistic materialism.

Hume attempted to rear on Berkeley's position an impregnable citadel of skepticism. He accepted Berkeley's conclusion that we know nothing of matter, and then attempted to show that inferences based on ideas might be equally illusory. Hume attacked the validity of the reasoning process itself. He endeavored to show that there is no such thing as cause and effect in either the mental or the material world.

Hume's *Treatise of Human Nature* (1739-1740), in which these views are stated, is one of the world's epoch-making works in philosophy. Its conclusion startled the great German metaphysician Kant and roused him to action. The questions thus raised by Hume have never been answered to the satisfaction of all philosophers.

Hume's skepticism is the most thoroughgoing that the world has ever seen; for he attacks the certainty of our knowledge of both mind and matter. But he dryly remarks that his own doubts disappear when he leaves his study. He avoids a runaway horse and inquires of a friend the way to a certain house in Edinburgh, relying as much on the evidence of his eyes and on the directions of his friend as if these philosophic doubts had never been raised.

Historical Prose. — In carefully elaborated and highly finished works of history, the eighteenth century surpasses

From the painting by Sir Joshua Reynolds.

E. Gibbon.

its predecessors. *The History of England* by David Hume, the philosopher, is the first work of the kind to add to the history of politics and the affairs of state an account of the people and their manners. This *History* is distinguished for its polished ease and clearness. Unfortunately, the work is written from a partisan point of view. Hume was a Tory, and took the side of the Stuarts against the Puritans. He sometimes misrepresented facts if they did not uphold his views. His *History* is consequently read more to-day as a literary classic than as an authority.

Edward Gibbon (1737-1794) is the greatest historian of the century. His monumental work, *The History of the Decline and Fall of the Roman Empire*, in six volumes, begins with the reign of Trajan, A.D. 98, and closes with the fall of the Eastern Roman Empire at Constantinople in 1453. Gibbon constructed a "Roman road" through nearly fourteen centuries of history; and he built it so well that another on the same plan has not yet been found necessary. E. A. Freeman says: "He remains the one historian of the eighteenth century whom modern research has neither set aside nor threatened to set aside." In preparing his *History*, Gibbon spent fifteen years. Every chapter was the subject of long-continued study and careful original research. From the chaotic materials which he found, he constructed a history remarkable as well for its scholarly precision as for the vastness of the field covered.

His sentences follow one another in magnificent procession. One feels that they are the work of an artist. They are thickly sprinkled with fine-sounding words derived from the Latin. The 1611 version of the first four chapters of the *Gospel* of John averages 96 per cent of Anglo-Saxon words, and Shakespeare 89 per cent, while Gibbon's average of 70 per cent is the lowest of any great writer. He has all the coldness of the classical school, and he shows but little sympathy with the great human struggles that are described in his pages. He has been well styled "a skillful anatomical demonstrator of the dead framework of society." With all its excellences, his work has, therefore, those faults which are typical of the **eighteenth century.**

From the painting by Sir Joshua Reynolds, National Portrait Gallery.

Political Prose. — Edmund Burke (1729-1797) was a distinguished statesman and member of the House of Commons in an important era of English history, — a time when the question of the independence of the American colonies was paramount, and when the spirit of revolt against established forms was in the air. He is the greatest political writer of the eighteenth century.

Burke's best productions are *Speech on American Taxation* (1774) and *Speech on Conciliation with America* (1775). His *Reflections on the Revolution in France* is also noteworthy. His prose is distinguished for the following qualities: (1) He is one of the greatest masters of metaphor and imagery in English prose. Only Carlyle (p. 487) surpasses him in the use of metaphorical language. (2) Burke's breadth of thought and wealth of expression enable him to present an idea from many different points of view, so that if his readers do not comprehend his exposition from one side, they may from another. He endeavors to attach what he says to something in the experience of his hearers or readers; and he remembers that the experience of all is not the same. (3) It follows that his imagery and figures lay all kinds of knowledge under contribution. At one time he draws an illustration from manufacturing; at another, from history; at another, from the butcher shop. (4) His work displays intense earnestness, love of truth, strength of logical reasoning, vividness of imagination, and breadth of view, all of which are necessary qualities in prose that is to mold the opinions of men.

It is well to note that Burke's careful study of English literature contributed largely to his success as a writer. His use of Bible phraseology and his familiarity with poetry led a critic to say that any one "neglects the most valuable repository of rhetoric in the English language, who has not well studied the English Bible. . . . The cadence of Burke's sentences always reminds us that prose writing is only to be perfected by a thorough study of the poetry of the language."

OLIVER GOLDSMITH, 1728-1774

Life and Minor Works. — Oliver Goldsmith was born of English parents in the little village of Pallas in the center of Ireland. His father, a poor clergyman, soon moved a short distance to Lissoy, which furnished some of the suggestions for *The Deserted Village*.

From the painting by Sir Joshua Reynolds, National Portrait Gallery.

Oliver Goldsmith

Goldsmith went as a charity student to Dublin University, where, like Swift, he graduated at the bottom of his class. Goldsmith tried in turn to become a clergyman, a teacher, a lawyer, and a doctor, but failed in all these fields. Then he wandered over the continent of Europe for a year and accumulated some experiences that he used in writing *The Traveler*. He returned to London in 1757, and, after an ineffectual attempt to live by practicing medicine, turned to literature. In this profession he at first managed to make only a precarious living, for the most part as a hack-writer, working for periodicals and filling contracts to compile popular histories of England, Greece, Rome, and *Animated Nature*. He had so much skill in knowing what to retain, emphasize, or subordinate, and so much genius in presenting in an attractive style what he wrote, that his work of this kind met with a readier sale than his masterpieces. Of the *History of Animated Nature*, Johnson said: "Goldsmith, sir, will give us a very fine book on the subject, but if he can tell a horse from a cow, that I believe may be the extent of his knowledge of natural history."

His first literary reputation was gained by a series of letters, supposed to be written by a Chinaman as a record of his impressions of England. These letters or essays, like so much of the work of Addison and Steele, appeared first in a periodical; but they were afterwards collected under the title, *Citizen of the World* (1761). The interesting creation of these essays is Beau Tibbs, a poverty-stricken man, who derives pleasure from boasting of his frequent association with the nobility.

It was not until the last ten years of his life that Goldsmith became famous. He certainly earned enough then to be free from care, had he but known how to use his money. His improvidence in giving to beggars and in squandering his earnings on expensive rooms, garments, and dinners, however, kept him always in debt.

From a drawing by B. Westmacott.
GOLDSMITH GIVES DR. JOHNSON THE MS. OF THE VICAR OF WAKEFIELD

One evening he gave away his blankets to a woman who told him a pitiful tale. The cold was so bitter during the night that he had to open the ticking of his bed and crawl inside. Although this happened when he was a young man, it was typical of his usual response to appeals for help. When his landlady had him arrested for failing to pay his rent, he sent for Johnson to come and extricate him. Johnson asked him if he had nothing that would discharge the debt, and Goldsmith handed him the manuscript of *The Vicar of Wakefield*. Johnson reported his action to Boswell, as follows:—

CANONBURY TOWER, LONDON, WHERE GOLDSMITH WROTE SOME OF HIS FAMOUS WORK

"I looked into it and saw its merit; told the landlady I should soon return; and having gone to a bookseller, sold it for sixty pounds."

During his last years, Goldsmith sometimes received as much as £800 in twelve months; but the more he earned, the deeper he plunged into debt. When he died, in 1774, at the age of forty-five, he owed £2000. He was loved because —

". . . e'en his failings leaned to virtue's side."

His grave by the Temple Church on Fleet Street, London, is each year visited by thousands who feel genuine affection for him in spite of his shortcomings.

Masterpieces. — His best work consists of two poems, *The Traveler* and *The Deserted Village;* a story, *The Vicar of Wakefield;* and a play, *She Stoops to Conquer.*

The object of *The Traveler* (1765), a highly polished moral and didactic poem, was to show that happiness is independent of climate, and hence to justify the conclusion : —

> "Vain, very vain, my weary search to find
> That bliss which only centers in the mind."

The Deserted Village (1770) also has a didactic aim, for which we care little. Its finest parts, those which impress us most, were suggested to Goldsmith by his youthful experiences. We naturally remember the sympathetic portrait of the poet's father, "the village preacher" : —

> "A man he was to all the country dear
> And passing rich with forty pounds a year.
>
> . . . .
>
> His house was known to all the vagrant train;
> He chid their wanderings but relieved their pain."

The lines relating to the village schoolmaster are almost as well known as Scripture. Previous to this time, the eighteenth century had not produced a poem as natural, sincere, and sympathetic in its descriptions and portraits as *The Deserted Village.*

The Vicar of Wakefield is a delightful romantic novel, which Andrew Lang classes among books "to be read once a year." Goldsmith's own criticism of the story in the *Advertisement* announcing it has not yet been surpassed : —

"There are an hundred faults in this Thing, and an hundred things might be said to prove them beauties. But it is needless. A book may be amusing with numerous errors, or it may be very dull without a single absurdity. The hero of this piece unites in himself the three greatest characters upon earth: he is a priest, an husbandman, and the father of a family. He is drawn as ready to teach and ready to obey; as simple in affluence, and majestic in adversity."

The Vicar of Wakefield has faults of improbability and of plot construction; in fact, the plot is so poorly constructed that the novel would have been almost a failure, had other qualities not insured success. The story lives because Dr. Primrose and his family show with such genuineness the

From a drawing by G. Patrick Nelson.
DR. PRIMROSE AND HIS FAMILY

abiding lovable traits of human nature, — kindliness, unselfishness, good humor, hope, charity, — the very spirit of the *Sermon on the Mount*. Goethe rejoiced that he felt the influence of this story at the critical moment of his mental development. Goldsmith has added to the world's stock of kindliness, and he has taught many to avoid what he calls "the fictitious demands of happiness."

Goldsmith wrote two plays, both hearty comedies. The less successful, *The Good-Natured Man* (acted 1768), brought him in £500. His next play, *She Stoops to Conquer*, a comedy of manners, is a landmark in the history of the drama. The taste of the age demanded regular, vapid, sentimental plays. Here was a comedy that disregarded the conventions and presented in quick succession a series of hearty humorous scenes. Even the manager of the theater predicted the failure of the play; but from the time of its first appearance in 1773, this comedy of manners has had an unbroken record of triumphs. A century later it ran one hundred nights in London. Authorities say that it has never been performed without success, not even by amateurs. Like all of Goldsmith's best productions, it was based on actual experience. In his young days a wag directed him to a private house for an inn. Goldsmith went there and with much flourish gave his orders for entertainment. The subtitle of the comedy is *The Mistakes of a Night;* and the play shows the situations which developed when its hero, Tony Lumpkin, sent two lovers to a pretended inn, which was really the home of the young ladies to be wooed.

It is interesting to note that his contemporary, **Richard Brinsley Sheridan** (1751-1816), produced, shortly after the great success of *She Stoops to Conquer*, the only other eighteenth-century comedies that retain their popularity, *The Rivals* (1775) and *The School for Scandal* (1777), which contributed still further to the overthrow of the sentimental comedy of the age.

General Characteristics. — Goldsmith is a romanticist at heart; but he felt the strong classical influences of Johnson and of the earlier school. In his poetry, Goldsmith used classical couplets and sometimes classical subject matter, but the didactic parts of his poems are the poorest. His greatest successes, such as the pictures of the village preacher and the schoolmaster in *The Deserted Village* and of Dr. Primrose and his family in *The Vicar of Wakefield*, show the warm human sympathy of the romantic school.

The qualities for which he is most noted are (1) a sane and saving altruistic philosophy of life, pervaded with rare humor, and (2) a style of remarkable ease, grace, and clearness, expressed in copious and apt language.

She Stoops to Conquer marks a change in the drama of the time, because, in Dobson's phrase, it bade "good-bye to sham Sentiment."

> ". . . this play it appears
> Dealt largely in laughter and nothing in tears."

SAMUEL JOHNSON, 1709-1784

Early Struggles. — Michael Johnson, an intelligent bookseller in Lichfield, Staffordshire, was in 1709 blessed with a son who was to occupy a unique position in literature, a position gained not so much by his writings as by his spoken words and great personality.

Samuel was prepared for Oxford at various schools and in the paternal bookstore, where he read widely and voraciously, but without much system. He said that at the age of eighteen, the year before he entered Oxford, he knew almost as much as at fifty-three. Poverty kept him from remaining at Oxford long enough to take a degree. He left the university, and, for more than a quarter of a century, struggled doggedly against poverty. When he was twenty-five, he married a widow of forty-eight. With the money which she brought him, he opened

SAMUEL JOHNSON

From the painting by Sir Joshua Reynolds.

a private school, but failed. He never had more than eight pupils, one of whom was the actor, David Garrick.

In 1737 Johnson went to London and sought employment as a hack writer. Sometimes he had no money with which to hire a lodging, and was compelled to walk the streets all night to keep warm. Johnson reached London in the very darkest days for struggling authors, who were often subjected to the greatest hardships. They were the objects of general contempt, to which Pope's *Dunciad* had largely contributed.

During this period Johnson did much hack work for the *Gentleman's Magazine*. He was also the author of two satirical poems, *London* (1738) and *The Vanity of Human Wishes* (1749), which won much praise.

Later Years. — By the time he had been for ten years in London, his abilities were sufficiently well known to the leading booksellers for them to hire him to compile a *Dictionary of the English Language* for £1575. He was seven years at this work, finishing it in 1755. Between 1750 and 1760 he wrote the matter for two periodicals, *The Rambler* (1750–1752) and *The Idler* (1758–1760), which contain papers on manners and morals. He intended to model these papers on the lines of *The Tatler* and *The Spectator*, but his essays are for the most part ponderously dull and uninteresting.

In 1762, for the first time, he was really an independent man, for then George III. gave him a life pension of £300 a year. Even as late as 1759, in order to pay his mother's funeral expenses, Johnson had been obliged to dash off the romance of *Rasselas* in a week; but from the time he received his pension, he had leisure "to cross his legs and have his talk out" in some of the most distinguished gatherings of the eighteenth century. During the rest of his life he produced little besides *Lives of the English Poets*, which is his most important contribution to literature. In 1784 he died, and was buried in Westminster Abbey among the poets whose lives he had written.

A Man of Character. — Any one who will read Macaulay's *Life of Johnson*[1] may become acquainted with some of Johnson's most striking peculiarities; but these do not constitute his claims to greatness. He had qualities that

---

[1] To be found in *Encyclopædia Britannica*, or in Macaulay's collected *Essays*.

made him great in spite of his peculiarities. He knocked down a publisher who insulted him, and he would never take insolence from a superior; but there is no case on record of his having been unkind to an inferior. Goldsmith said: "Johnson has nothing of a bear but the skin." When some one manifested surprise that Johnson should have assisted a worthless character, Goldsmith promptly replied: "He has

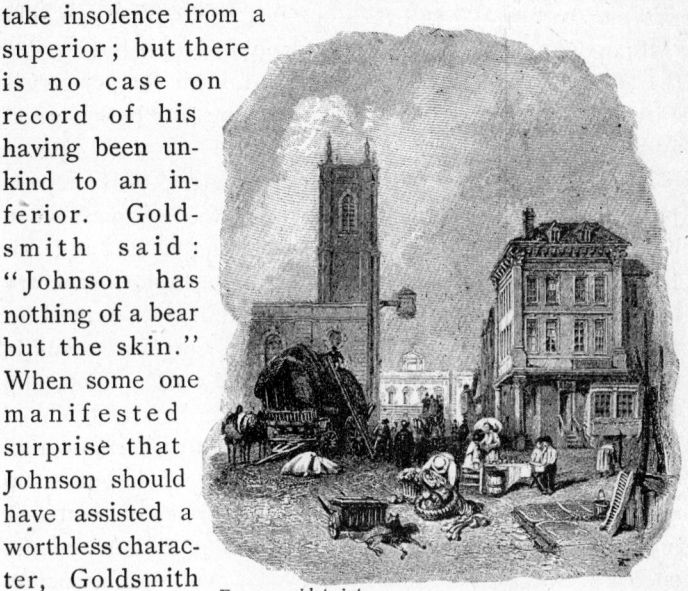

From an old print.

SAMUEL JOHNSON'S BIRTHPLACE

now become miserable, and that insures the protection of Johnson."

Johnson, coming home late at night, would frequently slip a coin into the hand of a sleeping street Arab, who, on awakening, was rejoiced to find provision thus made for his breakfast. He spent the greater part of his pension on the helpless, several of whom he received into his own house.

There have been many broader and more scholarly Englishmen, but there never walked the streets of London a man who battled more courageously for what he thought was right. The more we know of him, the more certain are we to agree with this closing sentence from Macaulay's *Life of Johnson:* "And it is but just to say that our intimate acquaintance with what he would himself have called the anfractuosities of his intellect and of his temper serves only to strengthen our conviction that he was both a great and a good man."

A Great Converser and Literary Lawgiver. — By nature Johnson was fitted to be a talker. He was happiest when he had intelligent listeners. Accordingly, he and Sir Joshua Reynolds, the artist, founded the famous Literary Club in 1764. During Johnson's lifetime this had for members such men as Edmund Burke, Oliver Goldsmith, Charles James Fox, James Boswell, Edward Gibbon, and David Garrick. Macaulay says : "The verdicts pronounced by this conclave on new books were speedily known over all London, and were sufficient to sell off a whole edition in a day, or to condemn the sheets to the service of the trunk maker and the pastry cook. . . . To predominate over such a society was not easy; yet even over such a society Johnson predominated."

He was consulted as an oracle on all kinds of subjects, and his replies were generally the pith of common sense. So famous had Johnson become for his conversations that George III. met him on purpose to hear him talk. A committee from forty of the leading London booksellers waited on Johnson to ask him to write the *Lives of the English Poets.* There was then in England no other man with so much influence in the world of literature.

Boswell's Life of Johnson. — In 1763 James Boswell (1740–1795), a Scotchman, met Johnson and devoted much time to copying the words that fell from the great Doctor's lips and to noting his individual traits. We must go to

Boswell's *Life of Johnson*, the greatest of all biographies, to read of Johnson as he lived and talked; in short, to learn those facts which render him far more famous than his written works.

Leslie Stephen says: "I would still hope that to many readers Boswell has been what he has certainly been to some, the first writer who gave them a love of English literature, and the most charming of all companions long after the bloom of novelty has departed. I subscribe most cheerfully to Mr. Lewes's statement that he estimates his acquaintances according to their estimate of Boswell."

JAMES BOSWELL

A Champion of the Classical School. — Johnson was a powerful adherent of classicism, and he did much to defer the coming of romanticism. His poetry is formal, and it shows the classical fondness for satire and aversion to sentiment. The first two lines of his greatest poem, *The Vanity of Human Wishes* —

> "Let observation with extensive view
> Survey mankind from China to Peru,"

show the classical couplet, which he employs, and they afford an example of poetry produced by a sonorous combination of words. "Observation," "view," and "survey" are nearly synonymous terms. Such conscious effort centered on word building subtracts something from poetic feeling.

His critical opinions of literature manifest his preference for classical themes and formal modes of treatment. He says of Shakespeare: "It is incident to him to be now and then entangled with an unwieldy sentiment, which he cannot well express . . . the equality of words to things is very often neglected."

Although there is much sensible, stimulating criticism in Johnson's *Lives of the Poets*, yet he shows positive repugnance to the pastoral references — the flocks and shepherds, the oaten flute, the woods and desert caves — of Milton's *Lycidas*. "Its form," says Johnson, "is that of a pastoral, easy, vulgar, and therefore disgusting."

General Characteristics. — While he is best known in literary history as the great converser whose full length portrait is drawn by Boswell, Johnson left the marks of his influence on much of the prose written within nearly a hundred years after his death. On the whole, this influence has, for the following reasons, been bad.

CHESHIRE CHEESE INN, FLEET STREET, LONDON

First, he loved a ponderous style in which there was an excess of the Latin element. He liked to have his statements sound well. He once said in forcible Saxon: "*The Rehearsal* has not wit enough to keep it sweet," but a moment later he translated this into: "It has not sufficient vitality to preserve it from putrefaction." In his *Dictionary* he defined "network" as "anything reticulated or decussated at equal distances with interstices between the intersections." Some wits of the day said that he used long words to make his *Dictionary* necessary.

In the second place, Johnson loved formal balance so much that he used too many antitheses. Many of his balancing clauses are out of place or add nothing to the sense. The following shows excess of antithesis: —

"If the flights of Dryden, therefore, are higher, Pope continues longer on the wing. If of Dryden's fire the blaze is brighter, of Pope's the heat is more regular and constant. Dryden often surpasses expectation, and Pope never falls below it. Dryden is read with frequent astonishment, and Pope with perpetual delight."

As a rule, Johnson's prose is too abstract and general, and it awakens too few images. This is a characteristic failing of his essays in *The Rambler* and *The Idler*. Even in *Rasselas*, his great work of fiction, he speaks of passing through the fields and seeing the animals around him; but he does not mention definite trees, flowers, or animals. Shakespeare's wounded stag or "winking Mary-buds" would have given a touch of life to the whole scene.

Johnson's latest and greatest work, *Lives of the English Poets*, is comparatively free from most of these faults. The sentences are energetic and full of meaning. Although we may not agree with some of the criticism, we shall find it stimulating and suggestive. Before Johnson gave these critical essays to the world, he had been doing little for years except talking in a straightforward manner. His constant practice in speaking English reacted on his later written work. Unfortunately this work has been the least imitated.

SUMMARY

The second part of the eighteenth century was a time of changing standards in church, state, and literature. The downfall of Walpole, the religious revivals of Wesley, the victories of Clive in India and of Wolfe in Canada, show the progress that England was making at home and abroad. Even her loss of the American colonies left her the greatest maritime and colonial power.

There began to be a revolt against the narrow classical standards in literature. A longing gradually manifested itself for more freedom of imagination, such as we find in *Ossian*, *The Castle of Otranto*, Percy's *Reliques*, and translations of the Norse mythology. There was a departure from the hackneyed forms and subjects of the preceding age and an introduction of more of the individual and ideal element, such as can be found in Gray's *Elegy* and Collins's *Ode to Evening*. Dr. Johnson, however, threw his powerful influence against this romantic movement, and curbed somewhat such tendencies in Goldsmith, who, nevertheless, gave fine romantic touches to *The Deserted Village* and to much of his other work. This period was one of preparation for the glorious romantic outburst at the end of the century.

In prose, the most important achievement of the age was the creation of the modern novel in works like Richardson's *Pamela* and *Clarissa Harlowe*, Fielding's *Tom Jones*, Sterne's *Tristram Shandy*, Smollett's *Humphrey Clinker*, and Goldsmith's *Vicar of Wakefield*. There were also noted prose works in philosophy and history by Hume and Gibbon, in politics by Burke, in criticism by Johnson, and in biography by Boswell. Goldsmith's comedy of manners, *She Stoops to Conquer*, won a decided victory over the insipid sentimental drama.

REFERENCES FOR FURTHER STUDY

HISTORICAL

For contemporary English history, consult Gardiner,[1] Green, Walker, or Cheney. For the social side, see Traill, V. Lecky's *History of the Eighteenth Century* is specially full.

LITERARY

The Cambridge History of English Literature.
Courthope's *History of English Poetry*, Vol. V.
Seccombe's *The Age of Johnson.*
Gosse's *History of English Literature in the Eighteenth Century.*
Stephen's *English Literature in the Eighteenth Century.*
Minto's *Manual of English Prose Literature.*
Symons's *The Romantic Movement in English Poetry.*
Beers's *English Romanticism.*
Phelps's *Beginnings of the English Romantic Movement.*
Nutt's *Ossian and Ossianic Literature.*
Jusserand's *The English Novel in the Time of Shakespeare.*
Cross's *The Development of the English Novel.*
Minto's *Defoe.* (E. M. L.)
Dobson's *Samuel Richardson.* (E. M. L)
Dobson's *Henry Fielding.* (E. M. L.)
Godden's *Henry Fielding, a Memoir.*
Stephen's *Hours in a Library* (Defoe, Richardson, and Fielding).
Thackeray's *English Humorists of the Eighteenth Century* (Fielding, Smollett, Sterne, Goldsmith).
Gosse's *Life of Gray.* (E. M. L.)
Huxley's *Life of Hume.* (E. M. L.)
Morrison's *Life of Gibbon.* (E. M. L.)
Morley's *Life of Edmund Burke.* (E. M. L.)
Woodrow Wilson's *Mere Literature* (Burke).
Boswell's *Life of Johnson.*
Stephen's *Life of Johnson.* (E. M. L.)
Macaulay's *Essay on Croker's Edition of Boswell's Life of Johnson.*
Irving's, Forster's, Dobson's, Black's (E. M. L.), or B. Frankfort Moore's *Life of Goldsmith.*

[1] For full titles, see p. 50.

SUGGESTED READINGS
WITH QUESTIONS AND SUGGESTIONS

The Romantic Movement. — In order to note the difference in feeling, imagery, and ideals, between the romantic and the classic schools, it will be advisable for the student to make a special comparison of Dryden's and Pope's satiric and didactic verse with Spenser's *Faerie Queene*, Milton's *Il Penseroso*, and with some of the work of the romantic poets in the next period. What is the difference in the general atmosphere of these poems? See if the influence of *Il Penseroso* is noticeable in Collins's *Ode to Evening* (Ward,[1] III., 287; Bronson, III., 220; *Oxford*, 531; Manly, I., 273; *Century*, 386) and in Gray's *Elegy* (Ward, III., 331; Bronson, III., 238; *Oxford*, 516; Manly, I., 267; *Century*, 398).

What element foreign to Dryden and Pope appears in Thomson's *Seasons* (Ward, III., 173; Bronson, III., 179; Manly, I., 255; *Century*, 369-372).

What signs of a struggle between the romantic and the classic are noticeable in Goldsmith's *Deserted Village* (Ward, III., 373-379; Bronson, III., 282; Manly, I., 278; *Century*, 463). Pick out the three finest passages in the poem, and give the reasons for the choice.

Read pp. 173-176 of *Ossian* (*Canterbury Poets* series, 40 cents; Chambers, II.; Manly, II., 275), and show why it appealed to the spirit of romanticism.

For a short typical selection from Walpole's *Castle of Otranto*, see Chambers, II. Why is this called romantic fiction?

In Percy's *Reliques*, read the first ballad, that of *Chevy Chase*, and explain how the age could turn from Pope to read such rude verse.

In place of Mallet's *Northern Antiquities*, twentieth-century readers will prefer books like Guerber's *Myths of Northern Lands* and Mabie's *Norse Stories Retold from the Eddas*.

From Chatterton's *Aella* read nine stanzas from the song beginning: "O sing unto my roundelay." His *The Bristowe Tragedy* may be compared with Percy's *Reliques* and with Coleridge's *The Ancient Mariner*. Selections from Chatterton are given in Bronson, III., Ward, III., *Oxford*, Manly, I., and *Century*.

The Novel. — Those who have the time to study the beginnings of the novel will be interested in reading, *Guy, Earl of Warwick* (Morley's

---

[1] For full titles, see p. 6.

Early Prose Romances) or *Sir Gawain and the Green Knight, Retold in Modern Prose, with Introduction and Notes*, by Jessie L. Weston (London: David Nutt, two shillings).

Two Elizabethan novels: Lodge's *Rosalynde* (the original of Shakespeare's *As You Like It*) and Greene's *Pandosto* (the original of *The Winter's Tale*) are published in *The Shakespeare Classics*, edited by Gollancz (Duffield & Company, New York, $1 each). *Pandosto* may be found at the end of the Cassell *National Library* edition of *The Winter's Tale* (15 cents). Selections from Lodge's *Rosalynde* are given in Craik, I., 544-549. These should be compared with the parallel parts of *As You Like It*. Selections from Nashe's *The Unfortunate Traveller* are given in Craik, I., 573-576, and selections from Sidney's *Arcadia* in the same volume, pp. 409-419. Deloney's *The Gentle Craft* and *Jack of Newberry* are given in his *Works*, edited by Mann (Clarendon Press).

For the preliminary sketching of characters that might serve as types in fiction, read *The Spectator*, No. 2, by Steele. Defoe's *Robinson Crusoe* will be read entire by almost every one.

In Craik, IV., read the following selections from these four great novelists of the middle of the eighteenth century; from Richardson, pp. 59-66; from Fielding, pp. 118-125; from Sterne, pp. 213-219; and from Smollett, pp. 261-264 and 269-272. Manly, II., has brief selections.

Goldsmith's *Vicar of Wakefield* should be read entire by the student (*Eclectic English Classics*, or *Gateway Series*, American Book Company). Selections may be found in Craik, IV., 365-370.

Sketch the general lines of development in fiction, from the early romance to Smollett. What type of fiction did *Don Quixote* ridicule? Compare Greene's *Pandosto* with Shakespeare's *Winter's Tale*, and Lodge's *Rosalynde* with *As You Like It*. In what relation do Steele, Addison, and Defoe stand to the novel? Why is the modern novel said to begin with Richardson?

Philosophy. — Two selections from Berkeley in Craik, IV., 34-39, give some of that philosopher's subtle metaphysics. The same volume, pp. 189-195, gives a selection from Hume's *Treatise of Human Nature*. Try stating in your own words the substance of these selections.

Gibbon. — Read Aurelian's campaign against Zenobia, which constitutes the last third of Chap. XI. of the first volume of *The Decline and Fall of the Roman Empire*. Other selections may be found in Craik, IV., 460-472; *Century*, 453-462.

What is the special merit of Gibbon's work? What period does he cover? Compare his style, either in description or in narration, with Bunyan's.

Burke. — Let the student who has not the time to read all the speech on *Conciliation with America* (*Eclectic English Classics*, or *Gateway Series*, American Book Company, 20 cents) read the selection in Craik, IV., 379-385, and also the selection referring to the decline of chivalry, from *Reflections on the Revolution in France* (Craik, IV., 402).

Point out in Burke's writings the four characteristics mentioned on p. 331. Compare his style with Bacon's, Swift's, Addison's, and Gibbon's.

Goldsmith. — Read his three masterpieces: *The Deserted Village, The Vicar of Wakefield* (*Eclectic English Classics*, or *Gateway Series*, American Book Company), *She Stoops to Conquer* (Cassell's *National Library*; *Everyman's Library*).

Select passages that show (*a*) altruistic philosophy of life, (*b*) humor, (*c*) special graces of style. What change did *She Stoops to Conquer* bring to the stage? What qualities keep the play alive?

Johnson. — Representative selections are given in Craik, IV., 141–185. Those from *Lives of the English Poets* (Craik, IV., 175–182; *Century*, 405–419) will best repay study. Let the student who has the time read Johnson's *Dryden* entire. As much as possible of Boswell's *Life of Johnson* should be read (Craik, IV., 482–495; Manly, II., 277–292).

Compare the style of Johnson with that of Gibbon and Burke. For what reasons does Johnson hold a high position in literature? What special excellences or defects do you note in his *Lives of the English Poets?* Why is Boswell's *Life of Johnson* a great work?

CHAPTER VIII

THE AGE OF ROMANTICISM, 1780–1837

History of the Period. — Much of the English history of this period was affected directly or indirectly by the French Revolution (1789). The object of this movement was to free men from oppression by the aristocracy and to restore to them their natural rights. The new watchwords were "Liberty, Fraternity, Equality." The professed principles of the French revolutionists were in many respects similar to those embodied in the American *Declaration of Independence*.

At first the movement was applauded by the liberal-minded Englishmen; but the confiscation of property, executions, and ensuing reign of terror soon made England recoil from this Revolution. When France executed her king and declared her intention of using force to make republics out of European powers, England sent the French minister home, and war immediately resulted. With only a short intermission, this lasted from 1793 until 1815, the contest caused by the French Revolution having become merged in the Napoleonic war. The battle of Waterloo (1815) ended the struggle with the defeat of Napoleon by the English general, Wellington.

The War of 1812 with the United States was for England only an incident of the war with France. England had become so powerful on the sea, as a result of the victories of Nelson, that she not only forbade vessels of a neutral power to trade with France, but she actually searched American vessels and sometimes removed their seamen, claiming that they were British deserters. The Americans won astonishing naval victories; but the war was concluded without any very definite decision on the points involved.

The last part of the eighteenth century saw the invention of spinning and weaving machines, the introduction of steam engines to furnish power, the wider use of coal, the substitution of the factory system for the home production of cloth, and the impairment of the home by the employment of women and children for unrestricted hours in the factories.

The long reign of George III., interrupted by periods of insanity, ended in 1820. The next two kings were his sons, George IV. (1820–1830) and William IV. (1830–1837). During these two reigns the spirit of reform was in the air. The most important reforms were (1) the revision of the criminal laws, which had prescribed death for some two hundred offenses, including stealing as much as five shillings; (2) the removal of political disabilities from Catholics, so that for the first time since 1673 they could hold municipal office and sit in Parliament; (3) the Reform Bill of 1832, which (*a*) extended the franchise to the well-to-do middle classes but not to those dependent on day labor, (*b*) gave a fairer apportionment of representatives in Parliament and abolished the so-called "rotten boroughs," *i.e.* those districts which with few or no inhabitants had been sending members to Parliament, while the large manufacturing cities in the north were without representatives; (4) the final bill in 1833 for the abolition of slavery; (5) child labor laws, which ordered the textile factories to cease employing children under nine years of age, prescribed a legal working day of eight hours for children between nine and thirteen, and of twelve hours for those between thirteen and eighteen; (6) the improvement of the poor laws.

The increased interest in human rights and welfare is the most important characteristic of this entire period, but most especially of the reigns of George IV. and William IV. Sir Robert Peel, the elder, although an employer of nearly a thousand children, felt the spirit of the time enough to call the attention of Parliament to the abuses of child labor. As we shall see, this new spirit exerted a strong influence on literature.

Influence of the New Spirit on Poetry. — The French Revolution stirred the young English poets profoundly. They proclaimed the birth of a new humanity of boundless promise. The possibilities of life again seemed almost as great as in Elizabethan days. The usually sober-minded Wordsworth exclaimed: —

> "Bliss was it in that dawn to be alive,
> But to be young was very heaven!"[1]

In the age of Pope, the only type of man considered worthy a place in the best literature was the aristocrat. The ordinary laborer was an object too contemptible even for satire. Burns placed a halo around the head of the honest toiler. In 1786 he could find readers for his *The Cotter's Saturday Night;* and ten years later he proclaimed thoughts which would have been laughed to scorn early in the century: —

> "Is there, for honest poverty,
>   That hangs his head and a' that?
> The coward slave, we pass him by,
>   We dare be poor for a' that!
>
> . . . .

[1] *Prelude*, Book XI.

> The rank is but the guinea stamp;
> The man's the gowd[1] for a' that."[2]

Wordsworth strikes almost the same chord:—

> "Love had he found in huts where poor men lie."[3]

The tenderness and sympathy induced by this new interest in human beings resulted in the annexation to English literature of an almost unexplored continent,—the continent of childhood. William Blake and William Wordsworth set the child in the midst of the poetry of this romantic age (pp. 356, 394).

More sympathy for animals naturally followed the increased interest in humanity. The poems of Cowper, Burns, Wordsworth, and Coleridge show this quickened feeling for a starved bird, a wounded hare, a hart cruelly slain, or an albatross wantonly shot. The social disorder of the Revolution might make Wordsworth pause, but he continued with unabated vigor to teach us—

> "Never to blend our pleasure or our pride
> With sorrow of the meanest thing that feels."[4]

New humanitarian interests affected all the great poets of this age. Although Keats was cut off while he was making an Æolian response to the beauty of the world, yet even he, in his brief life, heard something of the new message.

Growth of Appreciation of Nature. — More appreciation of nature followed the development of broader sympathy. Burns wrote a lyric full of feeling for a mountain daisy which his plow had turned beneath the furrow. Wordsworth exclaimed:—

---

[1] gold.
[2] *For a' That and a' That.*
[3] *Song at the Feast of Brougham Castle.*
[4] *Hart-Leap Well.*

"To me the meanest flower that blows can give
Thoughts that do often lie too deep for tears." [1]

For more than a century after Milton, the majority of references to nature were made in general terms and were borrowed from the stock illustrations of older poets, like Vergil. We find the conventional lark, nightingale, and turtledove. Nothing new or definite is said of them.

Increasing comforts and safety in travel now took more people where they could see for themselves the beauty of nature. In the new poetry we consequently find more definiteness. We can hear the whir of the partridge, the chatter of magpies, the whistle of the quail. Poets speak of a tree not only in general terms, but they note also the differences in the shade of the green of the leaves and the peculiarities of the bark. Previous to this time, poets borrowed from Theocritus and Vergil piping shepherds reclining in the shade, whom no Englishman had ever seen. In *Michael* Wordsworth pictures a genuine English shepherd.

The love for mountains and wild nature is of recent growth. One writer in the seventeenth century considered the Alps as so much rubbish swept together by the broom of nature to clear the plains of Italy. A seventeenth century traveler thought the Welsh mountains better than the Alps because the former would pasture goats. Dr. Johnson asked, "Who can like the Highlands?" The influence of the romantic movement developed the love for wild scenery, which is so conspicuous in Wordsworth and Byron.

This age surpasses even the Elizabethan in endowing Nature with a conscious soul, capable of bringing a message of solace and companionship. The greatest romantic poet of nature thus expresses his creed: —

[1] *Intimations of Immortality.*

> "... Nature never did betray
> The heart that loved her; 'tis her privilege,
> Through all the years of this our life, to lead
> From joy to joy."[1]

The Victory of Romanticism. — We have traced in the preceding age the beginnings of the romantic movement. Its ascendancy over classical rules was complete in the period between 1780 and the Victorian age. The romantic victory brought to literature more imagination, greater individuality, deeper feeling, a less artificial form of expression, and an added sense for the appreciation of the beauties of nature and their spiritual significance.

Swinburne says that the new poetic school, "usually registered as Wordsworthian," was "actually founded at midnight by **William Blake** (1757–1827) and fortified at sunrise by William Wordsworth." These lines from Blake's *To the Evening Star* (1783) may be given to support this statement: —

> "Thou fair-haired Angel of the Evening,
> . . . .
> Smile on our loves; and while thou drawest the
> Blue curtains of the sky, scatter thy silver dew
> On every flower that shuts its sweet eyes
> In timely sleep. Let thy West Wind sleep on
>   The lake."

We may note in these lines the absence of the classical couplet, the fact that the end of the lines necessitates no halt in thought, and a unique sympathetic touch in the lines referring to the flower and the wind.

Blake's *Songs of Innocence* (1789) and *Songs of Experience* (1793) show not only the new feeling toward nature, but also a broader sympathy with children and with all

---

[1] Wordsworth's *Lines composed a Few Miles above Tintern Abbey.*

suffering creatures. The chimney sweeper, the lost child, and even the sick rose are remembered in his verse. In his poem, *The Schoolboy*, he enters as sympathetically as Shakespeare into the heart of the boy on his way to school, when he hears the call of the uncaged birds and the fields.

These two lines express an oft-recurring idea in Blake's mystical romantic verse: —

> "The land of dreams is better far,
> Above the light of the morning star."

The volume of *Lyrical Ballads* (1798), the joint work of Wordsworth and Coleridge (see p. 390), marks the complete victory of the romantic movement.

The Position of Prose.—The eighteenth century, until near its end, was, broadly speaking, an age of prose. In excellence and variety the prose surpassed the poetry; but in this age (1780–1837) their position was reversed and poetry regained almost an Elizabethan ascendancy. Much good prose was written, but it ranks decidedly below the enchanting romantic poetry.

Prose writers were laying the foundations for the new science of political economy and endeavoring to ascertain how the condition of the masses could be improved. While investigating this subject, **Thomas Robert Malthus** (1766–1834), an Episcopal clergyman, announced his famous proposition, since known as the Malthusian theorem, that population tends to increase faster than the means of subsistence. Political economists and philosophers like **Adam Smith** (1723-1790), professor in the University of Glasgow, agreed on the "let-alone" doctrine of government. They held that individuals could succeed best when least interfered with by government, that a government could not set aside natural law, but could only impede it and cause harm, as for instance, in framing laws to tempt capital into forms of industry less productive than others and away from the employment that it would naturally seek. Many did not even believe in legislation affecting the hours of labor or the work of children. This "let-alone" theory was widely held until the close of the nineteenth century.

In moral philosophy, **Jeremy Bentham** (1748-1832), lawyer and philosopher, laid down the principle that happiness is the prime object of existence, and that the basis of legislation should be the greatest happiness to the greatest number, instead of to the privileged few. He measured the morality of actions by their efficiency in producing this happiness, and he said that pushpin is as good as poetry, if it gives as much pleasure. He was followed by **James Mill** (1773-1836), who maintained that the morality of actions is measured by their utility. The fault with many of the prevalent theories of government and morals lay in their narrow standards of immediate utility, their failure to measure remote spiritual effects.

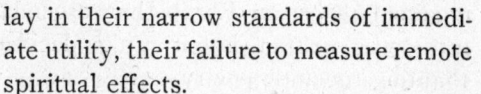

The taste of the age encouraged poetry. Scott, although a natural born writer of prose romance, made his early reputation by such poems as *Marmion* and *The Lady of the Lake*. **Robert Southey** (1774-1843), usually classed with Wordsworth and Coleridge as one of the three so-called Lake Poets, wrote much better prose than poetry. His prose *Life of Nelson* outranks the poetry in his *Curse of Kehama*. It is probable that, had he lived in an age of prose ascendancy, he would have written little poetry, for he distinctly says that the desire of making money "has already led me to write sometimes in poetry what would perhaps otherwise have been better written in prose." This statement shows in a striking way the spirit of those times. If Coleridge had not written such good poetry, his excellent critical prose would probably be more read to-day; but he doubtless continues to have a thousand readers for *The Ancient Mariner* to one for his prose.

Among the prose writers of this age, the fiction of Scott (p. 374) and Jane Austen (p. 382) seems destined to the longest lease of life and the widest circle of readers. De Quincey's work (p. 435), especially his artistic presentation of his thrilling dreams, has many admirers.

The *Essays of Elia* of **Charles Lamb** (1775–1834) still charms many readers. For over thirty years he was by day a clerk in the India House and by night a student of the Elizabethan drama and a writer of periodical essays, suggestive of the work of Addison and Steele.

From a drawing by Maclise.
CHARLES LAMB

Lamb's pervasive humor in discussing trivial subjects makes him very delightful reading. His well-known *Essays of Elia* first appeared in the *London Magazine* between 1820 and 1833. The peculiar flavor of his style and humor is shown in his *A Dissertation upon Roast Pig*, as one of the most popular of these *Essays* is called. Lamb relates how a Chinese boy, Bo-bo, having accidentally set his house on fire and roasted a litter of pigs, happened to acquire a liking for roast pig when he sucked his fingers to cool them after touching a crackling pig. It was considered a crime to eat meat that was not raw; but the jury fortunately had their fingers burned in the same way and tried Bo-bo's method of cooling them. The boy was promptly acquitted. Lamb gravely proceeds: —

From a drawing by B. Westmacott.
BO-BO AND ROAST PIG

"The judge, who was a shrewd fellow, winked at the manifest iniquity of the decision, and when the court was dismissed, went privily and bought up all the pigs that could be had for love or money. In a few days his lordship's town house was observed to be on fire. The thing took wing, and now there was nothing to be seen but fires in every direction. Fuel and pigs grew enormously dear all over the district. The insurance offices one and all shut up shop. People built slighter and slighter every day, until it was feared that the very science of architecture would in no long time be lost to the world. Thus this custom of firing houses continued, till in process of time, says my manuscript, a sage arose, like our Locke, who made a discovery that the flesh of swine, or indeed of any other animal, might be cooked (*burnt* as they called it) without the necessity of consuming a whole house to dress it. Then began the rude form of a gridiron."

Other enjoyable essays are *Old China*, a lovable picture of his home life with his sister, *Dream Children*, *New Year's Eve*, and *Poor Relations*.

The results of Lamb's Elizabethan studies appeared in the excellent *Tales from Shakespeare*, which he wrote with his sister, and in his *Specimens of English Dramatic Poets who wrote about the Time of Shakespeare.*

This age produced much prose criticism. Coleridge remains one of England's greatest critics, and Lamb and De Quincey are yet two of her most enjoyable ones. **Walter Savage Landor** (1775-1864) and **William Hazlitt** (1778-1830) also deserve mention in the history of English prose criticism. Both men were unusually combative. Landor was sent away from Oxford "for criticizing a noisy party with a shot gun," which he discharged against the closed shutters of the room where the roisterers were holding their festivities. He went to Italy, where most of his literary work was done. He avoided people, and even boasted that he took more pleasure with his own thoughts than with those of others. For companionship, he imagined himself conversing with other people. The titles of his best two works are *Imaginary Conversations* (1824-1848) and *Pericles and Aspasia* (1836), the latter a series of imaginary letters. His writings are notable for their style, for an unusual combination of dignity with simplicity and directness. A statement like the following shows how vigorous and sweeping his criticisms sometimes are: "A rib of Shakespeare would have made a Milton; the same portion of Milton, all poets born ever since." In spite of many splendid passages and of a style that suggests sculpture in marble, twentieth-century readers often feel that he is under full sail, either bound for nowhere, or voyaging to some port where they do not care to land.

Hazlitt is less polished, but more suggestive, and in closer touch with life than Landor. In seizing the important qualities of an author's works and summarizing them in brief space, Hazlitt shows the skill of a trained journalist. His three volumes, *Characters of Shakespeare's Plays* (1817), *Lectures on the English Poets* (1818), and *Lectures on the English Comic Writers* (1819) contain criticism that remains stimulating and suggestive. He loves to arrive somewhere, to settle his points definitely. His discussion of the frequently debated question, — whether Pope is a poet, shows this characteristic: —

"The question, — whether Pope was a poet, has hardly yet been settled, and is hardly worth settling; for if he was not a great poet, he must have been a great prose writer, that is, he was a great writer of some sort."

His two volumes of essays, *The Round Table* (1817) and *Table Talk* (1821-1822), caused him to be called a "lesser Dr. Samuel Johnson."

While the combative dispositions of Landor and Hazlitt did not make them ideal critics of their contemporaries, the taste of the age liked criticism of the slashing type. The newly established periodicals and reviews, such as *The Edinburgh Review* (started in 1802), furnished a new market for critical essays. **Francis Jeffrey** (1773–1850), editor of *The Edinburgh Review*, accused Wordsworth of "silliness" in his *Lyrical Ballads* (p. 390); and said vehemently of a later volume of the same poet's verse: "This will never do." *The Quarterly Review* in 1818 spoke of the "insanity" of the poetry of Keats. In 1819 *Blackwood's Edinburgh Magazine* gave a fatherly warning to Shelley that Keats as a poet was "worthy of sheer and instant contempt," advised him to select better companions than "Johnny Keats," and promised that compliance with this advice would secure him "abundance of better praise."

Even the more genial **Leigh Hunt** (1784-1859), the friend of Shelley and Keats, and the writer of many pleasant essays, called Carlyle's style "a jargon got up to confound pretension with performance." We like Hunt best when he is writing in the vein of the *Spectator* or as a "miniature Lamb." In such papers as *An Earth upon Heaven*, Hunt tells us that in heaven "there can be no clergymen if there are no official duties for them"; that we shall there enjoy the choicest books, for "Shakespeare and Spenser should write us *new ones*." He closes this entertaining paper with the novel assurance: "If we choose, now and then we shall even have inconveniences."

WILLIAM COWPER, 1731-1800

Life. — Cowper's life is a tale of almost continual sadness, caused by his morbid timidity. He was born at Great Berkhampstead, Hertfordshire, in 1731. At the age of six, he lost his mother and was placed in a boarding school. Here his sufferings began. The child was so especially terrified by one rough boy that he could never raise his eyes to the bully's face, but knew him unmistakably by his shoe buckles.

There was some happiness for Cowper at his next school, the Westminster School, and also during the twelve succeeding years, when he studied law; but the short respite was followed by the gloom of madness. Owing to his ungovernable fear of a public examination, which was necessary to secure the position offered by an uncle, Cowper underwent days and nights of agony, during which he tried in many ways to end his miserable life. The frightful ordeal unsettled his reason, and he spent eighteen months in an insane asylum.

Upon his recovery, he was taken into the house of a Rev. Mr. Unwin, whose wife tended Cowper as a son during the rest of her life. He was never supremely happy, and he was sometimes again thrown into madness by the terrible thought of God's wrath; but his life was

From the portrait by Sir Thomas Lawrence.

Wm Cowper

passed in a quiet manner in the villages of Weston and Olney, where he was loved by every one. The simple pursuits of gardening, carpentering, visiting the sick, caring for his numerous pets, rambling through the lanes, studying nature, and writing verse, occupied his sane moments when he was not at prayer.

Works. — Cowper's first works were the *Olney Hymns*. His religious nature is manifest again in the volume which consists of didactic poems upon such subjects as *The Progress of Error, Truth, Charity, Table Talk*, and *Conversation*. These are in the spirit of the formal classical poets, and contain sententious couplets such as

"An idler is a watch that wants both hands,
As useless if it goes as when it stands."[1]

"Vociferated logic kills me quite;
A noisy man is always in the right."[2]

The bare didacticism of these poems is softened and sweetened by the gentle, devout nature of the poet, and is enlivened by a vein of pure humor.

COWPER'S COTTAGE AT WESTON

He is one of England's most delightful letter writers because of his humor, which ripples occasionally over the stream of his constitutional melancholy. *The Diverting History of John Gilpin* is extremely humorous. The poet seems to have forgotten himself in this ballad and to have given full expression to his sense of the ludicrous.

From a drawing by R. Caldecott.
JOHN GILPIN'S RIDE

The work that has made his name famous is *The Task*. He gave it this title half humorously because his friend, Lady

[1] *Retirement.*   [2] *Conversation.*

Austen, had bidden him write a poem in blank verse upon some subject or other, the sofa, for instance; and he called the first book of the poem *The Sofa*. *The Task* is chiefly remarkable because it turns from the artificial and conventional subjects which had been popular, and describes simple beauties of nature and the joys of country life. Cowper says: —

"God made the country, and man made the town."

To a public acquainted with the nature poetry of Burns, Wordsworth, and Tennyson, Cowper's poem does not seem a wonderful production. Appearing as it did, however, during the ascendancy of Pope's influence, when aristocratic city life was the only theme for verse, *The Task* is a strikingly original work. It marks a change from the artificial style of eighteenth century poetry and proclaims the dawn of the natural style of the new school. He who could write of —

". . . rills that slip
Through the cleft rock, and chiming as they fall
Upon loose pebbles, lose themselves at length
In matted grass, that with a livelier green
Betrays the secret of their silent course,"

was a worthy forerunner of Shelley and Keats.

General Characteristics. — Cowper's religious fervor was the strongest element in both his life and his writings. Perhaps that which next appealed to his nature was the pathetic. He had considerable mastery of pathos, as may be seen in the drawing of "crazed Kate" in *The Task*, in the lines *To Mary*, and in the touchingly beautiful poem *On the Receipt of My Mother's Picture out of Norfolk*, beginning with that well-known line: —

"Oh that those lips had language!"

The two most attractive characteristics of his works are refined, gentle humor and a simple and true manner of picturing rural scenes and incidents. He says that he described no spot which he had not seen, and expressed no emotion which he had not felt. In this way, he restricted the range of his subjects and displayed a somewhat literal mind; but what he had seen and felt he touched with a light fancy and with considerable imaginative power.

ROBERT BURNS, 1759-1796

Life. — The greatest of Scottish poets was born in a peasant's clay-built cottage, a mile and a half south of Ayr. His father was a man whose morality, industry, and zeal for education made him an admirable parent. For a picture of his father and the home influences under which the boy was reared, *The Cotter's Saturday Night* should be read. The poet had little formal schooling, but under paternal influence he learned how to teach himself.

Until his twenty-eighth year, Robert Burns was an ordinary laborer on one or another of the Ayrshire tenant farms which his father or brothers leased. At the age of fifteen, he was worked beyond his strength in doing a man's full labor. He called his life on the Ayrshire farms "the unceasing toil of a galley slave." All his life he fought a hand-to-hand fight with poverty.

In 1786, when he was twenty-seven years old, he resolved to abandon the struggle and seek a position in the far-off island of Jamaica. In order to secure money for his passage, he published some poems which he had thought out while following the plow or resting after the day's toil. Six hundred copies were printed at three shil-

From the painting by Nasmyth, National Portrait Gallery.

Robert Burns

lings each. All were sold in a little over a month. A copy of this Kilmarnock edition has since sold in Edinburgh for £572. His fame from that little volume has grown as much as its monetary value.

Some Edinburgh critics praised the poems very highly and suggested a second edition. Burns therefore abandoned the idea of going to Jamaica and went to Edinburgh to arrange for a new edition. Here he was entertained by the foremost men, some of whom wished to see how a plowman would behave in polite society, while others desired to gaze on what they regarded as a freak of nature.

The new volume appeared in 1787, and contained but few poems which had not been published the previous

BIRTHPLACE OF BURNS

year. The following winter he again went to Edinburgh; but having shocked society by his intemperate habits, he was almost totally neglected by the leaders of literature and fashion.

In 1788 Burns married Jean Armour and took her to a farm which he leased in Dumfriesshire. The first part of this new period was the happiest in his life. She has been immortalized in his songs: —

> "I see her in the dewy flowers,
>   I see her sweet and fair:
> I hear her in the tunefu' birds,
>   I hear her charm the air:
> There's not a bonie flower that springs
>   By fountain, shaw, or green:
> There's not a bonie bird that sings,
>   But minds me o' my Jean."[1]

[1] *I Love My Jean.*

As this farm proved unprofitable, Burns appealed to influential persons for some position that would enable him to support his family and write poetry. This was an age of pensions, but not a farthing of pension did he ever get. He was made an exciseman or gauger, at a salary of £50 a year, and he followed that occupation for the few remaining years of his life.

Robert Burns wrote and did some things unworthy of a great poet; but when Scotland thinks of him, she quotes the lines which he wrote for *Tam Samson's Elegy:* —

> "Heav'n rest his saul, whare'er he be!
> Is th' wish o' mony mae than me:
> He had twa faults, or maybe three,
>   Yet what remead?[1]
> Ae social, honest man want we."

Burns's Poetic Creed. — We can understand and enjoy Burns much better if we know his object in writing poetry and the point of view from which he regarded life. It would be hard to fancy the intensity of the shock which the school of Pope would have felt on reading this statement of the poor plowman's poetic creed: —

> "Gie me ae spark o' Nature's fire,
> That's a' the learning I desire;
> Then tho' I drudge thro' dub an' mire
>   At pleugh or cart,
> My Muse, though hamely in attire,
>   May touch the heart."[2]

Burns's heart had been touched with the loves and sorrows of life, and it was his ambition to sing so naturally of these as to touch the hearts of others.

With such an object in view, he did not disdain to use in his best productions much of the Scottish dialect, the

---

[1] remedy.   [2] *Epistle to John Lapraik.*

vernacular of the plowman and the shepherd. The literary men of Edinburgh, who would rather have been convicted of a breach of etiquette than of a Scotticism, tried to induce him to write pure English; but the Scotch words which he first heard from his mother's lips seemed to possess more "o' Nature's fire." He ended by touching the heart of Scotland and making her feel more proud of this dialect, of him, and of herself.

Union of the Elizabethan with the Revolutionary Spirit. — In no respect does the poetry of Burns more completely part company with the productions of the classical school than in the expression of feeling. The emotional fire of Elizabethan times was restored to literature. No poet except Shakespeare has ever written more nobly impassioned love songs. Burns's song beginning: —

> "Ae fond kiss and then
> we sever"

seemed to both Byron and Scott to contain the essence of a thousand love tales. This

From the painting by James Archer.
BURNS AND HIGHLAND MARY

unaffected, passionate treatment of love had long been absent from our literature; but intensity of genuine feeling reappeared in Burns's *Highland Mary, I Love My Jean, Farewell to Nancy, To Mary in Heaven, O Wert Thou in the Cauld Blast,* which last Mendelssohn thought exquisite enough to set to music. The poetry of Burns throbs with varying emotions. It has been well said that the essence of the lyric is to describe the passion of the moment. Burns is a master in this field.

The spirit of revolution against the bondage and cold formalism of the past made the poor man feel that his place in the world was as dignified, his happiness as important, as that of the rich. A feeling of sympathy for the oppressed and the helpless also reached beyond man to animals. Burns wrote touching lines about a mouse whose nest was, one cold November day, destroyed by his plow. When the wild eddying swirl of the snow beat around his cot, his heart went out to the poor sheep, cattle, and birds.

Burns can, therefore, claim kinship with the Elizabethans because of his love songs, which in depth of feeling and beauty of natural utterance show something of Shakespeare's magic. In addition to this, the poetry of Burns voices the democratic spirit of the Revolution.

Treatment of Nature. — In his verses, the autumn winds blow over yellow corn; the fogs melt in limpid air; the birches extend their fragrant arms dressed in woodbine; the lovers are coming through the rye; the daisy spreads her snowy bosom to the sun; the "westlin" winds blow fragrant with dewy flowers and musical with the melody of birds; the brook flows past the lover's Eden, where summer first unfolds her robes and tarries longest, because of the rarest bewitching enchantment of the poet's tale told there.

In his poetry those conventional birds, — the lark and the

nightingale, — do not hold the chief place. His verses show that the source of his knowledge of birds is not to be sought in books. We catch glimpses of grouse cropping heather buds, of whirring flocks of partridges, of the sooty coot and the speckled teal, of the fisher herons, of the green-crested lapwing, of clamoring craiks among fields of flowering clover, of robins cheering the pensive autumn, of lintwhites chanting among the buds, of the mavis singing drowsy day to rest.

It is true that on the poetic stage of Burns, man always stands in the foreground. Nature is employed in order to give human emotion a proper background. Burns chose those aspects of nature which harmonized with his present mood, but the natural objects in his pages are none the less enjoyable for that reason. Sometimes his songs complain if nature seems gay when he is sad, but this contrast is employed to throw a stronger light on his woes.

General Characteristics. — More people often visit the birthplace of Burns near Ayr than of Shakespeare at Stratford-on-Avon. What qualities in Burns account for such popularity? The fact that the Scotch are an unusually patriotic people and make many pilgrimages to the land of Burns is only a partial answer to this question. The complete answer is to be found in a study of Burns's characteristics. In the first place, with his "spark o' Nature's fire," he has touched the hearts of more of the rank and file of humanity than even Shakespeare himself. The songs of Burns minister in the simplest and most direct way to every one of the common feelings of the human heart. Shakespeare surpasses all others in painting universal human nature, but he is not always simple. Sometimes his audience consists of only the cultured few.

Especially enjoyable is the humor of Burns, which usually

displays a kindly and intuitive sympathy with human weakness. *Tam o' Shanter*, his greatest poem, keeps the reader smiling or laughing from beginning to end. When the Scottish Muse proudly placed on his brow the holly wreath, she happily emphasized two of his conspicuous qualities, — his love and mirth, when she said: —

> "I saw thee eye the gen'ral mirth
> With boundless love." [1]

Burns is one of the great masters of lyrical verse. He preferred that form. He wrote neither epic nor dramatic poetry. He excels in "short swallow flights of song."

There are not many ways in which a poet can keep larger audiences or come nearer to them than by writing verses that naturally lend themselves to daily song. There are few persons, from the peasant to the lord, who have not sung some of Burns's songs such as *Auld Lang Syne, Coming through the Rye, John Anderson my Jo*, or *Scots Wha hae wi' Wallace Bled*. Since the day of his death, the audiences of Robert Burns have for these reasons continually grown larger.

WALTER SCOTT, 1771—1832

Life. — Walter Scott, the son of a solicitor, was born in Edinburgh in 1771. In childhood he was such an invalid that he was allowed to follow his own bent without much attempt at formal education. He was taken to the country, where he acquired a lasting fondness for animals and wild scenery. With his first few shillings he bought the collection of early ballads and songs known as Percy's *Reliques of Ancient English Poetry*. Of this he says, "I do not believe I ever read a book half so frequently, or with

[1] *The Vision.*

From the painting by William Nicholson.

half the enthusiasm." His grandmother used to delight him with the tales of adventure on the Scottish border.

Later, Scott went to the Edinburgh High School and to the University. At the High School he showed wonderful genius for telling stories to the boys. "I made a brighter figure in the *yards* than in the *class*," he says of himself at this time. This early practice of relating tales and noting what held the attention of his classmates was excellent training for the future Wizard of the North.

After the apprenticeship to his father, the son was called to the bar and began the practice of law. He often left his office to travel over the Scottish counties in search of legendary ballads, songs, and traditions, a collection of which he published under the title of *Minstrelsy of the Scottish Border*. In 1797 he married Miss Charlotte Carpenter, who had an income of £500 a year. In 1799, having obtained the office of sheriff of Selkirkshire at an annual salary of £300, with very light duties, he found himself able to neglect law for literature. His early freedom from poverty is in striking contrast to the condition of his fellow Scotsman, Robert Burns.

During the period between thirty and forty years of age, he wrote his best poems. Not until he was nearly forty-three did he discover where his greatest powers lay. He then published *Waverley*, the first of a series of novels known by that general name. During the remaining eighteen years of his life he wrote twenty-nine novels, besides many other works, such as the *Life of Napoleon* in nine volumes, and an entertaining work on Scottish history under the title of *Tales of a Grandfather*.

The crisis that showed Scott's sterling character came in the winter of 1825–1826, when an Edinburgh publishing firm in which he was interested failed and left on his shoulders a debt of £117,000. Had he been a man of less honor, he might have taken advantage of the bankrupt law, which would have left his future earnings free from past claims; but he refused to take any step that would remove his obligation to pay the debt. At the age of fifty-

ABBOTSFORD, HOME OF SIR WALTER SCOTT

four, he abandoned his happy dream of founding the house of Scott of Abbotsford and sat down to pay off the debt with his pen. The example of such a life is better than the finest sermon on honor. He wrote with almost inconceivable rapidity. His novel *Woodstock*, the product of three months' work, brought him £8228. In four years he paid £70,000 to his creditors. One day the tears rolled down his cheeks because he could no longer force his fingers to grasp the pen. The king offered him a man-of-war in which to make a voyage to the Mediterranean. Hoping to regain his health, Scott made the trip, but the rest came too late. He returned to Abbotsford in a sinking condition, and died in 1832, at the age of sixty-one.

SCOTT'S GRAVE IN DRYBURGH ABBEY

Poetry. — Scott's three greatest poems are *The Lay of the Last Minstrel* (1805), *Marmion* (1808), and *The Lady of the Lake* (1810). They belong to the distinct class of story-telling poetry. Like many of the ballads in Percy's collection, these poems are stories of old feuds between the Highlander and the Lowlander, and between the border lords of England and Scotland. These romantic tales of heroic battles, thrilling incidents, and love adventures, are told in fresh, vigorous verse, which breathes the free air of wild nature and moves with the prance of a war horse. Outside of Homer, we can nowhere find a better description of a battle than in the sixth canto of *Marmion: A Tale of Flodden Field:*—

> "They close, in clouds of smoke and dust,
>   With sword sway and with lance's thrust;
>   And such a yell was there,
>   Of sudden and portentous birth,
>   As if men fought upon the earth,
>   And fiends in upper air;
>
> . . . .
>
> And in the smoke the pennons flew,
> As in the storm the white sea mew."

The Lady of the Lake, an extremely interesting story of romantic love and adventure, has been the most popular of Scott's poems. Loch Katrine and the Trossachs, where the scene of the opening cantos is laid, have since Scott's day been thronged with tourists.

LOCH KATRINE AND ELLEN'S ISLE

The most prominent characteristic of Scott's poetry is its energetic movement. Many schoolboys know by heart those dramatic lines which express Marmion's defiance of Douglas, and the ballad of *Lochinvar*, which is alive with the movements of tireless youth. These poems have an interesting story to tell, not of the thoughts, but of the deeds, of the characters.

Scott is strangely free from nineteenth century introspection.

Historical Fiction. — Seeing that Byron could surpass him as a poet, and finding that his own genius was best adapted to writing prose tales, Scott turned to the composition of his great romances. In 1814 he published *Waverley*, a story of the attempt of the Jacobite Pretender to recover the English throne in 1745. Seventeen of Scott's works of fiction are historical.

When we wish a vivid picture of the time of Richard Cœur de Lion, of the knight and the castle, of the Saxon swineherd Gurth and of the Norman master who ate the pork, we may read *Ivanhoe*. If we desire some reading that will make the Crusaders live again, we find it in the pages of *The Talisman*. When we wish an entertaining story of the brilliant days of Elizabeth, we turn to *Kenilworth*. If we are moved by admiration for the Scotch Covenanters to seek a story of their times, we have Scott's finest historical tale, *Old Mortality*. Shortly after this story appeared, Lord Holland was asked his opinion of it. "Opinion!" he exclaimed; "we did not one of us go to bed last night — nothing slept but my gout." The man who could thus charm his readers was called "the Wizard of the North."

From a life sketch by Maclise.
WALTER SCOTT

Scott is the creator of the historical novel, which has advanced on the general lines marked out by him. Carlyle tersely says: "These historical novels have taught all men this truth, which looks like a truism, and yet was as good as unknown to writers of history and others till so taught: that the by-gone ages of the world were actually filled by living men, not by protocols, state papers, controversies, and abstractions of men."

The history in Scott's novels is not always absolutely accurate. To meet the exigencies of his plot, he sometimes takes liberties with the events of history, and there are occasional anachronisms in his work. Readers may rest assured, however, that the most prominent strokes of his brush will convey a sufficiently accurate idea of certain phases of history. Although the hair lines in his pictures may be neglected, most persons can learn more truth from studying his gallery of historic scenes than from poring over volumes of documents and state papers. Scott does not look at life from every point of view. The reader of *Ivanhoe*, for instance, should be cautioned against thinking that it presents a complete picture of the Middle Ages. It shows the bright, the noble side of chivalry, but not all the brutality, ignorance, and misery of the times.

Novels that are not Historical. — Twelve of Scott's novels contain but few attempts to represent historic events. The greatest of these novels are *Guy Mannering*, *The Heart of Midlothian*, *The Antiquary*, and *The Bride of Lammermoor*.

Scott said that his most rapid work was his best. *Guy Mannering*, an admirable picture of Scottish life and manners, was written in six weeks. Some of its characters, like Dominie Sampson, the pedagogue, Meg Merrilies, the gypsy, and Dick Hatteraick, the smuggler, have more life than many of the people we meet.

A century before, Pope said that most women had no characters at all. His writings tend to show that this was his real conviction, as it was that of many others during the time when Shakespeare was little read. *The Heart of Midlothian* presents in Jeanie Deans a woman whose character and feminine qualities have won the admiration of the world. Scott could not paint women in the higher walks of life. He was so chivalrous that he was prone to make such women too perfect, but his humble Scotch lass Jeanie Deans is one of his greatest creations.

SCOTT'S DESK AT ABBOTSFORD

When we note the vast number of characters drawn by his pen, we are astonished to find that he repeats so little. Many novelists write only one original novel. Their succeeding works are merely repetitions of the first. The hero may have put on a new suit of clothes and the heroine may have different colored hair, or each may be given a new mannerism, but there is nothing really new in character, and very little in incident. Year after year, however, Scott wrote with wonderful rapidity, without repeating his characters or his plots.

General Characteristics. — All critics are impressed with the healthiness of Scott's work, with its freedom from what is morbid or debasing. His stories display marked energy and movement, and but little subtle analysis of feelings and motives. He aimed at broad and striking effects. We do not find much development of character in his pages. "His characters have the brilliance and the fixity of portraits."

Scott does not particularly care to delineate the intense passion of love. Only one of his novels, *The Bride of Lammermoor*, is aflame with this overmastering emotion. He delights in adventure. He places his characters in unusual and dangerous situations, and he has succeeded in making us feel his own interest in the outcome. He has on a larger scale many of the qualities that we may note in the American novelist Cooper, whose best stories are tales of adventure in the forest or on the sea. Like him, Scott shows lack of care in the construction of sentences. Few of the most cultured people of to-day could, however, write at Scott's breakneck speed and make as few slips. Scott has far more humor and variety than Cooper.

Scott's romanticism is seen in his love for supernatural agencies, which figure in many of his stories. His fondness for adventure, for mystery, for the rush of battle, for color and sharp contrast, and his love for the past are also romantic traits. Sometimes, however, he falls into the classical fault of overdescription and of leaving too little to the imagination.

In the variety of his creations, he is equaled by no one. He did more than any other pioneer to aid fiction in dethroning the drama. His influence can be seen in the historical novels of almost every nation.

JANE AUSTEN, 1775–1817

Life and Works. — While Sir Walter Scott was laying the foundations of his large family estates and recounting the story of battles, chivalry, and brigandage, a quiet little woman, almost unmindful of the great world, was enlivening her father's parsonage and writing about the clergy, the old maids, the short-sighted mothers, the marriageable daughters, and other people that figure in village life.

From an original family portrait.

J. Austen

This cheery, sprightly young woman was Jane Austen, who was born in Steventon, Hampshire, in 1775.

She spent nearly all her life in Hampshire, which furnished her with the chief material for her novels. She loved the quiet life of small country villages and interpreted it with rare sympathy and a keen sense of humor, as is shown in the following lines from *Pride and Prejudice*: —

> "'Oh, Mr. Bennet, you are wanted immediately; we are all in an uproar! You must come and make Lizzy marry Mr. Collins, for she vows she will not have him; and if you do not make haste he will change his mind and not have her!'

"'Come here, child,' cried her father . . . 'I understand that Mr. Collins has made you an offer of marriage. Is it true?' Elizabeth replied that it was. 'Very well — and this offer of marriage you have refused?'

"'I have, sir.'

"'Very well. We now come to the point. Your mother insists upon your accepting it. Is it not so, Mrs. Bennet?'

"'Yes, or I will never see her again.'

"'An unhappy alternative is before you, Elizabeth. From this day you must be a stranger to one of your parents. Your mother will never see you again if you do not marry Mr. Collins, and I will never see you again if you do!'"

She began her literary work early, and at the age of sixteen she had accumulated quite a pile of manuscripts. She wrote as some artists paint, for the pure joy of the work, and she never allowed her name to appear on a title page. The majority of her acquaintances did not even suspect her of the "guilt of authorship."

She disliked "Gothic" romances, such as *The Mysteries of Udolpho* (p. 312), and she wrote *Northanger Abbey* as a burlesque of that type. In this story the heroine, Catherine Moreland, who has been fed on such literature, is invited to visit Northanger Abbey in Gloucestershire, where with an imagination "resolved on alarm," she is prepared to be agitated by experiences of trapdoors and subterranean passages. On the first night of her visit, a violent storm, with its mysterious noises, serves to arouse the most characteristic "Gothic" feelings; but when the complete awakening comes and the "visions of romance are over," Catherine realizes that real life is not fruitful of such horrors as are depicted in her favorite novels.

Pride and Prejudice is usually considered Jane Austen's best work, although *Sense and Sensibility, Emma, Mansfield Park*, and *Persuasion* have their ardent admirers. In fact, there is an increasing number of discriminating readers who enjoy almost everything that she wrote. During the last five years of the eighteenth century, she produced some of her best novels, although they were not published until the period between 1811 and 1818.

The scenes of her stories are laid for the most part in small Hampshire villages, with which she was thoroughly familiar, the characters being taken from the middle class and the gentry with whom she was thrown. Simple domestic episodes and ordinary people, living somewhat monotonous and narrow lives, satisfy her. She exhibits wonderful skill in fashioning these into slight but entertaining narratives. In *Pride and Prejudice*, for example, she creates some refreshing situations by opposing Philip Darcy's pride to Elizabeth Bennet's prejudice. She manages the long-delayed reconciliation between these two lovers with a tact that shows true genius and a knowledge of the human heart.

JANE AUSTEN'S DESK

A strong feature of Jane Austen's novels is her subtle, careful manner of drawing character. She perceives with an intuitive refinement the delicate shadings of emotion, and describes them with the utmost care and detail. Her heroines are especially fine, each one having an interesting individuality, thoroughly natural and womanly. The minor characters in Miss Austen's works are usually quaint and original. She sees the oddities and foibles of people with the insight of the true humorist, and paints them with most dexterous cunning.

William D. Howells, the chief American realist of the nineteenth century, wrote in 1891 of her and her novels:—

"She was great and they were beautiful because she and they were honest and dealt with nature nearly a hundred years ago as realism deals with it to-day. Realism is nothing more and nothing less than the truthful treatment of material."

She was, indeed, a great realist, and it seems strange that she and Scott, the great romanticist, should have been contemporaries. Scott was both broad and big-hearted enough to sum up her chief characteristics as follows:—

"That young lady has a talent for describing the involvements of feelings and characters of ordinary life, which is to me the most wonderful I ever met with. The big bow-wow strain I can do myself, like any one going; but the exquisite touch which renders commonplace things and characters interesting from the truth of the description and the sentiment is denied to me."

She died in 1817 at the age of forty-one and was buried in Winchester Cathedral, fourteen miles from her birthplace. The merit of her work was apparent to only a very few at the time of her death. Later years have slowly brought a just recognition of the important position that she holds in the history of the realistic novel of daily life. Of still greater significance to the majority is the fact that the subtle charm of her stories continues to win for her an enlarged circle of readers.

WILLIAM WORDSWORTH, 1770-1850

Early Life and Training. — William Wordsworth was born in Cockermouth, Cumberland, in 1770. He went to school in his ninth year at Hawkshead, a village on the banks of Esthwaite Water, in the heart of the Lake Country. The traveler who takes the pleasant journey on foot or coach from Windermere to Coniston, passes through

After the portrait by B. R. Haydon.

Hawkshead, where he may see Wordsworth's name cut in a desk of the school which he attended. Of greater interest is the scenery which contributed so much to his education and aided his development into England's greatest nature poet.

We learn from his autobiographical poem, *The Prelude*, what experiences molded him in boyhood. He says that the —

> ". . . common face of Nature spake to me
> Rememberable things."

In this poem he relates how he absorbed into his inmost

From mural painting by H. O. Walker, Congressional Library, Washington, D. C.
BOY OF WINANDER

being the orange sky of evening, the curling mist, the last autumnal crocus, the "souls of lonely places," and the huge peak, which terrified him at nightfall by seeming to stride after him and which awoke in him a —

> ". . . dim and undetermined sense
> Of unknown modes of being."

In his famous lines on the "Boy of Winander," Wordsworth tells how —

> ". . . the voice
> Of mountain torrents; or the visible scene
> Would enter unawares into his mind
> With all its solemn imagery, its rocks,
> Its woods, and that uncertain heaven, received
> Into the bosom of the steady lake."

At the age of seventeen he entered Cambridge University, from which he was graduated after a four years' course. He speaks of himself there as a dreamer passing through a dream. There came to him the strange feeling that he "was not for that hour nor for that place;" and yet he says that he was not unmoved by his daily association with the haunts of his illustrious predecessors, of —

> " Sweet Spenser, moving through his clouded heaven
> With the moon's beauty and the moon's soft pace,"

and of Milton whose soul seemed to Wordsworth "like a star."

Influence of the French Revolution. — His travels on the continent in his last vacation and after his graduation brought him in contact with the French Revolution, of which he felt the inspiring influence. He was fond of children, and the sight of a poor little French peasant girl seems to have been one of the main causes leading him to become an ardent revolutionist. *The Prelude* tells in concrete fullness how he walked along the banks of the Loire with his friend, a French patriot: —

> ". . . And when we chanced
> One day to meet a hunger-bitten girl,
> Who crept along fitting her languid gait
> Unto a heifer's motion, by a cord
> Tied to her arm, and picking thus from the lane
> Its sustenance, while the girl with pallid hands
> Was busy knitting in a heartless mood
> Of solitude, and at the sight my friend
> In agitation said, ''Tis against *that*
> That we are fighting.'"

Just as Wordsworth was prepared to throw himself personally into the conflict, his relatives recalled him to England. When the Revolution passed into a period of anarchy and bloodshed, his dejection was intense. As he slowly recovered from his disappointment, he became more and more conservative in politics and less in sympathy with violent agitation; but he never ceased to utter a hopeful though calm and tempered note for genuine liberty.

Maturity and Declining Years. — Although Wordsworth was early left an orphan, he never seemed to lack intelligent care and sympathy. His sister Dorothy, a rare soul, helped to fashion him into a poet. Their favorite pastime was walking and observing nature. De Quincey estimates that Wordsworth, during the course of his life, must have walked as many as 175,000 miles. He acted on his belief that —

"All things that love the sun are out of doors,"

and he composed his best poetry during his walks, dictating it after his return.

He must have had the capacity of impressing himself favorably on his associates or he might never have had the leisure to write poetry. When he was twenty-five, a friend left him a legacy of £900 to enable him to follow his chosen calling of poet. Seven years later, friends saw that he was appointed distributor of stamps for Westmoreland, at the annual salary of £400. Years afterward, a friend gave him a regular allowance to be spent in traveling.

The summer of 1797 saw him and Dorothy begin a golden year at Alfoxden in Somersetshire, in close association with Coleridge. The result of this companionship was *Lyrical Ballads*, an epoch-making volume of romantic verse, containing such gems as Wordsworth's *Lines composed a Few Miles above Tintern Abbey*, *Lines written in Early Spring*, *We Are Seven*, and Coleridge's *The Ancient Mariner*. "All good poetry," wrote Wordsworth in the *Preface* to the second edition of this volume, "is the spontaneous overflow of powerful feelings." This is the opposite of the belief of the classical school (pp. 259, 309).

In 1797, after a trip to Germany, he and Dorothy settled at Dove Cottage, Grasmere, in the Lake Country. She remained a member of the household after he married his cousin, Mary Hutchinson, in 1802. The history of English authors shows no more ideal companionship than that of these three kindred souls. Dove Cottage, where he wrote the best of his poetry, remains almost unchanged. It is one of the most interesting literary homes in England.

DOVE COTTAGE

In 1813 he moved a short distance away, to Rydal Mount, where he lived the remainder of his life. In 1843 he was chosen poet laureate. He died in 1850 and was buried in Grasmere Churchyard.

A Poet of Nature. — Wordsworth is one of the world's most loving and thoughtful lyrical poets of Nature. For him she possessed a soul, a conscious existence, an ability to feel joy and love. In *Lines written in Early Spring*, he expresses this belief: —

> "And 'tis my faith that every flower
> Enjoys the air it breathes."

All things seem to him to feel pure joy in existence: —

> "The moon doth with delight
> Look round her when the heavens are bare."

It was also his poetic creed that Nature could bring to human hearts a message of solace and companionship. His poem, *Lines composed a Short Distance above Tintern Abbey*, is a remarkable exposition of this faith.

He would have scorned to be considered merely a descriptive poet of nature. He satirizes those who could do nothing more than correctly apply the color "yellow" to the primrose: —

> "A primrose by a river's brim
> A yellow primrose was to him
> And it was nothing more."

He interprets the sympathetic soul of Nature, not merely her outward or her intellectual aspect. He says in *The Prelude*: —

> "From Nature and her overflowing soul
> I had received so much, that all my thoughts
> Were steeped in feeling."

If we compare Wordsworth's line —

> "This Sea that bares her bosom to the moon,"[1]

with Tennyson's line from *The Princess* —

> "A full sea glazed with muffled moonlight,"

we may easily decide which shows more feeling and which, more art.

Many poets have produced beautiful paintings of the external features of nature. With rare genius, Wordsworth looked beyond the color of the flower, the outline of the hills, the beauty of the clouds, to the spirit that breathed through them, and he communed with "Nature's self, which is the breath of God." He introduced lovers of his poetry to a new world of nature, a new source of companionship and solace, a new idea of a Being in cloud and air and "the green leaves among the groves."

Poetry of Man: Narrative Poems. — Wordsworth is a poet of man as well as of nature. The love for nature

---

[1] *Sonnet:* "The world is too much with us."

came to him first; but out of it grew his regard for the people who lived near to nature. His poetry of man is found more in his longer narrative poems, although in them as well as in his shorter pieces, he shows the action of nature on man. In *The Prelude*, the most remarkable autobiographical poem in English, he not only reveals the power in nature to develop man, but he also tells how the French Revolution made him feel the worth of each individual soul and a sense of the equality of all humanity at the bar of character and conscience. As his lyrics show the sympathetic soul of nature, so his narrative poems illustrate the second dominant characteristic of the age, the strong sense of the worth of the humblest man.

GRASMERE LAKE

Michael, one of the very greatest of his productions, displays a tender and living sympathy with the humble shepherd. The simple dignity of Michael's character, his frugal and honorable life, his affection for his son, for his sheep, and for his forefather's old home, appealed to the heart of the poet. He loved his subject and wrote the poem with that indescribable simplicity which makes the tale, the verse, and the tone of thought and feeling form together one perfect and indissoluble whole. *The Leech-Gatherer* and the story of "Margaret" in *The Excursion* also deal with lowly characters and exhibit Wordsworth's power of pathos and simple earnestness. He could not present complex personalities; but these characters, which belonged to the landscapes of the Lake District and partook of its calm and its simplicity, he drew with a sure hand.

His longest narrative poem is *The Excursion* (1814), which is in nine books. It contains fine passages of verse and some of his sanest and maturest philosophy; but the work is not the masterpiece that he hoped to make. It is tedious, prosy, and without action of any kind. The style, which is for the most part heavy, becomes pure and easy only in some description of a mountain peak or in the recital of a tale, like that of "Margaret."

An Interpreter of Child Life. — Perhaps the French Revolution and the unforgettable incident (p. 389) of the pitiable peasant child were not without influence in causing him to become a great poetic interpreter of childhood. No poem has surpassed his *Alice Fell, or Poverty* in presenting the psychology of childish grief, or his *We Are Seven* in voicing the faith of —

> ". . . A simple child,
> That lightly draws its breath,
> And feels its life in every limb,"

or the loneliness of "the solitary child" in *Lucy Gray:* —

> "The sweetest thing that ever grew
> Beside a human door."

In the poem, *Three Years She Grew in Sun and Shower*, Nature seems to have chosen Wordsworth as her spokesman to describe the part that she would play in educating a child. Nature says: —

> "This child I to myself will take ;
> She shall be mine, and I will make
> A lady of my own.
>
> . . . . . .

> ... She shall lean her ear
>   In many a secret place
> Where rivulets dance their wayward round,
> And beauty born of murmuring sound
>   Shall pass into her face."

One of the finest similes in all the poetry of nature may be found in the stanza which likens the charms of a little girl to those of: —

> "A violet by a mossy stone
>   Half hidden from the eye!
> Fair as a star when only one
>   Is shining in the sky."

Finally, in his *Intimations of Immortality from Recollections of Early Childhood*, he glorifies universal childhood, that "eye among the blind," capable of seeing this common earth —

> " Appareled in celestial light,
>   The glory and the freshness of a dream."

General Characteristics. — Four of Wordsworth's characteristics go hand in hand, — sincerity, feeling, depth of thought, and simplicity of style. The union of these four qualities causes his great poems to continue to yield pleasure after an indefinite number of readings. In his garden of poetry, the daffodil blossoms all the year for the "inward eye," and the "wandering voice of the cuckoo" never ceases to awaken springtime in the heart.

His own age greeted with so much ridicule the excessive simplicity of the presentation of ordinary childish grief in *Alice Fell*, that he excluded it from many editions of his poems. We now recognize the special charm of his simplicity in expressing those feelings and thoughts that "do often lie too deep for tears."

Wordsworth was most truly great when he seemed to

write as naturally as he breathed, when he appeared unconscious of the power that he wielded. When he attempted to command it at will, he failed, as in the dull, lifeless lines of *The Excursion*. Sometimes even his labored simplicity is no better than prose; but such simple and natural poems as *Michael, The Solitary Reaper, To My Sister, Three Years She Grew in Sun and Shower*, and the majority of the poems showing the new attitude toward childhood, are priceless treasures of English literature. Of most of these, we may say with Matthew Arnold, "It might seem that Nature not only gave him the matter for his poem, but wrote his poem for him."

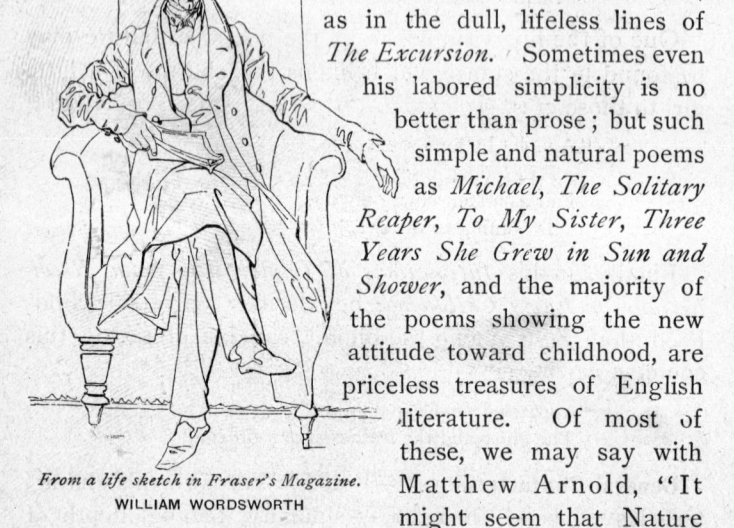

From a life sketch in Fraser's Magazine.
WILLIAM WORDSWORTH

Wordsworth lacks humor and his compass is limited; but within that compass he is surpassed by no poet since Milton. On the other hand, no great poet ever wrote more that is almost worthless. Matthew Arnold did much for Wordsworth's renown by collecting his priceless poems and publishing them apart from the mediocre work. Among the fine productions, his sonnets occupy a high place. Only Shakespeare and Milton in our language excel him in this form of verse.

Wordsworth is greatest as a poet of nature. To him nature seemed to possess a conscious soul, which expressed itself in the primrose, the rippling lake, or the cuckoo's song, with as much intelligence as human lips ever displayed in whispering a secret to the ear of love. This interpretation of nature gives him a unique position among

RYDAL MOUNT NEAR AMBLESIDE, THE HOME OF WORDSWORTH'S OLD AGE

English poets. Neither Shakespeare nor Milton had any such general conception of nature.

The bereaved, the downcast, and those in need of companionship turn naturally to Wordsworth. He said that it was his aim "to console the afflicted, to add sunshine to daylight." His critics often say that he does not recognize the indifference, even the cruelty of nature; but that he chooses, instead, to present the world as a manifestation of love and care for all creatures. When he was shown where a cruel huntsman and his dogs had chased a poor hart to its death, Wordsworth wrote:—

"This beast not unobserved by nature fell;
His death was mourned by sympathy divine.

"The Being that is in the clouds and air,
That is in the green leaves among the groves,

> Maintains a deep and reverential care
> For the unoffending creatures whom he loves."[1]

Whatever view we take of the indifference of nature or of the suffering in existence, it is necessary for us, in order to live hopeful and kindly lives, to feel with Wordsworth that the great powers of the universe are not devoid of sympathy, and that they encourage in us the development of "a spirit of love" for all earth's creatures. It was Wordsworth's deepest conviction that any one alive to the presence of nature's conscious spiritual force, that "rolls through all things"—

> "Shall feel an overseeing power
> To kindle or restrain."

SAMUEL TAYLOR COLERIDGE, 1772-1834

Life.—The troubled career of Coleridge is in striking contrast to the peaceful life of Wordsworth. Coleridge, the thirteenth child of a clergyman, was born in 1772 at Ottery St. Mary, Devonshire. Early in his life, the future poet became a confirmed dreamer, refusing to participate in the play common to boys of his age. Before he was five years old, he had read the *Arabian Nights*. Only a few years later, the boy's appetite for books became so voracious that he devoured an average of two volumes a day.

One evening, when he was about nine years old, he had a violent quarrel with his brother and ran away, sleeping out of doors all night. A cold October rain fell; but he was not found until morning, when he was carried home more dead than alive. "I was certainly injured;" he says of this adventure, "for I was weakly and subject to ague

[1] *Hart-Leap Well.*

From a pencil sketch by C. R. Leslie.

S. T. Coleridge

for many years after." Facts like these help to explain why physical pain finally led him to use opium.

After his father's death, young Coleridge became, at the age of ten, a pupil in Christ's Hospital, London, where he remained eight years. During the first half of his stay here, his health was still further injured by continuing as he was in earlier childhood, "a playless daydreamer," and by a habit of almost constant reading. He says that the food "was cruelly insufficient for those who had no friends to supply them." He writes: —

"Conceive what I must have been at fourteen; I was in a continual low fever. My whole being was, with eyes closed to every object of present sense, to crumple myself up in a sunny corner, and read, read, read, — fancy myself on Robinson Crusoe's island, finding a mountain of plumcake, and eating a room for myself, and then eating it into the shapes of tables and chairs — hunger and fancy!"

A few months after leaving Christ's Hospital, Coleridge went to Cambridge, but he did not remain to graduate. From this time he seldom completed anything that he undertook. It was characteristic of him, stimulated by the spirit of the French Revolution, to dream of founding with Southey a Pantisocracy on the banks of the Susquehanna. In this ideal village across the sea, the dreamers were to work only two hours a day and were to have all goods in common. The demand for poetry was at this time sufficiently great for a bookseller to offer Coleridge, although he was as yet comparatively unknown, thirty guineas for a volume of poems and a guinea and a half for each hundred lines after finishing that volume. With such wealth in view, Coleridge married a Miss Fricker of Bristol, because no single people could join the new ideal commonwealth. Southey married her sister; but the young enthusiasts were forced to abandon their project because they did not have sufficient money to procure passage across the ocean.

The tendency to dream, however, never forsook Coleridge. One of his favorite poems begins with this line: —

"My eyes make pictures when they are shut."[1]

He recognized his disinclination to remain long at work on prearranged lines, when he said, "I think that my soul must have preëxisted in the body of a chamois chaser."

In 1797–1798 Coleridge lived with his young wife at Nether-Stowey in Somerset. Wordsworth and his sister

[1] *A Day-Dream.*

Dorothy moved to a house in the neighborhood in order to be near Coleridge. The two young men and Dorothy Wordsworth seemed to be exactly fitted to stimulate one another. Together they roamed over the Quantock Hills, gazed upon the sea, and planned *The Rime of the Ancient Mariner*, which is one of the few things that Coleridge ever finished. In little more than a year he wrote nearly all the poetry that has made him famous.

Had he, like Keats, died when he was twenty-five, the world would probably be wondering what heights of poetic fame Coleridge might have reached; but he became addicted to the use of opium and passed a wretched existence of thirty-six years longer, partly in the Lake District, but chiefly in a suburb of London, without adding to his poetic fame. During his later years he did hack work for papers, gave occasional lectures, wrote critical and philosophical prose, and became a talker almost as noted as Dr. Johnson. It is only just to Coleridge to recognize the fact that even if he had never written a line of poetry, his prose would entitle him to be ranked among England's greatest critics.

COLERIDGE'S COTTAGE AT NETHER-STOWEY

Coleridge's wide reading, continued from boyhood, made his contemporaries feel that he had the best intellectual equipment of any man in England since Francis Bacon's time. Once Coleridge, having forgotten the subject of his lecture, was startled by the announcement that he would speak on a difficult topic, entirely different from the one he had in mind; but he was equal to the emergency and delivered an unusually good address.

Young men used to flock to him in his old age to draw on his copious stores of knowledge and especially to hear him talk about German philosophy. Carlyle visited him for this purpose and speaks of the "glorious, balmy, sunny islets, islets of the blest and the intelligible," which occasionally emerged from the mist of German metaphysics.

He spent the last eighteen years of his life in Highgate with his kind friend, Dr. Gillman, who succeeded in regulating and decreasing the amount of opium which Coleridge took. He died there in 1834 and was buried in Highgate Cemetery. Westminster Abbey does not have the honor of the grave of a single one of the great poets of this romantic age.

Poetry.— *The Ancient Mariner* (1798) is Coleridge's poetical masterpiece. It is also one of the world's masterpieces. The supernatural sphere into which it introduces the reader is a remarkable creation, with its curse, its polar spirit, the phantom ship, the seraph band, and the magic breeze. The mechanism of the poem is a triumph of romantic genius. The meter, the rhythm, and the music have well nigh magical effect. Almost every stanza shows not only exquisite harmony, but also the easy mastery of genius in dealing with those weird scenes which romanticists love.

The moral interest of the poem is not inferior to its other charms. The Mariner killed the innocent Albatross, and we listen to the same kind of lesson as Wordsworth teaches in his *Hart-Leap Well* (p. 397): —

> "'The spirit who bideth by himself
> In the land of mist and snow,

> He loved the bird that loved the man
> Who shot him with his bow.'"

The noble conclusion of the poem has for more than a hundred years continued to influence human conduct: —

> "He prayeth best who loveth best
> All things both great and small;
> For the dear God who loveth us,
> He made and loveth all."

His next greatest poem is the unfinished *Christabel* (1816). A lovely maiden falls under the enchantments of a mysterious Lady Geraldine; but the fragment closes while this malevolent influence continues. We miss the interest of a finished story, which draws so many readers to *The Ancient Mariner*, although *Christabel* is thickly sown with gems. Lines like these are filled with the airiness of nature: —

> "There is not wind enough to twirl
> The one red leaf, the last of its clan,
> That dances as often as dance it can,
> Hanging so light, and hanging so high,
> On the topmost twig that looks up at the sky."

In all literature there has been no finer passage written on the wounds caused by broken friendship than the lines in *Christabel* relating to the estrangement of Roland and Sir Leoline. After reading this poem and *Kubla Khan*, an unfinished dream fragment of fifty-four lines, we feel that the closing lines of *Kubla Khan* are peculiarly applicable to Coleridge: —

> "For he on honey dew hath fed
> And drunk the milk of Paradise."

Swinburne says of *Christabel* and *Kubla Khan:* "When it has been said that such melodies were never heard, such dreams never dreamed, such speech never spoken, the chief things remain unsaid, unspeakable. There is a charm upon these poems which can only be felt in silent submission and wonder."

General Characteristics of his Poetry.— Unlike Wordsworth, Coleridge is not the poet of the earth and the common things of life. He is the poet of air, of the regions beyond the earth, and of dreams. By no poet has the supernatural been invested with more charm.

He has rare feeling for the beautiful, whether in the world of morals, of nature, or of the harmonies of sound. The motherless Christabel in her time of danger dreams a beautiful truth of this divinely governed world: —

> " But this she knows, in joys and woes,
> That saints will aid if men will call:
> For the blue sky bends over all."

His references to nature are less remarkable for description or photographic details than for suggestiveness and diffused charm, such as we find in these lines: —

> ". . . the sails made on
> A pleasant noise till noon,
> A noise like of a hidden brook
> In the leafy month of June,
> That to the sleeping woods all night
> Singeth a quiet tune."

Wordsworth wrote few poems simpler than *The Ancient Mariner*. A stanza like this seems almost as simple as breathing: —

> " The moving moon went up the sky,
> And nowhere did abide:
> Softly she was going up,
> And a star or two beside."

Prose. — Coleridge's prose, which is almost all critical or philosophical, left its influence on the thought of the nineteenth century. When he was a young man, he went to Germany and studied philosophy with a continued vigor unusual for him. He became an idealist and used the idealistic teachings of the German metaphysicians to combat the utilitarian and sense-bound philosophy of Bentham, Malthus, and Mill (p. 358). We pass by Coleridge's *Aids to Reflection* (1825), the weightiest of his metaphysical productions, to consider those works which possess a more vital interest for the student of literature. His *Lectures on Shakespeare*, delivered in 1811, contained epoch-making Shakespearean criticism. We are told that every drawing-room in London discussed them. His greatest work on criticism is entitled *Biographia Literaria* (2 Vols., 1817). There are parts of it which no careful student of the development of modern criticism can afford to leave unread. The central point of this work is the exposition of his theory of the romantic school of poetry. He thus gives his own aim and that of Wordsworth in the composition of the volume of poems, known as *Lyrical Ballads* (p. 390): —

From a sketch made in Germany.
COLERIDGE AS A YOUNG MAN

" ... it was agreed that my endeavors should be directed to persons and characters supernatural, or at least romantic; yet so as to transfer from our inward nature a human interest and a semblance of truth sufficient to procure for these shadows of imagination that willing suspension of disbelief for the moment, which constitutes poetic faith.

Mr. Wordsworth, on the other hand, was to propose to himself as his object, to give the charm of novelty to things of every day, and to excite a feeling analogous to the supernatural by awakening the mind's attention from the lethargy of custom, and directing it to the loveliness and wonders of the world before us."[1]

Coleridge does not hold Wordsworth's belief that the language of common speech and of poetry should be identical. He shows that Wordsworth does better than follow his own theories. Yet, when he considers both the excellencies and the defects of Wordsworth's verse, Coleridge's verdict of praise is substantially that of the twentieth century. This is an unusual triumph for a contemporary critic, sitting in judgment on an author of an entirely new school and rendering a decision in opposition to that of the majority, who, he says, "have made it a business to attack and ridicule Mr. Wordsworth. ... His *fame* belongs to another age and can neither be accelerated nor retarded."[2]

GEORGE NOEL GORDON, LORD BYRON, 1788-1824

Life. — Byron was born in London in 1788. His father was a reckless, dissipated spendthrift, who deserted his wife and child. Mrs. Byron convulsively clasped her son to her one moment and threw the scissors and tongs at him the next, calling him "the lame brat," in reference to his club foot. Such treatment drew neither respect nor obedience from Byron, who inherited the proud, defiant spirit of his race. His accession to the peerage in 1798 did not tend to tame his haughty nature, and he grew up passionately imperious and combative.

Being ambitious, he made excellent progress in his studies

---

[1] *Biographia Literaria*, Chapter XIV.
[2] *Ibid.*, Chapter XXII.

From a portrait by Kramer.

at Harrow, but when he entered Cambridge he devoted much of his time to shooting, swimming, and other sports, for which he was always famous. In 1809 he started on a two years' trip through Spain, Greece, and the far East. Upon his return, he published two cantos of *Childe Harold's Pilgrimage*, which describe his journey.

This poem made him immediately popular. London society neglected its old favorite, Scott, and eagerly sought out the handsome young peer who had burst suddenly **upon** it. Poem after poem was produced by this lion of society, and each one was received with enthusiasm and delight. Probably no other English poet knew such instant widespread fame as Byron.

Suddenly and unexpectedly this adulation turned to hatred. In 1815 Byron married Miss Milbanke, an heiress, but she left him a year later. Although no reason for the separation was given, the public fastened all the blame upon Byron. The feeling against him grew so strong that he was warned by his friends to prepare for open violence, and finally, in 1816, he left England forever.

His remaining eight years were spent mostly in Italy. Here, his great beauty, his exile, his poetry, and his passionate love of liberty made him a prominent figure throughout Europe. Notwithstanding this fame, life was a disappointment to Byron. Baffled but rebellious, he openly defied the conventions of his country; and seemed to enjoy the shock it gave to his countrymen.

From a painting.
BYRON AT SEVENTEEN

The closing year of his life shone brightest of all. His main activities had hitherto been directed to the selfish pursuit of his own pleasure; and he had failed to obtain happiness. But in 1823 Byron went to Greece to aid the Greeks, who were battling with Turkey for their independence. Into this struggle for freedom, he poured his whole energies, displaying "a wonderful aptitude for managing the complicated intrigues and plans and selfishnesses which lay in the way." His efforts cost him his life. He contracted fever, and, after restlessly battling with the disease, said quietly, one April morning in 1824, "Now

NEWSTEAD ABBEY, BYRON'S HOME

I shall go to sleep." His relatives asked in vain for permission to inter him in Westminster Abbey. He was buried in the family vault at Hucknall, Nottinghamshire, not far from Newstead Abbey.

Early Works.—The poems that Byron wrote during his brilliant sojourn in London, amid the whirl of social gayeties, are *The Giaour, The Bride of Abydos, The Corsair, Parisina, Lara,* and *The Siege of Corinth.* These narrative poems are romantic tales of oriental passion and coloring, which show the influence of Scott. They are told with a dash and a fine-sounding rhetoric well fitted to attract **immediate attention;** but they lack the qualities of sincere feeling, lofty thought, and subtle beauty, which give lasting fame.

His next publication, *The Prisoner of Chillon* (1816), is a much worthier poem. The pathetic story is feelingly told in language that often displays remarkable energy and mastery of expression and versification. His picture of the oppressive vacancy which the Prisoner felt is a well-executed piece of very difficult word painting: —

CASTLE OF CHILLON

> "There were no stars, no earth, no time,
> No check, no change, no good, no crime —
> But silence, and a stirless breath
> Which neither was of life nor death;
> A sea of stagnant idleness,
> Blind, boundless, mute, and motionless!"

Dramas. — Byron wrote a number of dramas, the best of which are *Manfred* (1817) and *Cain* (1821). His spirit of defiance and his insatiable thirst for power are the subjects of these dramas. Manfred is a man of guilt who is at war with humanity, and who seeks refuge on the mountain tops and by the wild cataract. He is fearless and untamed in all his misery, and even in the hour of death does not quail before the spirits of darkness, but defies them with the cry: —

> "Back to thy hell!
> Thou hast no power upon me, *that* I feel!
> Thou never shalt possess me, *that* I know;

> What I have done is done; I bear within
> A torture which could nothing gain from thine :
>
> . . . .
>
> Back, ye baffled fiends !
> The hand of death is on me — but not yours !"

Cain, while suffering remorse for the slaying of Abel, is borne by Lucifer through the boundless fields of the universe. Cain yet dares to question the wisdom of the Almighty in bringing evil, sin, and remorse into the world. A critic has remarked that " Milton wrote his great poem to justify the ways of God to man; Byron's object seems to be to justify the ways of man to God."

The very soul of stormy revolt breathes through both *Manfred* and *Cain*, but *Cain* has more interest as a pure drama. It contains some sweet passages and presents one lovely woman,— Adah. But Byron could not interpret a character wholly at variance with his own. He possessed but little constructive skill, and he never overcame the difficulties of blank verse. A drama that does not show wide sympathy with varied types of humanity and the constructive capacity to present the complexities of life is lacking in essential elements of greatness.

Childe Harold, The Vision of Judgment, and Don Juan. — His best works are the later poems, which require only a slight framework or plot, such as *Childe Harold's Pilgrimage, The Vision of Judgment,* and *Don Juan.*

The third and fourth cantos of *Childe Harold*, published in 1816 and 1818, respectively, are far superior to the first two. These later cantos continue the travels of Harold, and contain some of Byron's most splendid descriptions of nature, cities, and works of art. Rome, Venice, the Rhine, the Alps, and the sea inspired the finest lines. He wrote of Venice as she —

"... Sate in state, throned on her hundred isles!

. . . .

She looks a sea Cybele, fresh from ocean,
Rising with her tiara of proud towers
At airy distance."

He calls Rome —

"The Niobe of nations! there she stands,
  Childless and crownless, in her voiceless woe;
An empty urn within her wither'd hands,
  Whose holy dust was scattered long ago."

The following description, from Canto III, of a wild stormy night in the mountains is very characteristic of his nature poetry and of his own individuality : —

"And this is in the night : — Most glorious night!
Thou wert not sent for slumber! let me be
A sharer in thy fierce and far delight —
  A portion of the tempest and of thee!
How the lit lake shines, a phosphoric sea,
And the big rain comes dancing to the earth!
And now again 'tis black, — and now, the glee
Of the loud hills shakes with its mountain-mirth
As if they did rejoice o'er a young earthquake's birth."

When George III. died, Southey wrote a poem filled with absurd flattery of that monarch. Byron had such intense hatred for the hypocrisy of society that he wrote his *Vision of Judgment* (1822) to parody Southey's poem and to make the author the object of satire. Pungent wit, vituperation, and irony were here handled by Byron in a brilliant manner, which had not been equaled since the days of Dryden and Pope. The parodies of most poems are quickly forgotten, but we have here the strange case of Byron's parody keeping alive Southey's original.

Don Juan (1819–1824), a long poem in sixteen cantos, is Byron's greatest work. It is partly autobiographic. The sinister, gloomy Don Juan is an ideal picture of the author, who was sore and bitter over his thwarted hopes of liberty and happiness. Therefore, instead of strengthening humanity with hope for the future, this poem tears hope from the horizon, and suggests the possible anarchy and destruction toward which the world's hypocrisy, cant, tyranny, and universal stupidity are tending.

The poem is unfinished. Byron followed Don Juan through all the phases of life known to himself. The hero has exciting adventures and passionate loves, he is favored at courts, he is driven to the lowest depths of society, he experiences a godlike happiness and a demoniacal despair.

Don Juan is a scathing satire upon society. All its fondest idols, — love, faith, and hope, — are dragged in the mire. There is something almost grand in the way that this Titanic scoffer draws pictures of love only to mock at them, sings patriotic songs only to add —

> " Thus sung, or would, or could, or should have sung
> The modern Greek in tolerable verse,"

and mentions Homer, Milton, and Shakespeare only to show how accidental and worthless is fame.

Amid the splendid confusion of pathos, irony, passion, mockery, keen wit, and brilliant epigram, which display Byron's versatile and spontaneous genius at its height, there are some beautiful and powerful passages. There is an ideal picture of the love of Don Juan and Haidee: —

> " Each was the other's mirror, and but read
> Joy sparkling in their dark eyes like a gem."

> " . . . they could not be
> Meant to grow old, but die in happy spring,
> Before one charm or hope had taken wing."

As she lightly slept—

> ". . . her face so fair
> Stirr'd with her dream, as rose-leaves with the air;
> Or as the stirring of a deep clear stream
> Within an Alpine hollow, when the wind
> Walks o'er it."

General Characteristics. — The poetry of Wordsworth and Coleridge shows the revolutionary reaction against classicism in literature and tyranny in government; but their verse raises no cry of revolt against the proprieties and moral restrictions of the time. Byron was so saturated with the revolutionary spirit that he rebelled against these also; and for this reason England would not allow him to be buried in Westminster Abbey.

As Byron frequently wrote in the white heat of passionate revolt, his verse shows the effects of lack of restraint. Unfortunately he did not afterwards take the trouble to improve his subject matter, or the mold in which it was cast. Swinburne says, "His verse stumbles and jingles, stammers and halts, where is most need for a swift and even pace of musical sound."

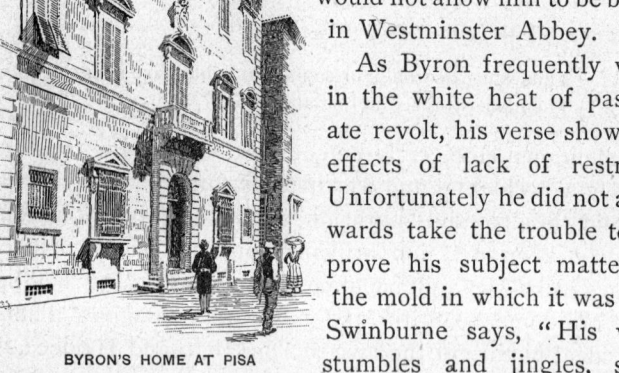

BYRON'S HOME AT PISA

The great power of Byron's poetry consists in its wealth of expression, its vigor, its rush and volume of sound, its variety, and its passion. Lines like the following show the vigorous flow of the verse, the love for lonely scenery, and a wealth of figurative expression:—

> "Mont Blanc is the monarch of mountains,
>   They crowned him long ago
> On a throne of rocks, in a robe of clouds
>   With a diadem of snow."[1]

Scattered through his works we find rare gems, such as the following—

> "... when
> Music arose with its voluptuous swell,
>   Soft eyes looked love to eyes which spake again,
> And all went merry as a marriage bell."[2]

We may also frequently note the working of an acute intellect, as, for instance, in the lines in which he calls his own gloomy type of mind—

> "... the telescope of truth,
> Which strips the distance of its phantasies,
> And brings life near in utter nakedness,
> Making the cold reality too real!"[3]

The answers to two questions which are frequently asked, will throw more light on Byron's characteristics:—

I. Why has his poetic fame in England decreased so much from the estimate of his contemporaries, by whom he seemed worthy of a place beside Goethe? The answer is to be sought in the fact that Byron reflected so powerfully the mood of that special time. That reactionary period in history has passed and with it much of Byron's influence and fame. He was, unlike Shakespeare, specially fitted to minister to a certain age. Again, much of Byron's verse is rhetorical, and that kind of poetry does not wear well. On the other hand, we might reread Shakespeare's

---

[1] *Manfred*, Act I. [2] *Childe Harold's Pilgrimage*, Canto III.
[3] *The Dream*.

Hamlet, Milton's *Lycidas*, and Wordsworth's *Intimations of Immortality* every month for a lifetime, and discover some new beauty and truth at every reading.

II. Why does the continent of Europe class Byron among the very greatest English poets, next even to Shakespeare? It is because Europe was yearning for more liberty, and Byron's words and blows for freedom aroused her at an opportune moment. Historians of continental literature find his powerful impress on the thought of that time. Georg Brandes, a noted European critic, says:—

"In the intellectual life of Russia and Poland, of Spain and Italy, of France and Germany, the seeds which he had sown, fructified. . . . The Slavonic nations . . . seized on his poetry with avidity. . . . The Spanish and Italian exile poets took his war cry. . . . Heine's best poetry is a continuation of Byron's work. French Romanticism and German Liberalism are both direct descendants of Byron's Naturalism."

Swinburne gives as another reason for Byron's European popularity the fact that he actually gains by translation into a foreign tongue. His faulty meters and careless expressions are improved, while his vigorous way of stating things and his rolling rhetoric are easily comprehended. On the other hand, the delicate shades of thought in Shakespeare's *Hamlet* cannot be translated into some European tongues without distinct loss.

PERCY BYSSHE SHELLEY, 1792-1822

Life. — Another fiery spirit of the Revolution was Shelley, born in 1792, in a home of wealth, at Field Place, near Horsham, Sussex. He was one of the most ardent, independent, and reckless English poets inspired by the French Revolution. He was a man who could face

From the portrait by Amelia Curran, National Portrait Gallery.

infamy and defy the conventionalities of the world, and, at the same moment, extend a helpful hand of sympathy to a friend or sit for sixty hours beside the sick bed of his dying child. Tender, pitying, fearless, full of a desire to reform the world, and of hatred for any form of tyranny, Shelley failed to adjust himself to the customs and laws of his actual surroundings. He was calumniated and despised by the public at large, and almost idolized by his intimate friends.

At Eton he denounced the tyranny of the larger boys. At Oxford he decried the tyranny of the church over freedom of thought, and was promptly expelled for his pamphlet, *The Necessity of Atheism.* This act so increased his hatred for despotic authority that he almost immediately married Harriet Westbrook, a beautiful school girl of sixteen, to relieve her from the tyranny of her father who wanted her to return to school. Shelley

SHELLEY'S BIRTHPLACE, FIELD PLACE

was then only nineteen and very changeable. He would make such a sudden departure from a place where he had vowed "to live forever," that specially invited guests sometimes came to find him gone. He soon fell in love with Mary Wollstonecraft Godwin, the brilliant woman who later wrote the weird romance *Frankenstein*, and he married her after Harriet Shelley had drowned herself. These acts alienated his family and forced him to forfeit his right to Field Place.

His repeatedly avowed ideas upon religion, government, and marriage brought him into conflict with public opinion.

Unpopular at home, he left England in 1818, never to return. Like Byron, he was practically an exile.

The remaining four years of Shelley's life were passed in comparative tranquillity in the "Paradise of exiles," as he called Italy. He lived chiefly at Pisa, the last eighteen months of his life. Byron rented the famous Lanfranchi Palace in Pisa and became Shelley's neighbor, often entertaining him and a group of English friends, among whom were Edward Trelawny, the Boswell of Shelley's last days, and Leigh Hunt, biographer and essayist.

On July 7, 1822, Shelley said: "If I die to-morrow, I have lived to be older than my father. I am ninety years of age." The young poet was right in claiming that it is not length of years that measures life. He had lived longer than most people who reach ninety. The next day he started in company with two others to sail across the Bay of Spezzia to his summer home. Friends watching from the shore saw a sudden tempest strike his boat. When the cloud passed, the craft could not be seen. Not many months before, he had written the last stanza of *Adonais*:—

> ". . . my spirit's bark is driven
> Far from the shore, far from the trembling throng
> Whose sails were never to the tempest given,
> The massy earth and sphered skies are riven!
> I am borne darkly, fearfully, afar;
> Whilst, burning through the inmost veil of heaven,
> The soul of Adonais, like a star,
> Beacons from the abode where the Eternal are."

Shelley's body was washed ashore, July 18, and it was burned near the spot, in accordance with Italian law; but the ashes and the unconsumed heart were interred in the beautiful Protestant cemetery at Rome, not far from where Keats was buried the previous year.

Few poets have been loved more than Shelley. Twentieth century visitors to his grave often find it covered with fresh flowers. The direction which he wrote for finding the tomb of Keats is more applicable to Shelley's own resting place:—

> "Pass, till the Spirit of the spot shall lead
> Thy footsteps to a slope of green access,
> Where, like an infant's smile, over the dead
> A light of laughing flowers along the grass is spread."[1]

Works. — *Alastor, or the Spirit of Solitude* (1816) is a magnificent expression of Shelley's own restless, tameless spirit, wandering among the grand solitudes of nature in search of the ineffably lovely dream maiden, who was his ideal of beauty. He travels through primeval forests, stands upon dizzy abysses, plies through roaring whirlpools, all of which are symbolic of the soul's wayfaring, until at last,—

> "When on the threshold of the green recess,"

his dying glance rests upon the setting moon and the sufferer finds eternal peace. The general tone of this poem is painfully despairing, but this is relieved by the grandeur of the natural scenes and by many imaginative flights.

GRAVE OF SHELLEY, PROTESTANT CEMETERY, ROME

[1] *Adonais*, Stanza xlix

The year 1819 saw the publication of a work unique among Shelley's productions, *The Cenci*. This is a drama based upon the tragic story of Beatrice Cenci. The poem deals with human beings, human passions, real acts, and the natural world, whereas Shelley usually preferred to treat of metaphysical theories, personified abstractions, and the world of fancy. This strong drama was the most popular of his works during his lifetime.

He returned to the ideal sphere again in one of his great poems, the lyrical drama *Prometheus Unbound* (1820). This poem is the apotheosis of the French Revolution. Prometheus, the friend of mankind, lies tortured and chained to the mountain side. As the hour of redemption approaches, his beloved Asia, the symbol of nature, arouses the soul of Revolution, represented by Demogorgon. He rises, hurls down the enemies of progress and freedom, releases Prometheus, and spreads liberty and happiness through all the world. Then the Moon, the Earth, and the Voices of the Air break forth into a magnificent chant of praise. The most delicate fancies, the most gorgeous imagery, and the

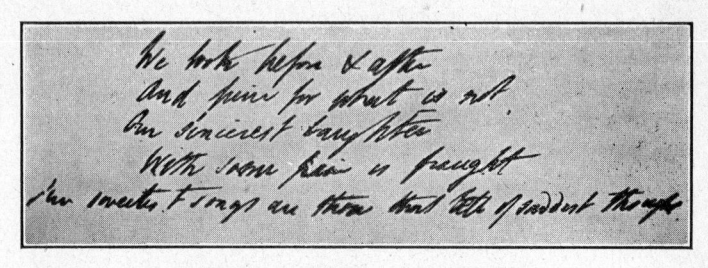

FACSIMILE OF STANZA FROM "TO A SKYLARK"

most fiery, exultant emotions are combined in this poem with something of the stateliness of its Greek prototype. The swelling cadences of the blank verse and the tripping rhythm of the lyrics are the product of a nature rich in rare and wonderful melodies.

The Witch of Atlas (1820), *Epipsychidion* (1821), *Adonais* (1821), and the exquisite lyrics, *The Cloud, To a Skylark*, and *Ode to the West Wind* are the most beautiful of the remaining works. The first two mentioned are the most elusive of Shelley's poems. With scarcely an echo in his soul of the shadows and discords of earth, the poet paints, in these works, lands —

> ". . . 'twixt Heaven, Air, Earth, and Sea,
> Cradled, and hung in clear tranquillity;"

where all is —

> "Beautiful as a wreck of Paradise."[1]

Adonais is a lament for the early death of Keats, and it stands second in the language among elegiac poems, ranking next to Milton's *Lycidas*. Shelley referred to *Adonais* as "perhaps the least imperfect of my compositions." His biographer, Edward Dowden, calls it "the costliest monument ever erected to the memory of an English singer," who

> ". . . bought, with price of purest breath,
> A grave among the eternal."

Mrs. Shelley put some of her most sacred mementos of the poet between the leaves of *Adonais*, which spoke to her of his own immortality and omnipresence: —

> "Naught we know dies. Shall that alone which knows
> Be as a sword consumed before the sheath
> By sightless lightning?
>
> . . . .
>
> He is a portion of the loveliness
> Which once he made more lovely."

Although some of Shelley's shorter poems are more popu-

---

[1] *Epipsychidion.*

lar, nothing that he ever wrote surpasses *Adonais* in completeness, poetic thought, and perfection of artistic finish.

Treatment of Nature. — Shelley was not interested in things themselves, but in their elusive animating spirit. In the lyric poem, *To Night*, he does not address himself to mere darkness, but to the active, dream-weaving "Spirit of Night." The very spirit of the autumnal wind seems to him to breathe on the leaves and turn them —

> "Yellow, and black, and pale, and hectic red,
>   Pestilence-stricken multitudes."[1]

In his spiritual conception of nature, he was profoundly affected by Wordsworth; but he goes farther than the older poet in giving expression to the strictly individual forms of nature. Wordsworth pictures nature as a reflection of his own thoughts and feelings. In *The Prelude* he says: —

> "To unorganic natures were transferred
>   My own enjoyments."

Shelley, on the other hand, is most satisfying and original when his individual spirit forms in night, cloud, skylark, and wind are made to sing, not as a reflection of his own mood, but as these spirit forces might themselves be supposed to sing, if they could express their song in human language without the aid of a poet. In the lyric, *The Cloud*, it is the animating spirit of the Cloud itself that sings the song: —

> "I bring fresh showers for the thirsting flowers,
>   From the seas and the streams;
> I bear light shade for the leaves when laid
>   In their noonday dreams.
>
> . . . .
>
> I sift the snow on the mountains below
>   And their great pines groan aghast."

[1] *Ode to the West Wind.*

He thus begins the song, *To a Skylark* —

> "Hail to thee, blithe spirit!
> Bird thou never wert,"

and he likens the lark to "an unbodied joy."

He peoples the garden in his lyric, *The Sensitive Plant*, with flowers that are definite, individual manifestations of "the Spirit of Love felt everywhere," the same power on which Shelley enthusiastically relied for the speedy transformation of the world.

> "A Sensitive Plant in a garden grew,
> And the young winds fed it with silver dew."

The "tulip tall," "the Naiad-like lily," "the jessamine faint," "the sweet tuberose," were all "ministering angels" to the "companionless Sensitive Plant," and each tried to be a source of joy to all the rest. No one who had not caught the new spirit of humanity could have imagined that garden.

In the exquisite *Ode to the West Wind*, he calls to that "breath of Autumn's being" to express its own mighty harmonies through him: —

> "O wild West Wind, thou breath of Autumn's being,
> . . . .
> Make me thy lyre, even as the forest is:
>   What if my leaves are falling like its own!
> The tumult of thy mighty harmonies
>   Will take from both a deep, autumnal tone,
> Sweet though in sadness."

We may fancy that the spirit forms of nature which appear in cloud and night, in song of bird and western wind, are content to have found in Shelley a lyre that responded to their touch in such entrancing notes.

General Characteristics. — Shelley's is the purest, the most hopeful, and the noblest voice of the Revolution. Wordsworth and Coleridge lost their faith and became Tories, and Byron was a selfish, lawless creature; but Shelley had the martyr spirit of sacrifice, and he trusted to the end in the wild hopes of the revolutionary enthusiasts. His *Queen Mab*, *Revolt of Islam*, *Ode to Liberty*, *Ode to Naples*, and, above all, his *Prometheus Unbound*, are some of the works inspired by a trust in the ideal democracy which was to be based on universal love and the brotherhood of man. This faith gives a bounding elasticity and buoyancy to Shelley's thought, but also tinges it with that disgust for the old, that defiance of restraint, and that boyish disregard for experience which mark a time of revolt.

The other subject that Shelley treats most frequently in his verse is ideal beauty. He yearned all his life for some form beautiful enough to satisfy the aspirations of his soul. *Alastor*, *Epipsychidion*, *The Witch of Atlas*, and *Prometheus Unbound*, all breathe this insatiate craving for that "Spirit of Beauty," that "awful Loveliness."

Many of his efforts to describe in verse this democracy and this ideal beauty are impalpable and obscure. It is difficult to clothe such shadowy abstractions in clear, simple form. He is occasionally vague because his thoughts seem to have emerged only partially from the cloud lands that gave them birth. At other times, his vagueness resembles Plato's because it is inherent in the subject matter. Like Byron, Shelley is sometimes careless in the construction and revision of his verse. We shall, however, search in vain for these faults in Shelley's greatest lyrics. He is one of the supreme lyrical geniuses in the language. Of all the lyric poets of England, he is the greatest master of an ethereal, evanescent, phantomlike beauty.

From the painting by Hilton, National Portrait Gallery.

John Keats

JOHN KEATS, 1795-1821

Life. — John Keats, the son of a keeper of a large livery stable, a man "fine in common sense and native respectability," was born in Moorfields, London, in 1795. He attended school at Enfield, where he was a prize scholar. He took special pleasure in studying Grecian mythology, the influence of which is so apparent in his poetry. While at school, he also voluntarily wrote a translation of much of Vergil's *Æneid*. It would seem as if he had also been attracted to Shakespeare; for Keats is credited with expressing to a young playmate the opinion that no one, if alone in the house, would dare read *Macbeth* at two in the morning.

When Keats was left an orphan in his fifteenth year, he was taken from school and apprenticed to a surgeon at Edmonton, near London.

When seventeen, he walked some distance to borrow a copy of Spenser's *Faerie Queene*. A friend says: "Keats ramped through the scenes of the romance like a young horse turned into a spring meadow." His study of Grecian mythology and Elizabethan poetry exerted a stronger influence over him than his medical instructor. One day when Keats should have been listening to a surgical lecture, "there came," he says, "a sunbeam into the room and with it a whole troop of creatures floating in the ray; and I was off with them to Oberon and fairy land."

He made a moderately good surgeon; but finding that his heart was constantly with "Oberon and the fairy land" of poesy, he gave up his profession in 1817 and began to study hard, preparatory to a literary career.

His short life was a brave struggle against disease, poverty, and unfriendly criticism; but he accomplished more than any other English author in the first twenty-five years of life. Success under such conditions would have been impossible unless he had had "flint and iron in him." He wrote:—

"I must think that difficulties nerve the spirit of a man. They make his Prime Objects a Refuge as well as a Passion."

Late in 1818, after he had published his first volume of verse, he met Fanny Brawne, a girl of eighteen, and soon fell desperately in love with her. The next six months were the happiest and the most productive period of his life. His health was then such that he could take long walks with her. In the first spring after he had met her, he wrote in less than three hours his wonderful *Ode to a Nightingale*, while he was sitting in the garden of his home at Wentworth Place, Hampstead, near London, listening to the song of the bird. Most of his famous poems were written in the year after meeting her.

In February, 1820, his health began to decline so rapidly that he knew that his days were numbered. His mother and one of his brothers had died of consumption, and he had been for some time threatened with the disease. He offered to release Miss Brawne from her engagement, but she would not listen to the suggestion. She and her mother tried to nurse him back to health. Few events in the history of English authors are tinged with a deeper pathos than his engagement to Miss Brawne. Some of the letters that he wrote to her or about her are almost tragic. After he had taken his last leave of her he wrote, "I can bear to die — I cannot bear to leave her."

Acting on insistent medical advice, Keats sailed for Italy in September, 1820, accompanied by a stanch friend, the

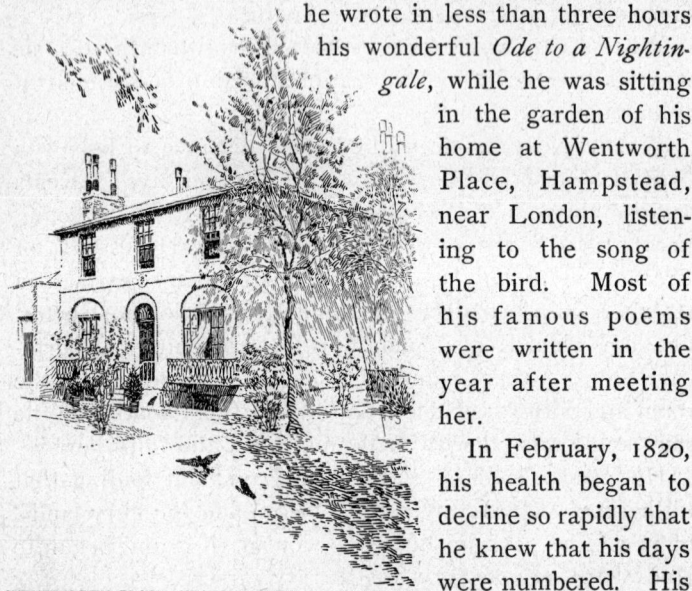

WENTWORTH PLACE, KEATS'S HOME IN HAMPSTEAD

artist Joseph Severn. On this voyage, Keats wrote a sonnet which proved to be his swan song: —

> "Bright star! would I were steadfast as thou art —
>   Not in lone splendor hung aloft the night
> And watching, with eternal lids apart,
>   Like Nature's patient, sleepless Eremite,
> The moving waters at their priestlike task
> Of pure ablution round earth's human shores."

While he lay on his sick bed in Rome, he said: "I feel the flowers growing over me." In February, 1821, he died, at the age of twenty-five years and four months. On the modest stone which marks his grave in the Protestant Cemetery in Rome, there was placed at his request: "Here lies one whose name was writ in water." His most appropriate epitaph is Shelley's *Adonais*.

Poems. — In 1817 he published his first poems in a thin volume, which did not attract much attention, although it contained two excellent sonnets: *On First Looking into Chapman's Homer* and *On the Grasshopper and Cricket*, which begins with the famous line: —

GRAVE OF KEATS, ROME

> "The poetry of earth is never dead."

We may also find in this volume such lines of promise as: —

> "Life is the rose's hope while yet unblown;
> The reading of an ever changing tale."

A year later, his long poem, *Endymion*, appeared. The inner purpose of this poetic romance is to show the search of the soul for absolute Beauty. The first five lines are a beautiful exposition of his poetic creed. *Endymion*, however, suffers from immaturity, shown in boyish sentimentality, in a confusion of details, and in an overabundance

> A thing of beauty is a joy for ever:
> Its Loveliness increases; it will never
> Pass into nothingness; but still will keep
> A Bower quiet for us, and a sleep
> Full of sweet dreams, and health and quiet breathing.

FACSIMILE OF ORIGINAL MS. OF ENDYMION

of ornament. This poem met with a torrent of abuse. One critic even questioned whether Keats was the real name of the author, adding, "we almost doubt whether any man in his senses would put his real name to such a rhapsody." Keats showed himself a better critic than the reviewers. It is unusual for a poet to recognize almost at once the blemishes in his own work. He acknowledged that a certain critic—

"... is perfectly right in regard to the 'slipshod' *Endymion* ... it is as good as I had the power to make it by myself. I have written independently, *without judgment*, I may write independently and *with judgment* hereafter."

The quickness of his development is one of the most amazing facts in literary history. He was twenty-three when *Endymion* was published, but in the next eighteen months he had almost finished his life's work. In that brief time, he perfected his art and wrote poems that rank among the greatest of their kind, and that have influenced the work of many succeeding poets, such as Tennyson, Lowell, and Swinburne.

From mural painting by H. O. Walker, Congressional Library, Washington, D. C.

ENDYMION

Nearly all his greatest poems were written in 1819 and published in his 1820 volume. *The Eve of St. Agnes* (January, 1819) and the *Ode to a Nightingale* (May, 1819) are perhaps his two most popular poems; but his other masterpieces are sufficiently great to make choice among them largely a matter of individual preference.

The Eve of St. Agnes is an almost flawless narrative poem, romantic in its conception and artistic in its execution. Porphyro, a young lover, gains entrance to a hostile castle on the eve of St. Agnes to see if he cannot win his heroine, Madeline, on that enchanted evening. The interest in the story, the mastery of poetic language, the wealth and variety of the imagery, the atmosphere of medieval days, combine to make this poem unusually attractive. The following lines appeal to the senses of sight, odor, sound, and temperature,[1] as well as to romantic human feeling and love of the beautiful: —

[1] For a discussion of the different sensory images of the poets, see the author's *Education of the Central Nervous System*, pages 109-208.

> ". . . like a throbbing star
> Seen mid the sapphire heaven's deep repose;
> Into her dream he melted, as the rose
> Blendeth its odor with the violet,—
> Solution sweet: meantime the frost-wind blows
> Like Love's alarum pattering the sharp sleet
> Against the window panes; St. Agnes' moon hath set."

The fact that Keats could write the *Ode to a Nightingale* in three hours is proof of genius. This poem pleases lovers of music, of artistic expression, of nature, of romance, and of human pathos. Such lines as these show that the strength and beauty of his verse are not entirely dependent on images of sense:—

> "Darkling I listen; and, for many a time
> I have been half in love with easeful Death,
> Call'd him soft names in many a musèd rhyme,
> To take into the air my quiet breath."

The *Ode on a Grecian Urn, To Autumn, La Belle Dame sans Merci, Ode on Melancholy, Lamia*, and *Isabella*,— all show the unusual charm of Keats. He manifests the greatest strength in his unfinished fragment *Hyperion*, "the Götterdämmerung of the early Grecian gods." The opening lines reveal the artistic perfection of form and the effectiveness of the sensory images with which he frames the scene:—

> "Deep in the shady sadness of a vale
> Far sunken from the healthy breath of morn,
> Far from the fiery noon, and eve's one star,
> Sat gray-hair'd Saturn, quiet as a stone,
> Still as the silence round about his lair;
> Forest on forest hung about his head
> Like cloud on cloud."

General Characteristics.— Keats is the poetic apostle of the beautiful. He specially emphasizes the beautiful in the world of the senses; but his definition of beauty grew to include more than mere physical sensations from attractive objects. In his *Ode to a Grecian Urn*, he says that "Beauty is truth, truth beauty," and he calls to the Grecian pipes to play —

> "Not to the sensual ear, but, more endeared,
> Pipe to the spirit ditties of no tone."

Those poets who thought that they could equal Keats by piling up a medley of sense images have been doomed to disappointment. The transforming power of his imagination is more remarkable than the wealth of his sensations.

His mastery in choosing, adapting, and sometimes even creating, apt poetic words or phrases, is one of his special charms. Matthew Arnold says: "No one else in English poetry, save Shakespeare, has in expression quite the fascinating felicity of Keats." Some of his descriptive adjectives and phrases, such as the "deep-damasked wings" of the tiger-moth, have been called "miniature poems." In the eighty lines of the *Ode to a Nightingale*, we may note the "*full-throated ease*" of the nightingale's song, the vintage cooled in the "*deep-delved* earth," the "*beaded bubbles winking* at the brim" of the beaker "*full of the warm South*," "the coming musk-rose, full of *dewy wine*," the sad Ruth "amid the *alien* corn," and the "*faery lands forlorn*."

A contemporary critic accused Keats of "spawning" new words, of converting verbs into nouns, of forming new verbs, and of making strange use of adjectives and adverbs. Some contemporaries might object to his "*torchèd* mines," "*flawblown* sleet," "*liegeless* air," or even to the "*calm-throated*" thrush of the immortals. Modern lovers of poetry, however, think that he displayed additional proof of genius by enriching the vocabulary of poetry more than any other writer since Milton.

Keats was not, like Byron and Shelley, a reformer. He drew his first inspiration from Grecian mythology and the romantic world of Spenser, not from the French Revolution or the social unrest of his own day. It is, however, a mistake to say that he was untouched by the new human impulses. There is modern feeling in the following lines which introduce us to the two cruel brothers in *Isabella* : —

> ". . . for them many a weary hand did swelt
> In torchèd mines and noisy factories.
>
> . . . .
>
> For them the Ceylon diver held his breath,
>   And went all naked to the hungry shark;
> For them his ears gushed blood; for them in death
>   The seal on the cold ice with piteous bark
> Lay full of darts."

In the last quarter of the nineteenth century Matthew Arnold wrote of Keats: "He is with Shakespeare." Andrew Bradley, a twentieth century professor of poetry in the University of Oxford, says: "Keats was of Shakespeare's tribe." These eminent critics do not mean that Keats had the breadth, the humor, the moral appeal of Shakespeare, but they do find in Keats much of the youthful Shakespeare's lyrical power, mastery of expression, and intense love of the beautiful in life. When Keats said: "If a sparrow comes before my window, I take part in its existence and pick about the gravel," he showed another Shakespearean quality in his power to enter into the life of other creatures. At first he wrote of the beautiful things that appealed to his senses or his fancies, but when he came to ask himself the question: —

"And can I ever bid these joys farewell?"

he answered: —

> "Yes, I must pass them for a nobler life,
> Where I may find the agonies, the strife
> Of human hearts."[1]

In *Isabella*, the *Ode to a Nightingale*, *Lamia*, and *Hyperion*, he was beginning to paint these "agonies" and "the strife"; but death swiftly ended further progress on this road. Before he passed away, however, he left some things that have an Elizabethan appeal. Among such, we may mention his welcome to "easeful death," his artistic setting of a puzzling truth: —

> "... Joy, whose hand is ever at his lips,
> Bidding adieu,"

his line to which the young world still responds: —

> "Forever wilt thou love and she be fair,"

and especially the musical call of his own young life, "yearning like a God in pain."

THOMAS DE QUINCEY, 1785-1859

Life. — Thomas De Quincey was born in Manchester in 1785. Being a precocious child, he became a remarkable student at the age of eight. When he was only eleven, his Latin verses were the envy of the older boys at the Bath school, which he was then attending. At the age of fifteen, he was so thoroughly versed in Greek that his professor said of him to a friend: "That boy could harangue an Athenian mob better than you or I could address an English one." De Quincey was sent in this year to the Manchester grammar school; but his mind was in advance of the instruction offered there, and he unceremoniously left the school on his seventeenth birthday.

[1] *Sleep and Poetry*.

From the painting by Sir J. W. Gordon, National Portrait Gallery.

Thomas de Quincey.

For a time he tramped through Wales, living on an allowance of a guinea a week. Hungering for books, he suddenly posted to London. As he feared that his family would force him to return to school, he did not let them know his whereabouts. He therefore received no money from them, and was forced to wander hungry, sick, and destitute, through the streets of the metropolis, with its outcasts and waifs. He describes this part of his life in a very entertaining manner in his *Confessions of an English Opium-Eater.*

When his family found him, a year later, they prevailed on him to go to Oxford; and, for the next four years, he lived the life of a recluse at college.

In 1808 he took the cottage at Grasmere that Wordsworth had quitted, and enjoyed the society of the three Lake poets (p. 358). Here De Quincey married and lived his happiest years.

The latter part of his life was clouded by his indulgence in opium, which he had first taken while at college to relieve acute neuralgia. At one time he was in the habit of taking an almost incredible amount of laudanum. Owing to a business failure, his money was lost. It then became necessary for him to throw off the influence of the narcotic sufficiently to earn a livelihood. In 1821 he began to write. From that time until his death, in 1859, his life was devoted mainly to literature.

ROOM IN DOVE COTTAGE OCCUPIED BY WORDSWORTH, COLERIDGE, AND DE QUINCEY

Works. — Nearly all De Quincey's writings were contributed to magazines. His first and greatest contribution was *The Confessions of an English Opium-Eater*, published in the *London Magazine*. These *Confessions* are most remarkable for the brilliant and elaborate style in which the author's early life and his opium dreams are related. His splendid, yet melancholy, dreams are the most famous in the language.

De Quincey's wide reading, especially of history, supplied the material for many of them. In these dreams he saw the court ladies of the "unhappy times of Charles I.," witnessed Marius pass by with his Roman legions, "ran into pagodas" in China, where he "was fixed, for centuries, at the summit, or in secret rooms," and "was buried for a thousand years, in stone coffins, in narrow chambers at the heart of eternal pyramids" in Egypt.

His dreams were affected also by the throngs of people whom he had watched in London. He was haunted by "the tyranny of the human face." He says: —

"Faces imploring, wrathful, despairing, surged upwards by thousands, by myriads, by generations, by centuries: my agitation was infinite, my mind tossed, and surged with the ocean."

Sound also played a large part in the dreams. Music, heart-breaking lamentations, and pitiful echoes recurred frequently in the most magnificent of these nightly pageants. One of the most distressing features of the dreams was their vastness. The dreamer lived for centuries in one night, and space "swelled, and was amplified to an extent of unutterable infinity."

To present with such force and reality these grotesque and weird fancies, these vague horrors, and these deep oppressions required a powerful imaginative grasp of the intangible, and a masterly command of language.

In no other work does De Quincey reach the eminence attained in the *Confessions*, although his scholarly acquirements enabled him to treat philosophical, critical, and historical subjects with wonderful grace and ease. His biographer, Masson, says, "De Quincey's sixteen volumes of magazine articles are full of brain from beginning to end." The wide range of his erudition is shown by the fact that he could write such fine literary criticisms as *On Wordsworth's Poetry* and *On the Knocking at the Gate in*

Macbeth, such clear, strong, and vivid descriptions of historical events and characters as *The Cæsars, Joan of Arc*, and *The Revolt of the Tartars*, and such acute essays on unfamiliar topics as *The Toilette of a Hebrew Lady, The Casuistry of Roman Meals*, and *The Spanish Military Nun*.

He had a contemplative, analytic mind which enjoyed knotty metaphysical problems and questions far removed from daily life, such as the first principles of political economy, and of German philosophy. While he was a clear thinker in such fields, he added little that was new to English thought.

The works which rank next to *The Confessions of an English Opium-Eater* are all largely autobiographical, and reveal charming glimpses of this dreamy, learned sage. These works are *Suspiria de Profundis* (*Sighs from the Depths*), *The English Mail Coach*, and *Autobiographic Sketches*. None of them contains any striking or unusual experience of the author. Their power rests upon their marvelous style. *Levana and Our Ladies of Sorrow* in *Suspiria de Profundis* and the *Dream Fugue* in the *Mail Coach* are among the most musical, the most poetic, and the most imaginative of the author's productions.

General Characteristics. — De Quincey's essays show versatility, scholarly exactness, and great imaginative power. His fame, however, rests in a large degree upon his style. One of its most prominent characteristics is precision. There are but few English essayists who can compare with him in scrupulous precision of expression. He qualifies and elaborates a simple statement until its exact meaning becomes plainly manifest. His vocabulary is extraordinary. In any of the multifarious subjects treated by him, the right word seems always at hand.

Two characteristics, which are very striking in all his works, are harmony and stateliness. His language is so full of rich harmonies that it challenges comparison with poetry. His long, periodic sentences move with a quiet dignity, adapted to the treatment of lofty themes.

De Quincey's work possesses also a light, ironic humor, which is happiest in parody. The essay upon *Murder Considered as One of the Fine Arts* is the best example of his humor. This selection is one of the most whimsical: —

> "For, if once a man indulges himself in murder, very soon he comes to think little of robbing; and from robbing he comes next to drinking and Sabbath breaking, and from that to incivility and procrastination. Once begin upon this downward path, you never know where you are to stop."

De Quincey's gravest fault is digression. He frequently leaves his main theme and follows some line of thought that has been suggested to his well-stored mind. These digressions are often very long, and sometimes one leads to another, until several subjects receive treatment in a single paper. De Quincey, however, always returns to the subject in hand and defines very sharply the point of digression and of return. Another of his faults is an indulgence in involved sentences, which weaken the vigor and simplicity of the style.

Despite these faults, De Quincey is a great master of language. He deserves study for the three most striking characteristics of his style, — precision, stateliness, and harmony.

SUMMARY

The tide of reaction, which had for some time been gathering force, swept triumphantly over England in this age of Romanticism.

Men rebelled against the aristocracy, the narrow conventions of society, the authority of the church and of the government, against the supremacy of cold classicism in literature, against confining intellectual activity to tangible commonplace things, and against the repression of imagination and of the soul's aspirations. The two principal forces behind these changes were the Romantic movement, which culminated in changed literary ideals, and the spirit of the French Revolution, which emphasized the close kinship of all ranks of humanity.

The time was preëminently poetic. The Elizabethan age alone excels it in the glory of its poetry. The principal subjects of verse in the age of Romanticism were nature and man. Nature became the embodiment of an intelligent, sympathetic, spiritual force. Cowper, Burns, Scott, Wordsworth, Coleridge, Byron, Shelley, and Keats constitute a group of poets who gave to English literature a new poetry of nature. The majority of these were also poets of man, of a more ideal humanity. The common man became an object of regard. Burns sings of the Scotch peasant. Wordsworth pictures the life of shepherds and dalesmen. Byron's lines ring with a cry of liberty for all, and Shelley immortalizes the dreams of a universal brotherhood of man. Keats, the poet of the beautiful, passed away before he heard clearly the message of "the still sad music of humanity."

While the prose does not take such high rank as the poetry, there are some writers who will not soon be forgotten. Scott will be remembered as the great master of the historical novel, Jane Austen as the skillful realistic interpreter of everyday life, De Quincey for the brilliancy of his style and the vigor of his imagination in presenting his opium dreams, and Lamb for his exquisite humor. In philosophical prose, Mill, Bentham, and Malthus made important contributions to moral, social, and political philosophy, while Coleridge opposed their utilitarian and materialistic tendencies, and codified the principles of criticism from a romantic point of view.

REFERENCES FOR FURTHER STUDY

HISTORICAL

Gardiner,[1] Green, Walker, or Cheney. For the social side, see Traill, V., VI., and Cheney's *Industrial and Social History of England.*

LITERARY

The Cambridge History of English Literature, Vols. XI., XII.
Courthope's *A History of English Poetry*, Vol. VI.
Elton's *A Survey of English Literature from 1780–1830*, 2 vols.
Herford's *The Age of Wordsworth.*
Brandes's *Naturalism in England* (Vol. IV. of *Main Currents in Nineteenth Century Literature*).
The Revolution in English Poetry and Fiction (Chap. XXII. of Vol. X. of *Cambridge Modern History*).
Hancock's *The French Revolution and the English Poets.*
Scudder's *Life of the Spirit in the Modern English Poets.*
Symons's *The Romantic Movement in English Poetry.*
Reynolds's *The Treatment of Nature in English Poetry between Pope and Wordsworth.*
Mackie's *Nature Knowledge in Modern Poetry.*
Brooke's *Studies in Poetry* (Blake, Scott, Shelley, Keats).
Symons's *William Blake.*
Payne's *The Greater English Poets of the Nineteenth Century* (Keats, Shelley, Byron, Coleridge, Wordsworth).
Stephens's *Hours in a Library*, 3 vols. (Scott, De Quincey, Cowper, Wordsworth, Shelley, Coleridge).
Dowden's *Studies in Literature*, 1879–1877.
Bradley's *Oxford Lectures on Poetry* (Wordsworth, Shelley, Keats).
Lowell's *Among my Books, Second Series* (Wordsworth, Keats).
Ainger's *Life of Lamb.* (E. M. L.)

---

[1] For full titles, see p. 50.

Lucas's *Life of Charles Lamb.*
Goldwin Smith's *Life of Cowper.* (E. M. L.)
Wright's *Life of Cowper.*
Shairp's *Robert Burns.* (E. M. L.)
Carlyle's *Essay on Burns.*
Lockhart's *Life of Scott*, Hutton's *Life of Scott.* (E. M. L.)
Yonge's *Life of Scott.* (G. W.)
Goldwin Smith's *Life of Jane Austen.* (G. W.)
Helm's *Jane Austen and her Country House Comedy.*
Mitton's *Jane Austen and her Times.*
Adams's *The Story of Jane Austen's Life.*
Knight's *Life of Wordsworth*, 3 vols., Myers's *Life of Wordsworth* (E. M. L.), Raleigh's *Wordsworth.*
Robertson's *Wordsworth and the English Lake Country.*
Traill's *Life of Coleridge* (E. M. L.), Caine's *Life of Coleridge* (G. W.), Garnett's *Coleridge.*
Sneath's *Wordsworth, Poet of Nature and Poet of Man.*
Mayne's *The New Life of Byron*, 2 vols., Nichol's *Life of Byron* (E. M. L.), Noel's *Life of Byron.* (G. W.)
Trelawney's *Recollections of the Last Days of Shelley and Byron.*
Dowden's *Life of Shelley*, 2 vols., Symonds's *Life of Shelley* (E. M. L.), Sharp's *Life of Shelley* (G. W.). Francis Thompson's *Shelley.*
Clutton-Brock's *Shelley: The Man and the Poet.*
Hogg's *Life of Percy Bysshe Shelley* (contemporary).
Angeli's *Shelley and his Friends in Italy.*
Colvin's *Life of Keats* (E. M. L.), Rossetti's *Life of Keats* (G. W.), Hancock's *John Keats.*
Miller's *Leigh Hunt's Relations with Byron, Shelley, and Keats.*
Arnold's *Essays in Criticism, Second Series* (Keats).
H. Buxton Forman's *Complete Works of John Keats* (includes the *Letters*, the best edition).
Masson's *Life of De Quincey.* (E. M. L.)
Minto's *Manual of English Prose Literature* (De Quincey).

SUGGESTED READINGS
WITH QUESTIONS AND SUGGESTIONS

Blake. — Some of his best poems are given in Ward, IV., 601–608; Bronson, III., 385–403; Manly, I., 301–304; *Oxford*, 558–566; *Century*, 485–489, and in the volume in *The Canterbury Poets.*

Point out in Blake's verse (*a*) the new feeling for nature, (*b*) evidences of wide sympathies, (*c*) mystical tendencies, and (*d*) compare his verses relating to children and nature with Wordsworth's poems on the same subjects.

Cowper. — Read the opening stanzas of Cowper's *Conversation* and note the strong influence of Pope in the cleverly turned but artificial couplets. Compare this poem with the one *On the Receipt of my Mother's Picture* or with *The Task*, Book IV., lines 1–41 and 267–332, Cassell's *National Library*, *Canterbury Poets*, or *Temple Classics* and point out the marked differences in subject matter and style. What forward movement in literature is indicated by the change in Cowper's manner? *John Gilpin* should be read for its fresh, beguiling humor.

For selections, see Bronson,[1] III., 310–329; Ward, III., 422–485; *Century*, 470–479; Manly, I., 285–294.

Burns. — Read *The Cotter's Saturday Night*, *For a' That and a' That*, *To a Mouse*, *Highland Mary*, *To Mary in Heaven*, *Farewell to Nancy*, *I Love My Jean*, *A Red, Red Rose*. The teacher should read to the class parts of *Tam o' Shanter*.

The *Globe* edition contains the complete poems of Burns with Glossary. Inexpensive editions may be found in Cassell's *National Library*, *Everyman's Library*, and *Canterbury Poets*. For selections, see Bronson, III., 338–385; Ward, III., 512–571; *Century*, 490–502; Manly, I., 309–326; *Oxford*, 492–506.

In what ways do the first three poems mentioned above show Burns's sympathy with democracy? Quote some of Burns's fine descriptions of nature and describe the manner in which he treats nature. How does he rank as a writer of love songs? What qualities in his poems have touched so many hearts? Compare his poetry with that of Dryden, Pope, and Shakespeare.

Scott. — Read *The Lady of the Lake*, Canto III., stanzas iii.–xxv., or *Marmion*, Canto VI., stanzas xiii.–xxvii. (American Book Company's *Eclectic English Classics*, Cassell's *National Library*, or *Everyman's Library*.) Read in Craik, V., "The Gypsy's Curse" (*Guy Mannering*), pp. 14–17, "The Death of Madge Wildfire" (*Heart of Middlothian*), pp. 30–35, and "The Grand Master of the Templars" (*Ivanhoe*), pp. 37–42. The student should put on his list for reading at his leisure: *Guy Mannering*, *Old Mortality*, *Ivanhoe*, *Kenilworth*, and *The Talisman*.

---

[1] For full titles, see p. 6.

In what kind of poetry does Scott excel ? Quote some of his spirited lines, and point out their chief excellences. How does his poetry differ from that of Burns ? In the history of fiction, does Scott rank as an imitator or a creator ? As a writer of fiction, in what do his strength and his weakness consist ? Has he those qualities that will cause him to be popular a century hence ? What can be said of his style ?

Jane Austen. — In Craik, V., or Manly, II., read the selections from *Pride and Prejudice*. The student at his leisure should read all this novel.

What world does she describe in her fiction ? What are her chief qualities? How does she differ from Scott ? Why is she called a "realist" ?

Wordsworth. — Read *I Wandered Lonely as a Cloud, The Solitary Reaper, To the Cuckoo, Lines Written in Early Spring, Three Years She Grew in Sun and Shower, To my Sister, She Dwelt among the Untrodden Ways, She Was a Phantom of Delight, Alice Fell, Lucy Gray, We Are Seven, Intimations of Immortality from Recollections of Early Childhood, Ode to Duty, Hart-Leap Well, Lines Composed a Few Miles above Tintern Abbey, Michael*, and the sonnets: "It is a beauteous evening, calm and free," "Milton, thou shouldst be living at this hour," and "The world is too much with us, late and soon." Some students will also wish to read *The Prelude* (*Temple Classics* or A. J. George's edition), which describes the growth of Wordsworth's mind.

All the above poems (excepting *The Prelude*) may be found in the volume *Poems of Wordsworth, chosen and edited by Matthew Arnold* (*Golden Treasury Series*, 331 pp., $1). Nearly all may also be found in Page's *British Poets of the Nineteenth Century* (923 pp., $2). For selections, see Bronson, IV., 1-54; Ward, IV., 1-88; *Oxford*, 594-618; *Century*, 503-541; Manly, I., 329-345.

Refer to Wordsworth's "General Characteristics" (pp. 393-396) and select the poems that most emphatically show his special qualities. Which of the above poems seems easiest to write ? In which is his genius most apparent ? Which best presents his view of nature? Which best stand the test of an indefinite number of readings ? In what do his poems of childhood excel ?

Coleridge. — Read *The Ancient Mariner, Christabel, Kubla Khan, Hymn before Sunrise in the Vale of Chamouni, Youth and Age* ; Bronson, I., 54-93; Ward, IV., 102-154; Page, 66-103; *Century*, 553-565; Manly, I., 353-364; *Oxford*, 628-656.

How do *The Ancient Mariner* and *Christabel* manifest the spirit of Romanticism? What are the chief reasons for the popularity of *The Ancient Mariner*? Would you call this poem didactic? Select stanzas specially remarkable for melody, for beauty, for telling much in few words, for images of nature, for conveying an ethical lesson. What feeling almost unknown in early poetry is common in Coleridge's *The Ancient Mariner*, Wordsworth's *Hart-Leap Well*, Burns's *To a Mouse, On Seeing a Wounded Hare Limp by Me, A Winter Night*, and Cowper's *On a Goldfinch Starved to Death in his Cage*?

The advanced student should read some of Coleridge's prose criticism in his *Biographia Literaria* (*Everyman's Library*). The parts best worth reading have been selected in George's *Coleridge's Principles of Criticism* (226 pp., 60 cents) and in Beers's *Selections from the Prose Writings of Coleridge* (including criticisms of Wordsworth and Shakespeare, 146 pp., 50 cents).

Note how fully Coleridge unfolds in these essays the principles of romantic criticism, which have not been superseded.

Byron. — Read *The Prisoner of Chillon* (*Selections from Byron, Eclectic English Classics*), *Childe Harold*, Canto III., stanzas xxi.–xxv. and cxiii., Canto IV., stanzas lxxviii., and lxxix., "Oh, Snatch'd away in Beauty's Bloom," "There's not a joy the world can give like that it takes away," and from *Don Juan*, Canto III., the song inserted between stanzas lxxxvi. and lxxxvii. All these poems will be found in the two volumes of Byron's works in the *Canterbury Poets'* series.

Selections are given in Bronson, IV., 125–174; Ward, IV., 244–303; Page, 170–272; *Oxford*, 688–694; *Century*, 586–613; Manly, I., 378–393.

From the stanzas indicated in *Childe Harold*, select, first, the passages which best illustrate the spirit of revolt, and, second, the passages of most poetic beauty. What natural phenomena appeal most to Byron? What qualities make *The Prisoner of Chillon* a favorite? Why is his poetry often called rhetorical?

Shelley. — Read *Adonais, To a Skylark, Ode to the West Wind, To Night, The Cloud, The Sensitive Plant*, and selections from *Alastor* and *Prometheus Unbound*. Shelley's *Poetical Works*, edited by Edward Dowden (*Globe Poets*), contains all of Shelley's extant poetry. Less expensive editions are in *Canterbury Poets, Temple Classics*, and *Everyman's Library*. Selections are given in Bronson, IV., 182–227; Ward, IV., 348–416; Page, 275–369; *Oxford*, 697–717; *Century*, 614–638; Manly, I., 394–411.

Under what different aspects do *Adonais* and *Lycidas* view the life after death ? Has Shelley modified Wordsworth's view of the spiritual force in nature ? Does Shelley use either the cloud or the skylark for the direct purpose of expressing his own feelings ? Why is he sometimes called a metaphysical poet ? What is the most striking quality of Shelley's poetic gift?

Keats. — Read *The Eve of St. Agnes, Ode to a Nightingale, Ode on a Grecian Urn, To Autumn, Hyperion* (first 134 lines), *La Belle Dame sans Merci, Isabella*, and the sonnets: *On First Looking into Chapman's Homer, On the Grasshopper and Cricket, When I Have Fears that I May Cease to Be, Bright Star! Would I Were Steadfast as Thou Art.* The best edition of the works of Keats is that by Buxton Forman. The *Canterbury Poets* and *Everyman's Library* have less expensive editions. All the poems indicated above may be found in Page's *British Poets of the Nineteenth Century.* For selections, see Bronson, IV., 230-265; Ward, IV., 427-464; *Oxford*, 721-744; *Century*, 639-655; Manly, I., 413-425.

By direct reference to the above poems, justify calling Keats "the apostle of the beautiful," in both thought and language. Give examples of his felicitous use of words and phrases. Show by illustrations his mastery in the use of the concrete. To what special senses do his images appeal ? Was he at all affected by the new human movement ? Why does Arnold say, " Keats is with Shakespeare "? In what respects is he like the Elizabethans ?

De Quincey. — Read *Levana and Our Ladies of Sorrow* (Craik, V., 264-270). The first chapters of *The Confessions of an English Opium-Eater* (*Everyman's Library; Temple Classics; Century*, 683-690; Manly, II., 357-366) are entertaining and will repay reading.

Does his prose show any influence of a romantic and poetic age? Compare his style with that of Addison, Gibbon, and Burke. In what respects does De Quincey succeed, and in what does he fail, as a model for a young writer ?

Lamb. — From the *Essays of Elia* (Cassell's *National Library; Everyman's Library, Temple Classics*) read any two of these essays: *A Dissertation upon Roast Pig, Old China, Dream Children, New Year's Eve, Poor Relations.* For selections, see Craik, V., 116-126; *Century*, 575-578; Manly, II., 337-345.

In what does Lamb's chief charm consist ? Point out resemblances and differences between his *Essays* and Addison's.

Landor, Hazlitt, and Hunt. — Good selections are given in Craik, V.; Chambers, III.; Manly, II. Inexpensive editions of Landor's *Imaginary Conversations* and *Pericles and Aspasia* may be found in the *Camelot Series*. Hazlitt's *Characters of Shakespeare's Plays*, *Lectures on the English Poets*, *Lectures on the English Comic Writers*, and *Table Talk* are published in *Everyman's Library*. The *Camelot Series* and the *Temple Classics* also contain some of Hazlitt's works. A selection from Leigh Hunt's *Essays* is published in the *Camelot Series*.

What are the main characteristics of Landor's style? Select a passage which justifies the criticism: "He writes in marble." Give some striking thoughts from his *Imaginary Conversations*. Compare his style and subject matter with Hazlitt's. Show that Hazlitt has the power of presenting in an impressive way the chief characteristics of authors. Select some pleasing passages from Leigh Hunt's *Essays*. Compare him with Addison and Lamb.

CHAPTER IX

THE VICTORIAN AGE, 1837–1900

History of the Period.—In the two periods of English history most remarkable for their accomplishment, the Elizabethan and the Victorian, the throne was occupied by women. Queen Victoria, the granddaughter of George III., ruled from 1837 to the beginning of 1901. Her long reign of sixty-three years may be said to close with the end of the nineteenth century.

For nearly fifty years after the battle of Waterloo (1815), England had no war of magnitude. In 1854 she joined France in a war against Russia to keep her from taking Constantinople. Tennyson's well-known poem, *The Charge of the Light Brigade*, commemorates an incident in this bloody contest, which was successful in preventing Russia from dismembering Turkey.

When the Turks massacred the Christians in Bulgaria in 1876, Russia fought and conquered Turkey. England again intervened, this time after the war, in the Berlin Congress (1878). In return for her diplomatic services and for a guaranty to maintain the integrity of certain Turkish territory, England received from Turkey the island of Cyprus. As a result of this Congress, the principalities of Roumania, Servia, and Bulgaria were formed, but the Turk was allowed to remain in Europe. A later English prime minister, Lord Salisbury (1830–1903), referring to

England's espousal of the Turkish cause, said that she had "backed the wrong horse." The bloody war of 1912-1913 between Turkey and the allied armies of Bulgaria, Servia, Montenegro, and Greece was the result of this mistake.

An important part of England's history during this period centers around the expansion, protection, and development of her colonies in Asia, Australia, Africa, and America. England was then constantly agitated by the fear that Russia might grow strong enough to seize India or some other English colonial possessions.

A serious rebellion in India (1857) led England to take from the East India Company the government of that colony. "Empress of India" was later (1876) added to the titles of Queen Victoria. Had India not been an English colony, literature might not have had Kipling's fascinating *Jungle Books* and Hindu stories. England's protectorate over Egypt (1882) was assumed in order to strengthen her control over the newly completed Suez Canal (1869), which was needed for her communication with India and her Australian colonies.

The Boer war in South Africa (1899-1902) required the largest number of troops that England ever mustered into service in any of her wars. The final outcome of this desperate struggle was the further extension of her South African possessions.

In the nineteenth century, England's most notable political achievement was "her successful rule over colonies, ranging from India, with its 280,000,000 subjects, to Fanning Island with its population of thirty." Her tactful guidance was for the most part directed toward enabling them to develop and to govern themselves. She had learned a valuable lesson from the American revolution.

Ireland, however, failed to secure her share of the benefits that usually resulted from English rule. She was neither regarded as a colony, like Australia, nor as an integral part of England. For the greater part of the century her condition was deplorable. The great prime minister, William E. Gladstone (1809-1898), tried to secure needed home rule for her, but did not succeed. Toward the end of the century, more liberal laws regarding the tenure of the land and more self-government afforded some relief from unjust conditions.

During the Victorian age the government of England became more democratic. Two reform bills (1867 and 1884) gave almost unrestricted suffrage to men. The extension of the franchise and the granting of local self-government to her counties (1888) made England one of the most democratic of all nations. Her monarch has less power than the president of the United States.

The Victorian age saw the rise of trades unions and the passing of many laws to improve the condition of the working classes. As the tariff protecting the home grower of wheat had raised the price of bread and caused much suffering to the poor, England not only repealed this duty (1846) but also became practically a free-trade country. The age won laurels in providing more educational facilities for all, in abridging class privileges, and in showing increasing recognition of human rights, without a bloody revolution such as took place in France. A rough indication of the amount of social and moral progress is the decrease in the number of convicts in England, from about 50,000 at the accession of Victoria to less than 6000 at her death.

An Age of Science and Invention. — In the extent and the variety of inventions, in their rapid improvement and utilization for human needs, and in general scientific progress, the sixty-three years of the Victorian age surpassed all the rest of historic time.

When Victoria ascended the throne, the stage coach was the common means of traveling; only two short pieces of railroad had been constructed; the electric telegraph had not been developed; few steamships had crossed the Atlantic. The modern use of the telephone would then have seemed as improbable as the wildest Arabian Nights' tale. Before her reign ended, the railroad, the telegraph, the steamship, and the telephone had wrought an almost magical change in travel and in communication.

The Victorian age introduced anæsthetics and antiseptic surgery, developed photography, the sciences of chemistry and physics, of biology and zoölogy, of botany and geology. The enthusiastic scientific worker appeared in every field, endeavoring to understand the laws of nature and to apply them in the service of man. Science also turned its attention to human progress and welfare. The new science of sociology had earnest students.

The Influence of Science on Literature. — The Victorian age was the first to set forth clearly the evolution hypothesis, which teaches the orderly development from simple to complex forms. While the idea of evolution had suggested itself to many naturalists, **Charles Darwin** (1809–1882) was the first to gain a wide hearing for the theory. After years of careful study of nature, he published in 1859 *The Origin of Species by Natural Selection*, an epoch-making work,

CHARLES DARWIN

which had a far-reaching effect on the thought of the age

The influence of his doctrine of evolution is especially apparent in Tennyson's poetry, in George Eliot's fiction, in religious thought, and in the change in viewing social problems. In his *Synthetic Philosophy*, **Herbert Spencer** (1820-1903), philosopher and metaphysician, applied the doctrine of evolution not only to plants and animals but also to society, morality, and religion.

Two eminent scientists, **John Tyndall** (1820-1893) and **Thomas Huxley** (1825-1895), did much to popularize science and to cause the age to seek a broader education. Tyndall's *Fragments of Science* (1871) contains a fine lecture on the *Scientific Use of the Imagination*, in which he becomes almost poetic in his imaginative conception of evolution:—

"Not alone the more ignoble forms of animalcular or animal life, not alone the nobler forms of the horse and lion, not alone the exquisite and wonderful mechanism of the human body, but the human mind itself,— emotion, intellect, will, and all their phenomena, — were once latent in a fiery cloud. . . . All our philosophy, all our poetry, all our science, and all our art,— Plato, Shakespeare, Newton, and Raphael,— are potential in the fires of the sun."

JOHN TYNDALL

Unlike Keats in his *Lamia*, Tyndall is firm in his belief that science will not clip the wings of imagination. In the same lecture he says:—

"How are we to lay hold of the physical basis of light, since, like that of life itself, it lies entirely without the domain of the senses? We are gifted with the power of imagination and by this power we can lighten the darkness which surrounds the world of the senses. . . . Bounded and conditioned by coöperant reason, imagination becomes the mightiest instrument of the physical discoverer. Newton's passage from a falling apple to a falling moon was at the outset a leap of the imagination."

Huxley was even a more brilliant interpreter of science to popular audiences. His so-called *Lay Sermons* (1870) are invigorating presentations of scientific and educational subjects. He awakened many to a sense of the importance of "knowing the laws of the physical world" and "the relations of cause and effect therein." Nowhere is he more impressive than where he forces us to admit that we must all play the chess game of life against an opponent that never makes an error and never fails to count our mistakes against us.

From the painting by Collier, National Portrait Gallery.

THOMAS HUXLEY

"The chess-board is the world, the pieces are the phenomena of the universe, the rules of the game are what we call the laws of Nature. The player on the other side is hidden from us. We know that his play is always fair, just, and patient. But we also know, to our cost, that he never overlooks a mistake, or makes the smallest allowance for ignorance. To the man who plays well, the highest stakes are paid, with that sort of overflowing generosity with which the strong man shows delight in strength. And one who plays ill is checkmated — without haste, but without remorse.

. . . .

"Well, what I mean by Education is learning the rules of this mighty game. In other words, education is the instruction of the intellect in the laws of Nature, under which name I include not merely things and their forces, but men and their ways; and the fashioning of the affections and of the will into an earnest and loving desire to move in harmony with those laws."[1]

We find the influence of science manifest in much of the general literature of the age, as well as in the special writings of the scientists. Science introduced to literature a new interest in humanity and impressed on writers what is known as the "growth idea." Preceding literature, with the conspicuous exception of Shakespeare's work, had for the most part presented individuals whose character was already fixed. This age loved to show the growth of souls. George Eliot's novels are frequently Darwinian demonstrations of the various steps in the moral growth or the perversion of the individual. In *Rabbi Ben Ezra*, Browning thus expresses this new idea of the working of the Divine Power : —

> "He fixed thee mid this dance
> Of plastic circumstance."

The Trend of Prose; Minor Prose Writers. — The prose of this age is remarkable for amount and variety. In addition to the work of the scientists, there are the essays and histories of Macaulay and Carlyle, the essays and varied prose of Newman, the art and social philosophy of Ruskin, the critical essays of Matthew Arnold and Swinburne.

One essayist, **Walter Pater** (1839–1894), an Oxford graduate and teacher, who kept himself aloof from contemporary thought, produced almost a new type of serious prose, distinguished for color, ornamentation, melody, and poetic thought. Even such prosaic objects as wood and brick were to his retrospective gaze "half mere soul-stuff, floated thither from who knows where." His object was to charm his reader, to haunt him with vague suggestions rather than

---

[1] *A Liberal Education and Where to Find It* (*Lay Sermons*).

to make a logical appeal to him, or to add to his world of vivid fact, after the manner of Macaulay. A quotation from Pater's most brilliant essay, *Leonardo Da Vinci*, in the volume, *The Renaissance : Studies in Art and Poetry*[1] (1873) will show some of the characteristics of his prose. This description of Da Vinci's masterpiece, the portrait of Mona Lisa, has added to the world-wide fame of that picture —

"Hers is the head upon which all 'the ends of the world are come,' and the eyelids are a little weary. It is a beauty wrought out from within upon the flesh, the deposit, little cell by cell, of strange thoughts and fantastic reveries and exquisite passions. Set it for a moment beside one of those white Greek goddesses or beautiful women of antiquity, and how would they be troubled by this beauty, into which the soul with its maladies has passed ! . . . She is older than the rocks among which she sits ; like the vampire, she has been dead many times, and learned the secrets of the grave ; and has been a diver in deep seas, and keeps their fallen day about her ; and trafficked for strange webs with Eastern merchants : and, as Leda, was the mother of Helen of Troy, and, as Saint Anne, the mother of Mary ; and all this has been to her but as the sound of lyres and flutes, and lives only in the delicacy with which it has molded the changing lineaments, and tinged the eyelids and the hands."

The period from 1780 to 1837 had only two great writers of fiction, — Scott and Jane Austen ; but the Victorian age saw the novel gain the ascendancy that the drama enjoyed in Elizabethan times.

In addition to the chief novelists, — Dickens, Thackeray, George Eliot, Stevenson, Thomas Hardy, George Meredith, and Kipling, — there were many other writers who produced one or more excellent works of fiction. In this class are the Brontë sisters, especially **Charlotte Brontë** (1816–1855) and **Emily Brontë** (1818–1848), the daughters of a clergyman, who lived in Haworth, Yorkshire. They had genius, but

[1] For suggested readings in Pater, see p. 584.

they were hampered by poverty, lack of sympathy, and peculiar environment. Charlotte Brontë's *Jane Eyre* (1847) is a thrilling story, which centers around the experiences of one of the great nineteenth-century heroines of fiction. This virile novel, an unusual compound of sensational romance and of intense realism, lives because the highly gifted author made it pulsate with her own life. Unlike *Jane Eyre*, Emily Brontë's powerful novel, *Wuthering Heights* (1847) is not pleasant reading. This romantic novel is really her imaginative interpretation of the Yorkshire life that she knew. If she had humanized *Wuthering Heights*, it could have been classed among the greatest novels of the Victorian age. She might have learned this art, had she not died at the age of thirty. "Stronger than a man, simpler than a child, her nature stood alone," wrote Charlotte Brontë of her sister Emily.

Among the other authors who deserve mention for one or more works of fiction are: **Bulwer Lytton** (1803–1873), a versatile writer whose best-known work is *The Last Days of Pompeii;* **Elizabeth Gaskell** (1810–1865), whose *Cranford* (1853) is an inimitable picture of mid-nineteenth century life in a small Cheshire village; **Anthony Trollope** (1815–1882), whose *Barchester Towers* is a realistic study of life in a cathedral town; **Charles Kingsley** (1819–1875), who stirs the blood in *Westward Ho!* (1855), a tale of Elizabethan seamen; **Charles Reade** (1814–1884), author of *The Cloister and the Hearth* (1861), a careful and fascinating study of fifteenth-century life; **R. D. Blackmore** (1825–1900), whose *Lorna Doone* (1869) is a thrilling North Devonshire story of life and love in the latter part of the seventeenth century; **J. M. Barrie** (1860–   ), whose *The Little Minister* (1891) is a richly human, sympathetic, and humorous story, the scene of which is laid in Kirriemuir, a town about sixty miles north of Edinburgh. His *Sentimental Tommy* (1896), although not so widely popular, is an unusually original, semi-autobiographical story of imaginative boyhood. This entire chapter could be filled with merely the titles of Victorian novels, many of which possess some distinctive merit.

The changed character of the reading public furnished one reason for the unprecedented growth of fiction. The spread of education through public schools, newspapers, cheap magazines, and books caused a widespread habit of reading, which before this time was not common among the large numbers of the uneducated and the poor. The masses, however, did not care for uninteresting or abstruse works. The majority of books drawn from the circulating libraries were novels.

The scientific spirit of the age impelled the greatest novelists to try to paint actual life as it impressed them. Dickens chose the lower classes in London; Thackeray, the clubs and fashionable world; George Eliot, the country life near her birthplace in Warwickshire; Hardy, the people of his Wessex (p. 3); Meredith, the cosmopolitan life of egotistical man; Kipling, the life of India both in jungle and camp, as well as the life of the great outer world. These writers of fiction all sought a realistic background, although some of them did not hesitate to use romantic touches to heighten the general effect. Stevenson was the chief writer of romances.

The Trend of Poetry; Minor Poets. — The Victorian age was dominated by two great poets, — Robert Browning and Alfred Tennyson. Browning showed the influence of science in his tendency to analyze human motives and actions. In one line of *Fra Lippo Lippi*, he voices the new poetic attitude toward the world: —

"To find its meaning is my meat and drink."

Browning advanced into new fields, while Tennyson was more content to make a beautiful poetic translation of much of the thought of the age. In his youth he wrote: —

"Here about the beach I wander'd, nourishing a youth sublime
With the fairy tales of science, and the long result of Time."

From merely reading Tennyson's verse, one could gauge quite accurately the trend of Victorian scientific thought.

The poetry of both Browning and Tennyson is so resonant with faith that they have been called great religious teachers. Rudyard Kipling, the poet of imperialistic England, of her "far-flung battle line," attributes her "dominion over palm and pine" to faith in the "Lord God of Hosts."

In the minor poets, there is often a different strain. Arnold is beset with doubt, and hears no "clear call," such as Tennyson voices in *Crossing the Bar*. Swinburne, seeing the pessimistic side of the shield of evolution, exclaims: —

"Thou hast fed one rose with dust of many men."

Arthur Hugh Clough (1819–1861), Oxford tutor, traveler, and educational examiner, was a poet who struggled with the doubt of the age. He loved —

"To finger idly some old Gordian knot,
    Unskilled to sunder, and too weak to cleave,
    And with much toil attain to half-believe."

His verse would be forgotten if it expressed only such an uncertain note; but his greatest poem thus records his belief in the value of life's struggle and gives a hint of final victory: —

"Say not the struggle nought availeth,
    The labor and the wounds are vain,

> The enemy faints not, nor faileth,
> And as things have been they remain.

> "If hopes were dupes, fears may be liars;
> It may be, in yon smoke concealed,
> Your comrades chase e'en now the fliers,
> And, but for you, possess the field."

Although he paid too little attention to the form of his verse, some of his poems have the vitality of an earnest, thoughtful sincerity.

Two poets, **W. E. Henley** (1849–1903) and **Robert Bridges** (1844–), although they do not possess Robert Browning's genius, yet have much of his capacity to inspire others with joy in "the mere living." Henley, a cripple and a great sufferer, was a poet, critic, and London editor. His message is "the joy of life": —

> "... the blackbird sings but a box-wood flute,
> But I love him best of all
> For his song is all of the joy of life."

His verse, which is elemental, full of enthusiasm and beauty, often reminds us of the work of the thirteenth-century lyrists (p. 71).

Robert Bridges, an Oxford graduate, physician, critic, and poet, also had for his creed: "Life and joy are one." His universe, like Shelley's, is an incarnation of the spirit of love: —

> "Love can tell, and love alone,
> Whence the million stars were strewn,
> Why each atom knows its own,
> How, in spite of woe and death,
> Gay is life, and sweet is breath."

He wishes for no happier day than the present one. Bridges has been called a classical poet because he often selects Greek and Roman subjects for his verse, and because he writes with a formality, purity, and precision of style. He is, however, most delightful in such volumes as *Shorter Poems* and *New Poems*,[1] wherein he describes in a simple, artless manner English rural scenes and fireside joys. In 1913 he was appointed poet laureate, to succeed Alfred Austin.

John Davidson (1857–1909), a Scotch poet, who came to London and wrestled with poverty, produced much uneven work. In his best verse, there is often a pleasing combination of poetic beauty and vigorous movement. Lines like these from his *Ballad of a Nun* have been much admired:—

> "On many a mountain's happy head
> Dawn lightly laid her rosy hand.
> The adventurous son took heaven by storm,
> Clouds scattered largesses of rain."

Davidson later became an offensively shrill preacher of materialism and lost his early charm. Some of the best of his poetry may be found in *Fleet Street Eclogues*.

Francis Thompson (1860–1907), a Catholic poet, who has been called a nineteenth-century Crashaw, passed much of his short life of suffering in London, where he was once reduced to selling matches on a street corner. His greatest poem, *The Hound of Heaven* (1893), is an impassioned lyrical rendering of the passage in the *Psalms* beginning: "Whither shall I go from thy Spirit? or whither shall I flee from thy presence?" While fleeing down "the long savannahs of the blue," the poet hears a Voice say:—

> "Naught shelters thee, who wilt not shelter Me."

William Watson (1858–   ), a London poet, looked to Milton, Wordsworth, and Arnold as his masters. Some of Watson's best verse, such as *Wordsworth's Grave*, is written in praise of dead poets. His early volume, *Epigrams*

---

[1] Pp. 225–364 of the Oxford University Press edition of his *Poetical Works*.

(1884), containing one hundred poems of four lines each, shows his power of conveying poetic thought in brief space. One of these poems is called *Shelley and Harriet Westbrook*:—

> "A star looked down from heaven and loved a flower,
> Grown in earth's garden — loved it for an hour:
> Let eyes that trace his orbit in the spheres
> Refuse not, to a ruin'd rosebud, tears." [1]

Many expected to see Watson appointed poet-laureate to succeed Tennyson. Possibly mental trouble, which had temporarily affected him, influenced the choice; for **Alfred Austin** (1835–1913) received the laureateship, in 1896. Like the Pre-Raphaelites, Watson disliked those whom he called a "phrase-tormenting fantastic chorus of poets." His best verse shows depth of poetic thought, directness of expression, and a strong sense of moral values.

The Victorian age has provided poetry to suit almost all tastes. In striking contrast with those who wrestled with the eternal verities are such poets and essayists as **Austin Dobson** (1840–   ), long a clerk of the London Board of Trade, and **Arthur Symons** (1865–   ), a poet and discriminating prose critic. Austin Dobson, who is fond of eighteenth-century subjects, is at his best in graceful society verse. His poems show the touch of a highly skilled metrical artist who has been a careful student of French poetry. His ease of expression, freshness, and humor charm readers of his verse without making serious demands on their attention. His best poems are found in *Vignettes in Rhyme* (1873), *At the Sign of the Lyre* (1885), and *Collected Poems* (1913).

In choice of subject matter, **Arthur Symons** sometimes suggests the Cavalier poets. He has often squandered

[1] Printed by permission of The Macmillan Company.

his powers in acting on his theory that it is one of the provinces of verse to record any momentary mood, irrespective of its value. His deftness of touch and acute poetic sensibility are evident in such short poems as *Rain on the Down, Credo, A Roundel of Rest,* and *The Last Memory.*[1]

The Pre-Raphaelite Movement. — In 1848 three artists, Dante Gabriel Rossetti (1828–1882), William Holman-Hunt (1827–1910), and John Everett Millais (1829–1896), formed the Pre-Raphaelite Brotherhood. Others soon joined the movement, which was primarily artistic, not literary. Painting had become imitative. The uppermost question in the artist's mind was, "How would Raphael or some other authority have painted this picture?" The new school determined to paint things from a direct study of nature, without a thought of the way in which any one else would have painted them. They decided to assume the same independence as the Pre-Raphaelite artists, who expressed their individuality in their own way. Keats was the favorite author of the new school. The artists painted subjects suggested

From the drawing by himself, National Portrait Gallery.
DANTE GABRIEL ROSSETTI

---

[1] Given in Stevenson's *Home Book of Verse* and *The Oxford Book of Victorian Verse.*

by his poems, and Rossetti thought him "the one true heir of Shakespeare."

When the Pre-Raphaelite paintings were violently attacked, Ruskin examined them and decided that they conformed to the principles which he had already laid down in the first two volumes of *Modern Painters* (1843, 1846), so he wrote *Pre-Raphaelitism* (1851) as the champion of the new school. It has been humorously said that some of the painters of this school, before beginning a new picture, took an oath "to paint the truth, the whole truth, and nothing but the truth."

The new movement in poetry followed this revolt in art. **Dante Gabriel Rossetti**, the head of the literary Pre-Raphaelites, though born in London, was of Italian parentage in which there was a strain of English blood. His poem, *The Blessed Damozel* (first published in 1850), has had the greatest influence of any Pre-Raphaelite literary production. This poem was suggested by *The Raven* (1845), the work of the American, Edgar Allan Poe. Rossetti said: —

"I saw that Poe had done the utmost it was possible to do with the grief of the lover on earth, and I determined to reverse the conditions, and give utterance to the yearnings of the loved one in heaven."

His Blessed Damozel, wearing a white rose, "Mary's gift," leaning out from the gold bar of heaven, watching with sad eyes, "deeper than the depth of waters stilled at even," for the coming of her lover, has left a lasting impression on many readers. Simplicity, beauty, and pathos are the chief characteristics of this poem, which, like Bryant's *Thanatopsis*, was written by a youth of eighteen.

Painting was the chief work of Rossetti's life, but he wrote many other poems. Some of the most characteristic of these are the two semi-ballads, *Sister Helen* and *The King's Tragedy*, *Rose Mary*, *Love's Nocturn*, and *Sonnets*.

One of the earliest of these Sonnets, *Mary's Girlhood*, describes the child as:—

> "An angel-watered lily, that near God
> Grows and is quiet."

His sister, **Christina Rossetti** (1830–1894), the author of much religious verse, shows the unaffected naturalness of the new movement. This stanza from her *Amor Mundi* (*Love of the World*) is characteristic:—

> "So they two went together in glowing August weather,
> The honey-breathing heather lay to their left and right;
> And dear she was to doat on, her swift feet seemed to float on
> The air like soft twin pigeons too sportive to alight."

William Morris (1834–1896), Oxford graduate, decorator, manufacturer, printer, and poet, was born near London. He was fascinated by *The Blessed Damozel*, and his first and most poetical volume, *The Defence of Guinevere and Other Poems* (1858), shows Rossetti's influence. The simplicity insisted on by the new school is evident in such lines as these from *Two Red Roses across the Moon:*—

> "There was a lady lived in a hall,
> Large in the eyes and slim and tall;
> And ever she sung from noon to noon,
> Two red roses across the moon."

Morris later wrote a long series of narrative poems, called *The Earthly Paradise* (1868–1870) and an epic, *Sigurd the Volsung* (1876). He turned from Pre-Raphaelitism to become an earnest social reformer.

In literature, the Pre-Raphaelite movement disdained the old conventions and started a miniature romantic revival, which emphasized individuality, direct expression, and the use of simple words. Its influence soon became merged in that of the earlier and far greater romantic school.

From the painting by Sir F. Grant, National Portrait Gallery.

THOMAS BABINGTON MACAULAY, 1800-1859

Life. — A prominent figure in the social and political life of England during the first part of the century was Thomas Babington Macaulay, a man of brilliant intellectual powers, strict integrity of character, and enormous capacity for work. He loved England and gloried in her liberties and her commercial prosperity. He served her for many years in the House of Commons, and he bent his whole energy and splendid forensic talent in favor of the

THOMAS BABINGTON MACAULAY

Reform Bill of 1832, which secured greater political liberty for England.

He was not a theorizer, but a practical man of affairs. Notwithstanding the fact that his political opinions were ready made for him by the Whig party, his career in the House was never "inconsistent with rectitude of intention and independence of spirit." He voted conscientiously for measures, although he personally sacrificed hundreds of pounds by so doing.

He was a remarkable talker. A single speech of his has been known to change an entire vote in Parliament. Unlike Coleridge, he did not indulge in monologue, but showed to finest advantage in debate. His power of memory was wonderful. He often startled an opponent by quoting from a given chapter and page of a book. He repeated long passages from *Paradise Lost;* and it is said he could have restored it complete, had it all been lost.

His disposition was sweet and his life altogether fortunate. His biographer says of him: "Descended from Scotch Presbyterians — ministers many of them — on his father's side, and from a Quaker family on his mother's, he probably united as many guaranties of 'good birth,' in the moral sense of the word, as could be found in these islands at the beginning of the century."

He was born at Rothley Temple, Leicestershire, in 1800. He was prepared for college at good private schools, and sent to Cambridge when he was eighteen. He studied law and was admitted to the bar in 1825; but, in the following year, he determined to adopt literature as a profession, owing to the welcome given to his *Essay on Milton.* As he had written epics, histories, and metrical romances prior to the age of ten, his choice of a profession was neither hasty nor unexpected.

He continued from this time to write for the *Edinburgh Review*, but literature was not the only field of his activity. He had a seat in Parliament, and he held several positions under the Government. He was never unemployed. Many of his *Essays* were written before breakfast, while the other members of the household were asleep.

He was a voracious reader. If he walked in the country or in London, he always carried a book to read. He spent some years in the government's service in India. On the long voyage over, he read incessantly, and on the return trip he studied the German language.

He was beyond the age of forty when he found the leisure to begin his *History of England*. He worked uninterruptedly, but broke down early, dying at the age of fifty-nine.

With his large, fine physique, his sturdy common sense, his interest in practical matters, and his satisfaction in the physical improvements of the people, Macaulay was a fine specimen of the English gentleman.

Essays and Poetry.—Like De Quincey, Macaulay was a frequent contributor to periodicals. He wrote graphic essays on men of action and historical periods. The essays most worthy of mention in this class are *Sir William Temple*, *Lord Clive*, *Warren Hastings*, and *William Pitt, Earl of Chatham*. Some of his essays on English writers and literary subjects are still classic. Among these are *Milton*, *Dryden*, *Addison*, *Southey's Edition of Pilgrim's Progress*, *Croker's Edition of Boswell's Life of Johnson*, and the biographical essays on *Bunyan*, *Goldsmith*, and *Johnson*, contributed to the *Encyclopædia Britannica*. Although they may lack deep spiritual insight into the fundamental principles of life and literary criticism, these essays are still deservedly read by most students of English history and literature.

Gosse says: "The most restive of juvenile minds, if induced to enter one of Macaulay's essays, is almost certain to reappear at the other end of it gratified, and, to an appreciable extent, cultivated." These *Essays* have developed a taste for general reading in many who could not have been induced to begin with anything dry or hard. Many who have read Boswell's *Life of Johnson* during the past fifty years say that Macaulay first turned their attention to that fascinating work. In the following quotation from an essay on that great biography, we may note his love for interesting concrete statements, presented in a vigorous and clear style: —

"Johnson grown old, Johnson in the fullness of his fame and in the enjoyment of a competent fortune, is better known to us than any other man in history. Everything about him, his coat, his wig, his figure, his face, his scrofula, his St. Vitus's dance, his rolling walk, his blinking eye, the outward signs which too clearly marked his approbation of his dinner, his insatiable appetite for fish sauce and veal pie with plums, his inextinguishable thirst for tea, his trick of touching the posts as he walked . . . all are as familiar to us as the objects by which we have been surrounded from childhood."

Macaulay wrote some stirring ballad poetry, known as *Lays of Ancient Rome*, which gives a good picture of the proud Roman Republic in its valorous days. These ballads have something of Scott's healthy, manly ring. They contain rhetorical and martial stanzas, which are the delight of many boys; but they lack the spirituality and beauty that are necessary for great poetry.

History of England. — Macaulay had for some time wondered why some one should not do for real history what Scott had done for imaginary history. Macaulay accordingly proposed to himself the task of writing a history that should be more accurate than Hume's and possess something of the interest of Scott's historical romances. In 1848 appeared the first two volumes of *The History of England from the Accession of James II.* Macaulay had the satisfaction of seeing his work, in sales and popular appreciation, surpass the novels. He intended to trace the development of English liberty from James II. to the death of George III.; but his minute method of treatment allowed him to unfold only sixteen years (from 1685 to 1701) of that period, so important in the constitutional and religious history of England.

Macaulay's pages are not a graveyard for the dry bones of history. The human beings that figure in his chapters have been restored to life by his touch. We see Charles II. "before the dew was off in St. James's Park striding among the trees, playing with his spaniels, and flinging corn to his ducks." We gaze for a moment with the English courtiers at William III.:—

"They observed that the King spoke in a somewhat imperious tone, even to the wife to whom he owed so much, and whom he sincerely loved and esteemed. They were amused and shocked to see him, when the Princess Anne dined with him, and when the first green peas of the year were put on the table, devour the whole dish without offering a spoonful to her Royal Highness, and they pronounced that this great soldier and politician was no better than a low Dutch bear."[1]

Parts of the *History* are masterpieces of the narrator's art. A trained novelist, unhampered by historical facts, could scarcely have surpassed the last part of Macaulay's eighth chapter in relating the trial of the seven Bishops. Our blood tingles to the tips of our fingers as we read in the fifth chapter the story of Monmouth's rebellion and of the Bloody Assizes of Judge Jeffreys.

[1] *History of England*, Vol. III., Chap. XI.

Macaulay shirked no labor in preparing himself to write the *History*. He read thousands of pages of authorities and he personally visited the great battlefields in order to give accurate descriptions. Notwithstanding such preparation, the value of his *History* is impaired, not only because he sometimes displays partisanship, but also because he fails to appreciate the significance of underlying social movements. He does not adopt the modern idea that history is a record of social growth, moral as well as physical. While a graphic picture of the exterior aspects of society is presented, we are given no profound insight into the interior movements of a great constitutional epoch. We may say of both Gibbon and Macaulay that they are too often mere surveyors, rather than geologists, of the historic field.[1] The popularity of the *History* is not injured by this method.

Macaulay's grasp of fact never weakens, his love of manly courage never relaxes, his joy in bygone time never fails, his zeal for the free institutions of England never falters, and his style is never dull.

General Characteristics. — The chief quality of Macaulay's style is its clearness. Contemporaries said that the printers' readers never had to read his sentences a second time to understand them. This clearness is attained, first, by the structure of his sentences. He avoids entangling clauses, obscure references in his pronouns, and long sentences whenever they are in danger of becoming involved and causing the reader to lose his way. In the second place, if the idea is a difficult one or not likely to be apprehended at its full worth, Macaulay repeats his meaning from a different point of view and throws additional light on the subject by varied illus-

[1] Morison's *Life of Macaulay*, p. 139.

trations. In the third place, his works abound in concrete ideas, which are more readily grasped than abstract ones. He is not content to write: "The smallest actual good is better than the most magnificent promise of impossibilities;" but he gives the concrete equivalent: "An acre in Middlesex is worth a principality in Utopia."

It is possible for style to be both clear and lifeless, but his style is as energetic as it is clear. In narration he takes high rank. His erudition, displayed in the vast stores of fact that his memory retained for effective service in every direction, is worthy of special mention.

While his excellences may serve as a model, he has faults that admirers would do well to avoid. His fondness for contrast often leads him to make one picture too bright and the other too dark. His love of antithesis has the merit of arousing attention in his readers and of crystallizing some thoughts into enduring epigrammatic form; but he is often led to sacrifice exact truth in order to obtain fine contrasts, as in the following: —

"The Puritan hated bear-baiting, not because it gave pain to the bear, but because it gave pleasure to the spectators."

Macaulay is more the apostle of the material than of the spiritual. He lacked sympathy with theories and aspirations that could not accomplish immediate practical results. While his vigorous, easily-read pages exert a healthy fascination, they are not illumined with the spiritual glow that sheds luster on the pages of the great Victorian moral teachers, like Carlyle and Ruskin. He has, however, had more influence on the prose style of the last half of the nineteenth century than any other writer. Many continue to find in him their most effective teacher of a clear, energetic form of expression.

From the painting by Emmeline Deane.

JOHN HENRY, CARDINAL NEWMAN, 1801-1890

Life. — Newman, who was born in London the year after Macaulay, represents a different aspect of English thought. Macaulay was thrilled in contemplating the great material growth and energy of the nation. Newman's interest was centered in the development of the spiritual life.

This son of a practical London banker was writing verses at nine, a mock drama at twelve, and at fourteen, "he broke out into periodicals, *The Spy* and *Anti-Spy*, intended to answer one another." Of his tendency toward mysticism in youth, he wrote: —

"I used to wish the Arabian Tales were true; my imagination ran on unknown influences, on magical powers and influences. I thought life might be a dream, or I an angel, and all this world a deception, my fellow angels by a playful device concealing themselves from me, and deceiving me with the semblance of a material world."

In his youth he imitated the style of Addison, Johnson, and Gibbon. Few boys of his generation had as much practice in writing English prose. At the age of fifteen years and ten months he entered Trinity College, Oxford, from which he was graduated at nineteen. Two years later he won an Oxford fellowship, and in 1824 he became a clergyman of the Church of England.

The rest of his life belongs mainly to theological history. He became one of the leaders of the Oxford Movement (1833–1841) toward stricter High-Church principles, as opposed to liberalism, and in 1845 he joined the Catholic Church. He was rector of the new Catholic University at Dublin from 1854 to 1858. In 1879 he was made a cardinal. Most of his later life was spent at Edgbaston (near Birmingham) at the Oratory of St. Philip Neri.

Works and General Characteristics. — Newman was a voluminous writer. An edition of his works in thirty-six volumes was issued during his lifetime. Most of these properly belong to the history of theological thought. His *Apologia pro Vita Sua*, which he wrote in reply to an attack by Charles Kingsley, an Episcopal clergyman, is really, as its sub-title indicates, *A History of His Religious Opinions*. This intimate, sympathetic account of his religious experiences won him many friends. He wrote two novels: *Loss and Gain* (1848), which gives an excellent picture of Oxford society during the last days of the Oxford Movement, and *Callista* (1852), a vivid story of an early Christian martyr in Africa. His best-known hymn, *Lead Kindly Light*, remains a favorite with all Christian denominations. *The Dream of Gerontius* (1865) is a poem that has been called "the happiest effort to represent the unseen world that has been made since the time of Dante."

Those who are not interested in Newman's Episcopal or Catholic sermons or in his great theological treatises will find some of his best prose in the work known as *The Idea of a University*. This volume, containing 521 pages, is composed of discussions, lectures, and essays, prepared while he was rector of the University at Dublin.

Newman's prose is worthy of close study for the following reasons:—

(1) His style is a clear, transparent medium for the presentation of thought. He molded his sentences with the care of an artist. He said:—

"I have been obliged to take great pains with everything I have ever written, and I often write chapters over and over again, besides innumerable corrections and interlinear additions."

His definition of style is "a thinking out into language," not an ornamental "addition from without." He employs his characteristic irony in ridiculing those who think that "*one* man could do the thought and *another* the style":—

"We read in Persian travels of the way in which young gentlemen go to work in the East, when they would engage in correspondence with those who inspire them with hope or fear. They cannot write one sentence themselves; so they betake themselves to the professional letter writer. . . . The man of thought comes to the man of words; and the man of words duly instructed in the thought, dips the pen of desire into the ink of devotedness, and proceeds to spread it over the page of desolation. Then the nightingale of affection is heard to warble to the rose of loveliness, while the breeze of anxiety plays around the brow of expectation. This is what the Easterns are said to consider fine writing; and it seems pretty much the idea of the school of critics to whom I have been referring."[1]

It was a pleasure to him to "think out" expressions like the following: —

"Ten thousand difficulties do not make a doubt."

"Calculation never made a hero."

"Here below to live is to change, and to be perfect is to have changed often."

(2) Like Macaulay, Newman excelled in the use of the concrete. In his *Historical Sketches*, he imagines the agent of a London company sent to inspect Attica: —

"He would report that the climate was mild; the hills were limestone; there was plenty of good marble; more pasture land than at first survey might have been expected, sufficient certainly for sheep and goats; fisheries productive; silver mines once, but long since worked out; figs fair; oil first rate; olives in profusion. . . . He would not tell how that same delicate and brilliant atmosphere freshened up the pale olive till the olive forgot its monotony, and its cheek glowed like the arbutus or the beech of the Umbrian hills."

A general statement about superseding "the operation of the laws of the universe in a multitude of ways" does not satisfy him. He specifies those ways when he records his belief that saints have "raised the dead to life, crossed the sea without vessels, multiplied grain and bread, cured incurable diseases."

(3) He modestly called himself a rhetorician, but he possessed also the qualities of an acute thinker. He displayed unusual sagacity in detecting the value of different arguments in persuasion. He could arrange in proper proportion the most complex tangle of facts, so as to make one clear impression. Such power made him one of the great Victorian masters of argumentative prose.

[1] *The Idea of a University* (*Literature: A Lecture*).

From the painting by James McNeil Whistler, Glasgow Art Galleries.

THOMAS CARLYLE, 1795-1881

Life.— Thomas Carlyle, who became one of the great tonic forces of the nineteenth century, was also most interested in spiritual growth. He specially emphasized the gospel of work as the only agency that could develop the atmosphere necessary for such growth, and, though deeply religious, he cared little for any special faith or creed.

The son of a Scotch stone mason, Thomas Carlyle was born in 1795 at Ecclefechan, Dumfriesshire. At the age of fourteen, the boy was ready for the University of Edinburgh, and he walked the eighty miles between it and his home. After he was graduated, he felt that he could not enter the ministry, as his parents wished. He therefore taught while he was considering what vocation to follow.

In 1821 he met Jane Welsh, a brilliant and beautiful girl, descended on her father's side from John Knox and on her mother's from William Wallace. With the spirit of Wallace, she climbed in her girlhood up to places that a boy would have considered perilous. When she was forbidden to take up such a masculine study as Latin, she promptly learned to decline a Latin noun.

CRAIGENPUTTOCK

Carlyle had much trouble in winning her; but she finally consented to be his wife, and they were married in 1826. In 1828 they went to live for six lonely years on her farm at Craigenputtock, sixteen miles north of Dumfries, where it was so quiet that Mrs. Carlyle said she could hear the sheep nibbling the grass a quarter of a mile away. Ralph Waldo Emerson visited them here and formed a lifelong friendship with Carlyle. It was here that Carlyle fought the intense spiritual battle of his early life, here that he wrote his first great work, *Sartor Resartus*, which his wife pronounced "a work of genius, dear."

It would be difficult to overestimate the beneficent influence which Mrs. Carlyle exerted over her husband in those trying days of poverty and spiritual stress. When her private correspondence was inadvisedly published after his death, she unwittingly became her husband's Boswell. For many years after the appearance of her letters, his personality and treatment of her were more discussed than his writings. Her references to marital unhappiness were for awhile given undue prominence; but with the passing of time there came a recognition

MRS. CARLYLE

of the fact that she was almost as brilliant a writer as her husband, that, like him, she was frequently ill, and that in expressing things in a striking way, she sometimes exercised his prerogative of exaggeration. "Carlyle has to take a journey always after writing a book," she declared, "and then gets so weary with knocking about that he has to write another book to recover from it." She once said that living with him was as bad as keeping a lunatic asylum.

Unfortunately, his early privations had caused him to have chronic indigestion. He thought that the worst punishment he could suggest for Satan would be to compel him to "try to digest for all eternity with my stomach." This disorder rendered Carlyle peculiarly irascible and explosive. His wife's quick temper sometimes took fire at his querulousness; but her many actions, which spoke much louder than her words, showed how deeply she loved him and how proud she was of his genius. After their removal to London, she would quietly buy the neighbors' crowing roosters, which kept him awake, and she prepared food that would best suit his disordered digestion. She complained of his seeming lack of appreciation. "You don't want to be praised for doing your duty," he said. "I did, though," she wrote.

Carlyle's lack of restraint was most evident in little things. A German who came from Weimar to see him was unfortunately admitted during a period of stress in writing. A minute later the German was seen rapidly descending the stairs and leaving the house. Carlyle immediately hurried to the room where his wife was receiving a visitor, and tragically asked what he had done to cause the Almighty to send a German all the way from Weimar to wrench off the handles of his cupboard doors. Carlyle did not then appear to realize that the frightened German had mistaken the locked cupboard doors for the exit from the room. On the other hand, when the great political economist, John Stuart Mill, was responsible for the loss of the borrowed manuscript of the first volume of *The French Revolution*, Carlyle said to his wife: "Well, Mill, poor fellow, is terribly cut up; we must endeavor to hide from him how very serious the business is to us." To rewrite this volume cost Carlyle a year's exhausting labor.

In 1834 Carlyle went to London, where he lived for the rest of his life in Cheyne Row, Chelsea. The publication of *The French Revolution* in 1837 made him famous. Other works of his soon appeared, to add to his fame. His essays, collected and published in 1839 under the title, *Critical and Miscellaneous Essays*, contained his sympathetic *Essay on Burns*, which no subsequent writer has surpassed. *Cromwell's Letters and Speeches, with*

Elucidations (1845) permanently raised England's estimation of that warrior statesman.

Carlyle's writings, his lectures on such subjects as *Heroes and Hero Worship* (1841), and his oracular criticism on government and life made him as conspicuous a figure as Dr. Samuel Johnson had been in the previous century. Carlyle's last great work, *History of Friedrich II.*, was fortunately finished in 1865, the year before his great misfortune.

In the latter part of 1865 the students of the University of Edinburgh elected Carlyle Lord Rector of that institution because they considered him the man most worthy to receive such high honor. In the spring of 1866, he went to Edinburgh to deliver his inaugural address. Before he returned, he received a telegram stating that his wife had died of heart failure while she was taking a drive in London. The blow was a crushing one. The epitaph that he placed on her monument shows his final realization of her worth and of his irreparable loss. He said truly that the light of his life had gone out.

During his remaining years, he produced little of value except his *Reminiscences*, a considerable part of which had been written long before. Honors, however, came to him until the last. The Prussian Order of Merit was conferred on him in 1874. The English government offered him the Grand Cross of Bath and a pension, both of which he declined. On his eightieth birthday, more than a hundred of the most distinguished men of the English-speaking race joined in giving him a gold medallion portrait. When he died in 1881, an offer of interment in Westminster Abbey was declined and he was laid beside his parents in the graveyard at Ecclefechan.

Sartor Resartus. — Like Coleridge, Carlyle was a student of German philosophy and literature. His earliest work was *The Life of Friedrich Schiller* (1823-1825), which won for him the appreciation and friendship of the German poet, Goethe.

Carlyle's first great original work, the one in which he best delivers his message to humanity, is *Sartor Resartus* (*The Tailor Patched*). This first appeared serially in *Fraser's Magazine* in 1833-1834. He feigned that he was merely editing a treatise on *The Philosophy of Clothes*, the work of a German professor, Diogenes Teufelsdröckh. This professor is really Carlyle himself; but the disguise gave him an excuse for writing in a strange style and for beginning many of his nouns with capitals, after the German fashion.

When *Sartor Resartus* first appeared, Mrs. Carlyle remarked that it was "completely understood and appreciated only by women and mad people." This work did not for some years receive sufficient attention in England to justify publication in book form. The case was different in America, where the first edition with a preface by Emerson was published in 1836, two years before the appearance of the English edition. In the year of Carlyle's death, a cheap London edition of 30,000 copies was sold in a few weeks.

Carlyle calls *Sartor Resartus* a "Philosophy of Clothes." He uses the term "Clothes" symbolically to signify the outward expression of the spiritual. He calls Nature "the Living Garment of God." He teaches us to regard these vestments only as semblances and to look beyond them to the inner spirit, which is the reality. The century's material progress, which was such a cause of pride to Macaulay, was to Carlyle only a semblance, not a sign of real spiritual growth. He says of the utilitarian philosophy, which he hated intensely:—

"It spreads like a sort of Dog-madness; till the whole World-kennel will be rabid."

The majority of readers cared nothing for the symbolism of *Sartor Resartus;* but they responded to its effective presentation of the gospel of work and faced the duties of life with increased energy. Carlyle seemed to stand before them saying:—

"*Do the Duty which lies nearest thee*, which thou knowest to be a Duty! Thy second Duty will already have become clearer. . . . The Situation that has not its Duty, its Ideal, was never yet occupied by man. Yes here, in this poor miserable, hampered, despicable Actual, wherein thou even now standest, here or nowhere is thy Ideal: work it out therefrom; and working, believe, live, be free. Fool! the Ideal is in thyself, the impediment too is in thyself: thy Condition is but the stuff thou art to shape that same Ideal out of . . . "

The French Revolution.—In 1837 when Carlyle finished the third volume of his historic masterpiece, *The French Revolution*, he handed the manuscript to his wife for her criticism, saying: "This I could tell the world: 'You have not had for a hundred years any book that comes more direct and flamingly from the heart of a living man.'" His Scotch blood boiled over the injustice to the French peasants. His temperature begins to rise when he refers to the old law authorizing a French hunter, if a nobleman, "to kill not more than two serfs."

Carlyle brings before us a vast stage where the actors in the French Revolution appear: in the background, "five full-grown millions of gaunt figures with their hungry faces"; in the foreground, one young mother of seven children, "looking sixty years of age, although she is not yet twenty-eight," and trying to respond to the call for seven different kinds of taxes; and, also in the foreground, "a perfumed Seigneur," taking part of the children's dinner. The scene changes; the great individual actors in the Revolution enter: the tocsin clangs; the stage is reddened with human blood and wreathed in flames. We feel that we are actually witnessing that great historic tragedy.

Carlyle had something of Shakespeare's dramatic imagination, which pierced to the heart of men and movements. More detailed and scholarly histories of this time have been written; but no other historian has equaled Carlyle in presenting the French Revolution as a human tragedy that seems to be acted before our very eyes.

He did not attempt to write a complete history of the time. He used the dramatist's legitimate privilege of selection. From a mass of material that would have bewildered a writer of less ability, he chose to present on the center of the stage the most significant actors and picturesque incidents.

Carlyle's "Real Kings." — Carlyle believed that "universal history, the history of what man has accomplished in this world, is at bottom the history of the great men who have worked here." In accordance with this belief, he studied, not the slow growth of the people, but the lives of the world's great geniuses.

In his course of lectures entitled *Heroes and Hero Worship* (1841), he considers *The Hero as Prophet*, *The Hero as Poet*, *The Hero as Priest*, and *The Hero as King*, and shows how history has been molded by men like Mohammed, Shakespeare, Luther, and Napoleon. It is such men as these whom Carlyle calls "kings," beside whom "emperors," "popes," and "potentates" are as nothing. He believed that there was always living some

Oliver Goldsmith 1728-74

1. Birthplace — Pallas
II. Education
   1. Charity School, Dublin
   2. European Travels
III. Occupations
   1. Medicine
   2. Literature
IV. Works
   1. Series of Letters — Citizen of the World
   2. Poetry
      A. The Traveler
      B. " Deserted Village
   3. Story — Vicar of Wakefield
   4. Play — She Stoops to Conquer
V. General Characteristics
   1. Romantic at heart
   2. Showed Classic influence
   3. Altruistic philosophy
   4. Rare humor
   5. Easy, graceful, and Clear Style

man worthy to be the "real king" over men, and such a kingship was Carlyle's ideal of government.

Oliver Cromwell was one of these "real kings." In the work entitled *Cromwell's Letters and Speeches, with Elucidations*, Carlyle was the first to present the character of the Protector in its full strength and greatness and to demonstrate once for all that he was a hero whose memory all Englishmen should honor.

The *Life of John Sterling* (1851) is a fair, true, and touching biography of Carlyle's most intimate friend, the man who had introduced him to Jane Welsh. After reading this book, George Eliot said she wished that more men of genius would write biographies.

Carlyle's next attempt at biography grew into the massive *History of Friedrich II.* (1858-1865), which includes a survey of European history in that dreary century which preceded the French Revolution. "Friedrich is by no means one of the perfect demigods." He is "to the last a questionable hero." However, "in his way he is a Reality," one feels "that he always means what he speaks; grounds his actions, too, on what he recognizes for the truth; and, in short, has nothing of the Hypocrite or Phantasm." Despite his tyranny and his bloody career, he, therefore, is another of Carlyle's "real kings." While this work is a history of modern Europe, Friedrich is always the central figure. He gives to these six volumes a human note, a glowing interest of personal adventure, and a oneness that are remarkable in so vast a work.

General Characteristics. — Carlyle's writings must be classed among the great social and democratic influences of the nineteenth century, in spite of the fact that he did not believe in pure democracy. It was his favorite theory that a great man, like Oliver Cromwell, could govern better than the unintelligent multitude. However much he rebelled against democracy in government, his sympathies were with the toiling masses. His work entitled *Past and Present* (1843) suggests the organization of labor and introduces such modern expressions as "a fair day's wages for a fair day's work." In *Sartor Resartus*, he specially honors "the toilworn Craftsman, that with earth-made implement laboriously conquers the Earth and makes her Man's."

Carlyle had a large fund of incisive wit and humor, which often appear in picturesque setting, as when he said to a physician: "A man might as well pour his sorrows into the long hairy ear of a jackass." As the satiric censor of his time, Carlyle found frequent occasion for caustic wit. He lashed the age for its love of the "swine's trough," of "Pig-science, Pig-enthusiasm and devotion." Although his intentions were good, his satire was not always just or discriminating, and he was in consequence bitterly criticized. The following Dutch parable is in some respects specially applicable to Carlyle: —

"There was a man once, — a satirist. In the natural course of time his friends slew him and he died. And the people came and stood about his corpse. 'He treated the whole round world as his football,' they said indignantly, 'and he kicked it.' The dead man opened one eye. 'But always toward the goal,' he said."

This goal toward which Carlyle struggled to drive humanity was the goal of moral achievement. Young people on both sides of the Atlantic responded vigorously to his appeals. The scientist John Tyndall said to his students: —

"The reading of the works of two men has placed me here to-day. These men are the English Carlyle and the American Emerson.

I must ever remember with gratitude that through three long, cold German winters, Carlyle placed me in my tub, even when ice was on its surface, at five o'clock every morning . . . determined, whether victor or vanquished, not to shrink from difficulty. . . . They told me what I ought to do in a way that caused me to do it, and all my consequent intellectual action is to be traced to this purely moral force. . . . They called out, 'Act!' I hearkened to the summons."

Huxley aptly defined Carlyle as a "great tonic, — a source of intellectual invigoration and moral stimulus."

Carlyle is not only a "great Awakener" but also a great literary artist. His style is vivid, forceful, and often poetic. He loves to present his ideas with such picturesqueness that the corresponding images develop clearly in the reader's mind. Impressive epithets and phrases abound. His metaphors are frequent and forceful. Mirabeau's face is pictured as "rough-hewn, seamed, carbuncled." In describing Daniel Webster, Carlyle speaks of "the tanned complexion, that amorphous crag-like face; the dull black eyes under their precipice of brows, like dull anthracite furnaces needing only to be blown, the mastiff-mouth, accurately closed." He formed many new compound words after the German fashion, such as "mischief-joy"; and when he pleased, he coined new words, like "dandiacal" and "croakery."

His frequent exclamations and inversions make his style seem choppy, like a wave-tossed sea; but his sentences are so full of vigor that they almost call aloud from the printed page. His style was not an imitation of the German, but a characteristic form of expression, natural to him and to his father.

The gift of verse was denied him, but he is one of the great prose poets of the nineteenth century. Much of *Sartor Resartus* is highly poetic and parts of *The French Revolution* resemble a dramatic poem.

From a photograph.

JOHN RUSKIN, 1819-1900

Life. — The most famous disciple of Carlyle is John Ruskin, the only child of wealthy parents, who was born in London in 1819. When he was four years old the family moved to Herne Hill, a suburb south of London, where his intense love of nature developed as he looked over open fields, "animate with cow and buttercup," "over softly wreathing distances of domestic wood," to the distant hills. His entertaining autobiography, *Præterita* (1885-1889), relates how he was reared: —

"I had never heard my father's or mother's voice once raised in any question with each other . . . I had never heard a servant scolded . . . I obeyed word or lifted finger, of father or mother, simply as a ship her helm . . . nothing was ever promised me that was not given; nothing ever threatened me that was not inflicted, and nothing ever told me that was not true. . . . Peace, obedience, faith; these three for chief good; next to these, the habit of fixed attention with both eyes and mind."

He grew up a solitary child without playmates. This solitude was relieved when his parents took him on occasional trips through England, Switzerland, and Italy. In *Præterita* he tells in an inimitable way how the most portentious interruption to his solitude came in 1836, when his father's Spanish partner came with his four beautiful daughters to visit Herne Hill. These were the first girls in his own station to whom he had spoken. "Virtually convent-bred more closely than the maids themselves," says Ruskin, "I was thrown, bound hand and foot, in my unaccomplished simplicity, into the fiery furnace." In four days he had fallen so desperately in love with the oldest, Clotilde Adèle Domecq, a "graceful blonde" of fifteen, that he was more than four years in recovering his equilibrium. She laughed at his protestations of love; but she repeatedly visited his parents, and he did not give up hope until 1840, when she married a French baron. His biographer says that the resulting "emotional strain doubtless was contributory to his breakdown at Oxford" and to his enforced absence for a recuperative trip on the continent.

His feminine attachments usually showed some definite results in his writing. Miss Domecq's influence during the long period of his devotion inspired him to produce much verse, which received such high praise that his father desired him to become a poet. Although some of Ruskin's verse was good, he finally had the penetration to see that it ranked decidedly below the greatest, and he later laid down the dictum: "with second-rate poetry *in quality* no one ought to be allowed to trouble mankind." In 1886, he had the humor to allude as follows to Miss Domecq and her influence on his rimes, " . . . her sisters called her Clotilde, after the queen-saint, and I, Adèle, because it rimed to shell, spell, and knell."

Before he was graduated from Oxford in 1842, he wrote the beautiful altruistic story, *The King of the Golden River* (1841) for Euphemia Gray, the young girl unhappily chosen by his mother to become his wife. He married her in 1848, but was divorced from her in 1854. In 1855 she was married to the Pre-Raphaelite artist, John Millais (p. 463).

Another attachment led to his writing some of the finest parts of his most popular work, *Sesame and Lilies* (1864). "I wrote *Lilies*," he says, "to please one girl." He is here referring to Rose La Touche, a bright, ardent, religious enthusiast, to whom he began to teach drawing when she was ten years old. His affection for her grew so strong that he finally asked her to become his wife. He was then a man of forty while she was scarcely grown. Her religious scruples kept her from definitely accepting him, because his belief was not sufficiently orthodox. The attachment, however, continued until her early death. She was in some respects a remarkable character, and he seems to have had her in mind when he wrote in *Sesame and Lilies* the "pearly" passage about Shakespeare's heroines.

Although Ruskin's wealth relieved him from earning a living, he was rarely idle. He studied, sketched, arranged collections of minerals, prepared Turner's pictures for the National Gallery, became professor of art at Oxford University, and wrote and lectured on art and social subjects.

His later activities, before his health gave way, were in many respects similar to those of a twentieth-century social-service worker. The realization of the misery that overwhelmed so much of human life caused him to turn from art to consider remedies for the evils that developed as the competitive industries of the nation expanded. He endeavored to improve the condition of the working classes in such ways as building sanitary tenements, establishing a tea shop, and forming an altruistic association, known as St. George's Guild. Nearly all his inheritance of £180,000 was expended in such activities. The royalties coming from the sale of his books supported him in old age.

Ruskin suffered from periods of mental depression during his last years, which were spent at Brantwood on Coniston Water in the Lake District. He died in 1900 at the age of eighty-one and was buried in the cemetery at Coniston.

Art Works. — Ruskin published the first volume of *Modern Painters* in 1843, the year after he was graduated from Oxford, and the fifth and last volume, seventeen years later, in 1860. Many of his views changed during this period; but he honestly declared them and left to his readers the task of reconciling the divergent ideas in *Modern Painters*. The purpose of this book was, in his own words, "to declare the perfectness and eternal beauty of the work of God; and test all works of man by concurrence with, or subjection to that."

Modern Painters contains painstaking descriptions of God's handiwork in cloud formation, mountain structure, tree architecture, and water forms. In transferring these aspects of nature to canvas, Ruskin shows the superiority of modern to ancient painting. He emphasizes the moral basis of true beauty, and the necessity of right living as a foundation for the highest type of art. Perhaps *Modern Painters* achieved its greatest success in freeing men from the bondage of a conventional criticism that was stifling art, in sending them direct to nature as a guide, and in developing a love for her varied manifestations of beauty.

Two of Ruskin's works on architecture, *The Seven Lamps of Architecture* (1849) and *The Stones of Venice* (1851-1853), had a decided effect on British taste in building. The three volumes of the *The Stones of Venice* give a history of the Venetians and of their Gothic architecture. He aims to show that the beauty of such buildings as St. Mark's Cathedral and the Doges' Palace is due to the virtue and patriotism of the people, the nobility of the designers, and the joy of the individual workmen, whose chisels made the very stones of Venice tell beautiful stories.

The most important of his many other writings on art is the volume entitled *Lectures on Art, Delivered before the University of Oxford, 1870*. In his famous *Inaugural* of this series, he thus states what he considers the central truth of his teaching: "The art of any country is the exponent of its social and political virtues."

Social Works. — By turning from the criticism of art to consider the cause of humanity, Ruskin shows the influence of the ethical and social forces of the age. In middle life he was overwhelmed with the amount of human misery and he determined to do his best to relieve it. He wrote: —

"I simply cannot paint, nor read, nor look at minerals, nor do anything else that I like, and the very light of the morning sky, when there is any — which is seldom, nowadays, near London — has become hateful to me, because of the misery that I know of, and see signs of, where I know it not, which no imagination can interpret too bitterly."[1]

[1] *Fors Clavigera*, Letter I.

After 1860 his main efforts with both pen and purse were devoted to improving the condition of his fellow men. His attempts to provide a remedy led him to write *Unto this Last* (1860), his first and most complete work on political economy, *Munera Pulveris* (1863), *Time and Tide by Weare and Tyne* (1868), *Fors Clavigera* (1871-1884), which is a long series of letters to workingmen, and a number of other works, that also present his views on social questions.

He abhorred the old political economy, which he defined as "the professed and organized pursuit of money." Instead of considering merely the question of the production and distribution of articles, his interest lay in the causes necessary to produce healthy, happy workmen. It seemed to him that the manufacture "of souls" ought to be "exceedingly lucrative." This statement and his maxim, "There is no wealth but life," were called "unscientific." In his fine book of essays, entitled *Sesame and Lilies* (1864), he actually had printed in red those pathetic pages describing how an old cobbler and his son worked night and day to try to keep a little home of one room, until the father died from exhaustion and the son had a film come over his eyes.

John Ruskin, social reformer, has an important place in the social movement of the nineteenth century. Many of his theories, which were considered revolutionary, have since become the commonplace expressions of twentieth-century social economists.

General Characteristics. — Ruskin was a champion of the Pre-Raphaelite school of art (p. 463). He used his powerful influence to free art from its conventional fetters and to send people direct to nature for careful loving study of her beautiful forms. His chief strength lies in his moral enthusiasm and his love of the beautiful in nature. Like his master, Carlyle, Ruskin is a great ethical teacher; but he aimed at more definite results in the reformation of art and of social life. He moralized art and humanized political economy.

Some of his art criticisms and social theories are fanciful, narrow, and sometimes even absurd. He did not seem to recognize with sufficient clearness the fact that immoral individuals might produce great works of art; but no one can successfully assail his main contention that there must be a connection between great art and the moral condition of a people. His rejection of railroads and steam machinery as necessary factors in modern civilization caused many to pay little attention to any of his social theories. Much of the gospel that he preached has, however, been accepted by the twentieth century. He was in advance of his time when he said in 1870 that the object of his art professorship would be accomplished if "the English nation could be made to understand that the beauty which is indeed to be a joy forever must be a joy for all."

At the age of fifty-eight, he thus summed up the principal work of his life: —

"*Modern Painters* taught the claim of all lower nature on the hearts of men; of the rock, and wave, and herb, as a part of their necessary spirit life. . . . *The Stones of Venice* taught the laws of constructive Art, and the dependence of all human work or edifice, for its beauty, on the happy life of the workman. *Unto this Last* taught the laws of that life itself and its dependence on the Sun of Justice; the *Inaugural Oxford Lectures*, the necessity that it should be led, and the gracious laws of beauty and labor recognized, by the upper, no less than the lower classes of England; and, lastly, *Fors Clavigera* has declared the relation of these to each other, and the only possible conditions of peace and honor, for low and high, rich and poor. . . ."

Ruskin has written remarkable descriptive prose. A

severe English critic, George Saintsbury, says of Ruskin's works ". . . they will be found to contain the very finest prose (without exception and beyond comparison) which has been written in English during the last half of the nineteenth century. . . . *The Stones of Venice* . . . is *the* book of descriptive prose in English, and all others toil after it in vain."

Ruskin could be severely plain in expression, but much of his earlier prose is ornate and almost poetic. The following description of the Rhone deserves to be ranked with the painter's art: —

"There were pieces of wave that danced all day as if Perdita were looking on to learn; there were little streams that skipped like lambs and leaped like chamois; there were pools that shook the sunshine all through them, and were rippled in layers of overlaid ripples, like crystal sand; there were currents that twisted the light into golden braids, and inlaid the threads with turquoise enamel; there were strips of stream that had certainly above the lake been mill streams, and were busily looking for mills to turn again."[1]

CHARLES DICKENS, 1812-1870

Life. — The first of the great Victorian novelists to make his mark was Charles Dickens. This great portrayer of child life had a sad painful childhood. He was born in 1812 at Landport, a district of the city of Portsmouth, Hampshire, where his father was a clerk in the Navy Pay Office. John Dickens, the prototype of Mr. Micawber, was a kind, well-intentioned man, who knew far better how to harangue his large household of children than how to supply it with the necessities of life. He moved from place to place, sinking deeper into poverty and landing finally in a debtors' prison.

[1] *Præterita*, Vol. II., Chap. V.

From a photograph taken in America, 1868.

The dreams of a fine education and a brilliant career, which the future novelist had fondly cherished in his precocious little brain, had to be abandoned. At the age of eleven the delicate child was called upon to do his part toward maintaining the family. He was engaged, at sixpence a week, to paste labels on blacking bottles. He was poorly clothed, ill fed, forced to live in the cheapest place to be found, and to associate with the roughest kind of companions. This experience was so bitter and galling to the sensitive boy that years after, when he was a successful, happy man, he could not look back upon it without tears in his eyes. Owing to a rupture between his employer and the elder Mr. Dickens, Charles was removed from this place and sent to school. At fifteen, however, he had to seek work again. This time he was employed in an attorney's office at Gray's Inn.

It was impossible, of course, for this ambitious boy to realize that he was receiving an education in the dirty streets, the warehouses, the tenements, and the prisons. Yet, for his peculiar bent of mind, these furnished far richer stores of learning than either school or college could have given. He had marvelous powers of observation. He noted everything, from the saucy street waif to the sorrowful prison child, from the poor little drudge to the brutal schoolmaster, and he transplanted them from life to fiction, in such characters as Sam Weller, Little Dorrit, the Marchioness, Mr. Squeers, and a hundred others.

While in the attorney's office, Dickens began to study shorthand, in order to become a reporter. This was the beginning of his success. His reports were accurate and racy, even when they happened to be written in the pouring rain, in a shaking stagecoach, or by the light of a lantern. They were also promptly handed in at the office, despite the fact that the stages sometimes broke down and left their passengers to plod on foot through the miry roads leading into London. These reports and newspaper articles soon attracted attention; and Dickens received an offer for a series of humorous sketches, which grew into the famous *Pickwick Papers*, and earned £20,000 for the astonished publishers. He was able to make his own terms for his future novels. Fame came to him almost at a bound. He was loved and toasted in England and America before he had reached the age of thirty. When, late in life, he made lecture tours through his own country, or through Scotland or America, they were like triumphal marches.

In his prime Dickens was an energetic, high-spirited, fun-loving man. He made a charming host, and was never happier than when engineering theatrical entertainments at his delightful home, Gads Hill. He was esteemed by all the literary men of London, and idolized by his children and friends. As his strong personality was communicated to his audiences and his readers, his death in 1870 was felt as a personal loss throughout the English-speaking world.

DICKENS'S HOME, GADS HILL

Works. — *Pickwick Papers* (1836-1837), Dickens's first long story, is one of his best. Mr. Pickwick, with his genial nature, his simple philosophy, and his droll adventures, and Sam Weller, with his ready wit, his acute observations, and his almost limitless resources, are amusing from start to finish. The book is brimful of its author's high spirits. It has no closely knit plot, but merely a succession of comical incidents, and vivid caricatures of Mr. Pickwick and his friends. Yet the fun is so good-natured and infectious, and the looseness of design is so frankly declared that the book possesses a certain unity arising from its general atmosphere of frolic and jollity.

Oliver Twist (1837-1838) is a powerful story, differing widely from *Pickwick Papers*. While the earlier work is delightful chiefly for its humor, *Oliver Twist* is strong in its pictures of passion and crime. Bill Sykes the murderer, Fagin the Jew, who teaches the boys deftness of hand in stealing, and poor Nancy, are drawn with such power that they seem to be still actually living in some of London's dark alleys. Little Oliver, born in the poorhouse, clothed by charity, taught by the evil genius of the streets, starved in body and soul, is one of the many pathetic portraits of children drawn with a sure and loving hand by Dickens. There are some improbable features about the plot and some overwrought sentimental scenes in this story. Dickens reveled in the romantic and found it in robbers' dens, in bare poverty, in red-handed crime. The touching pathos and thrilling adventures of *Oliver Twist* make a strong appeal to the reader's emotions.

With the prodigality of a fertile genius, Dickens presented his expectant and enthusiastic public with a new novel on an average of once a year for fourteen years; and, even after that, his productivity did not fall off materially. The best and most representative of these works are *Nicholas Nickleby* (1838-1839), *Barnaby Rudge* (1841), *Martin Chuzzlewit* (1843-1844), *Dombey and Son* (1846-1848), *David Copperfield* (1849-1850), *Bleak House* (1852-1853), *Hard Times* (1854), *A Tale of Two Cities* (1859), and *Our Mutual Friend* (1864).

Of these, *David Copperfield* is at once Dickens's favorite work and the one which the world acclaims as his masterpiece. The novel is in part an autobiography. Some incidents are taken directly from Dickens's early experiences and into many more of David's childish sorrows, boyish dreams, and manly purposes, Dickens has breathed the breath of his own life. David Copperfield is thus a vitally interesting and living character. The book contains many of Dickens's most human men and women. Petted Little Em'ly with her pathetic tragedy is handled with deep sympathy and true artistic delicacy. Peggotty and Mrs. Steerforth are admirably drawn and contrasted. Mrs. Gummidge's thoughtful care of Peggotty exhibits Dickens's fine perception of the self-sacrificing spirit among the very poor. Uriah Heep remains the type of the humble sycophant, and Mr. Micawber, the representative of the man of big words and pompous manners. These various characters and separate life histories are bound in some way to the central story of David.

General Characteristics.—England has produced no more popular novelist than Charles Dickens. His novels offer sound and healthy entertainment, hearty laughter, a wide range of emotions, and a wonderful array of personalities. He presents the universal physical experiences of life that are understood by all men, and irradiates this life with emotion and romance. He keeps his readers in an active state of feeling. They laugh at the broad humor in Sam Weller's jokes; they chuckle over the sly exposure of Mr. Pecksniff in *Martin Chuzzlewit;* they weep in *Dombey and Son* over poor Paul crammed with grown-up learning when he wanted to be just a child; they rejoice over David Copperfield's escape from his stepfather into the loving arms of whimsical, clever Aunt Betsey Trotwood; they shiver with horror in *Our Mutual Friend* during the search for floating corpses on the dark river; and they feel more kindly toward the whole world after reading *A Christmas Carol* and taking Tiny Tim into their hearts.

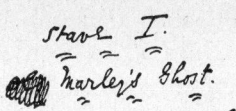

FACSIMILE OF MS. OF A CHRISTMAS CAROL

Dickens excels in the portrayal of humanity born and reared in poverty and disease. He grasps the hand of these unfortunates in a brother's clasp. He says in effect: "I present to you my friends, the beggar, the thief, the outcast. They are men worth knowing." He does not probe philosophically into complex causes of poverty and crime. His social creed was well formulated by Dowden in these words: "Banish from earth some few monsters of selfishness, malignity, and hypocrisy, set to rights a few obvious imperfections in the machinery of society, inspire all men with a cheery benevolence, and everything will go well with this excellent world of ours."

Every student of the science of society, however, owes a debt to Dickens. He did what no science or knowledge or logic can do alone. He reached the heart, awoke the conscience, and pierced the obtuseness of the public. He aroused its protests because his genius painted prisons and hovels and dens of vice so vividly that his readers actually suffered from the scenes thus presented and wanted such horrors abolished.

Dickens's infectious humor is a remarkable and an unfailing quality of his works. It pervades entire chapters, colors complete incidents, and displays the temper of the optimist through the darkest pictures of human suffering.

A hypocrite is an abomination to Dickens. Speaking of Mr. Pecksniff in *Martin Chuzzlewit*, Dickens says: "Some people likened him to a direction-post, which is always telling the way to a place, and never goes there." His humor can be fully appreciated only by reading long passages, such as the scene of Mr. Pickwick's trial, the descriptions of Mr. Micawber and of Miss Betsey Trotwood, or the chapter on Podsnappery in *Our Mutual Friend*. Dickens's humor has an exuberant richness, which converts men and women into entertaining figures of comedy.

Closely allied to his fund of humor is his capacity for pathos, especially manifest in his treatment of childhood. Dickens has a large gallery of children's portraits, fondly and sympathetically executed. David Copperfield, enduring Mr. Murdstone's cruel neglect, Florence Dombey pining for her father's love, the Marchioness starving upon cold potatoes, Tom and Louise Gradgrind, stuffed with facts and allowed no innocent amusement, and the waifs of Tom's-All-Alone dying from abject poverty and disease, are only a few of the sad-eyed children peering from the pages of Dickens and yearning for love and understanding. He wrings the heart; but, happily, his books have improved the conditions of children, not only in public asylums, factories, and courts, but also in schools and homes.

Dickens's chief faults arise from an excess of sensibility and humor. His soft heart and romantic spirit lead him to exaggerate. In such passages as the death of Little Nell in *The Old Curiosity Shop* and the interviews between Dora and David in *David Copperfield*, Dickens becomes mawkish and sentimental. While his power of portraiture is amazing, he often overleaps the line of character drawing and makes side-splitting caricatures of his men and women. They are remembered too often by a limp or a mannerism of speech, or by some other little peculiarity, instead of by their human weaknesses and accomplishments.

Dickens is not a master in the artistic construction of his plots. The majority of his readers do not, however, notice this failing because he keeps them in such a delightful state of interest and suspense by the sprightliness with which he tells a story.

He was a very rapid writer, and his English is consequently often careless in structure and in grammar. As he was not a man of books, he never acquired that half-unconscious knowledge of fine phrasing which comes to the careful student of literature. No novelist has, however, told more graphically such appealing stories of helpless childhood and of the poor and the outcast.

WILLIAM MAKEPEACE THACKERAY, 1811-1863

Life. -- Though nearly a year older than Dickens, Thackeray made his way to popularity much more slowly. These two men, who became friends and generous rivals, were very different in character and disposition. Instead of possessing the self-confidence, energy, and industry that brought Dickens fame in his youth, Thackeray had to contend with a somewhat shy and vacillating temperament, with extreme modesty, and with a constitutional aversion to work.

Born in Calcutta in 1811, he was sent to England to be educated. He passed through Charter House and went one year to Cambridge. He was remembered by his school friends for his skill in caricature sketching. He hoped to

From the painting by Samuel Laurence, National Portrait Gallery.

W M Thackeray

make painting a profession and went to Paris to study; but he never attained correctness in drawing, and when he offered to illustrate the works of Dickens, the offer was declined. Thackeray certainly added to the charm of his own writings by his droll and delightful illustrations.

When Thackeray came of age in 1832, he inherited a small fortune, which he soon lost in an Indian bank and in newspaper investments. He was then forced to overcome his idle, procrastinating habits. He became a literary hack, and contributed humorous articles to such magazines as *Fraser* and *Punch*. While his pen was causing mirth and laughter in England, his heart was torn by suffering. His wife, whom he had married in 1837, became insane. He nursed her patiently with the vain hope that she could recover; but he finally abandoned hope and put her in the care of a conscientious attendant. His home was consequently lonely, and the club was his only recourse. Here, his broad shoulders and kindly face were always greeted with pleasure; for his affable manners and his sparkling humor, which concealed an aching heart, made him a charming companion.

CARICATURE OF THACKERAY BY HIMSELF

It is pleasant to know that the later years of his life were happier. They were cheered by the presence of his daughters, and were free from financial worries. He had the satisfaction of knowing that, through the sales of his books and the returns from his lectures, he had recovered his lost fortune.

Novels. — *Vanity Fair* (1847–1848) is Thackeray's masterpiece. For the lifelikeness of its characters, it is one of the most remarkable creations in fiction. Thackeray called this work "A Novel without a Hero." He might have added "and without a heroine"; for neither clever Becky Sharp nor beautiful Amelia Sedley satisfies the requirements for a heroine. No perfect characters appear in the book, but it is enlivened with an abundance of genuine human nature. Few people go through life without meeting a George Osborne, a Mrs. Bute Crawley, or a Mrs. Sedley. Even a penurious, ridiculous, old Sir Pitt

Crawley is sometimes seen. The greatest stroke of genius in the book, however, is the masterly portrayal of the artful, scheming Becky Sharp, who alternately commands respect for her shrewdness and repels by her moral depravity.

In *Vanity Fair* certain classes of society are satirized. Their intrigues, frivolities, and caprices are mercilessly dealt with. Thackeray probes almost every weakness, vanity, or ambition that leads humanity to strive for a place in society, to long for a bow from a lord, and to stint in private in order to shine in public. He uncovers the great social farce of life, which is acted with such solemn gravity by the snobs, the hypocrites, and the other superficial *dramatis personæ*. Amid these satirized frivolities there appear occasional touches of true pathos and deep human tragedy, which are strangely effective in their unsympathetic surroundings.

THACKERAY'S HOME WHERE VANITY FAIR WAS WRITTEN

Thackeray gives in *Henry Esmond* (1852) an enduring picture of high life in the eighteenth century. This work is one of the great historical novels in our language. The time of Queen Anne is reconstructed with remarkable skill. The social etiquette, the ideals of honor, the life and spirit of that bygone day, reappear with a powerful vividness. Thackeray even went so far as to disguise his own natural, graceful style, and to imitate eighteenth-century prose. *Henry Esmond* is a dangerous rival of *Vanity Fair*. The earlier work has a freshness of humor and a spontaneity of manner that are not so apparent in *Henry Esmond*. On the other hand, *Esmond* has a superior plot and possesses a true hero.

In *The Newcomes* (1854-1855), Thackeray exhibits again his incisive power of delineating character. This book would continue to live if for nothing except the simple-hearted, courtly Colonel Newcome. Few scenes in English fiction are more affecting than those connected with his death. The accompanying lines will show what a simple pathos Thackeray could command:—

"At the usual evening hour the chapel bell began to toll, and Thomas Newcome's hands outside the bed feebly beat time — and just as the last bell struck, a peculiar sweet smile shone over his face, and he lifted up his head a little, and quickly said, '*Adsum*' — and fell back. It was the word we used at school when names were called; and, lo! he whose heart was as that of a little child had answered to his name, and stood in the presence of the Master!"

The History of Pendennis (1849) and *The Virginians* (1857-1859) are both popular novels and take rank inferior only to the author's three greatest works. *The Virginians* is a sequel to *Esmond*, and carries the Castlewood family through adventures in the New World.

Essays. — Thackeray will live in English literature as an essayist as well as a novelist. *The English Humorists of the Eighteenth Century* (1853) and *The Four Georges* (1860) are among the most delightful essays of the age. The author of *Henry Esmond* knew Swift, Addison, Fielding, and Smollett, almost as one knows the mental peculiarities of an intimate friend. In *The English Humorists of the Eighteenth Century*, Thackeray writes of their conversations, foibles, and strong points of character, in a most easy and entertaining way. There is a constant charm about his manner, which, without effort or display of learning, brings the authors vividly before the reader. In addition to this presentation of character, the essays contain appreciative literary criticism. The essence of the humor in these eighteenth-century writers is distilled in its purest, most delicate flavor, by this nineteenth-century member of their brotherhood.

The Four Georges deals with England's crowned heads in a satiric vein, which caused much comment among Thackeray's contemporaries. The satire is, however, mild and subdued, never venomous. For example, he says in the essay on George III.:—

"King George's household was a model of an English gentleman's household. It was early; it was kindly; it was charitable; it was frugal; it was orderly; it must have been stupid to a degree which I shudder now to contemplate. No wonder all the princes ran away from the lap of that dreary domestic virtue. It always rose, rode, dined, at stated intervals. Day after day was the same. At the same hour at night the King kissed his daughters' jolly cheeks; the Princesses kissed their mother's hand; and Madame Thielke brought the royal nightcap."

General Characteristics. — Dickens and Thackeray have left graphic pictures of a large portion of contemporary London life. Dickens presents interesting pictures of the vagabonds, the outcasts, and the merchants, and Thackeray portrays the suave, polite leisure class and its dependents.

Thackeray is an uncompromising realist and a satirist.

He insisted upon picturing life as he believed that it existed in London society; and, to his satiric eye, that life was composed chiefly of the small vanities, the little passions, and the petty quarrels of commonplace people, whose main objects were money and title. He could conceive noble men and women, as is proved by Esmond, Lady Castlewood, and Colonel Newcome; but such characters are as rare in Thackeray as he believed they were in real life. The following passage upon mankind's fickleness is a good specimen of his satiric vein in dealing with human weakness: —

"There are no better satires than letters. Take a bundle of your dear friend's letters of ten years back — your dear friend whom you hate now. Look at a pile of your sister's! How you clung to each other until you quarreled about the twenty-pound legacy! . . . Vows, love promises, confidence, gratitude, — how queerly they read after a while! . . . The best ink for Vanity Fair use would be one that faded utterly in a couple of days, and left the paper clean and blank, so that you might write on it to somebody else."

The phases of life that he describes have had no more subtle interpreter. He does not label his characters with external marks, but enters into communion with their souls. His analytic method of laying bare their motives and actions is strictly modern. His great master, Fielding, would have been baffled by such a complex personality as Becky Sharp. Amid the throng of Thackeray's men and women, there are but few who are not genuine flesh and blood.

The art of describing the pathetic is unfailing in Thackeray. He never jars upon the most sensitive feelings nor wearies them by too long a treatment. With a few simple but powerful expressions he succeeds in arousing intense emotions of pity or sorrow. He has been wrongly called a cynic; for no man can be a cynic who shows Thackeray's tenderness in the treatment of pathos.

Thackeray is master of a graceful, simple prose style. In its ease and purity, it most resembles that of Swift, Addison, or Goldsmith. Thackeray writes as a cultured, ideal, old gentleman may be imagined to talk to the young people, while he sits in his comfortable armchair in a corner by the fireplace. The charm of freshness, quaintness, and colloquial familiarity is seldom absent from the delightfully natural pages of Thackeray.

GEORGE ELIOT, 1819-1880

Life. — Mary Ann Evans, known to her family as Marian and to her readers as George Eliot, was born in 1819, at South Farm, in Arbury, Warwickshire, about twenty-two miles north of Stratford-on-Avon. A few months later, the family moved to a spacious ivy-covered farmhouse at Griff, some two miles east, where the future novelist lived until she was twenty-two.

She was a thoughtful, precocious child. She lived largely within herself, passed much time in reverie, and pondered upon deep problems. She easily outstripped her schoolmates in all mental accomplishments, and, from the first, gave evidence of a clear, strong intellect.

The death of her mother and the marriage of a sister left the entire care of the house and dairy to Marian before she was seventeen years old. Her labors were quite heavy for the next six years. At the end of that time, she and her father moved to Foleshill, near Coventry, where she had ample leisure to pursue her studies and music. At Foleshill, she came under the influence of free-thinking friends and became an agnostic, which she remained

From a drawing by Sir F. W. Burton, National Portrait Gallery.

through the rest of her life. This home was again broken up in 1849 by the death of her father. Through the advice of friends she sought comfort in travel on the continent.

Upon her return, she settled in London as assistant editor of the *Westminster Review*. By this time she had become familiar with five languages, had translated abstruse metaphysical books from the German into English, and had so thoroughly equipped her naturally strong intellect that she was sought after in London by such men as Herbert Spencer and George Henry Lewes. A deep attachment sprang up between Mr. Lewes and Miss Evans, and they formed an alliance that lasted until his death.

George Eliot's early literary labors were mainly critical and scientific, being governed by the circle in which she moved. When she came under the influence of Mr. Lewes, she was induced to attempt creative work. Her novels, published under the pen name of George Eliot, quickly became popular. Despite this success, it is doubtful whether she would have possessed sufficient self-reliance to continue her work without Mr. Lewes's encouragement and protecting love, which shielded her from contact with publishers and from a knowledge of harsh criticisms.

Their companionship was so congenial that her friends were astonished when she formed another attachment after his death in 1878, and married Mr. Cross. Her husband said that her affectionate nature required some deep love to which to cling. She had never been very robust, and, during her later years, she was extremely frail. She died in 1880.

Works. — George Eliot was fast approaching forty when she found the branch of literature in which she was to achieve fame. Her first volume of stories, *Scenes of Clerical Life* (1858), showed decisively that she was master of fiction writing. Three novels followed rapidly, *Adam Bede* (1859), *The Mill on the Floss* (1860), and *Silas Marner* (1861). Her mind was stored

GEORGE ELIOT'S BIRTHPLACE

with memories of the Midland counties, where her young life was spent; and these four books present with a powerful realism this rich rural district and its quaint inhabitants, who seem flushed with the warmth of real life.

Adam Bede is the freshest, healthiest, and most delightful of her books. This story leaves upon the memory a charming picture of peace and contentment, with its clearly drawn and interesting characters, its ideal dairy, the fertile stretches of meadow lands, the squire's birthday party, the harvest supper, and the sweet Methodist woman preaching on the green.

The Mill on the Floss also gives a fine picture of village life. This novel is one of George Eliot's most earnest productions. She exhibits one side of her own intense, brooding girlhood, in the passionate heroine, Maggie Tulliver. There is in this tragic story a wonderfully subtle revelation of a young nature, which is morbid, ambitious, quick of intellect, and strong of will, and which has no hand firm enough to serve as guide at the critical period of her life.

Silas Marner, artistically considered, is George Eliot's masterpiece. In addition to the ruddy glow of life in the characters, there is an idyllic beauty about the pastoral setting, and a poetic, half mystic charm about the weaver's manner of connecting his gold with his bright-haired Eppie. The slight plot is well planned and rounded, and the narrative is remarkable for ease and simplicity.

Romola (1863) is a much bolder flight. It is an attempt to present Florence of the fifteenth century, to contrast Savonarola's ardent Christianity with the Greek æstheticism of the Medicis, and to show the influence of the time upon two widely different characters, Romola and Tito Melema. This novel is the greatest intellectual achievement of its author; but it has neither the warmth of life, nor the vigor of her English stories. Though no pains is spared to delineate Romola, Tito, and the inspiring monk, Savonarola, yet they do not possess the genuineness and reality that are felt in her Warwickshire characters.

Middlemarch (1871–1872) and *Daniel Deronda* (1876) marked the decline of George Eliot's powers. Although she still possessed the ability to handle dialogue, to analyze subtle complex characters, and to attain a philosophical grasp of the problems of existence, yet her weakening powers were shown in the length of tedious passages, in an undue prominence of ethical purpose, in the more studied and, on the whole, duller characters, and in the prolixity of style.

George Eliot's poetry does not bear comparison with her prose. *The Spanish Gypsy* (1868) is her most ambitious poem, and it contains some fine dramatic passages. Her most beautiful poem is the hymn beginning:—

> "Oh, may I join the choir invisible
> Of those immortal dead who live again
> In minds made better by their presence!"

There is a strain of noble thought and lofty feeling in her poems, and she rises easily to the necessary passion and fervor of verse; but her expression is hampered by the metrical form.

General Characteristics. — George Eliot is more strictly modern in spirit than either of the other two great contemporary novelists. This spirit is exhibited chiefly in her ethical purpose, her scientific sympathies, and her minute dissection of character.

Her writings manifest her desire to benefit human beings by convincing them that nature's laws are inexorable, and that an infraction of the moral law will be punished as surely as disobedience to physical laws. She strives to arouse people to a knowledge of hereditary influences, and to show how every deed brings its own results, and works, directly or indirectly, toward the salvation or ruin of the doer. She throws her whole strength into an attempt to prove that joy is to be found only in strict attendance upon duty and in self-renunciation. In order to carry home these serious lessons of life, she deals with powerful human tragedies, which impart a somberness of tone to all her novels. In her early works she treats these problems with artistic beauty; but in her later books she often forgets the artist in the moralist, and uses a character to preach a sermon.

The analytical tendency is pronounced in George Eliot's works, which exhibit an exhaustive study of the feelings, the thoughts, the dreams, and purposes of the characters. They become known more through description than through action.

A striking characteristic of her men and women is their power to grow. They do not appear ready-made and finished at the beginning of a story, but, like real human beings amid the struggles of life, they change for the better or the worse. Tito Melema in *Romola* is an example of her skill in evolving character. At the outset, he is a beautiful Greek boy with a keen zest for pleasure. His selfishness, however, which betrays itself first in ingratitude to his benefactor, leads step by step to his complete moral degradation. The consequences of his deeds entangle him finally in such a network of lies that he is forced to betray "every trust that was reposed in him, that he might keep himself safe."

George Eliot occasionally brightens the seriousness of her works with humor. Her stories are not permeated with joyousness, like those of Dickens, nor do they ripple with quiet amusement, like the novels of Thackeray; but she puts witty and aphoristic sayings into the conversations of the characters. The scene at the "Rainbow" inn is bristling with mother wit. Mr. Macey observes:—

" 'There's allays two 'pinions; there's the 'pinion a man has of himsen, and there's the 'pinion other folks have on him. There'd be two 'pinions about a cracked bell if the bell could hear itself.' "[1]

Great precision and scholarlike correctness mark the style of George Eliot. Her vocabulary, though large, is too full of abstract and scientific terms to permit of great flexibility and idiomatic purity of English. She is master of powerful figures of speech, original, epigrammatic turns of expression, and, sometimes, of a stirring eloquence.

ROBERT LOUIS STEVENSON, 1850-1894

Life. — By preferring romantic incident to the portrayal of character, Stevenson differed from his great Victorian predecessors in the field of fiction. He was born in 1850 in the romantic city of Edinburgh, which he has described so well in his *Picturesque Notes on Edinburgh*. Being an invalid from early childhood, he was not sent regularly to school; yet he was ready at the age of seventeen to enter Edinburgh University. He says of himself that in college he neglected all the studies that did not appeal to him, to read with avidity English poetry and fiction, Scottish legend and history. During his summer vacations he

[1] *Silas Marner*, Chap. VI.

From a photograph.

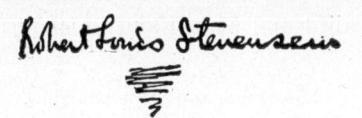

worked at lighthouse engineering. The out-of-door life was just what he liked; but the office work was irksome to him. When finally he made his dislike known, his father, although bitterly disappointed at his son's aversion to the calling followed by two generations of Stevensons, nevertheless consented to a change; and they compromised on the law. In 1875 Stevenson succeeded in gaining admission to the bar; but he soon realized that he would never feel at home in this profession. Moreover, he had always wanted to be a writer. He says: —

"All through my boyhood and youth . . . I was always busy on my own private end, which was to learn to write. I kept always two books in my pocket, one to read, one to write in. As I walked, my mind was busy fitting what I saw with appropriate words. . . . Thus I lived with words. And what I thus wrote was for no ulterior use; it was written consciously for practice."

STEVENSON AS A BOY

The next year, therefore, he decided to devote himself entirely to literature.

He was by heredity predisposed to weak lungs. For the greater part of his life he moved from place to place, searching for some location that would improve his health and allow him to write. He lived for a while in Switzerland, in the south of France, in the south of England, in the Adirondack Mountains, and in California. In 1880 he married in California, Mrs. Fanny Osbourne, of whom he wrote: —

"Steel-true and blade-straight,
The great artificer made my mate."

By a former marriage she had a son, who, at the age of thirteen, inspired Stevenson to write that exciting romance of adventure, *Treasure Island*, published in book form in 1883. This and the remarkable story, *The Strange Case of Dr. Jekyll and Mr. Hyde* (1886), made him so famous that when he visited New York in 1887, a newspaper there offered him $10,000 for a weekly article during the year.

He preferred to accept an offer of $3500 for twelve monthly articles for a magazine.

The most romantic part of his life began in 1888, when he chartered a yacht in San Francisco for a cruise among the South Sea Islands. He had the enthusiasm of a boy for this trip, which was planned to benefit his health. Almost as many adventures befell him as Robinson Crusoe. At one time Stevenson became so ill that he was left with his wife on one of the Society Islands while the yacht sailed away for repairs. Before the boat returned, both his food and money were exhausted, and he and Mrs. Stevenson were forced to live on the bounty of the natives, who adopted him into one of their tribes and gave him the name of Tusitala.

He wandered for three and a half years among the islands of the Southern Pacific, visiting Australia twice. On one trip he called at thirty-three small coral islands, and wrote, "Hackney cabs have more variety than atolls."

He finally selected for his residence the island of Samoa, where he spent the last three and a half years of his life. He died suddenly in his forty-fifth year, and was buried on the summit of a Samoan mountain near his home.

In 1893 he wrote to George Meredith: —

"In fourteen years I have not had a day's real health; I have wakened sick and gone to bed weary; and I have done my work unflinchingly. I have written in bed, and written out of it, written in sickness, written torn by coughing, written when my head swam for weakness . . ."

Many have found in Stevenson's life an inspiration to overcome obstacles, to cease complaining, and to bear a message of good cheer. These lines from his volume of poems called *Underwoods* (1887), are especially characteristic: —

"If I have faltered more or less
　In my great task of happiness;
If I have moved among my race
　And shown no glorious morning face;
If beams from happy human eyes
　Have moved me not; if morning skies,
Books, and my food, and summer rain
　Knocked on my sullen heart in vain: —
Lord, thy most pointed pleasure take
　And stab my spirit broad awake."

Works. — Stevenson wrote entertaining travels, such as *An Inland Voyage* (1878), the record of a canoe journey from Antwerp to Pontoise, *Travels with a Donkey through the Cévennes* (1879), and *In the South Seas* (published in book form in 1896). Early in life he wrote many essays, the best of which are included in the volumes, *Virginibus Puerisque* (*To Girls and Boys*, 1881) and *Familiar Studies of Men and Books* (1882). Valuable papers presenting his views of the technique of writing may be found in the volumes called *Memories and Portraits* (1887) and *Essays in the Art of Writing* (collected after his death). There is a happy blending of style, humor, and thought in many of these essays. Perhaps the most unusual and original of all is *Child's Play* (*Virginibus Puerisque*). This is a psychological study, which reveals one of his strongest characteristics, the power of vividly recalling the events and feelings of childhood.

"When my cousin and I took our porridge of a morning, we had a device to enliven the course of the meal. He ate his with sugar, and explained it to be a country continually buried under snow. I took mine with milk, and explained it to be a country suffering gradual inundation. You can imagine us exchanging bulletins; how here was an island still unsubmerged, here a valley not yet covered with snow; . . . and how, in fine, the food was of altogether secondary importance, and might even have been nauseous, so long as we seasoned it with these dreams."

The simplicity and apparent artlessness of his *A Child's Garden of Verse* (1885) have caused many critics to neglect these poems; but the verdict of young children is almost unanimous against such neglect. These songs

> "Lead onward into fairy land,
> Where all the children dine at five,
> And all the playthings come alive."

It is quite possible that the verses in this little volume may in the coming years appeal to more human beings than all the remainder of Stevenson's work. He and his American contemporary, Eugene Field (1850–1895), had the peculiar genius to delight children with a type of verse in which only a very few poets have excelled.

Boys and young men love Stevenson best for his short stories and romances. After a careful study of Poe and Hawthorne, the American short story masters, Stevenson made the English impressionistic short story a more artistic creation. Some of the best of his short stories are *Will o' the Mill* (1878), *The Sire de Malétroit's Door* (1878), and *Markheim* (1885). His best-known single production, *The Strange Case of Dr. Jekyll and Mr. Hyde*, is really a short story that presents a remarkable psychological study of dual personality.

The short stories served as an apprenticeship for the longer romances, of which *Treasure Island* is the best constructed and the most interesting. Among a number of other romances, the four which deal with eighteenth-century Scottish history are the best: *Kidnapped* (1886), *The Master of Ballantrae* (1889), *David Balfour* (*Catriona*, 1893), and the unfinished *Weir of Hermiston*, published two years after his death.

By Augustus St. Gaudens.
EDINBURGH MEMORIAL OF ROBERT LOUIS STEVENSON

General Characteristics. — Unlike the majority of the Victorian writers of fiction, Stevenson preferred the field of romance and adventure. It is natural to compare him with Scott, who showed a far wider range, both in subject matter and in the portrayal of human beings. Stevenson, however, surpassed Scott in swift delineation of incident, in pictorial vividness, and in literary form. Scott dashed off some of his long romances in six weeks; while Stevenson said that his printer's copy was sometimes the result of ten times that amount of writing. The year before he died, he spent three weeks in writing twenty-four pages.

Stevenson's romances are remarkable for **artistic style,**

clearness of visual image, and boyish love of adventure. He made little attempt to portray more than the masculine half of the human race. His simple verses possess rare power to charm children. The most evident quality of all his prose is its artistic finish.

GEORGE MEREDITH, 1828-1909

Life. — George Meredith was the only child of a Welsh father and an Irish mother. He was born in 1828 over his grandfather's tailor shop in Portsmouth, Hampshire. The father proved incompetent in handling the excellent tailoring business to which he fell heir; and he soon abandoned his son. The mother died when the boy was five years old, and he was then cared for by relatives. When he was fourteen, he was sent to school in Germany for two years; but he did not consider his schooling of much benefit to him and he was forced to educate himself for his life's work.

On his return to England, he was articled to a London solicitor; but by the age of twenty-one, Meredith had abandoned the law and had begun the literary life which was to receive his undivided attention for nearly sixty years. The struggle was at first extremely hard. Some days, indeed, he is said to have lived on a single bowl of porridge.

While following his work as a novelist, he tried writing for periodicals, served as a newspaper correspondent, and later became a literary adviser for a large London publishing firm. In this capacity, he proved a sympathetic friend to many a struggling young author. Thomas Hardy says that he received from Meredith's praise sufficient encouragement to persevere in the field of literature.

From the painting by G. F. Watts, National Portrait Gallery.

Meredith's marriage in 1849 was unhappy and resulted in a separation. Three years after his wife's death, which occurred in 1861, he married a congenial helpmate and went to live in Flint Cottage, near Burford Bridge, Surrey, where most of his remaining years were spent.

Not until late in life were the returns from his writings sufficient to relieve him from unceasing daily toil at his desk. He was widely hailed as a literary master and recognized as a force in fiction before he attained financial independence. After the death of Tennyson, Meredith was elected president of the Society of British Authors. Toward the end of the nineteenth century, his reply to the *Who's Who* query about his recreations was, "a great reader, especially of French literature; has in his time been a great walker." During his last sixteen years of life, he suffered from partial paralysis and was compelled to abandon these long walks, which had been a source both of recreation and of health.

He died in 1909 at the age of eighty-one and was laid beside his wife in the Dorking cemetery. The following words from his novel, *Vittoria*, are on his tombstone: "Life is but a little holding, lent to do a mighty labor."

Poetry. — During his long career, Meredith wrote much verse, which was collected in 1912 in a volume of 578 pages.

The quality of his poetry is very uneven. In such exquisite poems as *Love in the Valley*, *The Lark Ascending*, and *Melanthus*, the fancy and melody are artistically intertwined. Many have admired the felicity of the description and the romance of the sentiment in this stanza from *Love in the Valley*: —

> "Shy as the squirrel and wayward as the swallow,
>   Swift as the swallow along the river's light
> Circleting the surface to meet his mirrored winglets,
>   Fleeter she seems in her stay than in her flight.
> Shy as the squirrel that leaps among the pine-tops,
>   Wayward as the swallow overhead at set of sun,
> She whom I love is hard to catch and conquer,
>   Hard, but O the glory of the winning were she won!"

Some of his songs are pure music, and an occasional descriptive passage in his verse shows the deftness of touch of a skilled lyrical poet. Such poems as *Jump-to-Glory Jane*, *Juggling Jerry*, *The Beggar's Soliloquy*, and *The Old*

Chartist, are character sketches of humble folk and show genuine pathos and humor.

In his poetry, Meredith is, however, more often the moralist and philosopher than the singer and simple narrator. He treats of love, life, and death as metaphysical problems. He ponders over the duties of mankind and the greatest sources of human strength and courage. He roams through a region that seems timeless and spaceless. He "neighbors the invisible." The obscurities in many of these poems are due to the abstract nature of the subject matter, to excessive condensation of thought, to frequent omission of connecting words, and to an abundance of figurative language.

Novels. — Meredith's novels comprise the largest and most noteworthy part of his writings. His most important works of fiction are *The Ordeal of Richard Feverel* (1859). *The Egoist* (1879), and *Diana of the Crossways* (1885). *The Ordeal of Richard Feverel* is the story of a beautiful first love. The courtship of Richard and Lucy, amid scenes that inspire poetic descriptions, is in itself a true prose lyric. Their parting interview is one of the most powerfully handled chapters to be found in English novels. It is heart-rending in its emotional intensity and almost faultless in expression. *The Ordeal of Richard Feverel*, like most of Meredith's works, contains more than a love story. Many chapters of high-class comedy and epigrammatical wit serve to explode a fallacious educational theory.

The Egoist has for its special aim the portrayal and exposure of masculine egotism. This was a favorite subject with Meredith and it recurs frequently in his novels. The plot of *The Egoist* is slight. The interest is centered on the awakening of Clara Middleton and Laetitia Dale to the superlative selfishness of Sir Willoughby's egotism.

Scintillating repartee, covert side-thrusts, shrewd observations, subtle innuendoes, are all used to assist in the revelation of this egotism. One fair April morning, after his return to England from a three years' absence, Sir Willoughby met Laetitia Dale, an early sweetheart whom he no longer loved.

"He sprang out of the carriage and seized her hand. 'Laetitia Dale!' he said. He panted. 'Your name is sweet English music! And you are well?' The anxious question permitted him to read deep in her eyes. He found the man he sought there, squeezed him passionately, and let her go."

The delicate irony of this passage is a mild example of the rich vein of humor running through this work. *The Egoist* is the most Meredithian of the author's novels, and it displays most exuberantly his comic spirit, intent upon photographing mankind's follies. This book has been called "a comedy in narrative."

Diana, the heroine of *Diana of the Crossways*, is the queen of Meredith's heroines. She is intellectual, warm-hearted, and courageous. She thinks and talks brilliantly; but when she acts, she is often carried away by the momentary impulse. She therefore keeps the reader alternately scolding and forgiving her. Her betrayal of a state secret, which cannot be condoned, remains the one flaw in the plot. With this exception, the story is absorbing. The men and women belong to the world of culture. Among them are some of Meredith's most interesting characters, notably Redworth, the noblest man in any of the novels. The scene of the story is in London's highest political circle and the discussions sparkle with cleverness.

Evan Harrington (1861), the story of a young tailor, is one of the lightest and brightest of Meredith's novels. It presents in the author's most inimitable manner a comic picture of the struggle for social position. In two of the characters, Great Mel and Mrs. Mel, are found the pen portraits of Meredith's grandparents. *Rhoda Fleming* (1865) is in its style the simplest of his novels. The humble tragedy is related in the plain speech of the people, without the Gaelic wit usually characteristic of Meredith.

The first half of *The Adventures of Harry Richmond* has been called by some critics Meredith's best piece of writing, but the last half shows less power.

Meredith grew more introspective in his later years, as is shown in such long, analytical novels as, *One of Our Conquerors* (1891), *Lord Ormont and His Aminta* (1894), and *The Amazing Marriage* (1895).

General Characteristics. — Meredith's novels afford him various opportunities for an exposition of his views on education, divorce, personal liberty, conventional narrow-mindedness, egotism, sentimentalism, and obedience to law. His own personality creeps into the stories when he has some favorite sermon to preach; and he sometimes taxes the reader's patience by unduly delaying the narrative or even directing its course in order to accentuate the moral issue.

The chief excellences of his novels lie in the strong and subtle character portrayal, in the brilliant conversations, in the power with which intense scenes are presented, and in the well-nigh omnipresent humor.

Meredith's humor frequently arises from his keen intellectual perception of the paradoxes in life. One of his egotistical lovers, talking to the object of his undying affections, "could pledge himself to eternity, but shrank from being bound to eleven o'clock on the morrow morning." Meredith does not fly into a passion, like Carlyle, because society is sentimental and shallow and loves to pose. He proceeds in the coolest manner to draw with unusual distinctness the shallow dilletante, the sentimentalist, the egotist, and the hypocrite. By placing these characters in the midst of men and women actuated by simple and genuine motives, he develops situations that seem especially humorous to readers who are alert to detect incongruity. This veiled humor, which has been aptly styled "the laughter of the mind," gives to Meredith's works their most distinctive flavor.

His prose style is epigrammatic, rich in figures, subtle, sometimes tortuous and even obscure. He abhors the trite and obvious, and, in escaping them to indulge in witty riddles, fanciful expressions, and difficult allusions, he imperils his clearness. In the presence of genuine emotion, he is always as simple in style as he is serious in attitude; but there are times when he seems to revel in the extravagant and grotesque.

Meredith is the novelist of men and women in the world of learning, of letters, and of politics; he is the satirist of social shams; and he is the sparkling epigrammatist; but he is also the optimist with the sane and vigorous message for his generation, and the realist who keeps a genuine rainbow of idealism in his sky.

THOMAS HARDY, 1840-

Life. — The subtle, comic aspects of cosmopolitan life, which were such a fascination to Meredith, did not appeal to that somber realist, Thomas Hardy, whose genius enabled him to paint impressive pictures of the retired elemental life of Wessex (p. 3). Hardy was born in 1840 in the little village of Bockhampton, Dorsetshire, a few miles

From the painting by Winifred Thompson.

Thomas Hardy.

out of Dorchester. He received his early education at the local schools, attended evening classes at King's College, London, and studied Gothic architecture under Sir Arthur Blomfield. The boy was articled at the early age of sixteen to an ecclesiastical architect and, like the hero in his novel, *A Pair of Blue Eyes,* made drawings and measurements of old churches in rural England and planned their remodeling. He won medals and prizes in this profession before he turned from it to authorship. His first published work, *How I Built Myself a House,* was an outgrowth of some early experiences as an architect.

Hardy married Miss Emma Lavinia Gifford in 1874 and went to live at Sturminster Newton. Later he spent some time in London; but he returned finally to his birthplace, the land of his novels, and built himself a home at Max Gate, Dorchester, in 1885. His life has been a retired one. He always shunned publicity, but he was happy to receive in 1910 the freedom of his native town, an honor bestowed upon him as a mark of love and pride.

Works. — Thomas Hardy is one of the greatest realists in modern England, and also one of the most uncompromising pessimists. His characters are developed with consummate skill, but usually their progression is toward failure or death. These men and women are largely rustics who subsist by means of humble toil, such as tending sheep or cutting furze. The orbit of their lives is narrow. The people are simple, primitive, superstitious. They are only half articulate in the expression of their emotions. In *Far From the Madding Crowd*, for example, Gabriel Oak wished to have Bathsheba know "his impressions; but he would as soon have thought of carrying an odor in a net as of attempting to convey the intangibilities of his feelings in the coarse meshes of language. So he remained silent." On the other hand, the speech is sometimes racy, witty, and flavored by the daily occupation of the speaker.

The scenes usually selected for Hardy's stories are from his own county and those immediately adjacent, to which section of country he has given the name of Wessex. He knows it so intimately and paints it so vividly that its moors, barrows, and villages are as much a part of the stories as the people dwelling there. In fact, Egdon Heath has been called the principal character in the novel, *The Return of the Native* (1878). The upland with its shepherd's hut, the sheep-shearing barn, the harvest storm, the hollow of ferns, and the churchyard with its dripping water spout are part of the wonderful landscape in *Far From the Madding Crowd* (1874). This is the finest artistic product of Hardy's genius. It contains strongly-drawn characters, dramatic incidents, a most interesting story, and some homely native humor. The heroine, Bathsheba, is one of the brainiest and most independent of all Hardy's women. She has grave faults; but the tragic experiences through which she passes soften her and finally mold her into a lovable woman. Steady, resourceful, dumb Gabriel Oak and clever, fencing Sergeant Troy are delightful foils to each other, and are every inch human.

MAX GATE
The Home of Hardy near Dorchester (the Casterbridge of the Novels).

The Mayor of Casterbridge (1886) and *The Woodlanders* (1886-1887) deserve mention with *Far from the Madding Crowd* and *The Return of the Native* as comprising the best four novels of the so-called Wessex stories.

Hardy's later works exhibit an increasing absorption in ethical and religious problems. *Tess of the D'Urbervilles* (1892) is one of Hardy's most powerful novels. It has for its heroine a strong, sweet, appealing woman, whose loving character and tragic fate are presented with fearless vigor and deep sympathetic insight. The personal intensity of the author, which is felt to pervade this book, is present again in *Jude the Obscure* (1895), that record of an aspiring soul, struggling against hopeless odds, heavy incumbrances, and sordid realities.

General Characteristics. — Hardy's novels leave a sense of gloom upon the reader. He explains his view of modern life "as a thing to be put up with, replacing the zest for existence which was so intense in early civilization." His pessimistic philosophy strikes at the core of life and human endeavor. Sorrow appears in his work, not as a punishment for crime, but as an unavoidable result of human life and its inevitable mistakes. Events, sometimes comic but generally tragic, play upon the weaknesses of his characters and bring about entanglements, misunderstandings, and suffering far in excess of the deserts of these well-intentioned people. No escape is suggested. Resignation to misfits, mistakes, and misfortune is what remains.

Hardy is one of the great Victorian story-tellers. His personality is never obtruded on his readers. His humor is not grafted on his scenes, but is a natural outgrowth of his rustic gatherings and conversations. He relates a straightforward tale, and makes his characters act and speak for themselves. He selects the human nature, the rural scene, and the moral issue upon which his whole being can be centered. The result is a certainty of design, a somberness of atmosphere, and an intensity of feeling, such as are found in elegiac poetry. Natural laws, physical nature, and human life are engaged in an uneven struggle, and the result is usually unsatisfactory for human life. The novels are pitilessly sad, but they are nevertheless products of a genuine artist in temperament and technique. His novels show almost as much unity of plot and mood as many of the greatest short stories.

From the painting by G. F. Watts, National Portrait Gallery.

MATTHEW ARNOLD, 1822-1888

Life. — Matthew Arnold, Robert Browning, Alfred Tennyson, A. C. Swinburne, and the much younger Rudyard Kipling are the most noted among a large number of Victorian poets. All of these, with the exception of the two greatest, Browning and Tennyson, also wrote prose.

Matthew Arnold was born in 1822, at Laleham, Middlesex. His father, Dr. Thomas Arnold, was the eminent head master of Rugby School, and the author of *History of Rome, Lectures on Modern History,* and *Ser-*

mons. Under the guidance of such a father, Matthew Arnold enjoyed unusual educational advantages. In 1837 he entered Rugby, and from there went to Baliol College, Oxford. He was so ambitious and studious that he won two prizes at Oxford, was graduated with honors, and, a year later, was elected fellow of Oriel College. Arnold's name, like Thomas Gray's, is associated with university life.

From 1847 to 1851, Arnold was private secretary to Lord Lansdowne. In 1851 he married the daughter of Justice Wightman. After relinquishing his secretaryship, Arnold accepted a position that took him again into educational fields. He was made lay inspector of schools, a position which he held to within two years of his death. This office called for much study in methods of education, and he visited the continent three times to investigate the systems in use there. In addition, he held the chair of poetry at Oxford for ten years, between 1857 and 1867. One of the most scholarly courses of lectures that he delivered there was *On Translating Homer.* From this time until his death, in 1888, he was a distinguished figure in English educational and literary circles.

Poetical Works. — Matthew Arnold's poetry belongs to the middle of the century, that season of doubt, perplexity, and unrest, when the strife 'between the church and science was bitterest and each threatened to overthrow the other. In his home, Arnold was taught a devout faith in revealed religion, and at college he was thrown upon a world of inquiring doubt. Both influences were strong. His feelings yearned after the early faith, and his intellect sternly demanded scientific proof and explanation. He was, therefore, torn by a conflict between his emotions and reason, and he was thus eminently fitted to be the poetic exponent of what he calls —

> ". . . this strange disease of modern life,
> With its sick hurry, its divided aims,
> Its heads o'ertaxed, its palsied hearts."[1]

Arnold felt that there were too much hurry and excitement in the age. In the midst of opposing factions, theories, and beliefs, he cries out for rest and peace. We rush from shadow to shadow —

> "And never once possess our soul
> Before we die."[2]

Again, in the *Stanzas in Memory of the Author of " Obermann,"* he voices the unrest of the age —

> "What shelter to grow ripe is ours?
> What leisure to grow wise?
> Like children bathing on the shore,
> Buried a wave beneath,
> The second wave succeeds, before
> We have had time to breathe."

But Arnold is not the seer to tell us how to enter the vale of rest, how to answer the voice of doubt. He passes through life a lonely figure —

> "Wandering between two worlds, one dead,
> The other powerless to be born."[3]

The only creed that he offers humanity is one born of the scientific temper, a creed of stoical endurance and unswerving allegiance to the voice of duty. Many readers miss in Arnold the solace that they find in Wordsworth and the tonic faith that is omnipresent in Browning. Arnold himself was not wholly satisfied with his creed; but his cool reason refused him the solace of an unquestioning faith.

Arnold has been called "the poet of the Universities," because of the reflective scholarly thought in his verse.

---

[1] *The Scholar-Gypsy.* [2] *A Southern Night.* [3] *The Grande Chartreuse.*

It breathes the atmosphere of books and of the study. Such poetry cannot appeal to the masses. It is for the thinker.

The style of verse that lends itself best to Arnold's genius is the elegiac lyric. *The Scholar-Gypsy* and its companion piece *Thyrsis, Memorial Verses, Stanzas from the Grande Chartreuse,* and *Stanzas in Memory of the Author of "Obermann"* are some of his best elegies.

Sohrab and Rustum and *Balder Dead* are Arnold's finest narrative poems. They are stately, dignified recitals of the deeds of heroes and gods. The series of poems entitled *Switzerland* and *Dover Beach* are among Arnold's most beautiful lyrics. A fine description of the surf is contained in the last-named poem: —

> "Listen! you hear the grating roar
> Of pebbles which the waves draw back, and fling,
> At their return, up the high strand,
> Begin, and cease, and then again begin,
> With tremulous cadence slow, and bring
> The eternal note of sadness in."

Neither the movement of the narrative nor the lightness of the lyric is wholly congenial to Arnold's introspective melancholy muse.

Prose Works. — Although Arnold's first works were in poetry, he won recognition as a prose writer before he was widely known as a poet. His works in prose comprise such subjects as literary criticism, education, theology, and social ethics. As a critic of literature, he surpasses all his great contemporaries. Neither Macaulay nor Carlyle possessed the critical acumen, the taste, and the cultivated judgment of literary works, in such fullness as Matthew Arnold.

His greatest contributions to critical literature are the

various magazine articles that were collected in the two volumes entitled *Essays in Criticism* (1865-1888). In these essays Arnold displays great breadth of culture and fairness of mind. He rises superior to the narrow provincialism and racial prejudices that he deprecates in other criticisms of literature. He gives the same sympathetic consideration to the German Heine and the Frenchman Joubert as to Wordsworth. Arnold further insists that Frenchmen should study English literature for its serious ethical spirit, and that Englishmen would be benefited by a study of the lightness, precision, and polished form of French literature.

Arnold's object in all his criticisms is to discover the best in both prose and poetry, and his method of attaining this object is another illustration of his scholarship and mental reach. He says in his *Introduction* to Ward's *English Poets*:—

"Indeed, there can be no more useful help for discovering what poetry belongs to the class of the truly excellent, and can therefore do us most good, than to have always in one's mind lines and expressions of the great masters, and to apply them as a touchstone to other poetry."

When Arnold seeks to determine an author's true place in literature, his keen critical eye seems to see at a glance all the world's great writers, and to compare them with the man under discussion. In order to ascertain Wordsworth's literary stature, for example, Arnold measures the height of Wordsworth by that of Homer, of Dante, of Shakespeare, and of Milton.

Another essential quality of the critical mind that Arnold possessed, is "sweet reasonableness." His judgments of men are marked by a moderation of tone. His strong predilections are sometimes shown, but they are more often restrained by a clear, honest intellect. Arnold's calm, measured criticisms are not marred by such stout partisanship as Macaulay shows for the Whigs, by the hero worship that Carlyle expresses, or by the exaggerated praise and blame that Ruskin sometimes bestows. On the other hand, Arnold loses what these men gain; for while his intellect is less biased than theirs, it is also less colored and less warmed by the glow of feeling.

The analytical quality of Arnold's mind shows the spirit of the age. His subjects are minutely classified and defined. Facts seem to divide naturally into brigades, regiments, and battalions of marching order. His literary criticisms note subtleties of style, delicate shadings in expression, and many technical excellences and errors that Carlyle would have passed over unheeded. In addition to the *Essays in Criticism*, the other works of Arnold that possess his fine critical qualities in highest degree are *On Translating Homer* (1861) and *The Study of Celtic Literature* (1867).

General Characteristics. — The impression that Arnold has left upon literature is mainly that of a keen, brilliant intellect. In his poetry there is more emotion than in his prose; but even in his poetry there is no passion or fire. The sadness, the loneliness, the unrest of life, and the irreconcilable conflict between faith and doubt are most often the subjects of his verse. His range is narrow, but within it he attains a pure, noble beauty. His introspective, analytical poetry is distinguished by a "majesty of grief," depth of thought, calm, classic repose, and a dignified simplicity.

In prose, Arnold attains highest rank as a critic of literature. His culture, the breadth of his literary sympathies, his scientific analyses, and his lucid literary style make his critical works the greatest of his age. He has a light, rather fanciful, humor, which gives snap and spice to his style. He is also a master of irony, which is galling to an opponent. He himself never loses his suavity or good breeding. Arnold's prose style is as far removed from Carlyle's as the calm simplicity of the Greeks is from the powerful passion of the Vikings. The ornament and poetic richness of Ruskin's style are also missing in Arnold's. His style has a classic purity and refinement. He has a terseness, a crystalline clearness, and a precision that have been excelled in the works of few even of the greatest masters of English prose.

ROBERT BROWNING, 1812-1889

Life. — The long and peaceful lives of Browning and Tennyson, the two most eminent poets of the Victorian age, are in marked contrast to the short and troubled careers of Byron, Shelley, and Keats.

Robert Browning's life was uneventful but happy. He inherited a magnificent physique and constitution from his father, who never knew a day's illness. With such health, Robert Browning felt a keen relish for physical existence and a robust joyousness in all kinds of activity. Late in life he wrote, in the poem *At the Mermaid:* —

> "Have you found your life distasteful?
>   My life did, and does, smack sweet.
>
> . . . .
>
> I find earth not gray but rosy,
>   Heaven not grim but fair of hue.
> Do I stoop? I pluck a posy.
>   Do I stand and stare? All's blue."

Again, in *Saul*, he burst forth with the lines: —

From the painting by G. F. Watts, National Portrait Gallery.

Robert Browning,

"How good is man's life, the mere living! how fit to employ
 All the heart and the soul and the senses forever in joy?"

These lines, vibrant with life and joy, could not have been written by a man of failing vitality or physical weakness.

Robert Browning was born in 1812 at Camberwell, whose slopes overlook the smoky chimneys of London. In this beautiful suburb he spent his early years in the companionship of a brother and a sister. A highly gifted father and a musical mother assisted intelligently in the development of their children. Browning's education was conducted mainly under his father's eye. The boy attended neither a large school nor a college. After he had passed from the hands of tutors, he spent some time in travel, and was wont to call Italy his university. Although his training was received in an irregular way, his scholarship cannot be doubted by the student of his poetry.

He early determined to devote his life to poetry, and his father wisely refrained from interfering with his son's ambitions.

Romantic Marriage with Elizabeth Barrett Barrett. — Her Poetry. — In 1845, after Browning had published some ten volumes of verse, among which were *Paracelsus* (1835), *Pippa Passes* (1841), and *Dramatic Lyrics* (1842), he met Miss Elizabeth Barrett Barrett (1806-1861), whose poetic reputation was then greater than his own. The publication in 1898 of *The Letters of Robert Browning and Elizabeth Barrett Barrett* disclosed an unusual romance. When he first met her, she was an invalid in her father's London house, passing a large part of her time on the couch, scarcely able to see all the members of her own family at the same time. His magnetic influence helped her to make more frequent journeys from the sofa to an armchair, then to walk across the room, and soon to take drives.

From the painting by Field Talfourd, National Portrait Gallery.
ELIZABETH BARRETT BROWNING.

Her father, who might have sat for the original of Meredith's "Egoist," had decided that his daughter should be an invalid and remain with him for life. When Browning proposed to Miss Barrett that he should ask her father for her hand, she replied that such a step would only make matters worse. "He would rather see me dead at his feet than yield the point," she said. In 1846 Miss Barrett, accompanied by her faithful maid, drove to a church and was married to Browning. The bride returned home; but Browning did not see her for a week because he would not indulge in the deception of asking for "Miss Barrett." Seven days after the marriage, they quietly left for Italy, where Mrs. Browning passed nearly all her remaining years. She repeatedly wrote to her father, telling him of her transformed health and happy marriage, but he never answered her.

Before Miss Barrett met Browning, the woes of the factory children had moved her to write *The Cry of the Children*. After Edgar Allan Poe had read its closing lines:—

> ". . . the child's sob in the silence curses deeper
> Than the strong man in his wrath,"

he said that she had depicted "a horror, sublime in its simplicity, of which Dante himself might have been proud."

Her best work, *Sonnets from the Portuguese*, written after Browning had won her affection, is a series of love lyrics, strong, tender, unaffected, true, from the depth of a woman's heart. Sympathetic readers, who know the story of her early life and love, are every year realizing that there is nothing else in English literature that could exactly fill their place. Browning called them "the finest sonnets written in any language since Shakespeare's." Those who like the simple music of the heart strings will find it in lines like these:—

> "I love thee to the level of every day's
> Most quiet need, by sun and candlelight,
> I love thee freely, as men strive for right;
> I love thee purely, as they turn from praise.
> I love thee with the passion put to use
> In my old griefs, and with my childhood's faith.
> I love thee with a love I seemed to lose
> With my lost saints — I love thee with the breath,
> Smiles, tears, of all my life! — and, if God choose,
> I shall but love thee better after death."

After fifteen years of happy married life, she died in 1861, and was buried in Florence. When thinking of her, Browning wrote his poem *Prospice* (1861) welcoming death as —

> ". . . a peace out of pain,
> Then a light, then thy breast,
> O thou soul of my soul! I shall clasp thee again,
> And with God be the rest."

His Later Years. — Soon after his wife's death, he began his long poem of over twenty thousand lines, *The Ring and the Book*. He continued to write verse to the year of his death.

In 1881 the Browning Society was founded for the study and discussion of his works, — a most unusual honor for a poet during his lifetime. The leading universities gave him honorary degrees, he was elected life-governor of London University, and was tendered the rectorship of the Universities of Glasgow and St. Andrew's and the presidency of the Wordsworth Society.

During the latter part of his life, he divided most of his time between London and Italy. When he died, in 1889, he was living with his son, Robert Barrett Browning, in the Palazzo Rezzonico, Venice. Over his grave in Westminster Abbey was chanted Mrs. Browning's touching lyric: —

> "He giveth his belovèd, sleep."

Dramatic Monologues. — Browning was a poet of great productivity. From the publication of *Pauline* in 1833 to *Asolando* in 1889, there were only short pauses between the appearances of his works. Unlike Tennyson, Browning could not stop to revise and recast; but he constantly sought expression, in narratives, dramas, lyrics, and monologues, for new thoughts and feelings.

The study of the human soul held an unfailing charm for Browning. He analyzes with marked keenness and subtlety the experiences of the soul, its sickening failures, and its eager strivings amid complex, puzzling conditions. In nearly all his poems, whether narrative, lyric, or dramatic, the chief interest centers about some "incidents in the development of a soul."

The poetic form that he found best adapted to "the development of a soul" was the dramatic monologue, of which he is one of the greatest masters. Requiring but one speaker, this form narrows the interest either to the speaker or to the one described by him. Most of his best monologues are to be found in the volumes known as *Dramatic Lyrics* (1842), *Dramatic Romances and Lyrics* (1845), *Men and Women* (1855), *Dramatis Personæ* (1864).

My Last Duchess, *Andrea del Sarto*, *Saul*, *Abt Vogler*, and *The Last Ride Together* are a few of his strong representative monologues. The speaker in *My Last Duchess* is the widowed duke, who is describing the portrait of his lost wife. In his blind conceit, he is utterly unconscious that he is exhibiting clearly his own coldly selfish nature and his wife's sweet, sunny disposition. The chief power of the poem lies in the astonishing ease with which he is made to reveal his own character.

The interest in *Andrea del Sarto* is in the mental conflict of this "faultless painter." He wishes, on the one hand, to please his wife with popular pictures, and yet he yearns for higher ideals of his art. He says: —

> "Ah, but a man's reach should exceed his grasp,
>   Or what's a heaven for?"

As he sits in the twilight, holding his wife's hand, and talking in a half-musing way, it is readily seen that his love for this beautiful but soulless woman has caused many of his failures and sorrows in the past, and will continue to arouse conflicts of soul in the future.

Abt Vogler, one of Browning's noblest and most melodious poems, voices the exquisite raptures of a musician's soul: —

> "But God has a few of us whom He whispers in the ear;
>   The rest may reason and welcome: 'tis we musicians know."

The beautiful song of David in the poem entitled *Saul* shows a wonderful sympathy with the old Hebrew prophecies. *Cleon* expresses the views of an early Greek upon the teachings of Christ and St. Paul. *The Soliloquy of a Spanish Cloister* describes the development of a coarse, jealous nature in monastic life. *The Last Ride Together* is one of Browning's many passionate poems on the ennobling power of love. That remarkable, grotesque poem, *Caliban upon Setebos*, transcends human fields altogether, and displays the brutelike theology of a fiend.

In these monologues, Browning interprets characters of varying faiths, nationalities, stations, and historic periods.

He shows a wide range of knowledge and sympathy. One type, however, which he rarely presents, is the simple, commonplace man or woman. Browning excels in the portrayal of unusual, intricate, and difficult characters that have complicated problems to face, weaknesses to overcome, or lofty ambitions to attain.

The Ring and the Book. — When Browning was asked what he would advise a student of his poetry to read first, he replied: "*The Ring and the Book*, of course." He worked on this masterly study of human souls for many years in the decade in which his wife died. This poem (1868), which has been facetiously called "a Roman murder story," was suggested to him by a "square old yellow book," which he purchased for a few cents at Florence in 1860. This manuscript, dated 1698, gives an account of the trial of Guido Franceschini for the murder of his wife. Out of this "mere ring metal," Browning fashioned his "Ring," a poem twice the length of *Paradise Lost*.

The subject of the story is an innocent girl, Pompilia, who, under the protection of a noble priest, flees from her brutal husband and seeks the home of her foster parents. Her husband wrathfully pursues her and kills both her and her parents. While this is but the barest outline, yet the story in its complete form is very simple. As is usual with Browning, the chief stress is laid upon the character portrayal.

He adopted the bold and unique plan of having different classes of people in Rome and the various actors in the tragedy tell the story from their own point of view and thus reveal their own bias and characteristics. Each relation makes the story seem largely new. Browning shows that all this testimony is necessary to establish a complete circle of evidence in regard to the central truth of the tragedy. The poem thus becomes a remarkable analytic study of the psychology of human minds.

The four important characters, — Guido, the husband; Caponsacchi, the priest; Pompilia, the girl-wife; and the Pope, — stand out in strong relief. The greatest development of character is seen in Guido, who starts with a defiant spirit of certain victory, but gradually becomes more subdued and abject, when he finds that he is to be killed, and finally shrieks in agony for the help of his victim, Pompilia. In Caponsacchi there is the inward questioning of the right and the wrong. He is a strongly-drawn character, full of passion and noble desires. Pompilia, who has an intuitive knowledge of the right, is one of Browning's sweetest and purest women. From descriptions of Mrs. Browning, such as Nathaniel Hawthorne gave, we may conclude that she furnished the suggestion for many of Pompilia's characteristics. The Pope, with his calm, wise judgment and his lofty philosophy, is probably the greatest product of Browning's intellect.

The books containing the monologues of these characters take first place among Browning's writings and occupy a high position in the century's work. They have a striking originality, intensity, vigor, and imaginative richness. The remaining books are incomparably inferior, and are marked at times by mere acuteness of reason and thoroughness of legal knowledge.

A Dramatic Poet. — Although Browning's genius is strongly dramatic, his best work is not found in the field of the drama. *Strafford* (1837), *A Blot in the 'Scutcheon* (1843), and *Colombe's Birthday* (1844) have been staged successfully, but they cannot be called great acting plays. The action is slight, the characters are complex, the soliloquies are lengthy, and the climaxes are too often wholly dependent upon emotional intensity rather than upon great or exciting deeds. The strongest interest of these dramas lies in their psychological subtlety, which is more enjoyable in the study than in the theater.

Browning's dramatic power is well exhibited in poems like *In a Balcony* or *Pippa Passes*, in which powerful individual scenes are presented without all the accompanying details of a complete drama. The great force of such scenes lies in his manner of treating moments of severe trial. He selects such a moment, focuses his whole attention upon it, and makes the deed committed stand forth as an explanation of all the past emotions and as a prophecy of all future acts. *In a Balcony* shows the lives of three characters converging toward a crisis. The hero of this drama thus expresses his theory of life's struggles in the development of the soul: —

> ". . . I count life just a stuff
> To try the soul's strength on, educe the man."

Pippa Passes is one of Browning's most artistic presentations of such dramatic scenes. The little silk weaver, Pippa, rises on the morning of her one holiday in the year, with the intention of enjoying in fancy the pleasures "of the Happiest Four in our Asolo," not knowing, in her innocence, of their misery and guilt. She wanders from house to house, singing her pure, significant refrains, and, in each case, her songs arrest the attention of the hearer at a critical moment. She thus becomes unconsciously a means of salvation. The first scene is the most intense. She approaches the home of the lovers, Sebald and Ottima, after the murder of Ottima's husband. As Sebald begins to reflect on the murder, there comes this song of Pippa's, like the knocking at the gate in Macbeth, to loose the floodgates of remorse: —

> Song from "Pippa passes".
> The year's at the spring,
> The day's at the morn;
> Morning's at seven:
> The hill-side's dew-pearled:
> The lark's on the wing,
> The snail's on the thorn:
> God's in his Heaven —
> All's right with the world.

FACSIMILE OF MS. FROM PIPPA PASSES

His Optimistic Philosophy. — It has been seen that the Victorian age, as presented by Matthew Arnold, was a period of doubt and negation. Browning, however, was not overcome by this wave of doubt. Although he recognized fully the difficulties of religious faith in an age just awakening to scientific inquiry, yet he retained a strong, fearless trust in God and in immortality.

Browning's reason demanded this belief. In this earthly life he saw the evil overcome the good, and beheld injustice, defeat, and despair follow the noblest efforts. If there exists no compensation for these things, he says that life is a cheat, the moral nature a lie, and God a fiend. In *Asolando*, Browning thus presents his attitude toward life: —

" One who never turned his back but marched breast forward,
    Never doubted clouds would break,
Never dreamed, tho' right were worsted, wrong would triumph,
Held we fall to rise, are baffled to fight better,
    Sleep to wake."

There is no hesitancy in this philosophy of Browning's. With it, he does not fear to face all the problems and mysteries of existence. No other poet strikes such a resonant, hopeful note as he. His *Rabbi Ben Ezra* is more a song of triumphant faith than anything written since the Puritan days: —

> "Our times are in His hand
> Who saith, 'A whole I planned,
> Youth shows but half; trust God: see all, nor be afraid!'
>
> . . . .
>
> "Earth changes, but thy soul and God stand sure:
> What entered into thee,
> *That* was, is, and shall be:
> Time's wheel runs back or stops: Potter and clay endure."

General Characteristics. — Browning is a poet of striking originality and impelling force. His writings are the spontaneous outpourings of a rich, full nature, whose main fabric is intellect, but intellect illumined with the glittering light of spiritual hopefulness and flushed with the glow of deep human passion.

The subject of his greatest poetry is the human soul. While he possesses a large portion of dramatic suggestiveness, he nevertheless does not excel in setting off character against character in movement and speech, but rather in a minute, penetrating analysis, by which he insinuates himself into the thoughts and sensations of his characters, and views life through their eyes.

He is a pronounced realist. His verse deals not only with the beautiful and the romantic, but also with the prosaic and the ugly, if they furnish true pictures for the panorama of real life. The unconventionality and realism of his poetic art will be made manifest by merely reading through the titles of his numerous works.

Browning did not write to amuse and entertain, but to stimulate thought and to "sting" the conscience to activity. The meaning of his verse is, therefore, the matter of paramount importance, far overshadowing the form of expression. In the haste and carelessness with which he wrote many of his difficult abstruse poems, he laid himself open to the charge of obscurity.

His style has a strikingly individual stamp, which is marked far more by strength than by beauty. The bare and rugged style of his verse is often made profoundly impressive by its strenuous earnestness, its burning intensity, which seems to necessitate the broken lines and halting, interrupted rhythm. The following utterance of Caponsacchi, as he stands before his judges, will show the intensity and ruggedness of Browning's blank verse:—

> "Sirs, how should I lie quiet in my grave
> Unless you suffer me wring, drop by drop,
> My brain dry, make a riddance of the drench
> Of minutes with a memory in each?"

His lines are often harsh and dissonant. Even in the noble poem *Rabbi Ben Ezra*, this jolting line appears:—

"Irks care the crop-full bird? Frets doubt the maw-crammed beast?"

and in *Sordello*, Browning writes:—

> "The Troubadour who sung
> Hundreds of songs, forgot, its trick his tongue,
> Its craft his brain."

No careful artist tolerates such ugly, rasping inversions.

In spite of these inharmonious tendencies in Browning, his poetry at times shows a lyric lightness, such as is heard in these lines:—

> "Oh, to be in England
>   Now that April's there,
> And whoever wakes in England
>   Sees, some morning, unaware,

> That the lowest boughs and the brushwood sheaf
> Round the elm-tree bole are in tiny leaf,
> > While the chaffinch sings on the orchard bough
> > In England — now!"[1]

His verse often swells and falls with a wavelike rhythm as in *Saul* or in these lines in *Abt Vogler:* —

> "There shall never be one lost good! What was, shall live as before;
> > The evil is null, is nought, is silence implying sound;
>
> What was good shall be good, with, for evil, so much good more;
> > On the earth the broken arc; in the heaven, a perfect round."

While, therefore, Browning's poetry is sometimes harsh, faulty, and obscure, at times his melodies can be rhythmically simple and beautiful. He is one of the subtlest analysts of the human mind, the most original and impassioned poet of his age, and one of the most hopeful, inspiring, and uplifting teachers of modern times.

ALFRED TENNYSON, 1809-1892

Life. — Alfred Tennyson, one of the twelve children of the rector of Somersby, Lincolnshire, was born in that hamlet in 1809, a year memorable, both in England and America for the birth of such men as Charles Darwin, William E. Gladstone, Oliver Wendell Holmes, Edgar Allan Poe, and Abraham Lincoln.

Visitors to the Somersby rectory, in which Tennyson was born, note that it fits the description of the home in his fine lyric, *The Palace of Art:* —

> ". . . an English home, — gray twilight pour'd
> > On dewy pastures, dewy trees,
>
> Softer than sleep — all things in order stored,
> > A haunt of ancient peace."

His mother, one of the beauties of Lincolnshire, had

[1] *Home Thoughts from Abroad.*

From a photograph by Mayall.

twenty-five offers of marriage. Of her Tennyson said in *The Princess*: —

> "Happy he
> With such a mother! faith in womankind
> Beats with his blood, and trust in all things high
> Comes easy to him, and tho' he trip and fall,
> He shall not blind his soul with clay."

It is probable that Tennyson holds the record among English poets of his class for the quantity of youthful verse produced. At the age of eight, he was writing blank verse in praise of flowers; at twelve, he began an epic which extended to six thousand lines.

In 1828 he entered Cambridge University; but in 1831 his father's sickness and death made it impossible for him to return to take his degree. Before leaving Cambridge, Tennyson had found a firm friend in a young college mate of great promise, Arthur Henry Hallam, who became engaged to the poet's sister, Emily Tennyson. Hallam's sudden death in 1832 was a profound shock to Tennyson and had far-reaching effects on his poetic development. For a long time he lived in comparative retirement, endeavoring to perfect himself in the poetic art.

His golden year was 1850, the year of the publication of *In Memoriam*, of his selection as poet laureate, to succeed Wordsworth, and of his marriage to Emily Sellwood. He had been in love with her for fourteen years, but insufficient income had hitherto prevented marriage.

In 1855 Oxford honored him by bestowing on him the degree of D.C.L. The students gave him an ovation and they properly honored his greatest poem, *In Memoriam*, by mentioning it first in their loud calls; but they also paid their respects to his *May Queen*,

FARRINGFORD

asking in chorus: "Did they wake and call you early, call you early, Alfred dear?"

The rest of his life was outwardly uneventful. He became the most popular poet of his age. Schools and colleges had pupils translate his poems into Latin and Greek verse. Of *Enoch Arden* (1864), at that time his most popular narrative poem, sixty thousand copies were sold almost as soon as it was printed. He made sufficient money to be able to maintain two beautiful residences, a winter home at Farringford on the Isle of Wight, and a summer residence at Aldworth in Sussex. In 1884 he was raised to the peerage, with the title of Baron of Aldworth and Farringford.

He died in 1892, at the age of eighty-three, and was buried beside Robert Browning in Westminster Abbey.

Early Verse. — Tennyson published a small volume of poems in 1830, the year before he left college, and another volume in 1832. Although these contained some good poems, he was too often content to toy with verse that had exquisite melody and but little meaning. The "Airy, fairy Lilian" and "Sweet, pale Margaret" type of verse had charmed him overmuch. The volumes of 1830 and 1832 were severely criticized. *Blackwood's Magazine* called some of the lyrics "drivel," and Carlyle characterized the æsthetic verse as "lollipops." This adverse criticism and the shock from Hallam's death caused him to remain silent for nearly ten years. His son and biographer says that his father during this period "profited by friendly and unfriendly criticism, and in silence, obscurity, and solitude, perfected his art."

In his thirty-third year (1842), Tennyson broke his long silence by publishing two volumes of verse, containing such favorites as *The Poet, The Lady of Shalott, The Palace of Art, The Lotos Eaters, A Dream of Fair Women, Morte d'Arthur, Oenone, The Miller's Daughter, The Gardener's Daughter, Dora, Ulysses, Locksley Hall, The Two Voices,* and *Sir Galahad.*

Unsparing revision of numbers of these poems that had been published before, entitles them to be classed as new work. Some critics think that Tennyson never surpassed these 1842 volumes. His verse shows the influence of Keats, of whom Tennyson said: "There is something of the innermost soul of poetry in almost everything that he wrote."

One of Tennyson's most distinctive qualities, his art in painting beautiful word-pictures, is seen at its best in stanzas from *The Palace of Art* (p. 553). His mastery over melody and the technique of verse is evident in such lyrics as *Sir Galahad*, and *The Lotos Eaters*. When the prime minister, Sir Robert Peel, read from *Ulysses* the passage beginning:—

"I am a part of all that I have met,"

he gave Tennyson a much-needed annual pension of £200.

These volumes show that he was coming into touch with the thought of the age. *Locksley Hall* communicates the thrill which he felt from the new possibilities of science:—

"For I dipt into the future, far as human eye could see,
 Saw the Vision of the world, and all the wonder that would be.
 . . . .
 I the heir of all the ages, in the foremost files of time."

Hallam's death had also developed in him the human note, resonant in the lyric, *Break, break, break:*—

"But O for the touch of a vanish'd hand,
 And the sound of a voice that is still."

The Princess, In Memoriam, and Maud. — Tennyson had produced only short poems in his 1842 volumes, but his next three efforts, *The Princess* (1847), *In Memoriam* (1850), and *Maud* (1855), are of considerable length.

The Princess: A Medley, as Tennyson rightly called it, contains 3223 lines of blank verse. This poem, which is really a discussion of the woman question, relates in a half-humorous way the story of a princess who broke off her engagement to a prince, founded a college for women, and determined to devote her life to making them equal to men. The poem abounds in beautiful imagery and exquisite melody; but the solution of the question by the marriage of the princess has not completely satisfied modern thought. The finest parts of the poem are its artistic songs.

In Memoriam, an elegy in memory of Arthur Henry Hallam, was begun at Somersby in 1833, the year of Hallam's death, and added to at intervals for nearly sixteen years. When Tennyson first began the short lyrics to express his grief, he did not intend to publish them; but in 1850 he gave them to the world as one long poem of 725 four-line stanzas.

In Memoriam was directly responsible for Tennyson's appointment as poet-laureate. Queen Victoria declared that she received more comfort from it than from any other book except the *Bible*. The first stanza of the poem (quoted on page 9) has proved as much of a moral stimulus as any single utterance of Carlyle or of Browning.

This work is one of the three great elegies of a literature that stands first in elegiac poetry. Milton's *Lycidas* has more of a massive commanding power, and Shelley's *Adonais* rises at times to poetic heights that Tennyson did not reach; but neither *Lycidas* nor *Adonais* equals *In Memoriam* in tracing every shadow of bereavement, from the first feeling of despair until the mourner can realize that —

> ". . . the song of woe
>   Is after all an earthly song,"

and can express his unassailable faith in —

> "One God, one law, one element,
>   And one far-off divine event
>   To which the whole creation moves."

With this hopeful assurance closes Tennyson's most noble and beautiful poem.

Maud, a lyrical melodrama, paints the changing emotions of a lover who passes from morbid gloom to ecstasy. Then, in a moment of anger, he murders Maud's brother. Despair, insanity, and recovery follow, but he sees Maud's face no more. While the poem as a whole is not a masterpiece, it contains some of Tennyson's finest lyrics. The eleven stanzas of the lover's song to Maud, the —

"Queen Rose of the rosebud garden of girls,"

are such an exquisite blending of woodbine spice and musk of rose, of star and daffodil sky, of music of flute and song of bird, of the soul of the rose with the passion of the lover, of meadows and violets, — that we easily understand why Tennyson loved to read these lines.

The Idylls of the King. — In 1859 Tennyson published *Lancelot and Elaine*, one of a series of twelve *Idylls*, the last of which appeared in 1885. Together these form an epic on the subject of King Arthur and his Knights of the Round Table. Tennyson relied mainly on Malory's *Morte d'Arthur* for the characters and the stories.

These *Idylls* show the struggle to maintain noble ideals. Arthur relates how he collected —

"In that fair order of my Table Round,
A glorious company, the flower of men,
To serve as model for the mighty world,
And be the fair beginning of a time."

He made his knights swear to uphold the ideals of his court —

"To ride abroad redressing human wrongs,
To speak no slander, no, nor listen to it,
To honor his own word as if his God's,
To lead sweet lives in purest chastity,

> To love one maiden only, cleave to her,
> And worship her by years of noble deeds
> Until they won her."

The twelve *Idylls* have as a background those different seasons of the year that accord with the special mood of the story. In *Gareth and Lynette*, the most interesting of the *Idylls*, the young hero leaves his home in spring, when the earth is joyous with birds and flowers. In the last and most nobly poetic of the series, *The Passing of Arthur*, the time is winter, when the knights seem to be clothed with their own frosty breath.

Sin creeps into King Arthur's realm and disrupts the order of the "Table Round." He receives his mortal wound, and passes to rule in a kindlier realm that welcomed him as "a king returning from the wars."

Although the *Idylls of the King* are uneven in quality and sometimes marred by overprofusion of ornament and by deficiency of dramatic skill, their limpid style, many fine passages of poetry, appealing stories, and high ideals have exerted a wider influence than any other of Tennyson's poems.

Later Poetry. — Tennyson continued to write poetry until almost the time of his death; but with the exception of his short swan song, *Crossing the Bar*, he did not surpass his earlier efforts. His *Locksley Hall Sixty Years After* (1886) voices the disappointments of the Victorian age and presents vigorous social philosophy. Some of his later verse, like *The Northern Farmer* and *The Children's Hospital*, are in closer touch with life than many of his earlier poems.

He wrote also several historical dramas, the best of which is *Becket* (1884); but his genius was essentially lyrical, not dramatic. *Crossing the Bar*, written in his eighty-first year, is not only the finest product of his later years, but also one of the very best of Victorian lyrics.

Crossing the Bar.
Sunset & evening star,
  And one clear call for me.
And may there be no moaning of the bar,
  When I put out to sea.

FACSIMILE OF MS. OF CROSSING THE BAR

General Characteristics. — Tennyson is a poetic interpreter of the thought of the Victorian age. Huxley called him "the first poet since Lucretius who understood the drift of science." In these four lines from *The Princess*, Tennyson gives the evolutionary history of the world, from nebula to man: —

> "This world was once a fluid haze of light,
>   Till toward the center set the starry tides,
>   And eddied into suns, that wheeling cast
> The planets: then the monster, then the man."

Tennyson's poetry of nature is based on almost scientific observation of natural phenomena. Unlike Wordsworth, Tennyson does not regard nature as a manifestation of the divine spirit of love. He sees her more from the new scientific point of view, as "red in tooth and claw with rapine." The hero of *Maud* says: —

"For nature is one with rapine, a harm no preacher can heal;
  The Mayfly is torn by the swallow, the sparrow spear'd by the shrike,
And the whole little wood where I sit is a world of plunder and prey."

The constant warfare implied in the evolutionary theory of the survival of the fittest did not keep Tennyson from also presenting nature in her gentler aspects. In *Maud*, the lover sings —

> " .... whenever a March-wind sighs,
> He sets the jewel-print of your feet
> In violets blue as your eyes,"

and he tells how "the soul of the rose" passed into his blood, and how the sympathetic passion-flower dropped "a splendid tear." As beautiful as is much of Tennyson's nature poetry, he has not Wordsworth's power to invest it with "the light of setting suns," or to cause it to awaken "thoughts that do lie too deep for tears."

The conflict between science and religion, the doubts and the sense of world-pain are mirrored in Tennyson's verse. *The Two Voices* begins: —

> "A still small voice spake unto me,
> Thou art so full of misery
> Were it not better not to be?"

His poetry is, however, a great tonic to religious faith. The closing lines of *In Memoriam* and *Crossing the Bar* show how triumphantly he met all the doubts and the skepticism of the age.

Like Milton, Tennyson received much of his inspiration from books, especially from the classical writers; but this characteristic was more than counterbalanced by his acute observation and responsiveness to the thought of the age. *Locksley Hall Sixty Years After* shows that he was keenly alive to the social movements of the time.

Tennyson said that the scenes in his poems were so vividly conceived that he could have drawn them if he had been an artist. A twentieth century critic[1] says that

[1] A. C. Benson's *Alfred Tennyson*, p. 157.

Tennyson is almost the inventor of such pictorial lyrics as *A Dream of Fair Women* and *The Palace of Art*.

The artistic finish of Tennyson's verse is one of its great charms. He said to a friend: "It matters little what we say; it is how we say it — though the fools don't know it." His poetry has, however, often been criticized for lack of depth. The variety in his subject matter, mode of expression, and rhythm renders his verse far more enjoyable than that of the formal age of Pope.

Tennyson's extraordinary popularity in his own time was largely due to the fact that he voiced so clearly and attractively the thought of the age. As another epoch ushers in different interests, they will naturally be uppermost in the mind of the new generation. We no longer feel the intense interest of the Victorians in the supposed conflict between science and religion. Their theory of evolution has been modified and has lost the force of novelty. Theories of government and social ideals have also undergone a gradual change. For these reasons much of Tennyson's verse has ceased to have its former wide appeal.

Tennyson has, however, left sufficient work of abiding value, both for its exquisite form and for its thought, to entitle him to be ranked as a great poet. We cannot imagine a time when *Crossing the Bar*, *The Passing of Arthur*, and the central thought of *In Memoriam* —

> "'Tis better to have loved and lost
> Than never to have loved at all,"

will no longer interest readers. To Tennyson belong —

> "Jewels five words long
> That on the stretch'd forefinger of all Time
> Sparkle forever."

From the painting by Dante Gabriel Rossetti.

ALGERNON CHARLES SWINBURNE, 1837-1909

Life. — Swinburne was born in London in 1837. His father was an admiral in the English navy, and his mother, the daughter of an earl. The boy passed his summers in Northumberland and his winters in the Isle of Wight. He thus acquired that fondness for the sea, so noticeable in his poetry. His early experiences are traceable in lines like these: —

> "Our bosom-belted billowy-blossoming hills,
> Whose hearts break out in laughter like the sea."

He went to Oxford for three years, but left without taking his degree. The story is current that he knew more Greek than his teachers but that he failed in an examination on the *Scriptures*. He sought to complete his education by wide reading and by travel, especially in France and Italy.

When he was twenty-five, he went to live for a short time at 16 Cheyne Walk, Chelsea, in the western part of London, in the same house with Dante Gabriel Rossetti and George Meredith. Swinburne admired Rossetti's poetry and was much impressed with the Pre-Raphaelite virtues of simplicity and directness.

Swinburne never married. His deafness caused him to pass much of his long life in comparative retirement. His last thirty years were spent with his friend, the critic and poet, Theodore Watts-Dunton, at Putney on the Thames, a few miles southwest of London. Swinburne died in 1909 and was buried at Bonchurch on the Isle of Wight.

Works. — In 1864 England was enchanted with the melody of the choruses in his *Atalanta in Calydon*, a dramatic poem in the old Greek form. Lines like the following from the chorus, *The Youth of the Year*, show the quality for which his verse is most famous: —

> "When the hounds of spring are on winter's traces,
>   The mother of months in meadow or plain
> Fills the shadows and windy places
>   With lisp of leaves and ripple of rain."

The first series of his *Poems and Ballads* (1866) contains *The Garden of Proserpine*, one of his best known poems. Proserpine "forgets the earth her mother" and goes to her "bloomless" garden: —

> "And spring and seed and swallow
>   Take wing for her and follow

> Where summer song rings hollow
> And flowers are put to scorn."

Many volumes came in rapid succession from his pen. In 1904 his poems were collected in six octavo volumes containing 2357 pages. This collection includes the long narrative poems, *Tristram of Lyonesse* and *The Tale of Balen*, a faithful retelling of famous medieval stories. He, however, had more ability as a writer of lyrics than of narrative verse.

His poetic dramas fill five additional volumes. *Chastelard* (1865), one of the three dramas relating to Mary Queen of Scots, is the best of his plays. He had, however, neither the power to draw character nor the repression of speech necessary for a great dramatist. The best parts of his plays are really lyrical verse.

Many critics think that Swinburne's reputation would be as great as it now is, if he had ceased to write verse in 1866, at the age of twenty-nine, after producing *Atalanta in Calydon* and the first series of his *Poems and Ballads*. Although his interests widened and his poetic range increased, much of his work during his last forty years is a repetition of earlier successes. His *Songs before Sunrise*, however (1871), and the next two volumes of *Poems and Ballads* (1878 and 1889) contain some poems that rank among his best.

Later in life he wrote a large amount of prose criticism, much of which deals with the Elizabethan dramatists. His *A Study of Shakespeare* (1880) and his shorter *Shakespeare* (1905) are especially suggestive. In spite of the fact that the reader must make constant allowance for his habit of using superlatives, he was an able critic.

General Characteristics. — Swinburne's poetry suffers from his tendency to drown his ideas in a sea of words.

Sometimes we gain no more definite ideas from reading many lines of his verse than from hearing music without words. Much of his poetry was suggested by wide reading, not by close personal contact with life. His verse sometimes offends from disregarding moral proprieties and from so expressing his atheism as to wound the feelings of religious people. His idea of a Supreme Power was colored by the old Grecian belief in Fate. In exact opposition to Wordsworth, Swinburne's youthful poems show that he regarded Nature as the incarnation of a Power malevolent to man. He lacked the optimism of Browning and the faith of Tennyson. The mantle of Byron and Shelley fell on Swinburne as the poet of revolt against what seemed to be religious or political tyranny.

After Tennyson's death, in 1892, Swinburne was the greatest living English poet; but, even if his verse had not offended Queen Victoria for the foregoing reasons, she would not have appointed him poet-laureate after the misery of the Russians had moved him in 1890 to write, referring to the Czar: —

"Night hath naught but one red star — Tyrannicide.

"God or man, be swift; hope sickens with delay:
Smite and send him howling down his father's way."

Swinburne's crowning glory is his unquestioned mastery, unsurpassed by any poet since Milton, of the technique of varied melodious verse. This quality is evident, no matter whether he is describing the laughter of a child: —

"Sweeter far than all things heard,
Hand of harper, tone of bird,
Sound of woods at sundawn stirr'd,
Welling water's winsome word,
Wind in warm wan weather,"

or expressing his fierce hatred for any condition or place where —

> ". . . a curse was or a chain
> A throne for torment or a crown for bane
> Rose, moulded out of poor men's molten pain,"

or singing the song of a lover —

> "If love were what the rose is,
> And I were like the leaf,
> Our lives would grow together
> In sad or singing weather,
> Blown fields or flowerful closes,
> Green pleasure or grey grief;
> If love were what the rose is,
> And I were like the leaf,"

or voicing his early creed —

> "That no life lives forever;
> That dead men rise up never;
> That even the weariest river
> Winds somewhere safe to sea,"

or chanting in far nobler strains the Anglo-Saxon belief in the molding power of an infinite presence —

> "I am in thee to save thee,
> As my soul in thee saith,
> Give thou as I gave thee,
> Thy life-blood and breath,
> Green leaves of thy labor, white flowers of thy thought, and red fruit of thy death."

RUDYARD KIPLING, 1865-

Life. — Rudyard Kipling, the youngest of the great Victorians, was born in Bombay, India, in 1865. His parents were people of culture and artistic training, the father, John Lockwood Kipling, being a recognized authority on Indian art. Like most English children born in India,

From the painting by John Collier.

Rudyard Kipling.

Kipling, when very small, was sent to England to escape the fatal Indian heat. Afterwards in the story *Baa, Baa, Black Sheep*, Kipling told the tragic experience of two Anglo-Indian children when separated from their parents. If it is true that this story is largely autobiographical, the separation must have been a trying ordeal in Kipling's childhood. Later he spent several years at Westward Ho, Devonshire, in a school conducted mainly for the sons of Indian officials. *Stalky and Co.*, a broadly humorous book of schoolboy life, gives the Kipling of this period, in the character of the "egregious Beetle."

When only seventeen, he returned to India and immediately began journalistic work. For seven years, first at Lahore and later at Allahabad, he was busy with the usual hackwork of a small newspaper. During these impressionable years, from seventeen to twenty-four, he gained his intimate knowledge of the strangely-colored, many-sided Indian life. His first stories and poems, often written in hot haste, to fill the urgent need of more copy, appeared as waifs and strays in the papers for which he wrote. A collection of verse, *Departmental Ditties*, published at Lahore in 1886, was well received; and it was quickly followed by several volumes of short stories. His ability thus gained early recognition in India.

At the age of twenty-four, he left India for London. Here his books found a publisher almost at once, and he was hailed as a new literary genius. His work became so popular that he was able to devote his whole time to writing. It is doubtful whether any writer since Dickens has received such quick and enthusiastic recognition from all classes of the English-speaking race. Even the street-car conductors were heard quoting him.

In 1892 he married Miss Caroline Balestier, an American, and afterwards lived for four years at Brattleboro, Vermont. Later he settled in Sussex, England, whence he has made long journeys to South Africa, Canada, and Egypt, amassing more knowledge of the English "around the Seven Seas."

Probably the most remarkable feature of Kipling's career is the early age at which his genius developed. Before he left India he had published one book of verse and seven prose collections. By the time he was thirty, he had written *The Jungle Books*, most of his best short stories, and some of his finest verse.

Prose. — As a master of the modern short story, Kipling stands unsurpassed. His journalistic work helped him to acquire a direct, concentrated style of narrative, to find interest in an astonishing variety of subjects, and to seize on the right details for vivid presentation. He was fortunate in discovering in India a new literary field, in which his genius appears at its best. Some of his early tales of Indian life are marred by crudeness and by lack of feeling; but these faults decreased as he matured.

Kipling's stories depend for their interest on incident, not on analysis. He embodies romantic adventure and action in masterpieces as different as the terrible tragedy of *The Man Who would be King* (1888), the tender love story of *Without Benefit of Clergy* (1890), and the mystic dream-land of *The Brushwood Boy* (1895). He specially enjoyed potraying the English soldier. Perhaps his best-known characters are the privates Mulvaney, Ortheris, and Learoyd, whom we meet in such tales of mingled comedy and tragedy as *With the Main Guard* (1888), *On Greenhow Hill* (1890), *The Incarnation of Krishna Mulvaney* (1891), *The Courting of Dinah Shadd* (1891).

When Kipling traveled to new lands, he wrote stories of America, Africa, and the deep sea; but his later tales show an unfortunate increase in the use of technical terms and a lessening of his former dash and spontaneity. There are, however, readers who prefer such a delicate, subtle, story as *They* (1905), to his earlier masterpieces of strenuous action.

In *The Jungle Book* (1894) and *The Second Jungle Book* (1895), Kipling has accomplished the greatest of feats, — an original creation. From the moment the little brown baby, Mowgli, crawls into Mother Wolf's cave away from Shere Khan, the tiger, until the time for him to graduate from the jungle, we follow him under the spell of a fascination different from any that we have known before. The animals of the jungle have real personalities, from the chattering Bandar-log to the lumbering kindly Baloo. With all their intense individuality, they remain animals, each one true to his kind, hating or loving men, thinking mainly through their instincts, and surpassing human schoolmasters in teaching Mowgli the great laws of the jungle, — that obedience is "the head and the hoof of the Law," that nothing was ever yet lost by silence, that, in the jungle, life and food depend on keeping one's temper, that no one shall kill for the pleasure of killing.

By permission of Century Company.
MOWGLI AND HIS BROTHERS

Above all stands the character of Mowgli, the wolf-adopted man-cub, human and yet brother to the animals. With a touch of genius, Kipling revealed the kinship between Mowgli and the denizens of the jungle. Kipling's eyes could see both the harsh realism of animal existence and the genuine idealism of Mother Wolf and the Pack and the Jungle-law.

Just So Stories (1902), written primarily for children, but entertaining to all, is a collection of romantic stories, mostly of animals, illustrated by Kipling himself. One of the best of these tales is *The Cat that Walked by Himself*, which has distinct ethical value in showing how the cat through service won his place by the fireside.

Though Kipling has written four novels, only two, *The*

Light that Failed (1891) and *Kim* (1901), can compare with his best short stories. *The Light that Failed*, the tragedy of an artist who becomes blind, proves that Kipling was able to handle a long plot sufficiently well to sustain interest. *Kim* is an attempt to present as a more completed whole that India of which the stories give only glimpses. On the slenderest thread of plot is strung a bewildering array of scenes, characters, and incidents. His intimate knowledge of India and his photographic power of description are here used with remarkable picturesque effect.

Copyright, 1902, by Rudyard Kipling.
THE OAT THAT WALKED

Verse. — Kipling's poetry has many of the same qualities as his prose, — originality, force, love of action. In *Barrack Room Ballads* (1892), the soldier is again celebrated in vigorous songs with swinging choruses. *Mandalay, Fuzzy-Wuzzy, Danny Deever*, show what spirited verse can be fashioned from a common ballad meter and a bold use of dialect.

> "So 'ere's *to* you, Fuzzy-Wuzzy, at your 'ome in the Soudan;
> You're a pore benighted 'eathen, but a first class fightin' man;

An' 'ere's *to* you, Fuzzy-Wuzzy, with your 'ayrick 'ead of 'air —
You big black boundin' beggar — for you broke a British square!"

Much of his verse is political. His opinion of questions at issue is sometimes given with much heat, but always with sincerity and true patriotism. The best known of his patriotic songs, and perhaps his noblest poetic effort, *The Recessional* (1897), was inspired by the fiftieth anniversary of Victoria's reign. *The Truce of the Bear* (1898) is a warning against Russia. *The Native-Born* is a toast to the colonies in every clime.

Kipling's verse breaks with many of the accepted standards of English verse. He does not aim at such pure beauty of form as we find in Tennyson. He can handle skillfully many kinds of meter, as is shown in *The Song of the English*, *The Ballad of East and West*, *The Song of the Banjo*, and many sea lyrics. Yet he uses mostly the common measures, obtaining with these a free swing, a fitting of sound to sense, that are irresistible to the many —

"Common tunes that make you choke and blow your nose,
Vulgar tunes that bring the laugh that brings the groan —
I can rip your very heart-strings out with those." [1]

Some of his later work shows increasing seriousness of tone. *The Recessional* and the *Hymn before Action* are elevated in thought and expression. The bigness of *L'Envoi* shows poetic power capable of higher flights: —

"And only the Master shall praise us, and only the Master shall blame;
And no one shall work for money, and no one shall work for fame;
But each for the joy of the working, and each, in his separate star,
Shall draw the Thing as he sees It for the God of Things as They Are!" [1]

General Characteristics. — Kipling has carried to their highest development the principles of the Bret Harte

[1] Printed by permission of Rudyard Kipling and Doubleday, Page and Company.

School of short story writers. His style possesses those qualities necessary for telling a short tale, — directness, force, suggestiveness. Rarely has any writer so mastered the technique, the craftsmanship of this particular literary form. He has the gift of force and dramatic power, rather than of beauty and delicacy.

He excels in suggestive vivid description, and he draws wonderful pictures of all out-of-doors, especially of the sea; but nature remains merely the background for the human figures. Much of his vividness lies in the use of specific words. If he should employ the phraseology of his jungle laws to frame the first commandment for writers, it would be: "*Seven times never* be vague." Few authors have at the very beginning of their career more implicitly heeded such a commandment, obedience to which is evident in the following description from *The Courting of Dinah Shadd:* —

"Over our heads burned the wonderful Indian stars, which are not all pricked in on one plane, but preserving an orderly perspective, draw the eye through the velvet darkness of the void up to the barred doors of heaven itself. The earth was a grey shadow more unreal than the sky. We could hear her breathing lightly in the pauses between the howling of the jackals, the movement of the wind in the tamarisks, and the fitful mutter of musketry-fire leagues away to the left. A native woman from some unseen hut began to sing, the mail-train thundered past on its way to Delhi, and a roosting crow cawed drowsily."

Abundant and vivid use of metaphors serves to render his concreteness more varied and impressive. We find these in such expressions as "the velvet darkness," "the kiss of the rain," "the tree-road." His celestial artists splash at a ten-league canvas "with brushes of comet's hair." Five words from Mulvaney explain why he does not wish to leave his tent: "'Tis rainin' intrenchin' tools outside."

Kipling's spirit is essentially masculine. He prefers to write of men, work, and battle, rather than of women and love. Since his interest is mainly in action, he shows small ability in character drawing. His people are clear-cut and alive, but we do not see them grow and develop as do George Eliot's characters.

Above all, he stands as the interpreter of the ideals and the interests of the Anglo-Saxons of his time. Those tendencies of the age, which seem to others so dangerously materialistic, are the very causes of his zest in life. In an age of machinery, he writes of the romance of steam, the soul of an engine, the flight of an airship.

His is a work-a-day world; but in work well done, in obedience to the established law, and in courage, he sees the proving of manhood, the test of the true gentleman —

"Who had done his work and held his peace and had no fear to die."

Underlying all his thought is a deep belief in the "God of our fathers," a God just to punish or reward, whom the English have reverenced through all their history. Linked with this faith is an intense feeling of patriotism toward that larger England of his imperialistic vision.

These qualities justly brought Kipling the 1907 Nobel prize for idealism in literature. He is truly the idealist of a practical age, teaching the romance, the joy, the vision in the common facts and virtues of present-day life.

SUMMARY

The history and literature of the Victorian age show the influence of science. Darwin's conception of evolution affected all fields of thought. The tendency toward analysis and dissection is a result of scientific influence.

In describing the prose of the Victorian age, we have

considered the work of thirteen writers; namely, Macaulay, the brilliant essayist and historian of the material advancement of England; Newman, essayist and theologian, who is noted for clear style, acute thought, and argumentative power; Carlyle, who awoke in his generation a desire for greater achievement, and who championed the spiritual interpretation of life in philosophy and history; Ruskin, the apostle of the beautiful and of more ideal relations in social life; the essayist Pater, whose prose is tinged with poetic color and mystic thought; Arnold, the great analytical critic; Dickens, educational and social reformer, whose novels deal chiefly with the lower classes; Thackeray, whose fiction is not surpassed in keen, satiric analysis of the upper classes of society; George Eliot, whose realistic stories of middle-class life show the influence of science in her conception of character as an orderly ethical growth; Stevenson, an artist in style, writer of romances, essays, and poems for children; Meredith, subtle novelist, distinguished for his comic spirit and portrayal of male egotism; Hardy, realistic novelist of the lowly life of Wessex; Kipling, whose *Jungle Books* are an original creation, and whose short stories surpass those of all other contemporaries.

In poetry, the age is best represented by five men; namely, Arnold, who voices the feeling of doubt and unrest; Browning, who, by his optimistic philosophy, leads to impregnable heights of faith, who analyzes emotions and notes the development of souls as they struggle against opposition from within and without, until they reach moments of supreme victory or defeat; Tennyson, whose careful art mirrors in beautiful verse much of the thought of the age, the influence of science, the unrest, the desire to know the problems of the future, as well as to steal occasional glances at beauty for its own sake; Swinburne, the greatest artist since Milton in the technique of verse; and Kipling, the poet of imperialistic England, whose ballads sing of her soldiers and sailors, and whose lyrics proclaim the Anglo-Saxon faith and joy in working.

REFERENCES FOR FURTHER STUDY

HISTORICAL

Walker's *Essentials in English History*, Cheney's *A Short History of England*, McCarthy's *History of Our Own Times*, Cheney's *Industrial and Social History of England*, Traill's *Social England*, VI.

LITERARY

The Cambridge History of English Literature.
Walker's *The Literature of the Victorian Era.*
Magnus's *English Literature in the Nineteenth Century.*
Saintsbury's *A History of English Literature in the Nineteenth Century.*
Kennedy's *English Literature, 1880-1905.*
Walker's *Greater Victorian Poets.*
Brownell's *Victorian Prose Masters.*
Payne's *The Greater English Poets of the Nineteenth Century.*
Brooke's *Four Victorian Poets* (Rossetti, Arnold, Morris).
Perry's *A Study of Prose Fiction.*
Benson's *Rossetti.* (E. M. L.)
Noyes's *William Morris.* (E. M. L.)
Trevelyan's *Life and Letters of Macaulay.* Morrison's *Macaulay.* (E. M. L.)
Minto's *English Prose Literature* (Macaulay and Carlyle).
Barry's *Newman.*
Ward's *The Life of John Henry, Cardinal Newman*, 2 vols.
Newman's *Letters and Correspondence, with a Brief Autobiography.*
Carlyle's *Reminiscences.*
Froude's *Thomas Carlyle*, 2 vols. Nichol's *Carlyle.* (E. M. L.)
Garnett's *Thomas Carlyle.* (G. W.)
Froude's *Jane Welsh Carlyle*, 2 vols.
T. and A. Carlyle's *New Letters and Memorials of Jane Welsh Carlyle.*

Cook's *The Life of John Ruskin*, 2 vols.
Ruskin's *Præterita, Scenes and Thoughts of My Past Life*.
Benson's *Ruskin: A Study in Personality*.
Earland's *Ruskin and his Circle*.
Harrison's *John Ruskin*. (E. M. L.)
Birrell's *Life of Charlotte Brontë*.
Foster's *Life of Dickens* (abridged and revised by Gissing).
Kitton's *Dickens, his Life, Writings, and Personality*.
Gissing's *Charles Dickens: A Critical Study*.
Chesterton's *Charles Dickens*. Hughes's *Dickens as an Educator*.
Philip's *A Dickens Dictionary*.
Melville's *William Makepeace Thackeray*, 2 vols.
Trollope's *Thackeray*. (E. M. L.)
Merivale and Marzials's *Life of Thackeray*. (G. W.)
Mudge and Sears's *A Thackeray Dictionary*.
Cross's *George Eliot's Life as Related in her Letters and Journals*.
Browning's *Life of George Eliot*. (G. W.) Stephens's *George Eliot*. (E. M. L.)
Cook's *George Eliot: A Critical Study of her Life, Writings, and Philosophy*.
Olcott's *George Eliot: Scenes and People in Her Novels*.
Hamilton's *Robert Louis Stevenson*.
Balfour's *The Life of Robert Louis Stevenson*, 2 vols.
The Letters of Robert Louis Stevenson, edited by Sidney Colvin.
Raleigh's *Robert Louis Stevenson*. Hamerton's *Stevensoniana*.
Japp's *Robert Louis Stevenson*.
Hamerton's *George Meredith: His Life and Art in Anecdote and Criticism*.
Letters of George Meredith, 2 vols.
Sturge Henderson's *George Meredith*.
Bailey's *The Novels of George Meredith: A Study*.
Trevelyan's *The Poetry and Philosophy of George Meredith*.
Beach's *The Comic Spirit in George Meredith*.
Lionel Johnson's *The Art of Thomas Hardy*.
Macdonell's *Thomas Hardy*.
Abercrombie's *Thomas Hardy: A Critical Study*.
Saxelby's *Thomas Hardy Dictionary*.
Phelps's *Essays on Modern Novelists* (Hardy, Kipling, Stevenson).
Benson's *Walter Pater*. (E. M. L.)

Paul's *Matthew Arnold*. (E. M. L.)
Saintsbury's *Matthew Arnold*.
Letters of Robert Browning and Elizabeth Barrett Barrett.
Griffin and Minchin's *The Life of Robert Browning*.
Chesterton's *Robert Browning*. (E. M. L.)
Sharp's *Life of Browning*. (G. W.)
Symons's *An Introduction to the Study of Browning*.
Foster's *The Message of Robert Browning*.
Orr's *A Handbook to the Works of Robert Browning*.
Alfred, Lord Tennyson, A Memoir, by his son.
Benson's *Alfred Tennyson* (the best brief work).
Lyall's *Tennyson*. (E. M. L.)
Brooke's *Tennyson: His Art and Relation to Modern Life*.
Van Dyke's *The Poetry of Tennyson*.
Gordon's *The Social Ideals of Alfred Tennyson*.
Lockyer's *Tennyson as a Student and Poet of Nature*.
Luce's *Handbook to the Works of Alfred, Lord Tennyson*.
Woodberry's *Swinburne*.
Thomas's *Algernon Charles Swinburne: A Critical Study*.
Knowles's *Kipling Primer*.
Le Galliene's *Rudyard Kipling, A Criticism*.
Clemens's *A Ken of Kipling*.
Young's *Dictionary of the Characters and Scenes in the Stories and Poems of Rudyard Kipling*.
Canby's *The Short Story in English* (Kipling).
Cooper's *Some English Story Tellers* (Kipling).
Leeb-Lundberg's *Word Formation in Kipling* (excellent).

SUGGESTED READINGS
WITH QUESTIONS AND SUGGESTIONS

The Pre-Raphaelites. — Read Rossetti's *The Blessed Damozel, Sister Helen, The King's Tragedy, Love's Nocturne*, and *Mary's Girlhood*. All of these are given in Page's *British Poets of the Nineteenth Century*. Selections may be found in Bronson,[1] IV., *Century, Oxford Book of Victorian Verse*, and Manly, I. Selections from Christina Rossetti's Pre-Raphaelite verse are given in all except Page.

From William Morris, read *Two Red Roses Across the Moon, The*

---

[1] For full titles, see p. 6.

Defence of Guenevere (Page's *British Poets*), and the selections from *The Earthly Paradise* in either Page, *Century*, Bronson, IV., or Manly, I.

What part did Ruskin play in this new movement? Point out the simplest, the most affecting, and the most pleasing stanza in *The Blessed Damozel*. What Pre-Raphaelite qualities in this poem have made it such a favorite? What are the chief characteristics of Rossetti's other verse? Note specially Miss Rossetti's religious verse.

What Pre-Raphaelite qualities do Morris's *Two Red Roses across the Moon* (1858) and *The Defence of Guenevere* (1858) show? Compare this early verse with the selections from *The Earthly Paradise* (1868-1870).

Macaulay. — Read either the *Essay on Milton* or the *Essay on Addison* (*Eclectic English Classics* or *Gateway Series*) or the selections in Craik, V., Manly, II., *Century*, or Dickinson and Roe's *Nineteenth Century Prose*.

Read *History of England*, Chap. IX., or the selections in Craik V., or *Century*, or Manly, II.

What are some of the qualities that cause Macaulay's writings to outstrip in popularity other works of a similar nature? What qualities in his style may be commended to young writers? What are his special defects? Contrast his narrative style in Chap. IX. of the *History* with Carlyle's in *The French Revolution*, Vol. I., Book V., Chap. VI.

Newman. — The best volume of selections is edited by Lewis E. Gates (228 pages, 75 cents). Dickinson and Roe's *Nineteenth Century English Prose* contains Newman's essay on *Literature*. Selections are given in Craik V., *Century*, and Manly, II.

Compare his style with Macaulay's and note the resemblance and the difference. Why did Newman call himself a rhetorician? What qualities does he add to those of a rhetorician? Select passages that show his special clearness, concreteness, also his rhetorical and argumentative power.

Carlyle. — Read the *Essay on Robert Burns* (*Eclectic English Classics* or *Gateway Series*); *Sartor Resartus*, Book III., Chap. VI. (*Everyman's Library*); *The French Revolution*, Vol. I., Book V., Chap. VI. (*Everyman's Library*). Selections may be found in Craik, V., *Century*, Manly, II., and Evans's *Carlyle* (*Masters of Literature*).

What marked difference in manner of treatment is shown in Macaulay's *Milton* or *Addison* and Carlyle's *Burns*? What was Carlyle's **message** in *Sartor Resartus*? What did Huxley and Tyndale say of his influence? What are the most noteworthy qualities of *The French Revolution*? What are the chief characteristics of Carlyle's style?

Ruskin. — In Vol. I., Part II., of *Modern Painters*, read the first part of Chap. I. of Sec. III., Chap. I. of Sec. IV., and Chap. I. of Sec. V., and note Ruskin's surprising accuracy of knowledge in dealing with aspects of the natural world. *The Stones of Venice*, Vol. III., Chap. IV., states Ruskin's theory of art and its close relation to morality. Excellent selections from the various works of Ruskin will be found in *An Introduction to the Writings of John Ruskin*, by Vida D. Scudder. Selections are also given in *Century*, Manly, II., *Riverside Literature Series*, and Bronson's *English Essays* (*Modern Painters* and *Fors Clavigera*). *Sesame and Lilies*, *The King of the Golden River*, and *The Stones of Venice* are published in *Everyman's Library*.

What was the message of *Modern Painters*? of *The Stones of Venice*? of *Fors Clavigera*? Why is Ruskin called a disciple of Carlyle? Select a passage from Ruskin's descriptive prose and indicate its chief qualities.

Brontë, Bulwer Lytton, Gaskell, Trollope, Kingsley, Reade, Blackmore, and Barrie. — *Jane Eyre* (Charlotte Brontë), *Wuthering Heights* (Emily Brontë), *Last Days of Pompeii* (Lytton), *Cranford* (Gaskell), *Barchester Towers* (Trollope), *Westward Ho!* (Kingsley), *The Cloister and the Hearth* (Reade), and *Lorna Doone* (Blackmore) are all published in *Everyman's Library*. Barrie's *The Little Minister* is included in Burt's *Home Library*. The works of the Brontë sisters will be much more appreciated if Mrs. Gaskell's *Life of Charlotte Brontë* (*Everyman's Library*) is read first. The novels by the Brontë sisters, Mrs. Gaskell, Trollope, and Barrie record their impressions of contemporary life. The other novels are historical. Lytton gives a vivid account of the last days of Pompeii. Kingsley thrills with his story of the sailors of Elizabeth's time. Reade, who studied libraries to insure the accuracy of *The Cloister and the Hearth*, portrays vividly the oncoming of the Renaissance in the fifteenth century. Blackmore's great story, which records some incidents of the Monmouth rebellion (1685), is written more to interest than to throw light on history.

Dickens. — The first works of Dickens to be read are *Pickwick Papers*, *A Christmas Carol*, and *David Copperfield*. These are all published in *Everyman's Library*. Craik, V., gives "Mr. Pickwick on the Ice," "Christmas at the Cratchit's," and two scenes from *David Copperfield*.

Select passages that show (a) humor, (b) pathos, (c) sympathy with children, (d) optimism. Describe some one of the characters. Can you instance a case where a mannerism is made to take the place of other characterization? Is Dickens a master of plot? of style?

Thackeray. — Read *Henry Esmond* (*Eclectic English Classics*) and *The English Humorists of the Fifteenth Century* (Macmillan's *Pocket Classics*). Craik, V., and Manly, II. give selections.

Contrast the manner of treatment in Thackeray's historical novel, *Henry Esmond*, and in Scott's historical romance, *Ivanhoe*. Thackeray says: "The best humor is that which contains most humanity — that which is flavored throughout with tenderness and kindness." Would this serve as a definition of Thackeray's own style of humor? State definitely how he differs from Dickens in portraying character. Compare Thackeray's *English Humorists* with Macaulay's *Milton* and Carlyle's *Burns*. Which essay leaves the most definite ideas? Which is the most interesting? Which has the most atmosphere? How should you characterize Thackeray's style?

George Eliot. — Read *Silas Marner* (*Eclectic English Classics* or *Gateway Series*), or selections in Craik, V., or Manly, II. In what does the chief strength of *Silas Marner* consist, — in the plot, the characters, or the description? Does the ethical purpose of this novel grow naturally out of the story? Is the inner life or only the outward appearance of the characters revealed? Wherein do they show growth?

Stevenson. — Read *Treasure Island* (*Eclectic English Classics* or *Gateway Series*), *Inland Voyage*, and *Travels with a Donkey* (*Gateway Series*). From the essays read *Child's Play*, *Aes Triplex* (both in *Virginibus Puerisque*). Some of the essays and best short stories (including *Dr. Jekyll and Mr. Hyde*) are given in Canby and Pierce's *Selections from Robert Louis Stevenson*. From the volume of poems called *Underwoods*, read *The Celestial Surgeon* and *Requiem*. *A Child's Garden of Verse* may be read entire in an hour.

Compare *Treasure Island* with *Robinson Crusoe*. What are the chief characteristics of *An Inland Voyage* and *Travels with a Donkey?* Why is he called a romantic writer? As an essayist, compare him with Thackeray. What are the special qualities of his style?

George Meredith. — *The Egoist* is Meredith's most representative novel. *The Ordeal of Richard Feverel* and *Diana of the Crossways* are also masterpieces. From the *Poems* read *Love in the Valley*, *The Lark Ascending*, *Melanthus*, *Jump-to-Glory Jane*.

What is the central purpose of *The Egoist?* Select specially Meredithian passages which show his general characteristics. Can you find any other author whose humor resembles Meredith's? Would he naturally be more popular with men or with women?

Hardy. — Hardy's most enjoyable novel is *Far from the Madding Crowd.* *The Return of the Native* is one of his strongest works.

What are some of the most striking differences between him and Meredith? Which one is naturally the better story-teller? Where are the scenes of most of Hardy's novels laid? What is his theory of life?

Arnold. — Read *Dover Beach, Memorial Verses, Stanzas in Memory of the Author of "Obermann"* and *Sohrab and Rustum* (Page's *British Poets of the Nineteenth Century,* Bronson, IV., Manly, I.).

Is Arnold the poet of fancy or of reflection? How does his poetry show one phase of nineteenth-century thought?

Arnold's *Essays, Literary and Critical* are published in *Everyman's Library.* The best volume of selections from the prose writings of Arnold is the one edited by Lewis E. Gates (348 pages, 75 cents). Good selections are given in Craik, V., Manly, I. (*Sweetness and Light*), Century (*The Study of Poetry*). Arnold's *Introduction* to Ward, I., is well worth reading.

What quality specially marks Arnold's criticism? Compare him as a critic with Coleridge, Macaulay, Carlyle, and Thackeray. What are the advantages and disadvantages of a style like Arnold's?

Pater. — Read the essay, *Leonardo da Vinci* (Dickinson and Roe's *Nineteenth Century Prose,* pp. 338–368), from Pater's "golden book," *The Renaissance: Studies in Art and Literature.* E. E. Hale's *Selections from Walter Pater* (268 pages, 75 cents) gives representative selections. Manly, II., and Century give the essay on *Style.*

What are the chief characteristics of Pater's style? Compare it with Macaulay's, Newman's, Ruskin's, and Matthew Arnold's. Has Pater a message? Does he show the spirit of the time?

The Brownings. — From Elizabeth Barrett Browning, read *Cowper's Grave, The Cry of the Children,* and from her *Sonnets from the Portuguese,* Nos. I., III., VI., X., XVIII., XX., XXVI., XXVIII, XLI., XLIII.

Mrs. Browning's verse comes from the heart and should be felt rather than criticized. Fresh interest may, however, be given to a study of her *Sonnets from the Portuguese,* by comparing them with any other series of love sonnets, excepting Shakespeare's.

Robert Browning's shorter poems are best for the beginner, who should read *Rabbi Ben Ezra, Abt Vogler, Home Thoughts from Abroad, Prospice, Saul, The Pied Piper of Hamelin*. Baker's *Browning's Shorter Poems* (*Macmillan's Pocket Classics*) contains a very good collection of his shorter poems. Representative selections from Browning's poems are given in Page's *British Poets of the Nineteenth Century, Oxford Book of Victorian Verse*, Bronson, IV., Manly, I., and *Century*.

Browning's masterpiece, *The Ring and the Book* (*Oxford Edition*, Oxford University Press) would be apt to repel beginners. This should be studied only after a previous acquaintance with his shorter poems.

Define Browning's creed as found in *Rabbi Ben Ezra*. Is he an ethical teacher? Is there any similarity between his teaching and Carlyle's? What most interests Browning, — word-painting, narration, action, psychological analysis, or technique of verse? See whether a comparison of his *Prospice* with Tennyson's *Crossing the Bar* does not help you to understand Browning's peculiar cast of mind. What qualities in Browning entitle him to be ranked as a great poet?

Tennyson. — From his 1842 volume, read the poems mentioned on page 556. From *The Princess*, read the lyrical songs; from *In Memoriam*, the parts numbered XLI., LIV., LVII., and CXXXI.; from *Maud*, the eleven stanzas beginning: "Come into the garden, Maud"; from *The Idylls of the King*, read *Gareth and Lynette, Lancelot and Elaine, The Passing of Arthur* (Van Dyke's edition in *Gateway Series*); from his later poems, *The Higher Pantheism, Locksley Hall Sixty Years After*, and *Crossing the Bar*.

The best single volume edition of Tennyson's works is published in Macmillan's *Globe Poets*. Selections are given in Page's *British Poets of the Nineteenth Century*, Bronson, IV., *Oxford Book of Victorian Verse*, Manly, I., and *Century*.

In *The Palace of Art*, study carefully the stanzas from XIV. to XXIII., which are illustrative of Tennyson's characteristic style of description. Compare *Locksley Hall* with *Locksley Hall Sixty Years After*, and note the difference in thought and metrical form. Does the later poem show a gain over the earlier? Compare Tennyson's nature poetry with that of Keats and Wordsworth. To what is chiefly due the pleasure in reading Tennyson's poetry: to the imagery, form, thought? What idea of his faith do you gain from *In Memoriam* and *The Passing of Arthur*? In what is Tennyson the poetic exponent of the age? Is it probable that Tennyson's popularity will increase or wane? Select some of his verse that you think will be as popular a hundred years hence as now.

Swinburne. — Read *A Song in Time of Order, The Youth of the Year (Atalanta in Calydon), A Match, The Garden of Proserpine, Hertha, By the North Sea, The Hymn of Man, The Roundel, A Child's Laughter*.

The most of the above are given in Page's *British Poets of the Nineteenth Century*, Bronson, IV., Manly, I., *Century, Oxford Book of Victorian Verse*.

Compare both the metrical skill and poetic ideas of Swinburne and Tennyson. Can you find any poet who surpasses Swinburne in the technique of verse? What are his chief excellencies and faults?

Kipling. — Read *The Jungle Books*. The following are among the best of his short stories: *The Man Who Would be King, The Brushwood Boy, The Courting of Dinah Shadd, Drums of the Fore and Aft, Without Benefit of Clergy, On Greenhow Hill*.

From his poems read *Mandalay, Fuzzy-Wuzzy, Danny Deever, The 'Eathen, Ballad of East and West, Recessional, The White Man's Burden*; also *Song of the Banjo*, and *L'Envoi*, from *Seven Seas*, published by Doubleday, Page and Company.

Why is *The Jungle Book* called an original creation? What are the most distinctive qualities of Kipling's short stories? Point out in what respects they show the methods of the journalist. How does Kipling sustain the interest? What limitations do you notice? What is specially remarkable about his style? What are the principal characteristics of his verse? What subjects appeal to him? Why is his verse so popular?

Minor Poets. — Read the selections from Clough, Henley, Bridges, Davidson, Thompson, Watson, Dobson and Symons in either *The Oxford Book of Victorian Verse* or Stevenson's *The Home Book of Verse*. *The Poetical Works of Robert Bridges* is inexpensively published by the Oxford University Press. Dobson's verse has been gathered into the single volume *Collected Poems* (1913).

What are the chief characteristics of each of the above authors? Do these minor versifiers fill a want not fully supplied by the great poets?

CHAPTER X

TWENTIETH-CENTURY LITERATURE

Interest in the Present. — One result of the growing scientific spirit has been an increasing interest in contemporary problems and literature. At the beginning of the Victorian age, the chief part of the literature studied in college was nearly two thousand years old. When English courses were finally added, they frequently ended with Milton. To-day, however, many colleges have courses in strictly contemporary literature. The scientific attitude toward life has caused a recognition of the fact that he who disregards current literature remains ignorant of a part of the life and thought of to-day and that he resembles the mathematician who neglects one factor in the solution of a problem.

It is true that the future may take a different view of all contemporary things, including literature; but this possibility does not justify neglect of the present. We should also remember that different stages in the growth of nations and individuals constantly necessitate changes in estimating the relative importance of the thought of former centuries.

The Trend of Contemporary Literature. — The diversity of taste in the wide circle of twentieth-century readers has encouraged authors of both the realistic and the romantic schools. The main tendency of scientific influence and of the new interest in social welfare is toward realism. In his stories of the "Five Towns," Arnold Bennett shows how the dull industrial life affects the character of the individual. Much of the fiction of H. G. Wells presents matter of scientific or sociological interest. Poets like John Masefield and Wilfrid Gibson sing with an almost prosaic sincerity of the life of workmen and of the squalid city streets. The drama is frequently a study of the conditions affecting contemporary life.

Twentieth-century writers are not, however, neglecting the other great function of literature, — to charm life with romantic visions and to bring to it deliverance from care. The poetry of Noyes takes us back to the days of Drake and to the Mermaid Inn, where we listen to Shakespeare, Marlowe, and Jonson. The Irish poets and dramatists disclose a world of the " Ever-Young," where there is : —

"A laughter in the diamond air, a music in the trembling grass."

The influence of the great German skeptic, Friedrich Nietzsche (1844–1900), appears in some of Shaw's dramas, as well as in the novels of Wells; but the poets of this age seem to have more faith than Swinburne (p. 567) or Matthew Arnold (p. 536) or some of the minor versifiers of the last quarter of the nineteenth century.

Two prominent essayists, **Arthur Christopher Benson** (1862–   ) and **Gilbert K. Chesterton** (1874–   ) are sincere optimists. Such volumes of Benson's essays as *From a College Window* (1906), *Beside Still Waters* (1907), and *Thy Rod and Thy Staff* (1912) have strengthened faith and proved a tonic to many. Chesterton is a suggestive and stimulating essayist in spite of the fact that he often bombards his readers with too much paradox. Early in life he was an agnostic and a follower of Herbert Spencer, but he later became a champion of Christian faith. Sometimes Chesterton seems to be merely clever, but he is usually too thought-provoking to be read passively. His *Robert Browning* (1903), *Varied Types* (1903), *Heretics* (1905), *George Bernard Shaw* (1909), and *The Victorian Age in Literature* (1913) keep most readers actively thinking.

THE NOVEL

Joseph Conrad. — This son of distinguished Polish exiles from Russia, Joseph Conrad Korzeniowski, as he was originally named, was born in the Ukraine, in 1857. Until his nineteenth year he was unfamiliar with the English language. Instead of following the literary or military traditions of his family, he joined the English merchant marine. Sailing the seas of the world, touching at strange tropical ports and uncharted islands, elbowing all the races of the globe, hearing all the languages spoken by man, — such were Conrad's activities between his twentieth and thirty-seventh years.

JOSEPH CONRAD

At thirty-seven, needing a little rest, he settled in England and began to write. Short stories, novels, and an interesting autobiographical volume, *A Personal Record* (1912), represent Conrad's production. Among his ablest books are *Tales of Unrest* (1898), a volume of sea stories, and *Lord Jim* (1900), a novel full of the fascination of strange seas and shores, but still more remarkable for its searching analysis of a man's recovery of self-respect after a long period of remorse for failure to meet a momentary crisis. *Youth, A Narrative, and Two Other Tales* (1902), contains one of Conrad's strongest stories, *The End of the Tether*. This is a tender story of an old sea captain, who for the sake of a cherished daughter holds his post against terrific odds, including blindness and disgrace. *Typhoon* (1903) is an almost unrivaled account of a ship's fight against mad hurricanes and raging seas.

One of Conrad's prime distinctions is his power to visualize scenes. The terror, beauty, caprice, and mercilessness of the sea; the silence and strangeness of the impenetrable tropical forest; atmospheres tense with storm or brilliant with sunshine, — these he records with strong effect. But though he has gained his fame largely as a chronicler of remote seas and shores, his handling of the human element is but little less impressive.

Conrad's method is unusual. Though his sentences are sufficiently direct and terse, his general order of narration is not straightforward. He often seems to progress slowly at the start, but after the characters have been made familiar, the story proceeds to its powerful and logical conclusion.

Arnold Bennett. — Bennett was born in Hanley, North Staffordshire, in 1867. He studied law, but abandoned it to become for seven years an editor of *Woman*, a London periodical. In 1900 he resigned this position to devote himself entirely to literature. He went to France to live, and began to write novels under the influence of the French and Russian realistic novelists.

Bennett is the author of many works of uneven merit. Some of these were written merely to strike the popular taste and to sell. His serious, careful work is seen at its best in his stories of the *Five Towns*, so called from the small towns of his native Staffordshire. One of the best of these novels, *The Old Wives' Tale* (1908), is a painstaking record of the different temperaments and experiences of two sisters, from their happy childhood to a pathetic, disillusioned old age. The intimate, homely revelations and the literal fidelity to life in *The Old Wives' Tale* give it a high rank among twentieth-century English novels.

Clayhanger (1910) is another strong story of life in the "Five Towns" pottery district of Staffordshire. Although the hero, Edwin Clayhanger, is not a strong personality, Bennett's art makes us keenly interested in Edwin's simple, impressionable nature, in his eagerness for life, and in his experiences as a young dreamer, lover, son, and brother. *Hilda Lessways* (1911), a companion volume to *Clayhanger*, but a story of less power, continues the history of the same characters. Bennett reveals in these novels one of his prime gifts, — the skill to paint domestic pictures vividly and to invest them with a distinct local atmosphere. His art has won a signal triumph in arousing interest in simple scenes and average characters. He can present the romance of the commonplace, — of gray, dull monotonous, almost negative existence.

He has enlivened the contemporary stage with a few brisk comedies. *Milestones* was written in collaboration with Edward Knoblauch, an American author. Its characters, representing three generations, illustrate humorously the truth that what is to-day's innovation becomes to-morrow's august convention. *The Honeymoon* (1911) is a farce of misunderstandings adroitly handled.

Although Bennett has shown great versatility, yet his individual, strong, and vital work is found in the one field where he brings us face to face with the circumscribed, but appealing life of the "Five Towns" district of his youth.

John Galsworthy. — John Galsworthy was born in Coombe, Surrey, in 1867. He was graduated from Oxford with an honor degree in law in 1889 and was called to the bar in 1890. He traveled for a large part of two years, visiting, among other places, Russia, Canada, Australia, South Africa, and the Fiji Islands. On one of these trips he met Joseph Conrad, then a sailor, and they became warm friends. Galsworthy was twenty-eight when he began to write.

JOHN GALSWORTHY

Four of his novels deal with the upper classes of English society. *The Man of Property* (1906) treats of the wealthy class, *The Country House* (1907) presents the conservative country squire, *Fraternity* (1909) portrays the intellectual class, and *The Patrician* (1911) pictures the aristocrat. Galsworthy is the relentless analyist of well-to-do, conventional English society. As Frederic Taber Cooper well says, "British stolidity, British conservatism, the unvarying fixity of the social system, the sacrifice of individual needs and cravings to caste and precedent and public opinion, — these are the themes which Mr. Galsworthy never wearies of satirizing with a mordant irony."

Since his object is to present problems of life, many of his characters are but types. On the other hand, Soames Forsyte in *The Man of Property*, Lord Miltoun, Mrs. Noel, and Lady Casterley in *The Patrician*, are among the most brilliant and real characters in modern fiction. Galsworthy's style is clear, his plot construction is excellent, and his humor in caricaturing social types has many of the qualities of Dickens's.

Herbert George Wells. — Wells was born in Bromley, Kent, in 1866. He expected to be a shopkeeper and was apprenticed in his fourteenth year to a chemist; but this did not satisfy his ambition. Later, however, he won scholarships that enabled him to take a degree in science. While preparing himself to graduate from the University of London, he worked in Huxley's laboratory. The experiments there inspired him to write stories based on scientific facts and hypotheses, such as *The Time Machine* (1895) and *In the Days of the Comet* (1906). Wells is also vitally interested in problems of sociology. The *Discovery of the Future* (1902) and *The Future in America* (1906) present possibilities of scientifically planning man's further development. *Kipps: The Story of a Simple Soul* (1905) and *Marriage* (1912) are his best works, considered as actual novels of character. *Kipps* is a bitter but strong portrayal of the pretense and hypocrisy of society and of its inertia in responding to human needs, and *Marriage* is a subtle, psychological analysis of a conjugal misunderstanding and an attempted readjustment. Wells's study of man as a biological development and his preference of actual facts to sentimental conclusions are in accord with the trend of modern social science.

The work of Wells covers a wide range of subjects. He has written scientific romances, blood-curdling tales, strange phantasies, prophetic Utopias, and sociological novels. He shows an increasing tendency to depict the human struggle with environment, heredity, and the manifold forces that affect the earning of a livelihood. His characters are more often remembered as specimens exhibiting some phase of life than as attractive or repellent personalities. Increasing power of portraying character, however, is evident in his later work. He has a daring imagination, a sense of humor, satiric power, and a capacity for expressing himself in vivid and picturesque English.

Eden Phillpotts was born in India in 1862. His novels, however, are as definitely associated with Devonshire as Hardy's are with Wessex, and Bennett's with North Staffordshire. Phillpotts is noted for his power to paint "landscapes with figures." The "figures" are the farmers, villagers, and shepherds of that part of Devon, known as Dartmoor; and the landscapes are the granite crags, the moors; and farmlands of "good red earth." *Widecombe Fair* (1913) is the twentieth volume that he has published as a result of twenty years' work among these children of Devon. Sometimes the roughness and untutored emotions of the Dartmoor characters repel the readers; but these characters form strong, picturesque groups of human beings, and their dialect adds a pleasant flavor to the novels. Phillpotts's frequent use of coincidences weakens the effect and mars the naturalness of the plot, since their recurrence comes to be anticipated. *Children of the Mist* (1898) and *Demeter's Daughter* (1911) are among his ablest novels.

Maurice Hewlett was born in Kent in 1861, of an old Somerset family. He began writing in his boyhood, giving proof even then of his skill in catching the manner of other writers. His style to-day reëchoes his reading of many authors in Latin, French, Italian, and English.

The Life and Death of Richard Yea-and-Nay (1900) shows Hewlett's romantic fancy and love for historical characters and pageants. While this novel is full of life, color, and movement, it displays his proneness to allow the romantic vein to run to the fantastic in both episode and style. *The Stooping Lady* (1907) deals with the love of a lady of high degree for a humble youth whom her devotion ennobles.

Hewlett's style is finished and richly poetical, but often too ornate and too encrusted with archaic terms and other artificial forms.

Sir Arthur Quiller-Couch, born in Cornwall in 1863, is a fiction writer, critic, poet, and anthologist. Having much of Stevenson's love for romantic adventure, he was chosen to finish *St. Ives*, left incomplete by Stevenson. *The Splendid Spur* (1889), a spirited tale of romance and war in the perturbed time of Charles I., is one of his best stories of adventure.

Among his books on simple Cornish life may be mentioned *The Delectable Duchy* (1893). It is a collection of short stories and sketches. Quiller-Couch sees life without a touch of morbid somberness and he commands a vivacious, highly-trained style.

William Frend De Morgan was born in London, in 1839. He published his first novel, *Joseph Vance* (1906), at the age of sixty-seven. This plain, straightforward story of a little boy befriended by a generous-hearted London doctor won for De Morgan wide and hearty applause. While some contemporary writers fashion their style and select their material on the models of French or Russian realists, De Morgan goes to the great English masters, Thackeray and Dickens. Like them, De Morgan writes copiously and leisurely.

Alice-for-Short (1907) and *Somehow Good* (1908) are

strong novels, but *Joseph Vance*, with its carelessly constructed plot and power to awaken tears and smiles, remains De Morgan's best piece of fiction.

William John Locke was born in the Barbados in 1863. He gained much of his reputation from his tenth book, *The Beloved Vagabond* (1906). The book takes its charm from the whimsical and quixotic temperament of the hero. He is typical of Locke's other leading characters, who, like Hamlet's friend, Horatio, take "fortune's buffets and rewards with equal thanks." Like other novels by the same author, this story is pervaded by a distinctly Bohemian atmosphere, wherein the ordinary conventions of society are disregarded.

Locke's humor, his deft characterization, his toleration of human failings, largely compensate for his lack of significant plots. He is sometimes whimsical to the point of eccentricity, and his high spirits often verge on extravagance; but at his best he has the power of refreshing the reader with gentle irony, genial laughter, and love for human kind.

Israel Zangwill, the Jewish writer, was born in London in 1864. He first won fame by interpreting the Jewish temperament as he saw it manifested in London's dingy, pitiful Ghetto quarter. "This Ghetto London of ours," he says, "is a region where, amid uncleanness and squalor, the rose of romance blows yet a little longer in the raw air of English reality, a world of dreams as fantastic and poetic as the mirage of the Orient where they were woven."

In his volume, *The Children of the Ghetto* (1892), Zangwill admirably chronicles the lives of these people and the sharp contrasts between their quaint traditions and a great modern commercial city's customs.

POETRY

The Celtic Renaissance. — Some of the best recent English verse has been written by poets of Irish birth or sympathies. Because of the distinctive quality of both the poetry and prose of these Celtic writers, the term "Celtic Renaissance" has been applied to their work, which glows with spiritual emotion and discloses a world of dreams, fairies, and romantic aspiration. As Richard Wagner received from the Scandinavian folk-lore the inspiration for his great music, as Tennyson found the incentive for *The Idylls of the King* in Malory's *Morte d'Arthur*, so the modern Celtic poets turned back to the primitive legends of their country for tales of Cuchulain who fought the sea, Caolte who besieged the castle of the gods, Oisin, who wandered three hundred years in the land of the immortals, and Deirdre who stands in the same relation to Celtic literature as Helen to Greek and Brunnhilde to German literature. Some of the fascination that the past and its fairy kingdom exerted over these poets may be found in this stanza from Russell's *The Gates of Dreamland:* —

"Oh, the gates of the mountain have opened once again
And the sound of song and dancing falls upon the ears of men,
And the Land of Youth lies gleaming, flushed with rainbow light and mirth.
And the old enchantment lingers in the honey-heart of earth."[1]

William Butler Yeats. — One of the most talented and active workers in this Celtic Renaissance is William Butler Yeats, born in 1865 in Dublin, Ireland. He came from an artistic family, his father, brother, and sisters being either artists or identified with the arts and crafts movement. Yeats himself studied art in Dublin, but poetry was more attractive to him than painting.

[1] Printed by permission of The Macmillan Company.

He was greatly influenced by spending his youthful days with his grandparents in County Sligo, where he heard the old Irish legends told by the peasants, who still believed them. He translated these stories from Irish into English and wrote poems and essays relating to them. After reaching the age of thirty-four, he became engaged in writing dramas and in assisting to establish the Irish National Theater in Dublin (see p. 614). In thus reviving Ireland's heroic history, Yeats has served his country and his art.

WILLIAM BUTLER YEATS

The Wanderings of Oisin (1889) is his best narrative poem. Oisin, one of the ancient Celtic heroes, returns, after three hundred years of adventure, to find Ireland Christianized. St. Patrick hears him relate that he had been carried by his immortal wife, Niamh, to the land of the Ever-Young, —

> "Where broken faith has never been known,
> And the blushes of first love never have flown,"[1]

that he had battled for a hundred years with an undying foe, and that his strength had not waned during his stay on those immortal shores, although he had felt the effect of age when his foot again touched his native land. The days of "gods and fighting" men are brought back in this romantic poem. The battles, however, are not such gory conflicts as Scott and Kipling can paint. Yeats's contemplative genius presents bloodless battles, symbolic of life's continued fight, and accentuates the eternal hope and peace in the land of immortal youth.

[1] Printed by permission of The Macmillan Company.

Among his shorter narrative poems, which show some of the power of *The Wanderings of Oisin*, are *The Death of Cuchulain*, *The Old Age of Queen Maeve*, and *Baile and Aillinn*. Baille and Aillinn are the Irish Romeo and Juliet, each of whom hears from the baleful Aengus the false report that the other is dead. Each lover unhesitatingly seeks death in order to meet the other at once beyond these mortal shores. Yeats has also told simple stories in simple verse, as may be seen in *The Ballad of Father Gilligan* or in *The Fiddler of Dooney*.

The most striking characteristic of Yeats's work is the pensive yearning for a spiritual love, for an unchecked joy, and an unchanging peace beyond what mortal life can give. These qualities are strikingly illustrated by such poems as *Into the Twilight*, *The Everlasting Voices*, *The Hosting of the Sidhe* (Fairies), *The Stolen Child*. The very spirit of Celtic poetry is seen in these lines from *The Lake Isle of Innesfree*: —

"And I shall have some peace there, for peace comes dropping slow,
Dropping from the veils of the morning to where the cricket sings;
There midnight's all a glimmer, and noon a purple glow,
And evening full of the linnet's wings."[1]

Yeats's verse has been called "dream-drenched poems." The term is admirably descriptive of his romantic, lyrical verse.

George W. Russell. — Among the most prominent of these Celtic imaginative writers is George W. Russell (1867–   ), "the Irish Emerson," popularly known as "A. E." He is a poet, a painter, a mystic, and a dramatist. With Lady Gregory and Yeats, he has been one of the most active workers for the Irish National Theater (p. 614). He is an efficient member of those coöperative societies

[1] Printed by permission of The Macmillan Company.

which are trying to improve Ireland's industrial and agricultural conditions.

Russell's poetry is highly spiritual. Sometimes it is so mystical that like Prospero's messenger, Ariel, it vanishes into thin air. His shadowy pictures of nature and his lyrical beauty and tenderness are evident in two little volumes of his verse, *Homeward Songs by the Way* (1894) and *The Divine Vision* (1904). This stanza from *Beauty*, in *The Divine Vision*, shows his spiritual longing for quiet, peace, and beauty, in which to worship his Creator : —

> "Oh, twilight, fall in pearl dew, each healing drop may bring
> Some image of the song the Quiet seems to sing.
>
> My spirit would have beauty to offer at the shrine,
> And turn dull earth to gold and water into wine,
> And burn in fiery dreams each thought till thence refined
> It may have power to mirror the mighty Master's mind."[1]

Fiona Macleod. — All the work of **William Sharp** that he published under the pseudonym of "Fiona Macleod" belongs to this Celtic Renaissance. Born in 1856 at Paisley, Scotland, he settled in London in 1878, and became widely known as William Sharp, the critic. When he turned to his boyhood's home, the West Highlands of Scotland, for inspiration, he wrote, under the pen-name of Fiona Macleod, poetic prose stories and many poems about these Scotch Celts. He kept the secret of his identity so well that not until his death in 1905 was it known that Fiona Macleod, the mystic, was William Sharp, the critic.

Mountain Lovers (1895), a romantic novel of primitive people who live with nature in her loneliness, mystery, and terror, and who possess an instinctive, speechless, and poetic knowledge of her moods, is one of the earliest

[1] Printed by permission of The Macmillan Company.

and most interesting of his long novels. He excels in the short story. Some of his finest work in this field is in *The Sin Eater* (1895), which contains uncanny tales of quaint, strongly-marked highland characters with their weird traditions.

From the Hills of Dream (1901) and *The Hour of Beauty* (1907) are two small volumes of short poems full of the witchery of dreams, of death, of youth, and of lonely scenes. These poems come from a land far off from our common world. Delicacy of fancy, a freedom from any touch of impurity, a beauty as of "dew-sweet moon-flowers glimmering white through the mirk of a dust laden with sea-mist," are the qualities of Fiona Macleod's best verse.

John Masefield. — Instead of looking to the land of dreams and the misty past, like the Celtic writers, Masefield and Gibson, two younger English poets, have found in the everyday life of the present time the themes for their verse. Masefield was born in 1875 in Shropshire. He was a seafarer in his youth, and later, a traveler by land and sea. These varied experiences contributed color and vividness to his narrative verse.

He has written several long narrative poems on unromantic subjects. *Dauber* (1912) contains some of his best lines and its story is the most poetic. This poem follows the fortunes of a poor youth who, wishing to be a painter of ships, went to sea to study his mode at first hand. Masefield describes, with much power,

JOHN MASEFIELD

the young artist's ambition, his rough handling by the uncouth sailors, and his perilous experiences while rounding Cape Horn. *Dauber* exhibits the poet's power of vividly picturing human figures and landscapes. This poem, like most of Masefield's long narrative poems, is a story of human failure, — a dull prosaic failure, such as prose fiction presents in its pessimistic moods.

A strong and cheerful note is struck in some of Masefield's short lyrics, notably in *Laugh and be Merry, Roadways, The Seekers*, and *Being Her Friend*. In *Laugh and be Merry*, the song is almost triumphant: —

"Laugh and be proud to belong to the old proud pageant of man.

. . . .

Laugh and battle, and work, and drink of the wine outpoured
In the dear green earth, the sign of the joy of the Lord."[1]

Masefield's fancy does not busy itself with dreams and impossible visions. He paints life in its grayness and sordidness and dull mediocrity. Sometimes his verse is merely plain rimed prose, but again it becomes vigorous, picturesque, and vivid in description, as in the following lines from *Dauber:* —

". . . then the snow
 Whirled all about, dense, multitudinous cold,
Mixed with the wind's one devilish thrust and shriek
 Which whiffled out men's tears, deafened, took hold,
Flattening the flying drift against the cheek."[1]

Wilfred W. Gibson. — Gibson, who was born in Hexham in 1878, sings of the struggling oppressed work-a-day people: —

"Crouched in the dripping dark
 With steaming shoulders stark
The man who hews the coal to feed the fires."[1]

[1] Printed by permission of The Macmillan Company.

His poem, *The Machine*, awakens sympathy for the printer of Christmas story books and reveals Gibson as the twentieth-century Thomas Hood of *The Song of the Shirt*. One of the most richly human of his poems is *The Crane*, the story of the seamstress mother and her lame boy. His realistic volume of verse bearing the significant title, *Daily Bread* (1910), contains a number of narrative poems, which endeavor to set to music the "one measure" to which all life moves, — the earning of daily bread.

Gibson owes much of his popularity to his spirit of democracy and to the story form of his verse. Like Masefield, he sacrifices beauty to dull realism. Gibson manifests less range, less dramatic feeling, than Masefield, but avoids Masefield's uncouthness and repellent dramatic episodes.

These two poets illustrate a tendency to introduce a new realistic poetry. Wordsworth wrote of Michael and the Westmoreland peasantry, but Masefield and Gibson have taken as subjects of verse the toilers of factory, foundry, and forecastle. Closeness to life and simplicity of narration characterize these authors. They approximate the subject matter and technique of realistic fiction.

Alfred Noyes. — Alfred Noyes was born in 1880 in Wolverhampton, Staffordshire. He wrote verse while an Oxford undergraduate and he has since become one of the leading poets of the twentieth century. He has traveled in England and in America, reading his poems and lecturing on literary subjects.

The Flower of Old Japan (1903) is a fairy tale of children who dream of the pictures on blue china plates and Japanese fans. The poem is symbolic. The children are ourselves; and Japan is but the "kingdom of those dreams which . . . are the sole reality worth living and dying for."

The poet says of this kingdom : —

> "Deep in every heart it lies
> With its untranscended skies;
> For what heaven should bend above
> Hearts that own the heaven of love?"[1]

The Forest of Wild Thyme (1905) affords another

> "Hour to hunt the fairy gleam
> That flutters through this childish dream."[1]

ALFRED NOYES

There is also a deeper meaning to be read into this poem. The mystery of life, small as well as great, is found simply told in these lines : —

> "What does it take to make a rose,
>   Mother-mine?
> The God that died to make it knows
> It takes the world's eternal wars,
> It takes the moon and all the stars,
> It takes the might of heaven and hell
> And the everlasting Love as well,
>   Little child."[1]

Noyes has published several volumes of lyrical verse. Some of it possesses the lightness of these elfish tales. *The Barrel Organ*, *The Song of Re-Birth*, and *Forty Singing Seamen* are among his finest lyrics. They display much rhythmic beauty and variety. He strikes a deeply sorrowful and passionate note in *The Haunted Palace* and *De Profundis*. A line like this in *The Haunted Palace* —

> ". . . I saw the tears
> Bleed through her eyes with the slow pain of years,"[1]

indicates the strong emotional metaphor that occasionally deepens the passion of his verse.

[1] Printed by permission of The Macmillan Company.

England's sea power, immortalized in song from Beowulf to Swinburne, often inspires Noyes. His finest long poem is *Drake: An English Epic* (1908), which relates the adventures of this Elizabethan sea-captain and his victory over the Armada. The spirit of a daring romantic age of discovery is shown in these lines that tell how Drake and his men —

> ". . . went out
> To danger as to a sweetheart far away,
> Who even now was drawing the western clouds
> Like a cymar of silk and snow-white furs
> Close to her, till her body's beauty seemed
> Clad in a mist of kisses." [1]

Another volume of poems, *Tales of the Mermaid Tavern* (1913), brings us into the company of Shakespeare, Marlowe, Spenser, Jonson, Raleigh, and others of the great Elizabethan group that made the Mermaid Tavern their chosen resort. Greene's farewell to Shakespeare, —

> "You took my clay and made it live," [1]

shows that Noyes has caught something of the spirit that animated Elizabethan England.

Noyes is one of the most spontaneous and fluent writers of modern English poetry. Whether he is mystical, dramatic, playful, or marching along the course of a long narrative poem, he handles his verse with ease and facility. His language, his rhythm, and his thought are most happily blended in his graceful singing lyrics. The work of Noyes is inspired by the desire to show that all things and all souls are —

> "One with the dream that triumphs beyond the light of the spheres,
> We come from the Loom of the Weaver that weaves the Web of Years." [2]

[1] Printed by permission of Frederick A. Stokes Company.
[2] Printed by permission of The Macmillan Company.

THE MODERN DRAMA

The revival of the drama is a characteristic feature of the latter part of the nineteenth and the beginning of the twentieth century. The plays of the Norwegian, Henrik Ibsen (1828–1906), affected England profoundly in the last decade of the nineteenth century and proved an impetus to a new dramatic movement, seen in the work of men like Shaw.

The great literary school of dramatists passed away soon after the death of Shakespeare. While it is true that the writing of plays has been practically continuous since the time of the Restoration, yet for more than two hundred years after that event, the history of the drama has had little memorable work to record. There were two brief interesting comic periods: (1) the period of Congreve (p. 263) at the close of the seventeenth century, and (2) of Goldsmith and Sheridan (p. 337) nearly a hundred years later. The literary plays of the Victorians, — Browning, Tennyson, and Swinburne, — were lacking in dramatic essentials.

The modern drama has accomplished certain definite results. Pinero's work is typical of vast improvement in technique. Shaw is noted for his power of "investing modern conversation with vivacity and point." J. M. Synge has won distinction for presenting the great elemental forces that underlie the actions of primitive human beings. The playwrights are making the drama perform some of the functions that have been filled by the novel. The modern drama is also wrestling with the problem of combining literary form, poetic spirit, and good dramatic action. Some of the modern plays deal with unpleasant subjects, and some of the least worthy are immoral in their tendencies. Such plays will be forgotten, for the Anglo-Saxon race has never yet immortalized an unwholesome drama. Fortunately, however, the influence of a large proportion of the plays is pure and wholesome. In this class may be included the dramas of the Irish school and of Barrie, the majority by Galsworthy, and a number by Phillips and Shaw.

Jones and Pinero. — The work of Henry Arthur Jones and Sir Arthur Wing Pinero marks the advance of the English drama from artificiality and narrowness of scope toward a wider, closer relation to life. Henry Arthur Jones, both a playwright and a critic, was born in Grandborough, Buckinghamshire, in 1851. Contemporary English life is the subject of his numerous plays. *The Manœuvres of Jane* (1898) and *Mrs. Dane's Defence* (1900), are among his best works.

Sir Arthur Wing Pinero, born in 1855 in London, began his career as an actor. His real ambition, however, was to write for the stage. More than forty works, including farces, comedies of sentiment, and serious dramas of English life, attest his zeal as a dramatist. Among his most successful farces are *The Magistrate* (1885), *The School Mistress* (1886), and *The Amazons* (1893). Clever invention of absurd situations and success in starting infectious laughter are the prime qualities of these plays.

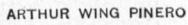

The Second Mrs. Tanqueray (1893) is by most critics considered Pinero's masterpiece. The failure of a character to regain respectability once forfeited supplies the nucleus for the dramatic situations. Excellent in craftsmanship as it is disagreeable in theme, this play contains no superfluous word to retard the action or mar the technical economy. Adolphus William Ward says: "With *The Second Mrs. Tanqueray* the English acted drama ceased to be a merely insular product, and took rank in the literature of Europe. Here was a play which, whatever its faults, was . . . an epoch-marking play."

One great service of Pinero and Jones to the twentieth-century drama has been excellent craftsmanship. Their technical skill may be specifically noted in the naturalness of the dialogues, in the movement of the characters about the stage, in the performance of some acts apparently trivial but really significant, and in the substitution of devices to take the place of the old soliloquies and "asides." Of the two, Pinero is the better craftsman, since Jones, in his endeavor to point a moral, sometimes weakens his dramatic effect.

George Bernard Shaw. — Shaw was born in Dublin, Ireland, in 1856. He was willful and took "refuge in idleness" at school. His education consisted mainly in studying music with his talented mother, in haunting picture galleries, and in wide reading. At the age of twenty, he went to London and began his literary career. He was at various times a journalist, a critic of art, music, and the drama, a lecturer, a novelist, and a playwright. Shaw describes himself as a man "up to the chin in the life of his times." He is a vegetarian, an anti-vivisectionist, an advocate for woman's suffrage, and a socialist.

Arms and the Man, Candida, You Never Can Tell, and

The Man of Destiny, published (1898) in the second volume of *Plays, Pleasant and Unpleasant;* and *The Devil's Disciple*, published (1900) in *Three Plays for Puritans*, are among his best dramas. With their stage directions and descriptions, they are as delightful to read as novels. Of these plays, *Candida* is first in character drawing and human interest. The dramatic action is wholly within the mental states of the three chief actors, but the situations are made intense through a succession of unique, absorbing, entertaining, and well-developed conversations.

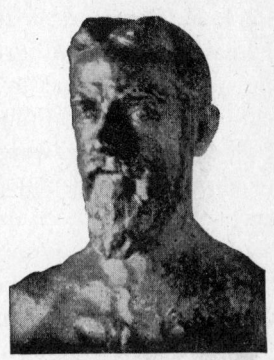

GEORGE BERNARD SHAW

Shaw is more destructive than constructive in his philosophy as expressed in his plays; and he criticizes so many of the institutions held sacred by society that people have refused to accept him seriously, even when he has written expository prefaces to his dramas. In *Arms and the Man*, he satirizes the romantic admiration for the soldier's calling; in *The Doctor's Dilemma* (1906), he attacks the professional man; in *Widowers' Houses* (1898), he assails the rich property holder with his high rents on poor people's houses; and in *Man and Superman* (1903), he dissects love and home until the sentiment is entirely taken out of them.

Shaw's chief object is to place before his audience facts, reasons, and logical conclusions. He will not tolerate romantic emotions or sentimentalism, which he ridicules with a reckless audacity, a literal incisiveness, and a satiric wit that none of his contemporaries can excel. His chief claim to his present important position among playwrights is based on his originality and fearlessness of thought, the unfailing sprightliness of his conversation, the infectious spirit of raillery in his comedies, and his mastery of the requirements of the modern stage.

J. M. Barrie. — With the successful stage production of *The Little Minister* (1897), Barrie passed from novelist to playwright. The qualities of humor, fancy, and quaint characterization, which were such a charm in his novels, reappear in his plays.

The Admirable Crichton, produced in 1903, is one of Barrie's most successful comedies. He displays skill and humor in handling the absurd situation of a peer's family wrecked on a desert island, where the butler, as the most resourceful member of the party, takes command. In *Peter Pan* (1904), the dramatization of the novel, *The Little White Bird*, care-free, prankish Peter Pan visits three children in their sleep and teaches them to fly away with him. He carries them to the little people of the fairy world, to the pirate ship, to other scenes dear to children's hearts, and finally to his home in the tree tops. The play is a mixture of fancy, symbolism, and realism. These are woven into a bright phantasy by an imagination that is near to childhood and has not lost its morning's brightness.

What Every Woman Knows (produced in 1908) shows Barrie's dramatic art at its height. He knows how to introduce variety and to give his characters an opportunity to reveal themselves. Every word, every movement of the heroine, Maggie Shand, adds to the unfolding of a fascinating personality. A period of intensely dramatic action may be followed by a comparative pause, such as occurs when the audience sees Maggie's husband slowly realize her cleverness and helpfulness,—qualities that had been long apparent to every one else.

Barrie shows the ability to present dramatically situations that are emotionally appealing or delightfully humorous. His plays exhibit admirably the deep feelings, the momentary moods, the resourcefulness, or the peculiar whimsicalities of men and women.

John Galsworthy. — As a means of presenting social problems, Galsworthy utilizes the drama even more than the novel. Faulty prison systems, discords between labor and capital, discrepancies between law and justice, are some of the themes he chooses to dramatize. *The Silver Box* (1906) ironically interprets Justice as blind rather than impartial. The poor man is often punished while the more fortunate man goes free. *Strife* (1909), in some respects the most powerful of his plays, illustrates the clash between capital and labor. In *The Eldest Son* (1912), the conflict is between two social orders. *Justice* (1910), which secured reforms in the English prison system, shows how a young man is affected by an inflexible but legal punishment; and how such a method fails to assist him humanely to a better manhood, but drives him to lower and lower depths.

In *Joy* (1907), a delightful play, Galsworthy momentarily relinquishes social problems for a drama of more personal emotion. In the mystical, poetical composition, *The Little Dream* (1911), he presents an allegory of the maiden in the Alps, dreaming first of the simple mountain life and then of the life in cities. With its spiritual note and delicate fancy, *The Little Dream* turns a golden key on the ideal world beyond the strife and gloom dramatized in the sociological plays.

Galsworthy has good stagecraft. His characterization

is distinct and consistent. His plays are simple in construction and direct in movement. He strictly avoids rhetorical and theatrical effects, but his dramatic economies often sacrifice all charm and æsthetic appeal. His gray world leaves no hope save the desperate one that conditions so grim may shame and spur society to reform.

Stephen Phillips. — This dramatist and poet was born at Somerton, near Oxford, in 1864. The boy was sent to Shakespeare's birthplace, Stratford-on-Avon, to attend school. He entered Cambridge; but at the end of his first term he left the university to join a company of Shakespearean players. His six years with them initiated him into the technique of stagecraft, which he later applied in the writing of his poetic dramas. He died in 1915.

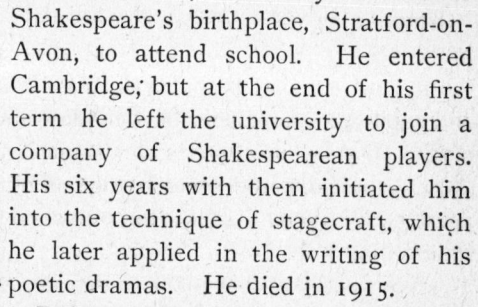

Before producing the plays for which he is known, he wrote some narrative and lyric verse. *Marpessa* (1890), a blank verse poem, is a beautiful treatment of the old Greek myth, in which Apollo, the god, and Idas, the mortal, woo Marpessa. Marlowe might have written the lines in which Apollo promises to take her to a home above the world, where movement is ecstasy and repose is thrilling. In some of his non-dramatic poems, *Christ in Hades* (1896), *Cities of Hell* (1907), and *The New Inferno* (1910), Phillips shows how the subject of life and punishment after death attracts him.

With the appearance of his *Paolo and Francesca* in 1899, the poetic drama seemed phœnix-like to arise from its ashes. Tennyson and Browning had failed to write successful plays. In fact, since the death of Dryden, poetry and drama had seemed to be afraid to approach each other.

Phillips effected at least a temporary union. His several plays have distinctly dramatic qualities and many passages of poetic beauty. From both a dramatic and a poetic point of view, *Paolo and Francesca* is Phillips's best play. Its dramatic values lie chiefly in its power to create and sustain a sense of something definitely progressing toward a certain point. The poetic elements of the play consist in the beauty of atmosphere and the charm of the lines. Giovanni Malatesta, the ugly tyrant of Rimini, being at war when his marriage draws near, sends his young brother Paolo to escort Francesca to Rimini. On the journey Paolo and Francesca fall in love with each other. When Giovanni discovers this, his jealous hand slays them. To such a tragic climax, Phillips drives steadily onward from the first scene, thus focusing the interest on a concrete dramatic situation.

Herod (1900) is a drama of ambition versus love. Herod, the great historic king of the Jews, though passionately in love with his wife Mariamne, sacrifices her brother Aristobulus to his suspicions, fearing that this young prince, the last of the Maccabees, may supplant him on the throne. This sacrifice, prompted by evil counselors, results in a train of tragic episodes, including Mariamne's death and Herod's madness. The lines in which Herod speaks of thinking in gold and dreaming in silver call to mind the hyperbole and music of Marlowe's mighty line.

Ulysses (1902), more of a panorama than a play, is founded on the Homeric story. Its scenes are laid in Olympus, in Hades, on Calypso's isle, and finally in Ithaca. Calypso tries to retain Ulysses upon her isle, beautiful —

> "With sward of parsley and of violet
> And poplars shimmering in a silvery dream."[1]

[1] Printed by permission of The Macmillan Company.

He struggles against her enchantment, returns home, finds his wife surrounded by her suitors, joins in their bow-drawing contest, and, in a most exciting and dramatic scene, surpasses all rivals and claims his faithful, beautiful Penelope.

The plays of Phillips not infrequently lack that clinching power that stretches the interest taut. Many scenes are admirably spectacular, suggestive of richly decorated tapestries, which hang separately in spacious rooms; but the plays need more forceful dramatic action, moving through changes to a climax. Phillips's diction, though sometimes rhetorical, is also often ornately beautiful and highly poetical. We feel that even in his plays, he is greater as a poet than as a dramatist.

Celtic Dramatists

Strong national feeling, interest in the folklore and peasant life of Ireland, and ambition to establish a national theater, have led to a distinct and original Irish drama. In 1899, with a fund of two hundred and fifty dollars, Lady Gregory, William Butler Yeats, G. W. Russell, and other playwrights and patrons succeeded in establishing in Dublin the Irish Literary Theater now known as the Irish National Theater.

The object of this theater is twofold. In the first place, it aims to produce "literary" plays, not the vapid, panoramic kind that merely pass away the time. In the second place, the Irish plays present fabled and historical Irish heroes and the humble Irish peasant.

Patriotism inspired many writers to assist in this national movement. Some gathered stories from the lips of living Irish-speaking peasants; others collected and translated into English the old legends of heroes. Dr. Douglas Hyde's translations of *The Five Songs of Connacht* (1894) and *The Religious Songs of Connacht* (1906) are valuable works and have greatly influenced the Irish writers.

Lady Augusta Gregory. — Lady Gregory, born in 1852, in Roxborough, County Galway, has made some of the best of these translations in her works, *Cuchulain of Muirthemna*, and *Gods and Fighting Men*. "These two books have come to many as a first revelation of the treasures buried in Gaelic literature, and they are destined to do much for the floating of old Irish story upon the world. They aim to do for the great cycles of Irish romance what Malory did for the Arthurian stories."[1]

Lady Gregory wrote also for the Irish Theater plays that have been acted successfully not only in Ireland but in England and in America. Among her best serious plays are *The Gaol Gate* (1906), a present-day play, the hero of which dies to save a neighbor, *The Rising of the Moon* (1907), and *Grania* (1912). *McDonough's Wife* (1913) is an excellent brief piece with an almost heroic note at the close. The great vagabond piper, McDonough, master of wonderful music, returns from wandering, to find his wife dead, and, because of his thriftlessness, about to be denied honorable burial. McDonough steps to the door, pipes his marvelous tunes, and immediately the village flocks to do homage to his wife.

Lady Gregory's farces have primarily made her fame. *Spreading the News* (1904), *Hyacinth Halvey* (1906), *The Image* (1910), and *The Bogie Men* (1913) are representa-

[1] Krans's *William Butler Yeats and the Irish Literary Revival.*

tive of her vigorous and well-constructed farces. They are varied in subject, the incidents are well developed, the characters are genuine Irish peasants and villagers, and the humor is infectious. It is interesting to note that Lady Gregory has continued to write farces because of the demand for them in the Irish National Theater, in order to offset the large number of tragedies by other authors.

William Butler Yeats. — In addition to delightful poetic fancy (p. 597), Yeats possesses considerable dramatic ability and stagecraft. In *The Countess Cathleen* (rewritten in 1912), the poor peasants are driven by a famine to the verge of starvation. Many die; but some are fed by the Countess Cathleen, while others sell their souls for the price of food to demons disguised as merchants. When these demons steal Countess Cathleen's stores in order to stop her charities, with instant Irish quickness and generosity, she sells her soul for a great price to the demons, in order to save her people here and hereafter. Such a tremendous sacrifice, however, is not permitted. Because of the purity of her motive, armed angels save her soul in the last impressive act. Supernatural powers, both pagan and Christian, participate in the play. Spirits haunt the woods, enter the peasants' cottages, and cast spells on the inhabitants. The play is Irish in story, in symbolism, and in the fancifulness of the conception.

The Land of Heart's Desire is another drama that has sprung from the soil and folklore of Ireland. This play was one of the first Celtic dramas to be produced, and in its present revised form (1912) it is one of the most engaging of the Irish plays. Partly in prose and partly in verse, it is the story of a young bride who tires of her monotonous life and calls upon the fairies to release her. The old parents tell her that duty comes before love of the fairies.

The good priest begs her not to forsake her faithful young husband; but the fairy wins, and, leaving a dead bride in the cottage, bears away the living bride to a land where —

> "The fairies dance in a place apart,
> Shaking their milk-white feet in a ring,
> Tossing their milk-white arms in the air;
> For they have heard the wind laugh and murmur and sing
> Of a land where even the old are fair,
> And even the wise are merry of tongue."[1]

Patriotic love for Ireland is the very breath of *Cathleen ni Hoolihan* (1902), a one-act prose play in which Cathleen symbolizes Ireland. *The Shadowy Waters* (1900) and *Deirdre* (1907) are more poetic than dramatic. The first of these with the mysterious harper, the far-sailing into unknown seas, the parting with everything but the loved one, shows Yeats in his deeply mystical mood. In *Deirdre* is dramatized part of a popular legend of the great queen by that name, who was too beautiful for happiness. She has seven long years of joy and then accepts her fate in the calm, triumphant way of the old heroic times.

Yeats's plays reflect the childlike superstitions and lively imagination of his country. He loves the fairies, the dreams of eternal youth, the symbolizing of things of the spirit by lovely things of earth. His plays are poetical, fanciful, and romantic.

John Millington Synge. — One of the most notable of the Irish writers, J. M. Synge, was born near Dublin in 1871 and died in that city in 1909. His brief span of life has yielded only scanty biographical data. He came of an old Wicklow family; he was graduated from Trinity College, Dublin; afterwards he wandered through much of Europe, finally settling in France.

[1] Printed by permission of The Macmillan Company.

In 1899, William Butler Yeats discovered him in Paris, a "man all folded up in brooding intellect," writing essays on French authors, — on Molière, for example, from whom he learned the trick of characterization; on Racine, who taught him concentration; on Rabelais, who infected him with love of deep laughter. Yeats, suspecting that Synge could be an original writer as well as an interpreter of others, persuaded him to go back to Ireland, to the Aran Islands, off Galway. Synge discovered there a lost kingdom of the imagination, a place where spontaneous feeling and primitive imagination had not been repressed by the outside world's customs and discipline, and where the constant voice of the ocean, the touch of the mysterious, all-embracing mist, and the gleam of the star through a rift in the clouds banished all sense of difference between the natural and the supernatural.

When Synge died in his thirty-eighth year, he had written only six short plays, all between 1903 and 1909. Two of these, *In the Shadow of the Glen* and *Riders to the Sea*, contain only one act. *The Tinker's Wedding* has two acts, and the rest are three-act plays.

In the Shadow of the Glen, *Riders to the Sea*, and *The Well of the Saints*, produced respectively in 1903, 1904, and 1905, show that Synge came at once into full possession of his dramatic power. Even in his earliest written play, *The Well of the Saints*, we find a style stripped of superfluous verbiage and vibrant with emotion. *In the Shadow of the Glen*, his first staged play, consumes only a half hour. The scene is laid in a cabin far off in a lonely glen, and the four actors, — a woman oppressed by loneliness, an unfeeling husband who feigns death, and two visitors, — make a singularly well-knit impressive drama.

Riders to the Sea has been pronounced the greatest drama of the modern Celtic school. Some critics consider this the most significant tragedy produced in English since Shakespeare. Simple and impressive as a Greek tragedy, it has for its central figure an old mother whose husband and five sons have been lost at sea. The simple but poignant feeling of the drama focuses on the death of Maurya's sixth and last son, Bartley. This tragic episode, simply presented, touches the depths of human sympathy. In old Maurya, Synge created an impressive figure of what Macbeth calls "rooted sorrow."

The Playboy of the Western World, produced first in 1907, is a three-act play. It is as fantastically humorous as the *Riders to the Sea* is tragical. Dread of his father ties this peasant to his stupid toil. A fearful deed frees the youth and throws him into the company of the lovely maiden, Pegeen, and admiring friends. The latent poetry and wild joy of living awake in him, and, under the spur of praise, he performs great feats. He who had never before dared to face girls, makes such love to Pegeen that poesy itself seems to be talking. The Playboy is one of the wildest conceptions of character in modern drama. His very extravagance compels interest. Pegeen is a fitting sweetheart for him. Her father is a stalwart figure, possessing a shrewd philosophy and rare strength of speech, as "fully flavored as nut or apple." Some critics object to such a boisterous play, but they should remember that it is intended to be an extravagant peasant fantasia.

Deirdre of the Sorrows, another three-act play, produced

first in 1910, tells the story of the beautiful princess Deirdre, of her isolated young life, and her seven years of perfect union with her lover Naisi. When her lover is slain, this true and tender queen of the North loosens the knot of life to accompany him.

Synge belongs in the first rank of modern dramatists. The forty Irish characters that he has created reveal the basal elements of universal human nature. His purpose is like Shakespeare's, — to reveal throbbing life, not to talk in his own person, nor to discuss problems. Synge has dramatized the primal hope, fear, sorrow, and loneliness of life. Although his plays are written in prose and have the distinctive flavor of his lowly characters, yet a recent critic justly says that Synge "for the first time sets English dramatic prose to a rhythm as noble as the rhythms of blank verse."

SUMMARY

The twentieth century shows two main lines of development, — the realistic and the romantic. The two leading essayists of the period, A. C. Benson and G. K. Chesterton, are both idealists and champions of religious faith.

Among the novelists, Conrad tells impressive stories of distant seas and shores; Bennett's strongest fiction gives realistic pictures of life in English industrial towns; Galsworthy's novels present the problems that affect the upper class of Englishmen; Wells writes scientific romances and sociological novels.

Some of the best poetry, full of the fascination of a dreamy far-off world, has been written by the Celtic poets, Yeats, Russell, and Fiona Macleod. Masefield and Gibson have produced much realistic verse about the life of the common toiler. Noyes has written *Drake*, a romantic epic, and a large amount of graceful lyrical verse, in some of which there is much poetic beauty.

The most distinctive work of recent times has been in the field of the drama. Pinero has improved its technique; Shaw has given it remarkable conversational brilliancy; Barrie has brought to it fancy and humor and sweetness; Galsworthy has used it to present social problems; Phillips has tried to restore to it the Elizabethan poetic spirit. The Celtic dramatists form a separate school. Lady Gregory, Yeats, and Synge have all written plays based on Irish life, folklore, or mythology. The plays of Synge, the greatest member of the group, reveal the universal primitive emotions of human beings.

CONCLUSION

Three distinctive moral influences in English literature specially impress us, — the call to strenuous manhood: —

> ". . . this thing is God,
> To be man with thy might,"

the increasing sympathy with all earth's children: —

> "Ye blessed creatures, I have heard the call,
> Ye to each other make,"

and the persistent expression of Anglo-Saxon faith. As we pause in our study, we may hear in the twentieth-century song of Alfred Noyes, the echo of the music from the loom of the Infinite Weaver: —

> "Under the breath of laughter, deep in the tide of tears,
> I hear the loom of the Weaver that weaves the Web of Years."[1]

REFERENCE FOR FURTHER STUDY

Kennedy's *English Literature*, 1880–1895 (Shaw, Wells, Fiona Macleod, Yeats).

[1] Printed by permission of The Macmillan Company.

Kelman's *Mr. Chesterton's Point of View* (in *Among Famous Books*).
Cooper's *Some English Story Tellers*.
Conrad's *A Personal Record*.
Phelps's *Essays on Modern Novelists* (De Morgan).
Yeats's *Celtic Twilight*.
Figgis's *Studies and Appreciations* (*Mr. W. B. Yeats's Poetry. The Art of J. M. Synge*).
More's *Drift of Romanticism* (Fiona Macleod).
Borsa's *The English Stage of To-day*.
Jones's (Henry Arthur) *The Foundation of a National Drama: A Collection of Essays, Lectures, and Speeches, Delivered and Written in the Years 1896–1912*.
Hamilton's *The Theory of the Theater*.
Hunt's *The Play of To-day*.
Hale's *Dramatists of To-day*.
Henderson's *George Bernard Shaw: His Life and Works*, 2 vols.
Chesterton's *George Bernard Shaw*.
Weygandt's *Irish Plays and Playwrights* (excellent).
Krans's *William Butler Yeats and the Irish Literary Revival*.
Howe's *J. M. Synge: A Critical Study*.
Yeats's *J. M. Synge and the Ireland of His Time* (in *The Cutting of an Agate*, 1912).
Bickley's *J. M. Synge and the Irish Dramatic Movement*.
Elton's *Living Irish Literature* (in *Modern Studies*).

SUGGESTED READINGS WITH QUESTIONS AND SUGGESTIONS

Essays. — From A. C. Benson, read one of these collections of essays: *The Altar Fire, Beside Still Waters, Thy Rod and Thy Staff*, and one or more of these biographies: *Tennyson, John Ruskin, Rossetti* (E. M. L.), *Walter Pater* (E. M. L.); from Chesterton, one of these collections of essays: *Varied Types, Heretics, Orthodoxy*, and one or more of these biographies: *George Bernard Shaw, Charles Dickens, Robert Browning* (E.M. L.). For other twentieth-century essays, see the preceding bibliography and the paragraph following this.

The Novel. — From Conrad, read *Youth, Typhoon, Lord Jim*; from Bennett, *The Old Wives' Tale, Clayhanger*; from Galsworthy, *The Man of Property, The Patrician*; from Wells, *The Time Machine*,

Kipps, The Future in America (essay); from Phillpotts, *Children of the Mist, Demeter's Daughter*; from Hewlett, *Life and Death of Richard Yea and Nay, The Stooping Lady*; from Quiller-Couch, *The Splendid Spur, The Delectable Duchy*; from De Morgan, *Joseph Vance, Somehow Good*; from Locke, *The Beloved Vagabond, The Adventures of Aristide Pujol*; from Zangwill, *The Children of the Ghetto, The Melting Pot* (play).

Poetry. — From *The Poetical Works of William B. Yeats* (Macmillan), read *The Wanderings of Oisin, The Lake Isle of Innisfree, The Hosting of the Sidhe*; from George W. Russell's *The Divine Vision and Other Poems* (Macmillan), *The Gates of Dreamland, The Master Singer, Beauty, The Call of the Sidhe, The Voice of the Waters*; from Fiona Macleod's *Poems and Dramas* (Duffield), *The Vision, The Lonely Hunter, The Rose of Flame*; from Masefield, the part of *Dauber* describing the rounding of Cape Horn, beginning p. 119, in *The Story of a Round-House* (Macmillan); from Gibson's *Fires* (Macmillan), *The Crane, The Machine*; from Noyes's *Poems* (Macmillan, 1906), *The Song of Re-Birth, The Barrel Organ, Forty Singing Seamen, The Highwayman*; Book II from his *Drake: An English Epic* (Stokes).

The Drama. — From Jones, read *The Manœuvers of Jane, Mrs. Dane's Defence* (Samuel French); from Pinero, *The Amazons, The School Mistress,* or *Sweet Lavender* (W. H. Baker); from Shaw's *Plays Pleasant and Unpleasant* (Brentano), *Candida, You Never Can Tell, Arms and the Man*; from Barrie, *Peter Pan, What Every Woman Knows*; from Galsworthy, *Strife, Joy, The Little Dream*; from Phillips, *Marpessa* (poem), *Ulysses* (Macmillan), *Herod*; from Lady Gregory's, *Seven Short Plays* (Putnam), *The Gaol Gate, Spreading the News*; from her *New Comedies* (Putnam, 1913), *McDonough's Wife, The Bogie Men*; from Yeats's *Poetical Works,* Vol. II. (Macmillan), *The Land of Heart's Desire, Countess Cathleen*; from Synge, *Riders to the Sea, The Playboy of the Western World, Deirdre of the Sorrows* (John W. Luce).

Questions and Suggestions. — Stevenson's *The Home Book of Verse* and *The Oxford Book of Victorian Verse* contain selections from a number of the poets. McCarthy's *Irish Literature,* 10 vols., gives selections from work written prior to 1904. The majority of the indicated readings can be found only in the original works of the authors.

Give an outline of the most important thoughts from one essay and one biography, by both Benson and Chesterton.

What distinctive subject matter do you find in each of the novelists? How do some reflect the spirit of the age?

What are the chief characteristics of each of the poets? What does the phrase "Celtic Renaissance" signify?

In brief, what had the drama accomplished from the time of the closing of the theaters in 1642 to 1890? What distinctive contributions to the modern drama have Pinero, Shaw, and Barrie made? Describe the work of Lady Gregory, Yeats, and Synge. In what does Synge's special power consist?

SUPPLEMENTARY LIST OF AUTHORS AND THEIR CHIEF WORKS

1400-1558

John Lydgate (1370?-1451?): *Falls of Princes.* Thomas Occleve (1370?-1450?): *Mother of God; Governail of Princes.* Sir John Fortescue (1394?-1476?): *Difference between an Absolute and Limited Monarchy. The Paston Letters* (1422-1509). Stephen Hawes (d. 1523?): *Pastime of Pleasure.* John Skelton (1460?-1529): *Bowge of Court; Philip Sparrow.* Alex. Barclay (1475?-1552): *Ship of Fools.* Sir Thomas More (1478-1535): *Utopia; History of Edward V. and Richard III.* Hugh Latimer (1485?-1555): *Sermon on the Ploughers.* Sir David Lindsay (1490-1555): *Satire of the Three Estates.*

1558-1603

John Knox (1505-1572): *Admonition; History of the Reformation of Religion within the Realm of Scotland; Sermons.* George Puttenham (d. 1590?): *Art of English Poesie.* Edward Dyer (1550?-1607): *My Mind to Me a Kingdom Is.* Samuel Daniel (1562-1619): *The Complaint of Rosamund; A Defence of Rhyme* (prose). Fulke Greville (Lord Brooke, 1554-1628): *Caelica.* Stephen Gosson (1555-1624): *The School of Abuse.* George Gascoigne (1525?-1577): *The Steele Glas.* William Warner (1558?-1609): *Albion's England.*

1603-1660

Prose Writers. — Robert Burton (1577-1640): *The Anatomy of Melancholy.* John Selden (1584-1654): *Table Talk.* Richard Baxter (1615-1691): *The Saints' Everlasting Rest.*

Poets and Dramatists. — Phineas Fletcher (1582-1650?): *The Purple Island.* William Drummond (1585-1649): *Sonnets; The*

Cypresse Grove (prose). Giles Fletcher (1588?–1623): *Christ's Victory and Triumph.* George Wither (1588–1667): *Juvenilia.* William Browne (1591–1643?) *Britannia's Pastorals.* Sir William D'Avenant (1606–1668): *Gondibert.* Edmund Waller (1606–1687): *Poems; Song*—"Go, lovely Rose." Richard Crashaw (1613?–1649): *Steps to the Temple; The Delights of the Muses.* Sir John Denham (1615–1669): *Cooper's Hill.* Abraham Cowley (1618–1667): *Anacreontiques.* Andrew Marvell (1621–1678): *The Garden.*

1660-1740

Dramatists of the Restoration. — Sir William D'Avenant (1606–1668): *Love and Honor.* George Etherege (1635?–1691?): *The Man of Mode.* William Wycherley (1640–1715): *The Plain Dealer.* Thomas Shadwell (1642?–1692): *Epsom Wells.* Thomas Otway (1652–1685): *Venice Preserved.* John Vanbrugh (1666?–1726): *The Confederacy.* Colley Cibber (1671–1757): *The Careless Husband.* George Farquhar (1678–1707): *The Beaux' Stratagem.*

Prose Writers. — Sir William Temple (1628–1699): *Essays.* Isaac Barrow (1630–1677): *Sermons.* Robert South (1634–1716): *Sermons.* Richard Bentley (1662–1742): *Epistles of Phalaris.* Gilbert Burnet (1643–1715): *History of My Own Time.* Francis Atterbury (1662–1732): *Sermons.* John Arbuthnot (1667–1735): *The History of John Bull.* Lord Bolingbroke (1678–1751): *Letter to Sir William Windham.* Bishop Berkeley (1685–1753): *Alciphron or the Minute Philosopher.* Lady Mary Wortley Montagu (1689–1762): *Letters.* Bishop Butler (1692–1752): *Analogy of Natural and Revealed Religion.* William Warburton (1698–1779): *The Divine Legation of Moses.*

Poets. — Matthew Prior (1664–1721): *Shorter Poems.* Isaac Watts (1673–1748): *Psalms and Hymns.* Thomas Parnell (1679–1718): *A Night-Piece on Death; The Hermit.* John Gay (1685–1732): *Fables; The Beggar's Opera.* Allan Ramsay (1686–1758): *The Gentle Shepherd.* John Dyer (1700?–1758): *Grongar Hill.*

1740-1780

Prose Writers. — Gilbert White (1720–1793): *Natural History of Selborne.* William Robertson (1721–1793): *History of the Reign of Charles V.* Adam Smith (1723–1790): *Wealth of Nations.* Sir Joshua Reynolds (1723–1792): *Discourses on Painting.* Thomas Warton (1728–1790): *History of English Poetry.* Sir Philip Francis (1740–1818): *Letters of Junius.* Fanny Burney (1752–1840): *Evelina.*

Poets. — Edward Young (1681–1765): *Night Thoughts.* Charles Wesley (1708–1788): *Hymns.* Mark Akenside (1721–1770): *Pleasures of the Imagination.* James Beattie (1735–1803): *The Minstrel.* Robert Fergusson (1750–1774): *Braid Claith; Ode to the Gowdspink.*

1780-1837

Philosophers. — William Paley (1743–1805): *Natural Theology.* Jeremy Bentham (1748–1832): *Principles of Morals and Legislation.* William Godwin (1756–1836): *Inquiry concerning Political Justice.* Thomas Robert Malthus (1766–1834): *Essay on the Principle of Population.* David Ricardo (1772–1823): *Principles of Political Economy.* James Mill (1773–1836): *Analysis of the Human Mind.*

Historians. — John Lingard (1771–1851): *History of England.* Henry Hallam (1777–1859): *Constitutional History of England.* Sir William Napier (1785–1860): *History of the Peninsular War.*

Essayists. — William Cobbett (1762–1835): *Rural Rides in England.* Sydney Smith (1771–1845): *Letters of Peter Plymley.* Francis Jeffrey (1773–1850): *Essays.* John Wilson (1785–1854): *Noctes Ambrosianæ.* John Gibson Lockhart (1794–1854): *Life of Sir Walter Scott.*

Novelists and Dramatists. — William Beckford (1759–1844): *Vathek.* Maria Edgeworth (1767–1849): *Castle Rackrent.* Jane Porter (1776–1850): *Scottish Chiefs.* John Galt (1779–1839): *The Annals of the Parish.* James Sheridan Knowles (1784–1862): *The Hunchback; The Love Chase.* Thomas Love

Peacock (1785–1866): *Nightmare Abbey.* Mary Russell Mitford (1787–1855): *Our Village.*

Poets. — George Crabbe (1754–1832): *The Borough.* Joanna Baillie (1762–1851): *Poems.* James Hogg (1770–1835): *Queen's Wake.* Thomas Campbell (1777–1844): *The Pleasures of Hope.* Thomas Moore (1779–1852): *Irish Melodies; Lalla Rookh.* Ebenezer Elliott (1781–1849): *Corn-Law Rhymes.* Bryan W. Procter (1787–1874): *English Songs.* John Keble (1792–1866): *The Christian Year.* Felicia Hemans (1793–1835): *Songs of the Affections.* Thomas Hood (1799–1845): *The Song of the Shirt: The Bridge of Sighs.* Winthrop Praed (1802–1839): *The Season; The Letter of Advice.* Thomas Beddoes (1803–1849): *Lyrics* from *Death's Jest Book* and from *The Bride's Tragedy.*

1837-1900

Philosophers and Scientists. — Sir William Hamilton (1788–1856): *Lectures on Metaphysics and Logic.* Michael Faraday (1791–1867): *Experimental Researches.* Sir Charles Lyell (1797–1875): *Principles of Geology; Antiquity of Man.* John Stuart Mill (1806–1873): *System of Logic; Utilitarianism.* George Henry Lewes (1817–1878): *A Biographical History of Philosophy; Problems of Life and Mind.* Sir Henry Maine (1822–1888): *Ancient Law; Village Communities.*

Historians. — Henry Hart Milman (1791–1868): *History of Latin Christianity down to the Death of Pope Nicholas V.* George Grote (1794–1871): *History of Greece.* James Anthony Froude (1818–1894): *History of England from the Fall of Wolsey to the Defeat of the Spanish Armada.* Henry Thomas Buckle (1821–1862): *History of Civilization.* Edward Augustus Freeman (1823–1892): *The History of the Norman Conquest.* William Stubbs (1825–1901): *The Constitutional History of England in its Origin and Development.* Samuel Rawson Gardiner (1829–1902): *History of England from the Accession of James I. to the Outbreak of Civil War,* 1603–1642; *History of the Great Civil War,* 1642–1649; *History of the Commonwealth and the Protectorate,* 1649–

1660. Justin M'Carthy (1830-1912): *A History of Our Own Times*. John Richard Green (1837-1883): *A Short History of the English People*. William Edward Hartpole Lecky (1838-1903): *History of England in the Eighteenth Century*. James Bryce (1838-): *The Holy Roman Empire; The American Commonwealth*. Rt. Rev. Abbot Gasquet, D.D., O.S.B. (1846-): *Henry VIII and the English Monasteries; The Greater Abbeys of England*. Wilfrid Ward (1856-): *Aubrey de Vere; Life and Times of Cardinal Newman*.

Essayists and Critics. — George Borrow (1803-1881): *The Bible in Spain; Lavengro*. Walter Bagehot (1826-1877): *Literary Studies; The English Constitution*. Leslie Stephen (1832-1904): *Hours in a Library; History of English Thought in the Eighteenth Century*. John Morley (1838-): *Studies in Literature; Edmund Burke; Life of Gladstone*. John Addington Symonds (1840-1893): *The History of the Renaissance in Italy*. Austin Dobson (1840-): *Eighteenth Century Vignettes; Henry Fielding, Samuel Richardson, Oliver Goldsmith;* also *Collected Poems*. Edward Dowden (1843-1913): *Shakespeare, His Mind and Art; Life of Shelley; Studies in Literature*, 1789-1877. Andrew Lang (1844-1912): *Letters to Dead Authors; Essays in Little; The Iliad in English Prose* (assisted by Leaf and Myers); also *Ballads and Lyrics of old France*. Augustine Birrell (1850-): *Obiter Dicta; Men, Women, and Books; In the Name of the Bodleian*. A. C. Bradley (1851-): *Shakespearean Tragedy; Oxford Lectures on Poetry*. Alice Meynell (1855-): *The Rhythm of Life; The Spirit of Place;* also *Collected Poems*. William Archer (1856-): *Poets of the Younger Generation; Masks or Faces: A Study in the Psychology of Acting*. John W. Mackail (1859-): *The Springs of Helicon; Life of William Morris*.

Novelists. — Wilkie Collins (1824-1889): *The Moonstone*. Dinah Maria Craik (1826-1877): *John Halifax, Gentleman*. Charles L. Dodgson (Lewis Carroll, 1832-1898): *Alice in Wonderland; Through the Looking Glass*. Joseph H. Shorthouse (1834-

1903): *John Inglesant.* Walter Besant (1836–1901): *All Sorts and Conditions of Men.* William Black (1841–1898): *A Daughter of Heth.* Canon W. Barry, D.D. (1849–   ): *The Two Standards.* Mrs. Humphry Ward (1851–   ): *Marcella.* Canon P. A. Sheehan, D.D. (1852–   ): *My New Curate; The Queen's Fillet.* Hall Caine (1853–   ): *The Manxman.* Rider Haggard (1856–   ): *King Solomon's Mines.* George Gissing (1857–1903): *New Grub Street; The Private Papers of Henry Ryecroft.* John Ayscough (Rt. Rev. Mgr. Bicherstaffe-Drew, 1858–   ): *Marotz.* Kenneth Grahame (1859–   ): *The Golden Age; Dream Days.* A. Conan Doyle (1859–   ): *The White Company; Adventures of Sherlock Holmes.* R. H. Benson (1871–   ): *By What Authority; The Queen's Tragedy.* Mrs. Wilfrid Ward: *Great Possessions.*

Poets. — Richard H. Barham (1788–1845): *Ingoldsby Legends.* James C. Mangan (1803–1849): *Selected Poems.* Edward Fitzgerald (1809–1883): *Rubaiyat of Omar Khayyam* (translation). Aubrey de Vere (1814–1902): *Irish Odes.* Coventry Patmore (1823–1896): *The Angel in the House; Amelia.* Sidney Dobell (1824–1874): *The Roman; Balder.* Adelaide Anne Procter (1825–1864): *Legends and Lyrics.* Jean Ingelow (1830–1897): *Poems.* Edwin Arnold (1832–1904): *The Light of Asia.* Lewis Morris (1833–1907): *Epic of Hades.* James Thompson (1834–1882): *The City of Dreadful Night.* J. B. L. Warren (Lord de Tabley, 1835–1895): *Poems: Dramatic and Lyrical.* Alfred Austin (1835–1913, appointed poet-laureate in 1896): *English Lyrics,* edited by William Watson. Theodore Watts-Dunton (1832–   ): *The Coming of Love.* Philip Bourke Marston (1850–1887): *Song-Tide and Other Poems; Wind Voices.* Oscar Wilde (1854–1900): *Ave Imperatrix; The Ballad of Reading Gaol; De Profundis* (prose).

1900–

Essayists. — Vernon Lee (Violet Paget, 1857–   ): *The Enchanted Woods and Other Essays; The Sentimental Traveler.*

Lawrence Pearsall Jacks (1860–   ): *Mad Shepherds, und Other Human Studies*. Arthur Symons (1865–   ): *William Blake; The Romantic Movement in English Poetry*. Edward Verrall Lucas (1868–   ): *Life of Charles Lamb; Old Lamps for New;* also the stories *Over Bemerton's* and *Mr. Ingleside*. Hilaire Belloc (1870–   ): *On Everything*.

Novelists.—Justin Huntley M'Carthy (1860–   ): *The Proud Prince; If I Were King.* W. W. Jacobs (1863–   ): *Many Cargoes; Ship's Company.* Anthony Hope Hawkins (Anthony Hope, 1863–   ): *The Prisoner of Zenda; Rupert of Hentzau.* Marie Corelli (1864–   ): *Thelma; Ardath.* Robert S. Hichens (1864–   ): *The Garden of Allah.* G. W. Birmingham (Rev. J. O. Hannay, 1865–   ): *Spanish Gold.* Seumas Macmanus (1870–   ): *The Chimney Corner; Donegal Fairy Stories.* J. C. Snaith (1876–   ): *Araminta; Broke of Covenden.* May Sinclair: *The Divine Fire.*

Poets.—A. E. Housman (1859–   ): *A Shropshire Lad.* Katherine Tynan Hinkson (1861–   ): *Collected Poems; New Poems* (1911). Arthur Christopher Benson (1862–   ): *Collected Poems; Paul The Minstrel.* Henry Newbolt (1862–   ): *Admirals All.* Herbert Trench (1865–   ): *Deirdre Wedded and Nineteen Other Poems; Collected Poems.* Ethna Carberry (1866–1902): *The Passing of the Gael.* Richard Le Gallienne (1866–   ): *Robert Louis Stevenson and Other Poems; Attitudes and Avowals* (essays); *The End of the Rainbow* (stories). Lionel Johnson (1867–1902): *Poems.* Lawrence Binyon (1869–   ): *London Visions; Atilla* (poetic drama). Nora Hopper Chesson (1871–1906): *Under Quicken Boughs.* Dora Sigerson Shorter (1873–   ): *Collected Poems.* John Drinkwater (1882–   ): *Poems of Love and Death; King Cophetua.* Richard Middleton (1882–1911): *Poems and Songs.* Lascelles Abercrombie: *Interludes.* James Stephens: *Hill of Vision; Crock of Gold* (prose fiction). T. Sturge Moore: *Aphrodite against Artemis; Poems.*

Celtic Dramatists.—George Moore (1853–   ): *The Bend-*

ing of the Bough. Edward Martyn (1859-   ): *The Heather Field.* William Boyle: *The Building Fund.* Padric Colum: *Thomas Muskerry; The Fiddler's House.* Lennox Robinson: *Patriots.* Rutherford Mayne: *The Turn of the Road.* H. Granville Barker (English dramatist, 1877-   ): *The Voysey Inheritance.*

INDEX

Diacritical marks. — VOWELS: ā in lāte, ă in făt, â in câre, ä in fär, ạ in fạll, ȧ in ȧsk; ē in mē, ĕ in mĕt, ẹ in vẹil, ẽ in tẽrm, ê in thêre; ī in fīne, ĭ in tĭn, ï in police; ō in nōte, ŏ in nŏt, ô in fôr, ǫ in wǫlf; ū in tūne, ŭ in nŭt, ṳ in rṳde, u̧ in fu̧ll; ў in hў̆mn. CONSONANTS: ç in çent, e in ean; g̑ in g̑em, g̅ in g̅et; s̱ in has̱; ŧh in wiŧh.

	PAGE
Abercrombie, Lascelles (lä-sĕl')	631
Ab'sa-lom and A-chit'o-phel	268
Abt Vogler (äpt fō'glĕr)	546, 553
Actors, in early plays	149
in Elizabethan theater	165
Adam Bede	512, 513
Addison, Joseph, collaborates with Steele	287
incidental references to	260, 290, 294, 300, 474, 508, 510
life of	285
references on	301
suggested readings in	302
works of	287–292
Admirable Crichton, The	610
Ad-o-nā'is	422, 429, 558
Advancement of Learning	132
Adventures of Harry Richmond	528
Ælf'ric	46
Aids to Reflection	405
Akenside, Mark	627
Alastor	420, 425
Alchemist, The	202, 204
Alexander's Feast	270
Alfred, King	44
Alice-for-Short	595
All for Love	269
Alysoun	71
Amazing Marriage, The	528
Amazons, The	607
Amelia	323
American Taxation, Speech on	330
Amorists	114
Ancient Mariner	359, 390, 401, 402
An'cren Riwle (rool)	69
Andrea (än-drā'ya) del Sar'to	546
An-dre-as	37
Anglo-Norman period and Chaucer's Age	53–98
characteristics of Normans	54
history	53
language	57
metrical romances	64
poets	67–73, 76–93
prose writers	66, 69, 73–76
references on	95
suggested readings and questions	96
summary	93

	PAGE
Anglo-Saxon Chronicle	47
Anglo-Saxon language	57–64
Anglo-Saxon period	7–52
history	14
home, migrations, and religion of Anglo-Saxons	11, 12
language	15
mission of English literature	8
poetry	16–43
prose	43–48
references on	50
subject matter and aim	7
suggested readings and questions	51
summary	48
Anglo-Saxons, earliest literature of	16
Annus Mirabilis (ăn'us mi-răb'i-lis)	266, 326
Antiquary, The	380
Apologia, Newman's	474
Apologie for Poetrie	123, 127
Ar'buth-not, John	626
Arcadia	123, 126
Archer, William	629
Ar-e-o-pa-git'i-ca	241
Arnold, Edwin	630
Arnold, Matthew, general characteristics of	539
incidental references to	107, 281, 455, 459, 461, 550, 577
life of	534
poetical works	535
prose works	537
quoted	260, 396, 433, 434
references on	579, 580
suggested readings in	584
Arnold, Thomas	534
Arthur, King	106
As'cham, Roger	123
Astræa Redux (as-trē'a rē'-duks)	267
As You Like It	184, 185, 190, 194
Atalanta in Calydon	565
Atterbury, Francis	626
Au'reng-zebe'	270
Austen, Jane, incidental references to	359, 441, 456
life and works of	382
references on	443
suggested readings in	445

633

634 INDEX

	PAGE
Austin, Alfred	462, 630
Autobiography, Franklin's	292
Ayscough, John	630
Bacon, Francis, incidental references to	123, 211, 255, 350
life of	128
references on	213
suggested readings in	215
works of	131
Bacon, Roger	56, 102
Bagehot, Walter	629
Baillie, Joanna	628
Balder Dead	537
Bale, John	19
Ballad of Agincourt	135
Ballads, English	312
in fifteenth century	110
Barchester Towers	457
Barclay, Alexander	625
Barham, Richard H.	630
Barker, H. Granville	632
Barnaby Rudge	499
Barrack Room Ballads	573
Barrie, incidental references to	457, 607, 610, 621
suggested readings in	582, 624
Barrow, Isaac	626
Barry, Canon W.	630
Battle of Bru'năn-burh	39
Battle of the Books	280
Baxter, Richard	625
Bĕat'tie, James	627
Beau'mont (bō'), Francis	137, 205, 212
Becket	560
Becket, Thomas à	85
Beckford, William	627
Beddoes, Thomas	628
Bede, *Ecclesiastical History*	31, 43
references on	50
suggested readings in	52
works of	43
Behn, Mrs. Aphra	318
Belloc, Hilaire	631
Bennett, Arnold	587, 590, 620
suggested readings in	622
Benson, Arthur Christopher	588, 620, 631
suggested readings in	623
Benson, R. H.	630
Bentham, Jeremy	358, 405, 442, 627
Bentley, Richard	626
Beowulf (bā'o-wulf)	24–30, 64
suggested readings in	51
Berke'ley, George	326, 626
Besant, Walter	630
Bible, King James version	223, 252
Tyndale's translation of	112
Wycliffe's translation of	75
Bickerstaff, Isaac	283, 287, 289
Bickerstaffe-Drew, Rt. Rev. Mgr.	630
Binyon, Lawrence	631
Bi-o-graph'i-a Lit-e-rā'ri-a	405
Birmingham, G. W. (Hanney, Rev. J. O.)	631
Birrell, Augustine	629
Black, William	630

	PAGE
Blackmore, Richard D.	457
suggested readings in	582
Blackwood's Edinburgh Magazine	362
Blake, William	354, 356, 357
references on	442
suggested readings in	443
Blank verse, in eighteenth century	308
introduction into England	114
Shakespeare's and Marlowe's use of	171
Bleak House	499
Blessed Damozel, The	464
Blot in the 'Scutcheon	548
Bol'ing-broķe, Lord	626
Bonduca	206
Book of Martyrs	123
Borrow, George	629
Boswell, James	342, 346, 469
Boy actors	166
Boyle, William	632
Bradley, Andrew	434
Brandes, Georg, quoted	416
Bret Harte	574
Bride of Lammermoor	380, 382
Bridges, Robert	460, 461
suggested readings in	586
Brontë, Charlotte	456
references for	579
suggested readings in	582
Brontë, Emily	456
Brooke, Stopford, quoted	36, 37, 38, 40, 42, 112
Brown, Charles Brockden	311
Browne, Sir Thomas	226
Browne, William	626
Browning, Elizabeth Barrett, life of	542
quoted	194
references on	580
suggested readings in	584
Browning, Robert, general characteristics of	551
incidental references to	9, 455, 458, 459, 534, 558, 567, 577, 606, 612
life of	540
optimistic philosophy of	550
references on	580
suggested readings in	584
works of	544–551
Brụt (Layamon's)	63, 67
Wace's	67
Bryce, James	629
Buckle, Henry Thomas	628
Bulwer Lytton	457
suggested readings in	582
Bunyan, general characteristics of	231
incidental references to	224, 252, 253
life of	228
references for	254
suggested readings in	255
works of	230
Burke, Edmund	330, 342, 346
references for	347
suggested readings in	350
Bur'net, Gilbert	626
Burney, Fanny	627
Burns, Robert, general characteristics of	373
incidental references to	353, 354, 441

INDEX

635

	PAGE
life of	367
love songs of	371, 372
poetic creed of	370
references on	443
suggested readings in	444
works of	370–373
Burton, Robert	625
Butler, Bishop	626
Butler, Samuel	256
Byron, Lord, compared with Shakespeare	415, 416
dramas of	410
general characteristics	414
incidental references to	146, 355, 371, 379, 425, 434, 540, 567
life of	406
references on	442, 443
suggested readings in	446
works of	409–414
Cǣd'mon	31–35
compared with Milton	33
Cǣd-mo'ni-an Cycle	31–35
Cain	410
Caine, Hall	630
Caliban upon Setebos	546
Camden, William	123
Campbell (căm'el), Thomas	628
Canterbury Tales	83–89
Carberry, Ethna	631
Ca-rew', Thomas	234, 235
suggested readings in	255
Car-lyle', Thomas, general characteristics of	485
incidental references to	331, 362, 380, 402, 455, 472, 488, 537, 539, 540, 558, 577
life of	477
quoted	380, 622
references on	578
Sartor Resartus	482, 483
suggested readings in	581
works of	480–487
Carols of fifteenth century	111
Carroll, Lewis	629
Castle of Indolence	309
Castle of O-trăn'to	311
Cathedrals, Gothic	55
Cato	286
Cavalier poets	234
Caxton, William	105
Celtic dramatists	614
Celtic imagery	42
Celtic Renaissance	597
Cenci (chen'chē), *The*	421
Cĕr-văn'tēs	316
Chapel Royal	154
Chapman, George	208
Charge of the Light Brigade	449
Chatterton, Thomas	312
suggested readings in	348
Chaucer, Geoffrey	80–93
Canterbury Tales	83–89
compared with Spenser	143
earlier poems of	82
incidental references to	57, 94, 97, 107, 324

	PAGE
influence on English language	93
life of	80
qualities of	89
quoted	66
references on	95
suggested readings in	97
Chaucer's age. See Anglo-Norman period.	
Chesson, Nora Hopper	631
Chester plays	148
Chesterton, Gilbert K.	588, 620
references on	622
suggested readings in	623
Childe Harold's Pilgrimage	407, 411
Child's Garden of Verse, A	521
Christ, Cynewulf's	36
Chris'ta-bel	403
Christmas Carol, A	506
Chronicle, The, Stow's	123
Chronicles of England, Ireland and Scotland	123, 187
Çibber, Colley	626
Citizen of the World	333
Clăr'en-don, Lord	225
Clarissa Harlowe	321
Classical couplet	343
Classic school	261, 268, 299, 309, 315, 343
Clive, Robert	305
Cloister and the Hearth	457
Cloud, The	422, 423
Clough (clŭf), Arthur Hugh	459
suggested readings in	586
Cobbett, William	627
Cole'ridge, Samuel Taylor, association with Wordsworth	390
general characteristics of	404
incidental references to	313, 323, 354, 357, 358, 361, 414, 425, 441, 442, 467, 482
life of	398
poetry of	402
prose of	404
quoted	11, 207
references on	442, 443
suggested readings in	445
Collier, Jeremy	264
Collins, Wilkie	629
suggested readings in	348
Collins, William	314, 316, 346
Collo'quium	47
Colombe's Birthday	548
Colum, Padric	632
Comedies, early	156
Comedy of Errors, The	185, 187, 193
Complete Angler	226
Co'mus	243
Conciliation with America, Burke's speech on	330
Conduct of the Understanding	259
Con-fes'sio A-man'tis	79
Confessions of an English Opium-Eater	436, 437
Congreve, William	263, 606
Conrad, Joseph	589, 620
references on	622
suggested readings in	623
Cooper, Frederic Taber, quoted	592
Corelli, Marie	631
Cornish, William	154, 155

INDEX

	PAGE
Cotter's Saturday Night	353, 367
Couplet, classical	261, 268, 299, 337, 343
"riming"	261
Court plays	154
Cov'en-try (kŭv') plays	148
Cowley, Abraham	626
Cowper, William, general characteristics of	366
incidental references to	354, 441
life of	363
references on	442, 443
suggested readings in	444
works of	364
Crabbe, George	628
Craik, Dinah Maria	629
Cranford	457
Cranmer's Bible	113
Crash'aw, Richard	236, 237, 255, 626
Critical writings, Addison's	290
Age of Romanticism	361
Arnold's	537, 539
Carlyle's	480, 481
Coleridge's	404
De Quincey's	438
Dryden's	268
Johnson's	345
Pope's	295
Swinburne's	566
Criticism, first essay on	127
Cromwell's Bible	113
Cross, John W.	512
Crossing the Bar	560, 562
Cry of the Children	543
Curse of Kehama	358
Cymbeline	67, 137, 186
Çȳn'e-wulf	35–38
Cynewulf Cycle	35–38
suggested readings in	52
Daniel Deronda	514
Daniel, Samuel	625
Darwin, Charles	452, 553, 576
D'ăv'en-ant, Sir William	626
David and Bathsabe	168
David Balfour	521
David Copperfield	499, 502
Davidson, John	461
suggested readings in	586
Deathe of Blanche the Duchesse	83
Decameron, framework of similar to *Canterbury Tales*	84
De-foe', Daniel, a journalist	273
incidental references to	300, 318
life of	271
references on	347
suggested readings in	302, 349
works of	273–276
Dekker, Thomas	209
Deloney, Thomas	123, 318
suggested readings in	349
De Morgan, William Frend	595
references on	622
suggested readings in	623
Denham, Sir John	626
Departmental Ditties	570
De Quincey, Thomas, general characteristics of	439

	PAGE
incidental references to	359, 361, 390, 441, 468
life of	435
references on	442, 443
suggested readings in	447
works of	437
Deserted Village, The	331, 335, 338
De Vere, Aubrey	630
Diana of the Crossways	526, 527
Diary, Evelyn's	256
Pepys's	263
Dickens, Charles, contrasted with Thackeray	508
general characteristics of	500
incidental references to	326, 456, 458, 577, 593, 595
life of	495
references on	579
suggested readings in	582
works of	498
Dictionary of the English Language, Johnson's	340
Didactic verse	269
Discovery of Guiana, The	123
Disdain Returned	235
Diurnall	273
Divine Vision, The	600
Dobell, Sidney	630
Dobson, Austin	462, 629
quoted	324, 338
suggested readings in	586
Dodgson, Charles L. (Lewis Carroll)	629
Dombey and Son	499
Don Ju'an	411, 412
Donne (don), John	137, 138
opposes sonnet	233
suggested readings in	215
Don Quix'ote (Span. pron. dōn kē-hō'tä)	316
Double Dealer, The	264
Doŭg'las, Gä'wain	109
Dover Beach	537
Dowden, Edward	629
quoted	195, 422, 501
Doyle, A. Conan	630
Dr. Faustus	170
Dr. Jekyll and Mr. Hyde	518
Drake: An English Epic	605, 621
Drama, English, and the Unities	156
actors in early	149
Beaumont and Fletcher in	205, 212
comedies, early	156
court plays	154
decline of	203
during Restoration	262
early religious	146
end of Elizabethan	210
interlude	155
Irish	614
Marlowe, founder of English	171
miracle and mystery plays	147
modern	606
morality plays	152
suggested readings in	216
See also Elizabethan Age, Jonson, Marlowe, Shakespeare, etc.	
Dramatic Lyrics, Browning's	542, 545

INDEX

Dramatic Romances and Lyrics, Browning's 545
Dramatic unities . . . 156, 172, 205
Dramatis Personæ 545
Drapier's Letters 284
Drayton, Michael 135
  suggested readings in 215
Dream Children 360
Dream of Fair Women, A . . 556, 563
Dream of Gerontius 475
Drinkwater, John 631
Drummond, William 625
Dryden, John, general characteristics of 271
  incidental references to 259, 262, 263, 300, 412, 612
  life of 265
  prose of 260, 267
  quoted 200
  references on 301
  suggested readings in . 301, 302, 348
  Spenser's influence on 146
  works of 260, 266–270
Duchess of Mäl'fi, The 209
Dun-bar', William 109
Dun'ci-ad 294, 298
Dyer, Edward 625
Dyer, John 626

Earthly Paradise 465
Edgeworth, Maria 627
Ed'in-burgh (-bŭr-ro) *Review* . . . 362
Edward II 170
Egoist, The 526
Eighteenth century, early literature. *See* Restoration period, etc.
Eighteenth century, later literature 304–350
  history 304
  literary characteristics 307
  novelists 311, 316–326, 336
  poets 309–316, 335
  prose writers 311, 316–345
  references on 347
  romanticism 307, 311, 312
  suggested readings and questions . 348
  summary 346
Elegy Written in a Country Churchyard 314
Elene 36
Eliot, George, general characteristics 514
  incidental references to 319, 453, 455, 456, 458, 485, 576, 577
  life of 510
  references on 579
  suggested readings in 583
  works of 512
Elizabeth, Queen 119
Elizabethan age 119–219
  history 119
  Jonson 199–210
  life of 121
  Marlowe 169–173
  minor dramatists 154–158, 167–169, 205–210
  miracle and mystery plays . 146–152
  morality plays 152

poetry (non-dramatic) . . . 134–146
presentation of Elizabethan plays 158–166
  prose writers 122–133
  references on 213
  Shakespeare 174–198
  suggested readings in 215
  summary 211
Elliott, Ebenezer 628
Emma 384
Endymion 430
England, origin of name of 11
English Humorists of the Eighteenth Century 326, 507, 508
English language, Chaucer's influence on 93
  emergence of modern 57–64
English literature, mission of . . . 8
  subject matter and aim of . . 7, 8
Epigrams, Watson's 461
Ep-i-psy-chĭd'i-on 422, 425
Epistle to Dr. Arbuthnot . . 294, 298
Ep-i-tha-lā'mi-on 140
Essay of Dramatic Poesy 268
Essay on Criticism 294, 295
Essay on Man 294, 297
Essays, Addison's 289
  Arnold's 455, 538
  Bacon's 129, 131
  Benson's 588
  Carlyle's 455, 480
  Chesterton's 588
  De Quincey's 439
  Goldsmith's 333
  Johnson's 340
  Lamb's 359, 360
  Macaulay's 455, 468
  Newman's 455
  Pater's 455
  Pope's 294
  Stevenson's 520
  Swinburne's 455
  Thackeray's 507
Essays in Criticism 538
Essays of E'li-a 359
Eth'er-ĕge, George 626
Ethical purposes, in literature. *See* Moral ideals
Eu'phu-es (ēz) 124
Euphuism 126
Evan Harrington 527
Eve of St. Agnes 431
Ev'e-lyn, John 256
Every Man in His Humor . . . 203
Excursion 393, 394
Ex'e-ter Book 19, 20, 22, 23
Expedition of Humphrey Clinker . 325

Fables, Ancient and Modern . . . 267
Fä'e-rie Queene . . . 140, 141, 309
Faithful Shepherdess 206
Familiar Studies of Men and Books . 520
Far From the Madding Crowd . 531, 532
Far Traveler, The 20
Fär'a-day, Michael 628
Far'quhar, George 626
Faustus, Dr. 170

INDEX

	PAGE
Fergusson, Robert	627
Field, Eugene	521
Fielding, Henry	309, 322, 324, 325, 326, 346, 508, 509
references on	347
suggested readings in	349
works of	323
Fight at Finnsburg	38
Fiona Macleod. *See* Sharp, William.	
Fitz-gĕr'ald, Edward	630
Fleet Street Eclogues	461
Fletcher, Giles	626
Fletcher, John	137, 205, 212
Fletcher, Phineas	625
Flower of Old Japan	603
Ford	210
Forest of Wild Thyme	604
Fors Cla-viḡ'e-ra	493
For'tes-cue, Sir John	625
Fortunes of Men	23
Four Georges	507, 508
Four P's	155
Fox, Charles James	342
Foxe, John	123
Fragments of Science	453
Francis, Sir Philip	627
Frankenstein	418
Franklin, Benjamin	292
Freeman, Edward Augustus	628
quoted	44, 329
French element in English	57–64
French Revolution, influence on literature	351, 389, 416
French Revolution (Carlyle's)	480, 483
Froude, James Anthony	628
Fuller, Thomas	225
Funeral Elegy	138
Galsworthy, John	592, 607, 611, 620
suggested readings in	623
Galt, John	627
Gammer Gurton's Needle	156
Gaol Gate	615
Gardiner, Samuel Rawson	628
Gardiner's Daughter, The	556
Găr'rick, David	342
Gas-coigne' (-coin'), George	625
Gas'kell, Elizabeth C.	457
suggested readings in	582
Gasquet, Rt. Rev. Abbot	629
Gates of Dreamland	597
Gă'wayne and the Green Knight	65
Gay, John	626
General reference list for English literature	6
Gentle Craft	123, 318
Geoffrey of Monmouth	66, 94, 96
Gib'bon, Edward	329, 342, 346, 349, 471, 474
quoted	296
suggested readings in	350
Gibson, Wilfrid	588, 602, 620
suggested readings in	623
Gissing, George	630
Gladstone, William E.	553
Gleeman	19
songs of	20–23
Globe Theater	158
Godwin, William	627
Goldsmith, Oliver, general characteristics of	337
incidental references to	210, 264, 342, 346, 510, 606
life of	331
quoted	341
references on	347
suggested readings in	348, 350
works of	331–338
Good-Natured Man, The	337
Gor'bo-duc	156
Gŏsse, Edmund, quoted	315, 326, 469
Gŏs'son, Stephen	625
Gower, John	79, 94, 97
suggested readings in	97
Grahame, Kenneth	630
Gray, Thomas	312, 314, 315, 346
references for	347
suggested readings in	348
Green, John Richard	629
Greene, Robert	124, 167, 169, 317, 318, 349
Gregory, Lady Augusta	599, 615, 621
suggested readings in	624
Gregory, Pope	45
Greville, Fulke (Lord Brooke)	625
Grote, George	628
Gulliver's Travels	276, 281, 284
Guy Mannering	380
Haggard, Rider	630
Hak'luyt, Richard	123
Hăl'lam, Arthur Henry	555, 557, 558, 627
Hamilton, Sir William	628
Hamlet	184, 185, 186, 187, 191, 195, 198
Handlyng Synne	72
Hard Times	499
Hardy, Thomas, general characteristics of	533
incidental references to	456, 458, 523, 577
life of	529
references on	579
suggested readings in	584
works of	531
Harleian, M.S.	70
Hawes, Stephen	625
Hawkins, Anthony Hope (Anthony Hope)	631
Hazlitt, William	361, 362
suggested readings in	448
Heart of Midlothian	380, 381
Hei'ne, Heinrich	25, 416, 538
Hĕm'ans, Felicia	628
Henley, W. E.	460
suggested readings in	586
Henry Esmond	506
Henry IV	184, 185, 187
Henry V	184, 185, 195
Henry VIII	205
Henryson, Robert	108
Herbert, George	236, 255
Hero and Leander	**171**

INDEX

	PAGE
Herod	613
Heroes and Hero Worship	481, 484
Herrick, Robert	234
suggested readings in	255
Hes-pĕr'i-des (-dēz)	234
Hewlett, Maurice	594
suggested readings in	623
Hey'wood, John	155
Heywood, Thomas	209
Hichens, Robert S.	631
Hilda Lessways	591
Hind and the Panther	270
Hinkson, Catherine Tynan	631
Historical prose	327
Historical Sketches, Newman's	476
History, English, Age of Romanticism	351
Anglo-Norman period	53
Anglo-Saxon period	14
Eighteenth century	256, 304
Elizabethan age	119
Puritan age	220
Renaissance	99
Restoration period	256
Victorian age	449
History of England, Hume's	328
Macaulay's	468–471
History of Friedrich II	481, 485
History of the Decline and Fall of the Roman Empire, The	329
History of the Great Rebellion	225
History of the Kings of Britain	66
History of the Reign of Henry VII	133
History of the World	225
History of the Worthies of England (Fuller's)	225
Hobbes, Thomas	224
Hogg, James	628
Hol'ins-hed, Raphael	124, 187
Holman-Hunt, William	463
Holy Dying	227
Holy Living	227
Holy War	231
Homer, Chapman's	208
Homer, Pope's translation of	292, 294, 296
Homeward Songs by the Way	600
Homilies	46
Hood, Thomas	603, 628
Hooker, Richard	123, 127, 211, 255, 268
references on	213
suggested readings in	215
Hope, Anthony (Hawkins)	631
Hor'ace, influence of	261
Hous of Fame	83
Housman, A. E.	631
Howells, William D., quoted	386
Hugo, Victor, quoted	307
Hume, David	326, 328, 346, 470
references on	347
suggested readings in	349
Humor, Addison's	291
Arnold's	540
Barrie's	610
Burns's	373
Carlyle's	486

	PAGE
Chaucer's	90
Cowper's	365, 367
De Quincey's	440
Dickens's	501, 502
Fielding's	323
Fuller's	215
Goldsmith's	338
Locke's	596
Meredith's	527, 528
Pope's	299
Sterne's	325
Swift's	283
Thackeray's	504, 505
Hundred Years' War	99
Hunt, Leigh (lē)	362, 363, 419
suggested readings in	448
Huxley, Thomas	453, 454
quoted	487, 561
Hyde, Dr. Douglas	615
Hydriota'phia	226
Hymns, Addison's	286
Hy-pe'ri-on	432
Ibsen, Henrik, influence of	606
Idea of a University	475
Ideals. See Moral ideals.	
Idler	340
Idylls of the King	556, 559, 597
Il Pen-se-ro'so	243
Iliad, Pope's translation of	292, 294, 296
Imaginary Conversations	361
In a Balcony	549
In Me-mo'ri-am	555, 557, 558, 562
In the South Seas	520
Induction (Sackville's)	157
In'ge-low, Jean	630
Inland Voyage	520
Interlude	155
Invention, age of	451
Irish drama	614
Irish National Theater	614
Isabella	432
I'van-hoe	55, 379
Jack of Newberry	318
Jacks, Lawrence Pearsall	631
Jacobs, W. W.	631
James I of Scotland	108
Jane Eyre	457
Jeffrey, Francis	627
Jew of Malta	170
John Gilpin	365
Johnson, Lionel	631
Johnson Samuel, Boswell's life of	342
converser and literary lawgiver	342
general characteristics of	344
incidental references to	292, 307, 315, 346, 355, 401, 474, 481
life of	338
quoted	293, 310, 311, 333, 334
references on	347
suggested readings in	350
works of	344, 345
Jonathan Wild the Great	323
Jones, Henry Arthur	607
suggested readings in	624

640 INDEX

	PAGE
Jonson, Ben, general characteristics of	205
incidental references to	129, 136, 137, 212, 605
life of	199
opposes sonnet	233
plays of	202
quoted	191, 196
references on	214
suggested readings in	215, 219
Joseph Andrews	323
Joseph Vance	595
Journal of the Plague Year	276
Journal to Stella	280
Jude the Obscure	533
Judith	39
Ju-li-an'a	36
Julius Cæsar	184, 185, 187
Jungle Books	450, 570, 571
Jury system, development of	55
Just So Stories	572
Kant	327
Keats, John, general characteristics	432
incidental references to	146, 244, 313, 354, 362, 422, 441, 453, 463, 540, 557
life of	426
poems of	429
references on	442, 443
suggested readings in	447
Kĕ'ble, John	628
Ken'il-worth	379
Kidnapped	521
Kim	573
King Lear	67, 185, 195
King of the Golden River, The	490
King's Quair, The	108
Kingsley, Charles	457, 474
suggested readings in	582
Kipling, Rudyard, general characteristics of	574
incidental references to	23, 450, 456, 458, 459, 534, 578
life of	568
Nobel prize awarded to	576
prose of	571
references on	579, 580
suggested readings in	586
verse of	573
Knighte's Tale, Chaucer's	88, 89
Knoblauch, Edward	591
Knowles, James Sheridan	627
Knox, John	625
Kubla Khan	403
Kyd, Thomas	169
Lady of the Lake	358, 377, 378
Lake Poets	358
L'Allegro (läl-lä'grō)	243
Lamb, Charles	359, 361, 441
quoted	208
references on	442, 443
suggested readings in	447
Lā'mi-a	432
Landor, Walter Savage	361, 362
suggested readings in	448
Lang, Andrew	335, 629

	PAGE
Läng'land, William	56, 76, 94, 97
references on	95
suggested readings in	95, 97
Language, new English	94
Languages, after Norman Conquest	57
Last Days of Pompeii	457
Lat'i-mer, Hugh	625
Lä'ya-mon	63, 67, 94
suggested readings in	96
Lay of the Last Minstrel	377
Lay Sermons, Huxley's	454
Lays of Ancient Rome	469
Lecky, William Edward Hartpole	629
Lectures on Art	492
Lectures on Shakespeare	405
Lee, Vernon (Violet Paget)	630
Le Gallienne, Richard	631
Legende of Good Women	83
Leviathan	224
Lew'es (-ĭs), George Henry	511, 628
Life and Death of Mr. Badman	231
Life of Johnson, Boswell's	469
Macaulay's	340, 342, 343
Life of Nelson	358
Light that Failed, The	573
Lindsay, Sir David	625
Lingard, John	627
Literary Club	342
Literary England	1–6
literary itinerary	2
references on	4
Literature, change in subject-matter after Restoration	259
childhood introduced into	354
definitions of	7, 8
influence of spirit of reform on	352, 353
Pre-Raphaelite movement	463–465
Reformation influences	112
Little Minister	457, 610
Little White Bird	610
Lives of the English Poets	293, 340, 342, 344, 345
Lives of the Saints	46
Locke, John	259
references on	301
Locke, William John	596
suggested readings in	623
Lockhart, John Gibson	627
Locksley Hall	556, 557
Locksley Hall Sixty Years After	560, 562
Lodge, Thomas	124, 127, 134, 167, 169, 317, 349
suggested readings in	215
London	340
Lord Ormont and His Aminta	528
Lorna Doone	457
Lounsbury, T. R., quoted	63, 93
Love lyrics	135
Love'lace, Richard	234, 236, 255
Love's Labor's Lost	186
Lōw'ell, James Russell, quoted	92, 295
Lucas, Edward Verrall	631
Lucrece	184
Luther, Martin	112
Lyç'i-das	243, 244, 558
Lydgate, John	625
Lyell, Sir Charles	628

INDEX

	PAGE
Lȳl'y, John . 123, 124, 139, 167, 168, 211, 255, 317	
references on	213
suggested readings in	215
Lyrical Ballads, Coleridge's	357, 405
Wordsworth's	357, 362, 390
Lyrical verse in Elizabethan age	134
Lytton, Edward Bulwer	457, 582
Macaulay, Thomas Babington, general characteristics of	471
History of England	468–471
incidental references to 268, 287, 340, 342, 455, 456, 476, 482, 537, 539, 577	
life of	466
quoted	140, 286
references on	578
suggested readings in	581
works of	468–471
Macbeth	184, 185, 187, 196
M'Carthy, Justin Huntley	629, 631
Mac Flecknoe	269
Mackail, John W.	629
Macleod, Fiona. *See* Sharp, William.	
Macmanus, Seumas	631
Macpherson, James	311
Magna Charta	55
Maid's Tragedy	206
Maine, Sir Henry	628
Mal'o-ry, Sir Thomas . 106, 115, 117, 255, 559, 597, 615	
Măl'thus, Thomas Robert . 357, 405, 442, 627	
Malthusian theorem	357
Mandeville, Sir John . 73, 94, 97, 255	
Manfred	410
Mangan, James C.	630
Mansfield Park	384
Marlowe, Christopher, general characteristics of	172
incidental references to . 136, 168,	

	PAGE
incidental references to . 456, 458, 565, 577	
life of	523
quoted	264
references on	579
suggested readings in	583
works of	525, 526
Metrical romances	64–66
Meynell, Alice	629
Michael	393, 396
Michaelmas Term	209
Middle Ages	102
Middlemarch	514
Middleton, Richard	631
Middleton, Thomas	208, 209
Midsummer Night's Dream	184, 185, 190, 194
Mill, James	358, 405, 442, 627
Mill, John Stuart	480, 628
Mill on the Floss	512, 513
Millais, John Everett	463, 490
Milman, Henry Hart	628
Milton, John, characteristics of poetry	247
compared with Shakespeare	247
incidental references to . 33, 114, 221, 252, 253, 268, 310, 314, 344, 348, 396, 422, 434, 461, 558, 567	
influence of *Paradise Lost*	250
life of	238
Macaulay's essay on	467
Paradise Lost	244
quoted	34
references on	254
Spenser's influence on	146
suggested readings in	254, 255
works of	241, 243, 244, 246, 251
Minstrelsy of the Scottish Border	376
Miracle plays	147
suggested readings in	217
Mitford, Mary Russell	628
Modern Painters	464, 491
Modest Proposal	284

INDEX

	PAGE
Morley, Henry, quoted	23, 34, 39, 40
Morley, John	629
Morris, Lewis	630
Morris, William	107, 465
references on	578
suggested readings in	580
Morte (môrt) *d'Ar'thur*	106, 556, 559, 597
Mourning Bride	264
Much Ado About Nothing	193, 194
Mysteries of Udolpho	312
Mystery plays	147
Nā′pi-er, Sir William	627
Nashe, Thomas	123, 167, 169, 317
suggested readings in	349
Nature, as depicted in Scottish poetry	108
Burns's, treatment of	372
Byron's, poetry of	411, 412
Chaucer's love of	91
Coleridge's treatment of	404
Cowper's poems of	366
Dunbar a student of	109
Gray's poetry of	314
growth of appreciation of	354
Keats's treatment of	432
poetry of	310
Ruskin's love of	488, 491, 493
Scott's treatment of	328
Shakespeare's treatment of	176
Shelley's treatment of	423
Tennyson's poetry of	561
Thomson's poetry of	310
Walton's love of	226, 227
Wordsworth's poetry of	391, 396
Navigations, Voyages, and Discoveries of the English Nation	123
Necessity of Atheism	418
New Atlantis	133
New Year's Eve	360
Newbolt, Henry	631
Newcomes, The	507
Newman, Cardinal John Henry, general characteristics of	474
life of	
references on	
suggested readings in	
works of	
"News books"	
"News letters"	

	PAGE
No′vum Or′ga-num	132
Noyes, Alfred	588, 603, 621, 622
suggested readings in	623
Nut-Brown Maid, The	111
O′bĕr-äm′mĕr-gau (-gou) Passion Play	147
Oc′cleve, Thomas	625
Ode on a Grecian Urn	432
Ode on the Passions	316
Ode to Evening	314
Ode to Mrs. Anne Killigrew	270
Ode to the West Wind	422, 424
Odyssey, Pope's translation of	294, 296
Of the Laws of Ecclesiastical Polity	123, 127
Old Bachelor, The	264
Old China	360
Old Curiosity Shop, The	502
Old Mortality	379
Oliver Twist	499
Olney Hymns	364
On the Morning of Christ's Nativity	243
On Translating Homer	535, 539
Ordeal of Richard Feverel	526
Origin of Species	452
Orm's *Or′mu-lum*	68
Oroonoko	318
O-ro′si-us (Alfred's)	45
Ossian (ŏsh′an)	311
Othello	185
Otway, Thomas	626
Our Mutual Friend	499
Palace of Art	553, 556, 557, 563
Paley, William	627
Pam′e-la	256, 321
Pandosto	123
Paracelsus	542
Paradise Lost	243, 248, 251
Paradise Regained	243, 246
Paraphrase, Caedmon's	31–35
Par′nell, Thomas	626
Passion Play at Oberammergau	147
Past and Present	486
	136
	455, 577
	579

INDEX

	PAGE		PAGE
Philosophical prose, of Puritan age	224	Recessional	574
Phœnix	37	References, historical and literary	50, 95,
Picaresque novel	169, 317	116, 213, 253, 300, 347, 442, 578, 622	
Pickwick Papers	497, 498	References for literary England	4
Piers Plowman	76, 97	Reflections on the Revolution in France	330
references on	95	Reformation	112, 120
suggested readings for	95, 97	Re-lig'i-o Lā'i-ci	270
Pilgrim's Progress	18, 230, 318	Religio Medici	226
Pinero, Sir Arthur Wing	606, 607, 621	Religion, effect of on literature	100, 115,
suggested readings in	624		453, 550
Pip'pā Passes	542, 549	Religious drama	146
Play of Noah's Flood	151	Rel'iques of Ancient English Poetry	312
Play of the Shepherds	151, 155	Reminiscences, Carlyle's	481
Playboy of the Western World	619	Renaissance	99–118
Plays, Pleasant and Unpleasant	609	causes and effects of the Renaissance	103
Plutarch's Lives	123, 187	culmination of	120
Poe, Edgar Allan, quoted	543	history	99
Poet, The	556	in Elizabeth's reign	119
Pope, Alexander, general characteristics of	298	influence on Chaucer	92
incidental references to	259, 261, 262,	invention of printing	105
300, 339, 348, 353, 362, 381, 412, 563		poets	108–112, 114
life of	292	prose writers	104, 106–108, 112, 113
references on	301, 442	references on	116
suggested readings in	303	suggested readings and questions	117
translation of Homer	292, 294, 296	summary	115
works of	293–298	Renaissance; Studies in Art and Poetry	456
Pope Gregory	45	Restoration period and early eighteenth-century literature	256–303
Porter, Jane	627	dramatists	262–264
Prāed, Winthrop	628	history	256
Præterita	488	poets	261, 265–270, 286, 292–300
Prelude, The	387, 389, 392, 393	prose writers	259–261, 271–292
Pre-Raphaelite movement	463, 493	references on	300
suggested readings in	580	suggested readings and questions	301
Pre-Raphaelitism	464	summary	299
Pride and Prejudice	384	Return of the Native	531
Princess, The	554, 557, 561	Review	273
Printing, invention of	105	Revolt of Islam	425
Prior, Matthew	626	Reynolds, G. F., quoted	160
Procter, Adelaide Anne	627	Reynolds, Sir Joshua	342, 627
Procter, Bryan W.	628	Rhoda Fleming	528
Pro-me'theūs Unbound	421, 425	Ri-car'do, David	627
Puritan age	220–255	Richard II	185
history	220	Richard III	184, 185
poets	233–252	Richardson, Samuel	256, 309, 320, 324,
prose writers	224–233, 241		325, 326, 346
references on	253	references on	347
suggested readings and questions	254	suggested readings in	349
summary	252	Ring and the Book	544, 547
Put'ten-ham, George	625	Rivals	210, 337
		Robert of Brunne	72, 96, 97
Quarterly Review	362	Robertson, William	627
Quiller-Couch (Cooch), Sir Arthur	595	Robin Hood	111
suggested readings in	623	Robinson Crusoe	273, 274
		Robinson, Lennox	632
Rabbi Ben Ezra	455, 551	Roderick Random	325
Radcliffe, Mrs. Anne	311	Romance, distinguished from modern novel	319
Ra'leigh, Sir Walter	121, 123, 140, 225, 605	Romance of the Forest	312
Rālph Royster Doyster	156	Romanticism	307, 315, 348, 351–449
Rambler, The	340	age of	351–449
Ramsay, Allan	626	appreciation of nature	354
Rape of the Lock	294, 295	history	351
Ras'se-las	340, 345	literary characteristics	353
Reade, Charles	457	poets	362–378, 386–435
suggested readings in	582	prose writers	357–363, 374–386, 398
Readings, suggestions for	59, 96, 117, 215,		436–440
254, 301, 348, 443, 580, 623			

INDEX

Romanticism, references on . . . 442
  suggested readings and questions . 443
  summary 440
Romaunt of the Rose 82
Romeo and Juliet . . . 185, 186, 187
Rŏm'o-la 513
Rosalynde . . . 123, 127, 169, 190
Ros-set'tĭ, Christina 465
Rossetti, Dante Gabriel . 463, 464, 565
  references on 578
Round Table 362
Rowley, Thomas 313
Rowley, William 209
Ruskin, John, art works of 491
  general characteristics of 493
  incidental references to . 455, 464, 472,
    539, 540, 577
  life of 488
  references on 579
  suggested readings in 582
  works of 491–493
Russell, George W. 597, 599, 620
  suggested readings in 623

Sackville, Thomas 156
Saintsbury, George, quoted 248, 250, 495
Samson Ag-o-nis'tes (-tēz) . . 243, 246
Sar'tor Re-sar'tus 478, 486
Satire, Addison's 289
  Carlyle's 486
  Dryden's 266, 268
  Fielding's 324
  Meredith's 529
  Pope's 294, 296, 298
  Swift's 280
  Thackeray's 506
Saul 546, 553
Saxon. *See* Anglo-Saxon.
Scenery, in early theater 163
Scenes of Clerical Life 512
Scholar-Gypsy 537
Scholemaster, The 123
School for Scandal 210, 327
School Mistress, The 607
Schoolmen 103
Science, age of 451
  influence on literature 452
Scop 19
  songs of 20–23
Scott, Sir Walter, general characteristics of 381
  incidental references to 312, 358, 359,
    371, 407, 441, 456, 469, 470, 522
  life of 374
  references on 442, 443
  suggested readings in 444
  works of 379–381
Seafarer, The 22
Seasons, The 310
Second Mrs. Tanqueray, The . . . 608
Selden, John 625
Sense and Sensibility 384
Sentimental Journey through France and Italy 325
Sentimental Tommy 458
Sesame (sĕs'a-mē) *and Lilies* . 490, 493
Seven Lamps of Architecture . . . 492

Shadwell, Thomas 269, 626
Shakespeare, William, amount and classification of work 184
  connection with London stage . . 179
  development as dramatist . . . 186
  general characteristics of . . . 190
  incidental references to 110, 114, 121,
    122, 124, 126, 137, 158, 163, 166, 168,
    212, 262, 263, 295, 310, 329, 349, 371,
    396, 415, 434, 484, 605, 619
  influence of Bible on 177
  life of 174
  publication of plays 183
  quoted . . . 7, 9, 10, 12, 54, 62, 99,
    126, 158
  references on 214
  sonnets 134, 135
  sources of plots 187
  suggested readings in . . . 215, 218
  table of plays 188
  variety of style 196
Sharp, William (Fiona Macleod) 600, 621,
    622, 623
  references on 622
  suggested readings in 623
Shaw, George Bernard . . 588, 606, 607,
    608, 621
  references on 622
  suggested readings in 624
She Stoops to Conquer 210, 335, 337, 338
Sheehan, Canon, P. A. 630
Shelley, Mrs. 422
Shelley, Percy Bysshe (bĭsh), general characteristics of 425
  incidental references to 146, 313, 362,
    429, 434, 441, 540, 558, 567
  life of 416
  lyrical genius 425
  references on 442, 443
  suggested readings in 446
  works of 420
Shepherd's Calendar 136, 140
Shĕr'i-dan, Richard Brinsley 210, 337, 606
Shirley, James 210
Shoemaker's Holiday 209
Short View of the Immorality of the Stage 264
Shorter, Dora Sigerson 631
Shorthouse, Joseph H. 629
Sidney, Sir Philip . . 121, 124, 126, 135,
    136, 211, 255, 317
  quoted 164
  references on 213
  suggested readings in 215
  works of 126
Sigurd, the Volsung 465
Silas Marner 319, 512, 513
Silent Woman, The 202, 204
Sinclair, May 631
Sir Charles Grandison 321
Sir Roger de Cov'er-ley Papers . 288, 290
Skeltin, John 625
Skylark, To a 422, 424
Smith, Adam 357, 627
Smith, Sydney 627
Smollett, To-bĭ'as 324, 325, 326, 346, 508
  references on 347

INDEX

	PAGE
Smollett, suggested readings in	349
Snaith, J. C.	631
Social movement of nineteenth century	493
Sohrab and Rustum	537
Somehow Good	595
Song of Roland	64
Songs before Sunrise	566
Songs of Experience	356
Songs of Innocence	356
Sonnets, in Elizabethan Age	134
introduction of	114
Jonson and Donne oppose	233
Keats's	244
Milton's	244
Shakespeare's	184
Sidney's	135
Spenser's	135
Wordsworth's	396
Sonnets from the Portuguese	543
Sordello	552
Southey, Robert	358, 400, 412
Spanish Gypsy, The	514
Spanish Tragedy, The	169
Specimens of English Dramatic Poets	360
Spectator, The	286, 288, 289
Spedding, James, quoted	130
Speech on American Taxation (Burke's)	330
Speech on Conciliation with America (Burke's)	330
Spencer, Herbert	453, 511, 588
Spenser, Edmund, chief characteristics of poetry of	144
Faerie Queene	140, 141, 309
incidental references to	121, 122, 211, 267, 309, 348, 434, 605
life of	139
references on	313
sonnets of	135
subjective poet	143
suggested readings in	215, 216
St. Francis	55
Stage, in early English theater	158, 164
Stalky and Co.	569
Steele, Richard	260, 264, 283, 287, 300
suggested readings in	302, 349
Stephen, Leslie	318, 629
quoted	298, 343
Stephens, James	631
Sterne, Laurence	324, 325, 326, 346
references on	347
suggested readings in	349
Stevenson, Robert Louis, general characteristics of	522
incidental references to	276, 456, 458, 577, 595
life of	516
references on	579
suggested readings in	583
works of	520
Stevenson, William	156
Stones of Venice, The	492, 495
Story, short	575
Stōw, John	123
Strafford	548
Strange Case of Dr. Jekyll and Mr. Hyde	518
Stubbs, William	628

	PAGE
Study of Celtic Literature	539
Suckling, Sir John	234, 236
suggested readings in	255
Suggested readings	59, 96, 117, 215, 254, 301, 348, 443, 580, 623
Summaries	48, 93, 94, 115, 210, 252, 299, 346, 440, 576, 620
Summer's Last Will and Testament	169
Surrey, Earl of	114, 116, 118
sonnets of	134
suggested readings in	118
Survey of London	123
Sweet, Professor, quoted	70
Swift, Jonathan, general characteristics of	283
incidental references to	276, 300, 318, 350, 508, 510
life of	276
references on	301
suggested readings in	302
works of	280–283
Swinburne, Al'ger-non Charles, general characteristics of	566
incidental references to	107, 416, 430, 455, 459, 534, 577, 606
life of	564
quoted	23, 314, 356, 403, 414
references on	580
suggested readings in	586
works of	565
Switzerland	537
Symonds, John Addington	629
quoted	102, 172
Symons, Arthur	462, 631
suggested readings in	586
Synge, John Millington	606, 617
references on	621, 622
Synthetic Philosophy	453
Table Talk	362
Taine, H. A., quoted	283, 290
Tale of a Tub	280
Tale of Two Cities	499
Tales from Shakespeare	360
Tales of a Grandfather	376
Tales of a Mermaid Tavern	605
Talisman	55, 379
Tam o' Shanter	374
Tam-bur-laine	170
Task, The	365
Tatler	283, 286, 287, 288
Taylor, Jeremy	227
Tempest, The	137, 184, 186, 192, 194
Temple, Sir William	626
Temple, The	237
Ten Brink, quoted	75
Tennyson, Alfred, general characteristics of	561
incidental references to	107, 392, 430, 449, 453, 458, 459, 534, 540, 545, 567, 574, 577, 597, 606, 612
life of	553
quoted	2, 65, 68, 83, 622
references on	580
suggested readings in	585
works of	555–561

INDEX

Tess of the D'Urberville's	532
Thackeray, William Makepeace, general characteristics of	508
incidental references to	287, 319, 326, 456, 458, 577, 595
life of	503
quoted	280, 298, 323
references on	579
suggested readings in	583
works of	503–508
Theater, Elizabethan	158–165
Thompson, Francis	461
suggested readings in	586
Thompson, James	630
Thomson, James	309
suggested readings in	348
Thoreau, quoted	29
Thyrsis	537
Time and Tide by Weare and Tyne	493
Tom Jones	323
Tottel's Miscellany	115
Tour-neur', Cyril	209
Traitor, The	210
Traveler, The	332, 335
Travels, Mandeville's	73
Travels with a Donkey	520
Treasure Island	276, 518, 521
Treatise of Human Nature	327
Trelawny, Edward	419
Trench, Herbert	631
Trick to Catch the Old One	209
Tristram and Iseult	64
Tristram of Lyonesse	566
Tristram Shandy	324
Troilus and Criseyde	83
Trollope, Anthony	457
suggested readings in	582
Twelfth Night	137, 184, 194
Twentieth-century literature	587–621
dramatists	606–620
essayists	588
novelists	589–596
poets	597–605
references on	622
suggested readings and questions	623
summary	620
trend of contemporary literature	587
Two Voices, The	556
Tyndale, William	116, 255
suggested readings in	117
Tyndall, John	453
quoted	486
U'dall, Nicholas	156
Ulysses	556, 557, 613
Underwoods	519
Unfortunate Traveler	123, 169, 317
Unities, dramatic	156, 172, 205
"University wits"	167
Unto this Last	493
Urn Burial	226
Utopia	104
Van-brugh' (-broo'), John	626
Vanity Fair	319, 505, 506
Vanity of Human Wishes	340, 343
Vaughan, Henry	236, 237, 255

Venus and Adonis	134, 180
Vercelli (vĕr-chel'le) Book	19
Vicar of Wakefield	338
Vice, in old plays	153
Victorian age	449–586
essayists	455, 456, 462, 466–495, 520, 538–540
history of	449
novelists	456–458, 495–533
poets	458–465, 469, 525, 535–537, 540–568, 573
references on	578
scientific writers	452–455
short stories	568–573
suggested readings and questions	580
summary	576
Vignettes in Rhyme	462
Virginians	507
Vision of Judgment	411
Vol-po'ne	202, 204
Voltaire	262
Vox Clamantis	79
Vulgar Errors	226
Wace	67
Wagner, Richard	597
Wallace, Professor C. W.	180
quoted	154
Waller, Edmund	262, 626
Walpole, Horace	311
suggested readings in	348
Walpole, Robert	304
Walton, Izaak	226
Wanderer, The	22
War'bur-ton, William	626
Ward, Mrs. Humphry	630
Ward, Mrs. Wilfrid	630
Ward, Wilfrid	629
Warner, William	625
Warren, J. B. L. (Lord de Tabley)	630
Wars of the Roses	100
Warton, Thomas	627
Watson, William	461, 630
suggested readings in	586
Watts, Isaac	626
Watts-Dunton, Theodore	565, 630
Waverley	376, 379
Way of the World	264
Webster, John	209
Weir of Hermiston	521
Wells, Herbert George	588, 593, 621
references on	622
suggested readings in	623
Wesley, Charles	627
Wesley, John	305
Westward Ho	457
What Every Woman Knows	610
White Devil, The	209
White, Gilbert	627
Whitefield, George	305
Widecombe Fair	594
Widsið (wĭd-sĭth)	20
Wilde, Oscar	630
Wilson, John	627
Winter's Tale	184, 186, 190
Witch of Atlas	422, 425
Wither, George	626

INDEX

Woman Killed with Kindness, A . . 209
Woodlanders, The 532
Woodstock 377
Wordsworth, William, general characteristics of 395
   incidental references to 114, 146, 244, 310, 312, 313, 354, 355, 356, 357, 358, 362, 402, 414, 423, 425, 441, 461, 538, 555, 561, 562, 567
   life of 386
   poet of child life 394
   poet of man 392
   poet of nature 391, 396
   quoted 8, 9, 353, 354
   references on 442
   suggested readings in 445
   works of 390–396
World, The 237

Wotton, Sir Henry, quoted 247
Wounds of Civil War 169
Wright 111
Wuthering Heights 457
Wyatt, Sir Thomas 114, 116, 118, 134
   suggested readings in 118
Wych'er-ley, William 626
Wyc'liffe, John, 57, 75, 93, 94, 97, 112, 255

Yeats, William Butler 597, 616, 618, 620
   references on 622, 623
   suggested readings in 623
York plays 148
Young, Edward 627
Youth of the Year 565

Zangwill, Israel 596
   suggested readings in 623